Jerry Bauer

About the Author

JOHN CROWLEY was born in 1942 on an Army Air Corps base and grew up in Vermont and Indiana. A recipient of the American Academy and Institute of Arts and Letters Award in Literature, Mr. Crowley's novels include *Ægypt*, *Love & Sleep*, *Dæmonomania*, and, most recently, *The Translator*. He teaches fiction and film writing at Yale, and lives in western Massachusetts with his wife and twin daughters.

Also by John Crowley

The Translator
Dæmonomania
Love & Sleep
Ægypt
Little, Big

Otherwise

THREE
NOVELS
BY
JOHN
CROWLEY

Perennial
An Imprint of HarperCollinsPublishers

First Perennial edition published 2002.

Designed by Donna Sinisgalli

Library of Congress Cataloging-in-Publication Data

Crowley, John.
Otherwise : three novels / by John Crowley.
p. cm.
Contents: The deep—Beasts—Engine summer.
ISBN 0-06-093792-0
1. Fantasy fiction, American. I. Title.
PS3553.R597 A6 2002
813'.54—dc21 2001055477

02 03 04 05 06 RRD 10 9 8 7 6 5 4 3 2 1

Contents

Otherwise

THE
DEEP

———

In memoriam
J.B.C.

PRINCIPAL CHARACTERS

The Blacks:
    King Little Black
    The Queen, his wife
    Black Harrah, the Queen's lover
    Young Harrah, his son
    A bastard son of Farin the Black

The Reds:
    Red Senlin
    Red Senlin's Son (later King)
    Sennred, Red Senlin's younger son
    Redhand
    Old Redhand, his father
    Younger Redhand, his brother
    Caredd, his wife
    Mother Caredd
    Fauconred

The Just:
    Nyamé, whose name is called Nod
    The Neither-nor
    Adar

The Grays:
    Mariadn, the Arbiter
    Learned Redhand, Redhand's brother and later Arbiter

Endwives, Ser and Norin

And a nameless one from Elsewhere called variously
    Visitor
    Secretary
    Recorder

Canst thou draw out Leviathan with an hook?
Or his tongue with a cord which thou lettest down?
Will he make a covenant with thee?
And wilt thou take him for a servant for ever?
Lay thine hand upon him,
Remember the battle, do no more.

JOB

ONE

VISITOR

1

After the skirmish, two Endwives found him lying in the darkness
next to the great silver egg. It took them only a moment to discover
that he was neither male nor female; somewhat longer to decide whether
he was alive or dead. Alive, said one; the other wasn't sure for how long;
anyway, they took him up on their rude stretcher and walked with him
nearly a mile to where a station of theirs had been set up a week before
when the fighting had started; there they laid him out.

They had thought to patch him up however they could in the usual
way, but when they began working they found that he was missing more
than sex. Parts of him seemed made of something other than flesh, and
from the wound at the back of his head the blood that flowed seemed
viscous, like oil. When the older of the two caught a bit of it on a glass,
and held it close to the lamplight, she gasped: it was alive—it flowed in
tiny swirls ever, like oil in alcohol, but finer, blue within crimson. She
showed her sister. They sat down then, unsure, looking at the figure on
the pallet; ghastly pale he was in the lamplight and all hairless. They
weren't afraid; they had seen too much horror to fear anything. But they
were unsure.

All night they watched him by lamplight. Toward dawn he began to move slightly, make sounds. Then spasms, violent, though he seemed in no pain—it was as though puppet strings pulled him. They cushioned his white damaged head; one held his thrashing arms while the other prepared a calming drug. When she had it ready, though, they paused, looking at each other, not knowing what effect this most trusted of all their secrets might have. Finally, one shrugging and the other with lips pursed, they forced some between his tightclosed teeth.

Well, he was a man to this extent; in minutes he lay quiet, breathing regularly. They inspected, gingerly and almost with repulsion, the wound in his head; it had already begun to pucker closed, and bled no more. They decided there was little they could do but wait. They stood over him a moment; then the older signaled, and they stepped out of the sod hut that was their station into the growing dawn.

The great gray heath they walked on was called the Drumskin. Their footsteps made no sound on it, but when the herds of horses pastured there rode hard, the air filled with a long hum like some distant thunder, a hum that could be heard Inward all the way to the gentle folded farmland called the Downs, all the way Outward to the bleak stone piles along the Drumsedge, outposts like Old Watcher that they could see when the road reached the top of a rise, a dim scar on the flat horizon far away.

They heard, dimly, that thunder as they stood at the top of the rise, their brown skirts plucked at by wind. They looked down into the gray grass bottom that last night's struggle had covered, a wide depression in the Drumskin that everywhere was pocketed with such hiding-places. This pocket held now four dead men or women; the burying spades of the Endwives, left last night; and an egg made of some dull silver, as high as a man, seemingly solid.

"What," said the younger then, "if no one knows of him but us?"

"We must tell his comrades, whichever they be, that we have him. It's the Way. We must tell the comrades of any survivor that he lives. And only his comrades."

"And how are we to know which—if either—were his comrades? I don't think either were."

The old one thought.

"Maybe," said the younger, "we should tell both."

"One side would probably gain an advantage, and the other probably not. The Protector Redhand might arrest him, and the Just be disadvantaged. The Just might kill him, and the Protector be disadvantaged. Worse: there might be a battle waged over him, that we would be the cause of."

"Well . . ."

"It's happened. That Endwives not taking care which side might be advantaged have caused death. It's happened. To our shame."

The other was silent. She looked up to where the Morning Star shone steadily. The home of the borning, as the Evening Star was of the dead.

"Perhaps he won't last the day," she said.

They called him Visitor. His strange wound healed quickly, but the two sisters decided that his brain must have been damaged. He spoke rarely, and when he did, in strange nonsense syllables. He listened carefully to everything said to him, but understood nothing. He seemed neither surprised nor impatient nor grateful about his circumstances; he ate when he was given food and slept when they slept.

The week had been quiet. After the battle into which the Visitor had intruded, the Just returned to the Nowhere they could disappear to, and the Protector's men returned to the farms and the horsegatherings, to other battles in the Protector's name. None had passed for several days except peatcutters from the Downs.

Toward the close of a clear, cold day, the elder Endwife, Ser, made her slow circular way home across the Drumskin. In her wide basket were ten or so boxes and jars, and ever she knelt where her roving eye saw in the tangle of gray grass an herb or sprout of something useful. She'd pluck it, crush and sniff it, choose with pursed lips a jar for it. When it had grown too dark to see them any more, she was near home; yellow lamplight poured from the open door. She straightened her stiff back and saw the stars and planets already ashine; whispered a prayer and covered her jars from the Evening Star, just in case.

When she stepped through the door, she stopped there in the midst of a "Well . . ." Fell silent, pulled the door shut and crept to a chair.

The Visitor was talking.

The younger Endwife, Norin, sat rapt before him, didn't turn when her sister entered. The Visitor, motionless on the bed, drew out words with effort, as though he must choose each one. But he was talking.

"I remember," he was saying, "the sky. That—egg, you call it. I was placed. In it. And. Separated. From my home. Then, descending. In the egg. To here."

"Your home," said Norin. "That star."

"You say a star," the Visitor said blankly. "I think, it can't have been a star. I don't know how, I know it, but, I do."

"But it circled the world. In the evening it rose from the Deep. And went overhead. In the morning it passed again into the Deep."

"Yes."

"For how long?"

"I don't know. I was made there."

"There were others there. Your parents."

"No. Only me. It was a place not much larger than the egg."

He sat expressionless on the edge of the bed, his long pale hands on his knees. He looked like a statue. Norin turned to her sister, her eyes shining.

"Is he mad now?" said Ser. Her sister's face darkened.

"I . . . don't know. Only, just today he learned to speak. This morning when you left he began. He learned 'cup' and 'drink,' like a baby, and now see! In one day, he's speaking so! He learned so fast . . ."

"Or remembered," Ser said, arising slowly with her eyes on the Visitor. She bent over him and looked at his white face; his eyes were black holes. She intended to be stern, to shock him; it sometimes worked. Her hand moved to the shade of the lamp, turned it so the lamplight fell full on him.

"You were born inside a star in the sky?" she asked sharply.

"I wasn't born," said the Visitor evenly. "I was made."

Ser's old hand shook on the lampshade, for the lamplight fell on eyes that had neither iris nor pupil, but were a soft, blank violet, infinitely deep and without reflection.

"How . . . Who are you?"

The Visitor opened his thin lips to speak, but was silent. Ser lowered the lampshade.

Then Ser sat down beside her sister, and they listened to the Visitor attempt to understand himself out loud to them, here and there helping with a guessed word or fact.

"When the egg opened," said the Visitor, "and I came out into the darkness, I knew. I can remember knowing. Who I am, what had made me, for what purpose. I came out . . . bearing all this, like . . . like a . . ."—pointing to Ser's basket.

"A gift," said Norin.

"A bundle," said Ser.

"But then, almost as soon as I arose, there were men, above me, dark, silent; I don't think they saw me; something long and thin strapped to each back . . ."

"Yes," said Norin. "The Just."

"And before I could speak to them, others came, with, with . . ."

"Horses," said Ser. "Yes. Protector Redhand's men."

"I ran up the—the bank, just as these two collided. There were cries, I cried out, to make them see me. There was a noise that filled up the air."

"A Gun," said Norin.

The Visitor fell silent then. The Endwives waited. The lamp buzzed quietly.

"The next thing I remember," he said at last, "is that cup, and drinking from it today."

Ser pondered, troubled. She would still prefer to think him mad; but the blank eyes, now velvet black, the viscous, living blood, the sexlessness . . . perhaps it was she who was mad. "How," she began, "did you learn to speak so well, so fast?"

He shook his head slowly. "It seems . . . easy, I don't know . . . It must be—part of what I was made to do. Yes. It is. I was made so, so that I could speak to you."

" 'You,' " said Ser doubtfully. "And who is 'you'?"

"You," said the Visitor. "All of you."

"There is no all of us," Norin said. "There are the Folk, but they aren't all of us. Because there are also the Just, with their Guns . . ."

"Warriors for the Folk," said Ser. "So they claim. They make war on the Protectors, who own the land, to take it from them and return it to the Folk. Secret war, assassination. They are known only to each other. And yet most Folk stand aside from the Just; and in hundreds of years of this nothing has changed, not truly. But the war goes on. You tried to speak to both of them, Just and the Protector's men, together; so you see."

"Even the Protectors," Norin said. "They own the land, they are the chief men . . ."

"They, then," said the Visitor.

"But they are divided into factions, intrigues, alliances. As bitter toward each other as they are toward the Just."

"The Reds and the Blacks," said Norin.

"Old quarrels." Ser sighed. "We Endwives come after battles, not before them. We help the hurt to live, and bury the dead."

"More often bury than help," said her sister.

"We are pledged neither to aid nor hurt in any quarrel. And . . . I suppose it can't be explained to you, but . . . the world is so divided that if anyone knew of you but us, you would be used for a counter in their game. And the death that came in the next moves—if death came—would be on our hands."

From his smooth face they couldn't tell if he had grasped any of this. "The Folk," he said at last.

Ser pursed her lips. He wouldn't leave it. "They aren't much used to being spoken to," she said drily. "Except by the Grays."

"Grays?"

"A brotherhood; lawyers and scholars; arbiters, priests, keepers of wisdom . . ." He had turned to her. "And what," she asked softly, "will you tell them then?"

She saw, not by any change in his face, but by the flexing of his long fingers, that he was in some torment of ignorance.

"I don't remember," he said at last.

"Well."

His pale hands ceased working and lay quiet on his sharp knees. His face grew, if possible, still more remote; he looked ahead at nothing, as though waiting for some internal advice. Then he said, with neither patience nor hope: "Perhaps, if I wait, something will return to me. Some direction, some other part of the way I am made, that will let me know the next thing to do."

Somewhere far off there grew a soft hum, indeterminate, coming from nowhere, growing louder that way, then louder this way. Riders on the Drumskin; the heath was speaking. Ser rose heavily, her eyes on the door, and moved to turn down the lamp.

"Perhaps it will," she said. "Until it does, you will stay here. Inside. And be silent."

The drumbeat grew steadily more distinct; the universal hum resolved itself into individual horses riding hard. Then cries, just outside. And Ser couldn't bar the door, because an Endwife's door is never barred.

Then there stood in the doorway a thick barrel of a man, bull-necked, shorn of all but a fuzz of steely hair. Dressed in leather, all colored red. Behind him two others in red carried between them a third, head bent back, open mouth moaning, red jacket brighter red with blood.

The barrel-man began to speak, but stopped when he saw someone sitting on the bed, pale and unmoving, regarding him with dark, calm eyes.

The Defender Fauconred disliked pens. He disliked paper and ink. On stormy days (which were growing more frequent as the year turned) or in the evenings after the horsegathering, he liked to stretch out on the pallet in his tent with a mug of blem-and-warm-water and stare at the pictures the living charcoal made in the brazier.

But once a week, every week, he must push his barrel shape into a camp chair and trim the lamp; sharpen two or three pens; lay out paper and mix ink; sit, sighing, humming, running thick fingers over his stubble of steel-gray hair; and finally begin.

"The Defender Fauconred to the Great Protector Redhand, greetings etc." That part was easy.

"We are this day within sight of Old Watcher, on a line between it and the Little Lake, as far from the lake as you can see a white horse on a clear day." He stopped, dipped his pen. "The herd numbers now one hundred five. Of these, forty-seven are stallions. Of the yearlings, the Protector will remember there were forty-nine in the spring. We have found thirty. Of all the horses, one is crippled, two have the bloat, and we have found three dead, one the old painted stallion the Protector mentioned.

"The Horse-master says the herd should number in all one hundred forty, counting in all dead & wounded & sick. He says the rains will be heavy in a week or two weeks. I think one. Unless other word comes from the Protector, we will be herding homeward in about ten days and reach the Downs before Barnolsweek. I will then come to the Hub with the Guard, bringing such horses as the Horse-master chooses, to the number twenty or as convenient."

Chewing on the end of the pen, Fauconred assembled the other news in his head, sighed, bent again over the paper.

"Also, the roan mare with the white eye the Protector mentioned has been found, and is in health.

"Also, we discovered one lying in ambush, with a Gun. When we questioned him he answered nothing, but looked always proud. He is hanged, and his Gun broken.

"Also, a man of my guard has been shot with a Gun, and though he will live, we are more alert.

"Also . . ."

Also. The Defender put down his splayed pen and looked to where the Visitor stood outside the tent, unmoving, patient, a dark shape in the brown Endwife's cloak against the growing thunderclouds.

Also. How could he be explained to the Protector? Fauconred drew out a fresh sheet, picked up a new pen. "Protector, I have found one sheltered by the Endwives, one neither male nor female, having no hair, who says he is not of the world but was made in the sky." He read it over, biting his lip. "I swear on my oaths to you and ours that it is true." The harder he swore, the more fantastical it sounded. "Perhaps," he began, and struck it out. It was not his place to perhaps about it. "He asks permission to come to the Protector. I know nothing to do but bring him to you." *Defender,* the old Endwife had said to him, *I charge you as you shall ever need me or mine, let no harm come to him.* He moved the pen above the paper in an agony of doubt. "I have promised him my protection. I hope . . ." Struck out. "I know the Protector will honor my promise." And he signed it: "The Drumskin, Bannsweek, by my hand, the Defender Fauconred, your servant."

He folded the letters separately, the ordinary and the preposterous, took wax, lit it in the lamp, and with his chin in his hand let the wax clot in bright crimson drops like blood on the fold of each. He pressed his ring, which showed a hand lifting a cup, into the glittering clots and watched them dry hard and perfect. He shook his head, and with a grunt pulled himself from his chair.

The Visitor still stood motionless, looking out over the gray evening heath. The wind had increased, and plucked at the brown cloak that the younger Endwife had wrapped him in; that was his disguise, for now, and Fauconred felt his sexlessness strongly seeing him in it.

"The herdsmen have returned," the Visitor said.

"Yes," said Fauconred.

They sat their ponies gracefully, wrapped to their eyes in dark windings that fluttered around them like bannerets. They moved the quick herd before them with flicks of long slim lashes and cries that, windborne, came up strangely enlarged to where Fauconred and the Visitor stood. Beyond, Old Watcher was lost in thick storm clouds that were moving over fast. The storm was the color of new iron, and trailed a skirt of rain; it was lit within by dull yellow lightnings. The roans and whites and painteds thundered before it, eyes panicky; the Drumskin's thunder as they ran was answered by the storm's drums, mocked by the chuckle of Fauconred's tent-cloths rippling.

"Beyond," said the Visitor, lifting his gentle voice against the noise. "Farther than Old Watcher. What's there?"

"The Outlands," said Fauconred. "Swamps, marshes, desolation."

"And beyond that?"

"Beyond that? Nothing."

"How, nothing?"

"The world has to end eventually," said Fauconred. "And so it does. They say there's an edge, a lip. As on a tray, you know. And then nothing."

"There can't be nothing," said the Visitor simply.

"Well, it's not the world," said Fauconred. He held out a lined palm. "The world is like this. Beyond the world is like beyond my hand. Nothing."

The Visitor shook his head. Fauconred, with an impatient sigh, waved and shouted to a knot of red-jacketed horsemen below. One detached himself from the group and started up the long rise. Fauconred turned and ducked back inside his tent.

He returned with the two letters under his arm, peering into a tiny goatskin-bound book, licking a thick thumb to turn its fine figured pages. He found his place, and turned the book into the light to read. The Visitor bent close to him to hear over the wind and the hooves. Carefully Fauconred made out words:

"The world is founded on a pillar which is founded on the Deep.

"Of the world, it is a great circle; its center is the lake island called the Hub and its margins are waste and desolate.

"Of the pillar, it is of adamant. Its width is nearly the width of the world, and no man knows its length for it is founded on the Deep. The pillar supports the world like the arm and hand of an infinite Servant holding a platter up."

He turned the page and with a finger held down its snapping corner. "The sky is the Deep above," he went on, "and as the Deep is heavy, so the sky is light. Each day the sun rises from the Deep, passes overhead, and falls again within the Deep; each night it passes under the Deep and hastens to the place where it arose. Between the world and the sun travel seven Wanderers, which likewise arise and descend into the Deep, but with an irregular motion . . ."

He closed the book. Up the rise came the red-jacketed man he had summoned. The rider pulled up, his horse snorted, and Fauconred took the bridle.

"It's possible," said the Visitor.

"Possible?" Fauconred shouted. "Possible?" He handed up the two letters to the beardless redjacket. "To the Protector Redhand, at his father's house, in the City."

The wind had begun to scream. "Tell the Protector," Fauconred shouted over the wind's voice. The boy leaned down to him. "Tell the Protector I bring him a . . . a visitor."

2

There are seven windows in the Queen's bedroom in the Citadel that is the center of the City that is on the lake island called the Hub in the middle of the world.

Two of the seven windows face the tower stones and are dark; two overlook inner courtyards; two face the complex lanes that wind between the high, blank-faced mansions of the Protectorate; and the seventh, facing the steep Street of Birdsellers and, beyond, a crack in the ring of mountains across the lake, is always filled at night with stars. When wind speaks in the mountains, it whispers in this window, and makes the fine brown bed hangings dance.

Because the Queen likes light to make love by, there is a tiny lamp lit within the bed hangings. Black Harrah, the Queen's lover of old, dislikes the light; it makes him think as much of discovery as of love. But then, one is not the Queen's lover solely at one's own pleasure.

If there were now a discoverer near, say on the balcony over the double door, or in the curtained corridor that leads to the servants' stairs, he would see the great bed, lit darkly from within. He would see the great, thick body of the Queen struggling impatiently against Black Harrah's old lean one, and hear their cries rise and subside. He might, well-hidden, stay to watch them cease, separate, lie somnolent; might hear shameful things spoken; and later, if he has waited, hear them consider their realm's affairs, these two, the Queen and her man, the Great Protector Black Harrah.

"No, no," Black Harrah answers to some question.

"I fear," says the Queen.

"There are ascendancies," says Black Harrah sleepily. "Binding rules, oaths sworn. Fixed as stars."

"New stars are born. The Grays have found one."

"Please. One thing at a time."

"I fear Red Senlin."

"He is no new star. If ever a man were bound by oaths . . ."

"He hates me."

"Yes," Harrah says.

"He would be King."

"No."

"If he . . ."

"I will kill him."

"If he kills you . . . ?"

"My son will kill him. If his sons kill my son, my son's sons will kill his. Enough?"

Silence. The watcher (for indeed he is there, on the balcony over the half-open double door, huddled into a black, watching pile, motionless) nods his head in tiny approving nods, well pleased.

The Queen starts up, clutching the bedclothes around her.

"What is it?" Black Harrah asks.

"A noise."

"Where?"

"There. On the stair. Footsteps."

"No."

"Yes!"

Feet grow loud without. Shouts of the Queen's guards, commands, clash of arms. Feet run. Suddenly, swinging like a monkey from the balcony, grasping handholds and dropping to the floor, the watcher, a tiny man all in black. Crying shrilly, he forces the great door shut and casts the bolt just as armed red-coated men approach without. The clash of the bolt is still echoing when armed fists pound from the other side:

"Open! In the name of the Great Protector Red Senlin!"

The watcher now clings to the bolt as though his little arms could aid it and screams: "Leave! Go away! I order you!"

"We seek the traitor Black Harrah, for imprisonment in the King's name . . ."

"Fool! Go! It is I who command you, I, your King, and as you truly owe me, leave!"

The noise without ceases for a moment. The King Little Black turns to the bed. Black Harrah is gone. The King's wife stands upright on the bed, huge and naked.

"Fly!" the King shouts. She stands unmoving, staring; then with a boom the door is hammered on with breaking tools. The Queen turns, takes up a cloak, and runs away down the servants' corridor, her screaming maidservants after her. The door behind the King begins to crack.

Because the island City lies within a great deep cup, whose sides are mountains, dawn comes late there and evening early. And even when the high spires of the Citadel, which is at the top of the high-piled City, are touched with light filtering through the blue-green forests, and then the High City around it and then the old-fashioned mansions mostly shuttered are touched, and then the old inns and markets, and the narrow streets of the craftsmen, and then the winding water-stairs, piles, piers, ramparts, esplanades and wharfs—even then the still lake, which has no name, is black. Mist rises from its depths like chill breath, obscuring the flat surface so that it seems no lake but a hole pierced through the fabric of the world, and the shadowy, broad-nosed craft that ride its margins—and the City itself—seem suspended above the Deep.

But when the first light does strike the Citadel, the whole world knows it's high morning; and though the watermen can still see only stars, they are about their business. The Protectorate has ever feared a great bridge over the lake that couldn't be cut down at need, and so the four bridges that hang like swaying ribbons from the High City gates are useless for anything but walkers or single riders. The watermen's business is therefore large, and necessary; they are a close clan, paid like servants yet not servants, owing none, singing their endless, tuneless songs, exchanging their jokes that no one else laughs at.

It was the watermen in their oiled goatskins who first saw that Red Senlin had returned from the Outlands, because it was they who carried him and his armed riders and his fierce Outland captains into the City. The watermen didn't care if Red Senlin wanted to be King; it's well-known that the watermen, "neither Folk nor not," care only for the fee.

Fauconred had put the Visitor on early watch, to make some use of him; but when the first chill beams silvered the Drum fog he woke, shivered with premonition, and went to find the Visitor.

He was still watching. Impervious apparently to loneliness, weariness, cold, he still looked out over the quadrant assigned to him.

"Quit now," Fauconred said to him hoarsely, taking his elbow. "Your watch is long over." The man (if man he was) turned from his watch and went with Fauconred, without question or complaint.

"But—what," he asked when they sat by Fauconred's fire, "was I to watch for?"

"Well, the Just," Fauconred said. "They can be anywhere." He leaned toward the Visitor, as though he might even here be overheard, and the Visitor bent close to hear. "They draw lots by some means, among themselves. So I hear. And each of them then has a Protector, or Defender, that he is pledged to murder. Secretly, if possible. And so you see, since it's by lots, and nothing personal, you'll never know the man. You can come face to face with him; he seems a cottager or . . . or anyone. You talk. The place is lonely. Suddenly, there is the Gun."

The Visitor considered this, touching the place on his head where he had been hurt. "Then how could I watch for one?" he asked.

Fauconred, confused, tossed sticks angrily into the fire, but made no other answer. Day brightened. Ahead lay the Downs at last . . .

It was a waterside inn.

"Secretly," the cloaked man said. "And quickly."

"You are . . ."

"A . . . merchant. Yes. What does it matter?" His old, lean hand drew a bag from within a shapeless, hooded traveler's cloak. It made a solid sound on the inn table.

The girl he spoke to was a waterman's daughter. Her long neck was bare; her blond, almost white hair cut off short like a boy's. She turned, looked out a tiny window that pierced the gray slatting of the inn wall. Above the mountains the sky had grown pale; below, far below, the lake was dark.

"The bridges?" she asked.

"Closed. Red Senlin has returned."

"Yes."

"His mob has closed the bridges."

"Then it must be illegal to ferry."

The other, after a moment, added a second bag to the table. The girl regarded neither. "Get me," the traveler said, "three days' food. A sword. And get your father to take me to the mountain road before daybreak. I'll double that."

The girl sat staring a moment, and then rose quickly, picking up the two bags. "I'll take you," she said, and turned away into the darkness of the inn. The traveler watched her go; then sat turning this way and that, looking ever out the tiny window at the pre-dawn sky. Around him a dark crowd of watermen sat; he heard bits of muttered conversation.

"There were oaths sworn."

Someone spat disgustedly.

"He's rightful King."

"Yes. Much as any."

"Black Harrah will hang him."

"Or maybe just hang."

Laughter. Then: "Where is Redhand?"

"Redhand. Redhand knows."

"Yes. Much as any."

Suddenly the girl was before him. Her long neck rose columnlike out of a thick cloak she had wrapped over her oiled goatskins—and over a bundle which she held before her.

"The sword?" he whispered.

"Come," she said.

There was a dank, endless stairway within the warren of the inn that gave out finally onto an esplanade still hooded in dark and fog. He followed her close, starting at noises and shapes.

"The sword," he whispered at her ghostly back. "Now."

"Here, the water-stairs. Down."

She turned sharply around the vast foot of pillar that supported waterfront lodges above, and started down the ringing stone stairway faster than he could follow. In a moment she was gone; he stumbled quickly after her, alone now, as though there were no other thing in the world than this descent, no other guide but the sound of her footsteps ahead.

Then her footsteps ceased. He stopped. There was a lapping of water somewhere.

"Stop," he said.

"I have," she answered.

"Where?"

"Here."

The last step gave out on a gravelly bit of shingle, barely walking space. He could see nothing ahead at first; took three timid steps and saw her, a tall blank ghost, indistinct, just ahead.

"Oh. There."

"Yes."

He crept forward. Her figure grew clearer: the paleness of her white head, the dark cloak, in her hand the . . .

In her hand the Gun.

"Black Harrah," she said.

"No," he said.

"Justice," she said.

The Gun she held in both hands was half as long as an arm, and its great bore was like a mouth; it clicked when she fired it, hissed white smoke, and exploded like all rage and hatred. The stone ball shattered Black Harrah; without a cry he fell, thrown against the stairs, wrapped in a shower of his own blood.

High above, on the opposite side of the City, by the gate called Goforth from which a long tongue of bridge came out, a young man commanded other men for the first time; a dark, small man destined by birth so to command; who felt sure now, as dawn began to silhouette the mountains against the sky, that he was in fact fitted for the work, and whose hand began to ease at last his nervous grip on his sword handle. He sighed deeply. There would be no Black reprisals. His men began to slouch against the ancient bridge pilings. One laughed. Day had come, and they were all alive.

The young man's name was Sennred; he was the younger of the two sons of Red Senlin, he who had come out of exile in the Outlands to reclaim his rightful place at the King's side by whatever means necessary.

That the Great Protector Red Senlin had been unjustly kept away from King Little Black's side by Black Harrah; that he came now to help the King throw off Black Harrah's tyranny; that his whole desire was to cleanse odiousness and scandal from the Citadel (and if that meant Black Harrah's arrest, so be it)—all this the young Sennred had by heart and would have argued fiercely to any who suspected his father's motives; but at the same time, as many can who are young and quick and loyal, Sennred could hold a very different view of things . . .

A century almost to the day before this pregnant dawn, a crime had torn the ancient and closely woven fabric of this world: a Great Protector, half-brother of King Ban, had seized from King Ban's heir the iron crown. King Ban's heir was the son of King Red. The Great Protector's name was Black. To the family Red and all its branches, allies, dependents, it mattered nothing that King Red's son was a foul cripple, a tyrannous boy in love with blood; he was Ban's heir. To the family Black and its equally extensive connections what mattered was that the crown had fitted Black's head, that the great legal fraternity, the Grays, had confirmed him, and his son, and his son's son. There had been uprisings, rebellions; lately there had been a brief battle at Senlinsdown, and King Little Black, childless, had accepted Red Senlin as his heir. So there had been no war —not quite; only, the world had divided itself further into factions, the factions had eaten up the unaligned, had grown paid armies each to protect itself from the other; the factions now waited, poised.

Red Senlin was King Red's true heir. He had learned that as a boy. He had never for a moment forgotten it.

And his younger son Sennred knew in his heart who was truly the King, and why Red Senlin had come back from the Outlands.

Around him, above him, the great City houses of the Protectorate had begun to awaken, such as were used; many were empty. There was, he knew, one sleeping army in the City large enough to decide, before noon, whether or not the world would change today; it was housed in and around that dark pile where now lamplight glimmered in tiny windows—the Harbor, the house of the family Redhand.

The Redhands would be waking to a new world, Sennred thought; and his hand tightened again on his sword handle.

At the head table in the great hall smoky with torches and loud with the noise of half a hundred Redhand dependents breaking their fast, Old Redhand sat with his three sons.

There was Redhand, the eldest, his big warrior's hands tearing bread he didn't eat, a black beard around his mouth.

There was the Gray brother, Learned, beside him. The gray that Learned Redhand wore was dark, darker than the robes of Grays far older than himself, dark and convoluted as a thundercloud, and not lightened by a bit of red ribbon pinned within its folds.

There was, lastly, Younger. Younger was huddled down in his chair, turning an empty cup, looking as though someone had struck him and he didn't know how to repay it.

When the red-jacketed messenger approached them they all looked up, expectantly; but it was only letters from the Drum, from Fauconred; Redhand tucked them away unread . . . "The Queen," he said to Learned, "has fled, Outward. No one knows how she escaped, or where Black Harrah is."

"Red Senlin let them slip."

"He would. Graceless as a dog among birds." Redhand's voice was a deep, gritty growl, a flaw left by the same sword that had drawn a purple line up his throat to his ear; he wore the beard to hide it.

"Where is Young Harrah?" Learned asked. The friendship between Black Harrah's son and Red Senlin's was well-known; they did little to hide it, though their fathers raged at it.

"Not imprisoned. At Red Senlin's Son's request—or demand. He will fly too; he must live. Join his father . . ."

"Will Red Senlin be King now?" Younger asked. "Does he wish it?"

"He could bring war with his wishing," Learned said. "He would."

"Perhaps," Redhand said, "he can be dissuaded."

"We can try," Learned said. "The reasons . . ."

Trembling with suppressed rage, his father cut across him. "You talk as though he were a naughty child. He is your uncle, and twice your age."

"He must listen, anyway," said Younger. "Because he can't do it without us. He knows that."

"*Must listen,*" Old Redhand said bitterly. "He will abide by your wishes." His hands were tight fists on the table.

"He will," Redhand said.

"And if he won't," Old Redhand shouted, rising out of his seat, "what then? Will you cut off his head?"

"Stop," Learned said. "The guests . . ."

"He is here because of you," Old Redhand shouted at his eldest son. "You, the Great Protector Redhand. Because of you and your army he thinks he can do this thing."

"He is rightful King," said Younger softly, drawing in spilled drink on the table.

"Little Black is King," said his brother Redhand.

"My King," said his father, "shortly to be murdered, no doubt, whom I fought for in the Outlands, and against the Just, and whom Red Senlin fought for and in the old days . . ."

"The old days," came his eldest's gritty voice, cold with disgust. "If time turned around, you could all be young again. But against the advice of the old, it keeps its course." He rose, took up his gloves. "And maybe it means to see Red Senlin King. If by my strength, then by my strength. You are gone foolish if you stand in our way."

His father rose too, and was about to speak, shout, curse; Redhand stood hard, ready to receive: and then there was a noise at the back of the hall; messengers, belted and armed, were making their way to the head table. Their news, rippling through the assembly as though from a cast stone, reached the head table before its bearers:

The Great Protector Black Harrah is dead. The richest man in the world, the Queen's lover, the King's King, has been shot with a Gun on the margin of the unplumbed lake.

The way from Redhand's house to the Citadel lay along the Street of Birdsellers, up the steep way through the Gem Market, along Bellmaker's Street; throngs of City people, lashed by rumor, called out to Redhand, and he waved but made no replies; his brother Younger and a crowd of his redjackets made a way for them through the frightened populace. "Redhand!" they called to him. "Redhand . . . !"

They said of the family Redhand that they had not walked far from the cottage door, which in an age-long scheme of things was true. Old Redhand's great-grandfather was the first Defender; he had been born merely a tenant of a Red lord whose line was extinguished by war and the assassinations of the Just. But it had always been so; there was no Protector, however great, who somewhere within the creases of history had not a farmer or a soldier or even a thief tucked.

Why one would wish to plot and strive to rise from the quiet pool of the Folk to be skimmed from the top by war, feud, and assassination was a question all the poets asked and none answered. The Protectorate was a selfish martyrdom, it had never a place empty. The laws and records of inheritance filled musty floors of the Citadel. Inheritance was the chief business of all courts of the Grays. Inheritance was the slow turning of this still world, and the charting of its ascendancies and declinations took up far more of the world's paper and ink than the erratic motions of its seven moons.

At Kingsgate, men Redhand recognized as old soldiers of Red Senlin's, wearing ill-fitting King's-men's coats, barred their passage. Redhand summoned an unshaven one with a pot in his hand. When the man came close, frankly comradely, but shaking his head, Redhand leaned over and took his collar in a strangling grip.

"Goat," he growled, "get your mummers out of my way or I'll ride them down."

He would almost have preferred them not to move.

Their hooves clattered down Kingsgate Alley between the walls of blank-faced, doorless mansions, pierced only far above by round windows. Somewhere above them a shutter clashed shut, echoing off the cool, shadowed stone walls.

Down at the puddly end of the alley was a tiny doorway called Defensible, a jackhole merely in the great curving wall of a rotunda: one of only three ways into the vastness of the Citadel.

The rotunda that Defensible let them into one by one was unimaginably old, crudely but grandly balconied, balustraded, arched and pierced. They said that this rotunda must be all that the Citadel was, once; that it was built up on older, smaller places that had left traces in its walls and doors. They said that the center of its figured stone floor was the exact center of the world; they said that the thousand interlaced pictures that covered the floor, once they were themselves uncovered of centuries of dirt, and explained, would explain all explanations . . . Two bone-white Gray scholars looked up from the space of floor they were methodically cleaning to watch the spurred men go through.

"Where will he be?" Younger asked.

"The King's chambers."

"The King. Has he . . ."

"He'll do nothing. Not yet."

"What will you tell him?"

Redhand tore off his bonnet and shook his thick hair. He pulled off his gloves and slapped them into the bonnet, gave them to Younger.

The doors of the Painted Chamber were surrounded by loafing guards who stood to some kind of attention when Redhand approached. Ignoring them, he hunched his shoulders as though disposing burdens on his back, left Younger and the redjackets at the door and went in, unannounced.

Red Senlin was there, and his two sons. The eldest was called simply Red Senlin's Son; it was he who was intimate with Young Harrah. The other Redhand had not been seen at court; his name was Sennred. At Redhand's entrance the three moved around the small room as though they were counters in some game.

The Painted Chamber had been an attempt of the ancients at gentility, no doubt once very fine; but its pictured battles had long since paled to ghostly wars in a mist, where they had not been swallowed up in gray clouds of mildew. And the odd convention of having everyone, even the stricken bleeding pink guts, smile with teeth made it even more weird, remote, ungentle.

With a short nod to the sons, Redhand extended his hand to his uncle. "Welcome home."

The Great Protector Red Senlin was in this year forty-eight years old. A battle in the Outlands, where he had been King's Lieutenant, had left him one-eyed. A scarf in the Outland fashion covered the dead one; the living was cold gray. His dress was the simplest, stout country leathers long out of fashion and ridiculous on any but the very high.

Redhand's father dressed so. Before him, Redhand wore his City finery self-consciously.

Red Senlin took his hand. "Black Harrah is dead."

"Yes."

"Shot by the Just."

"Yes?"

Red Senlin withdrew his hand. Redhand knew his tone was provoking, and surely no Protector, even against his greatest enemy, would have a hated Gun used—and no one of Red Senlin's generation would have a man slain secretly. "By a Gun, nephew," he said shortly.

"These are unlovely times." Behind him, Senlin's younger son, Sennred, stirred angrily. Redhand paid a smile to the dark, close-faced boy. So different from his tall, handsome older brother, whom nothing seemed to offend—not even the attentions of Black Harrah's son.

Red Senlin mounted the single step to the painted chair and sat. "Black Harrah's estates are vast. Half the Black Downs owes him. His treason forfeits . . . much of them."

"His son . . ."

One gray eye turned to the blond boy leaning with seeming disinterest at the mantel. And back to Redhand.

"Has fled, presumably to join his father's whore and other traitors. Understand me. The King will be at liberty to dispose of much."

It was an old practice, much hated by the lesser landowners and long considered dishonorable: seize the property of one's fallen enemies to pay the friends who struck them. Redhand, after the battle at Senlinsdown, had come into valuable lands that had been Farin the Black's. He chose not to visit them; had made a present of them to Farin's wife and children. But he had kept the title "Great" that the holdings carried. And certain incomes . . . It angered Redhand now more than anything, more than not being consulted at first, more than his father's maundering about the old days, more than the compromise to his oaths to the Blacks, to be so offered a price to make his uncle King.

"The Harrahs and their Black kin will not take it well, your parceling out of their property."

"Let them take it as they must."

"You make a war between Red and Black. And whoever dies in that war, on either side, will be kin to you."

"Life," said Sennred coolly, "is not so dear as our right."

"Your—right." Somehow Sennred reminded him of his brother Younger: that same quick anger, that look as of some secret hurt.

"Must I rehearse all of that again, nephew?" Red Senlin snapped. "Black took the crown by force from King Red's son . . ."

"As you mean to do?"

"My father's father was nearest brother to King Red's son . . ."

"And Black was half-brother to King Ban himself."

"But it was my father's father who in the course of things should have been King!"

"But instead swore oaths to Black."

"Forced oaths, that . . ."

"That he swore. That my grandfather's father swore too. That you and I in turn have sworn to Black's son's son."

"Can be set aside. Your brother Learned could sway the Grays to affirm me in this."

"And forfeit all credence with the world by such deceit?"

"Deceit? I am even now Little Black's heir, in default of heirs of his flesh!"

"You know the Queen is with child."

"By Black Harrah!"

"That matters nothing to the Blacks. They will swear oaths to Little Black's child with one hand on her great belly."

"Cousin." Red Senlin's Son spoke quietly from where he lounged at the mantel. "I think I have heard all this argued before, between my father and yours. The part you take your father took often."

Redhand felt his face grow hot suddenly.

"I don't know," the Son went on lazily. "It all seems of another day to me."

"It means nothing to me either, Defender," Redhand said fiercely. "But there are others . . ."

"It seems to me there are prizes to be won," said the Son, cutting across Redhand more sharply now. "It seems to me that Little Black is a cold pie left over from our ancestors' feasts. My oath to him makes him taste no better to me."

"He is weak-minded," Redhand growled, not sure whether he was accusing or excusing.

"Yes," said Red Senlin's Son. "We are fallen on evil days. The King goes mad, and old oaths no longer bind." He smiled a sweet smile of complicity at Redhand, who looked away. "We are protected only by our strength." He took Redhand's arm in a sudden strong grip. "We will be King. Tell us now whether you support us in this or not."

Redhand regarded the blue, uncaring eyes. Red Senlin might be grown evil, dishonorable, gone sour in repetition of old longings; might, in a passion of vanity, betray old alliances. He might, in his passion, be slain. Might well. But this blue boy was a new thing in the world; he would never lose, because he cared for nothing. And suddenly a dark wave rose under Redhand's heart: he didn't want to be an old man yet, sitting by the fire with his father, shaking his head over the coming of evil days without honor: he wanted suddenly very much to win while he could.

"Since oaths are thrown away," he said, releasing himself from the Son's grip and stepping back to face the three of them, "why, then I won't swear, and I ask no swearing from you. Until I see no further hope in you, I am yours." Red Senlin struck the throne arm triumphantly. "But this I do swear," he went on, raising his arm against them, his voice gravelly with menace. "I am no dog of yours. And if you kick me, I will bite you to the bone."

Later, when Sennred went unasked with the Redhands to the door Defensible, Redhand could almost feel his dark mistrustful eyes.

"If we must do this thing," he said at last when they stood in the ancient rotunda, "we must at least pretend to be friends."

"I don't pretend well."

"Then you must learn." He gestured to the beetling arcades above them. "If you would live here long."

When they had gone, Sennred watched the two Gray scholars working in the long, long shafts of dusty afternoon sun at their patch of floor, dusting with delicate brushes, scraping with fine tools, copying with colored inks what they uncovered.

"A pattern."

"Part of a pattern."

Crowned men with red tears running from their eyes held hands as children's cutouts do, but each twisted in a different attitude, of joy or pain he couldn't tell, for of course they all smiled with teeth. Behind and around them, gripping them like lovers, were black figures, obscure, demons or ghosts. Each crown had burning within it a fire, and the grinning black things tore tongue and organs from this king and with them fed the fire burning in the crown of that one, tore that one's body to feed the fire burning in this one's crown, and so on around, demon and king, like a tortured circle dance.

3

———

"If Barnol wets the Drum with rain," sang Caredd, the Protector Red-hand's wife, "then Caermon brings the Downs the same; if Caermon wets the Downs with rain, the Hub will not be dry till Fain; if Barnol leaves the Drum dry still, then . . . then . . . I forget what then."

"Each week has a name," the Visitor said.

"Each week," she said.

Barnol had wet the Drum with rain, and now, two weeks after, Caermon brought the same to Redsdown. Beyond the wide, open door of the barn, the hills, like folded hands, bare and wooded, marked with fence and harrow-cut, were curtained in silvery downpour. It whispered at the door, it ticked on the sloping roof, entered at chinks and holes, and tocked drop by drop into filling rain barrels. Safe from it in the wide, dim barn, Caredd searched for eggs in the hay that filled an old broken haywain. The Visitor followed, as he had almost continually since Fauconred had brought him there: always polite, even shy, but following anyway everywhere he was allowed, attending to her as a novice would to an ancient Gray.

"Why those names?" he asked. "What do the names mean?"

"I don't know." It was the answer she gave most often to the questions, but never impatiently. Where Fauconred would have thrown up his hands in red-faced exasperation, she merely answered, once again, "I don't know."

Caredd was more than ten years younger than her Protector husband, and seemingly as easy and fair as he was dark and troubled. Redsdown, his property, was her home, had been her father's and his father's father's—he a minor Defender who had married in turn one neighbor's widow and the other's only daughter, and became thereby Protector of wide and lovely holdings. Caredd, riding as soon as she could walk, knew all its mossy woodlands and lakelets, stony uplands and wide grainfields, and loved them as she loved nothing else. She had been few other places, surely, but surely had seen nothing to compare; and she who loved the gray vacancies of the glum fortress-house caught chills in the gray vacancies of her husband's town mansion.

For sure she loved Redhand too, in her fashion. Loved him in part because he had given her her home as a wedding gift when it seemed nearly lost. Her father and brother had been ambushed on a forest road by the Just, robbed and murdered; her weak-minded mother had flirted with one malcontent Red lord after another until she had been nearly tried for treason, and her estates—beloved Redsdown—had been declared forfeit to the King: thus to Black Harrah, in fact.

And then Redhand had come. Grave, dour almost, unfailingly polite, he had wooed the disoriented, frightened tomboy with rich gifts and impatient, one-sided interviews, explaining his power at court, her mother's jeopardy—till, in a stroke of grownup wisdom, she had seen that her advantage—thus her heart—lay with him.

So there had been held in the rambling castle a grand Redhand wedding.

Of that day she remembered disjunct moments only, like tatters of a vivid dream; remembered waiting in the tiny dark vestibule before the great hall for their cue to enter, pressed tight against him, surrounded protectively by his mother, his brothers, his sweating father, how she had felt at once safe and frightened, implicated yet remote; how Mother Redhand laughed, horns called from within, butlers whispered urgently from the narrow door, and how with a full rustle of many gowns the bright knot of them had unwound into the thronged hall hung with new red banners and filled with the resinous hum of many instruments.

She remembered how the guests had dusted them with salt and wound paper thorns around their wrists, and laughed though it meant suffering would come and must be endured; and how the country people gave them candied eggs for their pillow. And she remembered when later they had taken down her hair and taken away her cloudlike gown and she had stood shyly naked before him beneath a shadow of pale lace . . .

He had stayed long enough to meet and confuse the names and faces of his new tenants, Folk she knew as dearer than relatives; and he had ridden off, to court, to battle, to his other growing properties. Except for a fidgety week or two in summer, a politic ball at Yearend, he came to Redsdown little. Sometimes she felt it might be the better way. Sometimes.

She left one speckled egg from her basketful in a dark corner for the barn elf she knew lived there. She plucked a bit of straw from her autumn-auburn hair and let the Visitor take her basket. Stone steps worn to smooth curves took them out an arched side door into a breezeway that led to the kitchen; the leaves of its black vines were already gone purple with autumn, and the rain swept across its flagged path in gusts, sticking Caredd's billowing trousers to her flank. The Visitor tried clumsily to cover her with the old cloak he still wore, but she shook him off, ran tiptoe laughing through the puddles and up the kitchen stairs, brushing the clean rain from her cheeks, laughing at the Visitor making his careful, intent way toward her.

There were great rooms at Redsdown, chill halls lined with stiff-backed benches, tree-pillared places with fireplaces large as cottages, formal rooms hung with rugs and smelling of mildew. But when there was no one to entertain, nothing to uphold, Caredd and the rest stayed in the long, smoke-blackened kitchen with the Folk. There, there were four fireplaces hung with spits, hooks and potchains, with high-backed settles near and chimney corners always warm; there were thick tables worn so the smooth grain stood out, piled high with autumn roots to be strung or netted and hung from the black beams above. The rain tapped and cried at the deep small windows but couldn't come in.

Two ancient widows sat making thread in a corner, one of them meanwhile rocking ever with her naked foot a bagcradle hung there in the warmth. "If Barnol wets the Drum with rain," they sang, "then Caermon brings the Downs the same . . ."

"Rain indeed," said the Defender Fauconred from within his settle. He dipped a wooden ladle into a kettle steaming on the hob and refreshed his cup. "And when will it stop, ladies?"

"Could be tonight, Defender," said one, turning her distaff.

"Could be tomorrow," said the other, turning hers.

"Could turn to snow."

"Could continue wet."

Fauconred grunted and filled the cup of Mother Caredd, who took it with a slow, abstracted graciousness, set it on the settle-arm, and began to put up her cloudy white hair with many bone pins. It seemed that Mother Caredd's hair always needed putting up; Caredd rarely saw her but she was piling up, endlessly, patiently, its never-cut length.

"Now you see, Visitor," she said absently, "those are rainy-sounding names for weeks, is all; Barnol and Caermon, Haspen and Shen . . . as Doth is dry and Finn is cold . . ."

"I wondered about their origin," the Visitor said. He sat next to Caredd, looking from one speaker to the next as though in a schoolroom, teacher or pupil or both. Mother Caredd had no more lesson to say, and shrugged and smiled. The unhappy end of her playing at politics had left her vaguer even than she had always been, but also somehow calmer, more lovely, and gently accepting; where the Visitor disturbed and perplexed Fauconred, and fascinated Caredd, Mother Caredd just smiled at him, as though his dropping from heaven were the most natural of things.

"For any real answers," Caredd said, "you'll have to go to the Grays, in the end. For all old knowledge."

"They know?"

"They say they know. Help me here." She was trying with her long patient fingers to restring an old carved instrument.

"They say," Mother Caredd went on as though to herself, "that all the Just have names for their names. Is that so? Naming their names, and why . . . Their Guns have names too, all of them, don't they? I wonder if the Guns' names have names, and so on and on . . ."

"I don't know, Mother," Caredd said, laughing. "Could they remember all that?"

"I couldn't. But I wouldn't want to, would I?"

Caredd loved her mother fiercely, and though she allowed herself to smile at her rambling chatter, she let none mock her, and would die to keep her from being hurt again.

"The Just," the Visitor said, nodding; these he knew; but after a moment asked: "Who are they? How would I know them?"

"Murderers," Caredd answered simply. "These keys are warped."

"Bandits, as I told you," Fauconred said, frowning into his cup. "The men without law or honor; the women whores."

"Madmen," said Mother Caredd.

"Why Just, then?" the Visitor asked Caredd.

"A name from longer ago than anyone remembers. Perhaps once the name had a meaning. It's said they're dreamers." She plucked a dampened note. "Nightmare dreamers."

"Old names persist," Fauconred said. "Like Protector, Defender. Protectors and Defenders of the Folk, anciently."

"Protectors of the Folk against . . ."

Fauconred knitted his gray brows. "Why, against the Just, I suppose."

Caredd strummed a tuneless tune and put down the ancient instrument. The two widows went on spinning their eternal thread. "If it snows on Yearend Day," they sang, "then snow and rain will fall till Fain/Brings the New Year round again . . ."

By evening, the rain had blown away toward the City, leaving only a rent sash of clouds for the sun to color as it set. To watch, Caredd had climbed a hundred stairs to the long, fanged battlement that guarded Redsdown's Outward side, and then up between two broken castellations to where she knew of a flat, private place to sit. On the tower behind her, two forked banners, sunset-red, snapped tirelessly in rhythm with her own heavy cloak's blowing. She pulled it tighter around her, drew her knees up, wondered what Redhand was about tonight . . . There was a polite, introductory sort of noise on the battlement below. Caredd smiled down at the tireless Visitor.

"Even here?" she asked. "Those steps are long."

"I'm sorry," said the Visitor. "I'll go back."

"No. Stay. Better to talk to you than . . . Stay."

"I was wondering," he began, and Caredd laughed. He put his head down and went on carefully. "Wondering why no one of the Folk will talk with me." He had gone about the farms with Caredd, watching her stop everywhere to hug and talk and fondle babies, be cooed over herself by old ones who treated her as something between a cherished pet and a princess. But their happy chatter had ceased before him, turned to a cool reserve; he had never had any yield him anything but a nod and a wary, almost frightened smile.

"They think you are a creature of the Grays," Caredd said simply.

"A . . . creature?"

"Of old, the Grays could make combatants against the Seven Possessors. Creatures not anything but one of the Seven Strengths. The Folk have a thousand stories about such things, battles of the Seven Possessors against the Seven Strengths. Moral stories, you know; Gray knowledge or teaching made into a story about a battle. The Folk take them for real, the Sevens, real enough to see with eyes and touch."

"But the Gray in the village—he's just as afraid of me."

Caredd laughed again. "Old Driggory? He's afraid that you might have been sent to do battle against his own Possessor, the one named Blem." The Visitor looked puzzled. "Drunkenness. A good old man Driggory is, but a simple country clerk; he'd hardly know what the great Grays are capable of. Because it's from him, you see, and all his cousins, the village clerks and little Grays, that the Folk have learned their tales of the Sevens, from long ago."

The Visitor shook his head. "I wanted to talk with them. How can I explain I am no creature of the Grays?"

Caredd looked down at the strange personage below her, who looked up with his infinite blank eyes. Indeed, if there were Gray champions of the Right, they might look like this: or then Demons too. "Whose creature are you?" she asked.

The Deep had drunk the sun once more, and though the clouds Outward weren't yet drained of all color, the sky above had been swept clean of cloud, and on that blue-black ceiling already burned three of the Wanderers, pink, gold and red, all decrescent. "I can't remember," the Visitor said, as though for the first time.

"Perhaps," said Caredd, "you are no Strength, but Possessed; and the Possessor has eaten your memory and made your hair fall out. The Possessor Blem can do that; they show it in the pageants at Yearend." She was a wind-blown silhouette in the crack of battlement, and the Visitor couldn't see her little mocking smile.

"And if I am?" said the Visitor. "I don't think I am, but if I am?"

"If you are," Caredd said thoughtfully. "Well. I wouldn't know what then, and neither would Driggory. You'd have to go to Inviolable and ask."

"Inviolable?"

"The Grays' house in the mountains. Or"—a sudden thought that made her smile again—"wait till Fauconred takes you to my husband. His brother is a great Gray, oh very high." She would like to see Learned's unstirrable face, when this creature asked wisdom of him.

The Visitor turned his bald face to the deep sky he knew had made him. Had made him for—somewhere within him some formed thing tried to coalesce: a reason, a direction, the proper question, the name uncoded. He stood stock-still and watched it light up fitfully the structured regularity of his manufacture . . . and then dissolve as quickly into blank unknowing again.

"Very well," he said, when he was sure it was gone. "I'll wait, then. A little longer."

Learned Redhand was not particularly learned, though he was for sure Redhand. His family name had hardly hindered his quick rise through many degrees to the gray he wore, dark as rainclouds about to break; but still, it was due as much to his own efforts, to his subtlety if not depth of mind, to his unflappable grace of manner. Despite a certain cynicism in him, a smiling disregard for the dogmas of his Order that unsettled people, he had a deep affection for the elaborate systems, framed in ritual as though in antique, lustrous wood, that had taken the Grays countless centuries to create. But he had little interest in mastering those systems in all their complexity; was content to float on the deep stream of Gray knowledge, trailing one finger, buoyed by the immunity a Gray's unarmed strength gave him in the violent world of the court.

He did love without reservation, though, the house Inviolable, where he had first put on white linen, where he had grown up in the Grays and gained whatever wisdom he possessed. He loved the mountain that Inviolable had held since before any but they could remember, that looked down on the far-off City and Outward to the Downs, surrounded by the sounds and silence of sweet rocky woods. And he loved above all the ancient garden closed within its walls. Tended and nursed over centuries, its shadowed groves, vined walls, and sudden fountains had become a system of private places, singular yet unified, like states of mind.

The year was late now in the garden, that was its mood. The dark groves were mostly unleaved, and the intersecting paths were deep-strewn with black and brown. The air was clear and windy; the wind gathered leaves and the voices of distant boys at play, blew rippling waves through the coppery ivy, white-flecked the many fountains with foam.

How cold it must be now on the Drum, Learned Redhand thought, when even these fountains are blown black and gray . . . It had been some years now since he had had need to come back to Inviolable, and as he waited now in the garden for the interview he had asked for, he felt himself given over to an unaccustomed sweet nostalgia, a multiple sense of self and season, composed like a complex harmony out of the afternoon, the garden, the fountains—and himself, a boy, a man, in this same season but other years, with other selves in the same skin. It made him feel unreal, rich yet illusory.

The narrow, flinty archway that led into Inviolable from the garden, high as ten men, had neither door nor gate, only a great black drape of some ancient, everlasting stuff, so heavy that the restless air could barely lift it; it rose a bit and fell with a low solemn snap of one edge, filled again with breath and exhaled slowly. Learned watched go in and out of this door young scholars and country clerks in bone-white robes; smoky-gray lawyers and iron-gray lesser judges followed by white-robed boys carrying writing cases; thunder-gray court ministers and chamberlains with their lay petitioners . . . And then he stood as one came out, diminutive, and smaller still with age, in gray indistinguishable from black and little different from an old widow's black cowl, unaccompanied save for a thick cane. They stood aside on the steps for this shabby one, who nodded smiling side to side. Learned Redhand rose, but was waved away when he offered help; he made a graceful obeisance instead. The old, old Arbiter of all right and wrong, the grayest of all Grays, sat down on Learned's bench with care.

"It's not too cold, here in the garden?" Learned Redhand inquired.

"No, Learned, if you be brief." There was little about the Arbiter Mariadn that revealed gender, except the voice; all else had grown sexless with great age, but the voice somehow was still the young Downs farm girl she had been sixty years ago. "But before we speak, you must remove that." Her index, slim as bone, pointed to the bit of red ribbon Learned Redhand wore.

He knew better than to fence with the Arbiter. As though it were his own idea, he detached it and pocketed it even as he spoke: "I come to ask you to clarify for me a bit of ancient history," he said.

"You were ever nice in talk, Redhand," Mariadn said. "Be plainer.

Your faction—I'm sorry, your family's faction—wishes the oath sworn to the Blacks set aside."

"The Protectorate wish it."

"Yes?"

"It's complex," Learned said thoughtfully, as though considering the merits of the argument. "By all the old laws of inheritance, it seems Red Senlin's grandfather should have been King. In acknowledgment of those claims, he was named heir to Little Black. Now the Black faction seems ready to discredit the claim on the grounds that the Queen is with child, though none believes the King capable of such a thing after ten barren years of marriage. The Reds seem ready to force Red Senlin's claim, and crown him now in repayment for the Blacks' reneging."

"As a matter of principle, I suppose," said the Arbiter coolly. "Just to set the record straight."

Learned Redhand smiled. "Arbiter, there is doubtless much to be won. Little Black's reign has been long and dishonorable. The Red Protectorate suffered much from Black Harrah's ministry; I think they surely wish revenge. No. Not a matter of principle. The reverse."

"And they come then beforehand to have their hands washed at our fountain. Why should we be muddied by their revenge?"

Learned paused, looking into a pale, slate-colored agate he wore on one finger. The expert at circumlocution must first have his matter clear to himself: but when it was clear, he found no pretty way to say it. "Arbiter: Red Senlin means to be King. Many of the great support him in this. Even to war with the Queen. They wish their enterprise sanctioned by the Grays."

"And if we cannot sanction it? They must not ask for arbitration, Learned, unless they mean to abide by it."

"That's the hardest thing." He turned and turned the stone on his forefinger. "I needn't preach to you that the strong chain of oaths seems barely a thread in these bad times. But I feel sure that if the Grays decide against Red Senlin, the Reds . . . will lose adherents, yes. Will lose credence in the eyes of the Folk. Will give pretexts even to the Just, who grow strong lately. But will proceed, anyway."

Too old in judgment to be indignant, Mariadn considered, her eyes closed. "And will perhaps then be beaten by the Queen, and all hanged, and their sin made plain."

"Perhaps. But I think not. Black Harrah is dead. And the Great Protector Redhand and all his adherents are with Red Senlin."

"Dindred possesses them," the Arbiter said quietly. "Pride is their master, and what Strength can be called against him?"

"Arbiter," said Learned Redhand more urgently, "the question of succession is surely doubtful. It could be settled reasonably two ways; surely there is much in law to be said for the Senlin claim. But consider further the Order we owe. I think Red Senlin, without our help, has even chances of doing this thing. With a Gray word behind him, the thing is nearly certain. If he has our judgment and wins, we are the stronger for it. If without our judgment, then our judgment will have little power hence."

"The power of our judgment is in its Righteousness."

"Yes. Of old. And we must take care for that power. It is threatened. The Just speak Leviathan's name in the villages this year again. If the Protectorate act in disregard of us, then . . . then oaths far older than the Protectorate's to Little Black's kin are weakened, and begin to pass away."

The Arbiter Mariadn covered her old eyes with the long fingers of one hand. Only her finely lined mouth was visible; her voice held Learned Redhand like the gentlest of vices. "Learned. I am old. I see few visitors. Perhaps I can't any longer grasp the world's complexities: no, not these new heresies, I hate and fear them, so I am not qualified to speak. I must lean on you, on your worldliness, which I partly fear too . . . Only swear to me now, Learned, on all the ancient holy things there are, that what you advise you advise out of love and care for our Order. For our Order only."

"I do so swear," Learned said without hesitation. Mariadn breathed a little sigh, rose and took up her cane. She started slowly back toward the black-hung doorway into Inviolable.

"So," she said, not looking back. "It shall be as you advise, if I can sway others. And perhaps, after all, it's . . . only a little sin. Perhaps."

Learned Redhand sat a long time after she had gone, in the gathering evening, watching black leaves fall and float in the restless pool of the fountain. He should be in his carriage, taking news of his success to the Harbor: but it was success he suddenly felt little desire to announce.

Strange, he thought; she and he had talked so much of the new, oath-breaking way of the world, and yet when he swore to her, she accepted it unhesitatingly. It was inconceivable to her that he, a Gray, in no matter how disastrous a day, could swear falsely.

Perhaps indeed he hadn't. Without the Grays, Learned Redhand would be someone else's younger brother, nothing more, the Grays' strength and health were his. In any case, soon or late, there would be a testing of that oath, a reckoning. He wondered how he would bear.

He rose to go. The autumn evening had grown dense; the great age of the garden seemed to him suddenly palpable, and deeply melancholy.

Haspensweek Eve, and suddenly cold even in the City in its cup of mountains. That night they moved King Little Black from the Citadel to an old Black mansion, long shuttered, that sat inaccessible on a finger of rock, called Sping, just outside the High City gates.

For it had been decided, in a Whole-meeting of the Protectorate, that Red Senlin was Little Black's heir, and Viceroy too in times of the King's madness. The Black lords, of course, had stayed away from the meeting; so had many others. And even the Reds and Folk ombudsmen who had come, mostly dependents of Senlin's and Redhand's, were so glum and silent that Red Senlin had ended his brief screaming insults and arguments, his shouts echoing in the near-empty rotunda. No matter; It had been decided.

The small cavalcade, shielded by armed men, moved through the shadowed dark of the thousand-faced street. It had been decided that the King was indeed in his madness now, and for sure looked at least sickly and weak. He huddled on his nag, folded up in an old black cloak, and looked apprehensively from the silent crowd to the gleam of axes and spears, the smoky, flaring torches of his escort.

The Viceroy Red Senlin rode with his golden Son. It had been decided that the Son and his younger brother, dark Sennred, with a number of adherents, should ride toward Senlinsdown and rally there all the Protector's friends. Young Harrah, the Viceroy had learned, had gone off in quite another direction, toward the Black Downs and the Queen.

Redhand rode on the King's right side; on his left rode Redhand's father, Old Redhand. Around Old Redhand's neck hung an ancient chain, giltwork once, now worn again to the naked iron, that had ever been the sign of the chiefest of the vast Redhand clan. From this old chain hung now something new: the great carved beryl that is the City's seal, borne by the King's lieutenant, Master of the City—until recently, Black Harrah.

It had been decided that the family Redhand should inherit that rich honor.

It had been more than deference in Redhand that had insisted that not he but his father be given the City seal. Redhand knew that war with the Queen would come quick as anger, and he had hoped that the City seal would keep his father safe in the City while he and Red Senlin acted out the treasonous show they had trumped up together against the old man's wishes. But it hadn't worked. It had been instead decided—by Old Redhand, decided with all his remaining strength and will—that in case of sudden need the seal would devolve upon his son, and he, Old Redhand, would take command of the Redhand arms. He wasn't too old to fight for his friend.

Redhand tried to keep his eyes on the street, on the King, on the faces of the crowd—but they were drawn by his father's face. It was a face marked like a cliffside by wind and time, harder than his steel, and not softened by the halo of sparse hair he wore in the old fashion cropped close around his ears. His eyes, unlike his son's, were drawn to nothing, but looked ahead, farther than the end of the street or the end of the world.

When they passed through Farinsgate and out onto the Heights outside the City walls, the crowd became thinner. It wasn't a time for High City people to be outside their gates. The great mansions of this side, Farin's House, Blackharbor, were dark; only one house was lit, there, at the causeway's end, on the rock Spring, lit by the torches and watchfires of those assigned to guard close forever the little King.

Suddenly Old Redhand stopped his horse. Someone was pushing his way into the ranks ahead; the Viceroy Red Senlin leaned out to hear his news. A murmur went up from the armed men. Someone whispered to the King, and a pale smile grew on his face. Younger worked his horse to Redhand's side and told him the news.

The Queen had gathered an army on the Drumskin. She had turned Inward, had ceased to flee since none pursued, and unless a large force met her soon there was nothing to prevent her laying siege to the City itself. It hadn't happened in time out of mind. The Queen, seemingly, intended it.

Old Redhand, with only half a glance at his son, spurred forward to where Red Senlin summoned him.

It meant battle, and there was much to decide.

4

All day since before chill dawn the red-jacketed riders with their striped packs had come down the water-stairs toward the lake, guiding their mounts along the horse ramps. Shouted orders carried far in the still, cold air; captains perspired despite the frost steaming from their bellowing mouths. Great straining pulleys lowered painted wagons toward the ferries; horses reared and laughed; harried ostlers attempted to count off from lists, screaming at the watermen, whom no fee could hurry.

The girl had pulled and hauled since morning, somehow intensely elated by the first winey wrong-way breezes of the year; now the hard sunlight cast unaccustomed glitter on the stirred waters and heated her shorn blond head. She laughed out loud to see them struggle with their war there on the bank. Her laugh was lost in the uproar; whips snapped, and the oxen on the far bank lowed in misery as they began to turn the creaking winches once again.

Soldiers sitting atop piled bundles above her called down pleasant obscenities as she pushed to the forward end of the laden barge. She climbed up a crate that had Redhand's open-palm sign on it in new red paint, and, shielding her eyes, looked up to where the four tongues of bridges came out of the High City's gate-mouths. She thought probably there, at the gate called Goforth, the generals would come out—yes, there, for now, as she looked, their banners all burst forth from the Citadel onto the bridge-stairs, as though a giant had blown out from the gate a handful of petals. She couldn't see faces, but for sure they must be there, for there was Redhand's open palm, and the dried-blood red of Senlin marked with ancient words; the soldiers and the City cheered them, and she cheered too, laughing at the thought that the bridge might break under their great weight of pride and drop them, leaving their banners only, light as wind.

Something colder than his cold armor took hold on Redhand's heart, there where he stood among the gay flags with his brother Younger. Through Goforth his father, Old Redhand, with harsh pulls at the reins, forced his warhorse Dark Night. Through the cloud of banners before the gate, through the ribboned throng of riders, hearing no salutations, up to where his sons stood.

"Is our House all here?" he said, and then said again, over the great-throated war viols' endless chants.

"Yes," Redhand answered him. "Father . . ."

"Then give me the baton."

So many things, hurtful or too grownup for the child, had Redhand ever given up to his father: but never with such black presage, too cold for anger, as now when he lifted the slim general's stick to his father's outstretched hand.

"You can still stay," he growled. Both their hands held the baton. "Stay and see to the City . . ."

"You see to it," his father said. "Give it to me."

Redhand released it; Old Redhand tucked it into his sash and leaned out toward Younger, whose look clung desperately to his father's face. Old Redhand pulled Younger to him with a mailed hand, kissed him. He kissed him again, slapped his cheek lightly without word or smile. Turned away and tore from his old neck the Redhand chain with the City seal hung from it.

"Senlin!" he called out in a voice not his own. Red Senlin stood in his stirrups and waved to him. "Would you be *King*?" Red Senlin drew his

sword, pointed Outward. Old Redhand turned to Redhand his son. He
tossed him the chain. "Take care," he said. "Watch well."

Too proud to dismount to cross the two generals walked their heavy
steeds with infinite care over the swaying bridge. Redhand watched their
exertions till he could bear no more, and ran, his heart full, up the stairs,
through Goforth, into the silent City that the chain he held made him
master of.

That evening the first light snow was dusting Redsdown, blown in from
the Drum. From a window in the high headland tower that marked Redsdown's edge, Caredd and her mother watched the Protectors' horses, and
Fauconred and his redjackets, and the horsegatherers, and the Visitor too,
gather on the rutted road toward the mountains and the far-off City. They
were dim in the gusts of fine blown snow; there was the Visitor in his
brown Endwife's cloak. The horsegatherers flicked their lashes, and the
company unwound, their sharp hooves loud on the new-frozen ground.

"See how he drives them," Mother Caredd said.

"Fauconred?" Caredd asked.

"Yes, he is driven too."

"Who drives them, Mother?"

"Why, Rizna, Daughter," said her mother. "Surely you see him there,
so tall, with his black eye sockets, and the sickle hung on his neck . . .
See how he makes them step along!"

"Mother . . ."

"Like some great raggedy shepherd driving silly sheep . . . What
great steps he takes!"

"Mother, there's no such thing there." Yet she looked hard, holding
her throat where the blood beat.

"Why does he drive them, where, for what? See them look back, and
then ride on for fear . . ."

"There's nothing there, Mother! Stop!" She strained to see the caravan, strung out along the road; they were shadows already, and then
disappeared in a mist of blown snow. Mother Caredd began to put up her
hair with many bone pins . . .

If snow fell heavily in the mountains as they went up the high road
Cityward, they would be delayed till long after Yearend, holed up in some
bleak lodge or pilgrim house of the Grays, and Fauconred didn't want

that at all. He hurried as fast as he could through the black, leafless forest, had men ride ahead and behind to watch for the Just: these mountains were their castles and cities, they knew the rocky highlands and had a name for every thick ravine, could appear and disappear in them like the dream faces Fauconred saw in the knotted treeboles. He harried his riders till he was hoarse with it, and would have pushed them on through the nights, if he hadn't feared breaking some valued leg or his own neck in the dark even more than he feared the sounds and silence beyond the vague, smoky hole his campfires made.

He told himself, he told his men, that what made him afraid was ambush, the Guns of the Just. But the horsegatherers, Drumskin men, had their own tales of these mountain forests, and told them endlessly around the fire: stories of the Hollowed. "My grandfather's half-brother was taking horses to the City once, on this same road, and saw a thing, about dawn, running along beside the road, in the trees, making no sound, a thing—a thing as fearful as if you saw a great hooded cloak stand up and walk with no one in it, my grandfather's half-brother said . . ." The Hollowed, they said, were the bodies of the Possessors, abandoned by the Possessors themselves to their own malignant dead wanderings when the Strengths had driven the Possessors from the homeplaces of men into the Deep. Here the bodies wandered, Hollowed, unable to rest, empty cups still holding the dregs of poison, drinking up what souls they could seize on to sustain them, insect, animal, man.

Most days now they could see, far and dim, higher than any reaching crag, Inviolable in its high seat, placid and strong; even thought they heard, one cold still day, its low bells ring. But then they turned a twisting mile down the valley, between two high naked rocks men called the Knees, and the weather grew enough warmer to raise thick, bitter fogs; Inviolable was lost. By dawn on Lowday, the day before Yearend, the day of the Possessors' Eve, they were deep in the river Wanderer's rocky home.

Somewhere below their narrow way, Wanderer chased herself noisily through her halls, echoing in flumes and gorges, spitting at cave-mouths; but they could see nothing of her, for her breath was white and dense almost as haysmoke, and cold as Finn.

Fauconred wouldn't stop. It was baffling and frightening to try to pass this way in a fog, and hurry too, with the river's roar filling up your head; but it was worse to stop, so that the horses, stuck on a ledge, might panic and leap. It took all his strength and lungs to force them further down, to where at last the high wall beside them broke and a pass led down away, high-sided, obscure, but a pass: the Throat they called it, and it spoke with Wanderer's great voice even as it swallowed them. The Throat took away their own voices too, when they were inside it, amplified them in a weird way, so that every man who spoke looked behind him with a start for the source of his own words.

It was the Visitor, whose ears had proved sharp as a dog's, who first heard the other horsemen in the pass.

"It's only the Throat," Fauconred said, "our own hooves echoing."

"No. Make them stop, and listen. Down there, coming up."

Fauconred tried to read an imagining fear in the Visitor's face, but there was only attention. The fear was his own. He shouted a halt, and the horsegatherers sang out to still the herd. Then they waited for their own echoes to cease.

It was there, the noise of someone somewhere. The Visitor said ahead, Fauconred said behind, the horsegatherers and guard stared wildly here and there, their panic spreading to the horses and confusing every ear. Mist drawn into the Throat went by in ragged cloaks to hide and then reveal them to each other. And then they saw, far down the Throat, gray shapes moving at a mad pace toward them, gesticulating, pale as smoke.

A rasp of steel unsheathing. Fauconred knew that if they were men, they must be charged, hard, for he could not be forced back through the Throat and live. If they were not men . . . He shouted his redjackets forward and charged hard, hoping they dared follow.

The pale riders drew closer, coalescing out of fog and thunder of hooves. For sure they were men, yes, living men—were—were a war party, arms drawn, were a Red party—Redhand! "Redhand!" he shouted, and twisted his mount hard. They nearly collided. Fauconred just managed to keep his riders from tangling with his master's. He turned to laugh with Redhand out of relief, and looked into his face, a gray, frightening mask, eyes wide and mad. "Redhand . . ." He seemed a man, yet as Fauconred watched him stare around him unseeing, drawn sword clutched tight, he felt a chill of fear: Hollowed . . . some dream shape they could take . . .

The form Redhand spoke. "Turn your men." The harsh voice was an exhausted croak, expressionless. "Make for the Outward road."

Fauconred saw the iron chain of the Redhands hung on his neck. "What's happened?"

"War with the Queen."

"Red Senlin . . ."

"Slain. Slain before Forgetful . . . Why don't you turn?" he asked without inflection. Someone came up suddenly beside Fauconred, and Redhand flung out his sword arm with a cry: "Who is it . . . what . . ."

"The one I sent to tell you of. The . . . Visitor."

"Keep him for right's sake from me! . . ." The Visitor drew back, but Redhand's wide eyes still fixed him. Fauconred thought to speak, did not. There was a moment of freak silence in the Throat, and Redhand burst into strange, racking sobs.

He hadn't slept in days, had pressed every man he could into service, had flung them through the forest without mercy, once turning rebellious laggards at sword-point . . . Fauconred, taking command reluctantly, coaxed them all back through the Throat the way Redhand had come, had camp made and a precious cask broached, that calmed anger and fear both: and while Blem had his say, Drink-up, Sleep-fast, No-tomorrow, Fauconred drew from his master the tale, in words drunk with weariness and grief.

The Queen had led the Red army a quickwing chase across the plains toward the barren Drumsedge, Red Senlin desperately trying to cut her off from the Inward roads and her Outward strength both, until, weary with chase and no battle, he had made for Forgetful, watch castle of the Edge, where the garrison owed him. They had reached it Finnsweek Eve. They struck a truce with the Queen to last over Yearend. And then some of Red Senlin's men had been out foraging and been attacked by a marauding party of the enemy. Old Redhand and Red Senlin had issued from the castle to help—and been boxed by the mass of the Queen's army, who had thus drawn them out.

Red Senlin was among the first killed. Old Redhand had been killed or captured, none knew, none could tell him . . .

For two days Redhand had stayed in the Harbor in an agony of fear. And then another messenger arrived, a boy gaunt with cold and hunger, the red palm sign on his shoulder.

Old Redhand had been captured in the battle and imprisoned in Forgetful's belly where the day before he had been guest. Next day in the first light the boy watched them take him out into the courtyard, where snow fell; and a bastard son of Farin the Black chopped off his head with a sword.

The boy had fled then. He knew only that Young Harrah would be master at Forgetful, and that the Queen came Inward, behind him, with her army.

"They will be at the margin of the Downs tomorrow," Redhand said. "Red Senlin's Son is marching from Senlinsdown to stop her; we must go on, we must march before night . . ." He tried to rise, but Fauconred restrained him gently.

"Sleep," he said. "Sleep awhile."

Redhand slept.

They made a crown for Red Senlin of paper, and put it on his head; put the head on a pole and carried it before them as they streamed Inward across the Drum. Old Redhand they left in the courtyard of Forgetful where Young Harrah, its master now, could bury him or not, as he chose; but Red Senlin went before the Queen's army.

The immense, dull armor the Queen had had made for herself, wide-winged and endlessly riveted, crossed with chains and bristling with points, would have seemed comical if it hadn't first seemed so cruel. It took a great laborer of a stallion to bear both it and the Queen; her captain had paid high for it after she had ridden to death the strong black she had fled on. Beneath her visor, above the heavy veil she wore against the cold, her eyes, lampblack-soft and dark, made it seem that somewhere amid the massive flesh and unyielding armor a beautiful woman was held captive. It had been, at times, a useful illusion.

It had been Black Harrah who, ten years before, partly as a useful diplomacy, partly as a tool for his own use, and partly as a joke on the tiny weak-headed King, had brought back from the fastness of the Outlands the hulking, black-eyed girl, chieftain's daughter in a thousand brass spangles. Her bride-price, her own vast weight in precious metals, had made her father a rich man indeed.

And now Black Harrah is dead, slain she is sure by the Reds; and she, from ceaseless chase and fight, has miscarried his child in anguish: though none yet knows it. So at sunset near the Little Lake, those dark eyes look out on a thin line of Red horse and foot, Redhand's, Red

Senlin's Son's; she thinks of them slain, and her armed feet in their blood.

Her enemies had come together at the crossroads beyond Senlins-down. There they made a crown for Red Senlin's Son, a circle of gold riveted to his helmet, and Redhand put it on his head, and their two armies made a cheer muffled in Drumwind and cold; and they mounted again and rode for the Little Lake. At sunset they flew down the Harran road through the still, white Downs, Redhand's fast horsemen the van-guard, and Red Senlin's younger son Sennred fierce with grief. Lights were being lit in the last few cottages snowed in amid the folded land; sheep stamped and steamed, and ran huddling quick to their byres as they passed.

They came down between the milestones onto the frozen Drum again as the sun began to move into the smoky Deep ahead; the Queen, expect-ing them, had drawn up in the crisp snow before the Little Lake, and set her trophy there. When his sons see it, it is a week frozen, the flesh picked at by wind, the jaw fallen away.

They look toward each other there, and the scouts and captains point out which is which. The Queen on her stallion. Kyr, her cold Outland chief. Red Senlin's Son, tallest of his army. There, by the Dog banner, Sennred small and bent. Redhand—yes, she knows Redhand. Red Sen-lin's Son looks for someone, some banner, doesn't find it. They look a long time. The last sun makes them pieces in a game: the Queen's a black silhouette army, the King Red Senlin's Son's touched with crimson. They turn away.

The game is set. The first moves come at dawn.

How the word moved, that brought to a wind-licked flat above the battle plain so many of the brown sisterhood, the Endwives, none knows but they. But they have come; in the morning they are there, they have walked through the night or driven their two-wheeled carts or long tent-wagons; and they have come in numbers. For as long as any alive remem-bers, war with the Just has been harry and feint, chase and evade, search and skirmish, and tangle only at the last bitter moment. Now the End-wives look down through the misty dawn at two armies, Protectors and Defenders and all their banners, hundreds to a side, flanked by snow-bound cavalry, pushing through the drifts toward each other as though to all embrace.

"Who is that so huge on a cart horse, sister?"

"The Queen. Her enemy's head is her standard. See how she comes to the front . . ."

Redhand would not have the Visitor near him. Fauconred, knowing nothing better to do, has sent him to the Endwives to help. He stands with them, watching, listening.

"It'll snow again soon. It's darker now than at dawn."

"The wind blows toward the Queen."

"Whose is the Dog banner? They fall back from him."

"Sennred, the new King's stoop-shouldered brother . . . Ay, the murder they make."

Toward noon the snow does begin; the wind is Outward, blowing toward the Queen, who must fall back. The shifting line of their embrace wavers, moves toward the lake, then away, then closer; then the Queen's ranks part, here, there, and many are forced into the black water. If she had hoped fear of that frozen lake would keep her army from breaking, she was wrong; it looks a cruel gamble to the sisters; but then the wind and snow darken the field, put out the sun, and the Endwives listen, silent, to screams, cries, and the clash of metal so continuous as to be a steady whisper, drowned out when the wind cries or the Drum speaks with horse-sortie.

"Feed the fires, sisters. Keep torches dry. They make a long night for us here."

"Fall back!" And they do fall back, released from the maelstrom by his harsh croak, echoed by his captains; only Sennred and his wing hesitate, Sennred still eager. But they fall back.

"Regroup!" They force their panting mounts into a semblance of order behind him, the twisting hooves throwing up great clots of muddy snow. His red-palm banner is obscure in the snowy dark; but they see his snow-washed sword. His arm feels like an arm of stone: that numb, that obdurate. "Now on! Strike! Fall on them there!" and the force, in a churning, swirling storm of mud, beat the Drum.

He is outpaced by Sennred, is cut off by a flanking movement of near-spent horse, the stone arm flails with a stone will of its own; he can hear nothing but a great roar and the screaming of his own breath. Then the Black horses part, shattered, and fall away. The tireless snowstorm parts also, and the field grows for a moment ghastly bright, and he sees, amid the broken, fleeing Black cavalry, the Queen, shuffling away on her big horse, slim sword in her great mailed hand.

He shouts forward whoever is around him; the sight of her lashes through him, an icy restorative. Horror and hate, he would smash her like a great bug if he could. He flings from his path with a kind of joy some household people of hers, sees her glance back at him and his men, sees her urge the horse into a massive trot: does not see, in his single purpose, her man Kyr and his Outland spear racing for him. Someone shouts behind him; he wheels, suddenly breathless with the shock of collision; his horse screams under him, for the stone arm with its own eye has seen and struck, throwing the spear's point into his horse's breast. She leaps, turns in air spurting blood, catapulting Kyr away by the spear driven in her, falls, is overrun by Kyr's maddened horse, whose hooves trample her screaming head, trample her master, Redhand. He is kicked free, falls face down. His flung sword, plunged in mud, waves, trembles, is still. Redhand is still.

Blood frozen quickly stays as bright as when shed.

The Endwives, intent as carrion birds, move among the fallen, choosing work, turning over the dead to find the living caught beneath.

The Visitor's manufacture keeps him from weariness, but not from horror. He hears its cries in his ears, he stumbles over it half buried in bloody snow. His eyes grow wide with it.

His difficulty is in telling the living from the dead. Some still moving he sees the sisters examine and leave; others who are unmoving they minister to. This one: face down, arm twisted grotesquely . . . the Visitor turns him gently with more than man's strength, holds his torch near to see. "You're dead." A guess. The eyes look up at him unseeing. "Are you dead?" He wipes pink snow from the face: it is the man Redhand, who begins to breathe stertorously, and blows a blood-bubble from his gray lips. The Visitor considers this sufficient and lifts him easily in his arms, turning this way and that to decide what next. Redhand's breath grows less labored; he clings to the Visitor almost like a child in nurse's arms, his numb fingers clutching the brown cloak. Fauconred's tent: he sees its Cup banner far off as someone passes it with a torch. Even when it disappears into darkness again, he moves unerringly toward it, through that trampled, screaming field: and each separate cry is separately engraved on a deathless, forgetless memory.

Fauconred starts to see him. His day has been full of terrible things, but somehow, now, the Visitor's face seems most terrible: what had seemed changeless and blank has altered, the eyes are wide and deep-shadowed, the mouth thin and down-drawn.

"It's he, Redhand." The smooth, cool voice has not changed. "Help me. Tell me if he's dead. Tell me . . . He mustn't be dead. He mustn't be. He must live."

TWO

SECRETARY

1

____

An image of Caermon: a man, crowned with leaves, holding in one hand a bunch of twigs, and seated on a stone.

He found that though he came no closer to any Reason or Direction in his being, his understanding of his faculties grew, chiefly through the amazement of others. Fauconred had first noticed his hearing, in the Throat; his strength in lifting and carrying wounded Redhand had amazed the Endwives. Now Learned Redhand had observed him learn to read the modern and ancient languages in mere weeks—and remember everything he learned in them.

An image of Shen: a woman, weeping, seated in a cart drawn by dogs, wearing a crown.

The Visitor measured his growth in more subtle things: when he saw the King Red Senlin's Son, his head low, sword across his lap, attention elsewhere, he felt still the strength in him, no less than on the field. It gave him an odd thrill of continuity, a pleasurable sense of understanding: the King on the battlefield or here at his ease is one King. When the Visitor tried to describe the experience to Learned Redhand, the Gray failed to grasp what was marvelous in it. He found it much more compel-

ling that the Visitor could cause a stone thrown into the air to float slowly
to his own hand rather than fall on its natural course. The Visitor in turn
was embarrassed not to be able to understand the Gray's explanation of
why what he had done was impossible.

An image of Doth: a man carrying a lamp or pot of fire, old and ragged,
leaning on a staff.

Learned Redhand's head was beginning to ache. Perhaps he really
hadn't done it at all . . . This Visitor and the mystery of him grew
quickly more exacerbating than intriguing, like an answerless riddle.
Even in the bright winter light of the Harbor solarium, the Visitor made a
kind of darkness, as though the thick ambiguity of the far past, leaking
like a gas from the ancient writings he pored over, clouded him.

"These images," the Visitor said, marking his place with a careful
finger before looking up, "they're all of men or women. Why is that?"

"Well," Learned began, "the process of symbol-making . . ."

"I mean, for the names of weeks, it would seem one at least would
be, oh, a sheaf of wheat, a horse, a cloud . . ."

"The ancient mind . . ."

"Is it possible that these names were once truly the names of real
men and women?"

"Well . . . what men and women?" The Gray idea of the past, for-
mulated like their simple, stern moral fables out of long experience with
the rule of men's minds, was simply that before a certain time there were
no acts, men were too unformed or mindless to have performed any that
could be memorialized, and that therefore, having left no monuments,
the distant past was utterly unknowable. Time began, the Grays said,
when men invented it, and left records to mark it by; before then, it
didn't exist. To attempt to probe that darkness, especially through pre-
Gray manuscripts that claimed to articulate beginnings by unintelligible
"first images" and "mottoes" and "shadows of first things," was fruitless
certainly, and probably heretical. "No," he went on, "aids to memory I
think merely, however foolishly elaborate."

The Visitor looked at Learned's smooth, gracious face a moment, and
returned to his reading.

An image of Barnol carries this motto: Spread sails to catch the Light of
Suns.

An image of Athenol carries this motto: Leviathan.

"Leviathan," the Visitor said softly.

"An imaginary god or monster," said Learned. To the rational Gray mind the two were one.

Suddenly a servant stood in the solarium archway. The hall floors had been hushed with straw since Redhand had been brought home near dead; the servants moved like ghosts. "The Protector," he whispered, indicating the Visitor, "wishes to see you."

Leviathan . . .

The Visitor rose, nodded to Learned, went out behind the man and down twisting, straw-carpeted corridors.

Leviathan. It was as though the name had taken his hand in a darkness where he had thought himself alone. Taken his hand, and then slipped away. Gently, blindly he probed his darkness, seeking for its fearful touch again.

Redhand had grown older. He sat propped on pillows within a curtained bed; old, knowing servants made infusions and compresses, and the medicinal odor filled the high room. A large fire gave fierce heat, roaring steadily in the dim hush. Redhand's dark-circled eyes found the Visitor and guided him to the bed; he patted the rich coverlet and the Visitor sat.

"Do you have a name?" The Visitor could see in Redhand's face the unreasoning fear he had first seen in the forest; he could see too the broken body he had saved. Both were Redhand.

"They say—Visitor," he answered.

"That's . . ."

"It's sufficient."

"Fauconred has told me . . . incredible things. Which he apparently believes." His eyes hadn't left the Visitor. "I don't."

There was a gesture the Visitor had seen, had practiced privately when he had learned its vague but useful meaning. He made it now: a quick lift of shoulders and eyebrows, and return to passivity.

"You saved my life."

"I . . ."

"I want to . . . reward you, or . . . Is there anything you need?"

Everything. Could he understand that?

"There is a new King in the world. I have made him. Perhaps . . . it was wrong in me. Surely I have lost by it." *Take care,* his father had said.

Watch well. "But there it is. I am made great now in the world, and . . . ." He moved his knitting body carefully on the pillows. "Learned tells me you learn quickly."

"He tells me so too."

"Hm. Well. Learn, then. As long as you like. Anything you require . . . my house, servants are at your disposal." He tried to smile. "I will draw on your learning, if I may."

A silence, filled with the fire's voice. Already, it seemed to the Visitor, Redhand's thoughts were elsewhere. It was odd: he felt he had come a great distance, from somewhere no man had been, and carried, though he could not speak it, wisdom they could never here learn but from him. Yet they drifted off always into their own concerns . . . "You were at Redsdown," Redhand said. "You saw my lady there. She was well? Hospitable?" He looked away. "Did she . . . speak of me?"

"Often."

"She wrote me of you. This . . . airy talk."

The Visitor said nothing.

"I must regard you as a man."

"It's all I wish."

Redhand's eyes returned to him; it seemed they were again the eyes that had looked on him in horror in the Throat: alert with fear, yet dreaming.

"Who are you?" he asked.

Forgetful.

The Protectorate had built Forgetful as they had Old Watcher far away on the sunrise edge of the Drum, in the days after they had despaired of conquering the fierce, elusive tribes of the Outlands; built it to ensure that, if they could not conquer, at least they would not be conquered. The huge piles, strongly garrisoned, had made a semblance of diplomacy possible with the Outland chieftains; they had eventually accepted a king's lieutenant as their nominal ruler and only occasionally tried to murder him. Red Senlin had been one such; and before him, Black Harrah. The post at the moment remained unbestowed; but probably, Young Harrah thought, it will go to Younger Redhand for his infinite damned patience . . .

In Shensweek Young Harrah sat within the sweating, undressed stones of Forgetful, wrapped in a fur robe; completely safe, of course, but trapped in fact: it came to the same thing. With a lot of Outlanders for company, with spring coming but no help.

"Capitulate," he said.

"I don't see it," said the fat-cheeked captain he had taught to play War in Heaven—or at least move the pieces. The Outlander's thick fingers toyed with two sky-blue stones, moved them hesitantly amid the constellations pictured on the board. "Maybe you should capitulate."

"Move." Red Senlin's Son played at King in the City; the fat Queen, his father's whore, licked her wounds somewhere in the Outland bogs, whispering with the braid-beards who adored her; and Redhand's mastiff brother hung on here for life and would not be shaken. It had been for a while amusing to watch them out there, to make them endure a little privation before they took their ugly and useless prize, this castle. The game was no longer amusing. The Son played at King in the City . . . there was the game. The Outlander picked up the seven-stone, bit his lower lip, and set it down in the same place. Young Harrah sighed.

"Now, now," said the Outlander. "Now, now." At length he saw the trap and finessed gleefully. Young Harrah tapped his foot, his mind elsewhere, and threw a red stone across the sky without deliberating.

It was, of course, a struggle to the death. The Queen believed Black Harrah slain by the Reds. For sure she had slain Red Senlin the new King's father, and Old Redhand too. There could be no forgiveness for that. They must, he must, struggle with the King Red Senlin's Son till Rizna called a halt. Yes. And he could think of none else he would rather struggle with than the King's blond limbs . . . With one long-toed foot he overturned the War in Heaven in a clatter of stones. The Outlander looked up. Young Harrah combed his blond hair with his hand and said, "Surrender."

Along the wind-scoured Drumsedge, sterile land where the broken mountains began a long slide toward the low Outlands, it was winter still. The snow was a bitter demon that filled the wagon ruts, made in mud and frozen now, and blew out again like sand. Cloak-muffled guards paced with pikes, horsemen grimly exercised their mounts on the beaten ground. The wind snapped the pennons on their staves, snatched the barks of the camp dogs from their mouths—and carried from Forgetful's walls suddenly the war viol's surrender song, and blew it around the camp with strange alteration.

Young Harrah led the morose Outlanders down the steep gash in the rocks that was Forgetful's front way. He rode with his head high, listening to the distant cheers of his victors. At a turning he could see Younger Redhand and four or five others coming up toward him. He dismounted and walked to where Younger awaited him. He was amused to see that there had been time during the siege for Younger to grow a young man's mustache. The cheering troops were stilled by a motion of Younger's hand, and Young Harrah handed his sword up to him.

"Will I see the King?" he asked.

"Forgiveness," said the King. "Clemency."

The High City had been shaken out like a dusty rug till it was clean of the gloom and shadows of Little Black's reign. Great houses long shuttered were opened and aired, streets were widened and new-paved with bright stone. The City crafts, long in decline, suddenly had to seek apprentices to satisfy the needs of the great—for once more there were great in the City, their carriages flew to the Citadel, they were received by the King, they had audiences with Redhand; they were in need of all things fashionable, these Downsmen were, and their somnolent City houses were roused by a parade of tradesmen knocking at their thick doors. The cry of all stewards was for candles, good wax candles, but there were none: there were rushlights and tallows, torches and lamps and flambeaux—the candles had all been taken to the Citadel to spangle the Ball.

"No seizures, no treason trials," said the King. "Not now."

"If not now," said Learned Redhand, "then never. You can't try old crimes years later."

"I meant," said the King, turning a moment from his mirror, "no treason trials for these crimes. Later . . ."

The Ball is to be masked, a custom of ancient springs revived. The King will appear as the Stag Taken in a Grove—an image he discovered in an old Painted chamber, could not have conceived himself, there having been no stags in the forests for uncounted years—and as he was undressed and prepared he entertained Redhand and his Gray brother, and Redhand's Secretary. Learned would not go costumed, a Gray may not; but he carried a long-nosed vizard. Redhand wore domino only, blood-red. The King failed to understand why Redhand had to have a secretary with him at a ball, but insisted that if he must be here he must be masked. So the Secretary consented to domino—even enjoyed its blank privacy.

"The Protectorate," Redhand said, "will praise you for it."

"I know it."

"They are diminished in this war."

"I will rebuild them."

"Great landowners have been slain . . ."

"I will make new. Strictly"—bowing to Learned—"according to the laws of inheritance." He raised his arms for his dresser to remove his shirt. "Why do you suppose, Protector," he said idly, "that we have been able to do this thing?"

"What thing?"

"Pull down a king. Make a new king."

"Strength."

"Righteousness," Learned said graciously.

"Strength more nearly," said the King. "But private strength. The strength of great men whose allegiance to the old King lay only in an oath."

"Only?" said Learned.

The King smiled. "I mean that this that we have done could be done again." He watched in the mirror with dreamy interest as his dresser removed skirt and leggings. "I would prevent that."

"By . . ."

"By making a new kind of Protectorate. One whose loyalty lies here, in the Citadel. That looks for strength less to some distant Downs and dependents than directly"—turning to them naked—"to the King's person."

Redhand, folded in his domino, was unreadable.

The King's dresser, with a whisper of fine fabric, clothed the King in green, gorgeously pictured.

"The Grove," said the King. The room's candles played upon the stuff, making gold lights glitter in its leaves like noon sun. The King took from his dresser's hands a great head, contrived with golden horns that were as well a crown, and hung with ribbons.

"The Stag," he said. "The rose ribbons are its blood, these blue here its tears." He fitted the Stag's head to his own blond one, and was helped on with tall shoes that made dainty hooves beneath the Grove robe.

Despite himself, Redhand was moved by this splendor. Only—

"Where," he asked, "is the Hunter?"

There is a Rose with a Worm in its Breast, who laughs with a ghastly Suicide; there is a Cheese full of Holes who pretends fear of the Plate and Knife; there are two Houses Afire who are cool to one another; there is a Starry Night, there is a sheaf of wheat, a horse, a cloud.

There is a thing not man and not woman, made in a star: but he is disguised as Secretary to the Great Protector Redhand, and the Secretary is wrapped then in red domino like his master.

Where is the Hunter? He is all in green leather, belted and buckled, he has bow and ancient darts.

When the Stag sees him, he leaps to run, striding on his tiny hooves through the startled crowd. The music stumbles; the Chest of Treasure stops dancing with the Broken Jug, who turns to the Mountain; he jostles the Head without a Body so that his cup of drink is spilled.

Beneath a great circle of candles that overhang a dais, the Stag is brought to bay. He trembles; the candles as he trembles cast glitter through his moving Grove. The Hunter draws a dart and aims.

"What mummery is this?" Redhand asks, setting down his cup.

"Will he shoot the King?" asks his Secretary.

Redhand laughs shortly and pushes through the murmuring crowd of fantasies to where he can see.

"Strike now," says the Stag in a great voice. "I will no more fly thee; surely this day is made for thee, and thy hall shall rejoice in thy fortune."

The Hunter hesitates. "My arm refuses my command, my fingers rebel against my hand's wish."

"See," the Stag cries out, "thy spade has struck a red spring; the well is thine to make; make it quick."

The Secretary whispers in Redhand's ear: "The words. They are a song in the Thousand and Seven Songs."

"Yes?"

"Yes. It's a . . . love song."

"Why dost thou weep?" the Hunter asks, lowering his bow. "Have we not chased fair all the day long, and hast thou not eluded me time and again, when I thought all lost and might have departed, and is this now not well done, that I have brought thee by my strength to this?"

"It is well done."

"Weep not."

"I must."

"I cannot strike."

"Where are your black Hounds then, that have drawn so much red blood from me?"

" 'Black Hounds' is wrong," the Secretary whispers to Redhand. "There were no Hounds. In the song he does . . . strike."

"Watch," says Redhand. "I begin to understand this."

At the Hunter's signal, there leap forth seven black Hounds, who rush the Stag to worry him. From his Grove as the Stag cries out (or from the arras behind him) come forth seven red Wounds. The Starry Night beside Redhand cries out. The Hounds fall back then, covering their eyes.

"They are amazed," the Hunter cries. "They will do no further harm, seeing you in this distress."

"Command them."

"I cannot! My tongue rebels against my thought to say it!" Suddenly, as though in great agony, he rushes to the dais and falls before the Stag, making obeisance. "Noble, noble beast! Each wound you take is as a wound to me. Each Hound that savages you"—summoning them with his hand so they make obeisance too—"seems to make me bleed. Forgive me this and all outrages! I will do no murder on thee nor ever seek again to draw thy red blood!" He breaks across his knee his fragile play-bow. "And these mute"—indicating his cowering Hounds—"I ask in their names the forgiveness of the mute blood they have shed."

"Rise, brave Hunter!" cries the Stag joyfully. "Wear brown not green, for with these words my wounds begin to heal . . ." He makes a subtle cue, and the music strikes up; each of the Hounds embraces a Wound. "I do forgive you! You and all these brave, more than brave in this asking. Come!" He bends, takes up the Hunter; the music peals merrily. He draws off the Hunter's mask of green leather.

Young Harrah, flushed with his acting, turns smiling to the astonished company.

They are silent. The music trembles in a void.

Redhand, stepping forward, throwing back his domino to reveal himself, begins to applaud. His applause rings hollowly for a moment, a long moment, and then the Starry Night begins to clap; then the Cheese and the Suicide, the House Afire and the Chest of Treasure. The Stag, immensely pleased, draws Young Harrah and Redhand together to embrace. The fantasts push forward applauding to congratulate.

Redhand takes Young Harrah's arm. "Unfortunate," he says, "that the

Queen who was so eager in this same chase is not here to be forgiven."
Young Harrah looks at him, the smile wavering. "You found my brother
well?"

"He found me, Protector."

"Is he in health? I ask only because his health is not good, and the
winds of the Edge . . ."

"Protector," says Young Harrah with the faintest edge, "your brother
came to me as conqueror, not acquaintance. I did not inquire after his
welfare."

"Well. Well. Now if I read this show rightly, we are here both made
brothers of the Stag. I would have you be that to me, neither conquered
nor acquaintance."

He is granted a half-smile by the Hunter, who turns to take others'
hands.

"These others," Redhand says to the Stag. "I think I know them. Will
we see their faces?"

Dumbshow: each of the seven Hounds removes his hairy head, each
of the Wounds puts back his red-ribboned cloak.

"As I thought," Redhand says to his Secretary. "Young Black Defenders are the Hounds, younger sons of slain fathers, those who might have
been marked for seizure. The innocent Wounds—is that what they were?
—the King's brother Sennred, sons of intransigent fathers, small landowners, those . . ."

The last Hound has shown himself. A thick, brutish head, more
houndlike than his mask. It is a face Redhand vaguely knows: a certain
bastard son of Farin the Black.

The Stag has begun to speak again, of love, reconciliation, a new
bright order of things. Redhand turns away, pushing aside the murmuring guests, and leaves the floor.

"Sweet, come to bed."

None sees but the eyeless Stag's head, thrown upon a chair.

"I will not be mocked." Young Harrah drinks off the last of a cup,
naked by the curtained bed.

"No one mocks you." The King puts off the Grove robe, lets it fall
with a rustle. "Come to bed."

"Redhand."

"Redhand," the King says. "Redhand is a man of mine. He will love you for my sake."

"He would be your master."

"I have no master."

The room is smoky with incense; the bed hangings Harrah draws aside are fine as smoke. "None?"

"None other." He moves impatiently within the bed. "Love. Master me." He reaches out and draws Harrah down amid the clothes. "Master me. Master me . . ."

2

I t was as if, that spring, all eyes and ears turned Inward to the City on the Hub within its ring of mountains.

The King's appetite for shows, triumphs, displays grew larger; unappeased by the ragtail pageant-carts that on glum street corners gave shows everyone knew by heart, he commissioned his own, drawn out of ancient stories by eager young men, stories full of new wit and unheard-of spectacle. Guildsmen of the City put their tools to strange uses building the machinery for abductions, enthronements, clockwork miracles —and the cleverest of them were paid well, in bright coinage the King had struck showing not a crude denomination but his own profile—too lovely almost to spend.

He was, though, his own most striking show. With his crowd of young Defenders, all handsome, all proud, with a canopy over him and men-at-arms before him with fantastical pikes and banners, he rode through the City weekly, visiting the guildhalls and artisans' shops, viewing construction of arches and the preparation of plays, of *The Sword Called Precious Strength* or *The Grievances Brought to King Ban*; always on his right hand Young Harrah, on his left Redhand, Master of the City, with his shadow Secretary all in red domino; and behind, close behind, his brother Sennred.

The King's brother Sennred was as small and dark as the King was tall and fair; some said another man than Red Senlin must have been Sennred's father, that when Senlin was King's Lieutenant in the Outlands, some other . . . but none said it to his face.

Sennred's right shoulder was higher than his left, and they called him stooped for it; but it was only constant practice with the sword that made it so: practice that had made him a match for any man living, though not, he thought, therefore worthy of his brother's love.

The banner carried before Sennred in these pomps was the Dog; he had chosen it himself; he had made himself watchdog to his brother, and when the counselors departed, and the bodyguards slept, and the King was drunk and went abroad looking for his lover at dead of night, there was still one who watched, mute as a hound.

Who watched now, half-hearing the banter between Young Harrah and the King, and Redhand glum and unfashionable beside them.

Redhand. Sennred had once mistrusted Redhand, had thought that when danger came Redhand would turn on the Senlin clan. Then their fathers had died together at Forgetful, and Sennred had fought beside Redhand at the Little Lake: and he had yielded up to Redhand a share of his dark love. It hurt him now to see his brother turn from Redhand; hurt him more to see he turned to Young Harrah.

That Sennred longed to shed Young Harrah's blood, wound him in secret places, none knew, for none asked Sennred's opinions. It was as well.

They wound down Bellmaker's Street slowly, moving through throngs of people eager to touch the King (few had ever so much as looked up from their work to see Little Black pass); eager too for the new coins he dispensed.

It was as well. For Sennred knew where the King's love lay, and he would die rather than harm it. But Redhand . . . Now the tolling and tinkling drowned out the laughter of the King with Young Harrah; Sennred saw them turn laughing to Redhand, who turned away. Sennred pushed forward, waving aside the pikemen, and took Redhand's arm in the strong grip of his sword hand.

"There is another joke," he said to Redhand beneath the bells' voices. "They ask at court who holds the King's scepter now." He stared up at

Redhand unsmiling. "Do you understand? Who holds the King's scepter now."

Angry, red-faced, Redhand pulled himself from Sennred's grip and forced his way out of the procession, through the curious crowd, out and away down the Street of Goldsmiths, his Secretary close behind him.

A great yellow Wanderer came full that night and shone in the streets of the City, on closed carriages, on late carousers in rumpled costumery; calm, female, it stroked the narrow streets and high houses with pale light. It shone on two walkers, one in domino, turning their red to neutral dark.

Since being made King's Master of the City, Redhand had often walked away sleepless nights along its arching streets; had learned it like a footpad, knew its narrow places, its silences, its late taverns and late walkers—watermen and whores, watchmen and those they watched for, lovers alone together: found a comfort in it he never found in the silences of his Redsdown parks. No Master of the City knew the City as Redhand did; Black Harrah, when he went from the Citadel to his estates, went in a closed carriage.

They looked down, Redhand and his Secretary, onto the soundless lake from an ancient arched bridge.

If you kick me I will bite you to the bone.

In the row of shacks along the water's edge one light was lit. From that doorway a slim, tall figure came carrying a bundle, put it in a small boat and pushed off onto the lake, where the Wanderer's light trembled.

"The King," the Secretary began, "and Young Harrah . . ."

"They must know," Redhand growled. "They must know I will kill him if I can."

That Wanderer had set; another, palely blue, had risen when she reached the far margin of the lake. She nudged her boat in among the small craft sleeping there, and, stepping from deck to deck as though on stepping stones, came out on the wharf. Someone called out, and she answered in a waterman's singsong call; the someone needed to know no more, and was silent. She waited a long moment in the shadow of a winch piling, listening for other sounds than the lake's; heard none, and went quickly up the water-stairs to where they joined the highway into the mountains. There she did not approach the guardhouse for permission to enter the road, but, with a silence learned elsewhere than on the water, dropped into the brushy woods that ran along it.

The guardhouse torches that lit the road's wide mouth were far behind when she again stopped for a long moment, listening for other sounds than the forest's. Again she heard none, pulled herself up by the tangle of brush at the road's edge and stepped out onto the smooth blue highway, elated, walking with long strides at deep midnight.

Her name was Nyamé and the name of her name was Nod. Her Gun's name was Suddenly. She carried Suddenly in a pouch of oiled goatskin at her side, the kind watermen carry their belongings in, for she was a waterman's daughter: that is, Nyamé was. Nod was Just. Suddenly had said so.

Wet winds had bridged the days where Fain met Shen, and then had turned warm and dry; now beneath her feet the pavingstones were green with moss, and by the roadside tiny star-shaped flowers had sprung up. The hood of her no-color traveler's cloak, that covered goatskins, Gun, and all, was thrown back, and the nightwind tickled her shorn blond head; it seemed to speak a word in the budding forest, a word she could almost hear: *awake*, yet not that either. It bore her up; almost without knowing it, in answer to the hushing wind, she began to sing.

The tunes were tunes the Folk had always sung, so much alike that one slid into another at a change without her choosing. The words, though, were the Just's: mournful and hopeful, silly and sad. She sang of old, old things, of gods long asleep, of the Fifty-two, unborn, sky sailors; she sang, skipping a few steps, rhyming puns that mocked the King and all his lords, made them dance a foolish dance before they fell down dead, as fall they all must one by one: for she sang too of her Gun and its hunger. She sang of the Deep and its beings, of Leviathan curled around the pillar of the world, dreaming all things that were, old and memorious when even the Grays were young. She sang, tears starting in her eyes, of being young, and brave, and soon to die:

I lay on the hillside
I dreamed of Adar.
"King Red lies at Drumriven
But he'll rise up no more.
This one I call Shouter of Curses,

This one I call Shouter of Curses,
This is the flint, this the ball I will feed him
To spit in King Red's eye."

I woke on the hillside
The brothers and sisters were gathered.
"King Red lies at Drumriven
A stone ball in his forehead.
But the one called Shouter of Curses is broken
And Adar's flesh stills the hounds that mourn King Red."
Adar, the grass grows still on the hillside
The long, forgetful grass that covered us:
Why, why will you not come to where I lie waiting?

The paved highway soon gave way to dirt rutted with spring rain, and the dirt often to a lane, marked only by stern stone bridges the ancients had built to arch the deepest ravines. These she kept count of, and at the fifth, as the sun and a thin mist were rising together, she stopped; she looked quickly behind her and then went into the ravine beneath the bridge. A path, that might have been made by rain but hadn't been, led steadily downward, deep beneath the aged trees whose tops filled up the ravine. As she went, what seemed impassable from above became more and more an easy glen in the gloom below. She ate bread and cheese as she walked, listening to the birds awake; and before the mist had entirely burned away, she stood before the Door in the Forest.

Had there ever truly been one called Adar?

She knew of some who had named their names for him. Yet for sure King Red had died in his sleep at a great age, imprisoned in the Citadel.

Once, so long ago no one now knew his or the King's name, one of the Just had killed a king.

And now, she thought, the kings kill each other. May they, she prayed, go on doing so until the last of their line stands alone, deserted, with his prize that crown, alone before the Just; and may a Gun then speak intimately with him; and the Folk be at last made free.

In her lifetime, in her youth? How many of the Just had wondered that, since how long ago . . .

To any not allowed to pass through it, any not Just, the Door in the Forest would not have seemed a door. It was only a narrow way between the entangled roots of two elder trees, with impassable deadfalls on either side; yet she was careful to make all the proper signs to the Door's guardians she could not see but knew were watching there.

Beyond the Door was much the same as before it; here too was dim glen and the birds awaking. Yet she felt she had left all her fears at that Door, and had come at last home. When the path at length came out of the grove and opened out into a wide meadow, she could see far down the whole length of the valley; beyond this meadow another meadow and another went on like pools of grass in the forest, down to where the stony sides of the valley seemed to close a farther Door. Then sheer mountains rose up; far, far away was a pale glitter: sunlight striking the white stones of Inviolable. She could see it, but it couldn't see her: a thrill of private pleasure.

Here, at the edge of the meadow, new moss spangled with flowers made a bed, and she lay gratefully, suddenly exhausted; the Gun in its pouch she laid beside her, and her pack under her head, and slept.

She woke because she felt a presence. She had forgotten where she was, or when she had come there, or what time of day it now was: but she knew someone was near, and watching. She sat up with a start, and seemed at the same time to coalesce here: late afternoon, beyond the Door, and a boy, Just, before her, smiling.

A mirror image of her almost, he had her blond short hair, her pale eyes, her long limbs, and she smiled his smile. His homespun was faded to a blue like his eyes—as though it were part of him, it was creased for good, like his hands, smooth and useful as his naked feet. Across his back, as long almost as he, hung a black figured Gun.

From a pouch he drew a handful of gray withering leaves. "I gathered these for you."

"How did you know I was here?"

He smiled. "I found you hours ago. Gathered these. I've been watching you sleep."

As he said it, she seemed to remember dreaming of him. "What is your name called?"

"My name is called Adar."

"My name is called Nod." Not her name, but what her name was called. Why did it seem to reveal her more to say it than to say her name?

Adar had found a flat stone and laid the gray leaves on it; with flint and steel he started the little pile smoldering. Hungrily Nod bent over it, beckoning the smoke into her face with her hands and breathing it in. Adar did the same when Nod moved away satisfied; they bent over it in turns till it was all pale ash. And sat then together, looking out over the valley.

Though woolly clouds rose over and crossed the valley, to them now it seemed that the valley turned beneath still clouds, sharp and clear as though painted for some vast pageant. So the wind too, which moved the clouds, seemed to be rather the valley's passage through still air: they at its center watched the world turn beneath the sky.

Then the turning valley entered new country: the clouds it moved under were denser, gray as lamb's wool, and the valley moved faster through cool, wet air that stirred their hair and opened their nostrils. The valley groaned in its quickened passage, ground rocks perhaps that sparked pale lightnings: then its forward edge passed through a curtain of rain, and the fat drops filled up the air, startling them and dispelling their dream. They moved close, back into the dense grove that was suddenly noisy with rain; found themselves tasting each other's rain-wet flesh.

His hunger surprised her; she herself felt cool, poised, as she liked to feel before doing a dangerous thing, though often didn't; she relished the feeling now, helping his helpless-eager hands undo her. She let him feast on her, let herself by degrees expand with heat out of her reserve until she must cry out: letting herself cry out felt like falling backwards when something soft is sure to break the fall. Her cry stilled him, his hands grew less sure; so she began to take him, moving the smooth homespun from his smooth flesh.

Thunder beat on them. The grove grew wild and dark with storm.

It had always fascinated her, blind, eager, so helpless and vulnerable and then too imperious, not to be denied. She felt once again poised, but now on some higher peak, ready to leap yet delaying. He made some motion toward her, it didn't matter, this one held her with its blind eye: when she took it, it leapt in her hand as though startled.

Around her as she woke the grove let drops fall from leaf to shuddering leaf. Outside, the clouds were dark rags against pale night sky where only the brightest stars could be seen. Around the meadow sat many, in dark groups of two or three, the long black of their Guns sharp in the weird light. More came from the forest and the valley below, noiselessly, calling out in the voices of night things to announce themselves. Adar was gone.

It was this she had come for.

At the meadow's center, a pavilion, a gesture toward a pavilion—two slim stakes, a gauzy banner, a rug thrown over the wet grass. On the rug Someone to whom, singly, each in the meadow came. Nod waited, watching, till she felt some invisible motion in the whole of them that brought her to her feet, moved her in her turn to the pavilion.

Slim, soft, white as Death, maned with white hair, the Neither-nor perched upon the rug like an ungainly bright bird. Laid out on the painted board before It were the painted cards of an oblong deck.

The Neither-nor, neither man nor woman, arbiter of the Just, keeper of the Fifty-nine Cards and of all secrets. It—not-he-not-she—resolved in Its long, fragile body the contradictions that the rulers of this world (and their Gray minions especially) would keep at war: ruler and ruled; good and evil; chance and certainty; man and woman.

Since the Just had been, such a one had guided them; since the first appeared, ages ago, to free men from tyranny. That first Neither-nor had appeared out of nowhere, pure emanation of the Deep or the heavens, bearing in one hand the Cards, in the other a Gun—sexless, without orifice or pendants; birthless, without omphalos; deathless, who had only Departed and left nothing behind.

This Neither-nor, successor to the first, holy body of Chalah, Two Hands of Truth, threw down Its paint pot and bit of mirror in disgust. In this light, Its eyes could not be made to look the same. . . . Its anger passed, dispersed by a motion of the Two Hands. Nod came close to sit before It; It turned Its fabulous head to look at her; within the softness of Its face Its eyes were still fierce and male somehow. For this Neither-nor was not clean of sex, not truly neither, but only both, vestigially. It had been taken, soon after birth, by the Just, raised up to be successor to the old Neither-nor when It would die. So this one would die, too: was only human, however odd. But there was this Providence, and always (the Just believed) had been: the Neither-nor was Just, most Just of them all; wise; chose well from the Cards whom the Guns would speak to; watched their secrets well, and would die to keep them secret. It was enough. The Neither-nor received their love, and gave them Its love freely, even as It dealt Death.

"Child." With a jingle of bracelets It reached out a Hand to stroke Nod's shorn head. "Many have told me of Black Harrah." Its fluid fingers turned and turned the Cards. "Do you know. I have a stone, a leaf, a bit of earth from the places where six of your brothers and sisters lie, six who drew Black Harrah from my cards?" Nod could say nothing. The Neither-nor regarded her, a tiny smile on Its mauve lips. "Do you come again then so soon to draw another?"

"What else could I do, Blessed?" It was not bragging; in the winey, wind-blown night, chill after rain, here before fate, Nod felt transparent; her words to the Neither-nor seemed so truthful as not to be hers at all. The Neither-nor lowered Its head, made a tiny motion, turned a first card. Nod began to speak, telling what her life had been, plainly; what she had seen; who of the great she had been near. Once the Neither-nor stopped her, said over what Nod had said: "In Redhand's train, dressed in red domino . . ."

"A naked face, his eyes not like men's eyes. In the battle with the Queen, it was he who saved Redhand when he fell . . ."

She watched as the Neither-nor turned down a card: it was an image of Finn, with a death's head and a fire lit in his belly. It had this motto: *Found by the lost.* "Strange," the Neither-nor whispered. "But no, not him . . . Go on. Is there Young Harrah in it?"

No, Nod thought. Not both father and son. Let the cards say not so . . . She went on slowly, watching the silent fall of the cards.

"They call themselves Brothers of the Stag." She swallowed. "They are both Red and Black, and say they have put aside their quarrel to all serve the King. Young Harrah is their chief . . ."

The Neither-nor turned down a card. "Not Young Harrah, then. Here is Chalah."

The deck the Neither-nor read from contained fifty-two cards, each a week, and seven trumps. These trumps were they whom the Grays called the Possessors, whom the Seven Strengths did endless war with in the world and in men's hearts. The Just knew otherwise, that there were but Seven and Seven alone, and contained the contradiction that for their own ends the Grays had turned into open war so long ago. At the turn of each trump, the Neither-nor named it; for it was these Seven who ruled Time, which is the Fifty-two.

Chalah, who is Love and its redemption, is also Lust and its baseness.

Dindred, who is Pride, Glory, thus Greatness in the world's eyes, is also blind Rage, thence treachery and ingloriousness.

Blem, who is Joy and good times, Fellowship and all its comforts, is too Drunkenness, Incontinence and all discomforts.

Dir, who is Wit, is the same Dir who is Foolishness.

Tintinnar is the magnanimity of Wealth, the care for money, thus meanness and Poverty.

Thrawn is Strength and Ability, exertion, exhaustion, and lastly Weakness and Sloth.

These six, when they fall upon a name, shelter the one named, or throw obstacles in the path of the Just were they to pursue him; thus Chalah, for a reason the Neither-nor could not tell, protected Young Harrah. Nod went on, her heart beginning to tap at her ribs.

"Redhand stays apart from them, though he wears the badge too. He gathers strength. His brother Learned is a dark Gray. His brother Younger holds the castle Forgetful. His father is slain, all his father's honors and lands are his. He is greater than the King . . ."

Lips pursed, the Neither-nor turned down the last trump.

Rizna is Death. Death and Life, who carries the sickle and the seed-bag, and ever reaps what he continually sows.

"You are brave," It says in Its sweet, reedy voice.

"No."

"Implacable."

She cannot answer.

"Just."

"Yes."

"I think you are." It slides Rizna reversed toward Nod. "Are you afraid?"

"Yes." Till Death—his or hers—they have been wedded here.

Tears have suddenly begun to course down the Neither-nor's white cheeks. It is an ancient being; so many fates has It read, so many It has sent to death; weeps now because It can see nothing.

"Redhand," Nod says, trying to take him by the name. "Redhand."

The Arbiter Mariadn is dying.

The old, old grayest of all Grays lies propped on pillows within her chaste apartment. Its casement windows have been opened to the garden, though the doctors think it ill-advised, and a breeze lifts the edges of many papers on tables.

Her face is smooth, ashen, calm. Before sunset, before morning surely, her heart will stop. She knows it.

Through all this week they have come, the great Grays and the lesser, from every quarter, from the court, the law offices, the country seats, foregathering here like a summer storm. For a time she could feel their presence in Inviolable, in the chambers outside her still room; they have mostly faded now. Her world has grown very small; it includes the window, the bed, the servant ancienter even than herself, her dissolving body and its letting go—little else now.

The servant's face, a moon, orbits slowly toward her.

Has he come yet? she thinks she asks. When the servant makes no reply, she says again, with pain this time, "Has he come yet?"

"He is just here."

She nods, satisfied. The world has grown very small, but she has remembered this one thing, a thing expressed in none of the wills and instruments she has already forgotten. She would have it over; does not wish it, an oath in an autumn garden, a thing still left to do, to intrude on her dissolution, a process that has broken open all her ancient locked chests, torn down her interior walls, let past light in to shine on present darkness: the light of a farm on the Downs, in the spring, in seedtime, warming young limbs and brown earth . . .

He has been there some time when she again opens her eyes.

"Learned."

"Arbiter."

"They will not deny me . . ." She stops, her lips quivering. She must not ramble. There must be strength for this. There is: she draws on it, and the world grows smaller. She calls her servant. "Call them now. You know the ones. Those only."

She takes his warm hand in her cold. "Learned, lean close . . . Learned, my successor will be named by the Councils. Hush, hush . . ." He had begun some comforting words. There is no time for that; her time spills as from a broken clock. "Help me now. For our Order's sake. You must; you have no choice, no reason to deny me that can stand. Lift me up. They've come."

A cloud of smoke at the bed's end coalesces into faces, forms. Many she has known since they were boys and girls; it seems they have changed not at all. She must be firm with them. "I would have Redhand succeed me." She cannot tell if they are looking at her, at Redhand, at each other. It is too long ago to remember which is which, who would accede, who would be swayed by which other. It doesn't matter. "There is no time or strength left me to argue it. Take him at my word or do not. But let not one of you desire my place. Shun it. I place on Redhand only labor and suffering. Remember that. If you will not have him whom I name, let whomever you name have your pity and your love."

All done; and the last of her strength leaks away. She finds it hard to listen to the words spoken to her, Arbiter, Arbiter; she has forgotten why this man should not be excluded from her world like all else, except that his hand is warm and his voice pleasant though senseless.

Done. Sunset has come suddenly, the room is dark. Her little world with a grateful sigh shuts up small, smaller than a fist; it draws to a fine point and is gone.

And yet, and yet—strange: even when she is cool on the white-clothed bed, still the sunlight enters soundlessly in at the casements, the wind still lifts the corners of many papers on tables. In the garden trees still drop blossoms on the paths that go their ways; Learned Redhand at the casement can see them, and can feel on his face the hot, startling tears, the first he has shed since he put on Gray.

3

To my best-loved Caredd, at Redsdown:
He who bears this is known to you, and can tell you much that is too long for this.

You must know that the Arbiter Mariadn is dead. It was her wish, and the Grays in Council acceded to it, that my brother Learned be successor to her. This is great news and cause for celebration—no other in our family has risen so high in this. The ceremonies & all else attendant on this have been secret in part & I have heard of them only through Learned's hints, but it is all very solemn and grand.

So this must be celebrated! You write me that the lambs are fallen & the rabbits everywhere bold; well, then, there will be a feast at Redsdown, such as this soft age has not seen, that your father's father might have been satisfied to sit at. I leave it to your good judgment, & know that all you do will honor us.

If it cannot be Rokesweek Eve, write quickly and give it to Ham to carry. I will say Rokesweek Eve if I hear nothing.

*My duty etc. to our mother there, and kiss my girl for me. I
mean to set out this week eve.*

By he who bears it, at the Harbor, Devonsweek.

Beneath his signature, in his own tiny, long-tailed hand:

*Caredd, there are those here who say they are not enemies to me and
whom I do not fear but mistrust. They are partly the King's creations;
they are little men of no consequence, for all they wear the King's
badges and style themselves Brothers of the Stag. If such a feast as I
mean could show such ones what it is to be Protector of men and
lands, such would not be from my purpose. I know you know my
mind; you ever have. R.*

She folded the crackling paper and smiled at its bearer. "Welcome to
Redsdown," she said. "Welcome back."

"It's good to be back." This the Secretary knew to be the right response, but in fact it seemed to him odd in the extreme to have returned
here: it was the first place on his journey he had returned to, and he half-
expected that from here he would return to the horsegathering, the
Endwives' cottage, the egg . . . "And good to see you." It was: her au-
tumn-brown eyes and careful hands, her auburn hair stirred in him the
devotion he had felt that autumn. He watched her, feeling himself suddenly to be One, as he had felt the King and Redhand to be One . . .
no. Not wholly like.

She took his arm and led him up through the garden he had found
her in, the garden mad with spring and sun, toward the low dark of the
hall. "You are Secretary to my husband now."

"Yes."

"No longer Possessed, or some creature?"

He couldn't answer.

"You'll keep your secret, then."

"I don't know how to tell it."

"You must have many new ones now. City secrets, policy . . ." She
summoned up vague and dangerous knowledge with her hand.

"I am a Secretary," he answered. "It's not . . . what was intended, I
don't think. If I could, I would forget—all else. It's sufficient."

"Learned . . ."

"Taught me much. To read. To learn old knowledge." Like a shudder, he felt it come and pass again: *Leviathan.* "Yet never who or what I am. I intend now to serve Redhand."

She looked at him; his blank face still showed no trace of a man behind it, the eyes were still pools of unknowable dark.

"And serve you too," he said. "If I am allowed."

She smiled. "You have grown gracious in the City. Yes. Serve me. Tell me of these Brothers of the Stag and if there is danger to Redhand. Help me in this feast." Her smile faded. "Watch Redhand. You saved him in battle. You have strengths that frighten me. Watch Redhand, ever."

He would. If it were not the Task he had been made to do, not the Direction he had been made to take, it came from her. It would do.

Late, late, Redhand came to her. Below, the guests who had arrived with him at sunset went on with their play, though now it was near sun again. All night since his arrival, he had been with her only as master of Redsdown with its mistress; she had watched him shepherding his City friends and these Brothers of the Stag from drink to supper to drink again with a set and icy smile she had not known before. She had watched him, and Learned, for whom after all tomorrow's feast was made, left out of jokes or made the butt of them—so it seemed to her, though they both smiled, and Redhand poured cup after cup of drink, not drinking himself, as though he were afraid of Blem's indiscretion . . .

And then late, late, after she had been driven to bed by the malice and queerness she felt in the King and his young men, Young Harrah especially, Redhand came to her.

Plunged himself within her warm coverlets, silent, hasty, so needful it was hard for her to keep up with him, yet so fierce that he carried her along as in a storm.

Later, a chill summer rain began.

It seemed to Redhand that it always rained when he came to Redsdown. Always. Passion spent, he felt that fact weigh on him with an awful injustice, filling him with black self-pity, till he must get up from the bed and pull on his shirt, light a light and go to the gray window to watch it fall.

In a while, awakened by his absence, she called to him in a small voice.

"It was the rain," he said.

She stirred within the bedclothes. "What do they intend?"

"They?"

"Below. The King."

He said nothing, not knowing himself.

"Harm? To us?"

"And if they did?"

Rain fell with a constant sound. The darkness spoke to him again: "The King," she said. "Young Harrah is . . . They have some plan."

"They come at my invitation. To a feast. They have no plan." It put him in mind of them, hinting smugly at what they did not dare execute, at revenge they were too weak to take, power they could not seize. Not from Redhand. His head drew down to his wide shoulders, bull-like, as he thought of them. "Let him suck the King. Let them make their jokes, who holds the King's scepter. They are insects at a candle flame . . ."

She knew then, as she held still to hear his gritty voice, that she had been right, that the King intended if not her husband's death then his ruin; and that Redhand did not know it.

The feast day brightened; the rain began to blow away toward the City.

"Shall we go in, then?"

Fires had been lit in the apartments and anterooms of Redsdown, despite the new summer; the old house's chill was not to be banished by a few weeks' sun. Learned Redhand stood before one, his hand with its dark agate ring on the carved mantel. In his other hand he toyed with a bit of flame-red ribbon.

"He comes," Fauconred said, "to a feast, with an armed guard larger than his host's household."

"A king's prerogative," Redhand said.

"Do you suppose," Learned said, "he has come to steal our jewels? Ravish our pages?"

Fauconred ran his fingers through his burr of gray hair. "I do not suppose, Learned." He turned to Redhand. "If I may, I will take my feast with the guard."

Redhand shrugged. "Now let us go in. Caredd . . ." He took her arm.

Learned turned from the fire, discarding into it the bit of ribbon, which was consumed before it met the flame, so fine a stuff it was.

Wide doors were thrown open, and they entered the hall, and all assembled rose with a murmur for the grayest of all Grays.

The last juggler dropped his last ball and was not invited to pick it up again. The musicians, prettily arranged around the entrance arch on a scaffolding or trellis of beams, flower- and banner-decked, fell silent; the musicmaster glanced at the steward, who glanced at Redhand, but received no cue.

There was the King left, and Young Harrah at his left side, and a few of the Brothers of the Stag. There was Redhand on the King's right side; there were some few others at the great tables piled high with ravished roasts and pastries; some of them were asleep, face down on the wine- and grease-stained tablecloths.

"Splendid," the King said. "So . . . antique."

Alone at one long table from which the Arbiter and Caredd and the rest of Redhand's house had departed, the Secretary to Redhand sat, peeling a fruit he did not intend to eat.

"More of this?" Redhand asked, motioning a cup-bearer. The King motioned him away.

Also sitting alone, the King's brother Sennred watched the high table, keeping one hand on his sword. (Weapons, the feast-steward had said, were not allowed within the banquet hall. Sennred had not replied, and the steward had not repeated himself. Sennred's sword slept with him. For sure it would feast with him.)

"This," said the King, "is a man's place. Here, on land that is his, with his dependents around him. A good farmer, a good neighbor." Young Harrah giggled. "Your father and his must have sat here . . ."

"The land is mine by marriage," Redhand growled.

"Oh. I remember. The Red madwoman."

Redhand said nothing.

"I wonder," the King said, "what it is you find in the City so precious as this you leave behind."

Redhand felt a sudden chill of premonition. All this was another of their jokes, it had a cruel point to cut him with he hadn't seen yet. He saw, though, that Young Harrah had stopped toying with the remnants of his feast.

"My duty," he said carefully, "requires me in the City." The King was not looking at him. "I have the City's gem, given me by your father."

The King reached out and with his long, careless fingers lifted the heavy jewel that hung from Redhand's chain. "Will you give it to me, then?" He asked it coyly, teasingly, as one would a token from a lover.

"It is not mine to give."

"Is it, then," the King asked, "mine to give?"

"It is."

"And mine to take? It seems to me," he said, not waiting for reply, "that one with so many dependents, lands, a wife and daughter, might find this stone a heavy weight to bear."

Seeing at last what they intended, a weird calm subsumed Redhand's fears; he felt suddenly no further obligation to fence with them. Only let them not mock him further. "You've come for this."

"We will not leave without it." Young Harrah's voice was a light, melodic one; its tone never varied, no matter what he said with it. "I have seen enough of country pleasures for one year; the sooner gone the better."

"You see," the King said, "perhaps someone without these other responsibilities, someone . . ."

"Attached only to the King," Young Harrah said, smiling. "Someone . . ."

"Stop this." Redhand stood, tore the jewel from the chain and flung it down along the table. "I bought it with my father's blood. Can you return me that price?" He kicked back his chair the better to see Young Harrah where he sat; the chair's fall resounded in the high hall.

"You," he said. "Can you?"

Young Harrah regarded him. "Return you your father's death? I wish I could. It's not pleasant to remember."

"Not—pleasant." There was a sudden mad edge in Redhand's voice that made his Secretary stand.

"Your father," Harrah said coolly, "did not die well."

From the table Redhand snatched up a long bone-handled carving knife; the King stood to block his way, and Redhand threw him aside, reached Harrah and pulled him to his feet; slapped Harrah's face once, again.

Sennred was up, sword drawn. The King took Redhand's shoulder, Redhand pulled away and threw over the long table before them, dragged Harrah through the wreckage of dishes and cups to the center of the floor.

"Did not die well! Did—not—die well!" Redhand bellowed.

The Brothers of the Stag rushed forward shouting, and the King too, crying out, "Sennred!"

Redhand from a table took up another knife and thrust it into Young Harrah's hands. "Now fight me! Fight me, *woman*!" Again he slapped Young Harrah, and blood sprang from Harrah's nose.

Sennred reached them first, and turned to face the King and his Brothers, the quick sword against them. "Stand aside," he said quietly. "It is not your quarrel. Stand all aside." And they must.

Harrah held the knife before him, a quarry's fear in his eyes, and backed away, stumbling on spilled cups and rubbish; Redhand, heedless, moved on him, slashing with the unwieldy weapon, shouting at Harrah to fight. For a moment, desperate, Harrah stood, resisted; Redhand took a cut on the cheek, and at the same moment drove his blade deeply into Harrah's neck.

Harrah screamed, fell; his blood leapt, spattering Redhand. He twisted once, tried to rise, plucking at the blade in his throat; and then lay still, eyes wide.

There was a moment when no one moved, no one spoke.

Then someone struck Sennred from behind as he looked down, stunned, at Young Harrah; he fell sprawling across the floor, and the guests made for their host.

"Redhand!" The Secretary stood beneath the scaffolding at the archway. "Here!" He threw his arms around one of the thick beams that supported the structure and began pulling. It groaned, the musicians leapt and scrambled. Redhand ran through, with Farin's bastard son close behind. The Secretary strained, crying out with effort; the scaffolding swayed, splintered and collapsed before the archway, blocking pursuit.

Down the narrow corridors of Redsdown, doors slammed around Redhand, running feet pursued him, more doors opened and shut behind him. He didn't turn to look; he followed the fleet shape of his Secretary where it led, till at the top of a stair he stopped, gasping. Running feet came on behind, he could not tell how close. The Secretary ran down and flung open the door at the bottom of the stair, and late afternoon light poured through it. "Here."

There were horses, saddled, waiting in the kitchen court beyond the door. For a moment Redhand stood, unable to run, from his home, from his act.

"They are in the Long Hall of the old wing," the Secretary said in his passionless voice. "The servants will not hold them long."

"No."

"Do you know a place to run?"

"Yes."

Still he stood; the Secretary at last came to him, took him like a child, pushed him down and out the door and away.

There was a twilight gloom in the stables. Farin's son stumbled, cursing, calling for grooms, a light, his horse.

A lantern flickered into life at the dark back of the stables.

"Groom! Bring that light here! Have they come here?"

"They?"

"Your master. That other. Who is it there? Can you get me my horse? Your master, boy, has done a murder and fled."

The lantern moved forward. "Who are you?"

Farin touched his sword. "A King's man. Farin's son. Stand where I can see you . . . Your master has slain a man and run, I think toward the Drumskin. Will you get my horse and help me, or . . ."

"Yes." The lantern brightened, was hung on a peg. A person, slim in a cloak of no color, stood in its yellow light. "Let me ride with you. I . . . He came here, he did come here, and I saw the way he went."

"Quick, then."

They worked fast, saddling Farin's black and a nag the other found. From the castle above them they heard shouts, cries, alarms. Redhand's household struggled with the King's guard.

"The lantern," Farin's son said, reaching for it.

"Leave it," said the other. "He will see it better than we will see him by it."

In the stableyard some of the King's men fought with Redhand's redjackets, vying for the horses who kicked and showed teeth, maddened with excitement and the smell of blood. Some redjackets moved to stop Farin's son; he slashed at them, spurring his horse cruelly, and forced a way to the stablegate leading Outward. From there, they could see a troop of men, torches lit, riding Outward in another direction: King's horsemen. "There," said Farin's son. "We'll join them."

"No. They're taking the wrong way. It was this way he ran."

"But . . ."

"This way."

The nag began to canter, then broke into a swaying gallop; the cloak's hood was blown back, revealing short-cropped blond hair. Farin, looking after the others, stood indecisive.

"Come on, then! Would you have him?"

Farin turned his horse and caught up.

"Who was it murdered?"

"Young Harrah. There was not a finer, a sweeter gentleman . . ."

In the growing darkness he could not see her smile.

For a week she had concealed herself at Redsdown, in the woods at first, then on the grounds, finally within the house itself, stealing food, hiding, losing herself in the vast compound, not knowing even if Redhand were there. She had seen him come then with the King and the others, seen the feast prepared. It had ended thus. He was alone out there somewhere; alone, unarmed it might be.

"Stop," Farin's bastard said. "We go a quickwing chase here."

She had not thought this one would be fool enough to follow her so far.

A soft and windy night had come full. They stood on a knoll that overlooked grasslands, Redhand's grasslands that led Outward toward the Drum. They lay vast and featureless, whispering vague nothings made of grass and wind and new insects.

"Where are the others?" Farin said, standing in his stirrups. "I can't see their lights."

"No." She would need a better horse than this nag she rode; she would need other weapons, for silent work might need to be done. She must be quick; she must be the first to find Redhand.

"By now some of his people will have found him."

"Yes?"

"If we come upon them, they'll make a stand."

"Yes."

"We'll turn back then," Farin said.

She dismounted.

"Are you mad? We're alone here." She heard the jingle of his harness as he turned his horse, indecisive. "Will you search on foot? I'll return."

"Dismount, Farin."

"Stay, then!" she heard him shout at her turned back. "Join him, if that was your plan! Or have you led me away from him, knowingly?"

"Come, Farin. Dismount." Still her back was to him.

"You . . ." She heard him draw a sword, heard the horse turn on her. He meant to cut her down.

She turned. Suddenly.

It would have been easier if he had dismounted. She had but one chance, and must not hurt the horse. . . .

Night wind sent long shivers of light through the sea of grass. The land seemed flat, but everywhere was pocked with depressions, bowls, ditches. A man could be sought in them for days; there were narrow, deep places where two men and their horses could hide, and look out, and see pursuers a long way off.

Far off, a sharp sound broke the night, echoed, was gone. Redhand and his Secretary looked out, could see nothing but starlight moving through the grass. No further sound came to their hiding-place but the blowing of their spent horses. There was no pursuit.

Redhand knew many such places in the wide angle of grass and Drumskin that was in his Protection; had to know them, because the Just did, and from them at any time outlaws might attack.

Outlaws. Murderers of the Protectorate, hidden in holes.

He laughed, rolled on his back. Somehow Redhand felt cleansed, free. Young Harrah lay at Redsdown: of all the murder he had done, and it was much, he knew that that one face at least would not return to look at him in dreams.

Above him the floor of heaven was strewn with changeless stars. The Wanderers, gracious, benevolent, made procession through them.

"You were born there," Redhand said to his Secretary. It was a night to entertain such thoughts.

"Not born," the Secretary said. "Made."

"In a star?"

"No. In an . . . engine, set in heaven, set to circle like the Wanderers. I think."

Redhand pillowed his head on his hands. On so clear a night the stars seemed to proceed, if you stared at them, ever so slowly closer. Yet never came near.

"What did it look like from there? Could you see the City?"

"No." The Secretary turned from his watching to look upward with Redhand. "There were no windows, or I was blind, I forget . . ." Then the stars seemed to make a sudden, harmonious sound together, loud, yet far distant . . . He sat bolt upright.

"What is it? Do you hear pursuit?"

"No."

"Then what . . ."

"I did see it. I remembered, suddenly. Once. Many times, maybe, but it seems once. I saw it."

"And?"

So clear it was to him suddenly, as though it were his original thought, the ground of his being: "The world," he said, "is founded on a pillar, which is founded on the Deep."

"Yes," Redhand said. "So it is."

The Secretary watched the precious memory unfold within him; it seemed to make a sound, harmonious, loud yet far distant . . .

A chaos of dull darkness, unrelieved except by storms of brightness within it. Then a sense of thinning toward the top of view, and clarity. And then a few stars rose from the darkness, sparkling on a clear black of infinite dark sky.

"You arose from the Deep at morning," Redhand said.

Then there came far off a light, brighter than any star, rising up out of the dark and chaos, which seemed now to flow beneath him.

"Yes," Redhand said. "The sun, rising too out of the Deep."

The sun. It moved, rose up from the Deep blinding bright, cast lights down to the Deep below him. "Yes," Redhand said.

And there came the world. Merely a bright line at first, on the darkness of the horizon where the Deep met the black sky; then widening to an ellipse. The world, flat and round and glittering, like a coin flung on the face of the Deep. It came closer, or he grew closer to it—the sun crossing above it cast changing light upon it, and he watched it change, like a jewel, blue to white to green to veined and shadowed like marble.

Only it, in all the Deep that surrounded it, all the infinity of dense darkness, only it glowed: a circle of Something in a sea of nothing.

And when he drew close enough he could see that the disc of the
world rested on a fat stalk which held it up out of the nothingness, a
pillar which for an instant he could see went down, down, endlessly
down into the Deep, how far . . . but then the world was full beneath
him, cloudy, milky green and blue, like a dish the arm and hand of an
infinite Servant held up.

"Yes," Redhand said. "Just so."

The stars went by above, went their incomprehensible ways.

"Only," Redhand said, "you saw nothing of the Deep's beings."

"Beings?"

"Beneath the world. Oh, one's tail they say, the Just say, reaches
around the pillar that holds up the world, and so he clings on, like ivy."

"I saw no such one."

"His name," Redhand said, "is Leviathan." His horse made a sound,
and opened its nostrils to the night wind. Redhand turned to look across
the Downs.

And how, the Secretary thought, am I to come to him then, beneath
the world? And why has he summoned me?

"Riders," Redhand whispered.

They were a smudge only against the sky that lightened toward
dawn; it could not be seen how many of them there were, but they
moved slowly, searching; now two or three separated, went off, returned.
Always they grew closer.

Redhand's horse stamped, jingling its trappings. They watched, motionless, ready to ride and flee, hopeless though that seemed. One rider,
nearer to them than the rest, stopped, facing them. For a long moment he
stood; then they could see his heels kick, and the horse ambled toward
them. Stopped. And then faster, more deliberately, came for them.

Suddenly the Secretary was on his feet, running toward the rider, his
domino picked up by wind, red as a beacon. The rider pushed into a
canter.

"Stop!" Redhand cried.

"Fauconred!" the Secretary called.

"Redhand!" called Fauconred. He dismounted at a run and barreled
into the Secretary, then came sliding hallooing down the slope of Redhand's hiding-place.

"Fauconred!"

"We've found you first, then! I think the King's men have given up. Are you unhurt?"

"The others . . ." They were gathering now, and he could see the red leathers of Fauconred's men, and the men on farm horses with rakes, the boys with scythes, the kitchen folk with cutlery. At Fauconred's ordering, they arranged themselves into a rude troop.

"Caredd . . ." Redhand said.

"They thought to take some action," Fauconred said.

"They dared not," one from the House said. "Not with the Arbiter there."

"She is in his protection."

"The King rages mad with this," said another.

"There are many of our people slain," Fauconred said. "The King's men hold the house and grounds. He'll be following, with an army. Already men have gone to raise his friends near here."

Redhand looked far away down the dawn, but he could see nothing of his home; only some few stragglers hurrying across the Downs to join them.

"Now," Fauconred said.

"Now." Redhand mounted. "Outward."

"Outward?"

"To Forgetful."

They followed him, his outlaw army; soldiers, cooks, farmboys.

And one who just then joined them, a boyish figure in a cloak of no color, riding a fine black horse.

4

There was a single window in the room where they had prisoned Caredd the Protector Redhand's wife and Sennred the King's brother. It was a blue hole pierced in the sheer curtain wall. The bricks of the wall were roughly masoned and a skillful man might crawl down, with a rope, a rope made of bedclothes . . . . Sennred leaned far out and looked down, felt a weird fear grip his knees and pull him back. He hated high places, and hated his fear of them.

Below, in the dawn light of the courtyard of Redsdown, a knot of frightened servants was herded from the house by soldiers. Faintly he could hear pleas, orders. He turned from the window.

Caredd had ceased weeping.

She sat on the bed, eyes on the floor, hands resting in her lap.

"Lady," he said.

"Have they brought him back?" she asked, tonelessly.

"No," he said. "No, they have not."

He did not like to impose by sitting with her on the bed; he felt too implicated in her grief. So he had stood much of the night, trying in a helpless way to help, attempting lame answers to her unanswerable questions. Almost, at times, for her sake, he wished he had prevented what had happened in the banquet hall.

"Will they burn the house?" she asked.

"Never," he said, with almost too great conviction. "Never while the Arbiter is in it."

"And if he leaves?"

"He will not. Not till your safety is promised him."

They were silent awhile. The blue window brightened imperceptibly.

"What will they do to you?" she asked.

"I am the King's brother. Will you sleep, lady? No harm will come to you."

She had hardly looked at him, hadn't spoken except to question him; he could not tell if she hated him. For Young Harrah he had spared no thoughts. For himself he cared little. The thought that Redhand's lady suffered, because of him . . . her quiet weeping, nightlong, had been as knives to him.

"I think," she said quietly, "you must have done as you did . . . partly, at least . . . for his sake."

"I did," he said earnestly. "I did as I thought he wished me to, then." Was it so? "Perhaps I did wrong."

She looked up at him where he stood by the window. "I hope they will not harm you."

Perhaps the night's exhaustion, he didn't know, but suddenly he felt a rush of hot tears to his own eyes. He turned again to the window.

A troop of King's men were riding slowly up the road from the Downs. One man held the reins of a horse who plodded on, head down; over its back was flung a burden . . . "No!" he cried out, and then bit his lip in regret. But she had heard, and ran to the window beside him.

"They have brought him home," she whispered.

"Brought someone home."

"He was unarmed. There was no way he could have . . . ."

"Lady, he was resourceful. And brave."

"*Was.* Oh, gods . . ."

"Is that his horse?"

"His? No, not any I know . . ."

"Where is his Secretary? Fled?"

"He would not have."

"He is not there."

She had taken Sennred's hand, perhaps not knowing it; gripped it tight. "They must let me see him!"

"They . . ."

"No! I will not! I couldn't . . ."

The troop entered the courtyard. What was now clearly a body swayed will-less on the nag's back. Caredd stared wide-eyed, mouth down-drawn. A boot dropped from one lifeless foot, a green and cuffed boot, a fashionable tasseled boot. Caredd cried out: "That isn't his!"

"Not his boot?"

She laughed, or sobbed. "Never. Never would he wear such a thing."

Sennred leaned far out the window, calling and gesticulating. "Who is it? Who is the dead man?"

A soldier looked up. "It is Farin's bastard son."

"Who?" Caredd asked.

"Farin's bastard," Sennred exulted.

"Shot with a Gun," the soldier called.

"A Gun! Where is Redhand?"

"Fled. Fled Outward with his people."

"Fauconred!" Caredd said. She began to slump forward. Sennred caught her around the waist and helped her to the bed.

"A Gun," he marveled. "The lout! Strikes out to find a murderer, and finds one. Of all nights in the year, flushes out such game! The idiot! I should have realized it from the first! He had a habit of drooling; he is well out of his miserable life . . . and tripping on his boots . . ."

"His green boots," Caredd said. "With the ridiculous cuffs."

"And tassels."

She laughed. She laughed with relief, with amazement, with grief, a long and rich and lovely laugh, without any edge of hysteria or exhaustion; her whole body laughed, and her laughter poured over Sennred like cool water.

The bar on their door slid back with a grating sound.

There was the Arbiter, and ten or twelve guards, and two of the King's young favorites.

"Sennred," the Arbiter said. "They will take you to the City."

"I will speak to the King."

"The King will not see you," said one of the young Defenders.

"I will go nowhere without a word with the King."

"Sennred," Learned said, "I have taken a liberty. I have promised them your good conduct in exchange for the Lady Caredd's safety."

"And the house's safety," Sennred said. It had been mostly what she talked of through the night.

"He will guarantee nothing beyond . . ."

"Listen to me," Sennred said to the King's men. "Listen to me and tell the King. I am his heir. He will have no other. If ever I am King and I find that any part of this house, or any hair of this lady's head has been harmed, I will spend my life and my crown and all its powers to avenge it. Avenge it most terribly."

He looked once at Caredd, sitting shyly on the bed; he heard an echo of her laughter.

"And now. We will go to the City."

It was Rennsweek of the vine flowers, strange brief instant when all the world was summer, even the dun country far Outward.

The broken rock walls of the Edge were bearded with yellow-green; the ravines and crevasses, just for this one moment, ran with water; tiny sun-colored flowers nodded in the dry winds that would soon desiccate them. The few who lived this far Outward, solitary people, gem hunters, ore smelters, people dun-colored as the earth, smiled their one smile of the year this week, it seemed.

The watch-castle Forgetful seemed to grow out of the dull earth, made as it was of the same stone, undressed, undecorated, rectangular indeed, but hardly more so than the split and shattered cliffs of the Edge it guarded. It had few windows, fewer doors; blind and mute. Only now, in this week, the endless scrollwork of vines which lashed Forgetful to the earth flowered bright orange briefly, so orange that anciently the flower's and the color's name were one word; and bees were drawn up from the Outland valleys to feed on the nectar that dripped from the fat blossoms as from mouths. And Forgetful in this one week seemed rightly named: Forgetful old tyrant with vine leaves in his hair, drunk on honey wine and Forgetful of a life of sin.

A tent and cave village squatted at the fortress's feet, serving the soldiers with all that soldiers have always been served with; a few of its low buildings, in parody of their master, were covered too with vine flowers. Two soldiers, on this day in Rennsweek, climbed up the stone way that led back to Forgetful from the village.

"Is he as bad, then?" the ostler asked.

"Worse than he was," the quartermaster said.

"Didn't the Endwife say spring would bring him round, and . . ."

"She said it was a melancholy."

"A soldier's malady."

"And if it weren't that, would she know?"

They paused for breath. The perfume of the vine flowers was thick. Forgetful motioned to them, almost gaily, with its fingers of vine leaves.

"He has ordered," the quartermaster said, "more stone on the . . . in the courtyard. And belts and spikes."

"To hold down the stones," the ostler said.

"Hasn't slept these three days."

"Dreams while he's awake, then."

The quartermaster shuddered. "I wouldn't have his dreams," he said. "Not for the wealth of Tintinnar."

Far above their heads, the war viols called alarm from the battlements. The two scrambled up the rock walls to where they could see. Inward, Inward, the song called, and they looked Inward.

It could be no army; it had no wagons, no advance guard, no banners. It trailed out over the boulder-strewn plain in twos and threes; yet the ones in front wore red, and now as they looked a small detachment broke off and rode hard for Forgetful, unfurling as they rode a banner with a red open palm on it.

"Redhand."

"Come to pay his brother a visit."

"What are those weapons? A hoe?"

"A rake. Perhaps . . ."

"What?" the quartermaster said.

The ostler slid down from the rock. "Perhaps he's gone mad too. It should be a merry meeting."

In Forgetful's courtyard goats bleated, cookfires showed pale in the sun, curious soldiers lounged at doorways and looked down from parapets at the Army and Household of the Great Protector Redhand.

In Forgetful's courtyard, in the midst of this, there was a pile of stones half as high as a man. Over and through some of the stones ran leather straps and straw ropes, which were tied tight to stakes. The thing seemed weirdly purposeful, devised by a logic alien to the rest of the courtyard, the cooks, the goats, the soldiers, yet the center of all, like the altar of an ignorant, powerful cult.

Redhand's horse turned and turned in the wide sunstruck yard. They had opened the gates for him, but none had greeted him. His little crowd looked around themselves, silent, waiting for an order.

"You." Redhand called a grizzled man who stared openly at him. "Call your captain."

"Indisposed."

"How, indisposed?"

The soldier only stared at Redhand, grinning with sunlight, or at a private joke; chewing on a sliver of bone. Then he turned and went to climb worn stairs toward the slit of a doorway. Even as he approached it a man came from the darkness within, armed, helmeted.

"Younger!" Redhand dismounted, went to meet his brother. Younger came toward him down the stairs, unsmiling; his eyes had the blank, inward look of a child just wakened from a nightmare. Without a word he embraced his brother, clung to him tightly. In the grip of his embrace, Redhand felt fear.

He pulled himself away, experimented with a friendly smile, a slap on the shoulder, a laugh of greeting. Younger reacted to the slap as though stung, and the laugh died in Redhand's throat.

He turned to Fauconred. "Can you . . ." He waited for Fauconred to pull his gaze from Younger's face. "Can you find lodging, stabling? You'll get no help, I think." Fauconred nodded, glanced once at Younger, and began to shout orders to the men behind him.

Redhand put an arm tentatively, gently around Younger's shoulders. "Brother," he said. "Brother." Younger made no response, only sheltered himself, as he ever had in his great griefs, within the circle of Redhand's arm. "Come inside."

He walked with Younger toward the door he had come out of. All around them the garrison and its hangers-on looked on, some grinning, some fearful. His brother had been baited, Redhand knew. It had been so before; and always Redhand had hit out at them, beaten at their grinning, stupid faces, so much more mad-seeming than his brother's. And he would again, he vowed, memorizing the mockers, unappeased by his knowledge that they knew no better.

At the cairn, Younger stopped, staring, all his senses focused there as a rabbit's on a fox in hiding. "In winter," he began, in a thin, dreaming voice.

"Yes."

"In winter the ground was frozen."

"And."

"He lay still. Now . . ."

"He?"

"Father. Where they buried him. The ground was frozen hard, and he couldn't get out. Now he would push through. He must not, though; no, though he pleads with me." He started suddenly, staring at the pile, and it was as though Redhand could feel a surge of fear through the arm he held his brother with.

"It was Harrah's son," Younger said.

"Harrah?"

"Harrah's son who saw him slain. Harrah's son who threw him in a shallow hole, far too shallow, so shallow the birds would come and peck and scratch the ground. Harrah's son, that Father would get out to go find, but must not, must not . . ."

"Harrah's son," Redhand said slowly, "is dead. I have killed him."

Younger turned to him slowly. He took Redhand's arm in a mad, steel grip. "Dead." Tears of exhausted anguish rose in his eyes. "Then why do the stones move always? *Why does he squirm? Why will he not lie still?*"

In Rennsweek when he was ten years old it had begun, this way: when the vine flowers bloomed on the walls of Old Redhand's house, Younger had poured a child's pailful of dirt on his father's sleeping face, because, he said, tears in his eyes, anyone could see the man was dead . . .

Night along the Edge was cold even in Rennsweek. A fire had been lit; it was the huge room's only light. It lit Younger, who stared into it, lit lights within his eyes, though to Redhand it seemed he looked through his brother's eyes, and the lights he saw were flames within.

"There was a duel," Redhand said. "A kind of duel, with carving knives, in the banquet hall at Redsdown. I killed him. Then I fled."

Impossible to judge if Younger heard or understood. He only looked into the fire, flames gesturing within his eyes.

"Now I need you, Younger."

Always it had been that the faction that commanded a garrison of the Edge could forge it into a weapon for its use. After the battle at Senlinsdown in the old days, Black Harrah returned from Forgetful without orders to do so, with an unruly army and a new big wife for the King, and the Reds who had thought the King to be in their pockets backed away.

"The King Red Senlin's Son," Redhand said, "was Young Harrah's lover. He will send an army to invest Forgetful, once he deduces I am here. I would prevent that."

Yes, and Red Senlin too, Redhand thought. *He* had gone away to the Edge to be vice-regent then, and in his time *he* had returned with bought Outland chiefs and an army of Edge-outcast soldiers. And Black Harrah had turned and fled . . . Suddenly Redhand felt caught up in the turnings of an old tale, a tale for children, endlessly repetitious. Well, what other chance had he but to repeat what his fathers and their fathers had done? He would not wait here to be ferreted like a rabbit.

"I want to march first, Younger. I want you with me. Help me now, as ever I have done for you."

Younger said nothing, did not turn from the fire.

There was this flaw in it then. The old tale stopped here, the teller faltered at this turning.

That mob in the courtyard was no army. Fauconred had had to cut off some bandit's ear in order to find lodging for Redhand's household. He could flog them into order, a kind of order, with like means if he had weeks in which to do it. He did not have weeks.

"If flesh were stone," said Younger. "If all flesh were stone . . ."

No. He couldn't anyway face the King and the Folk with such a band. Outlanders, and men like these, had no strictures such as the Protectorate had concerning the Folk; they would take what they could. He must draw the country Defenders to his banners, keep the City open to him. It could not be done with marauders.

And they would not flock with any will to himself. He had no true friends; his strength lay in pacts, alliances, sealed with largesse. Red Senlin's Son had seen that, and vitiated it with his City courtiers and his own largesse.

There must be another banner to ride Inward with than his own.

"Her spies," Younger said, smiling. "The messages they take her. Songs, lies, jokes. What harm is there in that?"

With an instant, horrid clarity Redhand remembered the last time he had seen her: at the Little Lake, in the bloody snow, shuffling away on her big horse, riding Outward, looking back for fear.

No!

She must have had the child. Black Harrah's, doubtless. As he had said to Red Senlin (so long ago it seemed) that didn't matter. All the Outlands and half the world would kneel to kiss Little Black's heir.

No!

A joining of Red and Black. An end to the world's anguish. Despite his promises, the King had seized lands, divided them among his friends, who played in the City while farms rotted. The Downs would be his. And the City—well. He had been master of the City. He had friends. It would do.

No! No!

"What harm is there in it?" Younger said again, his voice beginning to quaver.

Redhand took hold of his revulsion and with an effort wrung its neck, stilling its protest. "No harm, brother," he said. "Can you find one of these spies? Do you know them?"

"I know them. Oh, I know them all."

"Send for one. Have him brought here. I . . . have a little joke myself to tell the Queen."

Younger returned to staring into the fire. "Only . . ."

"Only?"

"We will go Inward. But." He turned to Redhand. "Father *must not come!*" He beat his palm against the chair arm with each word. "They said he suffered from a soldier's melancholy. They said, the Endwives said, that spring would bring him round, and they would nurse him back to health. But those were lies."

As in one of the new pageants the King had caused to be shown in the City, the madman in the courtyard of Forgetful had an audience, an audience though of only one; and unlike those pageants' actors, he was unaware of being watched, for the drama unfolding within him took all his attention.

On the belvedere above, his brother, his audience, was attentive, though feeling he had lost the thread, the point, the plot; he shivered in the warm wind, dislocated, lost, feeling that at any moment some unexpected shock might happen. He leaned against the belvedere, tense with expectation, bored with awful expectation.

Now unlike those City pageants, this audience had an audience himself.

Again, an audience of one.

Only she knew the plot. This scene had been laid out in cards the troubled man she watched had never seen; it was a scene in a story begun she knew not how many millennia before she lived, whose end might come as long after her death; she only knew her part, and prayed now to many gods that she might play it right.

From a pouch beneath her cloak of no color she drew the Gun named Suddenly. She was behind a thick pillar of duncolored stone. There were stairs at her back. Beyond, Outward, yellow clouds encircled the setting sun like courtiers around a dying Red king, and as the sun set, the war-viols of Forgetful would start, calling the garrison to meat and meeting. She hoped the noise would cover Suddenly's voice. Afterwards, she would go quickly down those stairs, down to the stables, to Farin's black horse she had come to love, without, she hoped, arousing more suspicion than she had already. And after that—well: she didn't know. Nightfall. A curtain on this scene. She scarcely cared, if this was all played right.

She didn't know either that she, who watched the madman's audience, had herself an audience. Pageants upon pageants: she was observed.

He had come up the narrow stair to find his master. Had seen her at the top of the stair, dim, a blue shadow in the evening light. When she drew the thing from within her clothes, he at first did not recognize it; stood unmoving while a chain of associations took place within him.

So for a moment they all stood motionless; he on the stair, she with the Gun, he on the belvedere, he below biting his nails, and also he headless within the inconstant earth.

Then the one on the stair ran up.

She didn't know who or what had seized her, only that its strength was terrible. A hand was clamped over her face, she could not cry out or breathe; an arm encircled her, tight as iron bands, pressing the Gun against her so that if she fired she shot herself. She was picked up like a bundle of no weight, and before she was trundled away fast down the stair she saw that the man on the belvedere still looked down: he had not seen or heard.

They went quickly down. At a dim turning they paused; her captor seemed unsure. They turned down a tunnel-like hall, but stopped when the sound of men came from far off; turned back, slipped within a niche formed by the meeting of vast pillars, and waited.

She was beginning to faint; she could not breathe, and where the arm held her the pain had faded to a tingling numbness. Sheets of blank blackness came and went before her eyes. She tasted blood; the pressure of his hand had cut her mouth on her teeth.

When those coming up the hall had passed without seeing them, she was rushed out and down again. She saw evening light spilling from a door at the tunnel's end, and then it was extinguished, and she knew nothing for a time.

The thud of a door closing woke her. She woke gulping air, looking into a bald, blank face hooded in red, oddly calm. Its thin lips moved, and the words came as from a distance. "You won't cry out, struggle."

"No."

"If they found you. If I gave you to them, they would hang you."

"Yes. I won't." He was not "they," then?

His face withdrew. Her thudding heart slowed its gallop, and involuntarily she sighed a long, shuddering sigh.

The room was tiny, higher almost than wide; above her head a small window showed a square of summer evening; there was no other light. A wooden door, small and thick. A plain wooden pallet she lay on. A wooden chair he sat in; in one hand he held Suddenly by its barrel, loosely, as though it were a spoon.

"You are Just," he said.

"If you drop that," she said, her voice still hoarse, "they will know soon enough you have me."

He lifted the Gun, examined it without curiosity. "Does it have a name?"

"Why do you keep me?" she said. "I know you, I know you are a thing of his." She hoped to probe him, see if there was some disloyalty, some grudge she could play on . . . His face, though, remained expressionless. The same mask she had seen always beside Redhand in the City that spring. Who was he, then?

"I was told they have names."

"They do."

"I have an interest in names."

As though they had gathered here for some scholarly chat. She almost smiled. "And so what is yours?"

"I am called Secretary now."

"That's no name."

"No. I have no other."

She could not read him. There was nothing to grasp. His voice, cool and liquid, the strange nakedness of his face. His hideous strength. For the first time since he had seized her, she felt fear; yet could not imagine how to plead with him, beg him, felt that he knew nothing of mercy. A cold sweat sprang out on her forehead.

"I will say a name," he said, "if I can, and you will tell me if you know it."

What name? Some other she had slain? Some brother or sister? She would tell him nothing . . .

"Here is the name." It seemed to take all his strength to say it. "Leviathan."

She only looked at him in disbelief.

"Leviathan," he said again. "Do you know that name?"

Evening had deepened. The red cloak he wore was dark now as dried blood; his pale head shone like wax. And as it grew darker in the room, his eyes seemed to glow brighter, as precious stones do.

"Yes." In a whisper.

"Where he lives," the dark form said. "Where he lives, who he is, how to come to him."

He could not mean this; he must be mad.

And yet. "Yes." Again a whisper; he leaned forward to hear. "Yes, I know."

Slowly, as though not meaning to, he leveled Suddenly at her. "Do you pull this? The lever here? And it will kill you?"

She pressed herself against the stone wall behind her, but could not press through it.

"Listen to me," he said, the voice calm, liquid. "I will give you this choice. Take me to this one you know of, wherever, however far Outward. I will give you back this. If you refuse, tell me now, and I will kill you with it."

There was an old story she knew: a brother was surrounded by King's men, who closed in upon him with torches and dogs; he was utterly lost, yet had to escape. He did this, they say: he took a step Outward, a step Inward, and a step away, out and gone. The King's men when they closed the circle found only themselves; they never found him, nor did the Just ever see him again.

She took the step. "Yes. I'll take you. If we leave tonight. I'll take you to see him, I swear it, face to face."

THREE

RECORDER

1

How many skills he had learned since that distant morning on the Drum when with the young Endwife he had learned to say Cup and Drink! If there were wonder in him he would have wondered at it.

With Redhand he had learned secrecy, the gaining of ends unknown to others by means devised to seem other than they were. It was not a mode that suited him; he had this failing, a curiosity about others that made it hard for him to keep himself secret. Yet he had this virtue: it all meant little to him but the learning, and he never betrayed himself by eagerness or need.

Never till now.

For this mission was his only. No one had assigned it to him, as Caredd had the watching of her husband, or Redhand the keeping close of his alliances. This he had found within himself, this was the engine of his being, and he had used force and cunning and even the betrayal of his trust to Redhand to accomplish it.

And he feared for its success.

There were winds blowing in him then, awful winds he could hardly bear: this, he thought, is what they all feel, this singularity, this burden of unknown quest, that drives all else out, obscures other loyalties, causes their eyes and thoughts to drift away in conversation, their attention to wander: a mission, whose shape they cannot perceive, whose end they fear for, an end that may be a means, they don't know, or a lie, and yet they have no other.

He thought that in this he had become as fully a man as any of them. It gave him joy, and fear; a fierce resolution, and a strange vacillation he had known nothing of before.

He had stolen. Food from the kitchens, money from the purse he carried for Redhand, good boots and a lamp and a shelter from the quartermaster, a long knife and a short one. He would have stolen horses, but she said they would be useless till far beyond.

He had left the ravished purse and its papers for Redhand, without explanation—had thought to leave a note saying he was returning to the stars, but did not—and had crept away then with the girl, at midnight. Away from his master and the trusts given him. Away from the intrigues he had had some part in directing. Away from Younger's very instructive madness. Away from Forgetful's Outward wall, carrying the girl Nod on his back and her Gun in his belt, down the blind nighttime cliffs of the Edge, ever down, till dawn came and the girl slept and predatory birds circled the ledge they lay on, startled perhaps to see wingless ones there.

From there on the ledge at morning he looked over the Outlands, smoky with mist and obscured by coils of cloud. The paths of meandering rivers were a denser white than the greenshadowed land, which stretched flat and foggy to a great distance; far off the mists seemed to thicken into sky and gray rains could be seen moving like curtains in a wind. Except where low hills humped their backs above the mist, it was all shrouded. He woke her, they ate, and continued down.

He imagined this to be like his progress was from sky to earth, though he could remember nothing of that. As they went downward the air seemed to thicken, the sun's clarity was dimmed, the smooth-faced rocks became slippery with moss and the stone ground began to crumble into earth, sandy at first and cut with flood beds, and then darker and bound by vegetation.

By evening on the second day they were within the Outlands, up to their knees in its boggy grasp.

Late in the night Nod awoke, forgetting where she was, how she had come to be there. She sat upright in the utter darkness, hearing animal noises she did not recognize. Something very close to her grunted, and she inhaled sharply, still half asleep. Then the lamp came bright with a buzzing sound, and his familiar naked face, calm and inquisitive, was looking at her.

"Do we go on now?" he asked.

She blinked at him. "Do you never sleep?"

There was a halo of moisture around the lamp's glow, and clumsy insects knocked against it.

"How far is it?"

"Many days. Weeks." How would she know? How far is it to heaven, how long is death? There were a thousand spirits Nod believed in, prayed to, feared. Yet if someone had said to her, Let's go find the bogey who lives in the lake or the dryad of the high woods, she would have laughed. All that lay in some other direction, on a path you could put no foot on, somewhere at right angles to all else. If they wanted *you*, they would find you.

And perhaps then Leviathan wanted this one. Perhaps he walked that path, perhaps he was at right angles to all else.

"It will be dawn soon," he said.

Yes. That was it; and in spite of what they had agreed, *he* led *her*: to the edge of the world, to look over the edge, and call into the Deep.

Through the morning, mist in wan rags like unhappy ghosts rose up from the Outlands, drawn into the sun, but still lay thick along the river they followed. Gray trees with pendulous branches waded up to their knobby knees in the slow water.

"We must go up," she said. "We have to have dry ground, though we lose the way Outward." That she knew, that the rivers flowed Outward here as they flowed Inward on the other side of the Edge. But they would have to find another marker, or spend a lifetime in mud here.

They had begun to decide which way was up when the Secretary stopped still, listening. She stopped too, could hear nothing, and then sorted from the forest's murmur the knock of wood on wood, the soft slosh of water around a prow. A sound she knew well.

The Outlanders she had known were dour merchants she had ferried to the City, resplendent for the occasion but awed too: she had felt superior to them in her City knowledge. Here it was otherwise, and she sank behind the knees of a great tree. The Secretary followed; she was, after all, the guide.

The boat sounds grew closer, though they could see nothing through the shroud of mist; and then there came, walking on the water it seemed, a tall, tall figure, hideously purple of face with staring eyes . . . It took them a moment to see it was the boat's carved prow.

Dark men with long, delicate poles sounded the river channel, and called softly back to those who rowed. Deep-bellied, slow, with tiny banners limp in the windless air, it passed so close they could hear the oarsmen grunt, and its wake lapped their feet. Yards of it went by, each oarhole painted as a face with the oar its tongue, and each face looked at them unseeing.

In the stern, stranger than all the painted faces, there was a woman under a pavilion, a vast woman, a woman deep-bellied like the ship. She lay cushioned in her fat, head resting on an arm like a thigh, fast asleep. At her feet, in diverse attitudes, Outlanders, chiefs with brass spangles braided in their beards, slept too; one held to his softly heaving chest a grotesque battle-ax.

The boat passed with a soft sound, rolled slightly with the channel, which made the Queen list too, and was lost in the mist.

Other boats came after, not so grand but stuffed full of armed men, spiky and clanking with weapons. One by one they appeared and glided by. Deep within one boat, someone chuckled.

"Is the child strong?" Redhand asked. "Healthy? Is it male or female?"

The Queen said nothing, only continued with her refreshment. Before her was a plate like a tray, tumbled up in Outland fashion with cakes, fruits, cheese, and fat sausages.

"I would see the child," Redhand said.

"There are other things," the Queen said, "that must come first."

She was waited on by a lean, fish-eyed man, her companion and general, a man named Kyr: Redhand and he had exchanged names, looked long in each other's faces, both trying to remember something, but neither knew that it was Kyr who had nearly killed Redhand at the Little Lake. Kyr passed to his mistress a napkin; she took it, her eyes on her food.

So they waited—Redhand; Fauconred, who looked red-faced and furious as though he had been slapped; and Younger Redhand.

It had been an awful week. Redhand, with Fauconred's help, had locked his screaming brother in a tower room, at dead of night so no one saw. Then he had ordered the cairn in the courtyard dismantled.

He dug out of the garrison an unshaven, wispy man who said he was Gray, made him presentable, and then, with him presiding, had Old Redhand exhumed from the courtyard. He forced himself to look on, his jaw aching with nights of sleepless resolve; he made the garrison look on too, and they did, silent and cowed before his ferocity and his father's mortality.

He had found a quiet chamber within Forgetful, that once may have been a chapel, with dim painting on one wall he could not read, of a smiling, winged child perhaps; it would do. He had the great stones of the floor torn up, and a place made. From the dark wood of old chests a carpenter of his household had made a box.

"Wine," the Queen said. "No water."

When the last of the floor stones had been mortared back into place, and the same carpenter had tried an inscription on them, two or three ancient letters only that would stand for the rest, Redhand went to the tower and released Younger. Hesitant, his cheeks dirty with dried tears, Younger allowed himself to be taken and shown the empty place in the courtyard, and the quiet room and its secure stones. *Now,* Redhand had said, gripping his brother's shoulders, *now you have no more excuse to be mad. Please. Please . . .* They had embraced, and stood for a while together, and Redhand from exhaustion and confused love had wept too.

Whatever it was, the true burial, or Redhand's strength in doing this, or only that the vine flowers fell in that week: the horrid surgery worked. Younger slept for a day, worn out by his adventure, and woke calm: well enough to sit with his brother and Fauconred now, somewhat stunned, with the look of one returned from a long and frightening journey.

Kyr poured water from a ewer over the Queen's fingers, and only when she had dried them did she look up, with her marvelous eyes, at her new allies. "Have this cleared," she said, gesturing with a ringed hand at her pillaged feast, "and we will talk."

There had been little time for Redhand to worry over his Secretary and his weird disappearance, though now he felt in need of him. The man, if man he had been, was so fey that in a sense Redhand felt he had not ever been truly there: this though he had saved Redhand's life, twice. Well, there was no help for it. Redhand felt less that he had lost a friend or even an aide than that he had misplaced a charm, lucky but possibly dangerous too.

"Now, lady," Redhand said.

"We have conditions," she said. "We have drawn them up, you and whoever else will sign them."

"Conditions."

"Certain incomes I demand. Honors restored. There is a house near Farinsdown I wish for my summers." She took a paper from Kyr. "There are names here of those I want punished."

"Punished?"

"Much wrong was done me." As though it were a morsel, her fat hands unrolled the paper lovingly. "Red Senlin's Son, I have him here, and he must die."

"So must we all." Something like a smile had begun to cross Redhand's features. "Who else have you?"

She let the paper curl itself again, her dark eyes suspicious. "There are others."

"Half the Red Protectorate?"

"I will have revenge."

Redhand began to laugh, a hoarse, queer laugh that he owed to his old wound, and over his laughter the Queen's voice rose: "I will have revenge! They murdered Black Harrah, they imprisoned my husband, they took my crown, they killed my child!"

Redhand stopped laughing. "Your child."

The Queen stared at him defiantly.

"Where is the child?" he asked.

She rose slowly, raised her head, proud. "There is no child," she said quietly. "Red Senlin murdered him."

"Murdered a *child?*"

"His relentlessness. His constant harassment. I miscarried on the Drum."

Redhand too rose, and came toward the Queen, so malevolent that Kyr stepped close. "You have no child," Redhand said. "Then tell me, Lady, what you do here with your conditions, and your demands, and your revenges. Do you think we owe you now, any of us, anyone in the world? For your beauty only, did you think?"

She did not shrink, only batted her black lashes.

"These," he said, flicking her papers, hoarse with rage, "these will be our reason then to cross the Drum? Answer me, Lady. To kill the King, and any else who might have mocked you once or done you wrong?"

"No, Redhand."

"What reason, then?"

"To free my husband from the house they have prisoned him in. Free Little Black, and make him King again."

Redhand turned away, flung himself in his chair. But he said nothing.

"Send to the Black Protectorate," the Queen said. "Send word that you mean to do this. He has always been their King. They will rise."

Redhand glared at nothing, his jaw tight.

"It is your only hope, Redhand."

"The old man may be dead, or mad," Fauconred said.

"He is not dead. I have spies near him. And he is no more mad than he ever was."

"When the King learns of it," Redhand growled, "he will kill Little Black. It surprises me he has not yet."

The Queen sat heavily. "He will not learn of it. Send word to Blacks only, I will say whom, they will not reveal it. To your Red friends say only you want their help. Put it about that the child lives."

Redhand slowly shook his head.

"The notion brought me you," the Queen said lightly. "And before Red Senlin's Son learns that you mean anything but to save yourself, Little Black will be with us. I have people, Redhand, in the City, who have planned his escape, are ready to pluck Little Black from that awful place at my word."

"I have no faith in this," Redhand said.

"Nor I," said Fauconred.

The Queen's eyes lit fiercely. "Then you tell me, exiles, outlaws, what other chance you have. What other hope."

There was a long silence. Far away, from the courtyard, they could hear a fragment of an Outland song. Redhand, sunk in thought, looked less like a man weighing chances than one condemned reconciling himself. At last he said, almost to himself: "We will go Inward, then."

The Queen leaned forward to hear him. "Inward?"

"Send word to your people. Free the King, if you can."

She leapt up, flinging up her arms, and began a vast dance. "Inward! Inward! Inward!" She lunged at the table, reaching for her papers. "The conditions . . ."

"No."

"You must sign them."

"No. No more. Leave that."

She turned on them in fury. "You will sign them! Or I return!"

"Yes!" Redhand hissed. "Yes, go back to your bogs and lord it over your villages, weep storms over your wrongs. I will have no vengeance done. None." He raised his arm against her. "Pray to all your gods you are only not hanged for this. Make no other conditions."

"My incomes," she said, subdued. "What is due me."

"*If* this succeeds," Redhand said, "you will be treated as befits the King's loved wife. But all direction, now and hereafter, will be mine."

"You would be King yourself."

"I would be safe. And live in a world that does not hate me. You find that hard to grasp."

She rolled up her papers. "Well, for now. We will talk further of this."

"We will not." He turned to leave her; Fauconred and Younger stood to follow.

"Redhand," she said. "There is one further thing." Regal, on feet strangely small, she made progress toward them as though under sail. "You must kneel to me."

"Kneel!" Fauconred said.

"You must kneel, out there, before them all, or I swear I will return."

"Never, he never will," Younger whispered.

She only regarded them, waiting for her due. "Kneel to me, kneel and kiss my hand, swear to be my Defender."

Fauconred, and Younger with his whipped boy look, waited. Redhand, with a gesture as though he were wiping some cloud from before his eyes, only nodded.

It all took so long, he thought. So terribly long. Life is brief, they said. But his stretched out, tedious, difficult, each moment a labor of unutterable length. He wished suddenly it might be over soon.

Of all hard things Sennred had ever borne, imprisonment seemed the hardest. Adversity had never hurt him, not deeply; he seemed sometimes to thrive on it. The mockery of children at his misshapenness had made him not hard but resilient; death and war had made him the more fiercely protective of what he loved; the intrigues of his brother's brilliant court had made him not quick and brittle as it had the Son, but slow, long-sighted, tenacious. Though he was young, younger by years than the young King, Sennred had nothing left in him impetuous, half-made, loud.

What marked him as young was his love. He gave it, or withheld it, completely and at once. He had given it to his brother, and to Redhand. And then lastly to a young wife with autumn eyes and auburn hair, a free gift, without conditions, a gift she knew nothing of yet.

And what galled him in imprisonment, made him rage, was to be separated from those he loved, deprived of his watching over them; he could not conceive they could get on without him, it blinded him with anxiety that they were in danger, threatened, taking steps he could not see.

Where they had put him he could hardly see if it was night or day.

As though it were a maze made for the exercise of some small pet, most of the great house he had been shut in had been sealed off. The rest, windowless, doorless, he had his way in. It had been a Black mansion in some ancient reign; there were high halls where ghostly furniture still held conference, moldering bedrooms, corridors carved and pillared where his footsteps multiplied and seemed to walk toward him down other carved corridors. For days on end he went about it with candles cadged from his guards, exploring, looking he was not sure for what: a way out, an architectural pun somewhere that would double out suddenly and show him sky, blue and daylit.

His companions were a woman who brought food, deaf and evil-smelling—he thought sometimes her odor had got into his food, and he couldn't eat—and his guards, whom he would meet in unexpected places and times. He seemed rarely to see the same guard twice, and could not tell if there were multitudes of guards or if they were only relieved often. Anyway they were all huge, leather-bound, dull and seemingly well-paid; all he could get from them were candles, and infrequently a jug of blem, after which he would go around the great rooms breaking things and listening to the echoes.

And there was the ghost.

He had at first been a glimpse only, a shadow at the far edge of vision, and Sennred never saw more of him than a flick of robe disappearing around a corner. But the ghost seemed to delight in following him, and they began a game together through the dayless gloom of the house; Sennred supposed the ghost suffered as much from strangulating boredom as he did.

Natural enough that such a place would have a ghost, though Sennred suspected that this one was at least a little alive. Nor had it taken him long to deduce whose ghost it might be. He would have asked the guards, but he was afraid they would make new arrangements, and his only relief from the torment of imprisonment was his plan to catch this other one.

His trap was laid.

He had found a low corridor, scullery or something, with doors at each end of its lefthand wall. He learned that these were both doors of a long closet that ran behind the wall the length of the corridor. He learned he could go in the far door, double back through the closet, taking care not to stumble on the filthy detritus there, and come out the other door, just behind anyone who had followed him into the corridor.

Once he had discovered this, he had only to wait till his ghost was brave enough to follow him there. As near as he could measure time, it was a week till he stood listening at his trapdoor for soft, tentative foot-steps . . .

When he judged they had just passed him, he leapt out with a yell, filthy with cobwebs, and grappled with his ghost.

He had a first wild notion that it was truly a ghost, a greasy rag covering only a bundle of bones; but then he turned it to face him, and looked into the face he had expected, wildeyed, the mouth open wide in a soundless scream.

"Your Majesty," Sennred said.

"Spare me!" said the King Little Black in a tiny voice. "Spare me for right's sake!"

"And what will you give me?"

"What you most want," said the ghost.

"Freedom," Sennred said. "Freedom from this place. With the power of your crown, old man, grant me that."

He was old, and lived by lizard hunting. Perhaps the bloodstained boat was all his living; the Secretary, anyway, didn't think of that, though he did perceive the old man's terror when they appeared before him as though risen out of the mud. The coins they gave him must have been nearly useless to him; it didn't matter, they had been ready after days of mud to wrest the boat from him if need be, and the old one knew that.

The Secretary turned back once to look at him as the girl poled off. He stood unblinking, wrinkled as a reptile, his old claw clutching the gold.

Nod had long ago given up any idea of overpowering her captor, seizing the Gun from him, murdering him by stealth. Even to slip away, leaving the Gun, though it would have been like losing a limb, even that she had abandoned; he slept only when she slept, and her slightest stirring woke him.

So she went Outward, days into weeks, in a weird dream, the half dream the sleeper seems to know he dreams, and struggles restlessly to wake from. Yet she could not wake. Waking, she poled the boat. Sleeping, she dreamt of it.

It seemed they moved through the interior of some vast organism. It was dark always, except at high noon when a strange diffracted sunlight made everything glisten. The trees hung down ganglia of thick moss into the brown river slow with silt; the river branched everywhere into arteries clogged with odorous fungi and phosphorescent decay. At night they lay in their shelter listening to the thing gurgling and stirring.

They came once upon a place where a fresh spring had come forth in the scum and decay, like a singer at a funeral. The spring had swept clean a little lagoon, and even bared a few rocks of all but a slimy coat of algae.

She swam, dappled by sun through the clotted leaves.

He had some notion, abstract only, of men's bodies and their heats and functions, and had stored up court gossip and jokes to be explicated later. He watched her, faintly curious. She was made not unlike himself.

She wriggled up onto the rocks, laughing, brushing the water from her face, pale and glistening as a fish.

She saw him watching. "Turn away," she said sternly, and he did.

When at last the forest began to thin, and the tree trunks stood up topless and rotted like old teeth, and the rivers merged into a shallow acrid lake that seemed to have drowned the world, they had lost track of what week it was.

"Why are there no people?" His voice was loud in the utter silence. "Shouldn't there be villages, towns?"

"I don't know."

"There are Outlanders."

"Yes."

"Where?"

"Elsewhere."

"Do you know where we are?"

"No."

There was no line between water and sky; it was all one gray. The hooded sun burned dimly Inward, and a light like it burned within the lake.

There were no trees here; perhaps the shelf of the world below had grown too thin to contain their roots. There were only bunches of brown weed that stood up leafless and sharp, with a silver circle of wake around each stem. Only by these weeds could they tell their little boat moved at all.

They could see far off to their right a moving smudge of pink on the water. It rose up, settled again. Then a long boat gray as the lake crept from the weeds out there, and gray men with nets attached to long poles began to snare the pink birdlets that had floated away from the flock. When one was snared it cried out, and the pink clot rose, and then settled again nearby.

"Quickwings too stupid to fly all away," Nod said. It was the first time she had spoken that day, except to answer him.

"You will speak to them. Ask them . . ."

"No."

"Ask them . . ."

"I will not, not, not!" She looked around her, looking for escape, but there was only gray water, gray sky, indifferent, featureless. She sat down suddenly in the bows and began to weep.

He only stared at her, long hands on his knees, mystified.

Far off where the nets moved quick as birds in the gloom, men turned and pointed at their boat.

The birdmen had made themselves an island on that placeless lake; it was a raft, anchored to the bottom, an acre of lashed beams, platforms, rotten wood. All night the quickwings they had caught that day fluttered within long cages of wicker and string; all night the lake oozed up through the ancient beams of the raft. So old and big it was, their raft grew little groves of mushrooms, and fish lived out their lives amid the sheltering fronds that grew from its bottom. It was to this island they brought Nod and the Secretary, not quite prisoners, yet not quite guests either.

All night the one-eyed birdman sat next to Nod, talking in a language she didn't understand. He would slip off into the dark and return with some token, a stone, a rag of figured, moldered cloth, a lizard's tooth.

She told herself he wasn't there. She sat with her knees up, trying to clean from her feet the inexplicable sores that had begun to appear there.

She glanced up now and again; far off, in the muddy light of a lantern, the Secretary sat talking with some of them. They gestured, stood, pointed, sat again. He listened, unmoving. She had the idea he understood no more of their talk than she did.

When the one-eyed birdman, with a sudden gesture, slipped his moist hands beneath her clothes, she rose, furious, and made her way over incomprehensible bundles and slimy decks to where the Secretary sat, looking Outward.

"Protect me," she whispered fiercely, "or give me back my Gun."

Dawn was a gray stain everywhere and nowhere.

"Do you hear? I am helpless here. I hate it. Are you a man?"

"There." He pointed Outward. A light that might have been marsh-light flickered far away and disappeared. "There. The last house in the world, they said; and the one who lives there has spoken to Leviathan."

2

T he tower of Inviolable may be the highest place in the world. No one
 has measured, but no one knows a higher place.

There are many rooms in the tower, scholars' rooms, put there less
for the sublimity of the height than in the Order's belief that men who
spend their lives between pages should at least climb stairs for their
health. Because Inviolable has no need for defense, the tower is pierced
with broad windows, and the windows look everywhere, down the forests to the lake in the center of the world, a blue smudge of mist on
summer mornings. Outward over the Downs where the river Wanderer
branches into a hundred water fingers, to the Drum and farther still. But
when the scholars put down their pens and look up, their gaze is inward;
the vistas they see are in time not space.

One looks out, though, a slight and softly handsome man in black,
looking for something he probably could not anyway perceive at this
height, this distance . . . There is, far off, a tower of dark cloud, a last
summer storm walking Inward across the Drum to thresh the harvest
lands with hail; Learned Redhand can hear the mutter of its thunder. The
storm raises winds around the world; even here in the forests, wind turns

leaves to show their pale undersides as though it flung handfuls of silver coins through the trees. It will be here soon enough. Yes: the Black Protectorate raises an army on the Black Downs, Redhand's dependents unfurl, however reluctantly, their old battle banners: the storm will come soon Inward.

Was it this that old Mariadn died to avoid, this the burden she ordered the Grays never to envy him? Did she lay it on him only because he deserved to suffer it, or because she saw something in him that might mitigate it, some strength to make a shelter from this storm? If she did, he cannot find it in himself.

In another tower bells ring, low-voiced and sweet, reverberating through Inviolable, saying *day's end, day's end*. Around Learned, books close with the sound of many tiny doors to secret places, and there is the sound of speaking for speaking's sake, now that silence has been lifted. They pass behind Learned on their way downward, greeting him diffidently, expecting no reply, Arbiter, Arbiter, good evening, good day, Arbiter, our thoughts are with you . . . Against the sound of their many feet descending the stairs, he hears the sound of someone ascending; as those going down grow distant, one comes closer. He is alone now in the tower; the square of sunlight printed on the wall behind him is dimming, and the window before him rattles as the winds begin to enwrap Inviolable.

The unquestioning affection, the sincere hopes of his scholars, he knows to be less for him than for the black he wears; though, perhaps, by the end of his lifelong Arbitration, he may earn it for himself. Or they may call him, as they do some others of ancient times, a white Arbiter, foolish, useless to the world.

Or worse, a Red.

No. Not ever that.

A bone-white Gray at last achieves the room Learned sits in and comes to him, hesitant, unwilling to break Learned's meditation.

"Yes? Come in. What is it?"

"There is a rider below, Arbiter, all in red leather."

"I have expected him, I suppose."

"He says he comes from your brother the Protector. He brings you this."

It is a small piece of scarlet ribbon tied in a complex knot.

"Tell him to wait," Learned says, turning the ribbon in his fingers, "and see my carriage is made ready to travel."

Later that night, in a secret place in the forest far below Inviolable, white hands laid out cards on a board within a painted tent. The Neither-nor shivered, and the lamp flame too, when wind discovered the tent's hiding-place and made the tent-cloths whisper; but it was not only the wind that made the Neither-nor shiver.

For the seventh time It had turned down the card that bore an image of Finn: a death's head, with a fire burning in his belly, and this motto: *Found by the lost.*

The Neither-nor had chosen the card Roke to be the girl whose name was called Nod; and Roke should fall in some relation to the card Caermon, who was Redhand; should fall with the trump Rizna between, It had hoped. But Caermon hid within the pack, and Finn fell. Odd.

Where was Nod?

Dead . . . no; the cards did not seem to say so. Gone, lost. Anyway, her task remained undone, that was clear. Redhand hid. The Neither-nor snapped the Roke card's edge against the board.

The wind, with a sudden gust like a hand, picked up the tent's door flap. Outside, clouds raced across the Wanderers, or the Wanderers raced, it could not be said which; the forest, opulent in the windy darkness, gestured toward the Neither-nor's door.

Someone was coming up the secret way toward the Neither-nor's tent.

With a sudden rush of feeling, the Neither-nor thought it to be Nod. But in another moment the figure became a man, a boy really, who did look like the girl Nod. His name was called Adar, the Neither-nor remembered: a name chosen for great things.

As the Neither-nor had partly suspected, Adar had come to ask after the girl.

"No word, no word."

"The cards . . ."

"Silent, confused it may be."

They sat together as though afloat; the tent-cloths filled like sails, and the forest creaked and knocked and whispered continuously. The Neither-nor began to lay out cards, aimlessly, hardly watching, while the boy talked.

"The King has begun a tomb in the City. A hundred artisans are at work on it. He plays with this while the Queen gathers strength."

Doth, Haspen, Shen. Barnol, Ban, the trump Tintinnar, Roke and Finn again.

"I have watched near Fennsdown. They will not move without the King. Redhand . . ."

The Neither-nor's pack released the card Caermon.

"Redhand." The Neither-nor knew the next card. Adar fell silent. Whatever had become of Nod, whatever the chill card Finn spoke of, at least now It knew the next step.

"Redhand," said Adar, and the Neither-nor laid Rizna reversed before him, Rizna with sickle and seedbag, who constantly reaps what he forever sows.

"It will storm soon," the Neither-nor said. "Sit with me awhile before you go . . ."

All through that night, and through the next day and the next night, the Arbiter's closed black carriage rolled over the world, following the man in red leather.

Once out of the forest, they flew over the streets of Downs villages rain-washed and deserted nearly; along streets cobbled and dirt, past shuttered walls where loud placards of the Just were pasted, that the Folk would not or dared not remove; and on then, past the last cottage lamplit in the dark and stormy afternoon, on Outward.

Inside, the Arbiter, in a wide hat against the dripping from a leak in the roof, his hands on a stick between his knees, listened to the rattle of the fittings and the knocking of the wind against his door. Off and on, he turned over in his mind an old heretical paradox: if a man has two parents, four grandparents, eight great-grandparents, and so on endlessly back to the beginning of time, then how could it be that the world began with only fifty-two?

The carriage rolled; eight, sixteen, thirty-two, sixty-four, a hundred and twenty-eight, two hundred and fifty-six . . . In thirty generations or so the number would be almost beyond counting. And yet the world began with fifty-two . . .

The road went plainly on, wet and silvery between endless low retaining walls of piled fieldstone where rabbits lived. The few Folk left trying to gather in sodden hay in the rain turned to look as he passed.

High in a headland tower that looked out over Redsdown, in a room she never left any more, Mother Caredd sat by the window putting up her fine white hair with many bone pins. Far below her, on the Outward road, a carriage appeared as if conjured. It topped a rise and seemed to float down into a slough on the rainwings it cast up, and disappeared, only to appear, smaller, further on. She watched it go; it seemed to have some urgent appointment with the black clouds far Outward that the road between stone walls ran toward.

"Hurry," said Mother Caredd, and her servant looked up. "Hurry, hurry."

By nightfall of the next day, the man in red had brought the carriage within a vast circle of watchfires on the Drum, past sentries Red, Black and Outlander, into the Queen's encampment. It looked as though half the world had gone to war.

"And Caredd?" Redhand asked.

"Well. Untroubled. The house is guarded, but she is left in peace. Only she is not allowed to write, not even to me."

It was odd to think of, but Learned had never been within one of his brother's war tents, though his brother had lived as much in tents as he had in houses. It was large, shadowy, hung with tapestries. Rugs covered the Drumgrass underfoot; a charcoal brazier glowed on a tripod. There were chairs, chests, a bed, all cleverly contrived to be folded and carried on wagons. The furnishings seemed ancient, much used, battered like old soldiers. How long and well, Learned thought, we prepare for war, how thoughtfully and lovingly is it fitted out.

"Have you seen the Queen?" Redhand asked.

"No."

"You will wish to."

"No."

Redhand looked up from the papers he studied, pushed them aside. His reading lamp shone on armor, carefully polished, that stood up on a stand beside him like a second Redhand. "Learned." He smiled, his old, genuine smile. "I am grateful. It can't have been a pleasant ride."

"There was time to think."

Redhand got up, and Learned seemed to see for a moment another man, old, weary, to whom even the business of standing and sitting is too much labor. He poured steaming drink for the Arbiter from a pitcher by the brazier. "For the chill of the Drum.

"I would have come to you," he went on, "but I am an outlaw now, my name is posted in the towns like a horse thief's. You understand."

"Yes."

"What we wish of you," he said, turning his mug in his hands, "is simple, and doubtless you have suspected it. We wish only that you retract the decision of the old Arbiter in favor of the Senlin claims, and restore all to Little Black."

"Only."

"Say she was old, incapable. You know the words."

Learned wished suddenly he need not tell his brother what he must; he wished only to listen to that harsh voice, quick with authority. He savored the sound of it, carefully, as though he might never hear it more. "Do you remember," he said, "when first I went away, first put on Gray?"

Redhand smiled shortly. There was much to do.

"That Yearend when I came home, in my new white, so smug; I would take no orders from you, or turn the spit anymore when you said to."

"I remember."

"I was hateful. I bowed to Father, but only in a conditional sort of way. They had told me, you see, that my family had me no more, nor would I ever have any other: the Grays were all, and I owed them all."

"There was something about a horse."

"My painted. You said if I was Gray now, I had no more claim on any Redhand horse."

"We fought."

"Fought! You beat me pitilessly. I was never a fighter."

"Do you forgive me?" Redhand said, laughing.

"More important, brother, dear bully, you must forgive me, now, in advance."

Redhand put down his cup.

"I cannot do what you ask," Learned said softly. Terrible to see him so, stunned, helpless, in the power of a younger brother who had ever followed him. "Redhand, all my powers, resources are yours."

"All but this judgment."

"That is not mine to give. It belongs to Righteousness."

"Pious." He spat out the word. "Pious. When it was all lies, Learned, your judgment, and made at my bidding, at your House's bidding . . ."

"I know that. Don't go on. I cannot do this."

Redhand sat again. "Will you condemn me?"

"The old judgment stands."

"Call me traitor?"

"Are you not?"

They sat without looking at each other; the hostile silence was palpable between them. Outside, muffled drums marked the watch. Redhand poured cold water on his hands, wiped his face and beard, and sat then with his hands over his face.

"Redhand, if you leave this thing." It was hard to say. "Leave that tripes and her malcontents to their war, then . . . you will be under my protection. When the Queen is beaten, the King may forgive you. Return you Redsdown . . ."

Redhand looked up, but not at Learned, at nothing. "And what will I do at Redsdown? Pray?" With his knuckles he struck a gong that hung behind him. The sour sound hung in the tent. "That painted you spoke of. It died only last autumn, after a long life. He was a proud one, and fathered many."

"Yes."

"When we fought, it was because I was afraid you would have him gelded, and made a Gray's palfrey. You understand."

Two armed men showed themselves at the tent's door.

"Do you still play War in Heaven?" Redhand asked his brother.

"Rarely."

"Well. I have crossed the line, Learned. All my stones are on the board. If I must break rules I will break them. I am gone out to make a king again, and I suppose I can make an arbiter too." He motioned the armed men in. "Take the Arbiter," he said, "to some secure place, and keep him close."

"Redhand, don't do this."

"He shall have all comforts, but let him not escape."

The two men took Learned, tentatively, with respect. He stood, took up his wide hat against the rain outside. "You will have war."

"To the death, mine or his." It scarcely seemed to matter to him which. "It would help me to have this judgment. When you wish to render it, only tell me, and we will send you home." The guards began to lead Learned away. "Wait."

The light of the brazier lit two dull fires beneath Redhand's thick brow. He sat huddled in his camp chair, as though he, not Learned, were the prisoner. "A point of law," he said. "I would make a will. How can I make it so that Caredd will have all, and in safety?"

"I'll consider it," Learned said. "There are ways."

"Thank you."

"And I have a problem for you."

"Yes?"

"If a man has two parents, and four grandparents, eight great-grand-parents, and so on back to the beginning of time, how is it then that the world began with fifty-two?"

"Did the world?"

"So it is said."

Redhand regarded him, chewing on his thumbnail. "Do you know the answer?"

"Partly. We three, you and Younger and I, are part of it."

"Well." He put his hand on the papers before him. "I have other problems here."

"Perhaps," Learned said. "Perhaps, Redhand, and perhaps not."

"They will make me King again."

Oh, he was agile; he flew up back stairways Sennred had not known about, in the dark, as if by some other sense overstepping the rotten stairs. He climbed to porticos like a busy spider. Sennred for all his young strength could hardly follow him. No wonder he had eluded Senn-red for weeks; no wonder he could communicate with spies the King's men knew nothing of.

Upward they went, climbing the great house as though within a chimney.

At a crack, a window incompletely sealed, a fugitive ray shone in full of golden motes. The King Little Black stopped, and for the twentieth time drew out the paper, much folded, soft as kidskin. He read or spoke by rote the contents quickly: "Fear not, Sir, your deliverance is near. Redhand and the Queen's army is thousands now and the Son is on the march, and when you are with them their hearts will be high and you shall succeed in this. Be where we agreed before, on any night after you have this, we will watch every night. Sir, be quick if you can; we are in great danger here." He folded the note. "You see, you see?"

"Yes. Let's go on."

"You shall be rewarded," the King went on in his tiny voice. "I know the loyal, and you shall have reward. You shall be my minister. You shall see that their heads fall, yes, severed, every one." He paused to pry up a board that sealed the way, that Sennred would have thought immovable; when they had squeezed through, he pulled it carefully back into place. "Redhand, he shall have his neck cut quite through, yes, and Red Senlin too."

He seemed to confuse the war that had unseated him with this one, to want to slay his new allies and resurrect old enemies. It had always been thought that the executions during his reign had been all Black Harrah's doing, because the King had never shown himself. *If only Little Black knew,* the loyal used to say. But Sennred had for days been listening to his grisly tastes. He thought for sure the King had found in those days some secret niche to watch all from.

By a sudden echo of their footsteps in the dark, Sennred could tell that the back stairs had debouched into a wide high place, bare-floored, empty of furniture.

Beneath the smell of must and disuse in the room, there was another odor, intensely familiar to Sennred.

"Stop. Wait awhile."

"Hurry, hurry!"

That smell . . . Yes! He was sure now, and he stumbled with his arms outstretched to find the wall, and the racks on the wall he knew must be there . . . He stepped into some pieces of armor that rang like bells, and the King gave a frightened squeak.

But Sennred had found what he wanted.

How many hours he had spent in such a room, a room smelling of leather and steel polish, sweat and moldering straw targets, loud with weapons; how much of his life's little happiness he had got there! He gripped the sword's handle gratefully; it was like slipping into warm clothes after having been long naked.

"Lead on, Majesty," he said. "Your minister comes close after."

There was a suffocating hour when they had to crawl up between two close walls of crumbling brick, by elbow and knee and will. The

King went scrabbling first, and Sennred pushed him from below, his nose full of the smell of the old man's rusty clothes, hating him fiercely; and then there was a hole in the floor above them, and they crawled out into a tower room windowed and full of breeze.

Air. Light. Stars. Sennred stood panting, wiping the filthy sweat from his face.

They were near the very top of the house, up among its steep-pitched roofs and chimney stacks and fantastic cupolas. Below them the high-piled City was already starred with lamplight; all around, the lake lay like a hole pierced in the Deep.

The house stood outside the High City walls, on a finger of rock called Spring that was connected to the High City by a causeway; down there, watchfires burned, guards stood, they knew. On this side, though, the walls of the house went down and met the sheer walls of the rock Spring which went down, down to the lake and down then to the bottom of the world presumably.

"They will show a lantern," Little Black said. "Down there, where Spring meets the house. There are no guards there; they don't know there is a way there down the rock to the lake." He giggled. "They will know, one day, when they are all flung down Spring one by one. One by one."

"A lantern. And how will we get down to them then?"

"Crawl down, crawl down, swift as anything." He peered out over the window ledge into the gloom. "There are ways. There are handholds."

"And once down . . ."

"They have a boat, concealed at the bottom on the lake. Over there there is a path up the mountain that meets the High Road." He patted his hands together, gleeful. "And then free! Free!"

Sennred leaned out with the King. "Show me. Point it all out, how you will climb down."

The King's crooked finger traced the way down, along gutters, down roofs, clinging to gargoyles, walking ledges. With the horrid fear already biting into his knees, Sennred memorized it.

"There!" Little Black cried. "There they are!"

Down where the walls of the house met the walls of the rock Spring, a yellow light winked once, again.

Now, shouted all prudence in Sennred's mind, *do it now, here, there will be no other chance. . . .* He gripped the sword, staring at the King's back; the King's matted white hair stirred in the evening wind.

He could not do it; could not raise the sword, could not thrust it within the black cloak. The King turned and grinned wildly at him, and then slipped over the window ledge.

There was nothing for Sennred to do but follow. He didn't even know the way back into his prison.

A tiled roof went steeply down from the tower room, down to a gutter green with verdigris; the King let himself slip down the tiles, like a child at play, and caught himself on the gutter. Sennred, going slower, had a harder time; his caution caught him up on the tiles and nearly flung him into the night. He lay crouched at the gutter, panting, collecting himself. There is no way, he thought, to do this but fearlessly, I will fall otherwise . . . He tried to find in himself the fearlessness that the King (whispering urgently to him from around the roof's turning) had as a gift of his foolishness.

It was easier for a while around the roof's turning; they walked through a chute formed by two roofs' meeting, crept around clustered chimneys standing eerie and unconcerned in the moonlight, and stood then looking over a cornice. Here the wall went down sheer; there was only a ladder of stones, outcropping for some obscure mason's reason, that could be descended. With a little grunt of triumph, the King started down. Sennred could only follow because he was sure that he would fall, that caution was useless . . .

He stepped off the last stone onto a ledge, almost surprised.

They were in a valley between two wings of the house. A narrow chasm separated the ledge they stood on from a symmetrical ledge on the wall opposite; it must be jumped; they could not continue down on this side or they might be seen. The chasm was dark; how far down it went could not be seen, to the bottom of the house or further . . .

Outward, between the two wings of the house, was a narrow banner of night sky, still faintly green at the horizon but already starred. They could look down that way to the lake and the way that they had been promised was there; and even as they looked down, the yellow light winked again.

Across the chasm, a lizard, a stonecutter's fancy, clung to the wall above the ledge.

"Leap, leap," the King said. "Take hold of that thing when your foot strikes the ledge, and hold yourself to the wall." He prodded Sennred, who stood transfixed, looking down. "No!" the King said. "Look only at that, at that"—waggling his finger at the monster.

Sennred leapt.

His hand took hold of the lizard's foot as his foot took hold of the ledge; a weird sound came from his throat and he clung there a moment, stone himself, till the King's urgings made him let go and edge away.

The King poised himself a moment; his hair stirred in the air that sped through that narrow place; his hands moved like claws. Then he leapt too.

His hand took hold of the lizard's head, and gently, as though made of rotten wood, the head came away.

The King, looking faintly surprised, drifted backwards off the ledge, one hand spooning the air, the other holding the lizard's head as though it were a gift.

Sennred leaned over with a cry, almost falling himself, and snatched at the King's black cloak. It came away in his hand, rolling the King out as from a bag.

He fell soundlessly. It was Sennred who screamed, not knowing he did so, watching the King, storing up in a moment a lifetime of vertiginous dreams.

He stood a long time on the ledge, holding the cloak, staring down. Did the King live, clutching some ledge? He called out, his voice a croak. No sound answered. Then, down at the base of the house, the signal light winked again. Whoever was down there had seen nothing, heard nothing.

Would they expect some password, some sign?

No. All they looked for was a little man, dressed in black, alone and unarmed. Little. Dressed in black.

He looked at the greasy rag in his hands, and at the way he must go down, and a dark wave of fear and disgust washed over him.

3

Whenever Caredd the Protector Redhand's wife reined in her horse, the riders in King's livery reined in theirs not far off. The two had some difficulty in keeping with her as closely as their orders required, and out of pity for them she paused often to let them catch up.

It was that luminous harvest day when the world, dying, seems never more alive. A chill wind pressed against her, flushing her cheek like an autumn fruit. Dark, changeful clouds, pierced by sunrays that moved like lamp beams over the colored Downs, hurried elsewhere overhead; when they were gone they left the sky hard, blue, filled up with clean wind to its height.

She rode everywhere over Redsdown from white misty morning to afternoon, overseeing the slow wagons that toiled toward the barns under their great weight of harvest; planning the horse-gathering with the horsemaster as cheerfully as though no war were being waged; stopping everywhere to talk to the children who scared the birds from the grain and the old ones who sat in the year's last sun in their cottage doorways. She was Redsdown's mistress, servant, its reins were in her hands, and yet when she reined in a short way from where the road ran Outward screened by dusty trees, she had a mad impulse to fly to it, outrun her pursuers, make for her husband's tent.

As she stood there, she could hear, coming closer, the sound of wagons and many men. She turned her horse and rode for higher, nearer ground; those two followed.

It was an army that moved Outward, raising dust. Through the screen of trees along the road, she could see the long lances that stood up, bannered and glinting, and the tops of heavy war wagons, and the heads of a glum, endless line of footsoldiers. Boys like her own Redsdown boys, like the two who watched her. She stood in her stirrups and waved to her guards to come close. They were hesitant and, when they did canter up, deferential. They were both very young.

"Whose army is that?"

"The King Red Senlin's Son's, Lady."

"Where do they go?"

"To punish the outlaw Redhand."

"The Protector Redhand," the other said quickly. "And the Queen."

Her horse turned impatiently beneath her, and she steadied him with a gloved hand. In the midst of the line of march she could see a canopy, in the King's colors, moving like a pretty boat along the stream of men.

"Who is that carried in a litter?"

"The King, Lady."

"Taken sick," the other said.

"Will he die?"

"We will all die, Lady."

She thought suddenly of dark Sennred in the tower room: *When I am King* . . .

Around them in the yellow pasture wind threshed the ripened weeds, broadcast seed. Insects leaped at the horse's feet, murmuring. The sky had turned a lapidary green on the horizon, marbled faintly with wisps of cloud. Till it was nearly dark, the columns and wagons and mounted men and pennons went by.

She did not wish the King's death.

She shuddered, violently, with not wishing it. And turned her eager horse homeward.

Homeward.

———

The last house in the world was a squat tower of wood and stone on the lake's Outward shore. Patches of weed grew close around it as though for shelter, but there was no other life; beyond, the beach, undifferentiated, a rusted color, went on as far as could be seen.

There was no sign of the last man who lived there.

From the tower, a long tongue of pier stuck out over the water. Staying as far from the tower as they could, the birdmen piled up on the pier's end, silently and hurriedly, a large supply of food in oiled skins, and many bundles of sticks wrapped up too. They put off the girl and the Secretary and then rowed as fast as they could away.

Nod and the Secretary stood on the pier, waiting.

"The sticks are for a beacon," the Secretary said. He pointed to the closed door at the pier's end that led into the tower. "He lights it. To warn the birdmen when they come too near the shore."

"Why do they need such a warning?"

"It angers *him*, they said. This one who lives here is called Sop to His Anger."

"How long has he been here?"

"Since Old Fan died, they said. If he lives to be as old as Old Fan, they said, he will have to light the beacon only sixty summers more."

"Horrible."

"He will go mad soon. The madness will give him strength to live. They said it was his gift."

There was a curious wind here, blowing Inward, that they did not remember feeling on the lake. It was steady, insistent, like the gentle pressure of fingers pushing them away. It played within the tower, a penetrating, changeless note.

The door at the end of the pier began to open, squeaking, resisting, as though long unused.

The last man in the world was not a man; he was a boy, skinny as death and as hollow-eyed, with lank black hair down his back and a stain of beard on his white cheeks. He stared at them, hesitant, seeming to want to flee, or speak, or smile, or scream, but he said nothing; only his haunted eyes spoke; they were a beacon, but what they warned of could not be told . . .

On top of his tower the ashes of the previous night's beacon were still warm.

Since all around them was flat, the tower seemed a giddy height. Nothing anywhere stood up. Inward there was the lake and the sky like it; horizonless, empty, bleeding imperceptibly into night. Outward the featureless beach went on toward the Deep; out there was an occasional vortex of dust. The sun, setting, seemed huge, a distended ball, vaporous and red.

Nod felt poised between nothings, the world divided into two blank halves by the shoreline: the gray, misty half of the lake, and the rust-colored half of desert and dust. The sun frightened her. Almost without meaning to, she slipped her arm into the Secretary's, stood half-sheltered behind him, like a child.

"He'll give us food for a week, ten days. Fuel for the lamp," the Secretary said.

Why a week? Nod thought. How does he know the world will end in a week?

The last man in the world nodded, in assent or at something he saw Outward. The wind lifted his lank black hair, threw strands around his face that now and again he raised a hand to brush away slowly, abstractedly.

"I see his eye out there, sometimes," he said, in a voice thin and sweet as a quickwing's. "I see his eye, like a little moon. I hear him."

"What does he say?" the Secretary asked.

"He says *Silence,*" said the last man.

There is an edge, a lip, Fauconred had said to him on that day in the beginning of his life when they had stood together watching the horse-gathering; *an edge, as on a tray; and then nothing.*

For days the horizon seemed to draw closer, not as though they approached a ridge of mountains but as though the world steadily, imperceptibly foreshortened. When the sun set they could see a dark line at the horizon, a band of shadow that thickened each evening.

Beneath their feet, what had been in the first days recognizably sand changed character, became harder, less various; the occasional rain-cut ravine, even pebbles and earthly detritus, became scarcer. What they walked on was hard, infinitely wearying, like an endless flat deck; it seemed faintly, regularly striated, the striations leading Outward.

Somehow, impossibly, it seemed they came closer to the sun.

Each evening it set in a blank, cloudless sky; vast and shapeless, almost seeming to make a sound as it squatted on the horizon, it threw their shadows out behind them as far as they had come. It lit nothing; there was nothing to reflect it. The earth's faint striations deepened. Like stones across a game board, they rolled toward their Player.

Then on a night the setting sun lit something.

At the top of the band of shadow that was the world's edge something caught the sun's fire for a moment, lit up with its light, a spark only, and it faded quickly. If there had been anything, anything else to see in all that vastness, he would not have noticed its brief light.

"Look," he said, and she stopped. She would not raise her eyes; she could no longer bear the setting sun. When she did look up, the sign was gone. He could only tell her it had been there; she only looked from him to the fast-darkening edge whose shadow swept toward them; expressionless, faceless almost, like a brutalized child.

How was it, that as far Outward as she had gone, just so far within had she gone also? With every step a layer of her seemed to come away; something she had been as sure of as her name became tenuous, then untenable, and was shed like skin. She had not known how many of these layers she owned, how many she had to lose. When she felt she had been bared utterly, was naked as a needle of all notions, suppositions, wants, needs, she found there was more that the silence and emptiness could strip her of.

She had never hated him. Whatever in her could have hated him had been rubbed off, far away, on the cliffs of the Edge maybe. Now he was the only other in the world, and she found that the needle of being left her by solitude needed him utterly, beyond speaking, for they had spoken little lately; only there had come a day she could not go on unless he held her hand, and a night when she would not stop weeping unless he held her, held her tight.

So they had gone on, hand in hand.

They raised the shelter, there where he had seen the sign, though it was neither hot nor cold there. Partly they sought protection from the wind, which was not strong, only insistent and unceasing, like hopelessness; mostly, though, when it was pitched, they had a place amid placelessness.

They had not imagined, on the soundless lake, to what an unbearable pitch soundlessness could be tuned.

"What do you love?" she sobbed, muffled in his red robe late at night, curled within his arms. "What do you love? Tell me. What means more than love to you? What makes you laugh? What would you die for?" Her tears wet his chest, tears warmer than his flesh. He couldn't answer; he only rocked her in rhythm with her fast-beating heart, till she was quieter.

"What will you do," she asked then, "when you find him?"

"Ask him why he has summoned me."

"And what will he answer?"

Silence.

When the sun next day was overhead and they had no shadow, they came on the first step.

The step was low, cut sharp as though with tools, and it was wide, seemed to go on around the world, and it was so deep they could not see if it led to another. They stopped a moment, because it was a marker, and there had been no other all day. She tightened her grip on his hand and they stepped upward. Far, far behind a bird screamed, so startling they both jumped as though their stepping up had caused it; they looked back but could see no bird.

The next step when they came to it was perceptibly higher; beyond, closer, they could see the next, higher still.

Through the afternoon they climbed toward the top of the edge of the world, which lay above and ahead seeming sharp and flat as a blade. The steps grew shallower and higher in a geometric progression, each seeming to double the last, until toward sunset the steps they climbed were higher than they were deep, and the edge of the world was perpendicular above them. They were in its shadow.

Along the stair that circled the world there were huge flaws in its perfection: it seemed to slow the heart to imagine the shudderings of earth needed to crack and split that geometry, reduce its plated, flawless surface to glittering rubble. At an ungraspable distance away a pitted stone, a moon perhaps, something vast, had imbedded itself in the stair, blasting its levels for great distances. It was terrifying in its congruity, the unfathomable stair, the unfathomable stone.

It was they who were incongruous.

He was above her on the climb; sat on the stair holding his hand down to her to pull her up with him. Both wore the rags of the clothes they had left Forgetful in, his red domino, her hooded cloak, climbing steps never meant for anything like them; flesh in that desert.

The last step was a ledge barely wide enough to stand on and a sheer wall taller by far than he. He inched along it sidewise, she below him on the next stair, until they were nearer the catastrophic damage. There they

struggled up through a broken place, their hands and knees bleeding
from the malevolent surfaces, until he dragged himself groaning over the
last ledge and came out onto the last place in the world. He turned,
trembling, and drew her up with him.

It was nothing but the top of the last step. It was wide, but they
could see the edge of it, jagged, more broken than the stair. And beyond
that nothing, nothing, nothing at all. A veil of cloud extended Outward
from the edge like a ledge of false earth, and the sun stained it brown and
orange; but through the veil they could see that the Nothing went down,
down, thickening into darkness.

There were two things there with them at the edge. There was the
wind, stronger, filled with a presence they could not face into, though
they had sought it so long. And there was, not far from where they came
up, an egg of some soft silver, as high as a man, seamless, fired with
sunset light.

He had never been sure, not for a moment, that he had been right,
that he had saved from his damaged knowledge the right clues, the right
voice. Not till now.

He went to it, touched the hand that was a reflection of his own
hand in the glassy surface. Turned to look back to Nod: she crouched on
the shelf of the world, touching its surface with her hands, as though
afraid she might fall off.

"That," she said, and another would not have heard her tiny voice.

"A . . . Vehicle." He went to sit with her.

They watched the sunset fire fade from it in silence.

"What will you do?" she said at last.

"Eat," he said, and took from his pack a little of the food that the Last
Man had given them, broke it and gave her some.

The egg turned ghostly blue in the evening, then dark, seemed to
disappear. She threaded her thin arm in his which was cold as steel,
colder than ever.

"If you must return alone," he said.

"No."

"If you must . . ."

"No."

He said nothing further. It grew cold and she began to shiver, but
stopped then as through an effort of will.

In the night, it was almost possible to believe they were not where
they were. The stars, cold, distant, seemed familiar and near.

She felt him suddenly tense beside her, could almost feel the workings of his senses.

"*Yes,*" he said, and the wind snatched away his word.

The wind rose.

He went to the egg, touched the stars that seemed to cover its surface. The wind rose.

The wind rose, invaded him, filled him as though he were hollow, made him deaf then blind, then utterly insensate: calm in silence. The Blindness compressed itself into a voice, or the metaphor of a voice, speaking to senses he had not known he had; lovely, wise, murmurous with sleep.

You have come late, Recorder.

His being strove to speak, but he could find no voice.

Go, then, said his Blindness. *Go to him, he awaits you.*

Leviathan, he tried to say, *Leviathan.*

Blindness trembled, as though unsure, and withdrew in a roar of silence. The last place in the world congealed before the Recorder's eyes, like the false place of a dream though he had never dreamt, and he saw Nod on her knees, mouth open, an idiot's face.

He cried out, not knowing what he said, desperate that Blindness might not return. He pressed his naked cheek against the cold egg and waited. Waited . . .

Blindness, angry, inchoate, whipped through him.

Why are you not gone?

Now he found the voice to speak to that Voice: I know no way to go, he said. Do I trouble you?

Yes.

Only tell me then what I must do.

How am I to know if you do not? it asked.

You don't know?

Not what task he might have set you other than to Record, for which you were made, and could not but do.

It wasn't you . . . ?

I?

You who made me, you who summoned me.

Summoned, perhaps. Guided, as a beacon. But not made. No. What would I want with your Recording? I have forgotten more than he has ever created. It is my skill.

Who is he, then? Is he Leviathan?

I am Leviathan; so men call me. He is . . . other than me. A brother.
Where is he? How am I to come to him?

Where now? I cannot tell. Your Vehicle will find him. A journey of a thousand years. More. Less . . . Only go. Open that Vehicle. You have the key, not I.

I have no key, said the Recorder to his Blindness, feeling withered by an awful impatience pressing him to go: I have no key, Leviathan, I am damaged, I have forgotten everything; help me. Help me.

Help. I cannot . . .

Begin at the beginning, the Recorder said; and, as he had to the two Endwives on the Drum: perhaps something will return to me, some part of the way I am made, that will tell me what to do.

Beginnings, said Blindness. *You don't know what you ask. I have forgotten beginnings of worlds that were dead before this one was born.*

The Recorder heard no more then; but he waited, for he seemed to feel deep stirrings, a Thought drawn up painfully from some ancient gulf. *I have forgotten,* Blindness began again at last, *forgotten how it was I came here . . . But it was I who dropped the pillar into the placeless deeps . . . I who set this roof, to protect me from the heaven stones.*

You made the world.

My house this world; my roof, holding place, shelter. Beneath it I lived, down deep where it is hot and dense and changeless. I was alone. Then he brought them.

Men.

It was mine before they came. It will be mine when they are gone.

How did he bring them?

Sailed.

How, sailed . . .

He has sails, and I do not. We are not alike. He is busy and wide-ranging; I am sleepy and stationary. He has sails; sails like woven air, that fine; large as the world. Many of them. They are his speed.

Spread sails to catch the Light of Suns . . .

Yes, he did so. Bringing them.

From where?

Elsewhere. What could it matter? A journey of a thousand years. Less. More.

How did they survive?

He did not bring living men; no, they are too fragile for that; he brought instead a sliver of each, a grain, a seed, from which he could grow a whole man when he chose. These seeds or what you will could make the journey, though the men could not . . .

There were fifty-two.

Perhaps. And all their grasses, the green things proper to them, and their beasts too, one of each—no, two, one of each sex. And he set out each in turn to grow on my naked roof: increase and multiply. And set out the men last, new-grown.

And then.

And looked on it all, and saw that it was good.

The Recorder was desperate to pause, to assemble all this, to let it combine within him and form some answer; but Leviathan trembled at his hesitation. Wait, he said then; I have understood nothing; tell me who I am, what is to become of me; why he made me.

He does not trust me.

Not trust you . . .

I owed him a service, from another time. He put them in my charge. I have watched as well as I could, between sleepings. When he has not trusted me, he has had you.

Me?

You and others like you; recorders, adjusters. He has not forgotten. It is his chiefest toy, this world; no, not chiefest, not any longer. But he has not forgotten. And when he wishes to have senses here, he casts a recorder among men. A thing, his invention, his finger.

Why?

It must be kept in balance. That is the play, the whole jest. It is a small world, Recorder; my back only; it must be pruned, regulated. So there have been adjusters: warmakers, peacemakers, idiots, cardplayers. His invention is endless.

The Just.

The Just. A fine adjustment. The smaller wheel that justifies the large. He fashioned a Notion for them, you see; and when they gathered round it, he put the pruning knife into their hands. The Gun I mean. And so the thing is kept in balance . . .

The Recorder's utter attention had shifted, minutely: Nod . . .

Who is there with you?

She brought me.

Brought you?

I didn't know the Task, or how to come to you to ask what it was. She led me.

It doesn't matter. She cannot hear. Deaf. Deaf, blind, dumb; as they all are.

As I am.

Well. You are a thing of his. He will know if there is any use left in you.

I think . . . I will not go to him.

Recorder.

Why? Why did men agree to such a thing?

They asked it.

They could not have.

That is the tale, Recorder. He came to them on his endless, busy way; he found them on the last undesolated shelf of some wretched ruined stone. They worshiped him; that has always been his pleasure. He granted their desire.

What was their desire?

An end to Change. What other desire is there? "Take us away," they prayed, "to a new world, like the one our ancientest ancestors lived in, a small world where the sun rises and hastens to the place where he arose, where we can live forever and where nothing runs away." So I remember him telling it . . .

And he brought them here. Here.

They didn't know themselves. They made a bad bargain. We kept our part.

Did you?

They wanted eternal life; he gave them perpetual motion. It comes to the same thing, for such a race.

Why? What did he gain?

I don't remember. Some satisfaction. It had nothing to do with me. For the amusement of it only, perhaps, probably . . .

Does he know how men suffer?

Do they suffer?

I think, the Recorder said, I think I do not choose to return to him.

You think. You do not choose. Recorder! He has expended energy on your creation. He will not see it wasted. He wastes nothing. Every part of you is minutely inscribed; he will disentangle you utterly, leach from your every thread what it is dyed with. He looks forward to it.

I think I . . .

Recorder! I awoke from sleep to welcome you, awoke from depths and lengths of sleep you cannot imagine. Speaking to your ignorance is anguish. Go to him. If you can speak, then, ask him to illuminate you; if you can speak, perhaps he will answer you . . .

Unable to bear more, the Recorder sought within him for some barrier to hide from that lovely Voice behind, some refusal, some power . . . He found it. It would rise within him if he could find the strength to summon it: he found strength: it rose, blocking the blind madness.

As though far off, but coming closer, the last place in the world began to appear to him. And the nature of the wall he had found became clear:

He was screaming.

All his multiple strengths drew to his throat, drew in to be pressed into sound, a long, breathless, continual sound that grew louder as it rose higher until it ceased to be sound. The sound searched him, cleansed him, healed him, broke into places within him sealed since the Gun, and let out all his wounded knowledge.

With horror he remembered all. Who he was. What had made him. And why: he knew the whole Plot he had been made for, the reason for his hideous strength, the blood-hero he was to have been, the long war that would never happen now . . .

And with the great knowledges came a small one: he knew why it was he screamed, for at a certain pitch and loudness the egg before him opened soundlessly.

His scream had opened his Vehicle. It was the key.

He ceased; the sound lingered, ran away, died; he stood with his wide chest throbbing, done.

It was near dawn. Inward the stars faded in an empurpled sky. Nod lay before him, prostrate, hands against her ears, her face pressed against the ground. When the sound was gone she lifted her head, her tear-streaked face, looked at him, couldn't look away.

The wind had risen, pitiless, like no wind of the world. It tore at his ragged robe, urging him to discard it. He kicked off his cracked boots. He drew out the Gun, dropped it; undid his belt and let the garment go. It stepped away on the wind for a moment as though possessed, and then collapsed.

The wind could not touch him then. His skin shone, impervious, seamed with bright silver threads, knotted with weird muscle. Hairless, sexless, birthless, deathless.

"Neither-nor," Nod breathed, seeing him thus. "Neither-nor."

There was a part of himself, he knew now, that he had invented; had had to invent because of the damage done him. There was a Truth that his invention had allowed him to discover, that he was not meant or made to discover. That invented part wanted him to take up the girl, hold her as he seemed to remember he once had, speak comfort to her. That invented part, which his Maker could not have foreseen, wanted . . . it wanted.

He lifted Nod to her knees.

"Well, I will speak to him," he said, his hoarse voice nearly wind-lost. "I promise. Speak to him, ask him . . ."

"No!" she said. "Stay!"

He turned from her; that invented part was fading, disengaging; it was unnecessary now that he was whole again. Yet he would save one question. One question, over the whole length of his huge journey. He went to the open Vehicle, found a way to fit himself within it.

"No! you said *no* . . ."

The wind turned around, sucked suddenly into the Deep. It screamed as it ran down, bellowed, sobbed, shrieked. The ledge of earth trembled. As silently as it had opened, the Vehicle closed, closing the Recorder within it.

Nod, sobbing, unable to stand, searched for Suddenly on hands and knees; the wind, tortured, turned again and fled upward. The Vehicle began slowly to spin on its axis.

The Vehicle rose into the air, spinning faster.

And Leviathan arose from the Deep to bid his brother's thing farewell.

Mad, Nod ran toward the edge, toward the hugeness that rose from the Deep, screaming, screaming obscenities, pleading, reviling. As it rose it eclipsed each wavering star beyond; when it was so high it blotted out all the sky above her and looked, she thought, down toward her with an eye larger than night, she fired Suddenly toward the eye, trying to fling all of herself along the barrel with the little ball against that hatefulness.

For she had heard. Heard it all, all. She fell with the shock of the explosion; fell where his garment had come to rest on the ledge of earth; she clutched its worn stuff and knew nothing for a time.

But she had heard, and had recorded.

4
―――

They would say of the King Red Senlin's Son in later times that he was the tallest, the handsomest man of his age; that anyone who ever saw him in armor never forgot the splendor.

They would date an age's beginning from his reign, and cherish the glories of his new City, the wit of his poets, the loveliness of his artisans' work. They would forget his arrogance, his indulgence, his spendthrift luxury, and why should they not? They would remember only that he was handsome, and that his love was great, and that his reign was brief.

The tale told children would relate how with his architects he had worked in rain and by torchlight on the great Harran Stone and caught a fatal chill. It would not mention the traitor-god Blem, or the leaves called Sleep that he inhaled, or the violence of his lovers against him. It made no difference. Beneath the Stone he slept awhile and was no more; nor Harrah either. The Stone remained.

They woke him from a thick, feverish sleep, men masked in armor, whom he at first did not recognize.

"They are a mile out on the Drum," said one, his voice muffled by steel.

"Fifty watchfires. Stronger than we thought."

The King stared at them, sitting on the edge of his bed. "Redhand."

They looked one to another.

"This is all his work," the King said dully. "His crime."

They said nothing for a moment. Then: "The Queen is there too," one said.

He only looked at them. There were waves of familiar, enervating pain in him, and his limbs were cold. What had they said? "Bring me the drawings."

"Will you ride out?" one of them said. "See them there, see your army?"

"It would do them good to see you armed," the other said.

"Bring me the drawings," the King said. "Where is my brother?"

They surrendered then; one of them brought to him a wide, shallow wooden case stained with ink. The other stood at the tent door a moment, slapping one heavy glove into the other gloved hand, then turned and left.

The King fumbled with the lock, got it open; he turned up the lamp and spread out the drawings of the Harran Stone.

It was all there, from the first crude imagining in smudged charcoal to the final details of every carved figure cross-hatched in pale brown ink. He would never cease wondering at its calm, perfect volumes, its changeful expression of grief, strength, pride, quiet, solitude. How had they achieved it, through what magic? Behind it some of the drawings showed the old rotunda, a deadweight, gross, pig-eyed, with the chaotic towers of a thousand reigns bristling on its backside.

That must come down. He would see to it.

Down in the heart of that poised monument, down where every line drew the eye and every finger pointed, lay the Stone that covered Black Harrah. And here were drawn the carvings that covered that stone.

But how, the King thought for the thousandth time, how will he breathe there, beneath the stone? He felt his own breath constricted. "Redhand," he said again. He turned to the armed presence he felt hovering behind him. "Bring me my armor . . ."

He was alone in the tent.

He turned back slowly to the drawings, the thought of Redhand already leaking away from him. He turned the crackling, yellow sheets.

Down in the corner of a drawing that showed a mechanism for lifting stones, the architect had made another little sketch, a strange thing, something that had nothing to do with stones, it seemed. There was a diminutive figure, a man, strapped into a device of gears and pedals. Radiating out from the center of the device, made of struts and fabric, were the wings of a bird. A bird the size of a man.

For a long time the King stared at it. It would disappear in a cloud of pain and then appear again, still in its impossible flight.

How large is the world? the King thought, tracing the manwings with a trembling finger. How high up is the sky?

From the windows of his locked carriage the Arbiter could look out either side at the army that toiled Inward, gathering strength, through days that darkened toward winter.

It was not like one beast, as he had often thought an army would be, marching in time and with fierce purpose. No, men only; some hung back, contingents were lost, there were deserters and quarrels daily—especially in this army of new, uneasy allies. The whole parade was slung over a mile of Drumskin in an order that perhaps the captains understood, though he doubted it.

On a windy, cloud-striated day his carriage was stopped longer than usual in a stretch of country more desolate than usual. Perhaps another carriage had lost a wheel ahead; perhaps his brother and the Queen had had a falling-out . . .

Toward evening, a cheerless Barnolsweek evening, Fauconred came to his tent, unlocked its locks with some embarrassment.

"How is your war?" Learned asked.

"Not long now, Learned," Fauconred said gruffly. "We take up our positions here."

"And . . ."

"Wait for the King. It will not be long."

"Uncle," Learned said (and Fauconred lowered his eyes, though Redhand children had always called him that), "Uncle, will you give this to Redhand?" It was a folded paper, sealed with his ring.

"Is this . . ." Fauconred began, turning it in his hands.

"No. Only a task I could do, a will. Witness him signing it, and have it sent to Inviolable with this message." He gave Fauconred another paper. Fauconred looked doubtful, and Learned took his old hand. "I won't betray you. I can't help, but I won't betray."

Fauconred looked at him for a moment as though seeking some-thing, some word that would extricate them all from this; not finding it, he tapped the papers against his hand and turned away.

Learned watched him go, and wondered if he would, in his leather heart, rather win or lose against the King.

On Barnolsweek Eve the King Red Senlin's Son's battle came out of the Downs.

Learned Redhand, allowed to walk a ridge above the Queen's army within sight of a guard, watched as through the day they arranged them-selves there, a thousand strong, perhaps more. Tents were raised and banners raised above them, some the same banners that flew above the tents of Redhand's army. Families had been divided; the warriors of the King's father stood against the King; the sons of those who had fought Red Senlin stood beside his son.

He did not see the Son. He saw a royal tent pitched and no one enter it; no banner was raised above it. When it was pitched, Redhand and the Queen came out to see, but no one came forth, and they retired to their separate tents. Learned wondered why they did not mass their army sud-denly, and like some swift dagger stab into the King's army while it was in chaos. It was what he would have done. They intended to wait, appar-ently, like boxers, like the players of a game, wait for their opponents to settle themselves and the contest to begin. Odd . . .

At evening, from his vantage, he saw something that no one else seemed to notice. Off beyond the King's left wing, taking advantage of any cover, any patch of desiccated bush or rain-cut ravine, a young man made his way across the distance of gray heath that separated the two armies. Learned watched him, losing sight of him off and on, and looking away too so that no one would see what he looked at: he did not know this one's business, and like an Endwife wanted not to. He had made his last moves in this quarrel; in the silence of his confinement he had made his farewells to his brothers, had done what he had not before truly done: divested himself of his family. Like a trapped animal, he had escaped by gnawing away a part of himself. He had nothing further to do; but he watched this creeping one till clouded darkness cut him off, and won-dered: what if all the noise and clamor and great numbers were so much show, and this one held the game, and, like the single shot of a Gun, could resolve it?

When Redhand later found this boy hidden in the shadows of his tent, dark-hooded, his face smeared with ashes, he made a motion to call guards; but the boy laid a finger on his lips, and gave Redhand a folded paper.

There is a peat-cutter's house, the paper said, *less than five miles from us, along the edge of the Downs, on this side of a bog called Dreaded, by where the Harran Road comes out. On the night after you have this, come there. Come alone, or send only one other ahead to assure yourself there is no danger. Tell no one, most especially the Queen. I will be there, alone. I swear by our friendship no harm will come to you; I trust our friendship none will come to me. Redhand, there is much you should know that you do not.*

                                                                          Sennred

"This is lies," Redhand said, folding it carefully.

The boy said nothing.

"Sennred is prisoner in the City."

"I don't know his face," the boy said. "Only that he who gave that to me was a little man, dark, and one of his shoulders was higher than the other. And he said he was Sennred."

"Did he tell you," Redhand said, "that you will be hanged, and cut apart, and your body strewn before your army, to answer this?"

The boy said nothing.

"Why you? How were you chosen? Are you a man of Sennred's that he chose you?"

"I'm . . . no one. They asked for a volunteer. I chose myself."

"Whose household are you?"

"I come from Fennsdown."

Redhand read the letter again and fed it thoughtfully to the brazier. "How will you return? Have you thought of that?"

"I will not. Only allow me to escape, and I will go Outward. There are no sentries there."

"And what will he tell me in this house?"

"I can't read," the boy said. "I don't know what's written there."

An ash of the letter rose from the brazier and settled again like a bird. "Step back," Redhand said, striking the gong beside him, "back behind the curtains there."

A red-jacketed man entered as the boy hid himself.

"Go to the Defender Fauconred," Redhand said. "Send him to me." The guard turned to go. "Listen. Speak only to Fauconred. Tell him to come when the watch changes. Tell no one else."

When they were alone again, the boy came from behind the curtain. He had pulled back his hood to show short, blond hair and fair skin above the ashes smeared on his face.

"The watch will be changing," Redhand said. "Go now."

Unhooded, the boy reminded him of someone; he could not remember who, nor in what scene in his life; perhaps in a dream only. "You're brave," he said. "Will they reward you?"

The war-viols sounded. The boy hooded himself, turned into the shadows, lifted the edge of Redhand's tent and was gone.

In armor but without weapons, wrapped to their eyes in dark cloaks that blew as their horses' manes and tails blew, Fauconred and Redhand looked down at evening from a swell of Drumskin onto a thick-set peat-cutter's hovel. Dull light spilled from its single window into the little yard; its gate swung in the wind.

Fauconred pulled the cloak from around his mouth. "I'll go down."

Redhand looked behind him the way they had come; no one had followed.

"Wait here," Fauconred said. "Wait till I signal." He spurred his horse into a gentle trot and rode carefully down on the hut. At the yard he dismounted, led his horse around the turn of the wall out of sight.

Redhand's horse stamped, and the clash of his trappings was loud in the stillness.

The great gray heath, patent though glum by day, had grown moody and secretive as evening came on. There were glimmers and ripples of light somewhere at the edge of vision, that were not there when Redhand turned to look at them; evening light only, perhaps, changeful in the wind-combed grass. There were pockets of dark that bred fogs like dim slow beasts; there was the bog, Dreaded, prostrate beyond the little house; out there rotting things lit hooded candles that moved like conspirators, moved on him . . .

No. He was alone, utterly alone. For a moment he could even believe he was the only man alive anywhere.

Fauconred finished his inspection, came around the house and waved to him. As Redhand approached him, a cloaked ghost in the last light wary by the low door, he thought: what if he . . . in league with them . . . His hair stood on end. The idiot notion passed almost as it was born, but Redhand felt himself trembling faintly as he dismounted.

"No one," Fauconred said. "No one here but the Folk."

"Watch," Redhand said; he gave his reins to Fauconred and stooped to enter the little round doorway.

Two women cowled in shawls sat by a peat fire; they looked up when he entered, their faces minted into bright coins by the firelight. "Protector," said one, and they looked away. There was a movement in the house's only other room; Redhand turned, the wide boards of the floor cried out faintly; he could see someone, sick or asleep, in a loft in that room.

"Do you have a lamp?" he asked.

"There's the fire," the younger woman said. And the other quoted: "There's no lamp the foolish can see better by."

He sat then, in an old reed chair that groaned familiarly. Everything here spoke; the wind, twisted by a crack at the window, cried out in a little voice, the sleeping one stirred, sighed, the women sang: If Barnol wets the Drum with rain, then Caermon brings the Downs the same; if Caermon wets the Downs with rain, the Hub will not be dry till Fain brings the New Year round again; new year old year still the same . . .

At first Redhand started at every noise; but then the fire began to melt the chill of the Drum from him, and loosen too something tight that had held him. He sighed, inhaling the dark odor of the cottage.

There was a sentiment, among court poets, that this little life, cottage life, was the only true and happy one; filled up with small cares but without real burdens, and rich with the immortality of changelessness. Redhand had never felt so, had never envied the poor, surely not the peat-cutters and cottagers. No, there were no young people here, and Redhand knew why—they had escaped, probably to take up some untenanted farm, glad enough to get a piece of land, a share of the world, and to see their children then buy or inherit more, become owners, and their grandchildren perhaps Defenders, and so on and on till the descendants of these women singing the seasons entered the topmost spiral of the world and were flung Outward into pride, and war, and the Guns.

Two parents, Learned had said, four grandparents, eight great-grandparents, sixteen great-great-grandparents, thirty-two, sixty-four, one hundred and twenty-eight . . . We three, he had said, are part of it. Redhand, Learned, Younger.

Brothers. Well, that was easy, then; not every man needed all those ancestors, he shared them with others. Was that the solution? It wasn't sufficient; still the number of ancestors must be multiplied as you stepped back through the generations, how many thousands of them, each doubling the last, till the vast population needed to begin the world spilled over its edges into the Deep. It was mad . . .

It came to him as a sounding clarity, a benign understanding that made the close cottage order itself before his eyes and smile.

All those millions were dead; and when the Fifty-two began the world, the millions weren't yet born.

Yes, their shades crowded the edges of the world; yes, there were uncountable numbers of them. But they weren't alive, had never been alive all at once; they were simply all the people that had ever been, added up as though a farmer were to reckon his harvest by counting all the grain from all the seed he had ever sowed. Absurd that he could have been tricked into thinking that they needed all to live at once. Gratefully, the world closed up within him to a little place, a place of few; a handful at a time, who must give way to those who would come after.

Give way . . .

The structure of the burning peat was like a thousand tiny cities in flames. It held him; he watched ramparts crumble, towers fall, maddened populaces. Hung above the fire was a fat black kettle he hadn't noticed before. It had begun to boil; thick coils of steam rose from it. Now and again, the younger of the women took from within her clothes a handful of something, seeds or spices, and threw them in. The pot boiled more furiously each time she did so, frothing to its edges. The old one was anxious, cried out each time the pot began to seethe.

"Protector," she said, "help us here, or the pot will overflow."

"Why does she do that?" Redhand asked. "Let it subside."

"I must, I must," the younger said, and threw in more; a trickle of the froth this time ran over the kettle's edge and sizzled with an acrid odor. The old one gasped as though in pain. "Protector," she said, "remember your vows. Help the Folk."

He got up, not certain what he must do. Within the kettle a mass of stuff seethed and roiled; the younger woman flung in her seed, the stuff rose as though in helpless rage. Calmly then, with their eyes on him, he bent his head to the kettle to drink the boiling excess.

He started awake.

There was a horse in the courtyard. A man was dismounting. Fauconred threw open the door. "Sennred," he said. "Alone."

There was no kettle . . . The two women hurried away timidly into the other room when Sennred came in. His face, never youthful, looked old in the firelight. "I would have come sooner," he said, "only I wanted not to be followed." He held out his hand to Redhand, who hesitated, still addled with his dream. He got up slowly and took Sennred's hand.

"Does the King," he said, "know of this meeting?"

Almost imperceptibly, Sennred shook his head.

"Has he forgiven you?"

"I hope he has."

"He released you from prison."

"I broke from prison." He undid the cloak he wore, let it fall. He touched Redhand, gently, to pass by him, and sat heavily in the single chair. "I broke from prison with Little Black."

"With him?"

"He showed me the way out. We became . . . great friends in prison." A faint smile faded quickly; he cradled his pale forehead in his hand and went on, not looking at Redhand. "We climbed to the roof of our prison. And then down. At a certain point . . . at a certain point, Black fell . . ."

"Lies." With a sudden fierce anger, Redhand saw the story. "Lies."

"I grasped his cloak as he fell," Sennred went on, in the same tone, as though he hadn't been interrupted. "But the cloak wouldn't hold. He fell. I saw it."

"Who wrote this tale?" Redhand growled. "One of the King's urnings? And did you practice it then?"

"Redhand . . ."

"No. Sennred. It's a poor trick." But his neck thrilled; Sennred's look was steady, with an eerie tenderness; he didn't go on—it seemed inconsequential to him whether Redhand believed him or not. "Why," Redhand said, and swallowed, "why is the King not here then? Why is this done in secret? Shout it out to my army, to the Queen . . ."

"No. The Blacks would think their King was murdered . . ."

"Was he not?"

"They would fight. Redhand. Listen to me now. I want to begin with no war. This was never my quarrel. The King said to me: *burn Redhand's house, his fields; let nothing live.* I won't. It hurts me, Redhand, not to do what he asked. But I can't."

"What are you saying?"

"I'm asking you to desert the Queen. Take your army away. Decamp, by night. There will be no reprisals. I swear it."

A weird apprehension rose in Redhand's throat like spittle. "And who are you?" he said, almost whispered. "Who are you, Sennred, to swear such a thing?"

"Heir. Heir to it all: Black and Red. There's no other. Redhand, the King Red Senlin's Son is dead."

With a sudden whirr all Redhand's tense suspicions, doubts, plans took flight, left him for a moment blindly empty. Why had he not realized . . . ? With sickening certainty, he knew he was about to weep.

Give way, give way . . .

Toward dawn, Sennred rode away. Fauconred handed him up, and he and Redhand watched till he was gone.

"Go on, then," Redhand said. "We shouldn't return together."

"No." The old man mounted with clumsy grace and pulled his cloak around him. "The sun won't shine today."

"No. Fog, I think. A Drumskin fog."

"It will be easier then."

"Yes. Go now."

Fauconred stood his horse a moment; a cock crowed. He thought he knew what it was his cousin felt, but knew nothing to say to it. He saluted, and spurred his heavy horse.

Redhand stood a long time in the little yard, watching the air thicken around him. It was utterly still. A red dawn Inward was being extinguished as fast as it grew; Dreaded was thick with fog.

What if he was wrong?

All those boys and men, their loins rich with descendants, would escape death tomorrow. Perhaps it was wrong that they should live, perhaps their children's children, that might not be, would boil over the edges of the little world . . . He shrugged it all away. The truth he had glimpsed had grown tenuous and thin; he vowed not to touch it again. He was not one for notions; he was only grateful for what he felt now: calm, peaceful almost, for the first time in many weeks.

Behind him, sudden in the stillness, the shutters of the cottage

banged shut. He turned, saw a frightened face look out before the last
one closed. When he turned back, someone was coming toward him, out
of the fog, from Dreaded.

As the figure condensed out of the whiteness, he saw with a rush of
joy that it was his lost Secretary, of whom he had not thought in weeks.
But then, no, the figure came closer, changed; it wasn't him.

It was the blond boy who had brought him Sennred's message.

Redhand stepped toward him, was about to speak to him, tell him
what had come of his mission. Then he saw the Gun in the boy's hands.

They stood for a moment not far apart.

The boy's only thought was a hope that the old Gun not misfire in
the wet. Redhand felt only a faint resentment that the boy had told him
he couldn't read.

The shot made Fauconred's horse start, and Fauconred cry out. It
echoed long, rolling through the low country, almost reaching the place
of two armies before the fog drowned it at last.

There were two Endwives, a young girl named Norin, an old woman
named Ser, who had come several miles through the fog with a hospital
wagon, not sure of the way, getting down now and again to lead the
horses, who were afraid to go on; sure then that they had lost the way in
the fog. Toward night, though, which was a thickening of the fog only,
they came to high ground. There were lights, watchfires, dull gobbets of
flame in the wetness: their sisters.

Through the night, others arrived, fog-delayed; they prepared themselves, listening to the faint sounds of a multitude on the plain below
them, moving, stirring—arming themselves, probably. They talked little,
saying only what was necessary to their craft; hoping, without speaking
it, that the fog would hold, and there would be no battle.

Before dawn, a wind came up. They could feel it cold on their Outward cheeks; it began to tear at the fog. Their watchfires brightened; as
day came on, their wagons assembled there began to appear to them,
gradually clearer, as though they awoke from a drug.

When the sun rose the fog was in flight. Long bars of sunlight fell
across the plain where the battle was to be.

But there was no battle there.

There was one army of men, vast, chaotic, the largest army anyone had ever seen. There was a royal tent in its center, and a Dog banner above it; and there was a flag near it that bore a red palm. It was quiet; no war viols played; the Endwives thought they could hear faint laughter.

Opposite, where the other army should have been, there were a hundred guttering campfires. There were some tents of black, half dismantled. Soldiers, too, scattered contingents late in realizing what had happened in the night, but not many; the many were away over the Drum, a long raggedy crowd, no army, going Outward, not having planned on it, quickly.

By noon there was no one at all facing the world's largest army. All who had not joined it had fled it.

Only a single closed carriage remained. Beside it, a man in a wide black hat stood with his hands behind his back, the freshening breeze teasing the hem of his black coat. The carriage's dappled gelding quietly cropped the sparkling, sunlit grass.

EPILOGUE

When the snows came, the Neither-nor hibernated.

Deep in a rug-hung cave, in a bed piled with covers, pillows, furs, It dozed through week on week of storm that stifled Its forest, locked the Door.

In Rathsweek, pale and weak as an invalid, the Neithér-nor crept out from bed, to the cave-mouth, to look out. The forest glinted, dripped, sparkled with melting snow; the rock walls of the glen were ruined ice palaces where they were not nude and black.

It was a day, by Its reckoning, sacred to Rizna, a day when Birth stirs faintly below the frost, deep in the womb of Death. Not a day to look out, alone, on a winter forest, spy on its nakedness. But the Neither-nor was not afraid of powers; It owned too many for that; and when the figure in red appeared far off, like blood on the snow, the Neither-nor awaited it calmly, shivering only in the cold.

But when it came close, stumbling, knee-deep in snow, near enough to be recognized, the Neither-nor gasped. "I thought you were dead."

The girl's eyes stared, but didn't seem to see. Except for the shivers that racked her awful thinness, and the raggedy red cloak, real enough, the Neither-nor might have still thought her dead.

On feet bound in rags, Nod struggled toward It. Overcome with pity, the Neither-nor began to make Its way toward her, but Nod held up an arm; she would come alone.

When she stood before the Neither-nor she drew out Suddenly, and with all the little strength left her, struck the Gun against the rock wall, cracking its stock. "No," the Neither-nor said, taking Nod's shoulders in the Two Hands. "You haven't failed. You haven't. The task is done. Redhand is dead."

She stood, the broken Gun in her hands, a negation frozen on her dirty face, and the Neither-nor released her, frightened, of what It could not tell. And Nod began to speak.

He had not his brother's enthusiasm for works and words, but he had loved his brother deeply, and in his kingship the works would go forward. In that winter the Harran Stone was completed; there his brother lay, with Harrah, their flawed love made so perfect in their tomb that even in the darkest of winter days, shut up in the Citadel, Sennred had not sensed his brother's ghost was restless.

He had turned an old prison into a theater. A scheme for making books without writing them out by hand, that Sennred little understood or cared about, he had fostered anyway.

He looked after these things, and his peace, patiently through the winter of his mourning. And hers.

It had been easy to confirm her in sole possession, in perpetuity, of Redsdown; he had with pleasure expunged every lien, attachment, attainder on the old fortress and its green hills. To console her further was impossible, he knew; with grownup wisdom he had let time do that.

When spring, though, with agonizing delays began to creep forth, he sent gifts, letters impeccably proper, so tight-reined she laughed to read them.

And on a day when even in the cold old Citadel perfumey breaths of a shouting spring day outside wandered lost, he prepared to go himself.

There were seven windows in the chamber he sat in. Against six of them the towers of the castle and the City heights held up hands to block the light. The seventh, though, looked out across the lake and the mountains; its broad sill was warm where he laid his hand.

Out there, in those greening mountains, somewhere, the Woman in Red held her councils.

She was not Just, they said, though like the Just she spoke of the old gods—but when she spoke she cursed them. What else she spoke of the King couldn't tell; his informants were contradictory, their abstracts bizarre. Of the woman herself they said only that she wore always a ragged red domino, and that she was a waterman's daughter with cropped blond hair. The Grays thought her dangerous; the old ones' eyes narrowed as they glossed for him one or another fragment of her thought. The King said nothing.

People were stirred, in motion, that was certain. He gathered she spoke to all classes—Just, Defenders, Folk. Some he sent to hear her strange tale listened—and didn't return.

A spring madness. Well, he knew about that . . . almost, it seemed, he might have brought it forth himself, out of the indecipherable longings that swept him on these mornings: he felt himself melt, crumble within like winter-rotten earthworks before new rivulets. Sometimes he didn't know whether to laugh or cry.

Down on the floor of the old Rotunda as the King and his retinue went through, the patient Grays were still at their cleaning work. They had accomplished much since Sennred had first noticed them, that day Red Senlin had come to the City to be King. The tortured circle dance of kings he had seen them uncover then had proved to be not a circle but part of a spiral, part of a History they thought, emanating from a beginning in the center to an end—where?

You must learn to pretend, dead Redhand had said when they stood here together, *if you would live here long.* Well, he was learning: would learn so well, would live here so long that he could perhaps begin to lead that spiral out of its terrible dance, lead it . . . where?

In the center of the floor, the Grays had begun to uncover bizarre images—a thing with vast sails; stars, or suns; creatures of the Deep.

Didn't the Woman in Red talk too of suns, and sails, and the Deep? She had for sure talked of bringing her news to the King. Did he dare stop, on his way Outward, to speak to her, listen to her? They had all advised him against it. A spring madness, they said, people in motion.

He stepped carefully past the grinning kings to the door Defensible, newly widened that winter. His laughing servant held a brand-new traveling cloak for him.

And what if it was not madness at all, not ephemeral? What if Time had indeed burst out of his old accustomed round, gone adventuring on some new path? Would he know? And would it matter if he did?

He took the cloak from his servant. He would see Caredd soon, and that did matter, very much.

BEASTS

For my mother

CONTENTS

If thou wert the lion, the fox would beguile thee; if thou wert the lamb, the fox would eat thee; if thou wert the fox, the lion would suspect thee, when peradventure thou wert accused by the ass: if thou wert the ass, thy dullness would torment thee, and still thou livedst but as a breakfast to the wolf . . . What beast couldst thou be, that were not subject to a beast?

TIMON OF ATHENS, IV, iii

1

THE SHOT TOWER

Loren Casaubon thought of himself as a lover of solitude. He hadn't chosen fieldwork in ethology strictly for that reason, but he thought of it as an asset in his work that he could bear—and believed he preferred—the company of the wild and the inhuman. The old shot tower and its new ferocious inhabitants, which Loren was to spend a summer nurturing, suited him exactly. He had laughed aloud when he first saw it, responding immediately to its lonely intransigence: he felt he had come home.

Because it lay hidden in the last few folds of wooded hills before the low country began, the shot tower, despite its hundred-foot height, came into view without warning. It seemed to step suddenly out of the mountain granite and across the road to block the way; or to have stood up suddenly from sleep on hearing the approach of a man. For over two centuries it had had no human company. The vast lowlands pocked with marshes that slid from the mountains' margins down to the sea, which the tower guarded as though it were the utmost watchtower of a mountain warlord, were inhabited only by wild things.

Whatever foresightless pioneer it was who had planned this marsh-aborted industrial development here so long ago had gotten no further than the tower and a few stone outbuildings. All that had been made of wood was gone now. The canal that he had counted on to bring him into touch with the rest of the manufacturing world had ended in bankruptcy forty miles away. He must have been more dreamer than businessman anyway, Loren decided when he first encountered the tower. It should have been a purely utilitarian structure, a factory for the making of lead bullets; its striking slim height was necessary only so that molten lead, poured through sieves at the top, had time as it fell to form into perfect round balls like leaden raindrops before striking an annealing tank of water at the bottom. But the builder had been unable to resist the obvious romantic associations his tall, round, granite tower had, and in fact had made a castle keep, grimly Gothic, with narrow, ogive arrow slits and a castellated top. It was a fake feudal keep in a new world, whose only true affinity with real castles was its reason for being: war.

That reason had long passed. The ingenuity of the tower and its lead shot had been long supplanted by more horrid ingenuities. It had had, until Loren came, no function but its absurd picturesqueness. Loren brought it a new purpose: it was to be a substitute cliff for four members of a nearly extinct race of cliffdwellers.

He could feel motion inside the cardboard box when he lifted it from the carrier of his bike. He put the box on the ground and opened it. Inside, the four white birds, quilly and furious, set up a raucous squawking. Alive and well. Biking them in had been harrowing, but there was no other way to get into the area; the rutted road had brought his heart to his mouth at every carefully negotiated bump. He laughed at himself now for his scruples. Healthy and strong as young devils, the four immature peregrine falcons, two males and two females, looked harmful and unharmable. Their fiercely drawn brows and hooked beaks belied their infancy; their crying was angry and not pitiful. They, of course, couldn't know that they were among the last of their kind.

The process of breeding peregrine falcons in captivity and then returning them to the wild—a kind of reverse falconry, which in fact used many ancient falconers' techniques—had begun years ago in that rush of sentiment about wildlife and wild places that had rendered the word "ecology" useless. Like all rushes of sentiment, it was short-lived. The falcon-breeding program had been curtailed along with a thousand other, more ambitious programs—but it had not quite died. The handling of feral birds was a skill so demanding, a challenge so compelling, that like the old falconry it had proved self-perpetuating. The small band of corre-spondents engaged in it were a brotherhood; their craft was as difficult, esoteric, and absorbing as that of Zen monks or masters of Go. Their efforts were, almost certainly, all that kept peregrines in existence; just as certainly, if they stopped, extinction would follow. The falconers were too few; and the birds they released were too few to find each other easily to mate once they were free. Some studies Loren had read put the sur-vival rate for large aerial predators released from captivity at twenty per cent. Of these, perhaps a tenth mated and raised young. So, without Loren and the others, all sponsored by quixotic foundations or un-guarded university departments, the falcon would disappear from this continent. The proudest and most independent of winged things had become, in an odd sense, parasitic to man.

Holding the box carefully level, Loren ducked through the arched door and into the tower. Inside, not even the spooky, narrow bars of dust-filled sunlight from the arrow slits could disguise the fact that this place had after all been a factory. The narrow spiral staircase that went up to the top was iron; it rang dully beneath Loren's boots. At various levels the iron struts of platforms remained; from each level a different size of shot would have been dropped: dust shot from forty feet, bird shot from higher, buck shot still higher; musket balls from the topmost platform, which was still intact, though a large section of castellated wall had fallen away and the platform was only half roofed. It was here that Loren had built his nesting box, a barred cage for the birds' first weeks. He had placed it facing the gap in the wall so that the birds, even while caged, could look out over their domain.

The wind was strong at this height; it tossed Loren's thick, dark hair and tickled his beard. Without haste he opened the nesting box and one by one placed his four round feather-dusters inside. He could feel their quick heartbeats, and their young talons griped his hands strongly. Once inside, they ceased to cry out; they roused and shook down their dis-turbed plumage in miniature imitation of the way they would rouse when they were fully grown.

From his many-pocketed coat Loren took out the paper-wrapped bits of steak and the forceps. With the forceps he would feed them, and with the same forceps remove their droppings—"mutes" to the falconer—just as their parents' beaks would have done. They gulped the raw meat hun-grily, beaks wide; they ate till their crops were stuffed.

When he had finished, he locked the box and climbed to the gap. He stood there squinting into the wind, looking with his weak human eyes over the thousand acres of tree line, field, marsh, and sea coast that would be his falcons' hunting ground. He thought he could see, far off, a faint white glare where the sea began. There were probably three hundred species of bird and animal out there for his birds to hunt: rabbits, larks, blackbirds, starlings, and even ducks for the larger and swifter females to catch. "Duck hawk" was the old American name for the peregrine, given it by the farmers who shot it on sight as a marauder, just as they called the red-tailed hawk a chicken hawk. A narrow perspective; certainly neither the peregrine nor the nearly extinct red-tail had ever lived exclusively or even largely on domestic fowl; but Loren understood the farmer. Every species interprets the world in its own terms only. Even Loren, who served the hawks, knew that his reasons were a man's reasons and not a bird's. He looked around him once more, made certain that his charges lacked nothing, that their basin was full (they rarely drank, but soon they would begin to bathe), and then went clanking back down the iron stairway, pleased at the thought that he was settled in now, with a task to do, and alone.

Before bringing in the birds he had established himself at the tower. He had biked in supplies for a three-month stay: medicine, a bedroll, a heater and a stove, food, two shotguns and ammunition. The greater part of his duties over the next month or so would be to hunt for his falcons until they could do so for themselves. Unless they became familiar with the sight and taste of feral prey, they might be unable to recognize it as food—they might kill birds, because powerful instincts commanded it, but they might not know enough to eat what they killed. Loren must every day produce fresh-killed game for them to eat.

It was too late in the day now to go out, though; he would start the next morning. He had toyed with the idea of bringing in an adult trained hawk and hunting with it for his young ones; but—even though the immense difficulties of this plan intrigued him—in the end he decided against it; if for any of a thousand reasons the adult couldn't catch enough to feed the young, it would be his fault. The life his hawks must be prepared for was so arduous that they must have all his attention now.

He sat a long time outside the door of the stone building he had outfitted for himself, while the endless twilight lingered, fading from dusty yellow to lucent blue. Far above him in their tower his hawks would be grooming, tucking down their fierce heads, growing still, and at last sleeping. Loren had not enough duties to occupy his nights, and though he would go to sleep early, to be up before dawn, still he felt some anxiety over the blank hours of darkness ahead: anxiety that was causeless and that he never allowed to rise quite into consciousness. He made a simple meal meticulously and ate it slowly. He ordered his stores. He prepared for the next morning's hunt. He lit a lamp and began to look through the magazines.

Whoever it was that had camped here—last summer, he judged by the magazines' dates—had been an omnivorous reader, or looker anyway; they were mostly picture magazines. The camper had left few other traces of himself—some broken wine bottles and empty cans. From some impulse to purify his quarters for his own monkish purposes, Loren at first had thought to burn these magazines. They seemed intrusive on his solitude, freighted as they were with human wishes and needs and boredoms. He hadn't burned them. Now almost guiltily he began to leaf through them.

North Star was a government magazine he had not often bothered to look at. This issue was a fat one, "Celebrating a Decade of Peace and Autonomy." On its cover was the proud blond head of the Director of the Northern Autonomy, Dr. Jarrell Gregorius. Doctor of what? Loren wondered. An honorific, he supposed; just as it was an honorific to call the last ten years peaceful simply because they had not been years of total war.

Ten years ago the partition of the American continent had ended years of civil war. Almost arbitrarily—as quarreling parents and children retreat into separate rooms and slam doors on one another—ten large Autonomies and several smaller ones, independent city-states, mostly, had formed themselves out of the senescent American nation. They quarreled endlessly among themselves, and also with the stub of Federal government that still remained, supposedly as an arbitrator but in fact as an armed conspiracy of old bureaucrats and young technocrats desperately trying to retain and advance their power, like a belligerent old Holy Roman Empire intent on controlling rebellious princedoms. For young people of Loren's persuasion the long and still-continuing struggle had given rise to one great good: it had halted, almost completely, the uniform and mindless "development" of the twentieth century; halted the whole vast machine of Progress, fragmenting it, even (which had never in the old days seemed possible) forced its wheels to grind in reverse. All the enormous and prolonged sufferings that this reversal had brought on a highly civilized nation long dependent on resource management, on development, on the world of artifacts, could not alter Loren's pleasure in watching or reading about the old wilderness reclaiming a recreational facility or the grass covering silently the scars of strip mines and military bases.

So he looked kindly on the vain doctor. If it was only vanity and stupidity that had precipitated the partition, and kept these impotent little pseudonations alive and at one another's throats, then a theory of Loren's—not his alone—was proved out: that even the flaws of a certain species can contribute to the strength of the earth's whole life.

It may be now, though—the magazine gave some hints of it—that people had "learned their lesson" and felt it was time to consider plans for reunification. This same Dr. Gregorius thought so. Loren doubted whether the blood and the hatreds could be so quickly forgotten. "Independence," political independence, was a vast, even a silly myth; but it was less harmful than the myths of unity and interdependence that had led to the old wars: less harmful anyway to that wild world that Loren loved better than the lives and places of men. Let men be thrown onto their own resources, let them re-create their lives in small; let them live in chaos, and thus lose their concerted power to do harm to the world: that's what independence meant, practically speaking, whatever odd dreams it was dressed in in men's minds. Loren hoped it would last. Our great, independent Northern Autonomy. Long may it wave. He let the pages of *North Star* flutter together and was about to throw it back on the pile when a photograph caught his eye.

This might have been Gregorius as a boy. It was in fact his son, and there were differences. The father's face seemed to possess a fragile, commanding strength; the son's face, less chiseled, the eyes darker-lashed and deeper, the mouth fuller, seemed more willful and dangerous. It was a compelling, not a commanding, face. A young, impatient godling. His name was Sten. Loren folded the magazine open there and propped it beneath the lamp. When he had undressed and done his exercises, the boy watching, he turned down the lamp; the boy faded into darkness. When he awoke at dawn, the face was still there, pale in the gray light, as though he too had just awakened.

There is a certain small madness inherent in solitude; Loren knew that. He would soon begin to talk aloud, not only to the birds but to himself as well. Certain paths in his consciousness would become well-trodden ways because there was no other impinging consciousness to deflect him. A hundred years ago, Yerkes—one of the saints in Loren's brief canon—had said about chimpanzees that one chimpanzee is no chimpanzee. Men were like that too, except that eidetic memory and the oddity of self-consciousness could create one or a dozen others for a man alone to consort with: soon Loren would be living alone in company, the company of selves whom he could laugh with, chastise, chat with; who could tyrannize him, entertain him, bedevil him.

At noon he split with his sheath knife the skulls of the three quail he had shot and offered the brains to his charges: the best part. "Now look, there are only three among the four of you—none of that now—what's the matter? Eat, damn you—here, I'll break it up. God, what manners . . ." He let them tear at one of the quail while he dressed the other two for later. He watched the falcons' tentative, miniature voracity with fascination. He looked up; heavy clouds were gathering from the sea.

The next day it rained steadily, somberly, without pause. He had to light his lamp to go on with his magazines; he wore a hat against the dripping from the rotted ceiling. A chipmunk took refuge with him in the house, and he thought of trying to catch it for his hawks, but let it stay instead. Twice he splashed over to the tower and fed the birds steak and the remnants of quail, and returned through the puddles to his place by the lamp.

There was a fascination in the year-old news magazines, so breathlessly reporting transience, giving warnings and prophecies, blithely assuming that the biases and fashions of the moment were the heralds of new ages, would last forever. He speculated, turning the damp pages, on what a man of, say, a century ago would make of these cryptic, allusive stories. They would be—style aside—much like the stories of his own time in their portentous short sight. But they reflected a world utterly changed.

USE calls for quarantine of free-living leos. No search of this paper would reveal that USE stood for the Union for Social Engineering. What would his reader make of that acronym?

And what on earth would he make of the leos?

"It was a known fact—about mice and men, for instance—but the real beginning was with tobacco," the article began. Figure that out, Loren said to the reader he had invented. Opaque? Mysterious? In fact a cliché; every article about the leos told this tale. "They had long known, that is, that the protective walls of cells could be broken down, digested with enzymes, and that the genetic material contained in the cells could fuse to form hybrid cells, having the genetic characteristics of both—of mice and of men, say. This they could do; but they could not make them grow." Sloppy science, Loren thought, even for a popular magazine. He explained aloud about cell fusion and recombinant DNA to his non-plussed reader, then continued with the article: "Then in 1972"—just about the time Loren imagined this being read—"two scientists fused the cells of two kinds of wild tobacco—a short, shaggy-leafed kind, and a tall, sparse kind—and *made it grow:* a medium-tall, medium-shaggy plant which, furthermore, would reproduce its own kind exactly, without fur-ther interference. A new science—*diagenetics*—was born." Sciences are made, not born, Loren put in; and no science has ever been called diagenetics, except by the press. "In the century since, this science has had two important results. One is food: gigantic, high-protein wheat, tough as weeds." And as tasteless, Loren added. "Plants that grow edible fruits above ground, edible tubers below. Walnuts the size of grapefruits, with soft shells." And if anyone had listened to them, been capable, in those years, of Reason, had not preferred the pleasures of civil war, parti-tion, and religious zeal, the lowlands that Loren's tower commanded might now be covered with Walnato orchards, or fields of patent Whead.

"The other result was, of course, the leos," the article went on plac-idly. And without further explanation, having performed its paper-of-record duties, it went on to explicate the intricacies of the USE proposals for a quarantine. It was left up to Loren, in the rest of that wet, confining day, to try to make sense out of the leos for the reader he had summoned up and could not now seem to dismiss.

There had been cell-fusion experiments with animals, with verte-brates, with mammals finally. The literature was full of their failures. No matter how sophisticated the engineering, the statistical possibility of fail-ure in cell fusion, given all the possible genetic combinations, was virtu-ally limitless; it wouldn't have been surprising if only dead ends had resulted forever. But life *is* surprising; *your* era's belief that one sort of life is basically hostile to another has long been disproven, is in fact if you think about it self-evidently false. We are, each of us living things, noth-ing but a consortium of other living things in a kind of continual parlia-mentary debate, dependent on each other, living on each other, no matter how ignorant we are of it; penetrating each others' lives "like—like those hawks in the tower are dependent on me, and I am too on them, though we don't need to know it to get on with it. . . ."

So it happened that with skill and a growing body of theoretical knowledge, scientists (in a playful mood, Loren explained, having saved the world from hunger) created more grotesques than any old-time sideshow had ever pretended to exhibit. Most of them died hours after leaving their artificial wombs, unable to function as the one or as the other; or they survived in a limited sense, but had to be helped through brief and sterile lives.

The cells of the lion and the man, though, joined like a handshake, grew, and flourished. And bore live young like themselves. There was no way of explaining why this union should be so successful; the odds against a lion and a butterfly combining successfully were almost as high.

It was the Sun, the leos have come to believe, the Sun their father that brought them forth strong, and said to them: increase and multiply.

Loren stopped pacing out his small house. He realized that for some time he had been lecturing aloud, waving his arms and tapping his right forefinger against his left palm to make points. Faintly embarrassed, he pulled on his tall Irish rubber boots and stomped out into the wet to clear his head. It was unlikely that in this weather any rabbits would have visited his amateur (and very illegal) wire snares, but he dutifully checked them all. By the time he returned, the evening sky, as though with a sigh of relief, had begun to unburden itself of cloud.

Much later, moving with difficulty in the confines of his bag, he watched the horned moon climb up the sky amid fleeing cloudlets. He hadn't slept, still strung up from a day indoors. He had been explaining about the Union for Social Engineering to a certain John Doe dressed in a brown twentieth-century suit, with eyeglasses on. He understood that this person, invented by him only that day, had now moved in permanently to join his solitude.

"Welcome to the club," he said aloud.

It was raining softly again when Loren, at the end of the month, biked from the tower to the nearest town. He needed some supplies, and there might be mail for him at the post-office-store. The journey was also in the nature of a celebration: tomorrow, if it was fair, and it promised to be, he would open the nesting box for good. His falcons would fly: or at least be free to do so when the physical imperatives so precisely clocked up within them had come to term. From now on he would be chiefly observer, sometimes servant, physician possibly. They would be free. For a time they would return to the tower where they had been fed. But, unless they appeared to be ill or hurt, he wouldn't feed them. His job as parent was over. He would starve them till they hunted. That would be hard, but had to be; hunger would be the whip of freedom. And in two or three years, when they had reached sexual maturity, if they hadn't been shot, or strangled in electric wires, or poisoned, or suffered any of a thousand fates common to wild raptors, two of them might return to the tower, to their surrogate cliff, and raise a brood of quilly young. Loren hoped to be there to see.

His bike's tiny engine, which he shut off when the way was level and he could pedal, coughed as the tires cast up gauzy wings from the puddly road; Loren's poncho now and then ballooned and fluttered around him in the rainy breeze, as though he were rousing plumage preparatory to flight. He sang: his tuneless voice pleased no one but himself, but there was no one else to hear it. He stopped, as though hushed, when the raincut dirt road debouched onto the glistening blacktop that led to town.

He had a festive breakfast—his first fresh eggs in a month—and sipped noisily at the thick white mug of real coffee. The newspaper he had bought reported local doings, mostly, and what appeared to be propaganda generated by the Fed. This southernmost finger of the Northern Autonomy lay close to the coastal cities that, like the ancient Vatican States, huddled around the capital and enjoyed the Fed's protection. And the Fed's voice was louder than its legal reach. President calls for return to sanity. He laughed, and belched happily; he went out smoking a cheap cigar that burned his mouth pleasantly with a taste of town and humanity.

There was a single letter for him in his box at the store. It bore the discreet logo of the quasi-public foundation he worked for:

"Dear Mr. Casaubon: This will serve as formal notice that the Foundation's Captive Propagation Program has been dissolved. Please disregard any previous instructions of or commitments by the Foundation. We are of course sorry if this change of program causes you any inconvenience. If you wish any instructions on return of stores, disposal of stock, etc., please feel free to write. Yours, D. Small, Program Supervisor."

It was as though he had been, without knowing it, in one of those closets in old-time fun houses that suddenly collapse floorless and wallless and drop you down a wide, tumbling chute. Any inconvenience . . .

"Can I use your phone?" he asked the postmaster, who was arranging dry cereal.

"Sure. It's there. Um—it's not free."

"No. Of course. They'll pay at the other end."

The man wouldn't take this in; he continued to stare expectantly at Loren. With a sudden wave of displaced rage at the man, Loren chewed down on his cigar, glaring at him and fumbling furiously for money. He found a steel half-dollar and slapped it on the counter. The Foundation's money, he thought.

"Dr. Small, please."

"Dr. Small is in conference."

"This is Loren Casauban. *Dr.* Loren Casaubon. I'm calling long distance. Ask again."

There was a long pause, filled with the ghost voices of a hundred other speakers and the ticking, buzzing vacuum of distance.

"Loren?"

"What the hell's going on? I just came to town today—"

"Loren, I'm sorry. It's not my decision."

"Well, whose idiot decision was it? You can't just stop something like this in the middle. It's criminal, it's . . ." He should have waited to call, taken time to marshal arguments. He felt suddenly at a loss, vulnerable, as though he might splutter and weep. "What *reason* . . ."

"We've been under a lot of pressure, Loren."

"Pressure. Pressure?"

"There's a big movement against this kind of wildlife program just now. We spend public money . . ."

"Are you talking about USE?"

There was a long pause. "They somehow got hold of our books. Loren, all this is very confidential." His voice had grown dim. "A lot of money was being wasted on what could be called, well, unimportant programs." He cleared his throat as though to forestall Loren's objections. "A scandal might have brewed up. *Would* have brewed up: frankly, they intended to make an example of us. The Foundation couldn't afford that. We agreed to co-operate, you know, rationalize our programs, cut out the fat—"

"You bastard." There was no answer. "My birds will die."

"I put off sending the letter as long as I could. Isn't your first month's program complete? I tried, Loren."

His voice had grown so small that Loren's rage abated. He was angry with the wrong man. "Yes. The month is up. And if I spend another two months with them, it might—just *might* give them the edge to make it. No assurances."

"I'm sorry."

"I'm staying, Dr. Small. I never got this letter."

"Don't do that, Loren. It would embarrass me. This arrangement's very new. They're very—thorough, these USE people. It could harm you badly."

Till that moment, he hadn't thought of himself. Suddenly, his future unrolled before him like a blank blacktop road. There weren't many jobs around for solitary, queer, rageful ethologists with borderline degrees.

"Listen, Loren." Dr. Small began to speak rapidly, as though to overwhelm any objections; as though he were hurrying out a gift for a child he had just made cry. "I've had a request put to me to find a, well, a kind of tutor. A special kind. Someone like yourself, who can ride and hunt and all that, but with good academic qualifications. The choice is pretty much mine. Two children, a boy and a girl. A *special* boy and girl. Excellent benefits."

Loren said nothing. He understood of course that he was being bribed. He disliked the feeling, but some dark, fearful selfishness kept him from dismissing it angrily. He only waited.

"The trouble is, Loren, you'd have to take it up immediately." Still no surrender. "I mean right away. This man isn't used to having his requests lying around."

"Who is it?"

"Dr. Jarrell Gregorius. The children are his." This was meant to be the coup, the master stroke; and for an odd reason that Small couldn't know, it was.

With a sense that he was tearing out some living part of himself, a tongue, a piece of heart, Loren said tonelessly: "I'd have to have certain conditions."

"You'll take it."

"All right."

"What?"

"I said all right!" Then, more conciliatory: "I said all right."

"As soon as you can, Loren." Small sounded deeply relieved. Almost hearty. Loren hung up.

On the way back, tearing through thin rags of mist, Loren alternated between deep rage and a kind of heart-sinking expectation.

USE! If the old Federal government were the Holy Roman Empire, then the Union for Social Engineering was its Jesuits: militant, dedicated, selfless, expert propagandists, righteous proponents of ends that justified their means. Loren argued fiercely aloud with them, the crop-headed, ill-dressed, intent "spokesmen" he had seen in the magazines; argued the more fiercely because they had beaten him, and easily. And why? For what? What harm had his falcons done to their programs and plans? Not desiring power himself, Loren couldn't conceive of someone acting solely to gain it, by lying, compromise, indirection, by not seeing reason. If a man could be shown the right of a case—and surely Loren was right in this case—and then he didn't do it, he appeared to Loren to be a fool, or mad, or criminal.

Reason, of course, was exactly what USE claimed it did see: sanity, an end to fratricidal quibblings, a return to central planning and rational co-operation, intelligent use of the planet for man's benefit. The world is ours, they said, and we must make it work. Humbly, selflessly, they had set themselves the task of saving man's world from men. And it was frightening as much as angering to Loren how well their counter-reformation was getting on: USE had come to seem the last, best hope of a world helplessly bent on self-destruction.

Loren admitted—to himself, at least—that his secret, secretly growing new paradise was founded on man's self-destructive tendency, or at least that tendency in his dreams and institutions. He saw it as evolutionary control. USE saw it as a curable madness. So did many hungry, desperate, fearful citizens: more every day. USE was the sweet-tongued snake in this difficult new Garden, and the old Adam, whose long sinful reign over a subservient creation had seemed to be almost over, expiated in blood and loss, was being tempted to lordship again.

At evening he waited on top of the tower for the hawks to return. He had made up a box from the slatting of their outgrown nest boxes, and he carried a hood and wore a falconer's glove. He had brought the hood in with him in order to spend the long evenings embroidering and feathering it. Now he held it in his hand, not knowing whether it would mean betrayal or salvation for the hawk who would wear it.

They paid no attention to him when they arrived one by one at the tower. He was an object in the universe, neither hawk nor hawk's prey, and thus irrelevant: for they couldn't know he was the author of their lives. Hawks have no gods.

They hadn't eaten, apparently; none of their crops was distended.

They took a long time to settle, hungry and restless; but as the sun bloodied the west, they began to rest. Loren chose the smaller of the two males. To bind his wings he used one of his socks, with the toe cut off. He seized him, and had slipped the sock over his body before the bird was fully aware. He shrieked once, and the others rose up, black shapes in the last light, free to fly. They settled again when they had expressed their indignation, and by that time their brother was bound and hooded. They took no notice.

In the room where he had expected to spend the summer, Loren collected his few personal belongings: the guns, the clothes, the notebooks, let them worry about the supplies. If they wanted to make a cost accounting, they could do it without him.

The *North Star* magazine still stood propped under the lamp, open to the picture of Sten Gregorius. Beneath it on the floor was the box containing the tiercel peregrine falcon: tribute to the young prince. This one, anyway, would survive, taken care of, provided for. The three in the tower, free, might not survive. If they could choose, which life would they choose?

Which would he?

He put on his hat. There was still just enough light to start for town tonight. He didn't want to wake here in the morning, could not have borne seeing the hawks leave the tower at dawn under the press of hunger. Better to go now, and pedal his rage into exhaustion. Maybe then he could sleep.

He turned out the lamp and tossed the magazine into a corner with the others.

All right, he thought. I'll teach him. I'll teach him.

2

SPHINX

If a lion could talk, we would not understand him.

—WITTGENSTEIN

He called himself Painter.

It was rare to see a leo come so far north; Caddie had never seen one. She knew them only from the pictures in her schoolbooks: yellow sun, yellow land, the leo standing far off at a sod hut's door with one of his wives. The pictures were remote and unimpressive. But once she had dreamed of a leo. She had been sent to him on some business by her father. He lived in a place of stifling heat, which was lined with asbestos, as though to keep it from consuming itself. She panted, trying to draw breath, waiting with growing dread for the leo to appear. She felt the thunder of dream realization: she had come to the wrong house, she shouldn't be here, it wasn't the leo but the Sun who lived here: that was why it was so hot. She awoke as the leo appeared, suddenly, towering over her; he was simply a lion standing like a man, yet his face glowed as though made of molten gold, and his mane streamed whitely from his face. He seemed furious at her.

Painter was not a lion. He didn't tower over her; she kept her distance; yet he was massive enough. And he wasn't furious. He spent his time in his room, or at a table in the bar, and never spoke, except rarely to Hutt. She saw him take a telephone call, long distance; he said "Yes," holding the receiver slightly away from his head, and then only listened, and hung up without a farewell.

Tonight he sat at a table where she could see him from the laundry door. The bar was lit with smoky lanterns, and the smoke of the black cigarettes he smoked one after another rose into the lantern's light and hung like low clouds.

"I wonder where his wife is," she said to Hutt when he came to the door of the laundry. "Don't they always have a wife with them, wherever they go?"

"I'd just as soon not ask," Hutt said. "And neither had you better."

"Does he stink?"

"No more than me." Hutt grinned a gap-tooth grin at her and tossed her an armload of gray sheets.

Hutt was afraid of Painter, that was evident, and it was easy to see why. The leo's wrists were square and solid as beams, and the muscles of his arm glided and slid like oiled machinery when he merely put out a cigarette. Hutt got so few customers that he usually toadied up to any new face; but not this face. The leo seemed quite satisfied with that.

Later that evening, though, on her way out to the goat shed to lock up, she saw Hutt and the leo conferring in the deserted bar. Hutt was counting something off on his fingers. When she passed, both of them looked up at her. The eyes of the leo were as golden as lamps, as large as lamps, and as unwavering. What had he to do with her? When she looked questioningly at Hutt, he avoided her look.

Caddie's parents had been professionals—industrial relations, whatever that meant; when she was a kid she often recited it to herself, as an exiled princess might recite her lineage. They hadn't fared well as refugees when the civil wars started down south. Her father had cut his foot, stupidly, while chopping wood, developed an infection, and just quietly died from it, as though that were the best he could manage under the circumstances. Her mother wasn't long in following. When she stopped telling Caddie about the wealth and comfort and respect they all had had, back before Caddie could clearly remember, she began to resign from life as well. Once a month the doctor from town would come out and look at her and go away. She caught a cold when it snowed in May, and died from it.

That left Caddie, fourteen, with two choices: the whorehouse at Bend, or indenture. She had almost decided on the whorehouse, was almost in a fearful way looking forward to it, like a girl setting out for her first term at college, when Hutt made her the indenture offer. In ten years she'd be free, and he'd settle money on her. The sum, to Caddie in the north woods, seemed like a fortune.

He was good about the money. Every month he and Caddie would ride over to the J.P. and Hutt would make his deposit and she would sign his receipt. And he never treated her as anything but a servant. She soon learned about his taste for bully truck drivers and army boys; so that was all right. She didn't mind the work, though it was hard and continuous; she did it with a kind of quick contempt that annoyed Hutt; apparently, he would have preferred her to be cheerful as well as efficient and strong. And once she had gotten a certain ascendancy over the routine, the work could be gotten away from. In every direction there were miles of unpeopled forests she could escape into, alone or with a pack horse, for days.

She learned that she had a talent for bearing things: not only heavy packs and cold nights and miles of walking, but also the weight of the days themselves, the dissatisfaction that she carried always like a pack, the *waiting:* for that's what she felt she was doing, always—waiting—and she convinced herself that it was the end of her ten years' indenture she waited for. But it wasn't.

The next morning was cold for September, which this far north was nearly freezing. White steam rose from the pond, from the woolly pack horses Hutt kept for rent, and from the mounds of their droppings. When she went out to the goat shed, Caddie could see her breath, and steam rose too from the full milk pails. Everything warm, everything from the interior, steamed.

Coming back with the milk, she saw Ruta and Bonnie, the little pack horses, rearing and snorting, shunting each other against the corral walls. She came closer, calling their names, seeing now that their eyes were wide with fear. On the other side of the corral, the leo Painter leaned against the rail, smoking.

"What did you do to them?" she asked, putting down the milk. "Were you bothering them? What's wrong with you?"

"It's the smell," Painter said. His voice was thin, cracked, as though laryngitic.

"I don't smell anything."

"No. But they do."

How long could it have been since there was anything like a lion in these mountains? Last winter Barlo saw a bobcat, and talked about it for weeks. And yet maybe somewhere within Ruta and Bonnie the old fear lived, and could be touched.

"Trouble is," said Painter, "how are we going to use the damn animals if I scare them to death?" He threw down the cigarette with thick, golden-haired fingers. "We'll have a great time."

"We? Are you and Hutt going someplace?"

"Hutt?"

"Well, who do you mean, we?"

"You and me," Painter said.

She said nothing for a long moment. His face seemed expressionless, maybe because it wasn't completely human, or perhaps because he, like a cat, had nothing particular to express. Anyway, if he was making a joke, he didn't put it across. He only looked at her, steam coming from his narrow nostrils.

"What makes you think I'm going anywhere with you?" Caddie said. For the first time since she had seen Painter, she felt afraid of him.

He lit another black cigarette, clumsily, as though his hands were stiff with cold. "Last night I bought you. Bought your indenture from him—Hutt. You're mine now."

She only stared at him in disbelief. Then came a wave of anger, and she started up the muddy way toward the hotel, forgetting the milk pails. Then she turned on him. "Bought! What the hell does that mean? You think I'm a pair of shoes?"

"I'm sorry if I said it wrong," Painter said. "But it's all legal. It's in the papers, that he can sell the indenture. It's a clause." He opened his stubby hand wide, and the flesh drew back from his fingertips to show curved white nails.

She stood, confused. "How can he do that? Why didn't he tell me?"

"You sold him ten years of your life," Painter said. "On time. He owns it, he can sell it. I don't suppose he even has to tell you. That's not in the papers, I don't think. Anyway, it doesn't matter."

"Doesn't matter!"

"Not to me."

She wanted to run to Hutt, hurt him, hit him, plead with him, hold him.

Ruta and Bonnie had stopped their shunting, and only snorted occasionally and huddled at the far side of the corral. For a while they all stood there, triangulated, the horses, Caddie, the leo.

"What are you going to do with me?" Caddie said.

In the bar that night, Barlo and the two truck drivers stayed away from the table where Painter sat, though they glanced at him, one by one; he returned none of their looks.

The drivers had come up from the south. They wore uniforms of some kind, Caddie didn't know whose, their own invention maybe. They had the usual stories to tell, the refugees clogging the roads, the abandoned cars you had to avoid, the cities closed like fortresses. She had long ago given up trying to sort all that out. They had gone mad down there, had been mad since before she could remember anything. Painter's face showed no interest in them. But his ears did. His broad, high-standing ears were the most leonine, the most bestial, thing about his strange head. Partly hidden by his thick, back-swept hair, still they could be seen, pricking and turning toward the speakers with a will of their own. Perhaps he didn't even know they did so; perhaps it was only Caddie who saw it. She couldn't help glancing at him from behind the bar; her heart dove and rose again painfully each time she looked at him, sitting nearly immobile at his table.

"It don't matter to us," Barlo said. "We're independent anyways." This little chunk of north woods had seceded entirely, years before, and was now, officially, a dependency of Canada. "We got our own ways."

"That's all right," the elder said, "till they come to take you back again."

"The Fed," said the younger.

"Well, I ain't goin'," Barlo said, and grinned as though he had said something clever. "I ain't goin'."

Caddie was kept busy bringing beer for the drivers and rye for Barlo's coffee, and frying steaks, things Hutt usually did; but Hutt had gone over to the J.P.'s to get the papers notarized and a bill of sale made up: had left with a long angry mark on one cheek from Caddie's ring.

Until that morning, Caddie had thought she knew what shape the world had. She didn't like it, but she could stand it. She made it bearable by feeling little but contempt for it. Now, without warning, it had changed faces, expanded into a vertiginous gulf before her, said to her:

the world is bigger than you imagined. Bigger than you can imagine. It wasn't only that Hutt had cheated her, and apparently there was nothing she could do about it, but that the whole world had: the fear and confusion she felt were caused as much by life betraying the quick bargain she had long ago made with it as by her finding herself suddenly belonging to a leo.

Belonging to him. No, that wasn't so. She washed glasses angrily, slapping them into the gray water. She belonged to no one, not Hutt, and certainly not this monster. She had never been owned; one of her constant taunts to her mother, trying to bring Caddie up respectably in spite of exile and poverty, had been, "You don't own me." Maybe once she had been owned by her father, Sometimes she felt a long-ago adhesion, a bond in her far past, to that man who grew vaguer in memory every year. But he had freed her by dying.

"Getting hot down in the N.A.," said the older driver. "Getting real hot."

"I don't get it," Barlo said.

"They're trying to put it all back together. The Fed. The N.A.'s a holdout. Not for long, though. And if they join, where in hell will you be? They'll squeeze you to death."

"Well, we don't hear much up here," Barlo said uneasily. A silence occurred, made louder by the rattle of a loose window pane. The leo motioned to Caddie.

"I'd like some smokes."

The three at the bar turned to look at him, and then away again, as one. "We're out," Caddie said. "The truck won't come again till next week."

"Then we'll leave tomorrow," Painter said.

She put down the glass she had been wiping. She came and sat with Painter under the lantern, ignoring the alert silence at the bar. "Why me?" she said. "Why not a man? You could hire a man to do anything I can do, and more. And cheaper."

He reached over to her and raised her face to look at it. His palm was smooth, hard, and dry, and his touch was gentle. It was odd.

"I like a woman to do for me," he said. "I'm used to it. A man . . . it'd be hard. You wouldn't know."

Close to him, touched by him, she had thought to feel disgust, revulsion. What she felt was something simpler, like wonder. She thought of the creatures of mythology, mixed beasts who talked with men. The

Sphinx. Wasn't the Sphinx part human, part lion? Her father had told her the story, how the Sphinx asked people a riddle, and killed everyone who couldn't solve it. Caddie had forgotten the riddle, but she remembered the answer: the answer was Man.

Hutt sat at a table near the door with the coffee, pretending to do his accounts. She passed him and repassed, bringing down Painter's gear from his room, dumping it onto the barroom floor, kitting it up neatly, and taking it out to the pack ponies.

"You're lucky, really," Hutt said. "These drivers said in a month, two months maybe, they'll close the highway. There'll be no more trucks. How would I pay you?" He looked at her as though for some forgiveness. "How the hell am I going to live?"

She only shouldered the last pack, afraid that if she tried to speak she wouldn't be able to, that the hatred she felt then for him would stifle her; she picked up Painter's carbine, which had an odd-shaped stock, and went out.

When Ruta and Bonnie were ready, Painter tried to take the lead rope, but Bonnie shied and tried to rear. Painter's lip curled, and he made a sound, a shriek, a roar, and a sound that was all fierce impatience. He could have taken Bonnie's neck in one arm, but he seemed to gain some control of himself, and gave Caddie the rope. "You do it," he said. "You follow. I'll stay ahead or we'll never get there."

"Where?" she said, but he didn't answer, only took the carbine under his arm and started off with short, solid strides; as he walked, his shaggy head turned from side to side, perhaps looking for something, perhaps only from some half-instinct.

All that morning they went up the unfinished dirt truck road going north. The yellow earth-movers they passed were deserted, seemed to have been deserted for some time; apparently they had stopped trying to cut this road over the mountain. . . . From out of the constant forest sound there came a sound not quite of the forest, a dull, repeated sound, like a great quick watch. Ahead of her, Painter had stopped and was listening; he threw his head this way, then that. The sound grew more distinct, and suddenly he was running toward her, waving her off the road. "Why?" she said. "What's the matter?" He only made that harsh sound in his throat for answer, and pushed her down a crumbling embankment and into a tangle of felled trees and brush there. When Ruta and Bonnie pulled at the rope, reluctant to go down, he spanked them with his hand. The sound grew louder. Painter fingered his carbine, looking out from where they hid. Then, ghostly through the treetops, hovering like a preying dragonfly, a pale helicopter appeared. It turned, graceful and ominous; it seemed to quarter the area in its glance, as a searcher does. Then without a shift in its ticking voice it withdrew southward.

"Why did you hide?" she said. "Are they looking for you?"

"No." He smiled at her, something she hadn't known he could do, a slow and crooked smile. "But I wouldn't want them to find me. We'll go on now."

Mid-afternoon he had her make camp in a sheltered glade well off the road. "Eat if you want to," he said. "I won't today." He lay full-length on the heated ground pine, drawing up his muscled legs, resting his big head on his chin, and watching her work. She felt those lamplike eyes on her.

"I brought you cigarettes," she said. "I found a pack."

"Don't need them."

"Why did you say we had to leave when they were gone?"

"Men," he said. "Can't stand the smell. Not the men themselves, their places. The smell of, I don't know, their lives." His eyes began to close. "Nothing personal. The cigarettes block up the smell, is all." His eyes were slits; they closed entirely, then opened again. She had eaten and packed, and still he lay slipping in and out of sleep. Wherever it was he was going, he seemed in no hurry to get there.

"Lazy," he said, opening his eyes. "That's my trouble."

"You look comfortable," she said.

It would be many days before she understood that his direct, fierce stare more often than not looked at nothing; many days till in a fit of rage at being so intently regarded she stuck out her tongue at that gaze, and saw it drift closed without acknowledging the insult. He wasn't a man; he meant nothing by it.

Not a man. He was not a man. The men she had known, who had grasped and fumbled with her in a pleading, insistent way; the dark boy she had done the same with not long ago—*they* were men. Something leapt within her, at a thought she would not admit.

In the late afternoon he grew restless, and they went on. Perhaps by now the ponies had gotten used to him; anyway, they no longer shied from him, so Caddie could walk by his side.

"I don't want to pry," she said, even though she suspected irony would be lost on him, or perhaps because of that, "and you have the papers and all, but it'd be nice to know what's going on."

"It wouldn't," he said.

"Well," she said.

"Look," he said. "That copter we saw was looking for somebody. I'm looking for the same somebody. I don't know where he is, but I've got an idea, and a better idea"—pointing up—"than they have." He looked at her, expressionless. "If they find him first, they'll kill him. If I find him first, they might kill both of us."

"Both," she said. "What about me?"

He didn't answer.

What was it she felt for him? Hatred: a spark of that, a kind of molten core at the center of her feelings that warmed the rest, hatred that he had with so little thought snatched her from where she had been— well, comfortable anyway. Hatred of her own powerlessness was what it was, because he hadn't been cruel. The uses he put her to were what she was for; it was in the papers; there was no appeal from that and he made no bones about it. He obviously couldn't put a polite false face on the thing, even if it had occurred to him that it might make it easier for her.

Which it wouldn't have. She knew her own story.

And yet in using her he wasn't like Hutt had been. Not constantly suspicious, prying, attempting to snatch from her every shred of person she built for herself. No, he assumed her competence, asked for nothing more than she could do, said only when they would stop and where they would go, and left the rest to her; deferred, always, to her judgment. If she failed at anything he never showed anger or contempt, only left her to patch up her mistakes without comment.

So that slowly, without choosing to, resenting it, she became a partner in this enterprise that she couldn't fathom. Had he consciously so drawn her into it? She supposed not. He probably hadn't considered it that closely. *I like a woman to do for me,* he had said. *You wouldn't know.*

And touched her cheek with his hard, dry palm.

"You cold?" he said. The fire had died to coals. Her own sleeping bag was an old one, a grudging parting gift from Hutt. She said nothing, trying not to shiver. "Damn, you must be. Come over here."

"I'm fine."

"Come here."

It was a command. She lay coldly hating him for a while, but the command remained in the space between them, and at last she came, tiptoeing over the already rimy ground to where he lay large in his bag. He drew her down to him, tucked her efficiently within the cavity of his lean belly. She wanted to resist, but the warmth that came from him was irresistible. She thrust her damp cold nose into his furry chest, unable not to, and rested her head on his hard forearm.

"Better," he said.

"Yes."

"Better with two."

"Yes." Somehow, without her having sensed their approach, warm tears had come to her eyes, a glow of weeping was within her; she pressed herself harder against him to stifle the sudden sobs. He took no notice; his breathing, slow and with a burring undertone, didn't alter.

It was just light when she awoke. He had gone down to the quick stream they had camped by. She could see him, lightstruck, the fine blond hair of his limbs glistening in the sun as though he were on fire. He was washing, delicately, carefully; and from within her cave of warmth she spied on him. Her heart, whether from the invasion of his privacy or from some other reason, beat hard and slow. He bent, drew up silver strands of water, and swept his hands through his mane; he rubbed himself. He bent to drink, and when he arose, droplets fell from his beard. When he came back to the campsite, drying himself with an old plaid shirt, she saw that above his long lopsided testicles his penis was sheathed, like a dog's, held against his belly by gold-furred skin.

From somewhere to the south the copter's drone could be heard briefly, like the first faint roll of a storm. He glanced up and hurried to dress.

Through that day, walking by him or ahead of him (for she was the better walker, she knew that now, his strength wasn't meant for endurance, or his legs not made for walking, yet he no longer stopped for long rests as he had before), she felt come and go a dense rush of feeling that made her face tingle and her breasts burn. She tried to turn from him when she felt it, sure that he could read it in her face; and she tried to turn away from it herself, not certain what it was—it felt like clarity, like resolve, yet darker. Once, though, when he called out to her and she was above him on a hard climb, she turned to face him, and felt it rush up uncontrollably within her, as though she glowed.

"You're fast," he said, and then stood quiet, his wide chest moving quickly in and out. She said nothing, only stared at him, letting him see her, if he could; but then his unwavering gaze defeated her and she turned away, heart drumming.

Late in the afternoon they came on the cabin.

He had her tie up the ponies in the woods well away from the clearing the cabin stood in, and then for a long time watched the cabin from the cover of the trees; he seemed to taste, carefully, with all his senses, the gray, shuttered shack and its surroundings. Then he walked deliberately up to it and pushed open the door.

"No one's been here," he said when she came into the shuttered dimness. "Not for weeks."

"How can you tell?"

He laughed shortly—a strange, harsh sound, little like a laugh—and moved carefully through the two small rooms. In the afternoon light that filtered through the shutters she could see that the place was well furnished—no logger's cabin, but something special, a hideout, though from the outside it looked like any shack. She went to open a shutter. "Leave that," he said. "Light that fire. It's cold in here." He went from cupboard to cabinet, looking at things, looking for something that in the end he didn't find. "What's this?"

"Brandy. Don't you know?"

He put it down without interest.

"You were going to meet your somebody here."

"We'll wait. He'll come. If he can." The decision made, he ceased his prowling. The fire, a bottled-gas thing, boomed when she touched a match to it, and glowed blue. Why, she wondered, bottled gas in the middle of the woods? And realized: for the same reason that this place looks like a shack. Bottled gas makes no smoke. No smoke, nobody home.

"Where are we?"

"A place."

"Tell me."

The heat of the fire had seemed to soften him. He sat on the small sofa before it, legs wide apart, arms thrown across its back. On a sudden impulse she knelt before him and began to unlace his boots. He moved his feet to aid her, but made no remark on this; accepted it, as he did everything she did for him. "Tell me," she said again, almost coyly this time, looking up at his big head resting on his chest. She smiled at him and felt a dizzy sense of daring.

"We are," he said slowly, "where a certain counselor, a government counselor, comes, sometimes, when he wants to get away say from the office or town, and where he might come if he had to get away from the government. And we'll meet him here. If we're lucky."

It was the longest speech she had ever heard him make. Without hurry she took off his boot and rolled the sweat-damp sock from his long, neat foot.

"What then?" she said, more to hear him talk than because she cared or understood; anyway, the blood sounding in her ears made it hard to think.

"This counselor," he said lazily, seeming not to care either, watching her unlace the stiff thongs of the other boot, "this counselor is a friend of ours. Of our kind. And his government wasn't. And his government down there has just collapsed, which you may or may not know, partly because he"—she drew off the other boot—"undid it, you could say, and so he's had to leave. In a hurry."

"Want some?" she said, showing him the brandy bottle.

"I don't know," he said simply. He watched her as she went around the room, finding glasses, breaking the bottle's seal; watched her, she knew, differently now. She felt a fierce elation, having embarked on this thing; felt the danger like the sear of the brandy. "Warm," she said, putting the glass in his hands, touching his fingers lightly. He raised the glass to his face and withdrew it quickly, as though it had bitten him; his nostrils flared and he put it down.

"How come—" she had not sat but walked now before him, holding her glass in two hands, past him and back again—"how come you don't have a tail?"

"Tails," he said, watching her, "are for four-legs. I'm a two-legs." His voice had darkened, thickened. "Couldn't sit down, with a tail. A piece of luck."

"I'd like a tail," she said. "A long, smooth tail to move . . ." She moved it. He moved. She moved away, a sudden voice urgent in her ears: *you can't do this you can't do this you can't do it you can't.*

He rose. The way he did it made it seem as though he was doing it for the first time after aeons of repose, the way movement gathered in his muscles to lift his heavy weight, the way his hands took hold of the couch to help him up; it was like watching something inanimate come frighteningly, purposefully alive in a dream. As he stood, his eyes somehow caught the fire's light and the pupils glowed brilliant red.

She was in a corner, holding her glass before her breasts protectively, her daring gone. "Wait," she said, or tried to say, but it was a sound only, and he had her: it was useless to struggle because he was helpless. She was swallowed up in his strength but he was helpless, taking her because he no longer had a choice: and she had done that to him. An enormous odor came from him, dense as an attar, mingling with the smell of spilled brandy; she could hear his quick breath close to her ear, and her trembling hand fumbled with his at her belt. Her heart was mad, and another voice, shrill, drowned out the first: *you're going to do it you're going to do it you're going to.*

"Yes," she said. She yanked at her belt. A button tore. "Yes."

She had thought that a single act of surrender was all she needed to make, that having made it she would be deprived of all will, all consciousness by passion, and that whatever acts followed would follow automatically. Her heat hadn't imagined difficulties; her heat had only imagined some swift, ineluctable coupling, like contrary winds mixing in a storm. It wasn't like that. He wasn't a man; they didn't fit smoothly together. It was like labor; like battles.

And yet she did find the ways, poised at times between repugnance and elation, to bare herself to him; drowned at times, suffocated at times in him as though he plunged her head under water; afraid at times that he might casually, thoughtlessly kill her; able to marvel, sometimes, as though she were another, at what they did, feeling, as though through another's skin, the coarse hair of his arms and legs, thick enough almost to take handfuls of. For every conjunction they achieved, there were layers of shame to be fought through like the layers of their thick clothing: and only by shameless strategies, only by act after strenuous act of acquiescence, her voice hoarse from exertion and her body slick with sweat, did she conquer them: and entered new cities, panting, naked, amazed.

She began to sob then, not knowing why; her legs, nerveless, folded under his careless weight. She lay against his thick thigh, which trembled as though he had run a mile. She coughed out sobs, sobs like the sobs of someone who has survived a great calamity: been shipwrecked, suffered, seen death, but against all odds, with no hope, has survived, has found a shore.

She dreamed, toward dawn, curled against him, of muscle; of the tensed legs of his wives bearing him, of the fine bones and muscles of his hands, of her own slim arms wrapped in his, struggling with his. The soreness of her own muscles entered her dream, her own sinews tightening and slackening. She dreamed: *I did it I did it I did it.* She awoke exulting then for a moment and curled herself tighter against his deathlike sleep. She dreamed of his purring dreaming breath; it grew huge and menacing, and she awoke to the fast tick of the searching helicopter growing quickly closer. She moved to awake him, but he was awake already; all his senses pointed toward the growing sound. It became a roar, and its wind stirred in the cabin. It had landed outside.

He had a hand on her that she knew meant *keep still.* He turned, crouched and silent, toward the door, which was locked. Feet came across the pine needles toward the door with a sound they wouldn't have heard if they weren't all attention. Someone tried the door, paused, knocked, waited, pounded impatiently, waited again, then kicked in the door with a sudden crack. For a moment she could see a man silhouetted against the morning, could see him hesitate, looking into the shuttered gloom of the cabin, could see the gun in his hands. Then Painter, beside her, exploded.

She didn't see Painter move, nor did the one at the door, but there was a cry from his throat and a flurry of motion and he had seized the intruder, who made one sound, a sound Caddie would never forget— the desperate, shocked shriek of seized prey—and Painter had locked the man's head between his forearms. The man sank suddenly, as though punctured, his head loose on his body.

Painter, legs wide apart, supported him roughly—worried him, she would think later, like a cat, turning him this way and that to see if there was any life left in him—and then dropped him. "Sunless bastard," he said, or she thought he said. Beyond, in the tiny clearing, the copter's blades rotated lazily, not quite done.

———

"Come in TK24," the radio said. "Come in TK24. Have you achieved O1?" It spoke in quick, harsh bursts, all inflection lost in an aura of static. Getting no reply from TK24 (who was dead), it began a conversation with someone else; the someone else's voice couldn't be heard, was pauses only, long or short. "Roger your request to return to base." . . . "No, that hasn't been verified as yet. He doesn't come in." . . . "Negative, negative. Listen, you'd be the first to know." . . . "That's what I understand. The cabin was his O1. Then the wrecked plane." A laugh, strangled in static. "Government. A real antique. He wouldn't get far." . . . "Positive, that is O2 of TK24 and we'll hear soon." . . . "Right, positive, over. Come in TK24, TK24 . . ."

On the glossy seat of the copter were charts covered with clear plastic. On one of them were circles in red grease crayon: one circle was labeled O1. The other circle, from what Painter could read of the map, was about ten miles off, up a sharp elevation, and was labeled O2.

Caddie came toward him, passing slowly the folded body of TK24, and feeling as though she had entered somewhere else, somewhere totally other, and had no way to get back. "You killed him."

"You're staying here," he said. "Up there on the mountain a plane's crashed. It might be him. If it isn't, I'll be back tonight or tomorrow."

"No."

"Get my rifle."

"I'll get it. But I'm coming with you."

He looked at her for a moment, looked at her—in a new way, with that new bond between them, looked—no. She felt a chill wave of something like despair. He looked the same. Nothing had changed, not for him. All her surrender had been for nothing, nothing. . . . He turned away. "Get the horses, then. We'll take them as far as we can."

If he wasn't made for walking, he was made less for climbing. Only his strength hauled him up, his strength and a fierce resolve she didn't dare break by speaking, except to tell him where she had found the easiest ways up. He followed. Once, she got too far ahead, lost sight of him, and couldn't hear him coming after her. She retraced her steps and found him resting, panting, his back against a stone.

"Monkey," he said. "A damned monkey. I haven't got your strength."

"Strength," she said. "Two hours ago you killed somebody, with your hands, in about ten seconds."

"I saw him first. It would've taken him even less. He had a gun." For the first time since he had turned those yellow eyes on her at Hutt's place the night she was being sold, she felt that he was trying to read her. "They want to kill us all, you know. They're trying."

"Who?"

"The government. Men. You." Still his eyes searched her. "We're no use to them. Worse than useless. Poachers. Thieves. Polygamists. We won't be sterilized. There's no good in us. We're their creation, and they're phasing us out. When they can catch us."

"That's not right!" She felt deep horror, and shame. "How can they . . . You've got a right to live."

"I don't know about a right." He stood, breaking his look. "But I am alive. I mean to stay that way. Let's go."

The government. Men. You. What did she expect from him, then? Love? The leo had bought her as men hunt leos. They were not one kind; never, never could she and he be one. He could only use her, or not, as he liked. She climbed fiercely, tears (of rage or pity, for herself or for him, she didn't know) breaking the chill morning into stars.

They found O2 fitted snugly into the trees at the end of a rocky pasture. Its wings were folded back, neatly, looking at rest like a bird's; but bits of the plane were scattered over the pasture violently, and its wings were never made to bend. Painter went near it cautiously. The long shadows of the forest crept across the field, quicker as the sun sank further. One crazed window of the plane flared briefly in the last sun. There was an absolute stillness there; the wrecked plane was incongruous and yet proper, like a galleon at the bottom of the sea. There was no pilot, dead or alive; no one. Painter stood by it a long moment, turning his head slowly, utterly attentive; then, as though he had perceived a path, he plunged into the woods. She followed.

He didn't go unerringly to the tree; it was as if he knew it must be there, but not exactly where it was. He stopped often, turned, and turned again. The long blue twilight barely entered here, and they must go slowly through the undergrowth. But he had it then: an ancient monarch, long dethroned, topless and hollow, amid upstart pines. Insects and animals had deposited the powdered guts of it at the narrow door.

"Good afternoon, Counselor," he said softly.

"If you come any closer," said a little voice within the tree, "I'll shoot. I have a gun. Don't try . . ."

"Gently, Counselor," Painter said.

"Is that you? Painter? Good god . . ."

She had come up beside him and looked into the hollow. A tiny man was wedged into the narrow space. His spectacles, one lens cracked, glinted; so did the small pistol in his hands.

"Come out of there," Painter said.

"I can't. Something's broken. My foot, somewhere." From fear, exposure, something, his voice sounded faint and harsh, like fine sandpaper. "I'm cold."

"We can't light a fire."

"There's a cell heater in the plane. It might work." She could hear in his voice that he was trembling. Painter withdrew into the trees toward the blue dimness of the pasture, leaving her alone by the tree. She squatted there, alert, a little afraid; whoever was looking for this counselor would come and find him soon.

"You don't," said the tree, "have a cigarette." It was a remark only, without hope; and she almost laughed, because she did: the pack she had put in her shirt pocket, for Painter, a lifetime ago. . . . She gave them to him, and her tin of matches. He groaned with relief. In the brief, trembling light of the match she glimpsed a long, small face, thick, short red hair, a short red beard. His glasses flashed and went out again. "Who are you?" he said.

"His." Yes. "Indentured, from now till . . ."

"Not a bit."

"What?"

"Against the law. No leo could possibly employ a man. You're not obliged. 'No human being shall be suborned by or beholden and subservient to a member of another species.' " A tiny bark of a laugh, and he relapsed into exhausted silence.

Painter came back carrying the heater, its element already glowing dully. He put it before the tree's mouth and sat; the tension had slipped from him like a garment, and he moved with huge grace to arrange himself on the ground. "Get warm," he said softly. "We'll get you out. Down the mountain. Then we'll talk." His eyes, jewellike in the heater's glow, drifted closed, then opened slowly, feral and unseeing.

"He said," Caddie said, "that you can't own me. In the law."

He could at that moment have been expressing rage, contempt, indifference, jealousy: she had no way to tell. His glower was as vast as it was meaningless. "Warm," he said. He scratched, carefully. He slept.

"Of course," said the little mocking voice inside the tree, "he is King of Beasts. Or Pretender anyway. But that never applied to men, did it? Men are the Lords of Creation."

Painter was a shaggy shape utterly still. The law. What could it matter? The bond between them, which she had made out of total surrender since she had no other tool to forge it with, couldn't be broken now; not even, she thought fiercely, by him. "I suppose," he said, "a person could stop being a Lord of Creation. Surrender that. And be a beast." There was a tiny hammer beating within her thigh where he had stretched her. She felt it flutter. "Only another beast of his."

"I don't know." He was moving within the tree, trying to extricate himself. "Of course he has always been my king. No matter how often I have failed him." A small cry of pain. "Or fooled him. Help me here."

She went to the tree and he held out for her to take an impossibly tiny black-palmed hand, its wrist long and fine as a bunch of sticks tied together. If he hadn't gripped her hard, like a little child, she would have dropped the hand in fear. He pulled himself toward the opening, and she could see his long mouth grinning with effort; his yellow teeth shone.

"Who are you?" she said.

He ceased his efforts, but didn't release her. His eyes, brown and tender behind the glasses, searched her. "That's difficult to say, exactly." Was he smiling? She was close to him now, and an odor that before had been only part of the woods odor grew distinct. Distinct and familiar. "Difficult to say. But you can call me Reynard."

3

The flaying of Isengrim

The hardest work, Sten learned, was to carry the bird. Loren knew it was hard for a boy of fourteen to carry even a tiercel for the hours required, and he wore a glove, too, but Sten hated to give up the hawk; it was his hawk, he was the falconer, the hawk should be his alone to carry. If he rode, slowly, it was easier; but even on horseback Sten wanted desperately to lower his arm. Loren mustn't know that; neither must the hawk. As he rode, he spoke quietly, confidentially, to Hawk—he had never given him any other name, though Mika had thought of many: kingly, fierce names. Somehow, it seemed to Sten, any other name would be an excrescence, a boast about power and authority that a man might need but this bird didn't.

There had been a first frost that morning, and the leaves and brown grass they rode over were still painted with it; though the sun would be high soon and erase it, just for this moment it was lit with infinitesimal colored lights. Chet and Martha, the pointers, breathed out great clouds of frost as they studied the morning, padding with directness but no hurry toward the open fields that lay beyond the old stone farmhouse.

The farmhouse was mews, stable, and kennel, and Sten and Mika's private place. Their tutor, Loren, was allowed inside, but no one else. When their father had bought the long brown mansion whose roofs were still visible to them over the ridge, he'd wanted to pull down the old farmhouse and fill in the fulsome, duck-weedy pond. Sten had asked for an interview, and presented to his father the reasons for keeping them—for nature study, a place of their own to be responsible for, a place for the animals outside the house. He did it so carefully and reasonably that his father laughed and relented.

What his father had feared, of course, was that the place could be used for cover in an attack. The sensors around the grounds couldn't see through its walls. But he put aside his fears.

"Don't, Mika!" Sten hissed, but Mika had already kicked her bay pony into the proper gait. She took the low stone wall with great ease, gently, almost secretly, and quickly pulled up on the other side.

"Damn you," Sten said. His horse, seeing its cousin take off, had gotten restless to follow, and Sten had only one hand to settle him. Hawk bated on his wrist, the tassels of his hood nodding, his beak opening. He moved his feet on the glove, griping deeply; his bells rang. Furious, but careful, Sten picked his way through the fallen place in the wall. Mika was waiting for him; her brown eyes were laughing, though her mouth tried not to.

"Why did you do it? Can't you see . . ."

"I wanted to," she said, defensive suddenly, since he wasn't going to be nice about it. She turned her horse and went after Loren and the dogs, who were getting on faster than they.

It's Hawk, Sten thought. She's jealous, is all. Because Hawk is mine, so she's got to show off. Well, he *is* mine. He rode carefully after them, trying not to let any of this move Hawk, who was sensitive to any emotion of Sten's. Hawk was an eyas—that is, he had never molted in the wild; he was a man's bird, raised by men, fed by men. Eyases are sensitive to men's moods far more than are passage hawks caught as adults. Sten had done everything he could to keep him wild—had even let him out "at hack," after his first molt, though it was terrible to see him go, knowing he might not return to feed at the hack board. He tried to treat him, always with that gracious, cool authority his father used with his aides and officers. Still, Hawk was his, and Sten knew that Hawk loved him with a small, cool reflection of the passion Sten felt for him.

Loren called to him. Across the field, where the land sloped down to marshy places, Chet and Martha had stopped and were pointing to a ragged copse of brush and grapevine.

Sten dismounted, which took time because of Hawk; Mika held his horse's head, and then took up the reins. Sten crossed the field toward the place the dogs indicated, a thick emotion rising in him. When Loren held up his hand, Sten stopped and slipped Hawk's hood.

Hawk blinked, the great sweet eyes confused for a moment. The dogs were poised, unmoving. Loren watched him, and watched the dogs. This was the crucial part. A bad point from the dogs, bad serve from Sten, and Hawk would lose his game; if he missed it, he would sit glumly on the ground, or skim idly around just above the ground, looking for nothing; or fly up into a tree and stare at them all, furious and unbiddable; or just rake off and go, lost to them, perhaps forever.

Hawk shifted his stance on Sten's wrist, which made his bells sound, and Sten thought: he knows, he's ready. "Now!" he cried, and Loren sent the dogs into the bush. Hawk roused, and Sten, with all the careful swift strength he could put into his weary arm, served Hawk. Hawk rose, climbing a stair in the air, rose directly overhead till he was nearly as small as a swallow. He didn't rake off, didn't go sitting trees; it was too fine a morning for that; he hung, looking down, expecting to see something soon that he could kill.

"He's waiting on," Mika said, almost whispered. She shaded her eyes, trying to see the black neat shape against the hard blue sky. "He's waiting on, look, look . . ."

"Why don't they flush it?" Sten said. He was in an agony of anticipation. Had he served too soon? Was there nothing in the copse? They should have brought something bagged. What if it was a grouse, something too big . . . ? He began to walk, steadily, with long steps, so that Hawk could see him. He had the lure in his pocket, and Hawk would have to come to that, if he would deign to, if . . .

Two woodcock burst noisily from the copse. Sten stopped. He looked overhead. Hawk had seen. Already, Sten knew, he had chosen one of them; his cutout shape changed; he began to stoop. Sten didn't breathe. The world had suddenly become ordered before his sight, everything had a point, every creature had a purpose—dogs, birds, horses, men—and the beautiful straight strength to accomplish it: the world, for this moment, had a plot.

Both the woodcock were skimming low to the ground, seeking cover again. Sten could hear the desperate beating of their wings. Hawk, though, fell silently, altering his fall as the cock he had chosen veered and fled. The other saw cover and dove into a brake as though flung there; the one Hawk had chosen missed the brake, and seemed to tumble through the air in avoidance, and it worked, too: Hawk misjudged, shot like a misaimed arrow below the woodcock.

Mika was racing after them. Sten, watching, had missed his stirrup and now clambered up into the saddle and kicked the horse savagely. Loren was whistling urgently to Chet and Martha to keep them out of it. The woodcock wouldn't dare try for cover again. It could only hope to rise higher and faster than the falcon, so the falcon couldn't stoop to it. The "field"—Sten, Mika, Loren on foot, and the dogs—chased after them.

Hawk rose in great circles around the climbing woodcock. Far faster and stronger, he outflew it easily, but must gain sufficient altitude for a second stoop. They were only marks in the sky, but their geometry was clear to Sten, who shaded his eyes with the big glove he wore, to see.

"He's beaten, look!" Loren cried. "Look!"

The woodcock was losing altitude, dropping, exhausted, raking off. Beaten in the air, it was trying for cover again, falling fatally beneath the hawk, who gathered above it. There was a line of trees at the pasture edge and the woodcock plummeted toward it; but it was doomed. Sten wondered, in a moment of cold clarity, what the woodcock felt. Terror only? What?

It was close to the line of woods when the falcon exploded above it, transforming himself, with a wing noise they could hear, from bullet into ax. His foot struck the woodcock with the certainty of a million generations, killing it instantly. He bore it to the ground, leaving a cloud of fine feathers floating in the path they had taken.

Sten came close carefully, his heart hard and elated, his throat raw from panting in the cold air. Hawk tore at the woodcock, a bleeding bolus of brown plumage, needle beak open. Sten stood over them and his mouth was suddenly full of water. He fumbled in his pocket for the lure. "Should I lure him off?"

"Yes," Loren said.

Hawk turned from breaking the cock's pinion to look up at Sten. He mantled, not wanting to rise to the fist, but greeting Sten; rejoicing, Sten tried not to think, in his master. Then he cocked his liquid eye at the woodcock, and with foot and beak returned to it. His bells made sounds as he worked. Unwillingly, not wanting to spoil Hawk's enjoyment, but knowing he must, Sten took out the lure. He looked to Mika where she held the horses, and to Loren, who watched the dogs. "Hawk," he said, all he could think to say. "Hawk."

On the ride home, he let Loren carry the falcon, because his arm had begun to tremble with the weight, but he walked nearby, leading his horse, letting Mika chase on ahead. When they came near the farmhouse, they saw Mika looking out to the weedy road that went past the house and farther on joined the gravel drive up to the mansion. A slim black three-wheeler had come off the road and was approaching. It slowed as it came near them, seemed to consider stopping, but then didn't. It picked up speed silently and turned onto the elm-shaded drive toward the mansion.

"Was that that counselor?" Mika asked.

"I guess," Sten said.

"What did he want here? Anyway, he's not allowed."

"Why not? Maybe he is. Isn't it only other people who can't come in? If he's not exactly people . . ."

"He's not allowed." For some reason, not cold, though her legs were bare beneath leather shorts, Mika shivered.

The counselor wore an inverness cape because ordinary coats, even if they could be made to fit him, only emphasized his strangeness. His chauffeur opened the door of the three-wheeler's tiny passenger compartment and helped him out; he spoke quietly to the chauffeur for a moment and on tiny feet started up the broad stairs of the house, helping himself with a stick. The guards at the door neither stopped him nor saluted him, though they did stare. They had been instructed that it wasn't protocol to salute him; he wasn't, officially, a member of the Autonomy's government. They didn't stop him because he was unmistakable, there were no two of him in this world, and that also was why they stared.

Inside the mansion it was dim, which suited his eyes. He indicated to the servant who met him that he would retain cape and stick, and he was led down several halls to the center of the house.

Halls fascinated him. He enjoyed their odors of passage, their furniture no one ever used, their pictures not meant to be looked at—in this case, fox hunting in long-past centuries in all its aspects, at least from the hunter's point of view. He didn't mind when he was asked, with reserved apology, to wait for a moment in another hall. He sat on a hard chair and contemplated a black, sealed jar that stood on a—what? sideboard? commode?—and wondered what if anything it was pretending to be for.

The Director's appointments secretary, a woman of a certain lean nervosity common in powerful subordinates, greeted him without discernible emotion and led him through old, glossy double doors that had new metal eyes in them; past her own high-piled desk; across another metal thing set in the threshold of an arch; and into the Director's presence.

Hello, Isengrim, Reynard thought. He didn't say it. He made some conventional compliment, his voice thin and rasping like fine sandpaper drawn across steel.

"Thank you," the Director said, standing. "I thought it would be better to meet here. I hope I haven't inconvenienced you."

Jarrell Gregorius's voice was still faintly accented; he had learned English only as a schoolboy, when his father—whose portrait stood with the children's on an otherwise impersonally naked desk—came here with the international commission that had tried to arbitrate the partition. The commission had of course failed, though the idea of Autonomies remained, unlike as they were to the commission's complex suggestions. When the Malagasian member was kidnapped and executed, and it became obvious that the Autonomies were becoming, inevitably, disputing nations, the commission had disbanded, and Lauri Gregorius had gone home to ski, leaving them to their madness. Jarrell—Järl as he had been christened—stayed. The portrait on his desk was twenty years old.

"Will you take something? Lunch? A drink?"

"Early for both in my case."

"I'm sorry if we've called you too early."

Reynard sat, though the Director had not. It was among his privileges to be unbound by politenesses and protocol; people always assumed he couldn't understand them, didn't grasp the subtleties of human intercourse. They were wrong. "It's difficult to believe that any nocturnalism would have survived in me. But there it is. You can't have government solely at night."

"Coffee then."

"If convenient." He rested his red-haired tiny hands on the head of the stick between his knees. "I passed your children on my way up from the gate."

"Yes?"

"Someone, an adult, with them, with a bird on his wrist."

"A Mr. Casaubon. Their tutor."

"Beautiful children. The famous son resembles you as much as they say. Wasn't there a film . . ."

"A tape. I'm glad they're here now; the boy, I think, was beginning to be affected by the publicity. Here he can live a normal life."

"Ah."

"The girl has a different mother. Puerto Rican. She's only come to live here in the last—what?—eighteen months?" He had been pacing steadily in front of the tall windows seamed with metal that looked out toward raw concrete bunkers where men in Blue lounged. Gregorius would have looked well in Blue; its pure azure would have just set off his flawless, windburned skin and tawny hair. Instead, he wore black, noncommittal, well-tailored, somewhat abashing. "How," he said, "are we to behave today? Can we begin that way? The USE people will be here shortly."

"Will they bring the safe-conduct?"

"They say they will."

"And under what circumstances will they hand it over?"

"On receipt of a signed affidavit of mine endorsing the general aims of the Reunification Conference."

"As interpreted by USE."

"Of course."

"And you'll sign it?"

"I have no choice. USE's bargain with the Federal is that USE will accept the terms of reunification the conference arrives at, if USE can issue these safe-conducts."

"And since all the Autonomies must have representatives at the conference . . ."

"Exactly. They will arrive having, publicly at least, endorsed a USE view of reunification."

Reynard rested his long rufous chin on his hands, which held the stick between his knees. "You could refuse. Attempt to go down there without a safe-conduct . . ."

Gregorius stopped pacing. "Do you say that to test me, or what?" He picked up a small round steel box that lay on the desk and tapped its lid. "Without the safe-conduct I'd be detained at every border. With or without an armed guard. I certainly don't intend to battle my way down there." He opened the box, took a pinch of the glittering blue crystal it contained, and inhaled it. His eyes rested on his father's portrait. "I'm a man of peace."

"Well."

"I know," Gregorius said, "you're no friend of the Union for Social Engineering." He ran a hand through his proud hair. "You've kept me away from them. You were right. Those in the Directorate under their influence would have castrated me, with USE's help."

"But things have changed." Reynard could say such things without irony, without implication. It was a skill of his.

"*This* time," the Director said, "*this* time, reunification could work. Because of—well, my strength here, which you have helped me gain— I'm the logical choice, if a plan is arrived at, to direct. To direct it all." He sat; his look was inward. "I could heal."

Beyond the guardhouse the two children could be seen walking their horses; Gregorius looked out that way, but saw nothing, because, Reynard was astonished to see, his eyes glittered with tears.

Sten and Mika had begged one last ride before afternoon lessons began, and Loren had allowed it; he always did, the "one last" of anything, so long as it was truly the one last and not a ruse. That was their bargain, and the children mostly kept it.

"How can he be what you say?" Mika said.

"Well, he is. Loren said so."

"How." It was a command, a refusal, not a question.

"They made him. Scientists. They took cells from a fox. They took cells from a person . . ."

"What person?"

"What does it matter? Some person."

"It matters because that person would be his mother. Or his father."

"Anyway. They took these cells, and somehow they made a combination . . ."

"*Somehow.*"

"They *can!* Why do you want it not to be so?"

"I don't like him."

"Jesus. Some reason not to believe he's what he is. Anyway, they took the combination, is all, and they grew it up. And he came out."

"How could they grow it up? Loren says the deer and horses can't have children. Or dogs and foxes. How could a man and a fox?"

"It's not the same. It's not eggs and sperms. It's different—a mixture."

"Not eggs and sperms?" There was a sly, small laughter in her eyes.

"No." He had to keep this on a grown-up level. "A mixture—like the leos. You believe in them, don't you?"

"Leos. There are lots of them. They've got parents. And eggs and sperms."

"*Now* they do. But that's how they were first made: lions and men. The counselor is the same, except he's new. How do you think they first got leos?"

"Eggs and sperms," she said, abandoning reason, "eggsandsperms. Hey, Sperms. Let's play Mongol. Look!" She pointed with her gloved hand. Down the hill, across another collapsing stone wall—the vast property was seamed with them—they could just see Loren, who had come out of the stone farmhouse and was sweeping the yard with a great broom. He wore his long coat of Blue, which he called his teacher shirt. "Look. A poor peasant."

"Just gathered in his crop." He turned his horse. This was their favorite game. It was a dangerous game; that was the only kind Sten liked.

"Poor bastard," Mika said. "Poor eggsandsperms. He'll be sorry."

"Burn the women and children. Rape the huts and outhouses." He felt a lump in his throat, of laughter or ferocity he didn't know. He banged his hard heels against the pony's flanks. Mika was already ahead of him; she clutched her horse's bay ribs with thighs muscled and brown ("*trigueña*," she called the color: "Nutlike," Loren translated; "Like a nut is right," Sten said). She was streaking down on the wall; Sten would beat her to it. He gave his Mongol yell and bent low over his careening horse. The Mongol yell was a yell only, no words, sustained until his breath gave out; when it did, Mika took up the yell, a higher, clearer note with no male pubescent descant, and when she had to stop he had begun again, so that the sound was continuous, to keep Mongol spirits fierce and astound the cottagers. They ran as close together as they dared, to make an army, almost touching, the horses' feet a sound as continuous as their yell.

They took the wall together, Mika sitting neatly and confident, Sten losing his hold for a frightening moment, the yell knocked from him by impact. The farmer Loren looked up. He had been carrying wood back into the farmhouse to get a fire started for lessons, but he dropped it when he saw them and dashed across the yard, coat flying, for the broom. He had it in his hands when they rode down on him.

This was the scariest part, to ride hard right into the yard, without pulling up, as fast as they dared, as fast as the horses dared, coming as near as they dared to being thrown by the horses' excitement and as near as they dared to murdering the tutor they loved.

"Oh, no you don't," Loren shouted, "no you don't, not this year. . . ." He flailed with the broom at them, startling the horses, who wheeled around him, throwing up clots of farmyard, snorting.

"Give up, give up!" Mika cried, hoarse from yelling, striking at him with her little crop.

"Never, never, damn barbarians . . ." He was afraid, and afraid for the children, but not about to give in. He had to play as hard as they did. He gave Sten a swat on the shoulder with the broom, Sten's horse reared and wheeled, Mika laughed, and Sten went end-over onto the ground with a noise that brought a lump to Loren's throat.

"Peasants one, Mongols nothing," Loren said, rushing to Sten and holding him from getting up. "Wait a minute, let's see if any Mongol bones got broken."

"I'm all right." His voice was quavering. "Leamee alone."

"Shut up," Loren said. "Bend your legs up, slowly. All right, stand up. Bend over." He had to speak harshly, or Sten would cry, and hold it against him. "Oh, you're all right."

"That," Sten said with breathless dignity, "is what I said."

"Yes, all right." He turned to Mika. "Now the horses are good and lathered, are you happy?" She grinned down at him. "Go settle them down. And then let's go learn something." He pushed Sten toward the ramshackle stable. "Maybe next year, Genghis Khan."

"Loren," Mika said, "is that counselor what Sten says he is?"

"Tell her," Sten said, wanting this victory at least. "Once and for all."

"According to the journals of genetics, yes. If you mean is he half a fox, *vulpes fulva*, and half a man, *homo* sort of *sapiens*, whatever 'half' could mean in this context," he took a long breath, "yes."

"It's eerie." She slid from the saddle. "Why is he a counselor? Why does Daddy listen to him?"

"Because he's smart," Sten said.

Loren looked up to where the blank, bulletproof windows of the study could just be seen in the L of the house. "Yes, I suppose," he said, "or, as they used to say years ago, dumb like a fox."

———

Reynard pushed his coffee cup away with a delicate, long-wristed hand. "Supposing," he said carefully, "that the conference is a success. That reunification' is somehow arrived at, or its beginnings anyway. I think you're right that you would be the choice to direct it. But if you went down under the auspices of the Union for Social Engineering, it would be their plan that you would direct, wouldn't it? I mean 'make the world work' and the rest of their ideas."

"I don't expect you to agree."

"What do you expect?"

"I don't want to be bullied by them. Of course I have to sign this statement. But I want to preserve some independence."

Reynard pretended to consider this. "Do this," he said at last. "Tell them today that you are preparing a statement of your own, a statement of goals for the conference. You want it included with theirs."

"They will refuse."

"Assure them it won't contradict theirs. That you will sign theirs if they will accept yours. If they refuse still, throw a rage. Announce their intransigence. Threaten to break off negotiations."

"None of that will do any good. They'll want capitulation."

"Of course. And in the end you'll capitulate."

"What have I gained? They'll say I'm hesitating, malingering."

"If they say that, admit it. It's true."

"But . . ."

"Listen. They know you are the only possible representative at the conference from this Autonomy. Let them know you require this measure of independence—a separate statement. If they won't go that far, they will at least allow you to appear to negotiate for one."

"It seems like very little."

"You intend to sign. They know that."

Gregorius considered this, and his hand, which shook. "And where is this statement? They won't wait long."

"I'll prepare it. Tomorrow you'll have it."

"I'd like to discuss it."

"No time. Believe me, it will be mild enough." He rose. The appointments secretary, whose name was Nashe, approached. "Did you know, by the way," Reynard said, "that USE has recently developed a military arm?"

"Hearsay."

"Of course they are pacifist."

"I've heard the rumors."

"The USE people are here, Director," Nashe said.

"Five minutes," Gregorius said without looking at her. "They've denied everything. Assassinations, terror bombings—they've completely condemned all that, whenever they've been linked with it."

"Yes. But the rumors persist." He took up his stick. "As effective, it seems to me, as if they were true. Now, is there another exit here? I'd rather not pass the time with USE."

Gregorius laughed. "You amaze me. You hate them, but you show me how to surrender to them."

"Hate," Reynard said, smiling his long, yellow-toothed smile, "isn't the right word, exactly."

When his counselor had sticked away without farewell, Gregorius sat again in the deep chair behind the blank field of his desk. He should compose himself for the USE people. They would speak in that impenetrable jargon, dense as the priestly Latinate of ancient Jesuits, though half of it was invented yesterday; would speak of social erg-quotients and a holocompetent act-field and the rest of it, though what they wanted was clear enough. Power. He felt, involuntarily, an apprehensive reflex: his scrotum tightened.

That was why Reynard was invaluable. As invaluable as he was strange. He knew those ancient alterations of the spine and cortex, knew them when he saw them, though "saw" wasn't what he did. Unconfused by any intervening speech, he knew when a man was beaten, or unbeatable; he knew at what point fear would transmute within a man, alchemically, to anger. He had never been wrong. His advice must be taken. It had made Gregorius, and unmade his enemies.

Concerning USE, though, he couldn't be sure. How could a creature not quite a man tell Gregorius anything just, anything disinterested, about a force that wanted to make the world wholly man's? Perhaps at this point the fox ran out of usefulness to him.

And yet he had no choice. He no longer wholly trusted the fox, and yet there was no way now he could not follow his advice; he knew of nothing else to do. He felt a sudden rush of chemical hopelessness. The damn crystal. He looked at the silver cylinder on his desk, moved to pick it up, but did not.

He would be firm with them. It couldn't cost him anything to be intransigent for a day. It would be on record then that he was no thing of theirs to be slotted into their plans, or however they put it. He glanced at his watch. There would be no time today for his afternoon ride with Sten. He wondered if the boy would be disappointed. For sure he wouldn't show it.

"Nashe," he said in his beautifully modulated voice, "ask them to come in."

There was no way for Reynard to conceive of himself except as men had conceived of foxes. He had, otherwise, no history: he was the man-fox, and the only other man-fox who had ever existed, existed in the tales of Aesop and the fables of La Fontaine, in the *contes* of medieval Reynard and Bruin the bear and Isengrim the wolf, in the legends of foxhunters. It surprised him how well that character fitted his nature; or perhaps, then, he had invented his nature out of those tales.

The guards at the gate neither stopped his black car nor saluted it.

The foxhunters (like those in the aquarelles that lined Gregorius's walls) had discovered long ago a paradox: the fox, in nature, has no enemies, is no one's prey; why, then, is he so very good at escape, evasion, flight? They used to say a fleeing fox would actually leap aboard a sheep and goad it to run, thus breaking the distinctive trail of its scent and losing the hounds. The foxhunters concluded that in fact the fox enjoyed these chases as much as they themselves did, and used not natural terror in its flight but cunning practiced for its own sake.

And so they ran the fox to ground, and the dogs tore it to pieces, and the hunter cut off its face—its "mask," they used to say, as though the fox were not what it pretended to be—and mounted it on his hallway wall.

"What did he say?" the chauffeur asked when they were outside the grounds. "Will he give in to USE?"

"He will. Nothing I could say would move him."

"Then he'll have to die."

"Yes."

It had taken Reynard years to gather all the Directorate's power into Gregorius's hands, to eliminate, one by one, every other power center within the fluctuating, ill-defined government. When he was gone, the only person left in the Directorate capable of running the Autonomy would be the lean woman Nashe, who guarded his door.

Which is why, after years of self-effacing service, she had agreed to Reynard's plan.

She wouldn't, of course, last long. She was a servant only, however capable. She would fall, and there was no one else; factions only, like the crazy anarchist gang his chauffeur belonged to. There would be chaos.

Chaos. He couldn't, yet, deliver this realm in fealty to his king. He could bring to him, as fox Reynard did in the old tale, the skin of Isengrim the wolf. And make chaos. That was the best he could manage, and for the moment it would have to do.

Perhaps the old foxhunters hadn't been so wrong. A creature poised on some untenable line between predator and prey: that wouldn't be a bad school for cunning. For learning any art of preservation. For having no honor, none: not the innocence of prey, nor the predator's nobility. It was sufficient. If men wanted to create such a beast, he would be it; and he thanked them for at least having given him the means for survival.

"When do we get him?" the chauffeur asked.

"Tomorrow. When he rides out with the boy."

"We'll get the boy too."

"No. Leave the boy to me."

"We can't do that. He's too dangerous."

"I've given you your tyrant. Leave the boy to me, or we have no agreement." The chauffeur gave a suppressed cry of rage and struck the dashboard, but he said no more. Reynard found fanatics startling. Startling but simple: an equation, he might have said, had he understood anything but the simplest arithmetic, which he did not.

The tape about Sten that Reynard had seen had been immensely popular, had been shown continuously everywhere until its images had grown dim and streaky. It was as well known and worn as an old prayer, an old obeisance. Sten, a naked boy of eight or nine, a perfect Pan-god with flowers in his hair, leading folk to a maypole on donkeyback, laughing and happy in their adulation. Sten in stern black beside his father at some rally, his father's hand on his shoulder. Sten at the archery butts, careful, intent, somewhat overbowed, glancing now and again suspiciously into the recorder's eye as though its presence distracted him. Sten in Blue, playing with other boys; there seemed to be an aura around him, a kind of field, so that no matter how they all scrambled and chased together, the others always looked like his henchmen. The commentary was a praise-poem only. No wonder his father had tried to withdraw him from all this. "Sten Gregorius," it concluded, after describing his European ancestry, "son of a hundred kings."

Kings, Reynard thought. Kings are what they want. The desperate rationality of Directorates and Autonomies had satisfied no one; they wanted kings, to worship and to murder.

The day was colder. Afternoon seemed to be hurrying away earlier than it had yesterday. Through the deep windows of the farmhouse Reynard could see the moon, already risen, though the sun was still bright. A hunter's moon, he thought, and searched within himself for some dark response he was not sure would be there, or be findable if it were.

He wore no timepiece; he had never been able to correlate its geometry with any sense of time he felt. It didn't matter. He knew it was time, and though he doubted he would hear anything—should not, if his chauffeur and his comrades did their job right—his ears twitched and pointed with a will of their own.

He had never known a schoolroom, and its peculiar constellation of odors—chalk and children, old books and tape-players, pungency of an apple core browning somewhere—was new to him. He carefully pried into papers and fingered things. One of three butterfly nets remained in a rack. The other two, he knew, Mika and Loren had taken to a far pasture. He was glad of that. He felt capable of dealing with all three at once, but if he need not, so much the better.

He sat down on a hard chair with his back to a corner and rested his hands on his stick. He looked to the door just as it was flung open.

Sten, his chest heaving and his eyes wide, stood in the doorway with a drawn bow, its arrow pointed at Reynard.

"I'm unarmed," Reynard said in his small sandpaper voice.

"Someone's killed him," Sten said. His voice had a wild edge of shock. "I think he's dead."

"Your father."

"It was you."

"No. I've been to the house. I delivered a paper there. And came here to visit you." Sten's stare was fierce and frightened, and his arm that held the arrow had begun to tremble. "Tell me. Put down the bow. What was it that happened?"

Sten with a cry turned the bow from Reynard and released the arrow at full draw. It broke against a map of the old States, held with yellowing tape against the stone wall. He dropped the bow and fell, as much as sat, on the floor, his back against the wall. "We were riding. I wanted to go down to the beaver dam. He said he didn't have time, we'd just go the usual ride. We went through the little woods, along the wall." His face was blank now. "Why wouldn't he ride down to the dam?"

"He had no time." That noncommittal voice.

"There wasn't any sound. I didn't hear any. He just suddenly sat—straight up, and—" His face was suddenly distorted as a mental picture came clear. "Oh Jesus."

"You're quite sure he's dead." Sten said nothing. He was sure. "Tell me, then: Why did you come here? Why not to the house? Call the guard, call Nashe . . ."

"I was afraid." He drew up his knees and hugged them. "I thought they'd shoot me too."

"Well. They might have." A small elation began to grow in Reynard. He had taken a great chance, on slim knowledge, and it would work out. Knowing only Gregorius, and that tape—studying it, watching the boy Sten shrink from his father's hand on the podium, watching his self-possession, the self-possession of someone utterly alone—Reynard had learned that there was no love between Gregorius and his young heir. None. And when his father lay bleeding at his feet, dying, the boy had run, afraid for his own life: run not home for help but here. Here was home. "They still could." He watched fear, anger, withdrawal alternate within Sten. Alone, so terribly alone. Reynard knew. "Sten. What do you want now? Vengeance? I know who killed your father. Do you want to take up his work? You could, easily. I could help. You are much loved, Sten."

"Leave me alone."

"Is that what you want?"

For a long time Sten said nothing. He stared at Reynard, unable not to, and tried to pierce those lashless brown eyes. Then: "You killed my father."

"Your father was killed by agents of the Union for Social Engineering. I know, because one of them was my chauffeur."

"Your chauffeur."

"He'll deny it. Say he had other reasons. But the evidence linking him to USE is there to be found, in his apartment in my house, which will doubtless be ransacked."

They were like Hawk's eyes, Sten thought at first, but they weren't. Behind Hawk's eyes were only clear intelligence and pitiless certainty. These eyes were watchful, wanting, certain only of uncertainty, and with a fleck of deep fear animating them. A mammal's eyes. A small mammal's eyes. "All right," he said at last. "All right." A kind of calm had come over him, though his hands had begun to shake. "You killed my father. Yes. I bet that could be proved. But you didn't kill me, and you could have." He prayed to Hawk: help me now, help me to take what I want. "I don't want anything from you, any of that vengeance or his work or any of that. I don't want your help. I want to be left alone. Let me stay here. They won't want to kill me if I don't do anything."

"No. I don't suppose so." He hadn't moved; he hadn't moved a red hair since Sten had opened the door.

"I won't. I swear it." A tremor had started in his voice, and he swallowed, or tried to, to stop it. "Give me the house and the land. Let me stay here. Let Mika and Loren stay too. The animals. It's all I want."

"If it is," Reynard said, "then you have it. No one but you could ever hold this land. Your mark is on it." No hint, no betrayal that this was what he wanted from Sten, or even if such a plan had ever occurred to him. "And now I must flee, mustn't I? And quickly, since I no longer have a chauffeur; I'm a slow driver." He stood slowly, a tiny creature standing. "If you are careful, Sten, you need be neither predator nor prey. You have power, more maybe than you know. Use it to be that only, and you'll be safe." He looked around the stone place. It had grown dim and odorous with evening chill. "Safe as houses."

Without farewell, he left by the front door. Sten, still huddled by the back door, listened for the uncertain whine of the three-wheeler, and when it was gone, he stood. He had begun to shiver in earnest now. He would have to go up to the house, alert the guard, tell them what had happened. But not that he had come here: that he had stayed with his father, trying to stanch wounds . . .

Through the open door he could see, far off, Mika and Loren coming back across the field, Mika running, teasing Loren, who came carefully after with the collecting bottles. Their nets were like small strange banners. His only army. How much could he tell them? All, none? Would it have to be always his alone? Tears started in his eyes. No! He had to start for the house now, before they saw him, saw his horse.

He pulled up on the lawn before the white-stained perch where Hawk stood, preening himself, calm. In the growing twilight he looked huge; his great barred breast smooth and soft as a place to rest a baby's head.

How do you bear each day? Sten thought. How do you bear not being free? Teach me. How do you be leashed? Teach me.

"Sten will stay quietly on that estate," Reynard said to Painter. "For a time, anyway. The Union for Social Engineering is being blamed for Gregorius's death, though naturally they will deny it strenuously. And my poor chauffeur, who probably hated USE even more than he hated Gregorius, will never get out of prison. The documents that made him a USE agent were put in his apartment by me. I gave USE good reason for murdering Gregorius: the paper I wrote for him, which of course he never saw, was a violent denunciation of USE, and contained some— rather striking—premonitions that taking this stand might cost him much. The paper will stand as the moving last words of a martyr to independence.

"The Reunification Conference won't be held. Not this year, not next. No one will trust USE any longer: an organization capable of butchering a head of state for disagreeing with it is no arbiter of peace and unity. I don't, however, put it past the Federal to try some other means of getting power in the Autonomy. There will be pretexts . . ."

Caddie listened to him with fascination, though she didn't understand much of what he said. It seemed as though he had only a certain store of voice, and that it ran out as he spoke, dwindling to a thin whisper; still he went on, talking about betrayals and murders he had committed without emotion, saying terrible ironies without a shade of irony in his voice. Painter listened intently, without comment. When Reynard had finished, he said only: "What good has it done me?"

"Patience, dear beast," Reynard whispered, leaning his delicate head near Painter's massive one. "Your time is not yet."

Painter stood, looking down at the fox. Caddie wondered how many men had ever seen them together so. Herself only? The oddness of it was so great as to be unfeelable. "Where will you go now?" Painter asked.

"I'll hide," Reynard said. "Somewhere. There's a limit to how far they can pursue me here, in this dependency. And you?"

"I'll go south," Painter said. "My family. It's getting late."

"Ah." Reynard looked from Painter to Caddie and back again. "Just south of the border is the Genesis Preserve," he said. "Good hunting. No one can harm you there. Take that route." He looked at Caddie. "You?" he said.

"South," she said. "South too."

4

Go to the Ant, thou sluggard; consider her ways, and be wise

If they had lived on one of the lowest levels, the sun would already be setting for them; and down on the ground, only a few empurpled clouds would have been seen in a sky of lapidary clarity—if there had been anyone down on the ground to see them, and there wasn't, not for nearly a thousand square miles, which was the extent of Genesis Preserve. But up where they lived, above the hundredth level, they could still see the sun flaming crimson, and it wouldn't disappear from the highest terraces for minutes more. There was no other time when Meric Landseer felt so intensely the immense size of Candy's Mountain as when he looked down at evening into the twilight that extended over the plains, and watched it crawl level by level up toward him.

Sunlight pierced the glass he held, starting a flame in its center.

" 'You are the salt of the earth,' " Bree read, " 'and if the salt has lost its savor, wherewith shall it be salted?' What does that mean?"

"I don't know."

Bree sat upright on the chaise, her tawny legs wide apart, knees glossy with sun, with their extra share of sun. She scratched herself lazily, abstractly, turning the fine gold-edged pages. She was naked except for brown sunglasses and the thick gray socks she wore because, she said, her feet got cold first. The sun, striking lengthwise through the utter clarity of this air, drew her with great exactitude: each brown hair on her brown limbs was etched, every mole had highlight and shadow; even the serrations of her full, cloven lips were distinguished from the false wetness of the gloss that covered them.

Meric loved Bree, and she loved him, though perhaps she loved Jesus more. The sun made no distinctions, and in fact rendered the raw concrete of the terrace's edge as lovingly as it did the amber of Meric's drink or Bree's limbs. Jesus was unlightable; he made a darkness, Meric felt, fluorescing from the little book.

Shadow had climbed to their level. Bree put down the book. "Can you see them?" she asked.

"No." He looked out over the rolling grassland, fallow this year, that went on until evening swallowed it. Perhaps, if he had the eyes of the eagles who lived amid the clifflike roofs above, he could; he had watched the eagles, at his own terrace's height, floating on the complex currents, waiting for the movements of hares that dashed like fish through the sea of grass below. "No, I can't see them." Impossible for someone who lived here to fear heights, and Meric didn't; yet sometimes when he looked down a thousand feet he felt—what? wonder? astonishment?—some sudden emotion that waved him like a banner.

"It's cold," Bree said, almost petulant. A brief Indian summer had flamed and was going out again. Bree had taken it as a right, not a gift; she always felt wronged by the sun's departure. She stood, pulling a long robe of Blue around herself. Meric could look far down along the terraces that edged their level and see others, men and women, rising and drawing robes of Blue around themselves.

The sudden evening drop in temperature raised winds. The Mountain was designed not to intrude in any way upon the earth, to do no damage, none, to her body and the membrane of life stretched across it. Utterly self-contained, it replaced what it used of Earth's body exactly, borrowing and returning water and food by a nice reckoning. And yet the air was troubled by its mass; stuck up into the sea of air like an immense stirring-rod, it could raise and distort winds wildly. Once a year or so a vast pane of amber-tinted glass, faultily made, was sucked by wind from its place and went sailing out over the Preserve for hundreds of yards before it landed. When that happened, they went out and found it, every splinter, and brought it back, and melted it, and used it again.

But they couldn't cease troubling the air. A building a half mile broad and nearly as high, set amid rolling hills of grass, will do that; and it was not only Meric who felt bad about that, and as it were begged Wind's pardon.

"They're there, though, aren't they," Bree said. She closed the terrace doors behind her, but a wind had gotten in and went racing around the level, lifting rugs and drapes of Blue and making the wall panels vibrate.

"They're there somewhere."

She turned up the tapers at the low table and nudged the pillows close to it with her gray-socked feet. Beyond their doorless space, far off perhaps—the drafts and airs made it hard to judge—men and women began an antique hymn as they returned from work; Meric and Bree could hear the tune but not the words.

"Your show begins again tonight, doesn't it," Bree said as Meric laid out their plain supper. "Does it mention them?"

"No. We didn't have tape or film. It wouldn't have done much good."

"People don't know what to think, though." She tucked the robe between her brown thighs and knelt Japanese-fashion before the table. "Should they be here?"

"They're not men."

"You know what I mean." The Preserve—the land that Candy's Mountain owned—was strictly forbidden to hunters, hikers, trespassers —men.

"I don't know. There was talk sometime of putting them on a reservation. They have to live."

"You feel sorry for them?" Bree asked.

"Yes. They're not men. They don't have freedom of choice, I don't think. They can't decide, like we can, not to . . . not to be . . ."

"Carnivores."

"Yes. Not to be what they are."

"We thank Thee, O Lord," Bree said, her long-lashed eyes lowered, "for these gifts Thou hast given us, which we are about to receive, in Jesus's name, amen."

She took bread, broke it, and gave it to him.

When Meric had first come to live here, twenty years before, he was six years old and the great structure had not been inhabited for much longer than that. Its growth had begun to slow; it would never reach its two hundredth level. It would never, then, match exactly the exquisite model of it that Isidore Candy had made long before it had been begun. Among Meric's most deeply imprinted memories was his first sight of that model. In fact he remembered so little of his life before the Mountain—the fleeing, displaced life of refugees that burns an everlasting faint mark of insecurity on the soul but leaves few stationary objects in the mind—that it seemed as though his life began in front of that model.

"Look!" his mother said when their tiny, exhausted caravan was still miles away. "It's Candy's Mountain!" The enormous mass of it, blue with distance, rose like many great shoulders lifting themselves out of the earth; the skeleton shoulders of all the dead Titans coming forth together. Once it hove over the horizon, he saw it always no matter how the road they traveled twisted away from it; yet it was so big that it was a long time before they seemed to come any closer to it. It grew, and he must look always more sharply upward to see it, until they stood on the wide stairs of its threshold. The sea of grass they had crossed broke against those stairs in a foam of weed and flower, drowning the first tread, for no road or terrace led up to it. He stood on the stairs as though on a cliffy shore. When he tried to look up, though, the cliffs above were too huge to see. Around him, his people were mounting the stairs toward a hundred entrances that stood wide and waiting across the broken front; someone took his hand and he went up, but it was the Mountain itself that drew him in.

Their steps echoed in the vastest indoors Meric had ever seen or even dreamed of. The echoes had echoes, and those echoes fainter echoes. The whole arriving caravan was scattered across the chalky, naked stone of the floor, sitting on their bags or moving about, seeking friends, but they made no impression on the space, didn't diminish it at all. Yet at the same time its height and breadth were full of noises, people, activity, comings and goings, because the central atrium was strung all around with galleries, terraces, and catwalks; its depths were peopled, densely. Now that he was inside, it didn't seem to be a cliff on the seashore but the interior of the sea itself: life and movement, schools of busyness at every level.

He almost didn't dare to take steps there. There were so many directions to go, none marked and all seemingly infinite, that no decision was possible. Then a focus was given him: a girl, almost his age, in a dress of Blue, whose dark skin was like silk in the watery depths of this sunshot sea. She moved among the strangers as one who lived there, one of those who had taken the strangers in, one of those whom the weary, sad, desperate people he had traveled with wanted to become; and at that moment Meric wanted even more than that: he wanted to be her.

He hadn't ever quite stopped wanting that.

"Come see," she said to him, or at least to him and to others standing around him, grownups too distracted to hear her. He went with her, though, straight across the floor and into depths, following her. Beyond the central atrium, walls divided the space, bisecting it, halving and quartering it again and again as though he proceeded down some narrowing throat; and yet the heights and breadths remained, because most of these bisecting walls were transparent, an openwork of slats and suspended walks and cable-flown platforms, wood, metal, glass.

The place she brought him to, he knew now, years later, was in the very center of the Mountain. On a table there, standing nearly as high as himself, was the model of the Mountain. It was less like the model of a place than the idea of Place: space endlessly geometered by symmetries of lines, levels, limits. The sense grew only slowly in him that this was a model of the place he had come to live, that these dense accretions of closely set lines and serrated spaces modeled places large enough to live out lives in: were huge. The atrium he had stood stupefied in would not, in this model, have contained his fist; he could not have put a finger between the floors of any of the levels where multitudes lived and worked. Its tininess was the hugest thing he had ever seen. This, he thought, is how big it is. Its lines of wall and floor were made of materials whose fineness only made the idea of it grow bigger in his mind: gold wire and pins and grommets small as needles' eyes, steps made from single thicknesses of paper. Those steps he had mounted.

The girl pointed to a photograph suspended behind the model. An old man in a battered hat and a creased white shirt, with many pens in his shirt pocket; eyes kindlier than Santa Claus's and a beard like his too, which came almost to his waist.

"He built it," she said, and he knew that she meant both the model and in some sense single-handedly the place it was in as well. "His name was Isidore Candy. My name is Bree."

Around them as they ate, Bree and Meric heard the endless, wordless voice of their level and, though too faint to be distinguished, of others too. The panels of paper that were all that made this space theirs, panels that in every size, height, and extent were all that made any space a space on this level, vibrated like fine drumheads to the voices, the gatherings of people, and the noises of work and machinery, a noise so constant and so multiform in its variations that they really didn't hear it at all; nor were they heard.

"How many are there?" Bree asked.

"Nobody's sure." He took more of the dense, crumbling bread. "Maybe ten or so."

"What is it they call it?" Bree said. "I mean a family of lions. Do they use the same word?"

"Pride," Meric said. He looked at Bree. There was in her brown, gold-flecked eyes an unease he couldn't read but knew; knew well, though never how to make it pass. Was it fear? She didn't look at him. "A pride of lions. They use the same word."

She stood, and he suggested to himself that he not follow her with his eyes around the house ("house" they called it, as they called work-spaces "offices" and meeting-spaces "halls"; they knew what they meant). Something had been growing in her all day, he could tell it by her continual small questions, whose answers she didn't quite listen to.

Somewhere, clay bells rang, calling to meeting or prayer.

"Sodality tonight?" he asked. Why wasn't his tenderness a stronger engine against her moods?

"No."

"Will you come and see the show?"

"I guess."

He wasn't able not to look at her, so he tried to do so in a way that seemed other than pleading, though to plead was what he wanted to do; plead what, plead how? She came to him as though he had spoken, and stroked his cheek with the back of her hand.

Meric was so fair, his hair so pale a gold, that his sharp-boned face never grew a beard; his hair ran out along his ears like a woman's, and if he never shaved, a light down grew above his lip, but that was all. Bree loved that; it seemed so clean: She loved things she thought were clean, though she couldn't express just what "clean" meant to her. His face was clean. She had depilated herself because she felt herself to be cleaner that way. The softest, cleanest feeling she knew was when he gently, with a little sound like gratitude, or relief, laid his smooth cheek there.

She didn't want that now, though. She had touched him because he seemed to require it. She felt faintly unclean: which was like but different from feeling apprehensive.

She returned to her testament again, not as though to read it, but as though she wished to question it idly too. He wondered if she listened to Jesus's answers with any more attention than she did his.

"Why is it you want to know about them?" he asked. "What is it they make you feel? I mean when you think about them."

"I wasn't."

She perhaps wasn't. She might have meant nothing by her questions. Sometimes she asked aimless questions about his shows, or about technical matters he dealt with, tape, cameras. Sometimes about the weather. Maybe it was he who kept thinking about them; couldn't get the thought away from him. Maybe she only reflected an unease that he alone felt.

" 'Beware, watch well,' " Bree read, " 'for thine enemy like a roaring lion walketh about, seeking whom he may devour.' "

The Birthday Show began this way:

Isidore Candy's hugely enlarged, kindly face, or his eyes, rather, filled the screens. The face moved away, so that his hat and great beard came into view. There was a rising note of music, a single note only, that seemed to proceed outward as the face retreated into full view. Through some art, the whole image was charged and expectant. A woman's voice, deep, solemn almost, said without hurry:

> "There was an old man with a beard
> Who said: 'It is just as I feared.
> Two owls and a wren
> Three sparrows and a hen
> Have all built their nests in my beard.' "

At that moment the single note of music opened fanwise into a breath-snatching harmony, and the image changed: The eagles who had

aeries in the craggy, unfinished tops of the Mountain opened their ponderous wings in the dawn and ascended, one crying out its fierce note,
their shaggy legs and great talons seeming to grasp air to climb.

It was a moment Meric loved, not only because he was almost certain
of its effect, how it would poise the audience, at the show's beginning, on
some edge between wit, surprise, awe, glory, warmth; but also because
he remembered the chill dawn when he had hung giddy in the half light
amid the beams, clutching his camera with numb fingers, waiting for the
great living hulks within the stinking white-stained nest to wake and rise;
and the joy in which his heart soared with them when they soared, in full
light, in full view. He wasn't so proud of any image he had ever made.

The Birthday Show was all Meric's work. In a sense it was his only
work: shown each year on Candy's birthday, it was changed each year,
sometimes subtly, sometimes in major ways, to reinforce the effects Meric
saw—felt, more nearly—come and go in the massed audiences that each
year witnessed it. He had a lot of opportunity to check these reactions:
even in the huge multiscreen amphitheater it took nearly a month of
showings for everyone who lived in the Mountain to see it each year, and
nearly everyone wanted to see it.

Bree thought of it as his only work, though she knew well enough
that most of his year was taken up with training tapes, and a regular news
digest, and propaganda for the outside. Those things were "shows." This
was "your show." He asked her every year if she thought it was better
now, and laughed, pleased, when she told him it was wonderful but she
didn't notice that it was any different. She was his perfect audience.

Meric had acquired, or perhaps had by instinct, a grasp of the power
a progress of images had on an audience, of the rhythms of an audience's
perceptions, of what reinforcement—music, voice, optical distortion—
would cause a series of random images to combine within an audience's
mind to make complex or stunningly simple metaphors. And he made it
all out of the commonest materials: though it was all his work, in another
sense very little of it was, because he composed it out of scraps of old
footage, discarded tapes, ancient documentaries, photographs, objects—a
vocabulary he had slowly and patiently, with all the squirrelly ingenuity
that had built Candy's Mountain itself, hoarded up and tinkered with
over the years. The very voice that spoke to the audience, not as though
from some pillar of invisibility but as though it were a sudden, powerful
motion of the viewer's own mind, was the voice of Emma Roth, the
woman he worked with in Genesis Section: a voice he had first heard

speaking wildlife-management statistics into a recorder, a voice that made numbers compelling. A wizard's voice. And she completely unaware of it.

"Use it up," Emma's voice said in every ear, as they watched old tapes of the Mountain being built out of the most heterogeneous materials, "use it up, wear it out, make it do, do without": said no differently from the way she had said it one day to Meric when he asked about getting fresh optical tape. Yet she said it as though it were a faith to live by: as they did live by it.

Bree surrendered altogether to the mosaic of word and image, as she could surrender, at times, in prayer: in fact the Birthday Show was most like prayer. Some of it frightened her, as when over flaming and degraded industrial landscapes a black manna seemed endlessly to fall, and dogs and pale children seemed to seek, amid blackened streets, exits that were not there, and the sky itself seemed to have turned to stone, stained and eternally filthy, and Emma said in a voice without reproach or hope:

"The streams of Edom will be turned into pitch, and her soil into brimstone; her land shall become burning pitch. Night and day it shall not be quenched; its smoke shall go up forever. From generation to generation it shall lie waste; none shall pass through it for ever and ever. They shall name it No Kingdom There; and its princes shall be nothing."

For ever and ever! No, it could not be borne; Bree covered her mouth with her hands, hands ready to cover her eyes if she couldn't bear the scenes of war that followed: blackened, despairing faces, refugees, detention centers, the hopeless round of despair for ever and ever. . . . Only by stages was it redeemed; amaryllis in flower, cocoon opening, a butterfly's panting wings taking shape. Genesis Preserve: a thousand square miles stolen from Edom. Day rose over it, passed from it. She saw its fastnesses. Rapt, she let her hands slowly come to rest again. Emma spoke the words of an ancient treaty the Federal had made with the Indians, giving them the forests and plains and rivers in perpetuity, fine rolling promises; governments had made the same promises to the people of Candy's Mountain, and so there was warning as well as security in Emma's words. Then far off, seen from the unpeopled fastnesses of the Preserve, blue and shadowy as a mountain, remote, as though watched by deer and foxes, their home. Emma said again: "None shall pass through it for ever and ever; they shall name it No Kingdom There, and its princes shall be nothing," and Bree didn't know whether the change of meaning, which she understood in ways she couldn't express, made her want to laugh or cry.

Withdraw: that was what Candy had preached (only not preached, he was incapable of preaching, but he made himself understood, even as Meric's show did). You have done enough damage to the earth and to yourselves. Your immense, battling ingenuity: turn it inward, make yourselves scarce, you can do that. Leave the earth alone: all its miracles happen when you're not looking. Build a mountain and you can all be troll-kings. The earth will blossom in thanks for it.

A half century and more had passed since Candy's death, but there was as yet only one of the thousand mountains, or badger setts, or coral reefs that Candy had imagined men withdrawing into for the earth's sake and for their own salvation. The building of that one had been the greatest labor since the cathedrals; was a cathedral; was its own god, though every year Jesus grew stronger there.

All the world's miracles: Meric had combed the patronizing nature-vaudevilles of the last century and culled from them images of undiluted wonder. There was never a time that Bree didn't weep when from the laboring womb of an antelope, standing with legs apart, trembling, there appeared the struggling, fragile foreleg of its child, then its defenseless head, eyes huge and wide with exhaustion and sentience, and the voice, as though carried on a steady wind of compassion and wisdom, whispered only: "Pity, like a naked newborn babe," and Bree renewed her vows, as they all silently did, that she would never, never consciously hurt any living thing the earth had made.

Riding upward on the straining elevators, Bree felt that the taint of uncleanness was gone, washed away, maybe, by the sweet tears she had shed. She felt a great, general affection for the crowds she rode with; their patience with the phlegmatic elevator, the small jokes they made at it— "very grave it is," someone said; "Well, gravity is its business," said another—the nearness and warmth of their bodies, the sense that she was enveloped by their spirits as by breath: all this felt supremely right. What was the word the Bible used? Justified. That was what she felt as she rode the great distance to her level: justified.

She and Meric made love later, in the way they had gradually come most to want each other. They lay near each other, almost not touching, and with the least possible contact they helped each other, with what seemed infinite slowness, to completion, every touch, even of a fingertip, made an event by being long withheld. They knew each other's bodies so well now, after many years, since they were children, that they could almost forget what they did, and make a kind of drunkenness or dream between them; other times, as this time, it was a peace: it suspended them together in some cool flame where each nearly forgot the other, feeling only the long, retarded, rearising, again retarded, and at last inevitable arrival, given to each in a vacuum as though by a god.

Sleep was only a gift of the same god's left hand after these nearly motionless exertions; Bree was asleep before she took her hand from Meric. But, much as he expected sleep, Meric lay awake, surprised to feel dissatisfaction. He lay beside Bree a long time. Then he rose; she made a motion, and he thought she might wake, but she only, as though under water, rolled slowly to her side and composed herself otherwise, in a contentment that for some reason lit a small flame of rage in him.

What's wrong with me?

He went out onto the terrace, his body enveloped suddenly in wind, cold and sage-odorous. The immensity of night above and below him, the nearness of the sickle moon, and the great distance of the earth were alike claustrophobic, and how could that be?

Far off, miles perhaps, he could just see for a moment a tiny, clouded orange spark. A fire lit on the plains. Where no fire was ever to be lit again. For some reason, his heart leapt at that thought.

In the mornings, Meric moved comfortably in seas of people going from nightwork or to daywork, coming from a thousand meetings and masses, many of them badged alike or wearing tokens of sodalities or work groups or carrying the tools of trades. Most wore Blue. Some, like himself, were solitary. Not seas of people, then, but people in a sea: a coral reef, dense with different populations, politely crossing one another's paths without crossing one another's purposes. He went down fifty levels; it took most of an hour.

"Two or three things we know," Emma Roth told him as she made tea for them on a tiny burner. "We know they're not citizens of anywhere, not legally. So maybe none of the noninfringement treaties we have with other governments applies to them."

"Not even the Federal?"

"It's all *men* that are created equal," Emma said. "Anyway, what can the Federal do? Send in some thugs to shoot them? That seems to be all they know how to do these days."

"What else do we know?"

"Where they are, or were yesterday." She was no geographer; the maps she had pinned to the wall were old paper ones, survey maps with many corrections. "Here." She made a small mark with delible pencil. Meric thought suddenly that after all no mark she could make would be small enough; it would blanket them vastly.

"We know they're all one family."

"Pride," Meric said.

Emma regarded him, a strange level look in her hooded gray eyes. "They're not lions, Meric. Not really. Don't forget that." She lit a cigarette, though the nearly extinguished stub of another lay near her in an ashtray. Smoking was perhaps Emma's only vice; she indulged it continuously and steadily, as though to insult her own virtue, as a leavening. Almost nobody Meric knew smoked; Emma was always being criticized for it, subtly or openly, by people who didn't know her. "Well," she'd say, her voice gravelly with years of it, "I've got so much punishment stored up in hell for me that one more sin won't matter. Besides"—it was a tenet of the cheerful religion she practiced—"what's all this fear of sin? If God made hell, it must be heaven in disguise."

Meric returned to the recorder he was trying to fix. It was at least thirty years old and incompatible with most of his other equipment, and it broke or rather gave out in senile exhaustion frequently. But he could make it do. "Are they, what do you call it, poaching?"

"Don't know."

"Somebody ought to find out." With an odd, inappropriate sense that he was tattling, he said: "I saw a fire last night."

"A lot of people did. I've had pneumos about it all day." With comic exactness, the tube at her side made its hiccup, and she extracted the worn, yellowed-plastic container. She read the message, squinting one eye against the smoke rising from her cigarette, and nodded.

"It's from the ranger station," she said. "They are poaching." She sighed, and wiped her hands on her coat of Blue as though the message had stained them. "Dead deer have been found."

Meric saw her distress, and thought: there are nearly a hundred thousand of us; there can't be more than a dozen of them. There are a thousand square miles out there. Yet he could see in Emma the same fear that he sensed in Bree, and in himself. Who were they that they could rouse the Mountain this way?

"Monsters," Emma said, as though answering.

"Listen," he said. "We should know more. I don't mean just you and me. Everybody. We should . . . I'll tell you what. I'll go out there, with the H5 and some discs, and get some information. Something we can all look at."

"It wouldn't do any good. They're poaching. What else do we need to know?"

"Emma," he said. "What's wrong with you? Wolves aren't poachers. Hawks aren't poachers. You're losing your perspective."

"Wolves and hawks," Emma said, "don't use rifles." She picked up the message. "Shot with old-style high-caliber ballistic weapon. Liver, heart removed, and most of the long muscle. Rest in a high state of decomposition."

Meric saw in his mind an image from the Birthday Show, a bit of some long-dead family-man's home movies, he assumed: hunters, laughing and proud, in antique dress, surrounded a deer, shot, presumed dead. The deer suddenly twitched, its eye rolling, blood gushing from its mouth. The men appeared startled at first; then one drew a long blade, and as the others stood near, brave beside this thing so nearly dead, he slashed the deer's throat. It seemed easy, like slashing a rubber bag. Blood rushed out, far more than seemed likely. Emma's voice said: "As ye do unto these, the least of my brethren, you do unto me." He'd always (however often, with repugnance, he passed this scene in his workprints) wondered what those men had felt: any remorse, any disgust even? He had read about the joy of the hunt and the capture; but that was over, here. Shame? Dread? That blood: that eye.

"Let me go," he said. "I'd be back in a week."

"You'd have to be careful. They're armed." She said the word as though it took courage to say, as though it were obscene.

"*Enemy* is a name for someone you don't know." It was a proverb of the Mountain's. "I'll be careful."

The rest of that day he prepared his equipment, making as certain as he could that it would function, working from a checklist of emergency spares and baling-wire (a term he used, without knowing what it had once meant, for little things he found useful for making repairs, making do). In the evening he went to visit friends, borrowing things to make up a pack. He took a scabbard knife.

He lay that night sleepless as well.

"It makes me nervous," Bree said to him. "How long will you be?"

"Not long. A week." He took her wrist, brown and smooth as a sapling. "I'll tell you what," he said. "If I'm not back in a week, send a pneumo to Grady. Tell him something's up, and to come on if he thinks it's right."

Grady was a ranger whom Bree had once had an affair with: brown as she was, but humorless, dense, as hard and reliable as she was evanescent. He was a member of the small, highly trained team in the Mountain allowed weapons—net-guns, tranquilizing guns, theoretically only for wildlife.

Wildlife.

"Grady would know," Bree said, and withdrew her wrist from his hand. She didn't like to be touched while she slept.

He'd often wondered what Bree and Grady had been for each other. Bree had been frank about other lovers she'd had. About Grady, when he asked, she only said, "It was different," and looked away. He wanted to ask more, but he sensed the door shut.

He wanted to *see*. He wanted to enter into darkness, any darkness, all darkness, and see in it with sudden cat's eyes: nothing withheld. He realized, at the moment Bree took her wrist from him, that this was his nature: it was a simple one, but it had never been satisfied. Not so far.

Genesis Preserve occupied a space in the northwest of the Northern Autonomy about where the heart would be in a body. The multilane freeways that cut it into irregular chambers were used now only by crows, who dropped snails onto them from heights to break the shells. Two hundred years ago it had been farms, hard-scrabble Yankee enterprises on a difficult frontier. Never profitable, the farmers had mostly given up by the beginning of the twentieth century, though the stone houses they had made by gleaning glacier-scattered fieldstone from their pastures remained here and there, roofless and barnless, home for owls and swallows. It had never ranked high in the last century's ephemeral vacation places: no real mountains to ski in the cruel winters, and an unlovely, barren upland in summer. Yet, by count, its swamps and variegated woods, its rocky fields and dense meadows harbored more varieties of life than did most equivalent cuts of earth. And it belonged to no one but them.

Meric was no outdoorsman. It was a skill few in the Mountain possessed, though many held it up as an ideal; it was thought to require a special kind of careful expertise, like surgery. He bore his time on the ground well, though; life in the Mountain was austere enough that short rations of dull food, cold nights, long walking didn't seem to be hardship. That was more or less how life was most of the time. And the solitudes, the sense that he was utterly alone in an unpeopled place that didn't want him there and would take no notice if, say, he fell down rocks and broke a leg, the hostility of night and its noises that kept his sleep fitful, all this seemed to be as it should. He had no rights in the Preserve: its princes, who protected it, were, when they entered it, nothing.

On the second day, toward evening, he came in sight of the pride.

He stayed well away, behind cover of a brush-overgrown wall, on a rise above where they had made camp. From his pack he chose a telephoto lens and, with an odd shiver as though the false nearness it gave him could make them somehow conscious of him as well, he began his spying.

They had chosen one of the roofless stone farmhouses as a base or a windbreak. Smoke from a fire rose up from within it. Around it were two or three carelessly pitched tents; a paintless and ancient four-wheel van; a kind of gypsy wagon of a sort he'd never seen before, and a hobbled mule near it, cropping. And there was an expertly made construction of poles and rope, a kind of gallows, from which hung, by its delicate hind legs, a deer. A doe. Focusing carefully, Meric could see the carcass turning very slowly in the breeze. There was no other movement. Meric felt the tense expectancy of a voyeur watching an empty room, waiting.

What was it that suddenly made him snap his head around with a stifled cry? Perhaps while his eyes were concentrating on the camp, other senses were gathering small data from his surroundings, data that added up without his being aware of it till an alarm went off within him.

Some fifty feet behind him a young male leo squatted in the grass, long gun across his knees, watching him steadily, without curiosity or alarm.

"What is it you want?" Emma Roth said coldly, hoping to imply that whatever it was they wanted, they had no chance of getting it.

The three Federal agents before her, to whom she hadn't offered seats, looked from one to another as though trying to decide who should do the talking. Only the thin, intent one in a tight black suit, who hadn't produced credentials, remained aloof.

"A leo," one of them said at last, producing a dossier or file of some kind and exhibiting it to Roth, not as though he meant her to examine it, but only as a kind of ritual object, a token of his official status. "We have reason to believe that there is an adult male leo within the Preserve, who at one time called himself Painter. He's a murderer and a kidnapper. It's all here." He tapped the file. "He abducted an indentured servant north of the border and fled south. In the process he murdered—with his bare hands"—here the agent exhibited his own meaty ones—"an officer of an official Federal search party on other business."

"He murdered him on other business?" God, she hated the way they talked: as though it weren't they but some dead glum bureaucratic deity who spoke through them, and they were oracles only and had nothing to do with it.

"The officer was on other business," the agent said.

"Oh."

"We understand there is a formality to go through about getting safe-conducts or warrants to go into the Preserve and make an arrest. . . ."

"You don't understand." She lit a cigarette. "There are no formalities. What there is is an absolute ban on entering the Preserve at all, on whatever pretext. This is a protocol signed by the Federal and the Autonomy governments. It works this way: you ask permission to move onto the Preserve or enter the Mountain on what you call official business; and we refuse permission. That's the way it works." Twenty years of bribery, public pressure, and passive resistance had gone into those protocols and agreements; Roth knew where she stood.

"Excuse me, Director." The man in black spoke. It was a tight little voice with an edge of repressed fury in it that was alarming. "We understand about permission. We'd like to put in a formal request. We'd like you to listen to our reasons. That's what he meant."

"Don't call me Director," Emma said.

"Isn't that your title, your job description?"

"My name is Roth. And who are you?"

"My name is Barron," he said quickly, as though offering in return for her name something equally useless. "Union for Social Engineering, Hybrid Species Project. I'm attached to these officers in an advisory capacity."

She should have known. The cropped hair, the narrow, careless suit, the air of being a useful cog in a machine that had not yet been built. "Well." The word fell on them with the full censorious weight of her great voice. "And what are these reasons."

"How much do you know," the USE man asked, "about the parasociety the leos have generated since they've been free-living?"

"Very little. I'm not sure I know what a parasociety is. They're nomads . . ."

With a dismissive gesture whose impatience he couldn't quite hide, Barron began to speak rapidly, his points tumbling over one another, stitched together with allusions to studies and statistics and court decisions Roth had never heard of. Out of the quick welling of his certainty, though, she did gather facts; facts that made her uncomfortable.

The leos' only loyalty was to their pride. Whether they had inherited this trait from their lion ancestors or had consciously modeled themselves on lion society wasn't known, because they felt no loyalty to the scientific community that had given them birth, and had freed them in order to study them, and so no human investigators were allowed among them to verify hypotheses. No human laws bound them. No borders were respected by them. Again, it was impossible to tell whether these attitudes were deliberate or the result of an intelligence too low to comprehend human values.

Smug, thought Roth: "an intelligence too low . . ." Couldn't it be a heart too great?

Given a small population, Barron went on, and the fact of polygamy and extended families, young leos find it difficult to mate. At maturity, they usually leave or are thrown out of the pride. Their state of psychic tension can be imagined. Their connection to the pride, their only loyalty, has been broken. Aggressive, immensely strong, subhuman in intelligence, and out to prove their strength in the world, the young leos are completely uncontrollable and extremely violent. Barron could give her instances of violent crime—crime rates among this population as compared to an equivalent human group, resisting arrest for instance, assaulting an officer . . .

"Is this one you're after," Roth broke in, "one of these young ones?"

"That hasn't been determined yet."

"He is one of a pride, you know." She wished instantly that she hadn't said that. The officers exchanged looks; Roth could tell that in fact they hadn't known. Yet why should she want to keep it secret? Only because the Mountain never gave away anything, no scrap even of information, to the outside society from which they took nothing? Anyway, it was out. "How did you come to learn he was in the Preserve?"

"We're not at liberty to say," said the USE man. "The information is reliable." He leaned forward, lacing his fingers together; his eyes rifled earnestness at her relentlessly. "Director, I understand that you feel deeply about the inviolability of your area here. We respect that. We want to help you preserve it. This leo or leos are in violation of it. Now, you're very peace-loving here"—a fleeting smile of complicity—"and of course we interface with you there, USE is of course strictly pacifist. So we feel that these leos, who as we've pointed out are all armed and violent, can't be handled by the means you have, which are peaceful and thus inadequate. The Federal government, then, is offering you aid in removing this violation of your space.

"Of course," he concluded, "you do want the violation removed."

For some reason, Emma saw in her mind Meric Landseer's long patient fingers moving with fine sensitivity to find the flaw in an old, well-loved, much-used machine.

"I might point out also," Barron said, since she remained silent, "that it's part of your agreement with the Federal not to turn the Mountain into a refuge for criminals or lawbreakers."

"We aren't hiding them," Roth said. "We can deal with them."

"Can you?"

On her desk the ranger memo still lay: *most of the long muscle stripped away, the rest in a high state of decomposition . . .* She lit a cigarette from the stub of her last. "There's no way," she said, "that I can issue warrants or passports in my own name. You'll have to wait. It could take time." She looked at Barron. "We're not very efficient decision-makers here." She stood, strangely restless. She felt a hateful urgency, and wanted it not to show. "I suppose it's possible for you to stay here for a few days until our own rangers and—other investigators have returned with what they've learned. We have a kind of guest-house." In fact it was a quarantine quarters, as cheerless as a jail. That was fine with Roth.

Reluctantly, they agreed to wait. Roth began, with a slowness that obviously irritated them, to send messages and fill out passes. She thought: when bacteria invade you, you consciously invade your own body with antibiotics. Neither is pleasant. An ounce of prevention is worth a pound of cure. The pound of cure before her accepted glumly their highly restricted passes. Perhaps, possibly, thought Roth, the cure won't be needed. *Forgive us our trespasses,* she prayed, *as we forgive those who trespass against us; lead us not into temptation, but deliver us from evil. . . .*

The creature Meric looked at was young. He couldn't have said why that was apparent. He sat so calmly that Meric was tempted to stand up and walk over to him, smiling. He hadn't known what he would feel on coming close to a leo—he had seen photographs, of course, but they were for the most part distant and vague and had only made him curious. He hadn't expected, then, that his first impression would be of utter, still, unchallengeable beauty. It was an unearthly beauty that had something suffocating in its effect, an alien horror; but it was beauty.

"Hello," he said, smiling; both the little word and the fatuous gesture fell hollowly far short of the leo, Meric felt. How could he come to him? "I mean no harm." He was in fact harmless, defenseless even. He wondered whether it was possible for him to make himself clear to them. What if it wasn't? Why had he supposed he would be invisible to them? What, anyway, had he come out to learn?

The leo stood, and without prelude or greeting walked in short, solid strides to where Meric was crouched by the stone fence. He came with the unappeasable purposiveness of evil things in dreams, right at Meric, his intentions unreadable, and Meric, as in a dream, couldn't move or cry out, though he felt something like terror. He was about to fling his arms up before his face and cry out the nightmare-breaking cry, when the leo stopped and with an odd gentleness took the telephoto lens out of his hand. He looked at it carefully, batting a fly from before his face with a ponderous motion. Then he gave it back.

"It's nothing," Meric said. "A lens." The leo was close enough now for Meric to hear the faint whistle of air drawn regularly through his narrow nostrils; near enough to smell him. The smell, like the face, was alien, intensely real, and yet not anything he had expected: not monstrous.

"What did you want to see?" the leo said. At first Meric didn't understand this as speech; for one thing, the leo's voice was ridiculously small and broken, like an adolescent boy's with a bad cold. For another, he realized he had expected the leo to speak to him in some alien tongue, some form of speech as strange and unique as the creature itself.

"You," Meric said. "All of you." He began rapidly to explain himself, about the Preserve, about the Mountain, but in the middle of it the leo walked away and sat down on the stone fence, out of earshot. With his gun across his knees, he looked down the slope to where the camp lay.

Down there, where there had been no one before, there were leos. One, in a long loose coat like an antique duster, its head wrapped in a kind of turban, squatted by the door of the roofless farmhouse. Others— small, young ones apparently—came and went from her (why did he suppose the turbaned one to be female?). The young ones would run away together, playing, wrestling, and then return to her again and sit. She was passive, as though unaware of them. She appeared to be looking some way off. Once she shaded her eyes. Meric looked where she looked, and saw others: two more in long coats, carrying rifles resting upward on their shoulders, and another, behind them, in something like ordinary clothes, dressed like the young one who sat near Meric. One of the tur-baned ones carried a brace of rabbits.

The leo on the wall watched them intently. His nostrils now and again flared and his broad, veined ears turned toward them. If he was intended to be a guard, Meric thought, he wouldn't be watching them; he'd be watching everything else. Not a guard, then. He seemed, rather, to be in some kind of vigil. Everything that happened down below ab-sorbed him. But he made no move to go down and join them. He seemed to have forgotten Meric utterly.

Wondering whether it would be offensive to him, hoping it wouldn't, and not knowing how to ask, Meric put the lens to his eye again. The female by the door sat unmoving but attentive while the others came into camp. When they had come close enough to greet, though, no greetings were exchanged. The male—the one not in a long coat—came and sat beside her, lowering his great shape gracefully to the ground. She lifted her arm and rested it on his shoulder. In a moment they had so com-posed themselves that they looked as though they might have been rest-ing like that for hours.

Meric moved his field of view slightly. Someone could be just glimpsed in the broken doorway; appeared partly and went away; came out then and stood leaning against the jamb with arms crossed.

It wasn't a leo, but a human woman.

Astonished, Meric studied her closely. She seemed at ease; the leos paid her no attention. Her dark hair was cut off short, and he could see that her clothes were strong but old and worn. She smiled at those coming in, though nothing was said; when the one with the rabbits dropped them, she knelt, drew a knife worn down to a mere streak, and began without hesitation to dress them. It was something Meric had never seen done, and he watched with fascination—the lens made it seem that he was watching something happening elsewhere, on another plane, or perhaps he couldn't have watched as the girl expertly slit and then tugged away the skin, as though she were undressing a baby, who appeared skinny and red from within its bunting. Her fingers were soon bloodstained; she licked them casually.

The leo who sat near Meric on the wall stood. He seemed in the grip of a huge emotion. He started deliberately down the hill—they all seemed incapable of doing anything except deliberately—but then stopped. He stood motionless for a while, and then came back, sat again, and resumed his vigil.

Evening was coming on. The roofless house threw out a long tenuous shadow over the bent grass; the woods beyond had grown obscure. Now and again, clouds of starlings rose up and settled again to their disputatious rest. Their noise and the combing of the wind were all the sounds there were.

In an access of courage, feeling suddenly capable of it in the failing light, Meric stood. He was in their view now. One looked up, but started no alarm. Having then no choice—he had dived into their consciousness as a hesitant swimmer dives into cold water—he picked up his bag and started slowly but deliberately—in imitation, he realized, of their steady manner—down to the camp. He looked back at the leo on the wall; the leo watched but made no motion to follow or stop him.

Night within Candy's Mountain was as filled with the constant sound of activity as was day. There was no time when the machine was shut down, for too much had to be done too continually if it was to stay alive at all. Great stretches of it were dark now; ways along halls were marked only by phosphorescent strips, signs, and symbols. Where more light was necessary, there was more light, but it was husbanded and doled nicely. Power in the Mountain was as exactly sufficient to needs, without waste, as was food.

Bree Landseer lay awake on her bedmat in the darkness. She needed no light and used none. She listened to the multiplex speak: the soughing of the hydraulic elevators, the crackle of a welding torch being used on the level above her, which now and then dropped a brief fiery cinder past her window. Voices: freak acoustics brought an occasional word to her, clear as those sparks, through the paper partitions and drapes of Blue that made her house: careful, brooms, novena, Wednesday, cup, never again, half more, if I could . . . Where were those conversations? Impossible to tell . . .

If there had ever been a human institution in which life had been lived as it was within the Mountain, it wasn't any of the ones that the outside world compared it to. It wasn't like a prison, or a huge, self-involved family, or a collective farm, or any kind of collective or commune. It wasn't like a monastery, though Candy had known and revered Benedict's harsh and efficient rule. Yet there was one institution it was like, perhaps: one of those ancient Irish religious communities that never heard of Benedict and only rarely of Rome, great and continuously growing accretions of bishops, saints, monks, nuns, hermits, madmen, and plain people all clustered around some holy place and endlessly building themselves cells, chapels, protective walls, cathedrals, towers. Yes, it was like that. In the Mountain no one flogged himself daily or bathed cheerfully in brine for his soul's good; but they had in the same way rejected the world for the sake of their souls, while not the less—no, all the more —loving and revering the world and all things that lived and flew and crawled in it. They were as various and as eccentric here, as solitary, as individual, and as alone before God as those old Irishmen in their bee-hive cells; and in the same way joined, too: joined in a joyful certainty that they were sinners who deserved their keep but no more. And as certain too that the world blessed them for renouncing the world. Which saint had it been, Bree wondered, who stood one morning in prayer with his arms outstretched, and a bird came and settled in his hand; and so as not to disturb her he went on praying; and so she made her nest in his hand; and so he stood and stood (supported by grace) till the bird had hatched and raised her young? Bree laughed to think of it. A miracle like that would suit her very well. She stretched her arms open across the rough cloth of the mat.

It was on nights like this that Meric and she, wrapped in the delicate tissue of the Mountain's life-sounds, made their still love. She opened the robe of Blue and touched her nakedness delicately, following carefully to the end the long shivers that her fingers started. Meric . . . Like grace, the lovely feelings were suddenly withdrawn from her. Meric. Where was he? Out there, in the limitless darkness, looking at those creatures. What would they do? They seemed to her dangerous, unpredictable, hostile. She wished—so hard it was a prayer—that Meric were here in the shelter of the Mountain.

She surrendered to the anxious tightening of her body, rolling on her side and drawing up her knees. Her eyes were wide open, and she listened to the sounds more intently now, searching them. And—in answer to her prayer, she was certain of it—she sorted from the ambience footsteps coming her way, the sound altering in a familiar way as Meric turned corners toward her. It was his tread. She turned over and could see him, as pale as a wax candle in the darkness of the house. He put down his bundles.

"Meric."

"Yes. Hello."

Why didn't he come to her? She rose, pulling the robe around her, and tiptoed across the cold floor to hug him, welcome him back to safety. His smell when she took hold of him was so rank she drew back. "Jesus," she said. "What . . ."

He turned up the tapers. His face was as smooth and delicate as ever, but its folds and lines seemed deeper, as though filled with blown black dust. His eyes were huge. He sat carefully, looking around himself as though he had never seen this place before.

"Well," she said, uncertain. "Well, you're back."

"Yes."

"Are you hungry? You must be hungry. I didn't think. Wait, wait." She touched him, so that he would stay, and went quickly to make tea, cut bread. "You're all right," she said.

"Yes. All right."

"Do you want to wash?" she asked when she brought the food. He didn't answer; he was sorting through the bag, taking out discs and reading the labels. He ignored the tray she put before him and went to the editing table he kept in the house for his work. Bree sat by the tray, confused and somehow afraid. What had happened to him out there to make him strange like this? What had they done to him, what horrors had they shown him? He chose a disc and inserted it; then, with quick certainty, set up the machine and started it.

"Turn down the light," he said. "I'll show you."

She did, turning away from the screen, which was brightening to life, not certain she wanted to see.

A girl's voice came from the speakers: ". . . and wherever they go, I'll go. The rest doesn't matter to me anymore. I'm lucky . . ."

Bree looked at the screen. There was a young woman with short, dark hair. She sat on the ground with her knees drawn up, and plucked at the grass between her boots. Now and again she looked up at the camera with a kind of feral shy daring, and looked away again. "My god," said Bree. "Is she human?"

"No," the girl said in response to an unheard question. "I don't care about people. I guess I never liked them very much." She lowered her eyes. "The leos are better than people."

"How," Bree asked, "did she get there? Did they kidnap her?"

"No," Meric said. "Wait." He slid a lever and the girl began to jerk rapidly like a puppet; then she leapt up and fled away. There was a flicker of nothing, and then Meric slowed the speed to normal again. There was a tent, and standing before it was a leo. Bree drew her robe tighter around her, as though the creature looked at her. His gaze was steady and changeless; she couldn't tell what emotion it expressed: patience? rage? indifference? So alien, so unreadable. She could see the muscles of his heavy, squat legs beneath the ordinary jeans, and of his wide shoulders; at first she thought he wore gloves, but no, those were his own blunt hands. He held a rifle, casually, as though it were a wrench.

"That's him," Meric said.

"Him?"

"He's called Painter. Anyway, she calls him Painter. Not the others. They don't use names, I don't think."

"Did you talk to him? Can he talk?"

"Yes."

"What did he say?"

The leo began to move away from the tent door, but Meric reversed the disc and put him back again. He stood at the tent door and regarded the humans from his electronic limbo.

What had he said?

When Meric had gone down to where the leo stood broad and poised in the twilight, the leo hadn't spoken at all. Meric, in tones as pacific and self-effacing as he could make them, tried to explain about the Mountain, how this land was theirs.

"Yours," the leo said. "That's all right." As though forgiving him for the error of ownership.

"We wanted to see," Meric began, and then stopped. He felt himself in the grip of an intelligence so fierce and subtle that it made an apprehensive hollow in his chest. "I mean ask—see—what it was you'd come for. I came out. Alone. Unarmed."

The girl he had seen, and the females, had retreated into the shelter of the roofless farmhouse, not as though afraid but as though he were a phenomenon that didn't interest them and could be left for this male to dismiss. Someone within the walls was blowing a fire to life; spark-lit smoke rose over the walls. The young ones still played their silent games, but farther off. They looked at him now and again; stared; stopped playing.

"Well, you've seen," the leo said. "Now you can go."

Meric lowered his eyes, not wanting to be arrogant, and also not quite able to face the leo's regard. "They wonder about you," he said. "In the Mountain. They don't know you, what you are, how you live."

"Leos," said the leo. "That's how we live."

"I thought," Meric went on—it was exhausting to stand face to face like this, at a boundary, an intruder, and yet try to be intimate, carefully friendly, tentative—"I thought if I could just—talk with you, take some pictures, make recordings—just the way you live—I could take them back and show the others. So they could—" He wanted to say "make a decision about you," but that would sound offensive, and he realized at that moment that it was an impossibility as well: the creature before him would allow no decisions to be made about him. "So they could all see, you know," he finished lamely.

"See what?"

"Would you mind," Meric said, "if I sat down?" He took two careful steps forward, his heart beating hard because he didn't know just where he might step over some inviolable boundary and be attacked, and sat down. That was better. It gave the leo the superior position. Meric had made himself absolutely vulnerable, could be no threat here on the ground; yet he was now truly within their boundaries. He essayed a smile. "Your hunting went well," he said.

It would be a long time before Meric learned that such conversational ploys were meaningless to leos. Among men they were designed to begin a chat, to put at ease, to bridge a gap; were like a touch or a smile. The leo answered nothing. He hadn't been asked a question. The man had made a statement. The leo supposed it to be true. He didn't wonder why the man had chosen to make it. He decided to forget him briefly, and turned away into the enclosure, leaving Meric sitting on the ground.

Night gathered around him. He made up his mind to remain where he was as long as he could, to grow into the ground, become ignorable. He took a yoga position he knew he could hold for hours without discomfort. He could even sleep. If they slept, and let him sleep here, in the morning he might have become a fixture, and could begin.

Begin what?

The girl touched him and he roused, uncertain for a wild moment where he was. There was a burnt, smoky odor in the air.

"Do you want to eat?" she said. She put a plate of brown chunks before him. Then she sat too, a little way off, as though uncertain how he might respond.

"It's meat," he said.

"Sure." She said it encouragingly. "It's okay."

"I can't."

"Are you sick?"

"We don't eat meat." A broken, blanched bone protruded from one brown piece.

"So eat grass," she said, and rose to go. He saw he had rejected a kindness, a human kindness, and that she was the only one here capable of offering him that—and of talking to him, too.

"No, don't go, wait. Thank you." He picked up a piece of the meat, thinking of her tearing it bloody from its skin. "It's just—I never did." The smell of it—burned, dark, various—was heady, heady as sin. He bit, expecting nausea. His mouth suddenly filled with liquid; he was eating flesh. He wondered how much he needed in order to make a meal. The taste seemed to start some ancient memory: a race memory, he wondered, or just some forgotten childhood before the Mountain?

"Good," he said, chewing carefully, feeling flashes of guilty horror. He wouldn't keep it down, he was certain; he would vomit. But his stomach said not so.

"Do you think," he said, pushing away his plate, "that they'll talk to me?"

"No. Maybe Painter. Not the others."

"Painter?"

"The one you talked to."

"Is he, well, the leader, more or less?"

She smiled as though at some interior knowledge to which Meric's remark was so inadequate as to be funny.

"How do you come to be here?" he asked.

"His."

"Do you mean like a servant?"

She only sat, plucking at the grass between her boots. She had lost the habit of explanation. She was grateful it was gone, because this was unexplainable. The question meant nothing; like a leo, she ignored it. She rose again to go.

"Wait," he said. "They won't mind if I stay?"

"If you don't do anything."

"Tell me. That one up on the hill. What's his function?"

"His what?"

"I mean why is he there, and not here? Is he a guard?"

She took a step toward him, suddenly grave. "He's Painter's son," she said. "His eldest. Painter put him out."

"Put him out?"

"He doesn't understand yet. He keeps trying to come back." She looked off into the darkness, as though looking into the blank face of an unresolvable sadness. Meric saw that she couldn't be yet twenty.

"But why?" he said.

She retreated from him. "You stay there," she said, "if you want. Don't make sudden moves or jump around. Help when you can, they won't mind. Don't try to understand them."

Just before dawn they began to rise. Meric, stiff and alert after light, hallucinatory sleep, watched them appear in the blue, bird-loud morning. They were naked. They gathered silently in the court of the camp, large and indistinct, the children around them. They all looked east, waiting.

Painter came from his tent then. As though signaled by this, they all began to move out of the camp, in what appeared to be a kind of precedence. The girl, naked too, was last but for Painter. Meric's heart was full; his eyes devoured what they saw. He felt like a man suddenly let out of a small, dark place to see the wide extent of the world.

Outside the camp, the ground fell away east down to a rushy, marshy stream. They went down to the stream, children hurrying ahead. Meric rose, cramped, wondering if he could follow. He did, loitering at what he hoped was a respectful distance. As they walked down, he studied the strangeness of their bodies. If they were conscious of his presence, or of their own nakedness, they didn't show it; in fact they didn't seem naked as naked humans do, skinned and raw and defenseless, with unbound flesh quivering as they walked. They seemed clothed in flesh as in armor. A kind of hair, a blond down, as thick as loincloths between the females' legs, made them seem not so much hairy as cloudy. Walking made their muscles move visibly beneath the cloud of hair, their massive thighs and broad backs changing shape subtly as they took deliberate steps down to the water. In the east, a fan of white rays shot up suddenly behind down-slanting bars of scarlet cirrus, and upward into the blue darkness overhead. They raised their faces to it.

Meric knew that they considered the sun a god and a personal father. Yet what he observed had none of the qualities of a ritual of worship. They waded knee-deep into the water and washed, not ritual ablutions but careful cleansing. Women washed children and males, and older children washed younger ones, inspecting, scrubbing, bringing up handfuls of water to rinse one another. One female calmly scrubbed the girl, who shrank away grimacing from the force of it; her body was red with cold. Painter stood bent over, hands on his knees, while the girl and another laved his back and head; he shook his head to remove the water and wiped his face. A male child splashing near him attempted to catch him around the neck and Painter threw him roughly aside, so that the child went under water; Painter caught him up and dunked him again, rubbing his spluttering face fiercely. Impossible to tell if this was play or anger. They shouted out now and again, at each other's ministrations or at the coldness of the water, or perhaps only for shouting; for a spark of sun flamed on the horizon, and then the sun lifted itself up, and the cries increased.

It was laughter. The sun smiled on them, turning the water running from their golden bodies to molten silver, and they laughed in his face, a stupendous fierce orison of laughter.

Meric, estranged on the bank, felt dirty and evanescent, and yet privileged. He had wondered about the girl, how she could choose to be one of them when she so obviously couldn't be; how she could deny so much of her own nature in order to live as they did. He saw now that she had done no such thing. She had only acceded to their presence, lived as nearly as she could at their direction and convenience, like a dog trying to please a beloved, contrary, willful, godlike man, because whatever self-denial that took, whatever inconvenience, there was nothing else worth doing. Inconvenience and estrangement from her own kind were nothing compared to the privilege of hearing, of sharing, that laughter as elemental as the blackbird's song or the taste of flesh.

When they came back into camp they remained naked in the warming sunlight for a time, drying. Only the girl dressed, and then began to make up the fire. If she looked at Meric she didn't seem to see him; she shared in their indifference.

When he moved, though, there wasn't one of them who didn't notice it. When he went to his pack and got bread and dried fruit, all their eyes caught him. When he assembled his recorder, they followed his movements. He did it all slowly and openly, looking only at the machine, to make them feel it had nothing to do with them.

Painter had gone into his tent, and when Meric was satisfied that his recorder was in working order, he stood carefully, feeling their eyes on him, and went to the tent door. He squatted there, peering into the obscurity within, unable to see anything. He thought perhaps the leo would sense his presence and come to the door, if only to chase him off. But no notice was taken of him. He felt the leo's disregard of him, so total as to be palpable. He was not present, not even to himself; he was a prying eye only, a wavering, shuddering needle of being without a north.

"Painter," he said at last. "I want to talk to you." He had considered politer locutions; they seemed insulting, even supposing the leo would understand them as politeness. He waited in the silence. He felt the eyes of the pride on him.

"Come inside," Painter's thin voice said.

He took the recorder in a damp palm and pushed aside the tent flap. He went in.

Bree looked at the screen. The sun shone through the fabric of the tent, making the interior a burnt-ocher color; the walls were bright and the objects inside dark, bright-edged, as though the scene were inside a live coal. The leo was a huge obscurity, back-lit. The recorder was wide open, so values were blurred and exaggerated; dust motes burned and swam like tiny bright insects, the leo's eyes were molten, soft, alive.

"You shouldn't have eaten that meat, Meric," Bree said. "You didn't have to. You should have explained."

Meric said nothing. The pressure of her ignorance on him, ignorance he could never dispel, was tightening around his heart.

"What do you want?" the leo said. For a long time there was no answer; the leo didn't seem to await one. Then Meric, faint, off-mike said: "We think killing animals is wrong."

The leo didn't change expression, didn't seem to take this as a challenge. Meric said: "We don't allow it, anywhere within the Preserve."

Bree waited for the leo to make arguments, to say, "But all living things eat other living things"; or, "We have as much right to hunt as the hawks and the dragonflies"; or, "What right do you have to tell us what to do?" She had counterarguments, explanations, for all these answers. She knew Meric did too. She wanted to see it explained to the leo.

Instead the leo said: "Then why did you come out alone?"

"What?" Meric's voice, distant, confused.

"I said, why did you come out alone?"

"I don't understand."

"If you don't allow something, something I do, there ought to be more than one of you to make me stop."

As far as his emotions could be read, the leo wasn't being belligerent; he said it as though he were pointing out a fact that Meric had overlooked. Meric mumbled something Bree couldn't hear.

The leo said: "I have a living to get. It's got nothing to do with these —notions. I take what I need. I take what I have to."

"You have a right to that," Meric said. "As much as you need to live, I guess, but . . ."

The leo seemed almost to smile. "Yes," he said. "A right to what I need to live. That part's mine. And another part too for my wives and children."

"All right," Meric said.

"And another part as, what, payment for what I've gone through, for what I am. Compensation. I didn't ask to be made."

"I don't know," Meric said. "But still not all; there's still a part you have no right to."

"That part," the leo said, "you're free to take away from me. If you can."

Another long silence fell. Was Meric afraid? Bree thought, Why doesn't he say something? "Why didn't you *explain?*" she whispered. "You should have explained."

Meric pressed a lever on the editing table that froze the leo's unwavering regard, and the golden dust motes in their paths around him too. All along his long way home he had wondered how he would explain: to Bree, to Emma, to them all. All his life he had been an explainer, an expresser, a describer; a transformer, an instrument through which events passed and became meaningful: became reasons, programs, notions. But there was no way for him to explain what had happened to him in the leos' camp, because the event wouldn't pass through him, it would never leave him, he was in its grasp.

"I had nothing to say," he said to Bree.

"Nothing to say!"

"Because he's right." Right, right, how pointless. "Because if we want him not to do it, we have to make him. Because . . ." There was no way to say it, no way to pass it from him in words. He felt suffocated, as though he were caught in a vacuum.

When, after her affair with Grady, Bree had begun reading the Bible and talking and thinking about Jesus, she had tried to make Meric feel what she felt. "It's being good," she had said. Meric did his best to be good, to be Christlike, to be gentle; but he never felt it, as Bree did, to be a gift, a place to live, an intense happiness. He thought to say now that what he had felt in Painter's tent was what she had felt when she first knew Jesus, when she had glowed continually with it and been unable to explain it, when it made her weep.

But what could that mean to Bree? Her gentle Jesus, her lover who asked nothing of her but to stand with her and walk with her and lie down with her, what had he to do with the cruel, ravishing, wordless thing that had seized Meric?

"It's like Jesus," he said, ashamed, the words like dust in his mouth. He heard her breath indrawn, shocked. But it was true. Jesus was two natures, God and man, the godhead in him burning through the flesh toward his worshipers, burning out the flesh in them. Painter was two natures too: through his thin, strained voice pressed all the dark, undifferentiated world, all the voiceless beasts; it was the world Candy had urged us to flee from and Jesus promised to free us from, the old world returned to capture us, speak in a voice to us, reclaim us for its own. It was as though the heavy, earth-odorous Titans had returned to strike down at last the cloudy scheming gods, as though the circle had closed that had seemed an upward spiral, as though a reverse messiah had come to crush all useless hope forever.

As though, as though, as though. Meric looked up from the face on the screen, and drew a deep, tremulous breath. Tears burned on his dirty cheeks. The chains, as they had in Painter's tent, fell away from him. Nothing to say, yes, at last nothing to say.

Unable, despite a repugnance so deep it was like horror, to take her eyes from the screen, Bree heard unbidden in her mind the child's song she still sometimes sang herself to sleep with: *Little ones to him belong; they are weak but he is strong.* She shuddered at the blasphemy of it, and stood as though waking from an oppressive dream. "It doesn't matter," she said. "Pretty soon they'll be gone anyway."

"What do you mean?"

"Grady told me," she said. "There are Federal people here. One of those—animals committed a crime or something. The Feds want to go in and arrest him, or drive them off, or something."

He stood. She turned away from his look. "Grady's going with them. They were only waiting till you got back. What are you doing?"

He had begun to open cabinets, take out clothes, equipment. "I haven't come back," he said.

"What do you mean?"

He knotted together the laces of a pair of heavy boots so that they could be carried. "Do they have guns?" he asked. "How many are there? Tell me."

"I don't know. I guess, guns. Grady will be with them. It's all right." He seemed mad. She wanted to touch him, put a hand on him, restrain him; but she was afraid. "You have come back," she said.

He pulled on a quilted coat. "No," he said. "I came for this stuff." He was cramming recording tape, lenses, bits and pieces quickly into his pack. "I meant to stay a night, two nights. Talk to Emma." He stopped packing, but didn't look up at her. "Say good-bye to you."

A rush of fear contracted her chest. "Good-bye!"

"Now I've got to hurry," he said. "I've got to reach them before Grady and those." Still he hadn't looked at her. "I'm sorry," he said, quick, curt, rejecting.

"No," she said. "What's the matter?"

"I'm going back to them," he said. "I've got to—get it all down.

Record it all. So people can see." He slung the pack over his shoulder, and filled his pockets with the bread she had set out for him. "And now I've got to warn them."

"*Warn* them! They're thieves, they're killers!" She gasped it out. "They don't belong here, they have to go, they have to *stop it*!" He had turned to go. She grabbed at his sleeve. "What have they done to you?"

He only shook her off, his face set. He went out of their space and into the broad, low corridors that swept across the level. From the long high lines of clerestory windows, bars of moonlight fell across the ways. There was no other light. His footsteps were loud in the silence, but her naked feet pursuing him made no sound. "Meric," she whisper-called. "When will you come back?"

"I don't know."

"Don't go to them."

"I have to."

"Let Grady."

He rounded on her. "Tell Grady to stay away," he said. "Tell Emma. Don't let those men into the Preserve. They don't belong there. They've got no right."

"No *right*!" She stopped, still, at a distance from him, as though he were dangerous to approach. He stood too, knowing that everything he had said was wrong, knowing he was doing wrong to her, ashamed but not caring. "Good-bye," he said again, and turned down a corridor toward the night elevators. She didn't follow.

He went the night way down through the Mountain, following the spectral luminescent signs, changing from elevator to elevator—the banks of day elevators were shut down, and there were only one or two down-ward paths he could go; at every discharge level he had to interpret the way to the next, drifting downward side-to-side like a slow and errant leaf. How often he had dreamed he walked through night spaces like these, coming onto unfamiliar levels, finding with surprise but no won-der places he had never seen, vast and pointless divisions of space, im-passable halls, half-built great machines, processions of unknown faces, the right way continually eluding him and continually reappearing in a new guise—*oh now I remember*—until oppressed with confusion and strangeness he woke.

He woke: it seemed to him as he went down now that the Mountain had lost all solidity, had become as illusory as a thought, as a notion. The continual, sensible, long-thought-out divisions of its spaces, the plain, honest faces of its machines, its long black-louvered suntraps, its un-dressed surfaces, all showing the signs of the handiwork and labor that had brought them into being: it was all tenuous, had the false solidity of a dream. It couldn't contain him any longer, vast as it was.

He went out across the floor of the great, windy central atrium, past piles of supplies and materials—the place was never empty, always cluttered with things in progress from one condition into another under the hands of craftsmen, wood into walls, metal into machines, dirt into cleanliness, uselessness into use, use into waste, waste into new materials. Before him rose the transparent front, stories high, stone, steel, and pale green slabs of cast glass flawed and honest, through which a green, wrinkled moon shone coldly. He went out.

The moon was white and round. The grass before him bent, silvery, as it was mowed in long swaths by the wind. Behind him the Mountain was silent, a disturbance of the air only; its discreet lights didn't compete against the moon.

Certainty. That was what Painter offered him, only not offered, only embodied: certainty after ambivalence, doubt, uncertainty. He asked—no, not asked, could not ask; had no interest in asking, yet nevertheless he put the question—asked Meric to overthrow the king within himself, the old Adam whom Jehovah said was to rule over all creation. For even in the Mountain, King Adam was not overthrown, only in exile: still proud, still anxious, still throned in lonely superiority, because there was no new king to take up his abandoned crown.

That king had come. He waited out there in the darkness, his hidden kingship like a hooded sun. Meric had seen it, and had knelt before it, and kissed those heavy hands, ashamed, relieved, amazed by grace.

Give away all that you have, the leo said to men. Give away all that you have; come, follow me.

Meric stepped off the long steps into the whispering grass, not looking back, walking steadily north.

They took Painter at the end of that month, a gray day and very cold, with a few snowflakes blowing in the air like dust. It had been Barron's plan to encircle the whole pride, if they could, and negotiate a settlement, taking the one called Painter into custody and arranging for the movement of the others, under supervision, southeastward in the general direction of the Capitol and the sites of the new internment centers. But the man Meric Landseer had spoiled that. He, and the young leo appearing from nowhere. It was to have been a simple, clean, just act, location, negotiation, relocation. It became a war.

The leos for a while seemed to be fleeing from them along the foothills of the mountains that formed the northern boundary of the Preserve. Barron decided that if the mountains were keeping them from moving north, he could swing some of his men quickly ahead of them and cut them off in a C-movement with the mountains blocking retreat. When they did that, though, the slow-moving caravan turned north suddenly, toward the steep, fir-clad slopes. Yet Barron had been told they didn't like mountains. It must be Meric Landseer influencing them.

There was a river, and beyond it a sudden mountain. They abandoned their truck and the wagon beside the river. They were gathering at the river's edge, about to cross, when Barron and the ranger showed themselves. The Federal officers were staying out of sight, guns ready. Barron called to the leos through a bullhorn, setting out conditions, telling them to put down their guns. There was no answering motion. The ranger, Grady, took the bullhorn from him. He called out Meric's name, saying he should stay out of this, not be a fool, get away. No answer. The females in their long, dull dusters were hard to see against the dull, brown grass.

Barron, talking peaceably but forcibly through the bullhorn, and Grady, carrying a heavy, blunt weapon like a blunderbuss, started to walk down toward the river. The leos were entering the water. Barron began to hurry. He supposed that the tallest of them, in ordinary clothes, was the one they wanted. He called on him by name to surrender.

He saw then out of the corner of his eye a quick figure moving in the woods to his left. Saw that he had a gun. A leo. Who? Where had he come from? Grady dropped instantly to the ground, pulling Barron down with him. The leo's gun fired with a dull sound, and then came a sharp chatter of fire from where the officers were hidden.

The young leo dodged from tree to tree, loading his ancient gun and firing. There was a shriek or scream from behind Barron: someone hit. Barron caught a glimpse of the leo now and then when he dared to raise his head. The bullhorn had fallen some feet away from him. He squirmed over to it and picked it up. He shouted that the leo was to throw down his gun, or the officers would shoot to kill. The leos were in the river now, wading chest-deep in its brown current, holding the children up.

On the bank Painter still stood, and Meric, and another, the girl they had glimpsed during the chase, apparently the one he had kidnaped.

Suddenly the young one with the gun was racing, at an inhuman speed, out of cover, racing to put himself between the fleeing pride and the Federals. The guns behind Barron sounded. The leo fired blindly as he ran, and Barron and the ranger flattened themselves. He ran for a clump of bush. He seemed to stumble just as he reached it, then crawled to it, and fired again. The Federals covered the bush with fire.

Then there was a ringing silence. Barron looked up again. The young leo lay sprawled face up. The leo Painter had begun to walk alone away from the river toward where Barron and the ranger lay. He held a gun loosely in one hand. Barron thought he heard a faint voice, the girl's voice, calling him back. His hand trembling, Barron spoke through the bullhorn: put down the gun, no harm will come to you. The leo didn't look at the bush where the young one lay; he came toward them steadily, still holding the gun. Barron insisted he drop it. He said it again and again. He turned, and called out to the officers to hold their fire.

At last the leo threw down the gun, or dropped it, anyway, as though it were of no importance. At the river, the man was moving into the water with the girl, who was unwilling; she resisted, trying to turn back, struggling against the man, calling out to the leo. But the man made her go on. Some of the leos had already gained the far bank, and were climbing hand and foot up the fir-dark wooded slope. The ranger stood suddenly and raised his fat, blunt weapon.

He aimed well over the leo's head. The gun made a low boom, and instantly over the leo's head, like a hawk, there appeared a small amorphous cloud. There was a scream from the river, a girl's scream. The cloud flared open into a net of strong, thin cord, still attached to the gun by leads. It descended lazily, stickily, clingingly over the leo, who only as it touched him saw and tried to evade it. He roared out, pulling at the thing, and Grady at the other end hauled it tighter, shouting at the leo to relax, be quiet. The leo stumbled, his legs bound in the elastic cords. He was reaching for a knife, but his arms were enmeshed too tightly. He rolled over on the ground, the fine webbing cutting his face. Grady ran toward him and quickly, efficiently, like an able spider, made the cords secure.

Barron watched the two humans gain the opposite bank. The snow was still faintly blowing. What was wrong with them, anyway? Where did they think they were going?

He came to where the leo lay, no longer struggling. Grady was say-ing, "All right, all right," at once triumphant and soothing.

"What do you think you're doing?" Barron said to the leo. "What in *hell* do you think you're doing? I have a man dead here now." For some reason, shock maybe, he was furious. If the ranger hadn't been there, he would have kicked the leo again and again.

5

OF THE PACK

O keep the Dog far hence, that's friend to men

—T. S. ELIOT

Blondie was dead.

They didn't understand that for a time; they stood guard over her hardening body, fearful and confused. She had been the first to eat the meat, though in fact it was Duke who had found it. He had sniffed it and taken a quick nip or two before Blondie had come up, imperious, knowing her rights, and Duke had backed away.

By rights, Sweets, as her consort, should have been next at the meat, before the real melee began, but something had alerted him, some odor he knew; he had made warning sounds at Blondie, even whimpered to get her attention, but she was too old and too hungry and too proud to listen. Duke was young and strong; he had had spasms, and vomited violently. Blondie was dead.

Toward nightfall, the rest began to drift away, tired of the vigil and no longer awed by Blondie's fast-fading essence, but Sweets stayed. He licked Blondie's stiff, vomit-flecked face. He did run a way after the others, but then he returned. He lay by her a long time, his ears pricking at sounds, lonely and confused. Now and again one of the wild ones came near, circling their old queen carefully, no longer sure of her status or

Sweets's. They kept their distance when Sweets warned them off: he was still with her, she was still powerful, Sweets still shared that power. But his heart was cold, and he was afraid. Not so much of the wild ones, who, fierce as they were, were so afraid of men and so timid about wandering beyond the park that they could never lead. No, not the wild ones. Sweets was afraid of Duke.

Sweets had smelled Duke's sickness and weakness; Duke was in no mood for any struggle now. He had gone off somewhere to hide and recover from the poison. Then there would be battle. Both of them, deprived of the queen who had kept peace between them, knew, in fitful heart-sinkings of insecurity, that their status was altered and that it must be established newly.

By dawn, Sweets had slept, and Blondie had grown featureless with frost. Sweets awoke conscious of one thing only: not Blondie, but the acrid odor of Duke's urine, and the near presence of the Doberman.

The struggle had begun. From around the park the pack had begun to assemble, all of them lean and nervous with the oncoming of winter, their calls carrying far on the cold air. They were of every size and color, from a dirty-white poodle not quite grown fully shaggy and with the knot of a pink ribbon still in her topknot, to an aged Irish wolfhound, enormous and stupid. They each had a place in the pack, a place that had little to do with size or even ferocity, but with some heart they had or did not have. Places were of course eternally contested; only the old retriever Blondie had had no challengers. Between Sweets and Duke the issue was clear: who would be leader. For the loser, though, the battles would continue, until at least one other backed away from him and his place was found. It might be second-in-command. It could be, if his heart failed him, beneath the lowest of them.

If his heart failed him: when Sweets perceived Duke approach him, at once and in all his aspects, he felt a sudden overwhelming impulse to whimper, to crawl on his belly to the Doberman and offer himself up, to roll in and sniff up Duke's victorious urine in an ecstasy of surrender. And then quick as anger came another, fiercer thing, a thing that remade him all courage, that laid his teeth bare and drew back his ears, that erected his fur so that he appeared larger than his true size, that tautened his muscles and lashed him toward Duke like a whip.

———

Sweets's first pack had been a Chinese family on East Tenth Street, who had taken him milky and fat from his mother, the super's shepherd, and then put a sign on their door: PREMISES PROTECTED BY GUARD DOG. The whole block had been vacated by the provisional government shortly after that, before Sweets could yield up his whole allegiance to the shy, studious boy who was obviously the pack's leader. Sometimes, now, on garbage expeditions far south in the city, he would smell in the cans a faint odor of his earliest childhood.

The dogs on East Tenth Street who escaped the pound trucks were routinely shot by the paramilitary gangs, for hygienic reasons it was claimed, but chiefly so the boys could let off steam. Sweets had been among those impounded, and would have been destroyed with the rest of his snarling, terrified, famished cell if a fate in most cases usually worse hadn't befallen him: Sweets was one of those picked out by the laboratory of a city research center to see what he could teach them that might be of interest to the race that the race of dogs had taken as their leaders.

That was the first thing Sweets remembered, remembered that is not in his forgetless nerve and tissue but with the behind-his-nose, where he had come to locate his new consciousness: the laboratory of that research center. The ineluctable and eye-stabbing whiteness of its flourescence. The bright metal bands that held him. The itching of his shaven head where the electrodes were implanted. The strong, disinfected, and indifferent hands of the black woman who, one day soon after his awakening, released him—let him walk, stiff and ungainly as a puppy, into the welcoming arms of his new mistress: "Sweets," she said, "sweets, sweets, sweets, come to mama."

The experiments Sweets had been used in were concerned with frontal-lobe function enhancement. They had been judged a failure. Sweets's EEG was odd, but there was no interpreting that; nobody trusted EEG anymore anyway, and Sweets had been unable to perform at all significantly on any test devised for him; apparently he had experienced no enhancement of function, no increase in eidetic intelligence. The whole line of research was being closed up as a mistake. And Sweets, having no idea of what they were about, and altered in his mind only and not in the soul he had inherited from the gray shepherd, his mother, and the one-eyed mutt, his father, would not have thought to tell them, even if he could speak, that he had awakened. He only wallowed, tail frantic, in the kindness of his lady, a technician who had befriended him and claimed him when the experiment was done. To her he gave up as much of his love as had been left unshattered by his short life.

It had taken centuries for the bonding of men and dogs to come about, for dogs to come to accept men as of the pack. In the city that bond was being unraveled in a mere decade.

It was fair that those species who had chosen to share city-man's fate —dogs, cats, rats, roaches—should share in his tragedies too, and they always had; the dogs willingly, the cats with reproach, the rest blindly, starving with men, bombed with them, burned out with them, sacrificed to their famines and their sciences. But men had changed, quickly, far more quickly than their companion species could. The rats, who had so neatly matched man's filthy habits and who counted on his laziness, had suddenly been done in by his wits, and had nearly perished utterly: only now, in the loosening of man's hold over the world, forgotten in the mental strife that only man can engage in, the rats had begun to stage a small comeback: Sweets and his pack knew that, because they hunted them. Cats had been rigidly divided into two classes by the decline of the rat: sleek eunuchs who lived on the flesh of animals twenty times their own size, fattened for them and slaughtered and cut into dainty bits; and a larger class of their outcast cousins, who starved, froze, and were poisoned by the thousand.

Until men left the city entirely, of course, the roaches would flourish. But now, suddenly, that day seemed not far off.

Down Fifth from Harlem, the Renaissance fronts were stained and their windows blinded with sheets of steel or plywood. The park they had long regarded with calm possessiveness was rank and wild, its few attendants went armed with cattle-prods, and their chief duty was to guard the concrete playgrounds kept open during daylight hours for children who played glumly with their watchful nurses amid the tattooed seesaws and one-chain swings. Few people went into the wilder park north of the museums, where ivy had begun to strangle the aged trees with their quaint nameplates, and city stinkweed to crowd out their young; few, except at need. "We lost them in the park," the provisional police would report after a street fight with one or another faction; lost them in the woods and rocky uplands where they hid, wounded sometimes, dying sometimes. The occasional police sweep through the park uncovered, usually, one dead or in hiding, and a number of scruffy, wary dogs, seen at a distance, never within rifle-range.

It was there that Sweets first saw Blondie: up beyond the museum, at the southern edge of her territory.

The open spaces around the museum were now a universal dog run, despite the police notices, since there were hardly any people who would go into the park without a dog. Sweets grew to know many, and feared some; dainty greyhounds who shied at squirrels, rigid Dobermans and touchy shepherds who knew only Attack and no other games, St. Bernards clumsy and rank. The dog run was a confusing, exhausting place, a palimpsest of claims all disputed. Sweets feared it and was excited by it; he strained at his leash, barking madly like a dumb puppy, when his lady Lucille first brought him there, and then when she unchained him he stood stock still, unable to leave her, assaulted with odors.

Whatever sense Sweets and the rest could make of the place was aborted by the people. Sweets should have had the weimaraner bitch; she was in flaming heat and shouldn't have been brought there, but since she had been, why had his first triumph, his first, over others larger and meaner than himself, been taken from him? The bitch chose him. He had never had a female, and his heart was great; he would have killed for her, and she knew it. And then the big-booted man had come up and kicked them away, and left Sweets in his triumph unrelieved.

Exalted, buzzing with power that seemed to spring from his loins, he pranced away, hearing Lucille far away calling his name. They all faded behind him, and he was filled with his own smell only; he lowered his nose to the ground in a condescending way but nothing entered. He came to the top of the ridge, and in the bushes there Blondie rose up to meet him. He raised his head, not choosing to bark, feeling unapproachable, potent, huge, and she, though not in heat, acknowledged it. Bigger than he, she knew him to be bigger just then. She quietly, admiringly, tasted his air. And then lay down again to the nap he had roused her from, her tail making a soft thump-thump-thump on the littered ground.

And now Blondie is dead; murdered, he alone of them understands, by men's meat; and Lucille is gone, taken away unresisting in the night by big men in fear-smelling overcoats. Sweets, left locked in the bedroom, should have starved but did not, though Lucille in the relocation center wept to think of it; he knew well enough by then about doors and locks, and though his teeth and nails weren't made for it he opened the bedroom door, and stood in the ransacked apartment through whose open door came in unwonted night airs and odors.

He came to the park because there was nowhere else for him to go. If it hadn't been for Blondie, he would have starved that first winter, because he would no longer go near men, would never again look to them for food, or help, or any comfort. What the wild ones knew as their birthright, being born without men, he had as a gift of that eidetic memory men had given him by accident: he knew men were no longer of the pack. If he could he would lead his pack, all of them, away from men's places, somewhere other, though he had knowledge of such a place only as a saint has knowledge of heaven. He imagined it vaguely as a park without walls, without boundaries, without, most of all, men.

If he could . . .

When he rushed Duke, the Doberman didn't back away, though he himself didn't charge. His narrow, black face was open, his armed mouth ready. Duke had killed a man once, or helped to do it, when he was a guard dog in a jewelry store; the man's gun had shot away one of the ears the agency had so carefully docked when he was a pup. He feared nothing but noises and Blondie. He turned to keep facing Sweets as Sweets circled him in tense dashes, keeping the mouth facing him, wanting desperately to hurt him, yet unable to attack, which was Sweets's right.

When at last the courage within Sweets boiled over and he did attack, he was seized breathless by Duke's ferocity. They fought mouth to mouth, and Sweets tasted blood instantly, though he couldn't feel his cut lips and cheeks. They fought in a series of falls, like wrestlers, falls that lasted seconds: when Duke won a fall, Sweets would halt, paralyzed, offering his throat in surrender to Duke's wanting teeth, inches from his jugular. Then Duke would relent, minutely, and again they would be a blur of muscle and a guttural snarl, and Duke would be forced to freeze. Duke was the stronger: his nervous strength, teased up within him by his agency training, seemed ceaseless, and Sweets began helplessly—because he too had been doctored by men—to imagine defeat.

Then four sticks of dynamite took apart a temporary police headquarters on Columbus Avenue, and the sound struck them like a hand.

Duke twisted away, snapping his head in terror, seeking the sound to bite it. Sweets, surprised but not frightened, attacked again, drove Duke to yield; Duke, maddened, tried to flee, was made to yield again, and then lay still beneath Sweets, all surrender.

Sweets let him rise. He had to. He felt, irresistibly, an urge to urinate; and when he walked away to do so, Duke fled. Not far; from behind green benches along a walk he barked, letting Sweets know he was still there, still mean. Still of the pack. Only not leader.

Sweets, heart drumming, one leg numb, his lips beginning to burn in the cold air, looked around his kingdom. The others were keeping far from him; they were dim blurs to his colorless vision. He was alone.

There were four officers and a single prisoner in the temporary station on Columbus Avenue. The prisoner was in transit from up north, where he had been captured, to a destination undisclosed to the officers, who were city and not Federal; all they knew was that he was to be held and transferred. And, of course, that a report had to be made out. It was this report, on six thin sheets of paper the colors of confetti, that the sergeant had been typing out with great care and two ringed fingers when he was decapitated by the file drawer—K–L—behind which the charge had been hidden and which shot out like an ungainly broad arrow when it went off.

"Height: 6'2"," he had typed. "Weight: 190." He didn't look it; slim, compact, but mighty. "Eyes: yellow." He could almost feel those strange eyes, behind him in the cell, looking at him. "Distinguishing marks." The sergeant was a methodical, stupid man. He pondered this. Did they mean distinguishing him from others of his kind, or from men? He had seen others, in films and so on, and to him they all looked pretty much alike. He wasn't about to get near enough to look for scars and such. The species had existed for nearly half a century now, and yet few men— especially in cities—ever came near to one as the sergeant was now. They were shy, secretive, close. And they were all marked for extinction.

The form just didn't fit the prisoner. The sergeant knew well enough what to do when, say, a man's name was too large for the space it was to be put in. He could guess weights and heights, invent the glum circum- stances of an arrest. Distinguishing marks . . . He wrote: "Leo."

That certainly distinguished him. The sergeant used it twice more: in the Alias spot, and for Race. Pleased with himself, he was about to type it in for Nationality/Autonomy too, when the charge went off.

Two of the others had been in the foyer, and one was screaming. The third had been standing by the coffee urn, which was next to the cell door; he had been trying to catch a glimpse of their strange charge through the screened window. Now his head, face tattered by the screen, was thrust through the little window, wedged there, his eyes seeming to stare within, wide with surprise.

The leo shrieked in pain and rage, but couldn't hear his own voice.

What had happened? The night streets north of Cathedral Parkway were always dead quiet on winter nights like this one; the loudest noises were their own, overturning garbage cans and barking in altercation or triumph; only occasionally a lone vehicle mounted with lights would cruise slowly up the avenues, enforcing the curfew. Tonight the streets were alive; windows rose and were slammed down again, loud sirens and bullhorns tore at the silence, red lights at the darkness. Somewhere a burning building showed a dull halo above the streets. There were shots, in single pops and sudden handfuls.

With Blondie gone, Sweets had no one to interpret this, no one who with certitude would say *Flee*, or *Ignore that, it means nothing*. It was all him now. The pack was scattered by incident over two or three blocks when mistrust overwhelmed Sweets. He began to lope along the streets, swinging his head from side to side, nostrils wide, seeking the others. When he passed one, the fear smell was strong; they were all of a mind to run, and had all begun to turn toward the long darkness of the park to the south. Sweets, though, kept circling, unsure, unable to remember whom he had passed and whom he had not. Duke, Randy, Spike the wolfhound, Heidi the little poodle, the wild ones Blondie's daughter and another one . . . . He could bear it no longer. He turned to race across the avenue, meaning to go for the gate on 110th, when the tank turned the corner and came toward him.

He had never seen such a thing, and froze in fear in its path. Its great gun swiveled from side to side and its treads chewed the pavement. It was as though the earth had begun to creep. It churned a moment in one place, seeking with its white lights, which dazzled Sweets; then it started down on him, as wide almost as the street. It spoke in a high whisper of radio static above its thunderous chugging, and at the last moment before it struck him, there appeared on its top a man, popping up like a toy.

Somehow that restored Sweets to anger; it was after all only another man's thing to hurt him. He leapt, almost quick enough; some flange of the tank struck him in the last foot to leave its path. He went sprawling and then rose and ran three-legged, ran with red fury and black fear contesting within him, ran leaving bright drops along the street until cold closed his wound. He ran uptown, away from the park; he ran for darkness, any darkness. This darkness: an areaway, a stair downward, a bent tin doorway, a dank cellar. And silence. Blackness. Ceasing of motion. Only the quick whine of his own breath and the roar of anger retreating.

Then his fur thrilled again. There was someone else in the cellar.

Wounded beasts hide. It wasn't only that he, a leo, could never have passed unnoticed in the streets, certainly not coatless, and with an arm swollen, useless, broken possibly; not only that he knew nothing of the city. He had gone out into the streets still deafened by the blast, dazed by it; the street was dense with choking smoke. He began to hear people shouting, coming closer. Then the wail of sirens. And he wanted only and desperately silence, darkness, safety. The cellar had been nearest. He tore the sleeve of his shirt with his teeth, so that the arm could swell as it liked; he tried not to groan when it struck something and the pain flooded him hotly. He sat all day unmoving, wedged into a corner facing the door, the pain and shock ebbing like a sea that could still summon now and again a great wave to rush up the shore of his consciousness and make him cry out.

Only when evening began to withdraw even the gray light that crept into the cellar did he begin to think again.

He was free. Or at least not jailed. He didn't bother to marvel at that, just as he hadn't marveled at the fact of being taken. He didn't know why the fox had betrayed them—and he was sure that was how it had come about, no one else knew that he was within the Preserve, no one else knew what he had done up north—but he could imagine one motive at least for Reynard: his own skin. It didn't matter, not now, though when Reynard was before him again it would. Now what mattered was that he extract himself somehow from the city.

There was a river, he knew, west of here, and the only way out of the city was across that river. He didn't know which way the river lay; in any ordinary place he would have known west from east instantly, but the closed van they had brought him in, the blast, and the tangle of streets had distorted that sense. And if he knew how to find the river, he didn't know how to cross it, or if it could be crossed. And anyway, outside, the cruisers ran up and down the avenues and across the streets, making neat parallelograms around him endlessly: no path he knew how to find existed out there.

After nightfall, he began to hear the sounds of the reprisal against whoever it was that had bombed the station: the chug of tanks, the insistent, affectless voices of bullhorns. Guns. The sounds came nearer, as though bearing down on him. He drew the gun he had taken from a dead policeman; he waited. He felt nothing like fear, could not; but the steady rage he felt was its cognate. He had no reason to let them take him again.

When the dog growled at him, he snarled back instantly, silencing it. The dog could be theirs, sent to smell him out. But this dog reeked of fear and hurt, and anyway it wouldn't have occurred to Painter to shoot a dog. He put down the gun. As long as the dog made no noise—and if he was hurt and hiding, like Painter, he wouldn't—Painter would ignore him.

Sweets had thought at first: a man with a cat. But it was one smell, not two; and not a man's smell, only like it. He was big, he was hurt, he was in that corner there, but he didn't belong here—that is, this wasn't *his,* this cellar. Sweets knew all that instantly, even before his eyes grew accustomed to the place and he could see, by the gray streetlight that came through a high small window, the man—his eyes said "man" but he couldn't believe them—squatting upright in the corner there. Sweets retreated, three-legged, neck bristling, to a corner opposite him. He tried to lower his hurt leg, but when he put weight on it, pain seized him. He tried to lie, but the pain wouldn't allow it. He circled, whimpering, trying to lick the wound, bite the pain.

The small window lit whitely as a grinding noise of engines came close. Sweets backed away, baring teeth, and began to growl, helpless not to, answering the growl of the engines.

Men, he said, *men.*

No, the other said. *We're safe. Rest.*

The growl that had taken hold of Sweets descanted into a whimper. He would rest. The light faded from the window and the noise proceeded away. Rest . . . Sweets's ears pricked and his mind leapt to attention. The other . . .

The other still sat immobile in the corner. The gun hanging loosely in his hand glinted. His eyes, like a dog's, caught the light when he moved his head, and flared. Who is it?

Who are you? Sweets said.

Only another master of yours, the other said.

Sweets said: *No man is my master anymore.*

Long before you followed men, the leo said, *you followed me.*

(But not "said": not even Painter, who could speak, would have told himself he had been spoken to. Both felt only momentary surprise at this communication, which had the wordless and instant clarity of a handshake or a blow struck in anger.)

I'm hurt and alone, Sweets said.

Not alone. It's safe here now. Rest.

Sweets still stared at him with all his senses, his frightened and desperate consciousness trying to sort out some command for him to follow from the welter of fears, angers, hopes that sped from his nose along his spine and to the tips of his ears. The smell of the leo said, Keep away from me and fear me always. But he had been commanded by him to rest and be safe. His hurt leg said, Stop, wait, gather strength. The rivulets of feeling began, then, to flow together to a stream, and the substance of the stream was a command: Surrender.

Making as much obeisance as he could with three legs, he came by inches toward the leo; he made small puppy noises. The leo made no response. Sweets felt this indifference as a huge grace descending on him: there would be no contention between them, not as long as Sweets took him for master. Tentatively, nostrils wide, ready to move away if he was repulsed, he licked the big hand on the leo's knee, tasting him, learning a little more of the nature of him, a study that would now absorb most of his life, though he hadn't seen that yet. Unrepulsed, he crept carefully, by stages, into the hollow between Painter's legs, and curled himself carefully there, still ready to back off at the slightest sign. He received no sign. He found a way to lie down without further hurting his leg. He began to shiver violently. The leo put a hand on him and he ceased, the last of the shiver fleeing from the tip of his tail, which patted twice, three times against Painter's foot. For a time his ears still pricked and pointed, his nostrils dilated. Then, his head pressed against the hard cords of Painter's thigh and his nose filled with the huge, unnameable odor of him, Sweets slept.

Painter slept.

The sounds of a house-to-house search coming closer to where they hid woke them just before dawn.

Nowhere safe then, Painter said.

Only the park, Sweets said. *We'll go there.*

(It wouldn't happen often between them, this communication, because it wasn't something they willed as much as a kind of spark leaping between them when a charge of emotion or thought or need had risen high enough. It was enough, though, to keep the lion-man and the once-dog always subtly allied, of one mind. A gift, Painter thought when he later thought about it, of our alteration at men's hands; a gift they had never known about and which, if they could, they would probably try to take back.)

They went out into a thin dawn fog. Sweets, quick and afraid, still limping, stopped whenever he found himself outside the leo's halo of odor, paced nervously, and only started off again when he was sure the other followed. He lost the way for a time, then found traces of the pack, markings, which were to him like a man's hearing the buzz and murmur of distant conversation: he followed, and it grew stronger, and then the stone gateposts coalesced out of the fog. Between them a black shape, agitated, called out to him, unwilling to leave the grounds but pacing madly back and forth: Duke! Sweets yipped for joy and ran with him, not feeling the pain in his leg, snapping at Duke, sniffing him gladly, and stopping to be sniffed from head to toe himself and thus tell of his adventures.

Duke wouldn't come near the leo; he stood dancing on the lip of the hill while Sweets and Painter went slipping down the wet rotten leaves and beneath the defaced baroque bridge and through the dank culvert into the safety—the best safety Sweets knew—of their most secret den, where no man had ever been, where his wild ones by Blondie had been born and where she had tried, dying, to go.

Yours now, he said, and the great animal he had found fell gratefully into the rank detritus of the den, clutching his hurt arm and feeling unaccountably safe:

Winter had begun. Sweets knew it, and Painter. The others only suffered it.

One by one they had come to accept Painter as of the pack, because Sweets had. At night they gathered around him in the shelter of the den, which was in fact the collapsed ruins of a rustic gazebo where once old men had gathered to play cards and checkers and talk about how bad the world had grown. There was even a sign, lost somewhere in the brake of creeper and brush, which restricted the place to senior citizens. The pillars that supported it had failed like old men's legs, and its vaulted roof now lay canted on the ground, making a low cave. The pack lay within it in a heap, making a blanket of themselves. Painter, a huge mass in the middle of them, slept when they did, and rose when they rose.

He and Sweets provided for the pack. Painter had strengths they didn't have, and Sweets could hunt and scavenge as well as any of them, but he could think as well. So it was they two who were the raiders. They two executed the zoo robbery, which yielded them several gristly pounds of horsemeat intended for the few aged cats, senile with boredom, still cared for in the park cages. They two made the expeditions that began, paragraph by paragraph, to grow in the city newssheets: Painter was the "big, burly man" who had stolen two legs of beef from a restaurant supplier while the supplier had been held at bay by a maddened dog, and who had then loped off into the blowing snow with the legs over his shoulders, about a hundred and a half pounds of meat and bone; if the supplier hadn't seen it done, he wouldn't have believed it.

If there had been more of a man's soul in either Sweets or Painter they would have seen the partnership they had entered on as astonishing, the adventures they had as tales at once thrilling and poignant; they would have remembered the face of the tall woman whom Painter gently divested of an enormous rabbit-fur coat, which he then wore always, the coat growing daily fouler. They would have dwelt on the moment when Painter, in the zoo, stood face to face with a lion, and looked at him, and the lion opened his lips to show teeth, uncertain why he was being looked at but recognizing a smell he knew he should respond to, and Painter's lip curled in a kind of echo of the lion's. They remembered none of this; or if they did, it was in a way that men would never be able to perceive. When much later Meric Landseer would try to tell Painter's story, he wouldn't be able to discover much about this part of it; Painter had already discarded most of it. He survived. That's what he could do; that was what he bent his skills to.

They did, though, come increasingly to understand each other. Painter knew he had to find a path that led safely out of the city; he knew it was impossible for him to live in the now-naked park for long without being seen, and taken. He didn't know that a full search hadn't been begun only because the old building where he had been prisoner, weakened by the blast, had fallen in on itself, and, since no one seemed capable of an official decision to dig it out, he had been assumed buried beneath a ton of moldered brick and wallpapered plaster. He knew that Sweets, like him, wanted to escape the park; Sweets knew the pack only lived here on men's sufferance and men's neglect, and that they would eventually be hunted down and shot or imprisoned or taken away in vans, if they didn't starve first. So it grew between them that when Painter left, the pack would follow him. Sweets laid down before Painter the burden of leadership, gratefully, and his heart with it. He had no idea what the freedom was that Painter promised, and didn't try to envision it. Once he had taken the leo for master, all questions were for Sweets forever answered.

It was really all he had ever wanted.

The tunnel wasn't far north of the meat-packing houses the pack had used to haunt in the early morning, snatching scraps and suet from the discard bins, till the men armed with long stinging batons came out to chase them away. Since the time one of the pack had been cornered there by men and beaten and stung to death by those sticks, they had avoided the places. But Sweets remembered the tunnel. It was a dark, open mouth closed with barricades; above it, orange lights went on and off in sequence. The city streets swept down to it from several directions between stone bulwarks and then into its maw. Sweets had never speculated about where it led or why, though once he had seen a policeman mounted on a bike go in and not come out again.

By the time winter had grown old and filthy in the city, Painter had settled on the tunnel, of all the exits Sweets and he had investigated.

His and Sweets's breath rose whitely on the pale predawn air. Painter looked down into the tunnel from the shelter of the bulwark's lip. A broken chain of dim yellow lights went away down its center, but they lit nothing. Painter knew no more than Sweets what was in there, but he supposed it led to the Northern Autonomy; it was anyway the passage west, to the wild lands, and that was all the freedom he needed, just now, to imagine.

Why were there no guards, as there were at the bridges? Maybe there were, at the other end. Or maybe it was one of those ancient duties that had come to be neglected, left up to signs and fierce threats: DO NOT ENTER. NO THRU TRAFFIC. VIOLATORS SUBJECT TO ARREST DETENTION RELOCATION. PROVISIONAL REGIONAL GOVT. It's not in a leo's nature to speculate about threats, dangers, punishment for ventures. He had tried to work out what would happen once they were all inside, but nothing came. So he only waited for the pack to gather.

They had come downtown through the night in their way, separately, yet never disattached from another's odors and presence; they stopped to mark their way, stopped to investigate smells, food smells, rat smells, human smells. They circled downtown in a three-block quadrille. Sweets had stayed close to Painter in the vanguard, nervous over the direct, unhurried, unconcealed way he took but unwilling to be far from him. Now as the light grew he paced nervously, marked the place again, and kept his nose high for news of the others. In ones and twos and threes they assembled, all nervous at being so far from the smells of home as day broke; Duke especially was excited, his one proud ear swiveling for sounds.

Painter waited till he felt no further reluctance in Sweets to go (he'd never counted the pack or learned them all; only Sweets knew if they were all present) and then went down onto the tunnel approach, walking steadily through the yellow slush. The pack swarmed down behind him, staying close together now, not liking the tunnel but preferring its darkness to the exposed approach. Painter broke a place in the rotted wooden barricades; some of the pack had already slithered under, some clambered over. They were inside, moving quickly along the pale tiled wall. The clicking of the dogs' nails and the steady sound of Painter's boots were distinct, loud, intrusive in the silence.

The tunnel was longer than Painter had expected. It took wide, sinuous turns, as though they walked through the interior of a vast snake; the yellow lights glinted fitfully on the undersides of its scales. He thought they must be nearing the end when they had only passed the halfway mark, and he didn't know that at that mark—a dim white line at the river's center—their passage touched off a sensor connected to a police shack outside the far end of the tunnel.

Sweets ran on ahead, knowing he should around some turning see the daylight at the other end, wanting to be able to take Painter to it, to hurry him to it; but at the same time he wanted to be next to him. There was the pack also; impossible to keep them from lingering, from sounding when they passed through dark stretches where the light had failed. The best spur he could give them was to run on ahead and force them to follow; and it was when he had raced a distance ahead that he first heard the bike approaching them down the tunnel.

He stood stock still, fur standing, ears back. By the time the others had caught up with him the sound was loud. *No, keep on,* Painter said, and went on himself, drawing Sweets after him and the pack after Sweets, Now the noise was filling up the silence. Duke passed by Sweets, trembling, his face set, his odor loud and violent. The racket filled up every ear as they came to a turning; Sweets could hear nothing but it, and Painter's command to go on.

Around the turn the noise opened fanwise unbearably, and the black bike and its helmeted rider were bearing down on them. Whatever he had expected to find that had broken his sensor, it wasn't this; he had come up on them too fast; he backed off, braked, his engine broke into backfiring, and he skidded toward the animals. A black Doberman was flying through the air at him.

Duke, maddened by the noise, had attacked. He should have fled; he didn't know how. He only knew how to kill what attacked him. The noise attacked him and he leapt furiously to kill it. He struck with his mouth open as the bike twisted away like an animal in panic. Duke, the bike, and the man went down and spun in whipping circles sidewise violently into the wall. The noise was dead.

Go on, Painter said, beginning to run. *Run now, don't stop.* Sweets ran, blind fury behind his eyes; he didn't know how many of the others followed him, didn't care, didn't remember any longer where he ran, or why. He only knew that as he ran away a part of his being was left, caught, torn away, snared on the wreck of the bike and the broken body of Duke, brave Duke, mad Duke.

A half circle of light showed far off.

One after another, they pelted out of the tunnel, panicky; Heidi the poodle and Spike the wolfhound and Randy and the wild ones. All of them at last: leaping out, racing back within, running on away, and returning: all of them but Duke.

Painter came out, his broad chest heaving, the gun in his hand. His head snapped from side to side, looking for threats. There were none.

Sweets rushed to him, whimpering, lost now in sudden grief, entangling himself in Painter's legs, wanting Painter to somehow absorb him, solve his pain and anger. *All but Duke,* he said. *All but Duke.* But Painter only shrieked once in impatience and kicked him from underfoot; then he started away down the empty avenue. *Get on,* he said. *Quick, away from here. Follow.* And Sweets knew that all he could do was follow, that this was all the answer he would ever have for any fear, any grief: *follow.* It would do.

They had gone on for some time before Sweets began to see the place that Painter had led them into.

Years before, during the wars, this band of city had been cleared, a buffer zone between the fractious island city and the Northern Autonomy. Even then, there had not been many people to evacuate; it had been for a long time a failure as a city. Now it was as deserted and hollowed as if it had been under the sea. The streets ran in the old rectangles around carious buildings, but the only human faces were those smilers, blinded with rust or torn and flapping, pictured in huge ads for products mostly no longer made.

Sweets could not have read, and Painter didn't see, the new signs that announced that the Northern Autonomy was now a Federal protectorate, occupied by Federal troops, requiring Federal passports. All they both knew, with increasing certainty, was that they hadn't escaped the city. It poured on past them as they walked, identical block after block. The sky had grown larger, the buildings lower; but it was still only dead city. When in the silence Painter began to hear, overhead, the quick insistent ticking, which seemed to have been pursuing him for years, he wasn't surprised. He didn't look up or run for cover, though Sweets pricked up his ears and looked up at Painter, ready at any moment to run, to hide. Painter walked on. The copter hovered, watching, and retreated.

From the copter the officer radioed in what he saw: a big man, maybe not a man, walking with some purpose through the streets, heading due north. "A lot of dogs around."

"Dogs, over?"

"Dogs. Lots of them. Over . . ."

Painter reached an impassable valley: the empty cut of a sunken expressway. He turned northwest, walking along the edge of the expressway embankment. Far off as the road ran, but ahead, visible, the horizon could be seen, the true horizon, earth's, a bristle of leafless trees, soft rise of a brown hill, pale sun staining yellow a cape of winter clouds.

There, Painter said. *The freedom I promised you. Go now.*

Not without you.

Yes. Without me.

There were engines coming closer, coming through the maze of stone toward them. It must be toward them: they were the only living things here. The rest of the pack had fled along the intersecting streets. High above, the copter looked down, watching them flee away, watching the big one in the fur coat and the dog who stayed beside him walk on. The copter could see where they would intersect with the cruisers: at the cut there, steep as a chute, that led down onto the expressway. He watched them come together.

The cruisers climbed the chute toward Painter and Sweets. They stopped, tires shrieking. Men popped out of them, shouting, armed. Painter stopped walking. *Go now,* he said. *Go where I told you.*

Sweets, torn in two, wanting only to die at Painter's side, yet overwhelmed by Painter's command to go, stood, riveted. The rest of the pack had fled. His mind, stretched almost to breaking, insisted that to follow his master now he must flee, must do what he could not. *Must.*

Painter started down the cut toward the waiting men. Why had he thought there was any escape from them, anywhere to run where they were not? He tossed away the gun, which clattered on the stone and spun for a moment like a top. He had never escaped; only, for a time, escaped notice.

Sweets watched Painter raise his arms gently as he walked toward the men. Then, before he could see them touch him, before they slew him with their touch, he turned and ran. He bounded north, fast, forcing his legs to stretch, to betray: *betray betray betray* his feet said as they struck the hard, endless stone of the city street.

6

Vox clamantis in deserto

On Mondays Loren came in to meet the packet plane that flew in once a week with supplies and mail to a small town ten miles or so from his cabin. To get into town, he had to canoe from his river-island observation station, where he spent most of the week, downriver to his cabin. From there he went on muleback to town. He rarely got back to the cabin before midnight; the next morning he would start out before dawn, and canoe back upriver to the island. Then, as though the whole of this journey had set him vibrating on a wrong note, he would have to spend most of that day untuning himself so that he could once again turn all his attention to the flock of Canada geese he had under observation. If he brought whiskey back from town to the cabin, he would struggle with himself to leave it in the cabin, having sometimes to go so far as to pour it out, or what was left of it. He kept himself from ever bringing any to the island; but this struggle made his first day's work at the island that much harder.

There weren't, every week, enough reasons for him to make the journey into town, as far as supplies or necessities went. Yet he made it. He tried hard to stock up on things, to deprive himself of logical reasons for the trip; yet when he couldn't stock up, when some supply was short that week in town and he saw that he would have no choice but to return, he felt a guilty relief. And even when he had utterly subjugated all these tricks, and had no reason to come in that even self-deception would buy, he came in anyway. Always. Because there was one thing he couldn't stock up on, and that was mail. Each week, that was new; each week it bore the same promise, and like the stupid chickens he had experimented with in school, each time there was no mail, he responded more fiercely the next time.

"No mail" meant no letter from Sten. He got enough other things. Dross. Newspapers he soon became unable to read with any understanding. Letters from other scientists he corresponded with about technical matters, about the geese. They weren't what brought him to town. Nor was it the whiskey either, really. The whiskey more or less resulted from the mail or the lack of it; or, what brought him into town for the mail brought him later to the whiskey. It all came to the same impulse. A syndrome, he knew he had to call it; yet it felt more like a small, circumscribed suburb of hell.

Even Loren Casaubon, who had dissected many animals, from a nematode worm to a macaque monkey—which began to decay loathsomely in the midst of his investigations, insufficiently pickled—even he located the seat of his fiercest and most imperative emotions in his heart. He knew better, but that's where he felt them. And it seemed, over the last months, that his heart had suffered physical strain from the vast charge of emotion it continuously carried: it felt great, heavy, painful.

That Monday the packet was late. Loren had a not-quite-necessary reshoeing done on the mule, watching the smith work gracelessly and hastily and wondering if these old skills that had once meant so much to the world, and seemed to be becoming just as necessary again, would ever be done as well as they once had been. He picked up a box of raisins and a dozen pencils. He went down to the muddy end of the street, to the rusting steel pier, and waited. He had been born patient, and his patience had undergone training and a careful fine-tuning in his work. He could remember, as a kid, waiting hours for a dormant snail to put out its head or a hunting fox to grow accustomed to his stationary, downwind presence and reveal himself. And he used those skills now to await, and not attempt to hasten, the guttural far-off sound, the clumsy bird.

It appeared from the wrong direction, made maneuvers around the

skyey surface of the lake. Its ugly voice grew louder, and it settled itself
down with a racing of engines and a speeding and slowing of props that
reminded him of the careful wing-strategies of his landing geese. It must
be, he thought, as its pontoons unsteadily gripped the water's stirred
surface, the oldest plane in the world.

When the plane had been tied up, a single passenger got out. He
hardly needed to stoop, so short he was. Leaning on a stick, he made his
way down the gangway to the pier; sun and waterlight glinted from his
spectacles. When he saw Loren he came toward him in his odd, mincing
gait. Loren noticed that he limped now as well; he made the process of
walking look effortful and improbable.

"Mr. Casaubon." He removed the spectacles and pocketed them.
"We've met. Briefly."

Loren nodded guardedly. His small, week-divided world was shaken
by this creature's appearance. The beaten paths he had walked for
months were about to be diverted. He felt unaccountably afraid. "What
are you doing here?" He hadn't intended to sound hostile, but did; Reynard took no notice.

"In the first place, to deliver this." He took a travel-creased envelope
from within his cape and held it toward Loren. Loren recognized, at once,
the angular script; he had after all helped to shape it. Strange, he thought,
how terrific is the effect of a fragment of him, outside myself, a genuine
thing of his in the real world; how different than I imagine. This sense
was the calm, self-observant eye of a storm of feeling. He took the letter
from the strange, rufous fingers and put it away.

"And," Reynard said, "I'd like to talk to you. Is there a place?"

"You've seen Sten." The name caught in his throat and for a horrible
moment he thought it might not come out. He had no idea how much
the fox knew. He felt naked, as though even then telling all; as though his
racing pulse were being taken.

"Oh yes, I've seen Sten," Reynard said. "I don't know what he's written you, but I know he wants to see you. He sent me to bring you."

Loren hadn't risen, not certain his legs would hold him; still, within,
that calm eye observed, astonished at the power of a letter, a name, that
name in another's mouth, to cause havoc in the very tissues and muscles
of him.

"There's a bar up the street," he said. "The Yukon. Not the New
Yukon. A back room. Go on up there. I'll be along."

He watched Reynard stick his way up the street. Then he turned away and sat looking out across the water as though he still waited for something.

After Gregorius had been murdered, the three of them—Sten, Mika, and Loren—began gradually to move into the big house. They took it over by degrees as Gregorius's spirit seemed to leave it; the kitchen first, where they ate, where the cook stuffed Sten and Mika out of pity for their orphanhood (though what Mika felt was not grief but only the removal of something, something that had been a permanent blockage at the periphery of vision, a hobble on the spirit; she had hardly known Gregorius, and liked him less). Next they moved into the living quarters, spreading out from their own nursery wing like advancing Mongols into the lusher apartments. The movement was noticed and disapproved of by the maids and housekeepers, for as long as they remained; but Nashe, utterly preoccupied with her own preservation and the prevention of anarchy, hardly noticed them at all. Now and then they would see her, hurrying from conference to conference, drawn with overwork; sometimes she stopped to speak.

The government was finally withdrawn altogether from the house and moved back to the capital. Nashe hadn't the personal magnetism to rule from seclusion, as Gregorius had done; and she didn't have Reynard for a go-between. She knew also that she had to dissociate herself from Gregorius; the memory of a martyr—even if most people weren't sure just what he had been martyred for, there were reasons enough to choose from—could only burden her. And Sten Gregorius must not figure in her story at all. At all. A small number of men in Blue continued to patrol the grounds; the children saw them now and again, looking bored and left over. The house belonged to the three of them.

Loren continued to be paid, and continued to teach, though he became less tutor than father, or brother—something else, anyway, inexorably. There had been a brief meeting with Nashe in which the children's future was discussed, but Nashe had not had her mind on it, and it ended inconclusively. Loren felt unaccountably relieved. Things would go on as they had.

There was a sense in which, of course, Sten at least was not an inheritor but a prisoner. He knew that, though he told no one what he knew. Except when this knowledge bore down on him, paralyzingly heavy, he was happy: the two people in the world he loved most, and who loved him unreservedly, were with him constantly. There were no rules to obey except his own, and Loren's, which came to the same thing. Sten knew that, with his father dead and Nashe departed, Loren drew all his power from the children's consent. But Loren's rules were the rules of a wise love, the only Sten had ever known, to be haggled over, protested sometimes, but never resented. He wondered sometimes, times when he felt at once most strong and most horribly alone, when it would happen that he would overthrow Loren. *Never!* his heart said, as loud as it could manage to.

Still there were lessons, and riding; less riding when winter began to close down fully and snow piled up in the stony pastures and ravines. Loren spent a long time trying to repair an ancient motor-sled left in a garage by the mansion's previous inhabitants.

"No go," he said at last. "I'll call somebody in the capital. They can't refuse you a couple of motorsleds. . . ."

"No," Sten said. "Let's just snowshoe. And ski. We don't need them."

"They really more or less owe it to you."

"No. It's all right."

Later that month four new sleds arrived as a gift from a manufacturer; arrived with a hopeful photographer. Sten warily, ungraciously, accepted the sleds. The photographer was sent away, without Sten's picture, or his endorsement. The sleds were locked in the old garage.

Evenings they usually spent in the dim of the communications room, where deep armchairs deployed themselves around big screens and small monitors. They watched old films and tapes, listened to political harangues, watched the government and the religious channels. It didn't seem to matter. The droning flat persons were so far from them, so unreal, that it only increased their sense of each other. They could laugh together at the fat and the chinless and the odd who propounded to them the nature of things—Mika especially had no patience with rhetoric and a finely honed sense of the ridiculous—and the fat and the chinless and the odd, hugely enlarged or reduced to tininess by the screens, never knew they laughed. They could be extinguished by a touch on a lighted button. The whole world could be. It was a shadow. Only they three were real; especially when the heat failed in fuel shortages and they huddled together in a single thronelike chair, under a blanket.

Nashe was a fairly frequent shadow visitor in the communications room.

"Here's the straight pin," Mika said. Somehow this description of Mika's was hilariously apt, though none of them knew exactly why.

"She's got a hard job," Loren said. "The hardest."

"But look at that *nose.*"

"Let's listen a minute," Sten said, serious. They all knew their fate was, however remotely, connected to this woman's. Sten felt it most. They must, sometimes, listen.

She was being asked a question about the Genesis Preserve. "Whatever crimes may have been committed within its borders are no concern of the Federal government," she said in her dry, tight voice. "Our long-standing agreements with the Mountain give us sole authority—at the Mountain's request—to enter it and deal with criminal activities. . . . No, we have had no such request. . . . No, it doesn't matter that it's a so-called Federal crime, if that phrase has any legal meaning anymore. I can only interpret all of this as an attempt by the Federal and the Union for Social Engineering to gain some quasi-legal foothold within this Autonomy. As Director, I cannot countenance that." She seemed to have to do that—announce her status—fairly frequently. "We know, I think, too much about USE to countenance any such activities." At least, Sten thought, she'll keep USE out. She's got to fight them, take positions against them, because she benefited from their act, or what everybody thinks is their act. She can't make them illegal in the Autonomy, they're too strong for that. But she'll fight. Sten had inherited Loren's loathing of the intense men and women with their plastic briefcases and mechanical voices.

"What happens," Sten asked, "if Nashe can't hold it together?"

"I don't know. Elections?"

Sten laughed, shortly.

"Well," Loren said. "Supposedly the Federal can intervene if there's severe civil disturbance. Whatever that means." His leg ached where Sten lay on it, but he wanted not to move. He wanted never to move. He put a careful left hand, as though only to accommodate his bigness between the two of them, in the hollow between Sten's neck and his hard shoulder. He waited for it to be thrown off, willing it to be thrown off, but it wasn't. He felt, within, another self-made rampart breached; he felt himself sink further into a realm, a darkness, he had only begun to see when the children and he inherited their kingdom; when it was too late to withdraw from its brink.

"What happens to us, then?" Mika said.

"They don't care about us." Sten was quick, dismissive.

Yet later that night the old tape of him as a boy ran by again, on every screen; and the next night too. They watched it unroll. Not even Mika made fun of it. It seemed like a warning, or a summons.

There was an old-fashioned wooden sauna attached to what had been Gregorius's suite in the house. Here too, in the close, wood-odorous heat and dimness, they could hide together from whatever it was that seemed to press on them from the outside. When during the summer they had gone swimming together in the lakelets of the estate, Loren had been careful for their young shame; he'd worn a bathing suit, and so had they, until once on a humid night they'd gone without them and Mika had said that after all they'd only worn them for Loren's sake. After that they always went swimming naked, and later in the sauna too. They enjoyed the freedom of it, and they told each other that it was only sensible really; and forged without admitting it another bond between them.

"You start to feel," Sten said, "that you can't breathe, that the air's too hot to go in." He inhaled deeply.

"You're hyperventilating," Loren said. "You'll get dizzy."

Sten stood up, nearly fell, laughed. "I *am* dizzy. It feels weird."

Mika, feeling utterly molten within, as hot for once as she felt she deserved to be, rested her head against the wooden slatting. Drops of sweat started everywhere on her body and ran tickling along her skin. She watched Loren and Sten. Loren took Sten in a wrestler's hold around the middle and pressed; they were seeing how hyperventilated they could get, how giddy. Their wet feet slapped the floor. In the dim light their skin shone; they grappled and laughed like devils on a day off. At last they collapsed, gasping, weak. "No more, no more," Loren said.

Mika watched them. A man and a boy. She made comparisons. She seemed to be asleep.

"My father said," Sten gasped throatily, "that his father used to take a sauna, and afterward he ran out and rolled around in the snow. Naked."

"*Loco*," Mika said.

"No," Loren said. "That's traditional."

"Wouldn't you catch cold?"

"You don't catch cold," Loren said, "from cold. You know that."

"You want to do it?" Sten said.

"Sure." Loren said it casually, as though he did it often.

"Not me," Mika said. "I'm just starting to get warm at last."

In fact they had to egg each other on for a while, but then they went bursting out into the suite, halloing, through the French doors, and into the sparkling snow. Mika watched, hearing faintly through the glass their shouts—Loren's a deep roar, Sten's high and mad. She rubbed herself slowly with a thick towel. Loren wrestled Sten into a snowbank; she wondered if they were showing off for her. Loren was dark, thick, and woolly. Sten was lean, flaming pink now, and almost hairless; and shivering violently. Mika left the windows and went into the bedroom. She had already turned on her father's electric blanket; she always crawled beneath it after a sauna and slept. She glimpsed herself in one of the many tall mirrors, lean and brown and seeming not quite complete. She looked away, and slipped beneath the sheets.

She dreamed that she was married, in this bed, with her husband, whose features she couldn't make out; she felt an intense excitement, and realized that the mirrors in the room were her father's eyes, left there by him when he died just so he could witness this.

That winter was one of the hardest in living memory. Shortages made it harder: of fuel, of food, of everything. It didn't matter that Nashe and the few loyal ministers she had managed to keep around her blamed the Federal and USE for systematically blocking deliveries, causing delays at borders, issuing ambiguous safe-conducts or withholding them altogether: Nashe and the Directorate were whom the people blamed. There were mass demonstrations, riots. Blood froze on the dirty snow of city streets. USE journals and speakers, systematically and with charts and printouts, endlessly explained each crisis as a failure of human will and nerve, a failure to use human expertise, human reason—to make the world work. People listened. People marched for reason, rioted for reason. Along the borders of the Autonomy, troops—bands of armed men anyway, Federal men—kept watch, waiting. Candy's Mountain, self-sufficient and no hungrier this winter than another, felt, far-off, the pressure of envy.

Gregorius's house, too, felt far-off pressures. However they filled up the shortening days with activity, with hikes and study and snow castles, the days were haunted by the flickering hates and hungers they watched at night, as a day can be haunted by a bad dream you can't quite remember.

Every fine day that wasn't too bitterly cold, Hawk was set out on his high perch on the lawn. There was no way to fly him in this weather, so

he had to be exercised on the lure, which Sten found tiresome and difficult. He went about it doggedly, but if Hawk was fractious or unaccom-
modating, it was a trial for both of them. Loren began to take over the
duty, not letting Sten out of it, but "helping" just to keep him company
and keep him at it; then gradually taking over himself.

"See," Loren said, "now he's roused, twice."

"Yes." Sten tucked his hands into his armpits. The day was gray,
dense with near clouds; wind was rising. It would snow again soon.
Hawk looked around himself at the world, at the humans, in quick, stern
glances. His feathers filled out, his wings and beak opened, he shook
himself down: exactly the motion of a man stretching.

"Three times." It was an old rule of falconry that a hawk that has
roused three times is ready to be flown: Loren's falconry was a pragmatic
blend of old rules, new techniques, life science, observation, and patience.

"Do you want to work him?"

"No."

The skills involved in flying a falcon at lure were in some ways
harder to acquire than hunting skills. A sand-filled leather bag on a line,
with the wings and tail of a bird Hawk had slain last summer tied on
realistically, and a piece of raw steak, had to be switched from side to
side, swung in arcs in front of Hawk till he flew at it, and then twitched
away before he could bind to it. If Hawk bound to the lure, he would sit
to eat, or try to fly off with the lure, and the game would be over, with
Hawk the winner. If Loren swung the lure away too fast, giving him no
chance, Hawk would soon grow bored and angry. If Loren should hit
him with the heavy, flying lure, he'd be confused and perhaps refuse to
play—he might even be hurt.

Loren swung the lure before Hawk, tempting him, until Hawk, his
eyes flicking back and forth with the lure, threw directly into the air and
stooped to it, talons wide. Loren snatched it away and swung it around
his body like a man throwing the hammer; Hawk swooped in a close arc
around him, seeking the lure. Loren watched Hawk's every quick movement, playing with him, keeping him aloft, intent and careful and yet
reveling in his delicate control over this wild, imperious, self-willed being. He swung, Hawk stooped; the lure flew in arcs around Loren, and
Hawk followed, inches from it, braking and maneuvering, only a foot or
two off the ground. Loren laughed and cheered him, all his energies

focused and at work. Hawk didn't laugh, only turned and curved with his long wings and reached out with his cruel feet to strike dead the elusive lure.

Sten watched for a time. Then he turned away and went back into the house.

When Loren, breathless and satisfied, came into the kitchen to get coffee, something hot, some reward, he found Sten with a cold cup in front of him, his chin in his hands.

"You don't, you know," Loren said, "have to be best at everything. That's not required." As soon as he had said it, he regretted it bitterly. It was true, of course, but Loren had said it out of pride, out of success with Hawk, Sten's bird. He wanted to go to Sten and put an arm around him, show him he understood, that he hadn't meant what he said as crowing or triumph, just advice. And yet he had, too. And he knew that if he went to him, Sten would withdraw from him. That blond face, so whole and open and fine, could turn so black, so closed, so hateful. Loren made coffee, his exhilaration leaking away.

That night they turned away from the increasingly desperate government channels to watch "anything else," Mika said; "something not real—" something they could contain within the compass of their dream of three. But the channels were all full of hectoring faces, or were inexplicably blank. Then they turned on a sudden, silent image and were held.

The leo, with his ancient gun under his arm, stood at the flapping tent door. His great head was calm, neither inquisitive nor self-conscious; if he was aware his portrait was being taken he didn't show it. There was in his thick, roughly clothed body and blunt hands a huge repose, in his eyes a steady regard. Was it saintly or kingly he looked, or neither? The deep curl of his brow gave his eyes the easeful ferocity that the same curl gave to Hawk's eyes: pitiless, without cruelty or guile. He only stood unmoving. There was no sound but that peculiar electronic note of solitude and loneliness, the intermittent boom of wind in an unshielded microphone.

"Well," Mika said softly, "he's not real."

"Hush," Sten said. A mild boyish voice was speaking without haste:

"He was captured at the end of the summer by rangers of the Mountain and agents of the Federal government. Since that time he has not been heard of. The pride awaits word of him. They don't speculate about whether he was murdered, as he might well have been, in secret; whether

he's imprisoned; whether he will ever return. For leos, there is no specu-
lation, no fretting, no worry: it's not in their nature. They only wait."

Other images succeeded that lost king: the females around small
fires, in billowing coats, their lamplike eyes infinitely expressive above
their veiled mouths.

"God, look at their wrists," Mika said. "Like my legs."

The young played together, young blond ogres, unchildish, but with
children's mad energy: cuffing and wrestling and biting with intent purpose, as though training for some desperate guerrilla combat. The females
watched them without seeming to. Whenever a child came to a female,
leaping onto her back or into her broad lap, he was suffered patiently;
once they saw a female throw her great leg onto her child, pinning it
down; the child wriggled happily, unable to free himself, while the female went on boiling something in a battered pot over the fire, moving
with careful, wasteless gestures. No one spoke.

"Why don't they say anything?" Mika said.

"It's only humans who talk all the time," Loren said. "Just to hear
talk. Maybe the leos don't need to. Maybe they didn't inherit that."

"They look cold."

"Do you mean cold, emotionless?"

"No. They look like they're *cold*."

And as though he knew that his watchers would have just then come
to see that, the mild voice began again. "Like gypsies," he said, "like all
nomads, the leos, instead of adapting their environment, adapt to it. In
winter they go where it's warm. Far south now, other prides have already
made winter quarters. For these, though, there will be no move this
winter. The borders of this Autonomy are closed to them. They are, technically, all of them, fugitives and criminals. Somewhere in these mountains are Federal agents, searching for them; if they find them, they will
be shot on sight. They aren't human. Due process need not be extended
to them. They probably won't be found, but it hardly matters. If they
can't move out of these snow-choked mountains, most of them will starve
before game is again plentiful or huntable. This isn't strange; far from our
eyes, millions of nonhumans starve every winter."

In half-darkness, the pride clustered around the embers of a fire and
the weird orange glow of a cell heater. Some ate, with deliberate slowness, small pieces of something: dried flesh. In their great coats and
plated muscle it was hard to see that any were starving. But there: held

close in the arms of one huge female was a pale, desiccated child—no, it wasn't a child; she appeared a child within the leo's arms, but it was a human woman, still, dark-eyed: unfrightened, but seeming immensely vulnerable among these big beasts.

The image changed. A blond, beardless man, looking out at them, his chapped hands slowly rubbing each other. "We will starve with them," he said, his mild, uninflected voice unchanged in this enormous statement. "They are what is called 'hardy,' which only means they take a long time to die. They have strength; they may survive. We are humans, and not hardy. There's nothing we can do for them. Soon, I suppose, we'll only be a burden to them. I don't think they'll kill us, though I think it's within their right. When we're dead, we will certainly be eaten."

Again they saw the childlike girl within the leo's great protecting arms.

"We made these beasts," the voice said. "Out of our endless ingenuity and pride we created them. It's only a genetic accident that they are better than we are: stronger, simpler, wiser. Maybe that was so with the blue whale too, which we destroyed, and the gorilla. It doesn't matter; for when these beasts are gone, eliminated, like the whale, they won't be a reproach to our littleness and meanness anymore."

The lost king appeared again, with his gun, the same image, the same awesome repose.

"Erase this tape," the voice said gently. "Destroy it. Destroy the evidence. I warn you."

The king remained.

When the tape had run out, the screen flickered emptily. The three humans huddled in their chair together before the meaningless static glow, and said nothing.

(Far off, in the cluttered offices of Genesis Section, Bree Landseer too sat silent, shocked, motionless before a screen; Emma Roth's large arm was around her, but Emma could say nothing, too full of the bitterest shame and most sinful horror she had ever felt. She, she alone, had brought this about; she had opened the doors to the hunters, the killers, the voracious—not the leos, no, but the gunmen in black coats, the spoilers, the Devil. She had delivered Meric and those beasts into the hands of the Devil. She couldn't weep; she only held Bree, unable to offer comfort, knowing that for this sin she could not now ever see the face of God.)

"It's not right," Sten said. "It's not fair. It's not even legal."

"Well," Loren said. "We don't really know the whole story. We didn't even see the whole tape."

Sten walked back and forth across the communications room. The screen's voiceless note had changed to an inscrutable hum, and dim letters said TRANSMISSION DISCONTINUED.

"We could help," Sten said.

"Help how?" Loren said.

"We could call Nashe. Tell her . . ."

"What? Those are Federal agents, he said."

"We could tell her we protest. We could tell everybody. The Fed. I'll call."

"No, you won't."

Sten turned to him, puzzled and angry. "What's wrong with you? Didn't you see them? They'll starve. They'll die."

"In the first place," Loren said, trying to sound reasonable but succeeding only in sounding cold, "we have no idea what the situation is. I've seen that man before. Haven't you? He's been on. He's from Candy's Mountain. He puts out propaganda, I've seen it, about how we should love the earth and how all animals are holy. Maybe this is just propaganda. How, anyway, did they get that tape out from wherever they are? Did you think of that?" In fact it had just occurred to Loren. "If they had the means to do that, don't they have the means to get food in, or get out themselves?"

Sten was silent, not looking at Loren. Beside him in the chair, Mika had drawn up into a ball, the blanket drawn up around her nose. He felt that she shrank from him.

"In the second place, there's nothing we can do. If there are Federal agents on the Preserve, presumably the Mountain let them in. It's their business. And anyway, what do the Feds want with the leos? What do you know about leos, besides what this guy said? Maybe he's wrong. Maybe the Feds are right."

Sten snorted with contempt. Loren knew how remote a chance there was that the Fed was acting disinterestedly. He knew, too, that Sten did have power—not, perhaps, with Nashe, but a vaguer power, a place in people's hearts: stronger maybe because vague. "In the third place . . ." In the third place, Loren felt a dread he couldn't, or chose not to, analyze at the thought of Sten's making himself known to the government, or to anyone; that seemed to make Sten horribly vulnerable. To what? Loren pushed aside the question. The three of them must hide quietly. It was safest. But he couldn't say that. "In the third place, I forbid it. Just take my word. It would lead to trouble if we got involved."

Mika squirmed out from under the blanket and stood hugging herself. Never, never would she learn to bear cold; it would remain always a deep insult, a grievous wrong. Watching the leos around their little fires, she had felt intensely the cold that bit them. "It's horrible."

"He's wrong, too, you know," Loren said softly, "about their being better than we are." The children said nothing, and Loren went on as though arguing against their silence. "It's like dog-lovers who say dogs are better than people, because they're more loyal, or because they can't lie. They do what they have to do. So do humans."

Sten got out of the chair and went to the control panel. He began to punch up channels, idly. Each channel yielded only blank static or a whining sign-off logo.

"I don't mean it's right that they should be starved or hunted," Loren said. Between the three of them a connection had been strained; the children had been deeply scandalized by what they had seen, and he must help them to think rightly about it. There was a proper perspective. "They have a right to life, I mean insofar as anything does. There are no bad guys, you know, not in life as a whole; it's understandable, isn't it, that people might hate and fear the leos, or be confused about them, and . . . Well. It's just difficult." He shut up. What he said wasn't reaching them, and he felt himself trying to draw it back even as he said it; it all sounded lame and wrong after their eyes had looked into the eyes of those beasts, and those crazy martyrs. Smug, wrong-headed martyrs: as wrong as the domineering men who hunted the leos, or the USE criminals who had exiled his hawks. Taking sides was the crime; and guilt and self-effacement, taking on this kind of crazy "responsibility"—that was only the opposite of heedless waste and man-centered greed.

"What's wrong?" Sten said. None of the channels was operating. He stopped nervously switching from one blankness to another, and without looking at Loren, left the room.

Mika still stood hugging herself. She had begun to shiver. "I thought they were monsters," she said. "Like the fox-man."

"They are," Loren said. "Just the same."

She turned on him, eyes fierce, lips tight. He knew he should mollify her, explain himself; but suddenly he too felt rigid and righteous: it was a hard lesson, about men and animals and monsters, life and death; let her figure it out.

Mika, turning on her heel and making her disgust with him obvious, left the room.

So it was only Loren, left sitting rageful and somehow ashamed in the electronic dimness, who saw the drawn face of Nashe appear very late on every channel. She was surrounded by men, some in uniform, all wearing the stolid, self-satisfied faces of bureaucratic victors. Her voice was an exhausted whisper. Her hands shook as she turned the pages of her announcement, and she stumbled over the sentences that had been written for her. She told the Autonomy that its government was hereby dissolved; that because of serious and spreading violence, instability and disorder, the Federal government had been obliged to enter the Autonomy in force to keep the peace. The Autonomy was now a Federal protectorate. Eyes lowered, she said that she had been relieved of all powers and duties; she urged all citizens to obey the caretaker government. She folded her paper then, and thanked them. For what? Loren wondered.

When she was done, fully humiliated, she was led away from the podium and off-screen, with two men at her side, as nearly a prisoner as any thief in custody. A thick-faced man Loren remembered as having been prominent on the screens recently—one of those they had laughed at and extinguished—spoke then, and gave the venerable litany of the *coup d'état:* a new order of peace and safety, public order was being maintained, citizens were to stay in their homes; all those violating a sundown curfew would be arrested, looters shot, the rest of it.

They played the old national anthem then, a scratchy, dim recording as though it were playing to them out of the far past, and the new government stood erect and listened like upright sinners to a sermon. An old film of the Federal flag was shown, the brave banner waving in some long-ago wind. It continued to wave, the only further message there would be that night from the masters, as though they were saying, like a wolf pack, Here is our mark; it is all we need to say; this place is ours, you have been warned, defy it if you dare.

The waves that the packet plane had made in its landing continued to rebound from around the lake shore and slosh gently against the pilings in arcs of coming and going.

Loren saw that the letter began with his own name, but then he rushed along the close-packed lines so fearfully and voraciously that he understood nothing of the rest of it, and had to return, calm himself, and attend to its voice. "I hope you are doing all right where you are. I couldn't get any news for a long time and I wondered what had happened with you." Wondered how, how often, when, with what feelings? "I've heard about what you're doing, and it sounds very interesting, I wish we could talk about it. This is really very hard to write." Loren felt like a stab the pause that must have fallen before Sten wrote that sentence; and then felt well up from the stab a flood of love and pity so that for a moment the words he looked at glittered and swam illegibly. "For a lot of reasons I can't tell you exactly where we are now, but I wanted you to know that I'm all right and Mika is too. I know that's not much to say after so long, but when you're an outlaw and a murderer (that's what I'm called now) you don't write much down.

"I think a lot about what happened and about the fun we had alone in the house and how we were happy together. I wish it hadn't ended. But I did what I thought I had to, and I guess so did you. It's funny, but even though it was me who left, when I think about it it seems like it was you who ran out on me! Anyway I hope we can be friends again. As you will find out, I need all the friends I can get. I need your help. You always helped me, and whatever good I am, I owe to you. I've changed a lot." It was signed "Your good friend Sten."

Beneath his signature he had added another sentence, less like an afterthought than an admission that he had known all along he must make but which had been wrung from him only at the last moment: "I'm very very sorry about Hawk."

For a tense and ominous week after Nashe's fall the three of them waited for the new government to notice them. It would be like the Federal in its mindless thoroughness to attempt something against the heir of Gregorius, but nothing happened. They remained as free within the estate as they had been. People came, not sent by any government, but impelled by some need to gather at a center. They camped outside the walls or loitered in groups beyond the barred gates, looking in. They went away, others came. Still no official change in their status came.

But Sten felt a change. Where before he had felt isolated, hidden, protected even in his redoubt with Loren and Mika, safe from the consequences of his complicity in his father's murder, now he began to feel

imprisoned. The night when he had watched the leos, cut off and surrounded in their mountains, and listened to the pale powerless man admit that he and the girl would die with them, unable to struggle against
it, Sten had felt torn between contempt and longing: he wanted somehow
to help them; he knew he would never, never surrender like that, accede
to powerlessness as that man had; and at the same time he saw that
he too was as chained, as powerless as they were.

Now Nashe had given in, and the same Federal government that
hunted the leos surrounded Sten, strangling him, waiting for him to
starve to death. He felt a suffocating sense of urgency, a feeling that
wouldn't diminish; the more the invisible chains bound him, the harder
he pressed against them.

Even Loren, now, seemed interested only in restraining him. Where
before they had stood in a kind of balance, each, as it were, holding a
hand of Mika's to keep themselves stable, now they had begun to rock
dangerously. Loren issued commands; Sten flouted them. Loren lectured;
Sten was mum. Sten saw, shocked, that Loren was afraid; and not wanting to, he began to press Loren's fear, as though to see if it was really real.

"Are they still out there?" Mika asked.

"Don't acknowledge them," Loren said. "Don't encourage them.
Don't . . ."

Sten turned away from the bulletproof window of his father's office,
where he had been spying with binoculars at two or three silent,
overcoated people who could be seen beyond the gate. "Why is it," he
said to Loren coldly—it was his father's penetrating tone—"that you're
always hovering over me?"

Loren, knowing he couldn't say "Because I love you," said, "Don't do
anything dumb. It's all I meant," and left.

When he was gone, Sten took out the letter again. It had been given
to him by the man who brought provisions to the house, handed to him
without a word as the man left the kitchen. It wasn't addressed. It was
carelessly typed: *If after the manner of men, I have struggled with beasts at
Ephesus, what advantageth it me, if the dead rise not?* Beneath this, which
Mika thought was a quote from the Bible, was a series of numbers and
letters. Sten figured out, after much study, that these were geographical
co-ordinates, elevations, compass directions. Perhaps he wouldn't have
given it that much study, except that carefully, childishly, scrawled at the
bottom was a single letter for a signature: *R.*

"We should ask Loren," Mika said.

Sten only shook his head. Why should Reynard reveal to him the place where the leos were hiding? Because Sten was sure now that this was what it was. The maps kept in his father's office showed him the place Reynard had directed him to: a place in the mountains that bordered the Autonomy on the north, the crest of Genesis Preserve.

"Could it be," Mika said, "that he meant we should help them? Get to them somehow, and help?"

When, in the old schoolhouse, Reynard had given him this house and this safety, even, probably, his life, in exchange for silence, he had told him: be neither predator nor prey. If that was so, he was in growing trouble here, because he was fleeing, like prey, hiding: from the government, from the people out there—from Loren. If now Reynard had directed him to rise, as from the dead, was it for the leos he was to do so? And did he dare anyway? He did, desperately, want Loren's advice and help. But Loren had made himself clear about the leos.

"Would you dare?" he said to Mika. "Would you dare go up into the mountains, bring them food?"

Her black eyes grew round at the thought. "What will we tell Loren?"

"Nothing." Sten felt flooded with a sudden resolve. This would be the unbinding he had been waiting for: he had been called on, and he chose to answer. With Mika, if she dared; alone, if that was how it had to be.

Mika watched him fold the letter carefully, once, again, again, as though he were laying away a secret resolve. Without looking at her, he told her the story of how their father had been killed, and what he had done, and why they had been safe in the house.

"You could stay," he said. "You'd be safe, here, with Loren."

She sat silent a long time. It had begun to snow again, a sleety, quick-falling snow that could be heard striking, like a breath endlessly drawn. She thought of them naked, laughing in snow.

"We could use sleds," she said at last.

That week the telephone lines into the house were cut—perhaps by the snow, perhaps deliberately, they were given no explanation—and Loren began making weekly trips to the nearest town, nearly five miles off, to call their suppliers and to buy newspapers, to see if he could perceive some change in their status, guess what was to become of them. There was no one he trusted whom he could call, no old government official or family lawyer. He knew it was madness to try to hide this way;

it couldn't last. But when he contemplated bringing Sten to official attention, to try to get some judgment made, he shrank from it. Whatever
came of it, he was certain they would somehow take him away, somehow
part them. He couldn't imagine any other conclusion.

Returning from town, he pushed his way through the small knot of
people at the front gate and let himself in at the wicket. When questions
were asked he only smiled and shrugged as though he were idiotic, and
concentrated on passing quickly through the wicket and getting it locked
again, so as not to tempt anyone to follow, and went quickly up the
snow-choked road, away from their voices.

He stopped at the farmhouse and went in. A small cell heater had
been brought down from the house and was kept going here always,
though it barely took the chill from the stone rooms. That was all Hawk
needed.

Hawk was deep in molt. He stood on his screen perch, looking
scruffy and unhappy. Two primaries had fallen since Loren had last
looked in on him—they fell always in pairs, one from each side, so that
Hawk wouldn't be unbalanced in flight—and Loren picked them up and
put them with the others. They could be used to make repairs, if ever
Hawk broke a feather; but chiefly they were saved as a baby's outgrown
shoes are saved.

The day was calm and bright, the sun almost hot. He'd take Hawk up
to the perch on the lawn.

Speaking softly to him, with a single practiced motion he slipped the
hood over Hawk's face and pulled it tight—it was too stiff, it needed
oiling, there was no end to this falconer's job—and then pulled on his
glove. He placed the gloved hand beneath Hawk's train and brushed the
back of his legs gently. Hawk, sensing the higher perch behind him,
instinctively stepped backward, up onto the glove. He bated slightly as
Loren moved his hand to take the leash, and only when Hawk was firmly
settled on his wrist did Loren untie the leash that held him to the perch.
As between thieves, there was honor between falconer and bird only
when everything was checked and no possibility for betrayal—escape—
was allowed.

He walked him in the house for a time, stroking up the feathers on
his throat with his right forefinger till Hawk seemed content, and then
went out into the day, blinking against the glare from the snow, and up
to the perch on the wide lawn. From behind the house, he thought he

heard the faint whistle of the new motorsleds being started. He tied Hawk's leash firmly to the perch with a falconer's one-handed knot, and brushed the perch against the back of his legs so that Hawk would step from his hand up to the perch. He unhooded him. Hawk roused and opened his beak; the inner membranes slid across his dazzled eyes. He looked with a quick motion across the lawn to where three motorsleds in quiet procession were moving beyond a naked hedge.

"What's up?" Loren shouted, pulling off his glove and hurrying toward them. Mika, and Sten, to whose sled the third, piled up with gear wrapped in plastic, was attached, didn't turn or stop. Loren felt a sudden, heart-sickening fear. "Wait!" Damn them, they must hear. . . . He broke through the hedge just as the sleds turned into the snowy fields that stretched north for miles beyond the house. Loren, plowing through the beaten snow, caught Sten's sled before Sten could maneuver his trailer into position to gather speed. He took Sten's arm.

"Where are you going?"

"Leave me alone. We're just going."

Mika had stopped her sled, and looked back now, reserved, proud.

"I said *where*? And what's all this stuff?"

"Food."

"There's enough here for weeks! What the hell . . ."

"It's not for us."

"Who, then?"

"The leos." Sten looked away. He wore snow glasses with only a slit to look through; it made him look alien and cruel. "We're bringing it to the leos. We didn't tell you because you'd only have said no."

"Damn right I would! Are you crazy? You don't even know where they are!"

"I do."

"How?"

"I can't tell you."

"And when will you come back?"

"We won't."

"Get out of that sled, Sten." They had meant to sneak away, without speaking to him, without asking for help. "I said get out."

Sten pulled away from him and began to pull at the sled's stalled engine. Loren, maddened by this betrayal, pulled him bodily out of the sled and threw him away from it so that he stumbled in the snow. "Now listen to me. You're not going anywhere. You'll get this food back where it belongs"—he came up behind Sten and pushed him again—"and get those sleds out of sight before . . . before . . ."

Sten staggered upright in the snow. His glasses had fallen off, but his face was still masked, with something cold and hateful Loren had never seen in it before. It silenced him.

Mika had left her sled and came toward them where they stood facing each other. She looked at Loren, at Sten. Then she came and took Sten's arm.

"All right," Loren said. "All right. Listen. Even if you know where you're going. It's against the law." They made no response. "They're hunted criminals. You will be too."

"I am already," Sten said.

"What's that supposed to mean?"

"You wouldn't have helped, would you?" Mika said. "Even if we'd told you."

"I would have told you what I thought."

"You wouldn't have helped," she said with quiet, bitter contempt.

"No." Even as he said it, Loren knew he had indicted himself before them, hopelessly, completely. "You just don't throw everything up like this. What about the animals? What about Hawk?" He pointed to the bird on his perch, who glanced at them when they moved, then away again.

"You take care of him," Sten said.

"He's not my hawk. You don't leave your hawk to someone else. I've told you that."

"All right." Sten turned and strode through the snow to the perch. Before Loren could see what he was doing, he had drawn a pocketknife and opened it; it glinted in the snowlight.

"No!"

Sten cut Hawk's jesses at the leash. Loren ran toward them, stumbling in the snow.

"You little *shit*!"

Hawk for a moment didn't notice any change, but he disliked all this sudden motion and shouting. He was in a mood to bate—to fly off his perch—though he had learned in a thousand bates that he would only fall, flapping helplessly head downward. Sten had taken off his jacket, and with a sudden shout waved it in Hawk's face. Hawk, with an angry scream, flew upward, stalled, and found himself free; for a moment he thought to return to the perch, but Sten shouted and waved the jacket again, and Hawk rose up in anger and disgust. It felt odd to be free, but it was a good day to fly. He flew.

"Now," Sten said when Loren reached him, "now he's nobody's hawk."

With an immense effort, Loren stemmed a tide of awful despair that was rising in him. "Now," he said, calmly, though his voice shook, "go down to the farm and get the long pole and the net. With the sleds, we might be able to get him after dark. He's gone east to those trees. Sten."

Sten pulled on his jacket and walked past Loren back to the sleds.

"Mika," Loren said.

She stood a moment between them, hugging herself. Then, without looking back to Loren, she went to her sled too.

Loren knew he should go after them. Anything could happen to them. But he only stood and watched them struggle with the sleds, get them aligned and started. Sten gave Mika a quiet command and put his snow glasses on again. He looked back once to Loren, masked, his hands on the sticks of the sled. Then the sleds moved away with a high whisper, dark and purposeful against the snow.

"Yes," Reynard said. "It was I who told Sten where the leos were. It was very clever of him to have worked it out."

"And you had brought out the film, too, that we saw?"

"Yes."

"How did you get to them, find them, without being stopped? And back again?"

Reynard said nothing, only sat opposite Loren at the water-ringed table.

"You made Sten a criminal. Why?"

"I couldn't let the leos die," Reynard said. "You can understand my feelings."

Actually that was impossible. His thin, inexpressive voice could mean what it said, or the opposite, or nothing at all. His feelings were undiscoverable. Loren watched him scratch his whiskery chops with delicate dark fingers; it made a dry-grass sound. Reynard took a black cigarette from a case and lit it. Loren watched, trying to discover, in this peculiarly human gesture of lighting tobacco, inhaling smoke, and expelling it, what in Reynard was human, what not. It couldn't be done. Nothing about the way Reynard used his cigarette was human, yet it was as practiced, casual, natural—as appropriate—as it would be in a man.

"He saved them," Reynard said, "from death. Not only the leos, but two humans as well. Don't you think it was brave of him? The rest of the world does."

From his papers, reaching him usually a week late, Loren had learned of Sten's growing fame; it was apparent even here, far north of the Autonomy. "It was very foolhardy," was all he said.

"He took risks. There was danger. Unnecessary, maybe. Maybe if you'd been there, to help . . . Anyway, he brought it off."

Loren drank. The whiskey seemed to burn his insides, as though they had already been flayed open by his feelings. He couldn't tell the fox that he hated him because the fox had taken Sten from him. It wasn't admissible. It wasn't even true. Sten had gone on his own to do a difficult thing, and had done it. Mika, who loved him, had gone with him. Loren had been afraid, and so he had lost Sten. Was that so, was that the account he must come to believe?

"He had you, didn't he?" Loren said.

"Well. I'm not much good now. I was never—strong, really, and you see I'm lamed now."

"You seem to get around."

"I'm also," Reynard said as though not hearing this, "getting very old. I'm nearly thirty. I never expected a life-span that long. I feel ancient." Smoke curled from his nostrils. "There is a hunt on for me, Mr. Casaubon. There has been for a long time. I've thrown off the scent more than once, but it's growing late for me. I'm going to earth." He smiled—perhaps it was a smile—at this, and the ignored ash of his cigarette fell onto the table. "Sten will need you."

"What is it you wanted from Sten?" Loren asked coldly. He tried to fix Reynard's eyes, but like an animal's they wouldn't hold a stare. "Why did you choose him? What for?"

Reynard put out the cigarette with delicate thoroughness, not appearing to feel challenged. "Did you know," Reynard said, "how much Sten means in the Northern Autonomy? And outside it too?" He moved slowly in his chair; he seemed to be in some pain. "There is a movement—one of the kind that men seem so easily to work up—to make Sten a kind of king."

"King?"

"He'd make a good one, don't you think?" His long face split again in a smile, and closed again. "That he's an outlaw now, and hunted by the Federal, is only appropriate for a young king—a pretender. The Federal has mismanaged their chance in the Autonomy, as it had to. Sten seems to people everywhere to be—an alternative. Somehow. Some kingly how. Strong, and young, and brave—well. If there are kings—kings born—he's one. Don't you agree?"

From the time Loren had opened the *North Star* magazine he had been a subject of Sten's, he knew that. That Sten must one day pick up a heritage that lay all around him he had always known too, though he had tried to ignore it. He felt, momentarily, like Merlin, who had trained up the boy Arthur in secrecy; saw that what he had trained Sten to be was, in fact, king. There wasn't any other job he was suited for.

"It's a fact about kings," Reynard said, "That they must have around them a certain kind of person. Persons who love the king in the king, but know the man in the king. Persons for whom the king will always be king. Always. No matter what. I don't mean toadies, or courtiers. I mean —subjects. True subjects. Without them there are no kings. Of course."

"And you? Are you a king's man?"

"I'm not a man."

Already the northern afternoon was gathering in the light. Loren tried to count out the feelings contending in him, but gave it up. "Where is he now?"

"Between places. Nowhere long." He leaned forward. His voice had grown small and exhausted. "This is a difficulty. He needs a place, a place absolutely secret, a base. Somewhere his adherents could collect. Somewhere to hide—but not a rathole." Again, the long, yellow-toothed smile. "After all, it will be part of a legend someday."

Loren felt poised on the edge of a high place, knowing that swarming up within him were emotions that would eventually make him step over. He drank quickly and slid the empty glass away from him on a spill of liquor. "I know a place," he said. "I think I know a place."

Reynard regarded him, unblinking, without much interest, it seemed, as Loren described the shot tower, where it was, how it could be gotten to; he supposed the food, the cans anyway, and the cell heater would still be there.

"When can you be there?" Reynard said when he had finished.

"Me?" Reynard waited for an answer. "Listen. I'll help Sten, because he's Sten, because . . . I owe it to him. I'll hide him if I can, keep him from harm. But this other stuff." He looked away from Reynard's eyes. "I'm a scientist. I've got a project in hand here." He drew in spilled liquor on the table—no, not that name, he rubbed it away. "I'm not political."

"No." Reynard, unexpectedly, yawned. It was a quick, wide motion like a silent bark; a string of saliva ran from dark palate to long, deep-cloven tongue. "No. No one is, really." He rose, leaning on his stick, and walked up and down the small, smelly barroom—deserted at this hour— as though taking exercise. "Geese, isn't it? Your project." He stopped, leaning heavily on the stick, holding his damaged foot off the ground and turning it tentatively. "Isn't there a game, fox and geese?"

"Yes."

"A grid, or paths . . ."

"The geese try to run past the fox. He catches them where paths join. Each goose he catches has to help him catch others."

"Ah. I'm a—collector of that kind of lore. Naturally."

"My geese," Loren said, "are prey for foxes."

"Yes?"

"And they know it. They teach it—the old ones teach the young. It doesn't seem to be imprinted—untaught goslings wouldn't run from a fox instinctively. The older ones teach them what a fox looks like, by attacking foxes, in a body, and driving them off. The young ones learn to join in. I've seen my flock follow a fox for nearly a mile, honking, threatening. The fox looked very uncomfortable."

"I'll leave you now," Reynard said. If he had heard Loren's story he didn't express it. "The plane will be going. There are still a few things I have to do." He went to the door.

"No rest for the wicked," Loren said.

Reynard had been walking out of the bar without farewell. He turned at the door. "Teach your goslings," he said. "Only be sure you know who is the fox."

When he had gone out into the pall of the afternoon—tiny, old, impossible—Loren went to wake the bartender and have his glass filled again. The letter where it lay in his breast pocket seemed to press painfully against his heart.

Nothing is more soothing to a scientist than the duplication of another scientist's results. When Loren had left the empty brown mansion, he had thought only of a place to lose himself, a far, unpeopled place to hide; but he knew he would have to occupy himself as well, engage all his faculties in a difficult task, if he was to escape—even momentarily—the awful rain he seemed always to be standing in when he thought of Sten and Mika.

They meant what they had said: they didn't come back. He had known they wouldn't. After ten days had passed, and a new fall of snow had covered their traces, he called the Autonomy police and reported them suddenly missing. The police forces were in the process of being reorganized, and after some lengthy interrogations, in which he communicated as little as he could without arousing suspicion, the matter seemed to be dropped, or filed, or forgotten amid larger bureaucratic struggles. He thought once during a police interview (Federal this time) that he was about to be beaten into a confession, a confession of something; he almost wished for it: there was no one else to punish him for what he had done.

What had he done?

He drew his almost-untouched government salary, got a small, reluctant grant from Dr. Small, and went north out of the Autonomy to the breeding grounds of the Canada geese. One of the great ethologists of the last century had made extensive observations of the European greylag goose; his records were famous, and so were his conclusions, about men and animals, instinct, aggression, bonding. He had extended his conclusions to all species of the genus *Anser,* the true goose. The Canada goose isn't *Anser* but *Branta.* It would take months—healing, annealing months alone—to compare the century-old observations of *Anser* behavior with that of *Branta.* The resulting paper would be a small monument, a kind of extrusion out of misery, like an oyster's pearl.

Reading again the old man's stories—for that's what they seemed to be, despite their scientific apparatus, stories of love and death, grief and joy—what Loren felt was not the shocking sense its first readers had, that men are nothing more than beasts, their vaunted freedoms and ideals an illusion—the old, old reaction of the men who first read Darwin—but the opposite. What the stories seemed to say was that beasts are not less than men: less ingenious in expression, less complex in possibility, but as complete; as feeling; as capable of overmastering sorrow, hurt, rage, love.

The center of greylag life is the triumph ceremony, a startlingly beautiful enchainment of ritualized fighting, redirected aggression, a thousand interlocking, self-generating calls and responses. The geese perform this ceremony in pairs, bonded for life; bonded by the dance. The old man had said: the dance does not express their love; the dance is their love. When one of a pair is lost—caught in electric wires, shot, trapped—the other will search ceaselessly for it, calling in the voice a lost gosling calls its mother. Sometimes, after much time, they will bond again, begin again; sometimes never.

Mostly the pairs are male-female, but often they are male-male; in this case there is sometimes a satellite female, lover of one of the males, who will be satisfied to share their love, and can intrude herself sufficiently into their triumphs to be mounted and impregnated. This isn't the only oddity of their bonding: there are whole novels among them of attempted bondings, flawed affairs, losses, rivalries, heartbreaks.

Loren had seen much of this among his geese, though their social life seemed frozen at an earlier, less complex state; their ceremonies were less expressive; their emotions, therefore—from the observer's point of view —were less extensive. He had carefully noted and analyzed ritual behavior, knew his flock well, and had seen them court, raise young, meet threats, in a kind of stable, unexciting village life. Whether beneath the squabbles and satisfactions of daily life a richer current ran—as it does in every village—didn't interest him as a scientist. Unexpressed needs and feelings were either unfelt or unformed; they couldn't be analyzed.

Yet he wanted them to tell him more. Was *Anser* more human than *Branta,* or had the old man's stories been only parables in the end, like Aesop's?

He had told of two males, both at the top of the flock hierarchy, who had bonded, who danced only for each other. The proudest, the strongest, they had no rivals, no outsiders from whom to protect each other; few came near them. Their ceremony—change and change again—became more and more intense; they did it for hours. At last the weight of emotion that the ceremony carried became too great; the aggression that it modeled and ritualized became too intense, having no other outlet. The ritual broke into real, unmediated aggression; the birds bit and beat at each other with strong wings, inflicting real wounds.

The bond was broken. Immediately after, the two birds parted—went to opposite sides of the pond, avoided each other. Never performed for each other again. Once, when by error they encountered each other face to face in the middle of the pond, each immediately turned away, grooming excitedly, bill-shaking, in a state the old man said could only be described as intense embarrassment.

"Could only be described," Loren said aloud to the frosty night, "as intense embarrassment." The mule jogged, Loren swayed drunkenly. *"Intense. Embarrassment."*

How could he see Sten again? If they met, wouldn't there be between them an embarrassment that would make any communication impossible? Seeing him again, having him before his eyes again, had been Loren's obsession for months; but now that he had been invited to it, for real, he could only imagine that he would be full of shame and hurt and embarrassment. Better to let the enormous engine of his love, disengaged from its object, grind and spin on uselessly within him till it finally ran out of fuel or fell to pieces, to silence.

Yet Sten had sent for him. He groaned aloud at the stars. Far down within him he seemed to see—whiskey, only whiskey, he told himself—a possibility he had long discounted, a possibility for happiness after pain.

The next morning, to cleanse himself of shame and hope and the sour humors of the whiskey, he plunged naked up to his neck in the icy river, shouting, trying to shout out all the impurity he felt within; he splashed his face, rubbed his neck, waded onto the shore, and stood shivering fiercely. By an act of will he ceased shivering. There wasn't any weakness, any impatience, any badness in him that he couldn't, by a similar act of will, overcome.

Quieter then, he dressed, slipped the canoe, and started upriver. The river was low and slow; leaves floated on it, fell continuously on it, clogged its tributaries. Dense clouds were pillowed at the horizon, and overhead a high, fast wind, so high it couldn't be felt below, marked the October blue with chalk marks of cloud. Summer was long over here. Last night's frost had been hard.

During that week, his geese were restless, rising up in a body, circling for a time, realighting excited and nervous. It was as though his peaceful village had been swept by a bizarre religious mania. Old quarrels were forgotten. Nest sites were left unguarded. They were aligning themselves, making a flying force. The time had come for their migration. On Monday—the day that he would have gone into town—he awoke before dawn, and had barely time to dress before he saw that this would be the day of their leaving.

Loren had identified the commodore and his lieutenants (they were called that in his notes, though they would not be in his final paper) and noted their strategy meetings and route conferences. Now in the dawn the hair stood on Loren's neck: was it because, over the months, he had become almost one of them that he knew with such certainty that this was the day—had it been communicated to him as it had been to each of them, did his certainty add to the growing mass of their certainty, inciting them to fly?

All that morning he photographed and noted, ill almost with excitement, as they knitted their impulses together. Again and again small groups pounded into the air, circled, alighted, reascended. About noon the commodore and some of the ranking members of his staff, male and female, arose, honking, and sailed off purposefully, making a tentative, ragged V: maneuvers. They didn't return; with his glasses, Loren scanned from the crook of a tall tree, and saw them waiting in a water-meadow somewhat northeast. The rest still honked and argued, getting up nerve. Then the commodore and his staff flew back, sailing low and compellingly over the flock, going due south; and in a body the others were drawn after them, rising in a multiple fan of black and brown wings, attaching themselves.

For as long as he could, Loren followed them with the glasses, watched their V form neatly against the hard blue sky marked with wind. They were wind. They were gone.

Alone again, Loren sat in the crook of the tree. Their wings' thunder and their cries had left a new void of silence. Winter seemed suddenly palpable, as though it walked the land, breathing coldly. He remembered winter.

After Sten and Mika had gone out of sight, he had spent that day searching for Hawk on snowshoes, with lure and net and pole; walked himself to exhaustion through the woods, purposelessly, having no idea where Hawk might go and seeing no trace of him. If he had found a dead bird, if he had seen blood on the snow, he would have gone on, not eating, not sleeping; but he saw nothing. Night was full when he came back to the empty house, almost unable to stand; the pain, though, had been driven almost wholly to his legs and feet, where he could bear it.

Once inside, however, in the warm, lamplit emptiness, it took him again head to toe. He dropped the useless hawking gear. He would find, capture, hold, nothing, no one. He climbed the stairs, almost unable to bend his knees, and went to Sten's room. He didn't turn on the light. He smelled the place, the discarded clothing, the polished leather, the books, Sten. He felt his way to the narrow bed and lay down, pressing his face into the pillow, and wept.

All the wild things fly away from me, he thought now, in the crook of the tree by the empty river. Every wild thing that I love. If they don't know how to fly, I teach them.

Wiping the cold tears from his beard, he climbed down from the tree and stood in the suddenly pointless encampment. Stove, tent, supplies, canoe. Shirt drying on a branch. Camera, recorder, notebooks. He had tried to make a home in the heart of the wild, to be quiet there and hear its voice. But there was no home for him there.

Methodically, patiently, he broke camp. Like the geese, but far more slowly, he would go south. Unlike them, he was free not to; and yet he knew there was nothing else he could do.

7

IN AT THE DEATH

The last truck left Caddie off at an interchange a mile or more from the center of the city. The driver pointed out to her the slim white needle, impossibly tall, just visible beyond the river, and said this was as close as he came to it; so she swung down from the cab and began to walk toward it.

It had been terrifying at first to stand alone beside the vast spread of naked highway, waiting for the trucks. For a year she had rarely been out of the company of the pride, had forgotten, if she'd ever known, how to discount the terror of this inhuman landscape, stone and sounds and vast signs and speed. She wanted to run from it, but there was no one who could do this but she; certainly none of the leos, and Meric was known from the tape in which she had appeared only briefly. So she had stood waiting in a thin rain for the trucks—there was almost no other traffic—holding out her thumb in the venerable gesture. She recoiled when they bore down on her and barreled past, wrapped in thin veils of mist that their tires pressed out from the road's wet surface; but she stayed.

When at last one, with a long declension of gears, slowed and stopped fifty yards down from where she stood, her heart beat fast as she ran to it. She felt for the gun in her belt, under her jacket; she felt her breasts move as she ran.

They were only truck drivers, though, she came quickly to learn, the same she had dealt with every week in Hutt's bar. They talked a lot, but that didn't bother her. Only once did she feel compelled to mention the gun, casually, in passing: a person has to protect herself.

In a way, it was the small talk that was harder to answer: Where are you from? Why are you going to Washington? Who are you?

Looking for a relative. Promise of a job. Come from, well, north. Up there. Because she couldn't tell them that she had come hundreds of miles at the direction of the fox to try, somehow, to free the lion.

The last truck moved off, ascending stately through its gears. She turned up her jacket collar—it was still damp autumn here, not winter, as it was up north, and yet penetrating—and went down into the maze of concrete, trying to keep the white needle in sight.

She was nearing the end of the longest year of her life. It had been distended by loss, by suffering—by death, for it seemed to her that since she had seen she would die, in the mountains, and had accepted that, that she had in fact died; and when the ghostly sleds had appeared, creeping through the blowing snow with supernatural purpose and a faint wailing, it had taken her a time to understand that they had not come to signal the death she awaited but to thrust her back into life.

And then she had killed a man, an eternity later, when they had at last come down out of the mountains. A Federal man, one of the black coats, who still slogged through mud implacably toward her in dreams. That was a long moment, a year in itself. Yet it took her less time than it had taken Painter to kill the man who had come on them in the cabin in the woods, back at the beginning of her life.

Moving northwest with the widowed pride, always deeper into wilderness and solitude, always waiting for something, some word of Painter, some word from the fox, she felt her time expand vastly. Grief, waiting, solitude: if you want to live forever, she thought, choose those. In a way Caddie perceived but couldn't express, the pride did live forever, the females and the children: they lived within each moment forever, till the next moment. They took the same joy in the sunrise, hunted and played and ate with the same single-minded purpose, as they had when Painter had been with them; and their grief, when they felt it, was limitless, with no admixture of hope or expectation. She had explained to

Meric: leos aren't like Painter, not most of them. Painter has been wounded into consciousness, his life is—a little bit—open to us, something shines through his being which is like what shines through ours, but the females and the children are dark. You'll never learn their story because they have no story. If you want to go among them, you have to give up your own story: be dark like they are.

Caddie by now knew how to do that, to an extent, but Meric would never learn it, and in any case it wasn't allowed to either of them then, because with Painter gone they two must act as the bridge between the pride and the human world it moved through and lived in. They had to spend Reynard's money in the towns, they had to learn the safe border crossings, they had constantly to *think*. Caddie forced herself to struggle against the wisdom of the females, fight it with human cunning for their sakes, forced herself to believe that only by keeping her head above the dark water could she help save them, when all she wanted to do was give up the burden of cunning and sink down amid their unknowing forever. No: only to Painter could she resign that burden.

Then at one of the prearranged mail drops had come the summons from the fox. Suspicious, anxious, unable to believe that Reynard could really know all he pretended to know, she had nevertheless left Meric to shepherd the pride and followed her instructions. It was all she could do.

She soon lost sight of the monument. The littered, shabby streets urged her on, striking purposefully through the buildings but leading nowhere except to further streets. Alarmed by acrid odors that had come to mean danger to her, she began to see why Painter had smoked tobacco in towns. She walked aimlessly among crowds that seemed bent on pressing business, hurrying people with eyes intent, lugging heavy bags that perhaps they were carrying somewhere or perhaps had stolen from somewhere they were eager to get away from. Caddie thrust her hands into her pockets and walked on, unable to catch anyone's eye or hold his attention long enough to ask a question.

At a convergence of streets, stores were lit up, and the sallow globes of a few unbroken street lights were on. Lines of people stood patiently waiting to be let in one at a time to buy—what? Caddie wondered. In one barred store window, televisions: ranks of them, all showing the same image differently distorted, a man's head and shoulders, his mouth moving silently. Then, in an instant, they all changed, to show a street like this one. A black three-wheeled car. Two men in dark overcoats got out, looking wary and tired. Between them a third, a tiny limping creature, in a hat whose brim hid him from the camera, but whose manner revealed him to Caddie. She could almost smell him.

She went to the door of the store. A burly black guard, armed, stood in the doorway, looking bored. Caddie slipped past him, expecting to be seized, but the guard seemed not to care.

". . . has not revealed the identity of its witness, though he is believed to have been a high official in the Gregorius government. USE says facts revealed in the hearings will shed dramatic new light on the assassination of two years ago. . . ." He spoke with such a clipped, false intonation that she could barely understand him.

Someone stepped in front of her then; and another, coatless—he must work here, she thought—came to stand next to her. "This ain't a the-ayter," he said.

"What?"

The person in front of her stepped away. On the screen was an image that made her heart leap. Painter stood in front of his tent, his old shotgun in his hands. He looked at her—or at Meric, rather—calm, puzzled, faintly amused.

The store employee put his hand on Caddie's shoulder. "You ain't buyin'," he said. "Go home and watch it."

She pulled away from him, desperate to hear. The guard at the door glanced over, and proceeded toward her ponderously.

She heard the clipped, brisk voice say: "Government channels are silent." And Painter was replaced by a smiling woman standing next to a television, which showed the same woman and the same television, which showed her again.

The monument she found at last stood at the end of an oblong pool, empty now and a receptacle for the litter of those camped on the sward of brown grass around it. For the height of a man the monument was marked with slogans, most of them so covered with the other slogans as to be unreadable. It rose above these, though, to a chaste height. When Caddie looked up at it it seemed to be in the act of tumbling on her.

She went carefully around the perimeter of the park again and again, slowly, without much hope. Reynard between those men had obviously been a prisoner. How could he meet her here if he wasn't free? She studied the knots of people gathered around fires lit in corroded steel drums, looking for his small face, sure she wouldn't see it.

Night made it certain. She was trying to decide which of the fires she would approach, how she could buy food, when a bearded man, smiling, put a paper into her hand. WHERE IS HE NOW? the paper shouted, and beneath this was a grotesque picture of what might be a leo. Startled, she looked up. The man reminded her of Meric, despite the beard, despite the sunken chest and long neck: something gentle and self-effacing in his eyes and manner. She tried to read the paper, but could only pick out words in the last light: civil rights, nature, leo, crimes, USE, freedom, Sten Gregorius.

He must have seen the look of wonderment on her face, because he turned back to her after handing out more of the sheets. "Here," he said, digging into a pocket, "wear a button." He wore one like the one he gave her: the cartoon of the leo, and under it the words BORN FREE.

She didn't know how any of this had come about, but this man must be a friend. She wanted desperately to tell him, to ask him for help; but she didn't dare. She only looked at him, and at the button. He turned to go. She said: "Will you be here tomorrow?"

"Here or over there," he said, pointing to where a pillared shrine was lit garishly by spotlights. "Every day. If I'm not in jail." He made a sudden, aggressive gesture with upraised fist, but his inoffensive face still smiled. She let him go, with a sinking heart.

She was not alone. There were others who knew about Painter. Many others. She didn't know if that was good or bad. She slipped in among a silent crowd around a fire at the base of the monument, the strange button clutched in her hand like a token, and rested her back against the stone. Her last meal had been hours ago, but she hardly noticed that she was hungry; hunger had come, over the months, to seem her natural state.

"They'll bring him out in a moment," Barron said. "Yes. There. There he is."

The room they stood in was a consulting room of what had once been a public mental hospital meant for the dangerous insane. It was empty now, except for its single prisoner or patient; he had been installed here because no one could think of anywhere else to put him: no other cage.

The window of the consulting room looked out on the exercise yard, a high box of blackened brick, featureless. The single rusted steel door that led into the yard opened. Nothing could be seen within. Then the leo came out.

Even at this distance, and even though he was draped in an old army greatcoat, Reynard could see that he was thin and damaged. He walked aimlessly for a moment, taking small steps. He seemed constricted; then Reynard saw that his wrists were shackled. He wondered briefly if they had had to smith special shackles for those wrists. Painter went to the one corner of the blind court where thin sunlight fell in a long diagonal, and sat, lowering himself carefully to the ground. He rested his back against the blank brick and looked out at nothing, unmoving. Now and again he moved his arms within the shackles, perhaps because they chafed, perhaps because from moment to moment he forgot they were on him.

"What have you done to him?" Reynard asked.

"His condition is his own fault," Barron said quickly. "He won't eat, he won't respond to therapy." He turned from the window. "As far as we can tell, he's physically unimpaired. Just weak. Of course he makes difficulties when we try to examine him."

"I think," Reynard said, "your prisoner is dying."

"Wrong. He has injections daily. Almost daily." As though trying to draw Reynard with him away from the window, he went to the far end of the room and perched on a dusty metal desk. "And he's not a prisoner. He's a subject of the USE Hybrid Species Project research arm. Technically, an experimental subject."

"Ah."

"Anyway, you've seen him. Now can we begin? You understand," he went on, "that I don't have any governmental authority. I can't make any legal deals."

"Of course."

"I can only act as a mediator."

"I think it'll do."

"This shouldn't enter into it," Barron said, looking at his knuckles, "but you, you personally, have made enormous difficulties for the government. Just enormous. It would be completely within their rights just to seize you and try you, or . . ."

"Or toss me down there. I know that. I think that what I have to offer will outweigh any vengeful feelings."

"Sten Gregorius."

"Yes. Where he is now, who his people are, the evidence against them, everything."

"We don't have much reason to believe you know all of that."

"My information regarding him"—he gestured toward the yard below the window—"was accurate enough."

"It put us to a lot of trouble. Unnecessary trouble."

"Well."

"You might be merely planning to confuse us, tell lies. . . ."

"I've voluntarily put myself in your hands this time," Reynard said. "I'm helpless. I know that if I mislead you now, the full weight of your authority will fall on me. I'm sure also that you have, well, experimental methods of extracting truths. The research arm."

"That's an odious slander."

"Is it?"

"We wouldn't let you renege, that's true enough," said Barron testily.

"It's all I meant."

"And what you want in exchange. It doesn't seem enough. Not for such a betrayal."

Reynard turned to the window again and looked out. "Perhaps you feel more deeply about betrayal than I do." Barron had to lean out over the desk now to catch his hoarse whisper. "The answer is that I'm at the end of my powers. I've eluded your government so far because of a large fortune I managed to assemble working for Gregorius. That's gone now. I'm old, not well. I've spent my life in motion, but I can't run anymore. Eventually I'd be cornered, taken—" He paused, staring down into the yard. "Rather than have that happen, I'd prefer to trade the last of what I have for peace. For time to die peacefully in." He turned to Barron. "Remember," he said. "I'm not a man. I am the only, the first and last of me there will ever be. You know I'm sterile. I have no loyalties. Only advantages."

Barron didn't speak for a moment; the affectless voice had seemed to paralyze him. Then he cleared his throat, opened his briefcase and looked inside, closed it. Himself again. "So," he said briskly, "in exchange for immunity, and a pension or the like—we'll negotiate details—you're willing to give evidence that Sten Gregorius and yourself planned the murder of Gregorius; that USE had nothing to do with it; that the murderers weren't USE agents; that Sten Gregorius is still conspiring against the Federal provisional government in the Northern Autonomy. Nashe?"

"Nashe, I hear, is dead."

"Then what you have to say about her can't hurt her."

"There's the other thing I require," Reynard said.

"Yes."

"The leo."

Barron straightened. "Yes, I think that's odd."

"Do you?"

"It's also probably impossible. He's committed several crimes; he's very dangerous."

Reynard made a noise that might have been a laugh. "Look at him," he said. "I think you've broken his spirit. At least."

"The criminal charges . . ."

"Come now," Reynard said almost sharply. "You've said yourself he's not a prisoner. An experimental subject only. Well. Put an end to the experiment."

"He's still dangerous. It would be like . . . like . . ." He seemed to search unused places for a forgotten image. "Like releasing Barabbas to the populace."

Reynard said nothing. Barron supposed he had spoken over the creature's head. "He's part of the conspiracy, in any case," he said.

"A very small part," Reynard said. "He never understood it. He was used, first to help me, then to distract your attention. He worked well enough."

"He and his kind have gotten completely bound up together in the public mind with Sten Gregorius. That may have been an accident. . . ."

"No accident. It was due to your stupidity in persecuting the leos so —so artlessly. Sten took up their cause. It was ready-made. By you." He limped toward the desk where Barron still sat, and Barron drew back as though he were being approached by something repugnant. "Maybe I can put this so that you can see the advantage to you. You're planning a reservation somewhere for the leos, a kind of quarantine."

"In the Southeastern Autonomy."

"Well then. Once Sten is in your hands, and the leo has gone voluntarily to this reservation, the union will evaporate."

"He would never go voluntarily," Barron said. "These beasts never do anything voluntarily except make trouble."

"Let me talk to him. I could persuade him. He listens to me. I've been his adviser, his friend." No irony. This was presented as an argument only. Barron marveled: no thin skin of pretense was drawn over this creature's amorality. It made him easy to deal with. Only—

"Why," he said, "do you insist on this? It can't be just to make things easier for us."

Reynard sat on the edge of a metal folding chair. Barron wondered if he was at a loss. It seemed unlikely. He moved his hands on the head of his stick. His long feet just touched the floor. "Do you go to zoos?" he said at last.

"When I was a kid. In my opinion, zoos . . ."

"You might have noticed," Reynard went on, "that according to a curious human logic, the cages are proportionate in size to the creatures they contain. Small cages for small animals—weasels, foxes—big ones for big animals. In old zoos, anyway."

"Well?"

"People go to zoos. They pity the lions, noble beasts, caged like that, with hardly room to move. In fact the lion is relatively comfortable. He's a lazy beast and exerts himself only when he must—if he doesn't have to, he rests. Other animals—foxes, notably—have a natural urge for movement. In the wild, they may cover miles in a night. They pace endlessly in their little cages. All night, when the zoo is closed, they pace—two body lengths this way, two that way. For hours. They probably go mad quite quickly. A madness no one notices.

"To put it baldly: I would do anything to avoid the cage. I hope you grasp that. He—down there—probably doesn't care. So long as he has a cage suited to his dignity."

"The reservation."

"It's the least I can do for him," Reynard said, again with no irony. "The very least."

Barron stood and went to the window. The leo still sat; his eyes appeared to be closed. Was he sleeping? Maybe the fox was right. Barron had felt, though he had ignored, a certain pity for the leos who would be committed to quarantine. Left over from guilt over the Indian reservations, perhaps. But the Indians were, after all, men. Maybe the USE plan, besides being the only practicable one, was the kindest too.

"All right," he said. "When do you want to talk to him? I make no promises. But I agree in principle."

"Now," Reynard said.

Face upward into the weak sun, Painter watched brilliance expand and deliquesce on his eyelids. Entranced by hunger, he had entered into a fugue of sleep, memory, waking, rough dream.

Coalescing in sunlight, fat, strong; taste of blood from cut lips, a haze of fury, then some victory—ancientest childhood. Sun and darkness, warmth of light and then warmth of flesh in lightlessness, amid other bodies. Sleep. Consciousness spring by spring flaring like anger along flesh wakened roughly, nothing father Sun could do against the father before him, his battle only, only perceived in enormous flashings of feeling, the possibility of victory, the battle prolonged, unacknowledged, he shackled and . . . Shackled. He raised his arms and opened his eyes. Vision of nothing. Still shackled. Stains of ancient rains ran across the yard, meeting at the drain in the center, rays from a minute black sun, tears from a deadeye.

Wandering. Nothing to do, nothing he couldn't do, coursing the stream of his own blood, turning and spinning on its currents. But bounded: banks of men, channeling him. He pressing on their united faces, passing through, they coalescing again behind and in front, rebounding him. Towns and roads. Strength for sale: cold steel half-dollars and paper as fine as shed snakeskin. As though in disguise he wore them. Smells burned him, tobacco burned smells, half-dollars bought both, language crept in between his eyes and came out his mouth tasting of tobacco. At a touch, anger could flare; they pressed so tightly together, how could they bear themselves? Learning how to bind down strengths and knit them up, twigs bound too tightly to burn. Until he was packed and pregnant as bound dynamite, faceless as quarried walls: the stone walls he square-cut in quarries, faceted walls all of one stone, like the faces that looked at him, faceted, unyielding, nothing could move them except dynamite.

The walls around him now were black; those had been pale. Would he die here? Sun had withdrawn from him. He would die here when Sun withdrew altogether; day by day it had grown narrower, a few minutes' blessing only now, tenderly feeling the brick wall brick by brick as it ascended away from him. Winter, and he would die in prison.

In prison. That was where he had been cut in two, years ago, in the darkness. Feeling the manskin peel away in the darkness like a separate being. Solitary. No place else to put you. Steel doors closing like cryings-out. Rage at the darkness. Too dumb to know better. Half a man, they said. Like the blond boy who kissed his hands for it, wept before him: not a man. They didn't know he had a man concealed on his person. Carrying a concealed weapon, resisting arrest, solitary: and in the darkness feeling the man peel away, as though he were a skin, and the manskin in darkness acquired his own life.

How long? Day after dark day he descended stairs, kept descending further stairs into further darkness, illuminating it with unyielding will, following the manskin that led the way. Solitary. Not alone though. Because the manskin led him. Down to the bottom of the darkness, his being held up before him like a torch, the manskin always just ahead, hair streaming from his head like language from his mouth; stepless darkness where they went down in the halo of his light-bearing aliveness. In the end, the bottom, and he made the manskin turn. No retreat. You are me. In the terrible dry light of understanding looking into his face, drawing close to his face, reaching for him, he for him, coupling ravishing, beast with two backs but ever after that one face only. He did not die in prison.

The fox came to him in prison. He thought at first he had invented him too. Not a prison like this one: white, naked, without surfaces, only the cryings-out of steel doors shrieking closed together. Get you out of here. What did he want? Nothing. Out of there: away from darkness, through the shrieking doors, into Sun's face again. Why?

Accept it as your due, the fox had said. Only accept it. You deserve my service; only accept it.

"Painter," said the fox.

Take me as your servant, he had said. Only go by my direction for a while. For a long while, maybe. Take what you deserve; I'll point it out to you.

"Painter," said the fox.

If this were the fox before him now in the black prison, he would kill him. The fox had betrayed him, freed him from the white prison so that he could die in the black; had given him over to the men. Had killed his son. Would kill him. Sun alone knew why he wanted such deaths. And if this were the fox

"Painter."

before him now he would

"Your servant," said the fox.

"You."

"I've come to get you out. Again."

"You put me here." His long-unused voice was thick.

"An error. A piece of planning that went badly. My apologies. It's worked out for the best."

"My son is dead."

"I'm sorry."

Painter moved his arms against the shackles. Reynard, hardly taller than he, though he stood, bent over him, leaning on his stick. "How ill are you?"

"I could still kill you."

"Listen to me now. You must listen. There is a way out of this."

"Why? Why listen?"

"Because," Reynard said, "you have no one else."

From the window of the consulting room, Barron looked down on them. Like a scene from some antique cartoon or fairytale, seeing them together. Hideous, in a way. Misdirected ingenuity. Frankenstein. He wondered at the fox, though; had he been right, about his own nature? It would be interesting to see what limits there were to his intelligence. Certainly he was cunning, cold, in a way no man could be; but still he apparently had been unable to see that the price he had asked for his betrayal was too high, and that to leave him in peace was something the government couldn't possibly do. Once Reynard was of no more use to them, he certainly couldn't be set free to do more mischief.

Tests, maybe. It would be interesting to see. A misdirected experiment, perhaps, and yet perhaps something could be learned from it.

What were they saying? He cursed himself for not having forseen this, not having the courtyard bugged.

In the morning, Caddie found a food shop and ate, pressed in among other bodies, watching the windows steam up and the steam condense to tears that streaked the panes. An argument started and threatened to become a fight. Everyone here seemed touchy, frustrated, at flashpoint. What did they want so badly, which they weren't getting? What was it that goaded them?

She began her circuit of the park again, carefully studying faces and places, wondering what she could do alone, if she couldn't find Reynard. Nothing. She had no idea where Painter was. *Government channels are silent.* But she couldn't give up, not after having come so far, counted so much on this plan, readied herself so carefully for any sacrifice. . . . She found that she was hurrying, not searching, driven by anxiety. She stopped, and closed her eyes. No hope, she must have no hope. When her heart was calm, she opened her eyes. At an intersection of streets not far off was a slim, black three-wheeler, closed and faceless.

She approached it by stages, uncertain, and not wanting to reveal herself. When she passed by it, walking aimlessly and not looking at it, as though passing by chance, the passenger door was pushed open by a stick. "Get in," Reynard whispered.

His traveling den smelled richly of him, though he himself was obscure in the shuttered darkness. The man up front was uniformed. Caddie looked from him to Reynard, uncertain.

"My jailer," Reynard said. His harsh sandpaper voice was fainter than ever. "On our side, though. More or less."

Still not knowing how freely she could speak, Caddie gave him the paper the bearded man had given her. She saw Reynard's spectacles glint as he bent over it, his nose almost touching it. He folded it, thoughtful.

"It's Meric Landseer who's done this," he said at last. "Yes. His tapes. Prepare ye the way of the Lord. Well. It'll do. Yes." He put the paper back in her hand, and leaned close to her, seizing her wrist in the strong, childlike grip she had first felt in the woods, in the hollow tree. "Now listen to me and remember everything I say. I'm going to tell you where Painter is. I'm going to tell you what he must do to be free, and what the price is, and what you must do. Remember everything."

When he had told her, though, she refused. He said nothing, only waited for her answer. She felt she would weep. "I can't," she said.

"You must." He stirred, impatient or uncomfortable. "We don't have time here to talk. If I'm missed, they'll suspect something. They'll prevent this. Now I'll tell you: it was I who sent the Federals to the Preserve, to arrest Painter. Do you understand? Because of me he's where he is. He might have died. He will die, now, if he's not freed. His son. I murdered him. By what I did. Do you understand? All my fault. You might have starved. His wives and children. All my fault. Do you understand?"

He had taken her wrist again, and squeezed insistently. She looked at his black shape, feeling well up in her a disgust so deep that saliva gathered in her mouth, as though she would spit at him. Alien, horrid, as unfeeling as a spider. She wanted desperately to leave, to do this without him, but she knew she couldn't. "All right," she said thickly.

"You'll do it."

"Yes."

"Exactly as I said."

"Yes."

"Remember everything."

"Yes." She pulled her wrist from his fingers. He pushed open the door with his stick.

"Go," he said.

She went across the street to the park, pulling up her jacket collar against the cold wind, which blew papers and filth against her ankles as she walked. She wouldn't weep. She'd think of Painter and Painter's son only. As though she were an extension of the gun and not the reverse, she would execute its purposes. She wouldn't *think*.

The pillared shrine contained only an enormous seated figure Caddie thought she should know but couldn't remember. His name, most of his left leg, and some fingers had been erased by a bomb. The black rays of the blast still flashed up the pillars and across the walls as though frozen at the moment of ignition. The same desperate and illegible slogans marked this monument, sprayed across the slogans cut in stone. With malice toward none, and justice for all.

Vengeance.

At the side of the building the bearded man sat on the steps, eating hard-boiled eggs from a paper and talking animatedly to a group of men and women gathered around him. The step was littered with eggshell and his beard was flecked with yolk.

"Brutality," he was saying. "What does that mean? It doesn't matter what *they* do. Their morality isn't ours, it can't be. It's enough that *we* see the right in our terms, and if we see it we *must* act on it. The basis of all political action . . ."

He turned and looked at her, munching. She gave him back the paper he had given her, with the picture of the leo on it.

"I know where he is," she said.

"Without the shackles," Reynard said.

"We can't," Barron said. "How do we know what he'll do?"

"A crowd of people is outside," Reynard said. "They've been waiting all night. Do you want them to see him shackled?"

"Well, why did you delay us all night?" Barron's voice was a tense whisper attempting a shout. It was hideously cold in the corridors of the old hospital; he felt tremors of anxiety and cold and sleeplessness contract his chest. The corridors were dim; only every third or fourth light was lit, glaring off the particolored green enamel of the walls, as though the place were lit with fading flares. "We'll take him out a back way."

"I think they've discovered all the exits."

The guards and overcoated marshals whom Barron had brought in to organize this release stood around looking stupidly efficient, waiting for orders to execute. "We'll have to get the van around to the back."

"They'll follow that for sure. Leave the van where it is. Send some people out the front way, to make it look as though he were coming out that way. Then we'll go out the back. The car that brought me is across the street; one of your people is driving it. Use that."

"That's crazy," Barron said. He was in an agony of indecision. "How did all those people *find* this place? What do they want?"

"However they did," Reynard said, almost impatiently, "they certainly won't go away until the leo is gone. In fact, more are collecting." He looked at the marshals, who nodded. "You'll have a mass demonstration if you don't act quickly."

Barron looked from the marshals to the door through which the leo was to come. He had meant it all to be so simple. The leo would walk freely out of the building and into a waiting van. A single camera would record it. Tomorrow, his arrival at the barracks in Georgia. The news would show it, with understated commentary. Later, when a fully articulated program had been developed, the film would be a powerful incentive to other leos.

All spoiled now. The leo refused to leave unless Reynard was present. Reynard fussed and delayed. The crowd condensed out of the city like fog. And Barron was frightened. "All right," he said. "All right. We'll do that. We'll take him to that car. You'll remain here." He steeled himself. "I'll go with him."

Reynard said nothing for a moment. Then his pink tongue licked his dark lips: Barron could hear the sound it made. "Good," he said. "It's brave of you."

"Let's get it over with." He signaled to the marshals. From the car he could radio to be met somewhere. He wouldn't have to be alone with the leo for more than ten minutes. And the driver would be there. Armed.

They opened the heavy doors along the corridor, and signals were passed down. A dark figure appeared at the hallway's end, and came toward them. Two guards on each side, and two waiting at each branching corridor. He passed beneath the glare of the lights, in and out of pools of darkness. The men at his side, since they chose not to touch him as guards usually do, appeared more like attendants. The leo, draped in his overcoat, seemed to be making some barbaric kingly progress past the guards, beneath the lights.

He stopped when he reached Reynard.

"Take off the shackles," Reynard whispered. The attendants looked from the fox to Barron. Barron nodded. He must retain control of this situation; his must be the okay. He chose not to look at the leo; a glimpse showed him that the leo's face was passive, expressionless.

The shackles fell to the floor with a startling clatter.

"Down here," Barron said, and they began a procession—marshals, Barron, Reynard, the leo, more marshals, a hurried, undignified triumph: only the leo walked a measured pace.

Through the dirty glass of the back exit they could see the deserted street lit by a single dim streetlight and the pale light of predawn. Across the street, down another street, they could just make out where the three-wheeler was.

"Can't we get him closer?" Barron said. "You. Go over and tell him . . ." A knot of people appeared in the street, searching. Someone pointed to the door they stood behind; then the group turned away, running, apparently to summon help.

"Don't wait," Reynard said. "Do it now."

Barron looked up at the leo's huge, impassive face, trying to discover something in it. "Yes," he said; and then, loudly, as people do to someone they aren't sure will understand, he said: "Are you ready now?"

The leo nodded almost imperceptibly. Reynard, at his elbow—he came not much higher, stooped as he was now—said: "You know what to do." The leo nodded again, looking at nothing.

Barron took hold of the bar that opened the door. "You," he said, sectioning out with his hand some of the marshals, "Watch here till we get off. The rest of you take him"—Reynard—"to the front, to the van. If they want something to look at, they can look at him. Quick."

With some bravado, he pushed open the door and held it for the leo, who went out and down the steps without waiting. From both ends of the street, people appeared, sudden masses, as though floodgates had been opened. Barron saw them; his head swiveling from side to side, he skipped to catch up with the leo. He reached up as though to take the beast's elbow, but thought better of it. The car was just ahead. The crowd hadn't yet seen them.

Good-bye, Barron, Reynard thought. Exhaustion swept him; he felt faint for a moment. The marshals collected around him and he raised a hand to make them wait a moment. He leaned on the stick. Only one more thing to do. He summoned strength, and straightened himself, leaning against the glass door facing the marshals. "All right," he said. "All right." Then he raised the stick, as though to indicate them.

The charge in the stick killed one marshal instantly, hurtling him into the others; two others it wounded. It threw Reynard, wrist broken, out the door and into the street. He began to scuttle rapidly across the pavement, his mouth grimacing with effort, his arms outstretched as though to break an inevitable fall. The crowd had swollen hugely in an instant; when it heard the blast and saw Reynard come stumbling out, it flowed around him as he went crabwise down the street opposite the way Barron and Painter had gone. Behind him, the marshals, guns drawn, came running; the crowd shrieked as one at the guns and the blood, and tried to stop their motion, but they were impelled forward by those behind.

The cameraman turned on his lights.

One person pushed out of the crowd toward the hurrying figure, ran toward him as the marshals ran after him, the marshals unable to fire because of the crowd. The swiveling, jostled blue light turned them all to ghastly sculptured friezes revealed by lightning.

Caddie reached the fox first. The crowd, impelled by her, surged close to the wounded, spidery creature. He grasped Caddie's arm.

"Now," he whispered. "Quick."

Quick, secret as a handshake, unperceived clearly by anyone—later the police would study the film, trying to guess which one of the fleeting, flaring, out-of-focus faces had been hers, which hand held the momentary glint of gun—she fired once, twice, again into the black creature who seemed about to embrace her. The gun sounds were puny, sudden, and unmistakable; the crowd groaned, screamed as though wounded itself, and struggled to move back, trampling those in back. Caddie was swallowed in it.

They made a wide circle around the fox. The blue light played over him; his blood, spattering rapidly on the pavement, was black. He tried to rise. The marshals, guns extended, shouting, surrounded him like baying hounds. His spectacles lay on the pavement; he reached for them, and stumbled. His mouth was open, a silent cry. He fell again.

Far off, coming closer, sirens wailed, keening.

8

HIERACONPOLIS; SIX VIEWS FROM A HEIGHT

Very soon he would start south. His children had already departed, and he saw his wife less and less often as she scouted farther south. That evening she would not return; and soon winter would pinch him deeply enough to start him too toward the warmth. He lingered because he was ignorant; he had never made the journey, didn't know from repetition that the summons he felt was that summons. His first winter he had spent in the warmth of an old farmhouse; the second he had been flung into late, and he had only managed, mad with molt and cold and near-starvation, to come this far before spring saved him.

Returning at evening to the empty tower over the brown and suddenly unpopulated marshes, he had seen the big blond one arrive on foot; watched him tentatively explore the place. Then he slept. Men were of little interest to Hawk, though they didn't frighten him; he had lived much in their company. The following day another arrived, smaller, dark. The first visitor pointed Hawk out to the second where he stood on the tower top. Hawk went off hunting, deeply restless, and caught nothing all day. He stood sleepless long into the night, feeling the pressure of the wheeling stars on his alertness.

Below him in the shed, Caddie pressed herself against Painter, squirmed against him as though trying to work herself within the solidity of his flesh; tears of relief and purgation burned her eyes and made her tremble. She stopped her ears, too full of horrors, with the deep, continual burr of his breath, pressed her wet face against the drum of his chest. She wanted to hear, smell, touch, know nothing else now forever.

The next morning she was awakened by the growing burr of an engine. Painter was awake and poised beside her. She thought for a moment that she was in Reynard's cabin in the woods, where in her dream she had been sleeping. The engine came close—a small motor-bike, no, two. Painter with silent grace rose, stepped to the boarded window, and peered through the slats.

"Two," he said. "A blond boy. A dark girl."

"Sten," Caddie said. "Sten and Mika!"

She rose, laughing with relief. Painter, uncertain, looked from her to the door when it opened. Morning light silhouetted the bearded youth for a moment.

"Sten," Caddie said. "It's all right."

Sten entered cautiously, watching Painter, who watched him. "Where's Reynard?" he said quietly.

Painter said: "Shut the door."

Mika slipped in behind Sten, and Sten shut the door. The leo sat, slowly, without wasted motion, reminding Sten of an Arab chief taking a royal seat on the rug of his tent. The room was dim, tigered by bars of winter sunlight coming in through holes in the boarded windows, spaces in the old walls.

"You're Painter," Sten said. The leo's eyes seemed to gather in all the light there was in the room, to glow in his big head like gems cut cabochon. They were incurious.

"All right," he said.

"We thought you were dead," Mika said.

"I was." He said it simply.

"Why did you come here?" Sten said. "Did Reynard . . . How did you get away from them?" He looked from the leo to the girl, who looked away. "Where is Reynard? Why are you here and not him?"

"Reynard is dead," Caddie whispered, not looking up.

"Dead? How do you know?"

"She knows," Painter said, "because she killed him."

Caddie's face was in her hands. Sten said nothing, unable to think of the question that would make sense of this.

Eyes still covered, unwilling to look at them, Caddie told them what had happened; she told them about the capital, about the hospital, the bearded man, tonelessly, as though it had happened to someone else. "He made me," she said at last, looking up at them. "He made me do it. He said there was no other way of getting Painter free except to trade him for you, Sten. And there was no way he could keep from telling all he knew about you unless he was dead. So we planned it. We made a distraction at the hospital—the crowd—so Painter could get away. He said it was the only way." She pleaded with them silently. "He said he longed for it. He said, 'Do it right; do it well.' Oh, Jesus . . . ."

Mika came to her and sat beside her, put her arm around her, moved to pity. Horrible. She thought Caddie would weep, but she didn't; her eyes were big, dark, and liquid as an animal's, but dry. She took Mika's hand, accepted absently her comfort, but was uncomforted.

No one spoke. Her brother sat down warily opposite Painter. Mika felt, in spite of the golden, steady regard in the leo's eyes, that he saw nothing, or saw something not present, as though he were a great still ghost. What on earth was to become of them? They lived at the direction of beasts. Reynard had used Caddie as he might a gun he put into his mouth. In the mountains with the leos she had witnessed inexplicable things. Now in the shuttered shack she felt intensely the alien horror that Reynard had inspired in her the first time she had seen him; the same horror and wrongness she felt when she thought of certain sexual acts, or terrible cruelties, or death.

"He sent us both here," Sten said softly to the leo. "He must have meant for us to meet." He raised his head, tightened his jaw in a gesture Mika knew meant he was uncertain, and wanted it not to show. "It's my plan, when things are—further along, to protect you. All of you. To offer you my protection."

Mika bit her lip. It was the wrong thing to say. The leo didn't stir, but the charge that ran between him and her brother increased palpably. "Protect yourself," he said. Then nothing more.

They were engaged in some huge combat here, Mika felt, but whether against the leo or beside him, and for what result, she didn't know. And the only creature who could resolve it for them was dead.

There are bright senses and dark senses. The bright senses, sight and hearing, make a world patent and ordered, a world of reason, fragile but lucid. The dark senses, smell and taste and touch, create a world of felt wisdom, without a plot, unarticulated but certain.

In the hawk, the bright senses predominated. His scalpel vision, wide and exact and brilliantly hued, gave him the world as a plan, a geography, at once and entire, without secrets, a world that night (or—in his youth—the hood) annihilated utterly and day recreated in its entirety.

The dog made little distinction between day and night. His vision, short-sighted and blind to color, created not so much a world as a confusion, which must be discounted; it only alerted him to things that his nose must discover the truth about.

The hawk, hovering effortlessly—the merest wing shift kept him stable above the smooth-pouring, endlessly varied earth—perceived the dog, but was not himself perceived. The dog held little interest for him, except insofar as anything that moved beneath him had interest. He recorded the dog and its lineaments. He included the dog. He paid him no attention. He knew what he sought: blackbird on a reed there, epaulet of red. He banked minutely, falling behind the blackbird's half circle of sight, considering how best to fall on him.

Through a universe of odors mingled yet precise, odors of distinct size and shape, yet not discrete, not discontinuous, always evolving, growing old, dying, fresh again, the dog Sweets searched for one odor always. It needed to be only one part in millions for him to perceive it; a single molecule of it among ambient others could alert his nose. Molecule by molecule he had spun, with limitless patience and utter attention, the beginnings of a thread.

The thread had grown tenuous, nearly nonexistent at times; there were times he thought he had lost it altogether. When that happened, he would move on, or back, restless and at a loss until he found it again. His pack, not knowing what he sought or why, but living at his convenience —usually without argument—followed him when he followed the thread of that odor. Somewhere, miles perhaps, behind him, they followed; he had left a clear trail; but he had hurried ahead, searching madly, because at last, after a year, the thread had begun to thicken and grow strong, was a cord, was a rope tugging at him.

Some days later. Flying home from the margins of the gray sea, weary, talons empty. From a great height he saw the man moving with difficulty over the marshy ground: followed his movements with annoyance. Men caused the world to be still, seek cover, lie motionless, swamp-colored and unhuntable, for a wide circle around themselves: some power they had. The man looked up at him, shading his eyes.

Loren stopped to watch the hawk fall away diagonally through the air as cleanly and swiftly as a thrown knife. When he could see him no longer, he went on, his boots caught in the cold, sucking mud. He felt refreshed, almost elated. That had been a peregrine: it had to be one of his. At least one bird of his had lived. It seemed like a sign. He doubted he would ever read its meaning, but it was a sign.

The tower seemed deserted. There was no activity, no sign of habitation. It seemed somehow pregnant, waiting, watching him; but it always had, this was its customary expression. Then his heart swelled painfully. A tall, bearded boy came from the tower door, and saw him. He stopped, watching him, but didn't signal. Loren, summoning every ounce of calm strength he owned, made his legs work.

As he walked toward Sten, an odd thing happened. The boy he had carried so far, the Sten who had inhabited his solitude, the blond child whose eyes were full of promise sometimes, trust sometimes, contempt and bitter reproof most times, departed from him. The shy eyes that met his now when he came into the tower yard didn't reflect him; they looked out from Sten's real true otherness and actuality, and annihilated in a long instant the other Sten, the Sten whom Loren had invented. With relief and trepidation, he saw that the boy before him was a stranger. Loren wouldn't embrace him, or forgive him, or be forgiven by him. All that had been a dream, congress with phantoms. He would have to offer his hand, simply. He would have to smile. He would have to begin by saying *hello*.

"Hello," he said. "Hello, Sten."

"Hello, Loren. I hoped you'd come."

So they talked there in the tower yard. Someone seeing them there, looking down from a height, would not have heard what they said, and what they said wasn't important, only that they spoke, began the human call-and-response, the common stichomythy of strangers meeting, beginning to learn each other. In fact they talked about the hawk that floated far up, a black mark against the clouds.

"Could it be one you brought in, Loren?"

"I think it must be."

"We can watch it and see."

"I doubt if I could tell. They weren't banded."

"Could it be Hawk?"

"Hawk? I don't think so. No. That would be . . . That wouldn't be likely. Would it."

A silence fell. They would fall often, for a while. Loren looked away from the blond boy, whose new face had already begun to grow poignantly familiar to him, terribly real. He ran his hand through his black hair, cleared his throat, smiled; he scuffed the dead grass beneath his feet. His heart, so long and painfully engorged, so long out of his body, began to return to him, scarred but whole.

Painter lay full length on his pallet at the dark end of the building Loren had once lived in. The cell heater near him lit his strange shape vaguely. He lifted his heavy head when they came in, easeful, careful. If he had been observing them in the tower yard he gave no sign of it.

"A friend," Sten said. "His name is Loren Casaubon. My best friend. He's come to help."

The leo gazed at him a long time without speaking, and Loren allowed himself to be studied. He had often stood so, patiently, while some creature studied him, tried to make him out; it neither embarrassed nor provoked him. He stared back, beginning to learn the leo, fascinated by what he could see of his anatomy, inhaling his odor even as the leo inhaled his. Half-man, half-lion, the magazines and television always said. But Loren knew better, knew there are no such things as half-beasts: Painter was not half-anything, but wholly leo, as complete as a rose or a deer. An amazing thing for life to have thrown up; using man's ceaseless curiosity and ingenuity, life had squared its own evolution. He almost laughed. Certainly he smiled: a grin of amazement and pure pleasure. The leo was, however he had come about, a beautiful animal.

Painter rose up. His prison weakness had not quite left him; now, when he stood, a sudden blackness obtruded between him and the man who stood before him. For a brief moment he knew nothing; then found himself supported by Sten and Loren.

"Why did you come here?" he said.

"Reynard sent me. To help Sten."

The leo released himself from them. "Can you hunt?"

"Yes."

"Can you use those?" He pointed to Loren's old rabbit wires hung in a corner.

"I made them," Loren said.

"We'll live, then," Painter said. He went to where the snares were hung and lifted them in his thick graceless fingers. Traps. Men were good at those. "Can you teach me?" he asked.

"Teach you to be a trapper?" Loren smiled. "I think so."

"Good." He looked at the two humans, who suddenly seemed far away, as though he looked down on them from a height.

Since the moment in the dead city when he had seen that there was no escape from men, no place where their minds and plans and fingers couldn't reach, a flame had seemed to start within him, a flame that was like a purpose, or a goal, but that seemed to exist within him independently of himself. It was in him but not of him. It had nearly guttered in the black prison, but it had flamed up brightly again when he had taken the man Barron in his grip. In the days he had lain with Caddie on the pallet here in the darkness he had begun to discern its shape. It was larger than he was; he was a portal for it only. Now when he looked at the men and saw them grow small and far-off, it flared up hotly, so hotly that it blew open the doors of his mouth, and he said to them, not quite knowing why or what he meant: "Make me a trapper. I will make you hunters of men."

Furious, Hawk broke his stoop and with a shriek of bitter rage flung himself toward the prongs of a dead tree. The rabbit struggling on the ground, hurt, helpless, had been the first edible creature he had seen all day. And just as he was diving to it with immense certainty, already tasting it, the big blond one had stamped out of the weeds with a shout.

Hawk observed the intruder mantle over the rabbit. He roused, and his beak opened with frustrated desire. They were driving him off: from his home, from his livelihood. The wind, too, pressed him to go, creeping within his plated feathers and causing the ancient tree to creak. Unknown to him, a family of squirrels lay curled inside the tree, not far below where he sat, utterly still, nosing him, alert with fear. Hawk didn't see the squirrels: there were no squirrels there.

Painter slit the twitching rabbit's throat neatly and then attempted to take it from the snare. He knew he must think, not pull. There was a plan to this. His unclever fingers moved with slow patience along the wire. He could learn this. He suggested that the man within him take a part: help him here.

He gutted the rabbit, and slit its ankle at the tendon; then he slipped one foot through the slit he had made so that the rabbit could be carried. The hitch was neat, satisfying, clever. He wouldn't have thought of it: the boy Sten had shown it to him.

The long prison weakness was sloughing away from him; and even as his old strengths were knitting up in him, cables tempered somehow by loss, by imprisonment, he felt his being knitted together too, knitted into a new shape. Carrying the rabbit, enjoying the small triumph of the snare, he went up a low hill that gave him a view over the wide marshland. The feeble sunlight warmed him. He thought of his wives, far off somewhere; he thought of his dead son. He didn't think anything about them; he came to no conclusions. He only thought of them. The thoughts filled him up as a vessel, and passed from him. He was emptied. Wind blew through him. Wind rushed through him, bright wind. Something brilliant, cold, utterly new filled him as with clear water. He knew, with a certainty as sudden as a wave, that he stood at the center of the universe. Somehow—by chance even, perhaps, probably, it didn't matter—he had come to stand there, be there, be himself that center. He looked far over the winter-brown world, but farsighted as he was he couldn't make out the shape of what lay at his frontiers, and didn't attempt to. From all directions it would come to him. He thought: if I were raised up to a high place, I would draw all men to me.

His wide gaze turned the world. He saw, far off, the dog, coming toward him, squirming through the reeds and mud. Even as he looked, the dog barked, calling to him.

Sweets didn't need to call again, he already lived within Painter; the dark shape far off on the hill was only the rich, imperious center of him, he extended infinitely out from it; Sweets had been drawn to him by only the faintest, the most tenuous, the farthest-extended atoms of his being. It had been enough. Now Sweets needed only to plunge into that center, taste it with his tongue, to forget that anything else existed.

Painter waited on the hill, watching the dog hunching and leaping and struggling toward him.

Winter deepened toward the death of the sun. On the eve of the solstice, Hawk could refuse the insistent summons no more. He had come back to his evening rest, but perceived as he approached it that there was someone there in the tower. He circled it for a time. He didn't, anyway, want to rest; he wanted to fly, soar, beat away night with long wings. This world had grown old. He rose up in easy stages, seeking a quick current.

As he went, Loren and Sten watched him, passing back and forth Loren's binoculars.

"The glint," Sten said. "When the light catches it . . . See?"

"Yes."

"His jesses. The grommets in them."

"It must be."

"It *was* Hawk."

"I think it was. I don't know how."

"Next year, will he come back?"

"Maybe."

"We could take him, take him up."

"No." Loren had read the sign. "Not after he's been free. There's no caging him now. He's nobody's hawk now, Sten." He didn't say: and neither are you.

He shifted the binoculars. Far off, something hovered: not a bird. It seemed to dart, searching, like a preying dragonfly. Then, moving straight toward them, swiftly: they could hear it.

All of them in the tower heard it. Below, Mika looked out the slats of the windows; Sweets lifted his ears and growled deep in his throat, till Painter stilled him.

"It's coming here," Mika said. "It's black."

Like a hawk, it hung for a time thoughtfully overhead, moving only slightly, looking (they all felt it) down on prey it knew was there, however concealed. Then it dropped; its noise grew loud and its vortex hurtled away dead leaves and chaff, dust of weeds and winter detritus. Its blades slowed, but continued to slice air. Its bubble face was tinted, they couldn't see anything within. Then it opened.

The pilot leapt out. Without looking around him he began to haul out boxes, crates, stores. He threw them out anyhow; one box of shiny aluminum containers broke open and spilled its contents like treasure. He pulled out three long guns and added them to the pile. He put his head within the interior. He stood aside while his passenger, with some difficulty, got out; then he clambered quickly back in and closed the bubble. The blades roared; their visitor bent over, closing his eyes against the machine's rising, his cape snapping around him. Then he straightened, tidying himself.

Reynard stood in the tower courtyard, leaning on a stick, waiting.

They came slowly from their hiding places. Reynard nodded to them as they came forth, pointing to each one with his stick. "Mika," he said. "And Caddie. Sten, and, and Loren. Where is the leo, Painter?"

"You're dead," Caddie said, staying far from him. "I killed you."

"No," he said. "Not dead." He walked toward her, not limping now, and she retreated; he seemed brisk, young, almost gay.

"I shot you." She giggled, a mad, strangled laugh.

"The one you shot," Reynard said, "was my parent. I am his—child. In a sense. In another sense, I am he almost as much as he was." He looked around at them. "It would be convenient for you to regard me as him." He grinned, showing the points of yellow teeth. "How anyway could Reynard the Fox die?"

Painter had come out of the shed, and Sweets, who curled his lip at the fox's odor. Painter came across the yard to where the little figure awaited him.

"Good evening, Counselor," he said.

"Hello, Painter."

"You're supposed to have died."

"Well, so I did. It's wrong, I know, for Judas to be the one to rise from the grave. But there it is." He looked a long time up at the massive face he had so often heard described and seen in tapes, but had never confronted. Even in the first moments of encounter he saw his parent's mistake, and wondered at it. "You shouldn't feel cheated," he said. "The one who betrayed you suffered death. But he wanted you to have his services still. My services. Forever.

"You see," he said, including them all, but looking at Painter intently, and at Sten, "I am sterile. Sexless, in fact. Therefore, in order to go on, I must be recreated—cloned—from a cell of my own. My parent understood the impasse he had come to, and saw that the only way out of it was his own death. I had been prepared to succeed him. My education was to have been longer, but I was released when he died." He looked up at the wide sky. "It was a long wait."

Loren said: "He did that in secret? Matured a clone? And nobody knew?"

"He was—I am—rich enough. There are men I pay well. Skilled. All that. I am immortal, if I'm careful." He smiled again. "A less delightful prospect than you might imagine."

Sten said: "You know what he knows."

"I am he."

"You know his plans, then. Why we're here."

"He had no plan." Reynard's voice had grown thin and almost inaudible. Small plumes of frost came from his nostrils. Evening—the longest of the year—had gathered by degrees around them.

"No plan?"

"No." Slowly, as though crumpling, he sat. A tiny folded figure. "Men plan," he said. "I'm not a man. The appearance is a deception. All lies. Talk." He said the word like a tiny bark. "Talk."

Mika shivered violently. When she spoke, she felt her throat constricted. "You said Sten was to be a king."

"Yes? Well, so he is, I suppose."

Sten said: "What am I supposed to do?"

"That's up to you, isn't it? If you are a king."

Caddie said: "You said Painter was King of Beasts."

"I did. How was I to know it was the truth? My parent died learning it."

They had come close, to hear his delicate, rasping, exhausted voice. "I make no plans," he said. "I discern what is, and act accordingly. You can never trust me. I must act; it's my nature. I'll never stop. You. You make the future. You know yourselves. I will act in the world you make. It's all up to you." One by one, they sat or squatted around him, all but Painter, who still stood, remote, unmoving as an idol with eyes of jewel. It was still not yet night, though it had been twilight most of the day. They could still see one another's faces, strange, matte, like the faces of people asleep. Tomorrow, the day would be imperceptibly longer. The sun would stir in his long sleep.

"Whatever we are to do," Reynard said, "we are at least all here. Everyone I know of. All but Meric. Well. He prepares the way. Some way." He offered, with a tiny, long-wristed hand, a place in the circle to Painter. He waited while the leo sat. The dog crept in beside him.

"Shall we begin?" Reynard said.

ENGINE
SUMMER

———

For Lance Bird,
who also thinks that the snake's-hands
in a story can be the best part.

. . . a man once said: Why such reluctance? If you only followed the parables, you yourself would become parables and with that rid of all your daily cares.

Another said: I bet that is also a parable.

The first said: You have won.

The second said: But unfortunately only in parable.

The first said: No, in reality; in parable you have lost.

FRANZ KAFKA
From "Parables and Paradoxes" by Franz Kafka. Reprinted by permission of Schocken Books, Inc.

THE FIRST CRYSTAL

MANY LIVES

First Facet

Asleep? *sleep?* No. Awake. I was told to close my eyes. And wait, he said, till you're asked to open them.

Oh. You can open them now . . . What do you see?

You.

Am I . . .

You're like . . . a girl I know. Taller. Are all the angels tall?

What else do you see?

This grass we sit on. Is it grass?

Like grass.

I see the sky. Through your roof of glass, oh, angel, can it be?

It is.

I'm here, then. Here. He was right, that I could come here . . . Angel! I see the clouds below us!

Yes.

I've found you, then. I've found the greatest thing that was lost.

Yes. We were lost and you found us. We were blind, and you made us see. Now. You can only—stay—a short time, so . . .

What is it you want from me?
Your story.

That's all I am, now, isn't it: my story. Well, I'll tell it. But it's long. How can I tell it all?

Begin at the beginning; go on till you reach the end. Then stop.

The beginning. . . . If I am only a story now, I must have a beginning. Shall I begin by being born? Is that a beginning? I could begin with that silver glove you wear; that silver glove, and the ball . . . Yes, I will start with Little Belaire, and how I first heard of the glove and ball; and that way the beginning will be the ending too. I would have to start with Little Belaire anyway, because I started with Little Belaire, and I hope I end there. I am in Little Belaire somehow always. I was created there, its center is my center; when I say "me" I mean Little Belaire mostly. I can't describe it to you, because it changed, as I changed; changed with me as I changed. But you'll see Little Belaire if I tell you about me—or at least some of the ways it can be.

I was born in my Mbaba's room. My Mbaba is my mother's mother, and it was with her mostly that I spent my baby years, as the custom is. I remember Mbaba's room better than any other of Little Belaire's thousand places; it was one that never changed, whose boundaries stayed the same, though it seemed to move from place to place as I grew up, because the walls and rooms around it were always being changed. It wasn't one of the oldest rooms, the old warren built by St. Andy that is the center of Little Belaire (tiny rooms of porous-looking square-cut gray angelstone, the old rooms where all secrets are kept); nor yet was it one of the airy, nonexistent rooms of the outside, with light translucent walls that change every day and fade into the woods till Little Belaire ends without a sign and the world begins. Mbaba's was on the Morning side, not far from Path, with walls of wood and a dirt floor covered with rugs, and many beetles and once a blacksnake that stayed nine days. And skylights that made it gleam in the mornings as though moist and fade slowly in the evening before the lamps were lit. You can see Mbaba's room from the outside, because it has a little dome, and on its sides red-painted vents that wave in the wind.

It was afternoon, in late November, when I was born. Already nearly everyone had revolved back into the close warm insides of Little Belaire, and went out rarely; smoke and food had been laid up for the winter season. In my Mbaba's room my mother sat with my Mbaba and Laugh Aloud, a gossip and a famous doctor too. They were eating walnuts and drinking red raspberry soda when I started to be born. That's the story I have been told.

The gossip named me Rush that Speaks. I was named for the rush that grows in water, that on winter days like the day I was born seems to speak when the wind goes through its dead hollow stem.

My cord is Palm cord, the cord of St. Roy and St. Dean. A lot of Palm cord people have names about words and speaking. My mother's name was Speak a Word; my Mbaba's name was So Spoken. There are hand names too—the cord is Palm, after all—like Seven Hands and Thumb. Since I have always been Palm, the Little Belaire I can tell you of is Palm's and is like my cord. But ask someone of Leaf cord or Bone cord and he'd tell you about a different place.

The silver ball and glove. I was seven, and it was a day in November; I remember, because this was also the first day I was taken to see a gossip, as that happens in the time of year when you were born, when you're seven.

Inside Mbaba's room, the vents in the little dome made a soft clack-clack-clack above my head. I watched Mbaba climb down the rope ladder that hung from a door set in the dome; she was coming back from feeding the birds. A sparrow flew in with her, fluttering noisily against the skylights and dropping white droppings on the rug below. It was cold this day I am telling you of, and Mbaba looked out from a thick shaggy shawl that ended in clicking tassels, though her feet wore only rings.

My mother had told me that Mbaba was growing solitary, the way old people do; and it was true that as I grew up, Mbaba came to spend most of her time in this room. But she wasn't ever really alone. Because around the walls were Palm cord's carved chests, of which Mbaba was the keeper. The carved chests are like—like honeycombs. What they are most like is Little Belaire itself: interrelated, full of secrets, full of stories. Each of the hundred drawers is marked with signs and carved in a different shape, depending on what's in it: each drawer was designed to hold just what it holds in the chest and to tell things about it: how it came here, what it has done, and what stories it can tell. Mbaba was never alone, because of all the souvenirs in the drawers of Palm cord's carved chests.

I lay naked under the thick rugs on Mbaba's bed, watching and listening. Mbaba, talking to herself, went around the room; she pressed one long finger to her collapsed toothless mouth, as though trying to remember something. She gave it up and came to busy herself about the pipe. The pipe in Mbaba's room is old and very beautiful, made of green glass, shaped like an onion, and hung on chains from the dome above. There are four stems hung around it in loops, woven in bright colors like snakes; and there is a metal bowl at the top in the shape of St. Bea's head, her mouth wide open to accept the chips of St. Bea's-bread.

Mbaba struck a match and held it lit in one hand while with the other she filled St. Bea's mouth with blue-green chips of bread from her barrel. She touched the match to the bread, took down one of the long stems, and inhaled; a dark bubble ascended from the bottom of the pipe to the top above the liquid level, where it burst and let out its smoke. Above the metal mouth ropes of thick, rose-colored smoke twined up around the chains, ascending to the dome; all around Mbaba was a rosy mist, the smoke coming from her nostrils and mouth. The smell of St. Bea's-bread is a good smell, dry and spicy, toasted, warm, a smell with a lot of insides. It doesn't taste like it smells; it tastes . . . like everything. Like anything. All at once. It tastes like other things to eat: dried fruit sometimes, or sour grass, or hazelnuts. And charred wood too, and dandelions; grasshopper's legs; earth, autumn mornings, snow. And thinking of it then and smelling it made me jump out of bed with the rug around me and run across the cold floor to where Mbaba motioned to me, grinning. I wriggled down next to her; she grunted as she took down a stem of the pipe for me. And so we two, me and my mother's mother, sat and smoked and talked.

"When we wandered," Mbaba said, and a bubble of laughter rose inside me because she was going to tell when-we-wandered. It could have been any story on this morning, because Mbaba knew as many stories as there were things in the carved chests, but this is the one she told:

"When we wandered, and this was a great long time ago, before any now alive were thought of or their cords thought of or even Little Belaire itself thought of, St. Andy got lost. St. Andy got lost seven times when we wandered, and this was one of the times. He got lost because he had to pull St. Roy's wagon and the treasures of Big Belaire that were kept in it, and the whole of our fires burning where people sat to warm themselves. St. Andy's wagon was a source of great amazement to them, even though they couldn't figure out how to get a lot of the drawers open. St. Andy would have liked to sit down and warm himself too, and maybe have a bite to eat, but he was kept busy by the people of the place showing off the ingenious wagon. Finally he said, 'If you'll let me sit down and thaw out a little, I can work a miracle or two and entertain you.' Well, they let St. Andy sit, but didn't offer him any food or drink. St. Andy got tired of waiting for them to offer and decided to put everybody in good spirits with a miracle.

"This was the first miracle he did. He took from a drawer of the wagon a silver glove that whistled when you wore it, and a ball that whistled the same note. St. Andy showed them both off, and the people were interested, I imagine. But then St. Andy threw the whistling silver ball as hard as he could off into the darkness. They could hear it clattering in the trees. St. Andy stood holding out his hand with the glove on it. And pretty soon back comes the ball and lands in St. Andy's hand again, as gently as a bird. Everyone was astonished. St. Andy threw the ball again and again as the people whistled and clapped. But the ball took a long time to get back each time, and soon the whistling and clapping stopped, and finally people said, 'Well, we're very bored with this miracle, let's have a different one.' St. Andy thought there were a lot of tricks you could do with the silver ball and glove, but he didn't know how any were done; the men were prodding him with sticks and making remarks, so St. Andy put aside the ball and glove and said, 'I'll show you another miracle. I'll show you a man eat raw meat who has no teeth.' And he opened his mouth to show them he was toothless as a melon, just like me.

"They agreed that might be interesting, but said they had no raw meat, only cooked meat. St. Andy was very hungry and said that would be fine. They brought the meat and set it before him—and he suddenly threw open his mouth to show a full set of perfect luminous white teeth. He chomped and tore the meat with his mouth open, gnashing the amazing teeth so all could see and hear.

"After he had eaten his fill, he stood up to leave while everyone was still impressed. They weren't too overcome not to take the silver ball and glove for themselves, so I can't prove to you that part of the story is true. But for the rest, see here":

And, as often at the end of a story, Mbaba got up and went to the carved chests, her eyes flitting over the drawers, touching the signs with her fingers till she found the right one. From it she drew out a wooden case carved in the shape of a mouth; and from the mouth case, her eyes sparkling, Mbaba drew out St. Andy's perfect, luminous white teeth.

"False teeth," she said. "Fits all." And she popped them in her mouth, fit them in with her tongue, and opened wide for me to see. I was screaming with laughter. She looked like she had a huge mouthful of something, and when she opened her mouth it was—teeth! "That's how he did it, that's how," she said, "with these very teeth, which are as old as anything and still good as new."

That was at my birth-time, in my seventh year; almost ten years ago now.

What is it?

Nothing. Go on now.

What was it I said that startled you?

Go on.

Well . . . Seventh years. Every seventh year, you visit a gossip who knows your cord well, to have the System looked at for you, and learn what state you're in. I don't know why it happens every seventh year, except that there are a lot of things we count off by sevens. And it seems —from the two sevens I've lived through—that seventh years are the ones where you are, somehow, most yourself. There are other times you could consult a gossip; for the untying of a knot, or anytime you don't understand yourself. But everyone goes in their first seventh year, and every seventh year thereafter—fourteen, twenty-one, twenty-eight—and the first seventh year is a rose year as well.

But to explain about the rose year, I have to tell you about the Four Pots, and Dr. Boots's List who makes them, and before that about the League, and the Storm which ended the angels' world . . . maybe my story doesn't really have any beginning after all.

SECOND FACET

The gossip Mbaba took me to was an old woman named Painted Red, who was a friend of Mbaba's from youth. Painted Red was, Mbaba remembered, of Water cord when she was young, and her name had been Wind, before she learned to read the System and gossip.

"She hasn't always known our cord," Mbaba said as she got me ready to go. Her breath was faintly visible in the cold. "Only in the last few years has she studied it."

"Not since I was born?"

"Well, yes, since before that," Mbaba said. "But that's not really so many years, you know." We were ready. "She's very wise, though, they all say, and knows Palm well, and all its quirks."

"What are its quirks?"

"You!" she said, and tugged my ears. "You should know, of anyone."

"She lives near Path," Mbaba said as we went along, "because she likes to feel the feet of those going by."

St. Roy—I mean Little St. Roy, of course, not Great St. Roy—said that Path is drawn on your feet. Little Belaire is built outward from a center in the old warren where it began, built outward in interlocking rooms great and small, like a honeycomb, but not regular like a honey-comb. It goes over hills and a stream, and there are stairs and narrow places, and every room is different in size and shape and how you go in and out of it, from big rooms with pillars of log to tiny rooms all glit-tering with mirrors, and a thousand other kinds, old and changeless at the center and new and constantly changing farther out. Path begins at the center and runs in a long spiral through the old warren and the big middle rooms and so on to the outside and out into the aspen grove near Buckle cord's door on the Afternoon side. There is no other way through Little Belaire to the outside except Path, and no one who wasn't born in Little Belaire, probably, could ever find his way to the center. Path looks no different from what is not Path: it's drawn on your feet. It's just a name for the only way there is all through the rooms which open into each other everywhere, which you could wander through forever if you didn't know where Path ran.

Painted Red's room was deep in toward the center. There in the ancient small stone rooms, cool in summer and warm and snug in winter, the gossips sit and feel their cords run out linking and tying like a web all through Little Belaire. It was dim; there was no skylight as Mbaba had, but a pale green lens full of bubbles set into the roof. Mbaba spoke from outside, her hand on my shoulder. "Painted Red," she said. Someone within laughed, or coughed, and Mbaba drew me in.

This was the oldest place I had ever been in. The walls were of the gray blocks we call angelstone. Here and there a block was turned on edge, and the oval piercings that (they say) go through every such block's insides made four small windows in the wall. Through these I could glimpse the little falls of the stream, lit by the slabs of glass that are set in the roof above it.

Mbaba sat me down, and I tried not to fidget, aware and expectant. When she came forth from a farther room, Painted Red looked first to Mbaba and laughed low, her hands making welcoming movements that set her bracelets clicking. She was older than Mbaba, and wore a huge pair of spectacles that glittered as she nodded to Mbaba's greeting. She sat opposite me, drew up her naked feet, and rested her arms on her knees. She didn't speak to me, but her eyes behind the quick glasses studied me as she listened to Mbaba talk. When she spoke herself, her voice was rich and slow as running oils, thick with inflection I only partly understood.

While they talked, Painted Red drew from a small pouch some flakes of St. Bea's-bread, which she rolled into a blue paper to make a fat cigar. She took a long match from her pocket and motioned for me to come sit by her. I went slowly, Mbaba's hands encouraging me. Painted Red gave me the match, and watched me as I struck it on the rough wall and held it with both hands to light her cigar. Her cheeks hollowed and a rosy cloud ascended as she inhaled noisily. The frank and friendly curiosity of her look made me smile and blush at the same time. When she had smoked, she said, "Hello, you're a graceful fellow, I'm in a mood to talk to you. Don't expect me to reveal too much of myself, though I'm sympathetic and can be helpful. Be at ease with me; I know it's strange here, but soon we'll be easy together, and then friends. . . ."

No, of course she said nothing like that, but it was all in what she did say, in her greeting, for she spoke truthfully, and was very, very good at it; so good that, speaking, she couldn't hide from my knowledge of what she meant. Of course my knowledge then was very slight; when she talked with Mbaba, they both said things I couldn't hear.

"You are not," Painted Red said, "a truthful speaker."

"No," I said.

"Well, you will be soon." She put her hand on my shoulder and raised her curling brows at me. "I will call you Rush, as your Mbaba does, if I may; your name Rush that Speaks is too much a mouthful for me." I laughed at that. too much a mouthful! She said a word to Mbaba that meant she and I must be alone, and when Mbaba was gone, she stubbed out the flat end of her crackling cigar and motioned me to come with her into the small farther room.

There she took from a chest a small narrow box that just fit in her lined palm. "Your Mbaba tells me good things about you, Rush," she said. She opened the box. Inside were four small round pots with snug lids, each a different color: a black one, a silver one, a bone-white one, and one the pure blue of a sunset winter sky. "She says you like stories."

"Yes."

"I know a huge number." Her face was gently grave but her eyes were sly behind the glittering glasses. "All true." We both laughed at that; her laugh made me shiver with the weight and fullness of it, light and low though it was. I knew then that Painted Red was very holy; possibly she was a saint.

Why do you say holy?

Holy. Blink told me once that in ancient times they said a thing was holy if it made you hold your tongue. We said a thing was holy if it made you laugh. That's all.

Painted Red now chose the little black pot, opened it, and rubbed her thumb in the rose-colored stuff that it contained; then she rubbed her thumb on my lips. I licked it off. It had no taste at all. She took from another place in her chests a set of nesting black boxes and tubes with tiny lenses, and these she assembled in her larger room beneath the big lens, setting the tubes to point at a white space on the wall. She drew a string that closed the pupil of the green lens in the ceiling until its light fell in a tiny bright spot onto a mirror which she placed at the back of the boxes. The light from the lens was reflected through the tube; a circle of pale green shone on the wall.

She opened carefully a long box and, after some thought, drew out one of the many thin squares of glass it contained. I could see as she held it to the light that it was inscribed with a pattern, and when she slipped it into place, there was suddenly the same pattern projected onto the wall, greatly enlarged and as clear as though drawn there.

"Is it the Filing System?" I asked in a whisper.

"It is."

Years later, Blink told me the full name of the Filing System, and I made him say it over and over till I could say it too, and then I went on saying it, like a nonsense rhyme. Sometimes at night I say it over to myself till I fall asleep: Condensed Filing System for Wasser-Dozier Multiparametric Parasocietal Personality Inventories, Ninth Edition. Blink tried to explain what all that meant, but I forget now what he said; and even the gossips who sit and look at it all day call it only the Filing System. It's from the Filing System that the cords are derived, though the angels who created the System knew nothing of cords, and the System is hundreds of years older than the cords which the gossips found there. "In ancient times," Blink told me, "it wasn't supposed to yield knowledge, only to keep facts straight; but the angels who thought it up had created more than that, and although whatever facts the System was to have kept straight are lost now, this new knowledge of the cords was found in it, which its makers didn't know how to see there. It's often so."

I looked at the wall where the figures glowed that meant my cord, and a great cord it is, with two great saints in it. "My cord has two saints in it," I said.

"You're very clever," said Painted Red. "Perhaps you can tell me more." She spoke kindly, but I was abashed then, having spoken up before this thing I knew so little about. She waited politely a moment for me to speak again, and laughed gently at my silence; and then, turning to the System, after a long moment she began to talk, partly to me, partly to herself, about our cord and its ways and how Palm cord goes on with the business of life; and as she talked she put her hand over mine where I sat beside her on her couch. There was nothing in the room to see except the bright pattern on the wall, nothing to hear but Painted Red's soft voice. When my lips began to grow oddly numb and loose, I hardly noticed. What I did notice was that Painted Red's questions, and then my answers, began to take on bodies somehow. When she talked about something, it wasn't only being talked about but called into being. When she asked me about my mother, my mother was there, or I was with her, on the roofs where the beehives are, and she was telling me to put my ear against the hive and hear the low constant murmur of the wintering bees inside. When Painted Red asked me about my dreams, I seemed to dream them all over again, to fly again and cry out in terror and vertigo when I fell. I never stopped knowing that Painted Red was beside me talking, or that I was answering; but—it was the rose-colored stuff that did it, of course, but I wasn't aware even of that—though I knew that I hadn't left her side and that her hand was still on mine, still I went journeying up and down my life.

It seemed to take as long as my life had, too; but gradually the solid-seeming incidents of my life became thinner and more tenuous, less real than the face of Painted Red beside me; and I returned, a little surprised, yawning a huge yawn and feeling I had slept a whole night's refreshing sleep, to the little room where the pattern still burned on the wall.

"Rush that Speaks," Painted Red said to me gently. "You are Palm for sure, and doubly Palm."

I said nothing to that, because in my growing up I had learned it was regarded as something secret, not to be spoken of, and possibly shameful, that my father Seven Hands was Palm cord as my mother was. It doesn't happen often that both your parents are of the same cord; it's almost as rare as when they are sister and brother. The gossips warn against it; it makes, they say, for knots.

"When will Seven Hands leave?" she said.

"I don't know," I said, not surprised that she knew Seven Hands's secret; she seemed to know everything. I wasn't surprised either that she knew it was my greatest sorrow. "Soon, he says, is all."

"And you want him not to go."

Again I said nothing, afraid of what would show in my speech. Seven Hands was my best friend, though I saw little enough of him; and when in the middle of some game or story he would fall silent, and sigh, and talk about how big the world is, a fear would take hold of me. The fear was that the world—outside Little Belaire—*was* big; it was vast, and unknown; and I wanted not to lose Seven Hands in it.

"Why does he want to go?" I asked.

"Perhaps for the untying of a knot." She rose up, her joints cracking, and took from the long box another thin square of glass. She put this before the mirror in the box with the first and drew out the tube a little to make the picture clear. And suddenly it was all changed. The fine-lined pattern was altered, colored, darkened, obscured.

She looked at it in her dreamy, attentive way. "Rush," she said, "lives come in many shapes, did you know that? There are lives that are like stairs, and lives that are like circles. There are lives that start Here and end There, and lives that start Here and end the same. There are lives full of stuff, and lives that will hold nothing."

"What shape is mine?"

"Don't know," she said simply. "But not the same as the man Seven Hands's. That's certain. Tell me: when you are grown up, and a truthful speaker, what will you do?"

I lowered my head, because it seemed presumptuous; as it wouldn't if I were to say that I wanted to make glass, or keep bees, or even gossip. "I'd like to find things," I said. "I'd like to find all our things that are lost, and bring them back."

"Well," she said. "Well. There are some things that are lost, you know, that may be better unfound." But I heard her say too: don't lose your thought, Rush, it's a good one. "Did you tell Seven Hands about it?"

"Yes."

"What did he say?"

"He said that things that get lost—get lost for good—all end up in the City in the Sky."

She laughed at that; or perhaps not at that but at something she saw in the tangled figure on the wall. "Palm cord," she said, and was absorbed for a long time. "Do this, Rush that Speaks," she said then. "Ask Seven Hands if he will take you with him when he leaves."

My heart leaped. "Will he?"

"No," she said. "I don't think so. But we'll see what happens. Yes. It's best." And she pointed to the figure on the board. "There's a path out of that. Its name is Little Knot, and the path isn't so long . . ."

She had seen enough; she seemed to rouse herself from a kind of sleep. She rose, picked out the two squares of glass and wiped them clean; then she took out the little mirror and wiped that clean too, and put them all away. As she did so, I saw that drawn on the end of the long box was the palm sign that signifies my cord. So the entire box was my cord. I hadn't seen my cord at all, but only a fraction of a part of the ways it can be. "How," I said, pointing to the box, "how does it . . ."

"It would take you till you are as old as me," she said, "to know how does it do it, if that's what you mean." She stowed it all, without haste, and returned to me. "But think," she said. "They are all of glass, like the two you saw, thin and clear."

"So you could put three at once in the tube," I said, "and the light would shine through all three, and you could see how it changes, how it . . ."

Painted Red clapped her hands, smiling at me. "Or seven, or ten, however many you're clever enough to read at once." She knelt down near me and looked at me closely. "They all have names, Rush, and each has its knowledge to add about you as you are Palm. Each added to the rest changes the whole and makes a difference. The Filing System is very wise, Rush, far wiser than I am."

"What are the names?" I asked, knowing I would not be told.

"Well," she said, "there will be time to learn that, if you want to learn it. Listen, Rush: How would you like to come see me, often? There are a few other children who come often. I tell stories, and we talk, and I show them things. Does that sound like fun?"

Fun! She had just seen that I was Palm cord, and that in this room I was in the presence of knowledge far beyond me. "Yes," I managed to say, hoping the little truthful speaking I had would let her know how I felt.

Her spectacled face was crinkled in smiles. "Good," she said. "When you've spoken to Seven Hands, and done—listen to me now—done exactly as he asks you or tells you, and when you are done with it, come and see me. I don't think it will be long." She ran her hand through my hair. "Go now, Rush that Speaks. Untangle yourself. Then come back."

She could see my wonder and confusion and excitement, and her laugh rolled out into the room, saying a thousand things and distilling a thousand years of holiness.

When I went out, Mbaba was gone. That was all right; Painted Red's rooms were near Path, and though there were places in Little Belaire I have never been, there was nowhere there that I was lost, because Path was drawn on my feet.

THIRD FACET

There are places in Little Belaire where you're likely to find people of a certain cord. By the stream and out by the willows on the Morning side you'll find Water cord, that's easy; but Water cord is an easy cord, they always do what you expect they will. Palm cord isn't as predictable, but of course I knew where to look, and I found Seven Hands among friends in one of the old arched rooms with dirt floors that were built toward the Afternoon side for meeting rooms hundreds of years ago when we still had meetings. Light fell from great slabs of glass that faced the afternoon sun, and smoke arose into the sun like thunderclouds from the noisy little group that sat in the warmth talking.

They were all Palm. It wasn't that people of other cords weren't allowed among them, but other cords get tired quickly of Palm cord's endless talk, which is full of qualifications and snake's-hands and complicated jokes other people don't find very funny. They go on: like I go on.

I was shy to speak up before all of them, and I asked Seven Hands if I could talk to him alone. He looked at me and grinned, but I guess I spoke so seriously that he got up with a grunt and went off with me around one of the big beams that supported the glass of the roof. He was still grinning; nothing embarrasses Palm cord more than intrigue, and secrets, and being asked about themselves and not about the world in general. So I asked him flatly:

"When you leave Belaire," I said, with a lump in my throat and all the little truthful speaking I knew in my words, "will you take me with you?"

"Well, big man," he said. He called me big man, which I knew was a joke, but I enjoyed it anyway. He pulled his skirts around him and sat down with his back against a pillar. He had a way of hanging his long arms over his knees when he sat, and holding the thumb of one hand in his other hand; and I did it too, in imitation of him.

He looked at me, nodding thoughtfully, waiting I think for me to ask again so that he could determine a little more of why I asked this of him; but I said nothing more. It had seemed important to Painted Red that I ask, even though she thought he wouldn't take me; so I only waited.

"I'll tell you," he said at last. "It'll probably be a long time till I go. Really go. There are—well, a lot of preparations to make. So. Maybe, when I'm ready to go, you'll be ready too."

There was something in what he said beyond what he said. I was truthful speaker enough to hear it, but not enough to know what it was. He reached over and slapped my thigh lightly. "I'll tell you what, though," he said. "If you're ever to go, you've got to make preparations too. Listen: we'll start by taking a little trip together."

"A trip?"

"Yes. A little hike. In preparation, sort of. Have you ever seen Road?"

"No."

"Would you like to?"

I said nothing, made a few shruggings that could mean I would like to if that was what was required of me.

"You ask Mbaba," said Seven Hands, "and if she says it's all right, and she will, we'll go tomorrow if it doesn't rain or something. I'll come find you early."

Painted Red had said I must do exactly as Seven Hands asked me; she'd said she didn't suppose he'd take me with him, but he hadn't said he wouldn't. I should have been pleased at that, and pleased he'd invited me to make his preparations with him; but still I felt troubled and un-easy. That's what it's like having a knot with someone. Nothing—not even the simplest feelings—seem to cross between you without somehow getting tangled.

Anyway, that's how it came to be that the next day I was in the middle of a bridge that goes across the river called That River, the bridge made of red rusted iron bars only, the only bridge there is since the one with the road that could be walked on fell down before I was born. There had been a frost the night before, and the cold wind was bitter over That River.

We went carefully from bar to bar across the bridge, looking down—or trying not to look down—through the gaps between the bars at the black, angry water. The ancient metal creaked and whined in a wind that was picking up. I followed Seven Hands, my hands taking hold where his did; our hands and clothes were covered with red rust, thick and grimy, and mine were dead cold from the iron.

Then there was a break. Seven Hands stopped ahead of me and looked. Soon the bridge would be no use: here, a beam had fallen out at last, and soon the whole bridge must follow. The wind whipped Seven Hands's long hair into his face and waved his long knotted sleeves as he looked up and down, thinking, and all the time the bridge was swaying and creaking and the black water was rushing by below. Seven Hands looked at me, grinning, rubbed his hands together and blew on them, poised himself and jumped.

I think I cried out. But Seven Hands had thrown his arms around the upright, and clung; he moved his hand to a better place *slap* on the cold metal, and pulled himself around to face me, his chest heaving and his face smeared with rust.

"Come on, Rush, come on," he said between pants, but I just stood there looking at him. He straddled the beam then, and hooked his feet under it. "Sit down," he said, so I did. I was shorter, so my feet couldn't get a grip. Seven Hands reached out his long arms toward me, his big hands motioning me to lean to him. I grabbed his wrists, hard with bone and tendon, and when he gave me the signal, pushed off. I kept my eyes on the beam and not on the water, and swung out over air, and felt a snap in my shoulders, and then up; one leg reached and slipped off the beam, and then I was struggling on and felt my balance return, and with my face pressed against Seven Hands's chest I held on tight till I knew for sure I was there, and even then I kept my hold on his wrists. I heard him laughing. His big face was close to my face, exulting, and I was laughing too between pants, and at last slowly let go of his wrists and sat there on my own.

"Preparations," he said. "You see? If you're going to go somewhere, you have to believe you can get there. Somehow, some way."

We got to the end of the bridge and let ourselves down its struts, and sat for a while not speaking but looking back up at the bridge we had beaten; and suddenly I wanted more than anything to go with him when he truly left, and share all his adventures.

"You *will* take me," I said, "if I'm grown up enough? When will it be?"

"Well, big man, well." Again I heard the shadow behind his speech, almost a regret; but I knew now that it wasn't for me. He stood up. "We have to get to Road while it's still day, if we want to see it," he said.

We were some time climbing upward, through woods filled with fallen leaves frosted and aged-looking, till the woods thinned and we climbed gray-lichened foreheads of stone onto stony uplands. The sky hung low, solid and gray above us; as we climbed, we seemed to come closer to it. When we had come out onto the crest of the hill, we could see that above the gray, spiky distant hills, a thin crack of blue sky lit the hem of the clouds with silver. Seven Hands pointed to a line of evergreens ahead. "Beyond there," he said, "we'll see Road."

The wind was boring an icy spot in my windward cheek and beginning to tear the solid fabric overhead as we broke through the line of evergreens and came out onto a rocky height that overlooked a valley. Above the hills across the valley, the sky was all pink and blue as the clouds moved fast away; as they rushed over our heads they left the sky high, infinitely high and deeply blue—what winds must be there! Soon the late sun reached where we stood, lighting the valley before us; and lighting, too, Road.

For there was Road. It followed the Valley, but curtly; it dug itself through the valley's gentle folds with an imperious, impossible straight sweep away that was the hugest thing I had ever seen. There were so many wonders about it: how can I tell you I saw them all at once?

First of all it wasn't one road, but two. Two roads, each wide enough for twenty men to stand easily across it. And matched to race away like two racing gray squirrels, and as gray as that. They ran together as far as you could follow, not varying their width or the distance between them, eye to eye to—where?

Miles down the valley it turned a somersault, curling in and out of itself, running up and down bridges and ramps, making of itself what looked, from where we stood, like an immense leaf of clover, just, it seemed for the fun of it, like a vast child doing a thundering, earth-shaking cartwheel.

As far off as I could see, it ran smack into a high hill where it must stop; and here was the last wonder—it didn't stop. Its two parts each found a perfect, high-arched cave or cleft to run into. And then no doubt out the other side and on and on, leaping and curling in bows and straightening the lumpy, bumpy earth with its angel-made straight lines.

"Where does it go?" I asked.

"Everywhere," Seven Hands said simply, letting himself down to a squat. "From This Coast to the Other Coast, and when it reaches the Other Coast it turns and comes back again to This Coast by a different way, and back again. And crosses and recrosses a thousand times, and doubles back and radiates out like a spider's web in a thousand ways."

"Is it all like this?"

"Like this or bigger."

"More than two?"

"No. Always two. One to go this way on, one to go that way on. Bigger across, and curling around like you see there, but in huge flowers. And mixing it up in Cities, with bridges on its back and tunnels under its belly. So I've heard. One day I'll see."

"What was it . . . for?"

"To kill people with," Seven Hands said, simply as before. "That's what the saints said. The cars used to go on it, you see. At night you could have seen them from here, all lit; I know they were all lit, with white lights in front and red in back, so that the road to go this way on would be white, and the road to go that way on would be all red."

"And how did Road kill them?"

"Oh, Road didn't kill them. The cars killed them. People were inside them, and there was only room in them to sit with arms and legs just so, so they were easy to break; the whole thing could sort of fold up and break you like a nutcracker.

"They went fast, you see, faster than bats but not so carefully, and so they collided all the time. St. Clay said he heard from Great St. Roy—and St. Roy had seen Road in the last days when there were millions of these cars, like ants along a path, like shoals of minnows—St. Roy said that Road killed in a year as many people as there are in Little Belaire, twice over."

I started out over that proud, dove-gray thing. Nearby, its stone could be seen to be cracked by weeds, and the ditch that separated its parts was filled with saplings growing tall. You could stand in the middle of one half and be aimed right at the Other Coast, the angels knew how far away; you could pass things that the truthful speakers have forgotten for hundreds of years, and come to the Other Coast at last, and then cross to the other side and be pointed home, and never once leave Road. And yet it killed people.

Now the whole sky was clear, and the wind that filled up the air to its blue height was dying away. Seven Hands got up and started down the steep slope toward Road, and I followed him. "Why didn't they just stop, then," I asked, "and just walk along it? Or just—just look at it?"

"They did, eventually, when everything went off," said Seven Hands, finding footing. "But in the ancient days, they didn't mind much; they weren't afraid; they were angels. And besides, there were millions of them; they didn't mind a few thousand killed."

We reached its edge and walked out to the middle of its near part, and faced the huge knot in it miles away, and the Other Coast far farther than that. "We came along Road," Seven Hands said, stamping lightly on its smooth surface. "St. Bea and St. Andy came along it in the saints' days, and left Road just here. And went to rebuild Big Belaire. But you knew all that."

I knew some of it. I hadn't known this was the place, or this the Road we had left. "Tell me," I said.

"Well," he said, "help me make a fire." We gathered sticks and kindling and made a fire in the middle of Road, and Seven Hands took matches from his sleeve and lit it. When it was a small bright blaze we sat near it, and bound our hands in our sleeves, and pulled over our hoods, and Seven Hands began to talk.

"There were nearly a thousand of us. We had wandered, oh, I don't know, a hundred years, a hundred and a half, and had never forgotten the Co-op Great Belaire or truthful speaking in all those years after the Storm had passed; we had stayed together; others had joined us. And now we had come here. It was spring then; we had stopped for the night, and sat here on Road and put up tents and unloaded things, and St. Bea and St. Andy opened the old wagon, and there were fires lit; well, imagine a thousand and their fires here.

"St. Bea talked late with St. Andy that night. They talked about the children there, and the old people; they spoke over and over the things they knew from Big Belaire and from the old times, and how it might be that the wagons would be lost and with them many memories of those times. Already a lot had been forgotten. And I suppose they looked out at Road, which they had come along, as we do now. And, St. Andy said, that was when St. Bea got the idea. You know what the idea was."

"Little Belaire."

"She said: 'It's spring now. And this part of the country is very nice, and fertile, and very scenic too.' And she wondered if maybe they hadn't wandered far enough, far enough from the angel's death and ruin, who had never hurt this land around here much; and mightn't it be time to stop? There would be no danger of St. Andy getting lost for good with the precious wagon. It had been a long time since the Storm had passed, the going-off of the world the angels made; perhaps all those sins had been forgiven, perhaps long ago. They had learned a lot, St. Bea thought, and maybe it was time to stop learning and start living a little.

"But St. Andy didn't know. He knew how to keep moving. He said: 'We fly the angels. The League is no friend of ours. There are a lot of people who don't love us at all.' And St. Bea said: 'The angels are dead and gone. For the others,' she said, 'we can plan against them.'

"And she drew in the ashes by the fire the circle that is Little Belaire today, with its secret door and its Path no one knows but the speakers, and she said: 'We'll build it all of angelstone, and it will have no windows, and will all be joined, just like Big Belaire was.'

"Well, she convinced St. Andy. 'She's a very persuasive woman,' he used to say. And so they called the gossips together around their fire, and toward morning it had been decided to rebuild the Co-op as well as they could, here, in this country the angels had left alone except for Road, which ran through it almost without stopping.

"And so that day the truthful speakers left Road and never took it again."

Now the sun was low, and the wind had died away almost as suddenly as it had risen. It was colder than it had been. I pulled my hooded cloak more tightly around me. "You'll take it, though," I said. "One day."

"Yes, big man," he said softly. "One day."

And when he said it—I don't know how, whether because we had shared this adventure, or because of the story he had told, or because now for the first time he knew it to be true himself—I saw that Seven Hands wouldn't leave Little Belaire and follow Road where it led. That had been the knot between us, that I had believed him when he said it, and resented and admired him for having decided to do it; and he, who knew in his heart of hearts that he never would, had disliked me for believing him capable of it when he wasn't. He had spoken truthfully of all this to me even as he told me of his plans to go and his dreams of what he would see; but till now I hadn't been able to hear it. With something like an audible whisper, the knot came untied in me, and left me sad. "One day," I said. Beneath his hood his face was grave, and sad too; for I had in those two words just told him what I had learned.

Around us, and stretching away and behind, Road seemed to glow faintly in the quick-fading light, as though it spent an old radiance of its own. The sky was huge over the valley. I wondered then if there were truly cities in the sky; and if there were, could they see us here—two little men and their fire, whose thread of smoke rose straight up on the spot where St. Bea stopped, white smoke mixed now with the rose smoke of her Bread that we lit and passed; two men in the middle of the vast road where millions had raced. It was evening, it was November. There were two, there had been millions. Did the angels in their city in the sky weep to think of it?

No.

No. The angels don't weep.

The angels weep, but for themselves. And never saw you there.

—

FOURTH FACET

It was another day till I went along Path alone to Painted Red's room. I left Mbaba still asleep, and ate an apple as I hurried along the still-dim way. If you could have hung in the air above like an angel and looked in, you would have seen me run around Little Belaire in a long, slow spiral, save for one short cut that had me stepping over sleeping bodies.

When I came within sound of the stream, people were awake and dressing; I passed a room where six sat smoking, laughing and talking. Little Belaire was waking up. On ladders men opened skylights and smelled the sharp morning air, climbed down again. I was walking against many who were going to the outside. It was warmer than it had been the day Seven Hands and I went to see Road, and people would stay in the sunny outer rooms today, and at evening bring back with them something they would need for the winter, like a set of Rings or tools or a big pipe that had been hung up in the outer rooms for summer. Some would make expeditions to gather the last of the year's nuts in the woods; or they would meet each other in the outside rooms to weave and talk, if they were Leaf cord. Or climb to the top of Belaire and do sealing-work for the winter, if they were Buckle cord. Or discuss the affairs of their cord, if they were Whisper, or the affairs of others' cords, if they were Water, or the affairs of the world if they were Palm; and gossip about all the things they remembered and knew about and had heard of from the saints back when we wandered and before that back to Big Belaire and before to ancient times, so none of it would be forgotten.

There are always a thousand things to see and stop for along Path, snake's-hands to explore and people to listen to. In a snake's-hand near Painted Red's room I found some friends playing whose-knee, and I waited for a turn to play. . . .

Stop a moment. When you said it before, a snake's-hand was something in talk. Now it's a place. And tell me about whose-knee, too, since you're stopped.

All right. I told you about Path: Path is like a snake, it curls around the whole of Little Belaire with its head in the middle and the tip of its tail by Buckle cord's door, but only someone who knows Little Belaire can see where it runs. To someone else, it would seem to run off in all directions. So when you run along Path, and here is something that looks to be Path, but you find it is only rooms interlocking in a little maze that has no exits but back to Path—that's a snake's-hand. It runs off the snake of Path like a set of little fingers. It's also called a snake's-hand because a snake has no hands, and likewise there is only one Path. But a snake's-hand is also more: my story is a Path, too, I hope; and so it must have its snake's-hands. Sometimes the snake's-hands in a story are the best part, if the story is a long one.

Whose-knee. I've never been that good at whose-knee, but like every kid in Belaire I carried my ball and tweezers everywhere; it's part of every kid's equipment. My ball was a cherry stone tightly wrapped in some string; the tweezers are a rush almost as long as your forearm that's split almost all the way down and pegged just right so you can pick up a ball. You can play it a lot of different ways, with one ball or several, with two people or with as many sitting in a circle as you can reach with your tweezers. Whatever way you play, the ball is balanced on your knee— you draw up your knees like this—and another person picks the ball off your knee with his tweezers and places it on someone else's knee. The different ways to play are different ways of calling whose knee will be played, and who will move.

It has to be played very fast—that's the fun of it—and if you drop a ball or move out of turn three times, you have to ask to stay in, and the others can say Yes or No. . . .

How do you win?

Win?

How do you beat the others?

Beat them? You're not fighting, you're playing a game. You just try to keep the ball in motion and stay out of the way of other people; and keep your ball on your knee, too. It takes a lot of concentration, and you can't laugh too much, though it can get very funny. Buckle cord plays it very well; they all wear very intent, serious faces and the tweezers fly around, snicksnicksnick. Also Buckle cord people all seem to have flat, broad knees.

Anyway, a place in this circle became empty, and I sat down. The girl opposite me, whose knee I would play, looked up at me once with eyes startlingly blue; startling because her hair was deeply black and thick, and her eyebrows too; they curved down and almost met above her nose. She only glanced at me, to make certain it was I whose knee she was playing, and set her ball.

"Whose knee?" they said, and we began. Little yelps of anxiety or triumph: "Miss! He has two." The girl opposite me played with a kind of abstracted intentness, as though utterly aware of a game, but a game she was playing in a dream. Her down-turned full mouth was partly open; her tiny teeth were white.

"Whose knee?" we said. "Big Bee moves Whisper cord," the leader said, and a lanky, laughing Leaf cord boy, after only the quickest glance around the circle, moved the ball of the girl opposite me. Whisper cord: yes, I would have chosen her too. Not only for her abstraction, her appearance of not being wholly present; not only that she seemed—to me, anyway—the center of this circle without having to claim that. Something else: some whisper. When it came my turn to move her, she suddenly raised her impossible blue eyes to me. The ball dropped.

"Miss!"

She retrieved the ball, not looking again at me. I tried to play well, now, but I stumbled over myself, missed my cord when it was called. I was soon out.

And all that, about the game, was a snake's-hand in my story; but just as there are snake's-hands that look like parts of Path, so there are parts of Path that look like snake's-hands. When I stood up, so did she; behind us others were calling out the words that meant they had claim on our places. When I came onto Path, she was ahead of me, going toward Painted Red's room; I followed at a distance. At a turning, she stopped and waited for me.

"Why are you following me?" she said. Her down-turned eyebrows gave her a permanent angry sulk that was only occasionally the way she felt, but I knew nothing of that then.

"I wasn't. I was going to a gossip named Painted Red. . . ."

"So am I." She gazed at me without much curiosity. "Aren't you a little young?"

That was annoying. She was no older than I. "Painted Red doesn't think so."

She crossed her pale arms, thin and downed with dark hair. "Come on, then," she said, as though I needed her protection, and she reluctantly had to give it. Her name, she said when I asked it, was Once a Day; she didn't bother to ask mine.

Painted Red was still asleep when we came into the larger of her two rooms; we sat down amid the others gathered there, who looked at me and asked my name. We waited, trying to be quiet, but that was hard, and soon we heard her moving around in her other room. She looked out sleepily, blinking without her spectacles, and disappeared again. When she finally came out we had stopped trying to be quiet, and she sat down in the middle of the hubbub and calmly rolled herself a blue cigar. Someone lit it for her, and she inhaled deeply, looking around and feeling better. She smiled at us, and patted the cheek of the girl who lit her smoke. And my first morning with Painted Red began.

"When we wandered," she said, and began the story about St. Gary and the fly that I had heard Mbaba tell. She brought us a basket of apples, and as we ate them she told the story in her Water way, full of false beginnings and little ironies which if you stopped to think about you lost the thread; and the story was not quite the story I knew. When, at the end of the story, St. Gary let the fly go, nobody laughed. It seemed to have become, in Painted Red's telling, a riddle or something meant to be solved; and yet at the same time you felt that the answer lay within the story—that it wasn't a riddle but an answer, an answer to a question you didn't know you'd asked.

Big Bee, the Leaf cord boy, his mouth full of apple, asked Painted Red why she had told us that story. Leaf cord doesn't like mysteries.

"Because a saint told it," Painted Red said. "And why are the saints saints?" She looked around at us, smiling and waiting for an answer.

"Because," someone said, "we remember the stories of their lives."

"How do we remember the stories of their lives?"

"Because—because they told them in a way that couldn't be forgotten."

"In what way?"

"They spoke truthfully," a Water cord girl named Rain Day said.

"And what is it to speak truthfully?" Painted Red asked her.

She began to answer like Water cord, saying, "There was the Co-op Great Belaire," and, "But there was a beginning almost before that," and how in ancient times most people had no homes they lived in all their lives. Except for the people in the Co-op Great Belaire. There, in its thousand rooms, people lived a little as they do now in Little Belaire. "But they were angels, too," she said. "Their co-op was high, they rode in elevators, they talked on phones. . . ."

"Yes," Painted Red said. "Phones. It seemed, in those days, that the more the angels had to ride on, and talk over distances with, and get together by, the more separate they became. The more they made the world smaller, the greater the distance between them. I don't know how the people of the Co-op Great Belaire escaped this fate, but the children who grew up there, if they left, would find nowhere else to be as happy as they had been there, and they would bring their own children back with them to live there. And so it went on over many lifetimes.

"Now," she said, raising one finger as gossips do, "now in those days everyone talked to everyone else by the phones. Every room in the Co-op had a phone, every person had his own to call and be called on. A phone is only your voice, carried by cords over distance, just as a tremor is carried over the whole length of a taut string if you pluck one end. The people of the Co-op, as they grew closer together, began to learn about this engine: that to talk to someone with a phone is not like talking to him face to face. You can say things to a phone you wouldn't say to a person, say things you don't mean; you can lie, you can exaggerate, you can be misunderstood, because you're talking to an engine and not a man. They saw that if they didn't learn to use the phones right, the Co-op couldn't exist, except as a million others did, just places to put people. So they learned."

We weren't silent as she told us this; each of us knew a piece of this story and wanted to put it in, and some were contradicted by others. Only Once a Day said nothing: but no one expected her to. Rain Day told how there were gossips then too, old women who knew everyone and everything, and who had advice on all matters; but not listened to as carefully as now. Somebody else said that there were locks to every door at first, and every set of rooms was the same in size and shape, but by the time St. Roy led them all away, there were no locked doors, and all the inside of the Co-op had been changed to great and tiny rooms, like Belaire today. Painted Red listened to each of us, and nodded, and folded in what we said with little motions of her head and hands to what she was explaining, seeming not to care how long it took.

"What they learned," she went on, "was to speak on the phones in such a way that your hearer couldn't help but understand what you meant, and in such a way that you, speaking, had no choice but to express what you meant. They learned to make speech—transparent, like glass, so that through the words the face is seen truly.

"They said about themselves that they were truthful speakers. In those days people who thought alike were a church. And so they were the Truthful Speakers' Church.

"The truthful speakers said: We really mean what we say and we say what we really mean. That was a motto. They were also against a lot of things, as churches were; but nobody now can remember what they were.

"The Co-op Great Belaire survived for a long time, raised its children and learned speaking. But of course the day came when first the lights and finally, at last, the phones went off. And Great St. Roy led them out onto Road. And we wandered. That's when the saints were, who took the speech begun in the Co-op and finished it, when we wandered and while the warren was building, in the stories they told of their lives, which we remember and tell.

"And I have to tell you now: before there was truthful speaking, and you talked on the phones with others, and a confusion resulted, and someone was hurt or two people set against each other, the gossips would say, 'There must have been a knot in the cord.' A knot in the cord! That makes me laugh." And she did laugh, her big liquid laugh, and we laughed with her.

Once a Day wasn't laughing. She was looking at me, steadily, not curiously; just looking.

FIFTH FACET

There were times during those winters that I sat with Painted Red when I thought that to be a gossip must be the most wonderful and strangest way to live. In those ancient rooms near the center of Belaire all our wisdom originates, born in the gossip's mind as she sits to watch the Filing System or think on the saints. Things come together, and the saint or the System reveals a new thing not thought before to be there, but which once born spirals out like Path along the cords, being changed by them as it goes. As I got older, the stories of the saints which Painted Red told absorbed me more and more; when one day I stayed after everyone else had gone, hoping to hear more, Painted Red said to me: "Remember, Rush, there's no one who would not rather be happy than be a saint." I nodded, but I didn't know what she meant. It seemed to me that anyone who was a saint would have to be happy. I wanted to be a saint, though I told no one, and the thought gave me nothing but joy.

But perhaps to others I might not have looked happy, a shy, slight kid, a Palm cord kid too much in love with knowledge, with a secret desire that made me inattentive and silent; maybe it was that desire that left me with what seems an odd set of memories of those years. Leaf cord remembers expeditions, achievements, summers they went naked and winters they built snow warrens. Buckle cord remembers skills and Thread cord remembers puzzles and Water cord remembers people: everyone's memories are of things, it seems, but mine aren't, not really; they are memories of things unspeakable, that I only remember because there are no words to put them in that could be forgotten. And remembering Painted Red, I know now I don't want to be a saint—I'd rather be happy. Do you know what I mean at all?

I think I do a little. And I know someone who would know what you mean, well.

He's Palm cord, probably. Except there are no cords here. . . .

Yes. In a way. I think he would be Palm cord.

Are you crying? Why?

No. Go on. Was that all your education was, the stories about the saints?

Oh no. There were other things. Painted Red told us stories about ancient times, long and fabulous stories impossible to remember all of, unless your memory is like a gossip's. The longest I remember her telling was called Money, and it went on for days and covered great stretches of time, and was full of angles. It was hard to believe it was all true, but it was told by a truthful speaker, and there was proof, though not very impressive for all the fantastic comings and goings and great powers of the stuff. It was just an oblong piece of paper, worn and limp like skin, with tiny figures all over it, and leaves I think, and a face in the leaves. It looked magical for sure, but not something to die for, as Painted Red insisted so many had.

But mostly, what Painted Red said wasn't as important as the speaking of it; she would talk to us often about nothing really, and gradually and with a skill I only see in looking back and couldn't ever explain to you, she made us truthful speakers. We were honest when we were young and came to see her, there's no other way for kids to be, even when they're not telling the truth; but when we went out from Painted Red's room at the end of a year or two years or five years, however long Painted Red thought each of us needed, then we were truthful speakers: in the ancient way, which we could not have explained but always thereafter did, we Really Meant what we Said and we Said what we Really Meant.

Even Once a Day, St. Olive's dark child, Whisper cord keeper of secrets—even she learned, almost against her will, to speak truthfully. She could not then lie to me, not truly. If she could have—if she weren't a truthful speaker—then it may be my life would not now be utterly bound up in hers, and her story my story.

The day the Money story was finished, Once a Day came up beside me as I was going along Path and slipped her arm in mine. I was too astonished to speak; she had done it as though she always did it, though in fact she had hardly spoken to me since the first day.

"Do you think Painted Red is wise?" she asked me.

I said, of course, that I thought she was very wise; perhaps the wisest person in the world.

"She knows a lot," Once a Day said. "She doesn't know everything."

"What doesn't she know?"

"There are secrets."

"Tell me."

She glanced sidelong at me, smiling slightly, but said nothing more. Then at a turn of Path she drew me into a curtained room there. It was dark, and crowded with things I couldn't make out; someone asleep was snoring softly. "Do you think she knows all about Money?"

I didn't answer. For some reason my heart had started to beat fast. Once a Day, watching my face, took from a pocket an object that seemed to glow in the darkness. She held it up before me.

"This is Money too," she said. "Painted Red didn't say anything about this Money."

It was a small disc of silver. On its surface was a head, not drawn but cut so that it seemed to be coming forth from the glittering surface; its eyes caught the little light in the room and seemed to study me. She turned it in her hands and showed me the other side; a hawk with open wings. She took my hand and placed the disc in it. It was warm from her flesh. "If I give you Money," she said, "you must do what I say." She closed my fingers around it. "You've taken it now," she said. Painted Red had said people had once given others Money to do their bidding. I felt as though I were participating in a sin as old as the earth. But I didn't want to refuse the Money in my hand. "What," I said, and found my throat almost too dry to speak, "what do you want me to do?"

She laughed, as though a joke had been told or a trick played. Without answering, she ran out. Under my thumb I could feel the face on the Money she had given me, its features and the upswept brush of its hair.

The next days she didn't come to Painted Red's; I glimpsed her with grownups of her cord, on errands of their own, and if she saw me she didn't acknowledge it; and when one day she slipped late among us in

Painted Red's room she said nothing to me. It was as if nothing at all had happened between us; perhaps, as she saw it, nothing had. I rubbed the Money in my pocket and thought of nothing but her. What was the word Painted Red used? An ancient word—I was *bot*.

The way people revolve back into the crowded warm interior of the warren in winter is matched by the way they come out as it gets warm again, slowly, the old ones staying in wrapped up till late in the spring, but the kids running out before the snow melts and catching crocuses and colds. I spent days in the woods, exploring with Seven Hands, gathering with Speak a Word, my mother, but often by myself; and one raw evening, carefully screened by a winter deadfall, I saw something that might unlock Once a Day to me.

I found her wrapped in red playing Rings with another girl of her cord. I couldn't tell her what I wanted with someone else present, so I sat and watched and waited. A game of Rings can take days, depending on what cord is playing it; Whisper cord uses it to tell the future in a way I never understood, and Once a Day had even further rules which the other girl got mad at, and at last left. I was alone with her.

She tossed the linked rings across the figured board, pouting, and gathered them up again. "It's hot in here."

"Outside it's nice," I said.

"Is it?" she said, half-watching her aimless throws.

"I could show you something you'd like. Out in the woods."

"What?"

"It's a secret. If I take you, you have to not tell anybody."

Well, they're lovers and collectors of secrets, and she questioned me further, but I wasn't telling, and at last she stood up and told me to take her.

The woods were budding pale green, and the streams were swollen with spring, the ground soft and growing. Thin clouds whipped away in the cold sky, but the sun was warm as afternoon went on, and we carried our shaggies over our shoulders, stumbling through ancient dead leaves and wet roots deep in the woods. On wet black branches new leaves glowed like glass and shook off water from the morning's rain as we pushed through them. "Here," I whispered when we had come to the place.

"What?"

"Climb up. I'll help you."

She climbed, clumsy-graceful, up the great fallen logs that spring had forced a few new shoots from. Her thighs tensed with effort, which made hollows in her flanks; her smooth pale legs were smeared with bark-rot, and there a tiny ruby scratch. At the top we crowded together into a narrow crotch that let us see, down in a cave protected by the tangled roots, a family of foxes. The mother and her cubs were just discernible, and no doubt invisible from everywhere but the one place where we stood. And as we watched, we saw the bright-tailed male return with a dead animal swaying from his jaws.

We watched in silence the wiggling cubs at their mother's belly, taking a few blind halting steps and turning to nuzzle her again. I was pressed close to Once a Day, who in order to see better had thrown an arm around my neck and lay against my back with her cheek pressed to mine. I could tell by her rapt silence that she was impressed with my secret. One of my legs was going to sleep, but I wanted her never to move.

"How many are there?" she whispered.

"Three."

"And she has them all at once?"

"Like twins."

"Twins?"

"When a woman has two babies at the same time."

"I've never heard of that."

"Mbaba told me it happens. Sometimes."

She pushed away from me at last, and climbed down. At the bottom she watched me descend; she shook her hair from her eyes as I jumped from the last big log, and walked toward me, commanding me with her eyes to do the same; we met, and she took my face in her hands, smiling, and kissed me. I think I surprised her by how fiercely I responded, and she pushed me away at last, holding me at arm's length, and, still smiling, wiped her mouth with the back of her hand. "I'll show you a secret now," she said.

"What?"

"Come on." She took my hand and led me back through the greening wood to where the twenty-three towers of Little Belaire were growing among the trees.

She took me quickly along Path where it led to the deepest center of old warren. "Where?" I asked as we ran. She pointed but said nothing, only flicking her head back in a flash of smile. Soon all the walls around us were of angelstone, and the lights were few, the doors small. It was warm here too; we were walking above the tanks and the stones that warm Little Belaire. There was a turn where she paused, uncertain; then she pushed through an ancient curtain, and we were inside a tiny stone-walled bare room, gloomy and warm, with a single small skylight in one corner. Through it the afternoon made a diamond shape on the rough wall.

My eyes grew big: on a chest near one wall stood a leg. Once a Day turned to me and laughed very small. It wasn't, I realized after a moment, a real leg, but a false one, yellow and waxy like dead flesh, with corroded metal parts and ancient straps. I stared at it.

"What is it?" I whispered.

"It's a leg," she said, and took my hand in hers and squeezed it. I wanted to ask whose it was, but only stood with my hand growing wet in hers.

"Come here," she said, and tugged me to the other side of the room where above us a thing hung on the wall. She pointed at it. "You must never, never tell anyone you came in here and saw this," she said to me in an urgent, commanding whisper. "It's a very secret thing in my cord. I'm going to tell you about it even if I shouldn't." Her blue eyes were grave, and I nodded gravely too.

The thing on the wall was made of plastic. It was like a tiny house with a high-peaked roof; but it was flat, with only a little shelf that stuck out in front of it. It had two doors, one on each side. Three people lived in the house, one of whom—I watched with hair rising on my neck—at that moment was backing into the right-hand doorway with tiny jerking motions, while the other two came jerking out the left-hand door. The one disappearing inside was an old woman, bent and hooded and gnarled, leaning on a stick; the two who began to appear were children, with their arms around one another.

"How do they move?" I said.

"That's the secret," Once a Day said.

In the space between the two little doors was pasted a strange pink and blue picture; it showed a great mountain (you could tell because tiny people were shown standing below looking up at it) that was four heads, four men's heads; four heads as big as mountains—four heads that were a mountain—with great grave faces and one with, it seemed, spectacles.

"This one," Once a Day said, pointing to the old woman whose hooked nose could just be seen inside the door, "hides when the sun shines. And these two"—pointing to the children—"come out." She looked up at the bright skylight. "You see? And when the weather changes, they move. It's ancient as anything. There are lots of secrets."

"Those four," I said. "Who are they?"

"Those are the four dead men. And are they mad."

We stared at the four stony faces, with the sky behind them falsely pink and blue. "It's their own fault," Once a Day said.

It was warm in the room, and a prickly heat was all over me, but in spite of it I shivered. The false leg. The thing on the wall that moved when it was light and dark, that only Whisper cord knew the secret of. And her small hot hand in mine.

A cloud went over the sun just then, and the diamond of sun disappeared from the wall. I watched the tiny children and the old woman, but they didn't move.

Sixth facet

How am I to tell you all of this? How? In order to tell you any single thing I must tell you everything first; every story depends on all the stories being known beforehand.

You can tell it; it can be told. Isn't that what it is to be a saint? To tell all stories in the single story of your own life?

I'm not a saint.

You are the only saint. Go on: I'll help if I can. Before nightfall it will be told; before moonrise at least.

I wanted to say: Whisper cord lay coiled within the cords of Belaire like an old promise never quite broken, or a piece of dreaming left in your mind all day till night comes and you dream again. But to say that I must tell you about cords. About the Long League of women, and how it came to be and came to be dissolved. About St. Olive and how she came to Belaire, and found Whisper cord. About Dr. Boots's List, and the dead men; about how I come to be here now telling this.

Cords. Your cord is *you* more surely than your name or the face that looks out at you from mirrors, though both of those, face and name, belong to the cord you belong to. There are many cords in Little Belaire, nobody knows exactly how many because there is a dispute among the gossips about cords which some say aren't cords but only parts of other cords. You grow into being in your cord; the more you become yourself, the more you become the cord you are. Until—if you aren't ordinary— you reach a time when your own cord expands and begins to swallow up others, and you grow out of being in a single cord at all. I said Painted Red had been Water cord, and her name was Wind; now she was larger than that and she had no cord that could be named, though in her way of speaking, in the motions of her hands, the manner of her life, in small things, she was still Water.

Water and Buckle and Leaf; Palm and Bones and Ice; St. Gene's tiny Thread cord, and Brink's cord if it exists. And the rest. And Whisper. And was it because of her secrets that I loved Once a Day, or because of Once a Day that I came to love secrets?

She liked night more than day, earth more than sky—I was the reverse. She liked inside better than outside, mirrors better than windows, clothes better than being naked. Sometimes I thought she liked sleeping better than being awake.

In that summer and the winter that followed it, and the next summer, we came to own Little Belaire. That's how it's put. When you're a baby you live with your mother, and move with her if she moves. Very soon you go to live with your Mbaba, especially if your mother's busy, as mine was with the bees; Mbabas have more time for children, and perhaps more patience, and especially more stories. From your Mbaba's room you make expeditions, as I did up to the roofs where the beehives are or along the learnable snake of Path—but always you return to where you feel most safe. But it's all yours, you see—inside to outside—and as you grow up you learn to own it. You sleep where you're tired, and eat and smoke where you're hungry; any room is yours if you're in it. When later on I went to live with Dr. Boots's List I saw that their cats live the way we lived as children: wherever you are is yours, and if it's soft you stay, and maybe sleep, and watch people.

We had our favorite places—tangles of rooms with a lot of comings and goings and people with news, quiet snake's-hands in the warm old warren where there were chests that seemed to belong to no one, full of rags of old clothes and other oddities. She liked to dress up and play at being people, saints and angels, heroes of the Long League, people in stories I didn't know.

"I must be St. Olive," she said, holding up to the light of a skylight a bracelet of blue stones she had found in a chest, "and you must be Little St. Roy and wait for my coming."

"How do I wait?"

"Just wait. Years and years." She dressed herself in a long sad cloak and moved away with stately steps. "Far away the League is meeting. They haven't met since the Storm passed long, long before. Now they meet again. Here we are, meeting." She sat slowly and put her hand to her brow; then she glanced up at me and spoke more naturally. "While we meet, you hear about it," she said. "Go on."

"How?"

"Visitors. Visitors come and tell you."

"What visitors?"

"This was hundreds of years ago. There were visitors."

"All right." I adopted a listening position. An imaginary visitor told me that the women of the Long League were meeting again. "What are they deciding?" I asked him.

"He doesn't know," Once a Day said, "because he's a man. But his women have gone to the meeting, bringing their babies and helping the old ones, all the women."

"But not the women of Belaire."

"No. No." She raised a hand. "They just wait. All of you wait, to hear what the League has decided."

I waited more while the League met. "Somehow you know," Once a Day said, "that someone is to come, to come to Little Belaire from that meeting, though it might be years, and bring news . . ."

"How do I know?"

"Because you're Little St. Roy," she said, losing patience with me. "And he knew."

She rose up, and taking tiny slow steps to lengthen the journey, came toward me. "Here is Olive, coming from the meeting." She progressed slowly, her eyes fixing mine where I waited for years in the warren, knowing she was to come.

"It's night," she said, her steps so slow and small she tottered, "When you least expect it, and then . . . Olive is there." She drew herself up, looked around surprised to find herself here. "Oh," she said. "Little Belaire."

"Yes," I said. "Are you Olive?"

"I'm the one you waited for."

"Oh," I said. "Well." She looked at me expectantly, and I tried to think what Little St. Roy would say. "What's new? With the League?"

"The League," Olive said solemnly, "is dead. I've come to tell you that. And I have a lot of secrets only you can hear, because you waited and were faithful. Secrets the League kept from the speakers, because we were enemies." She knelt next to me and put her mouth to my ear. "Now I tell them." But she only made a wordless buzzing noise in my ear.

"Now," she said, getting up.

"Wait. Tell me the secrets."

"I did."

"Really."

She shook her head, slowly. "Now," she said, commanding, "we must go and live together in your little room ever after." She took the cloak from her sharp shoulders, let it fall; she knelt beside me, smiling, and pressed me backward till I lay down. She lay down next to me, her downy cheek next to mine and her leg thrown over mine. "Ever after," she said.

"Why were the Long League and the speakers enemies?" I asked Seven Hands. "What secrets did they keep from us?"

He was at work making glass—the glass of Little Belaire is famous, traders still come to deal for it—and all morning had been mixing beechwood ash and fine sand with bits of angel-made glass from all over; now he threw in a broken bottle green as summer and said, "I don't know about secrets. And the speakers were never the League's enemies, though the League thought it to be so. It goes back to the last days of the angels, when the Storm came. That Storm was like any storm, on a day when the air is still and hot and yellowish, and big clouds are high and far away in the west; and as the storm comes closer it comes faster, or seems to, and suddenly there is rain in the mountains, and a cold wind, and it is on top of you. The Storm that ended the angels was like that: even when they were strongest the Storm was coming on, perhaps it had always been coming on, from the beginning. But few seemed to see it, except the League of women, who prepared themselves.

"And so when the Storm at last came in a thousand ways, multiplying, it seemed very sudden. But the League wasn't surprised."

He trod on the bellows that made his fire roar. "The Storm took years to pass; and when everything was going off and the millions were left alone without help, and great death and vast suffering, multiplying as the Storm multiplied, were visited on every part of the land, it was to the Long League fell the task of helping, and saving what and who could be saved, and cutting away the rest; repairing the angel's collapse where it could be repaired, and burying it forever where it could not. And for this huge task the League broke its old silence, and all the women acknowledged one another, because you see it had always been secret before. And for years the Long League of women saved and buried, till the world was different. Till it was like it is now."

His molten glass was ready, and he took up his long pipe and fixed a ball of it, turning and turning it with great care.

"Did everyone do what the League told them? Why?"

"I don't know. Because they were the only ones who were prepared. Because they had a new way to live, to replace the angel's way. Because people had to listen to somebody." He began to blow, his face red and his cheeks impossibly round. The green ball grew into a balloon. When it was the right size, working quickly he snipped off the end of it, and began to spin the pipe in his hands. What had been a balloon widened, flattened into a dish, seeming at every moment about to fall from the pipe.

"But the speakers didn't listen."

"No. During those years, we were wandering, and building Belaire. The women of Belaire had never been of the League, had never acknowledged that the League included them, though the League was said to be a league of all women everywhere. But our women were indifferent to almost everything but their speech and their histories and their saints. That angered and frustrated the women of the League, I guess, angered them because they needed all the help they could get and frustrated them because they were sure that the League knew what was best for the world."

"Did they?" Seven Hands's dish had become a plate, faintly green and striated with its cooling.

"Maybe they did. I guess our women thought it was only none of our business.

"What's odd though," he said, as he took the plate of glass from the pipe, "is that in hiding the terrible learning of the angels from everyone, so that the world had to become different, the League was left alone with it. They, who hated the angels most, were in the end the only ones who knew what the angels knew."

"Like what?"

He held his circle of glass, flecked with bubbles and green, like the stirred surface of a tiny pond, up before his face. "Don't ask me," he said. "Ask women."

Mbaba asked me: "Is it your Whisper cord girl who makes you ask all this?" I didn't answer. Of all the cords, Whisper is the one that stays most to itself. Knots happen with others.

"Well," Mbaba said. "I don't know any secrets Little St. Roy knew. I think he told all he knew. Little St. Roy wanted to be a gossip, you know, but in the end he said he wasn't smart enough. All his life he spent with them, though, serving them and carrying for them, and running Path with their messages. And listening to them talk. Little St. Roy said he was like an idea in the gossips' minds, and ran through Belaire with pails full of water and a head full of notions.

"Later when he lived with Olive he told hard stories. But he always had, though maybe he didn't think so, nobody knows.

"In those days the Filing System was just being learned, and Olive came to learn it as well as any; Little St. Roy said, 'Remember, Olive, it's time to stop when hunting for your identity turns into hunting it down.'

"He said, about Olive, that when she was dark she was very, very dark, and when she was light, she was lighter than air. I don't know what that meant. Maybe Whisper cord does."

When I asked Painted Red, she said: "I don't know what angel's secrets Olive might have brought. They aren't in the story I know. There is a cat in it, and a Light. That's all.

"It was a night in the middle of October," she went on, "when Little St. Roy was sitting near the outside to watch the full moon. The big many-paned skylight that these days is deep in was in those days nearer to the outside, and was the best place to sit and see the moon. He was busy watching for the full moon when, just as Little Moon came over, tiny and white, presaging Big Moon, a noise startled him, and he looked up to see before him a huge yellow cat. Little St. Roy said he felt the hair on his nape rise as he watched the cat regarding him frankly. And as the cat regarded him there came floating through the door from the outside a ball of light.

"A round ball of white light, as big as a head, floating at about a man's height, gently as a milkweed seed. It floated to a stop above the cat's head, and then there was a gust of wind and the Light drifted till it hung over Little St. Roy's head. Now, like all his cord, Little St. Roy could see things that no one else saw, and he looked at these signs and waited for what was to happen, which he guessed: and as he sat unmoving, a person followed the globe of light: a tall, lean woman, beak-nosed, her gray hair cut off short.

" 'Oh,' she said when she saw Little St. Roy. 'I'm here.'

" 'Yes,' said Roy, for he knew now who she was: that she was she whom he had waited for. 'At last.'

"Her huge cat had sunk slowly to the floor and placed his head on his paws, and she went and sat with him, gathering her cloak around her. 'Well,' she said, 'now you must take me within, and call together everyone who should hear what I've come to tell.'

" 'Please,' Roy said. 'In a minute I could take you deep within, and I know everyone who should hear your message, who first, who last; but . . .' Well, the woman waited. The great moon now lit the room and eclipsed her light. St. Roy spoke at last: 'It's been a long time since the League's meeting, since we learned that someone, or some news would come. It was I who learned that, and told Little Belaire about it, and waited for this day. And what I ask now is just for all that. I would like to know first what the news is. Now, before the others.'

"The woman looked at him a long time, and then laughed gently. 'It was always the story,' she said, 'that the Long League was much feared here, and its news ignored. Has it changed?'

"St. Roy smiled too. 'There are old things,' he said, 'and there are new things. I think the Long League must be changed now too.'

" 'No,' she said. 'No. There is no new thing with the League any longer. That's what I've come to tell you, as others have gone to tell all the old enemies of the League—everywhere we made enemies in the old, old days—to all of them women had gone to tell them: the League is done. It's all done now. For a long time our strength has withered, as any great strength must and should; and nothing has come up to challenge its strength and make it grow again. The world is different now. What it matters that we all came together to say this I don't know; but perhaps that last acknowledgment is the greatest success. Anyway. That's what I've come for. Just to tell you. The Long League of great memory is dead. My name is Olive, and I've come with this news, and if you'll have me, to stay and help.'

"Then the only noise in the room was the cat's and the moon's."

Painted Red took the claws of her spectacles from behind her ears and wiped them carefully. "What secrets she brought to Roy that Whisper cord inherits, I can't say," she said. "I know this though about Whisper cord: that for them a secret isn't something they won't tell. For them, a secret is something that can't be told."

Seventh facet

There's a time in some years, after the first frosts, when the sun gets hot again, and summer returns for a time. Winter is coming; you know that from the way the mornings smell, the way the leaves, half-turned to color, are dry and poised to drop. But summer goes on, a small false summer, all the more precious for being small and false. In Little Belaire, we called this time—for some reason nobody now knows—engine summer.

Maybe because summer seemed endless; but in that season of that year it seemed Once a Day and I could never be parted either, any more than Buckle cord could untangle sun from a crystal, no matter what unhappiness we might cause each other, no matter even if we wanted to be parted. When we weren't together we were looking for each other. It isn't strange that you think love, which is so much like a season, will never end; because sometimes you think a season will never end—no matter that you tell yourself you know it will.

In engine summer we went with an old breadman of Bones cord named In a Corner to gather in St. Bea's-bread. He allowed us to come as a favor to Once a Day's Mbaba, whom he had known long; a favor, because we were too young to be much help. We slept with him in his room near the outside, waking when dawn light came through his translucent walls of yellow. A misty engine summer morning, which would turn dry and hot and fine. Once a Day, shivering and yawning at once, stood pressed to me for warmth as we waited in the white dawn for everyone to gather, many carrying long poles with big hooks at their tips. After some head-counting and consultation, we moved away into the woods, following the stream up into the misty, sun-shot forest.

We would reach the stand of bread-trees at sundown, In a Corner thought, at the time when they were largest. "At night when it's cool, they grow smaller," he said. "Like morning glories; except that instead of closing up, they shrink. That's only one of the funny things about them."

"What are the other funny things?" Once a Day asked.

"You'll see," said In a Corner. "This afternoon, tonight. Tomorrow. You'll see all the funny things."

There was no path to follow to the stand; the other breadmen had spread out so that only occasionally did we see one or two moving beside us through the woods. Many besides the speakers smoke St. Bea's-bread, but it remains our secret where it lives, and we were careful not to stamp a path to that place. When we had harvested it and prepared it, then others would come to Belaire to trade for it; which was fun and I guess to everyone's advantage.

We came out of the forest late in the afternoon, came out from under big sighing pines into a wide field of silvery grass stirred by wind. The other breadmen were stretched out in a long line to our right and left, sometimes hidden up to their shoulders, making dark furrows in the grass. There was a high wave in the ground, and on top of it some of the breadmen already stood, waving and shouting to us. "From the top you can see them," In a Corner said; "you hurry on." And we did, racing to the top of the ridge where tall concrete posts stood at intervals like guardians.

"Look," Once a Day said, standing by a concrete post, "oh, look."

Down in a little river valley, sun struck the water, bright as silver. And struck, too, the stand of St. Bea's-bread, which lived there and (I think) nowhere else in this world.

Did you ever blow soap bubbles? When you blow softly, and the soap is sticky, you can grow a great pile of bubbles, large and small, from the cup of the pipe. Well: imagine a pile of bubbles as large as a tree, the big bubbles on the bottom as large as yourself, the small ones at the top smaller than your head, than your hand, trailing off in an undulating tip; a great irregular pile of spheres, seeming as insubstantial as bubbles, but the weight of them great enough to press down the bottom bubbles into elliptical sacks. And imagine them not clear and glassy like soap bubbles, but translucent, the upper sunside of them a pale rose color, the undersides shading into blue-green at the bottom. And then imagine as many of these piles of bubbles as fir trees in a grove, all leaning gently, bulging and bouncing as in a solemn dance, the ground around them stained colors by the afternoon sun striking through their translucence. That's what Little Belaire lives on.

We ran down to where they stood, across great fractured plazas of concrete, past ruined roofless buildings laid out angelwise in neat squares with the neat lines of weed-split roads between them, and into the stand itself. "They really *are* bubbles," Once a Day said, laughing, amazed. "Nothing. Nothing at all." They were membranes, dry and scored into cells like a snake's skin, and inside, nothing but air. The odor as we stood among them was spicy and dusty and sweet.

The breadmen were all gathering in the rosy light the bubble-trees made. They smiled to each other, slapped each other's backs, pulled and pinched at the skin of the bottom bubbles, coarse and thick, and shaded their eyes to look up at the pale, fine tops. It had been a good summer, humid and hot, and there would be no skimping next winter. The hooked sticks they carried were laid in a heap for the next day, and coils of thin rope were handed out from a big sack. Then we all dispersed—Once a Day and I following In a Corner—to circle the whole stand, and work inward till we met in the center.

In a Corner would choose a short length of rope and tie it very tightly around the feathery neck of a stem beneath the bottom bubbles. The stems were chest-high to Once a Day and me, and there were many of them supporting each tree.

"Except they're not supporting them, not really," said In a Corner. "That's another funny thing about them. The stems don't support the bubbles as much as they keep them from flying away. See, when the sun heats up the air inside, the whole tree grows huge, like now; and gets lighter. Hot air is lighter than cold air. And if they weren't tied down by the stems—"

"They'd float away," said Once a Day.

"Float right away," In a Corner said. His tough old hands drew the cord tight, tying off the stem. We were deep in now, moving slowly toward the center; all around us the blue-green undersides bulged and swayed in the slightest breezes. It was exhilarating; it made you want to jump and shout. "Lighter than air," Once a Day said laughing. "Lighter than air!"

In the center of the stand was a clearing, and in the center of the clearing were the ruins of low buildings and tall metal towers bent and rusted, some fallen to their knees; all faced a great pit in their midst, and in this pit, as though designed to fit there, there sat a squat, complex mass of black metal, high and riveted, from which struts shot out to grip the broad concrete lip of the pit—a great spider climbing from a hole. Machinery of unfathomable design protruded everywhere from its hump. The buildings and towers seemed to have fallen asleep in attendance on it.

"Is it the planter?" I asked.

"It is," In a Corner said. He coiled the last of his rope over his shoulder and motioned us to follow; Once a Day held back till I took her hand, and she pressed close behind me as we walked up to it.

"It went to the stars," I said.

"It did. And came back again." It and a hundred more like it, gone to the stars; and when they returned, after how many centuries, full of knowledge of the most outlandish kind—nobody was left to receive them. Of any left on earth, they were the only ones who still knew their purposes; and without men to receive it, their knowledge was locked within them. And they sat, with endless patience, but no one came, because they were all on the road or dead or gone. And at last the planters died where they sat, rusted, decayed; their memories disintegrated, their angel-made minds became dust.

"And how odd to think," In a Corner said, "that they were called planters because they were to have been the first of a system of machines that planted men on other stars. Instead, here it sits, having become a planter in truth: it planted the little balloon-tree from elsewhere here, on this earth, and is its planter, like an old black pot an mbaba plants marigolds in."

Up close, it was huge; it rose up, flat black, and glowered down at us. The couplings and devices that held it in place were of a strength that was hard to really believe in: metal that thick, that rustless, a hold that perfectly crafted, that tenacious. In its center what might have been a door had broken open; and from that door there foamed like a mouthful of great grapes the misshapen bubbles of the first of the trees, mother of them all. From this mother-plant, blue-green shoots had been sent out, and had found a way down through the struts and plates of the planter and then gone underground, like roots; and then had surfaced again, In a Corner said, as the other stems in the stand. "It's all one plant," he said, "if it is a plant at all."

Our work for that day was finished, and while the sun set we gathered wood and built fires on the concrete plazas beyond the bread.

"I don't know where it comes from," In a Corner said, laying the logs Once a Day and I brought in a circle that would keep us warm all night. "But I think things, about that place. It's a cold place, I think, and much larger than this one; these trees never grow so large there, and living things move slowly or not at all."

We looked out over the bread, which had already diminished as the chill of evening came on. "Why do you think that?" I said.

"Because from boyhood I have been smoking it. Because it has grown me up to be a man, and my eyes and my blood and my brain are partly made of its stuff, now. And I think I know: I think it has told me."

They say that the planters were far wiser than any human. I wonder: if this planter returned from who knows where and found that no one would ever learn what it knew, could it have let out its load on purpose, hoping (could it hope?) that someday men would learn a little, as In a Corner had? I suppose not. . . . In a Corner from his pouch drew a handful of last year's bread with knobby fingers.

It was all blue-green, without the rose color of the spheres; it shone with a strange interior light as he sifted it into the bowl of the big gourd pipe he carried hung around his neck. "It used to be thought, you know, not good to smoke it all the time. And later that if you did smoke it all the time, it must be piped through water, as in the great pipes. But you young ones pay no attention. And I think you know best. It won't harm you: hasn't harmed anyone. But it changes you. If you spend your life a man, and eat not only men's food, but this."

The reason it was thought, in the old days, to be bad, was because of St. Bea, of course. It was after the first hard winter at Little Belaire that she found the stand of bubbles, which smelled so nice when the sun warmed them; and St. Bea was hungry. And it wasn't even that eating the bread made her die, or even sicken; but when St. Andy found her, weeks later, still beneath the trees, her clothes had all gone to rags, she ate of the bread when she was hungry, and had forgotten him and the speakers and the new Co-op that was her own idea. And though she lived for some time after that, she never said another three words together that made sense to St. Andy.

That pipe you smoked from, in your Mbaba's room . . .

Yes. For a long time after it was learned to smoke it, hundreds of years ago, the pipes' mouths were made in the shape of St. Bea's head, her mouth open to receive it.

Her bread hissed and bubbled as In a Corner put match to it, hollowing his cheeks around the old chewed stem. The first rosy cloud billowed up. He gave the pipe to Once a Day, and she inhaled, and a thin rosy mist came out from her lungs, through her nose and mouth, and I shuddered with a sudden wonder at this odd consumption—odd though I'd seen it and done it almost all my life.

The first stars were winking on in the near blue sky. A breeze made the bowl of the pipe glow, and snatched away the smoke. One star, perhaps one we could see from here, was its home. But no matter how high the wind took it, it would never go there again.

Next morning was heavy with clouds, and the rafts came up the river from the south. All day the breadmen worked, pulling away the vast clusters from the strangled stems with their hooked sticks, and lifting them (on this cloudy day they weren't lighter than air, but almost as light) and maneuvering them to the rafts with shouts and directions, and tying them to the rafts with hooks and ropes through their skins. Once a Day and I weren't much help, but we ran and pushed and pulled with the rest as hard as we could, for they had all to be taken today, or they would collapse like tents and be unmovable.

When the last of them had been floated away to where Buckle cord burned maple for charcoal to dry it, and where it would be shattered then and sifted and packed to haul, and the whole glade stood naked, only the blue-green stems left, and the men from the rafts were left to cover those stems with sacks for the winter, and others were winding plastic and cloths around the planter to keep the mother-tree safe from snow, well, then the harvest was over; and Once a Day and I had helped; and we rode back on the next-to-last raft.

Exhausted, she laid her head in my lap, and we wrapped ourselves in a shaggy cloak someone gave us, for the wind was cold; blown leaves floated on the river's gray surface.

"Winter's coming," I said.

"No," she said sleepily. "No, it's not."
"It has to sometime."
"No."
"Well, if winter . . ."
"Hush," she said.

EIGHTH FACET

In a winter of rain, long after this, after my year with a saint, after my letter from Dr. Boots, a winter that I spent alone and often asleep, there was a trick I learned my mind can do: sometimes, halfway between waking and sleep, it would grow young again. How can I explain it? As though, for a brief moment, I would be a younger self; or as though a whole moment of my past would be given back to me, complete, no part of it missing, and so suddenly that often I wouldn't know which moment it was; before I could learn, I would fall asleep, or the effort of concentration would bring me awake and it would be lost.

Well, this was interesting, and I had time to practice it—in fact I had nothing else at all to do—and there were times I could do it for some time together, all my being reliving a past time, except for a small watching eye to marvel at it. I thought I was at the end of my life in that endless winter, and it seemed right that I should be allowed to review, in bits and glances, my short life, which seemed so long to me: like Mbaba going through the contents of her carved chests. I had no choice about when I find myself; I could be two or ten. I could be on the roofs in summer, my head thumping with heat under a hat and a veil, tending the bees with my mother. I could be deep in, in winter, in the stuffy warmth, learning Rings with Once a Day, my head full of that winter's notions, with that winter's flavor: because each season of each year—could it be each day, each morning and evening?—has its own taste, distinct, entirely forgotten, till you taste it again.

I could be listening to Painted Red weave the stories of the saints in her rich roomy voice, and beginning to see how all those stories were in some way one story: a simple story about being alive, and being a man; a story that, simple as it was, couldn't itself be told.

And once I closed my eyes, and waited, and didn't move, and found myself in my tenth spring, sitting with the others at Buckle cord's door, looking out at the flowering trees that littered with petals the way that led to the south, and watching come up that way, stark in their black clothes against the pink and white spring, a band of travelers, come to trade for bread. Around me the translucence of Buckle cord's walls pale yellow in the sun; beneath me the dirt of the floor, laid with bright rugs; beside me in their figured cloaks Water cord's traders and the pale sacks of bread. And next to me, just then slipping her hand from mine, Once a Day. I came awake in winter, wide-eyed, cold, my heart beating; and listened to the cold rain falling.

For many weeks that spring Once a Day had talked of nothing but the traders of Dr. Boots's List, who were to come; when she wasn't talking of them she was silent. The traders of the List came every year in the spring, they were almost our only visitors, and their arrival was a great event, but to Whisper cord they were more than visitors. "They're my cousins," Once a Day said, a word I didn't understand; when I asked her what she meant, she couldn't explain, except that it tied her closely to them.

"How can that be?" I said. "They aren't truthful speakers. They aren't your cord. You don't even know their names. Not one name."

"My cord is Olive's," she said, "and Olive was of the League. So is Dr. Boots's List. That's what 'cousins' means."

"The League is over and dead," I said. "Olive said so."

"Don't talk," she said, "about what you don't know."

There were a dozen or more coming up the way now, mostly men in wide low black hats ringed around with flowers. As they came closer we could hear their singing: or perhaps not singing, for there weren't any words, and no tune either, only a low humming in different tones and volumes, a burr here and a rumble there, changing as one left off or another started, each with his own sound. The old men and women of Water cord went down the hill to meet them, and the younger after to take their burdens, intricately tied packs and cases and bundles. There were greetings all around, quiet and formal, and the black-hatted men and tall women came up through Buckle cord's door into the pretty rooms they make near the outside, where I waited with Once a Day and the others come out to greet them. The bells they wore jingled and they talked in odd burring accents and old blurred speech, and their bundles were laid aside till fruit sodas and winter nuts were brought. Once a Day wouldn't take her eyes from them, though if one in his survey of those sitting there happened to look at her she looked away; I hadn't before seen the smile she smiled at them.

From a distance, black and bearded, they had seemed severe, but when they were close it was otherwise; their long straight robes were minutely decorated in gold and colors, and caught in complex folds for show, and their bells were tied on at surprising places that made you laugh when they rang. In their jingling, slow-smiling midst, you felt them to be people of immense ease and comfort, with grace and energy enough to sit forever. They reminded me of Painted Red telling about St. Olive's cat.

Bread from the fall gathering was handed around by the Water cord traders to the visitors, whose bells and bracelets sounded as they passed the glittering handful of flakes from hand to hand to be felt and sniffed and looked at. Old In a Corner threw handfuls of it into the great brass mouth of St. Bea—almost as large as life—that topped a huge amber glass pipe, moved here to the outside on a tripod the day before in expectation of guests. It was hundreds of years old, and one of Buckle cord's chief treasures, even though it had no story about it except how old it was, so Palm cord wouldn't have thought it such a wonder.

One of the traders came and lowered himself gracefully to sit next to Once a Day. He was a brown, wrinkled man like a nut, his wrists and hands gnarled and rooty, but his smile was broad and his eyes alert and smiling too as he looked down at Once a Day, who looked away from him, overcome. When he looked away, she looked up at him; when he looked down at her, she looked away. Then she undid from her wrist the bracelet of blue stones she had found in an old chest and claimed as her own.

She held it up to him, and he took it lightly in his yellow-nailed fingers. "This is nice," he said. He turned it, and held it to the light; he smiled "What do you want to trade for it? What do you want?"

"Nothing," she said.

He lifted his eyebrows at her, passing the bracelet from hand to hand; then he smiled, and clasped the bracelet around his own wrist, and without a word, giving it a brief shake to settle it among the others he wore, attended to the trading again. Once a Day, with a secret smile, took up in her hand a corner of his black robe that lay near her, and held it.

Through the afternoon the men and women of the List opened their cases, laid out their goods, and the Bread was measured out. They had brought Four Pots, each set of four in its own case; it was the black one of these, which contained a rose-colored stuff, that had made me dream with Painted Red, and the others are for other uses; the List calls them "medicine's daughters," and they alone know the secret of them. They had implements and odd pieces of angel silver, which they called "stainless steel." They had boxes and jars filled with sweet herbs and dried spices, sugar made from beets, and flea powder for cats; for Buckle cord, old things to fix, edged tools, angel-made nuts with their own bolts attached; for Palm cord, ancient found things, keys, whistles, and a ball of glass inside which a tiny house was snowed on.

For these we traded glass bowls and other glass, spectacles bound in plastic, papers for smoking, rose, yellow, and blue, honeycomb, turtle-shell polished to look like plastic, and yards and yards of translucent plastic ribbon on which were hundreds of square pictures, good for belts. And of course Bread, in sacks, as valuable to them as the medicines they brought were to us. In two or three rooms the trading went on filled with sweet smoke, a murmur of talk, and the deepening color from the yellow walls; so many wanted to trade, or just to see the visitors and hear them, that I had to give up my place, but Once a Day kept hers near the brown man who wore her bracelet.

The visitors slept that night with Whisper cord, in twos and threes in rooms far from Path and near the outside—these were ancient precautions, just forms now, but still observed—and late at night, if you passed the rooms where they were, you saw them deep in talk, or laughing together. And I did pass by, not daring to enter their circles though no one had said I was forbidden, and loitered outside, trying to overhear what passed between them.

In the first dawn I awoke alone, crying out because I saw a sudden

face looking down at me, but there was no one there. As though summoned, and too much still asleep to ignore the summons, I followed Path
quickly toward Buckle cord's door, running from dim pool to dim pool of
blue light which poured from skylights above; no one was awake. But
when I came near Buckle cord's door there were other shapes coming
onto Path, and I hid and watched.

Dr. Boots's List was leaving, guided out by a woman of Whisper
cord, their big packs on their shoulders altering their shapes in the dimness. The door was shown them, a square of blue dawn growing brighter,
and the woman withdrew without farewell. They waited a moment till
they had all collected, and started toward the door; and someone small
darted out from Path to overtake them.

I stepped out from where I hid and took Once a Day's arm, somehow
not surprised now though I hadn't for a moment suspected it. "Wait," I
said.

"Let me go," she said.

"Tell me why."

"No."

"Will you come back?"

"Don't ask me."

"Tell me you'll come back. Promise. Or I'll follow you. I'll tell Seven
Hands, and In a Corner, and your Mbaba, and we'll follow you and bring
you back." I spoke in a frantic, rapid whisper, only half-aware of what I
said. I hadn't released her, and now she took hold of my arm that held
her, and so we stood joined, staring at each other's half-seen faces.

"I gave you Money," she said, quiet but intent. The Money was in my
sleeve; I was never without it. "I gave you Money and you must do what I
say." She took my hand from her. "Don't follow me. Don't tell anyone
where I've gone, not today, not tomorrow, not till I'm far away. Don't
think about me any more. By the Money I gave you."

I was stilled, hopeless and afraid; and she turned away. The last of
Dr. Boots's List, the brown, rooty man, glanced back at her as she hurried
to catch him.

"In the spring," I said. "You'll come back."

"This is spring," she said, not looking back; and she was gone. I went
to the door and watched them, cloaked and hatted in the misty dawn, go
single-file away to the south; and Once a Day in a blue dress, her black
hair flying, running to catch them; and I thought, before the mist, or
tears, made them invisible, I saw one take her hand.

I hid that day, for there was no one I could go to who wouldn't question me, no one I could talk to that my speech wouldn't betray me to. Almost, almost, in an agony of doubt, I went to Seven Hands; but I didn't. She wouldn't be missed unless I raised the alarm, for she could be anywhere, and safe anywhere, in the tangle of Belaire; but I didn't know if it was best. I knew nothing, and so I left the decision to her. I thought: it's been arranged; Whisper cord arranged it; grownups decided on it. I didn't know if this was true, but I tried to believe it; and I hid.

Seeking places where I would be alone, I dug deeper into the old warren, and came, late, to the room Once a Day had led me to the spring before, the room that on its walls of angelstone bore the little house where the two children and the old woman went in and out their little doors according to the weather, and the false leg stood in a corner.

How could it be that I hadn't known? We had been like two fingers of the same hand; we were truthful speakers; yet I hadn't known, any more than I understood now. Perhaps, I thought, it hadn't been till that very moment, that dawn, that she had decided; but I couldn't believe that. She had known, and planned it, and thought about it, thought—it must be—about nothing else for days; and yet I hadn't known.

I thought about what she had said: cousins; and how she, who was Whisper, was of the League even as Dr. Boots's List was, however distantly. I thought that whatever secrets Olive had brought from the League that Whisper cord knew, Dr. Boots's List must know more, just as they knew medicine and traveled, as the old League had; I thought about what Painted Red had said, that for Whisper cord a secret isn't something you won't tell, but something which can't be told.

I thought about all that, but none of it combined to make a sense I understood. I studied the little plastic house on the wall. On its ledge there now stood the old woman, alone; the two children hid.

The old woman comes out when it's dark, she said, and the two children when the sun shines. And when the weather changes, they change. And four dead men. Are they mad, she said.

But overhead the sun shone, and spring was full.

I understood nothing at all, and cried a long time in the dim little room, hiding, left alone with the house and the leg and every untold secret.

It was a barometer.

What?

A barometer. The little house on the wall; it was a barometer. A thing which tells about the weather. An engine, is all.

Yes. About the weather. But don't you see . . .

Wait. This crystal is finished.

THE SECOND CRYSTAL

THE LAUGHTER OF
THE LEGLESS MAN

First facet

W hat is it?
A crystal. A crystal with eight sides: you see? I've replaced it with another. We can go on now.

I don't understand. Why did we stop?

The crystals record what you say. Everything you've said was—was cut, or impressed, on the facets of this crystal; I can't explain how. Then it can be recaptured, with another engine, and we can hear again exactly what you said; the very words, as you spoke them.

Like the Books that Blink had.

Yes. In a way. . . .

But why would you want such a thing? I'm only a thing like that now myself; I know that, though I feel myself to be truly here. I'm a sort of crystal only, or—or a fly trapped in a block of plastic. . . .

What?

A fly. Inside a block of plastic. That was a thing Blink had. . . . Tell me. Who is it that I am?

Rush that Speaks.

That's not an answer.

It's the only one that's true now.

It's very confusing. I feel myself to be me, and only me; but that can't be so.

Go on with your story; it's less confusing. It's best just to tell the story, beginning to end—that's something we know about you. Will you tell about Blink?

Blink.

If Blink was a saint, then I'm not; if Blink wasn't a saint, then perhaps it's true that I could be one. Transparent: that's what Painted Red said the saints were, or tried to be; and that's what I am now, isn't it?

She said: "The saints found that truthful speaking was more than just being understood; the important thing was that the better you spoke, the more other people saw themselves in you, as in a mirror. Or better: the more they saw themselves through you, as though you had become transparent."

It was the end of my second seventh year, and I had come to have the System read for me again; and before she began work with her lenses and squares of glass we sat talking, eating apples which reminded me of the first day I had come to learn with her.

"Why are there no saints now?" I asked.

"Well," she said, "perhaps there are. Saints aren't known to be saints, you know, till long after they're dead, and people see that their stories have lived. So if there are saints now, we don't know it."

"But there haven't been saints. Not for many lives."

"That's true," she said. "Little St. Roy and St. Olive were the last; and St. Gene, if he's a saint, as Thread cord thinks. But there are quiet times, you know, centuries long they can be, where the task is only to learn what the busy times discovered; and then there will come a time of new discovery. People in motion."

"Seven Hands thinks one is beginning now."

"Does he?"

"He talks about leaving Belaire, 'going to meet it and not wait,' he says."

"Yes?"

I knew by the way she spoke that she doubted Seven Hands truly knew of a new thing, or meant to go out and discover it. "And Once a Day left," I said.

"Who is that?" Painted Red said. "Ah, the Whisper cord girl . . ." She looked at me closely. "Do you suppose she left to learn to be a saint?"

"I don't know."

"Will you follow where she went?"

"I don't know," I said. "No."

When Once a Day had at last been found to be missing, I was questioned. I said I knew she had gone with the List, and of her own accord, but not why, or whether she would return; and they saw that this was the truth. The news went quickly all through Belaire, and there were reproaches, and a meeting was nearly held; messages flew along Path, and gossips met, but no one could determine whether the grownups of Whisper cord had known beforehand what Once a Day would do, or not, or if the List had asked her to come, or how it had come about. It ought to be, among truthful speakers, that such mysteries couldn't occur, but they can. Little St. Roy said: "Truthful speaking would be a simple way to tell the truth, if the whole truth were simple, and could be told."

When the traders of the List came next spring, she wasn't among them. Waiting for them to come, I had imagined a lot of things: that she would return, but would be changed beyond recognition, unable to speak truthfully; that she would not be changed at all, would greet me as she always had, and share with me all the wonders she had seen; that she would be sorry she had run away, and ask us humbly to take her back; that she would have sickened and died amid the alien surroundings of the List, and they would bring back her white, sad corpse amid them. But she didn't come back at all; and they would only say that she was well, and happy enough, and they forgot what else, nothing important, and could the trading begin?

We counted our children, that spring, after they had gone.

Every spring I waited for her, but she didn't return. Every year, waiting for the List to come, waiting for her, became part of waiting for spring. It made the need for spring more urgent, the boredom of winter's end more maddening; made the signs—snow torrents, birds returning—spur me more terribly. She, who was so autumnal, so indoor, came to mean spring to me.

"You won't follow her," Painted Red said. "Then where will you go?"

"Well, I don't know," I said. "Not exactly."

"For someone who's to be a saint," she said, "you don't know a lot of things." She smiled. "That's a good sign."

That Painted Red knew, though I had not told her or anyone, that I meant to leave Little Belaire and learn to live a life that could be told in stories—that I meant to be a saint—didn't surprise me. I *had* told her. There was nothing now that I knew or wanted or thought that I could keep from telling her: for I spoke truthfully, and it was she who had taught me.

"A life," she said, folding her hands and regarding the first slide of the System which shone on her wall, "is circumstances. Circumstances are encirclings, they're circles. The circle of a saint's life, all its circumstances, is contained in the story of his life as he tells it; and the story of his life is contained in our remembering it. The story of his life is a circumstance in ours. So the circle of his life is contained in the circle of our lives, like circles of ripples rising in water."

She rose, leaving the marks of her skirts on the hard dirt floor. From the long box that was Palm cord, she drew out a second square of glass and put it in place with the other. The board changed; colors mixed and became other colors; masses changed shape, became newly related to other masses.

"Do you see?" she said. "The saints are like the slides of the System. Their interpenetration is what reveals, not the slides themselves."

"It's like the saints," I said, "because they made their lives transparent, like the slides; and their lives can be placed before our own, in our remembering their stories, and reveal things to us about ourselves. Not the stories or the lives themselves, but their—"

"Interpenetration, yes," Painted Red said. "They're saints not because of what they did, especially, but because in the telling of it, what they did became transparent, and your own life could be seen through it, illuminated.

"Without the Co-op Great Belaire there would be no truthful speaking. Without truthful speaking there could be no transparent life. And in transparent life, the saints hoped that one day we might be free from death: not immortal, as the angels tried to become, but free from death, our lives transparent even as we live them: not through a means, you see, like the Filing System or even truthful speaking, but transparent *in their circumstances:* so that instead of telling a story that makes a life transparent, we will ourselves be transparent, and not hear or remember a saint's life, but live it: live many lives in the moment between birth and dying."

"How could that come about?" I said, unable to grasp it, or even imagine it.

"Well," she said, "If I knew, perhaps I would be a great saint. Perhaps if you discover it . . . But tell me this, Rush that Speaks: how anyway is truthful speaking itself done?"

I must know that; I was a truthful speaker, the craft could never be taken from me; and yet . . . How: Painted Red's question reverberated within me, as a thing held up between two mirrors multiplies itself endlessly; as though my mind were crossing as my eyes can cross. I laughed, helpless. "I don't know," I said. "I don't know how it's done."

She laughed with me. She leaned forward, as though to impart a secret, and almost whispered to me: "Well, well, you know, Rush, I don't know either!"

Still chuckling, she picked up the long box which contained Palm cord's slides, to continue her preparations. A thought struck her as her fingers moved over the tabs. "You asked me once, Rush," she said, "what the names of these slides are, and how they go together."

"Yes."

"Do you still want to know?"

"I do."

"It's the day for it," she said, regarding me for a long time with a tenderness that was like a farewell. "The one you see," she said, "the first slide, is Fourth Finder, Palm cord's slide: you see, in the center, where the lines meet, a figure like the palm of a hand? And the other placed over it is called Little First Slot. Together, they make Little Knot." She took a third slide from the box and placed it behind the others. "Little Knot and Hands make Little Knot Unraveled." She put two more with them. "Little Knot Unraveled and the two Stair slides make Great Knot." Carefully she drew out and inserted the thin, thin pieces of glass. "Great Knot and First Trap make Little Trap. Little Trap and the Expedition make Little Second Gate, or Great Trap Unlocked in Leaf cord. Little Second Gate and the Ball Court make Gate."

The figures on the wall had grown tangled and dark, infinitely intertwining. When one slide seemed to make a pattern of the previous ones, the next distorted the pattern. And now I could see nothing in it. Painted Red's hands lingered over the rest of the slides in her box. "It's thought," she said, "that Gate and the second and great Slot slides, together with the Broken Heart and the Shaken Fragments slides, all make Great Knot Unraveled. But no one can read that much; no one who can begin to understand Gate can even begin to read that much." She touched the lens tube to sharpen the figures; sharpness came and went amid the overlayed figures as she moved the tube. She came and sat by me again. "The gossips know, now, after many years of searching, that it can't be read past Gate, not packed all together; and if Great Knot Unraveled is the whole set, then Great Knot Unraveled can never be read."

"Does that mean," I asked, "that it's no longer any use? Since you know that? It doesn't, does it?"

"Oh no," she said. "No, no. It will be a long time before we have learned everything there is to learn even from Little Knot. But . . . well. It seemed, when the System was first being truly searched, in St. Olive's time, it seemed that . . . it seemed there was a promise, that one day it would be seen all together, and answer all questions. Now we know it won't, not ever. When that was first understood, there were gossips who broke up their Systems, and some who left Belaire; that was a sad time."

She pushed her spectacles back along her nose. "For me: well, I know there are enough byways, and snake's-hands, and things to be learned from the System to last many lifetimes. And work enough to do with its wisdom among the cords, in their knots and troubles." She looked at Gate, and its lights were reflected from her spectacles. "And the whole answer is there, you know, Rush, though I can't read it; it knows everything, about people, though I never will. That's enough to keep me in its presence."

She was silent a long time, and seemed to grow older. Then: "When will you leave?" she asked me.

"In the spring," I said. "I think I'll be ready then."

"A saint," she said. "You know, Rush, the first time you came to see me, seven years ago, you had a different thought. You were going to go out and find all our things that were lost, and bring them back to us."

"Yes."

"Is your Whisper cord girl one of those things that was lost?"

I said nothing. Painted Red had not looked at me, only at Gate. "Well, perhaps after all it's not a different thought, not really. . . ." She struck her knees with her palms. "No," she said. "No, I won't read for you this year. I think, if you mean to do this, it could hurt as much as help. Do you mind?"

"If you think it's right."

"I do," she said. She had me help her up. "I do." Could it be that I had—almost instantly—grown taller than she, or had she somehow just as quickly shrunk? She took my shoulders in her strong hands. "When you go," she said, "never forget us and our needs. Whatever you find, if it's useful to us, save it; make the knowledge you got here into a box to carry it, it can be used for that. And however far away you go, come back with what you find to us."

And so she embraced me, and I left her, and ran away down the puzzle of Path that I knew by heart, through rooms and passages that seemed also to have grown smaller suddenly. I wondered about the reading of the System, and what it might have shown for me and my endeavor, what possibilities, what failures; and I felt a cord cut that had tied my childhood to Little Belaire, and a little lost, and a little free. She must have known best, though: if she knew nothing else (and she did, much else) she knew when and when not to tell what the System revealed.

But forget Little Belaire! She could not have thought I could forget it. The longer I'm away, the more it grows in my mind, the stream that runs through it speaking, its bugs and birds and berry bushes, the mystery at the heart of it hidden perhaps in the Filing System or the saved things of the Carved Chests; and now, now after I have lived in a tree and gotten a letter from Dr. Boots and been dark and light and lived as an avvenger and been taken apart and put back together any number of ways, though now I think sometimes that that place in the woods is imaginary and I am not a truthful speaker at all, do not really mean what I say or say what I really mean, and have invented all of it: still, even if it's a dream, it's a dream dictated by a voice that speaks truthfully: a voice that cannot lie.

SECOND FACET

Y ou did, though, really set out to find Once a Day again. Didn't you?

I don't know. Perhaps I did. I didn't know it.

When I was a kid, I wanted to find our things that were lost; as I grew up, and heard the stories of the saints, and listened to Seven Hands talk, I had another ambition: I wanted to be a saint. I wanted to have strange adventures, which I could tell of; and learn forgotten secrets, secrets stronger than the ones Once a Day kept from me; and make sense of the world in the stories I told.

Painted Red suspected that what I really wanted to do was follow Once a Day; that perhaps she was the lost thing I most wanted to find.

And she told me that what saints attempt to do is to become transparent.

How could I know, that spring, what it was I most wanted, or what would become of me? And how was I to know that all of those things were true, that they would all happen to me, every single one?

Well, I didn't. What I thought was this: that despite what Painted Red had said about saints nowadays, somewhere in the world there must

be a saint, a saint like the saint I wanted to become; and that what I
ought to do first was to find such a saint, and sit down before him, and
study him, and learn from him how to go about being what I couldn't
imagine being: transparent.

Seven Hands and I had made many expeditions together, sometimes
spending a week outside Belaire, just seeing what we could see. I had
learned to climb rocks, to make fires with wet wood, tell directions, and
to walk all day without worrying that I didn't know just where I was
walking to. Preparations, Seven Hands called these; and as my resolve to
leave Little Belaire grew stronger, I made these preparations more eagerly,
with greater attention. And Seven Hands came to know—though we
never spoke of it—that the preparations we made were in the end mine,
and not his.

I had a shaggy blue shirt, and bread and a pipe and some dried fruit
and nuts; I had a string hammock, light and strong, that Seven Hands
had made for me, and a sheet of plastic to hang above it to make a tent. I
had Four Pots and some other doses; I had my new spectacles that My
Eyes had made for me. They were yellow, and turned the white May
morning into deepest summer; I took them off and put them on again for
entertainment, looking now and then up into the trees for saints.

In the trees?

Because the saints always lived apart from us, and often in houses
built into trees. I don't know why. I thought, one day, I would live in a
tree as those old saints had; I would choose a great low-branching oak
or maple, like some I passed. I loved already the saint I knew I would
be, saw with strange clarity that old man, could almost, though not quite,
hear the compelling stories he would tell. . . . When the sun was high,
I crept into a little woods that bordered a marshy stream where wild cows
sometimes could be seen drinking, and smoked. Then there was nothing
to do but keep on. With only a morning of my adventure passed so far, it
began to seem impossibly long; and I decided I would lighten that load.

Of the Four Pots, it is the silver one that lightens a load. It contains
many small black granules like cinders, of different sizes; I knew this
because I had seen Mbaba open it and swallow one. I knew also that to
lighten the load of a journey, you must know clearly before you lighten
your load just where you are going, how you will get there, and when
you intend to arrive. I knew the way to That River, and that it would take
me till nearly sunset to find it and the bridge of iron that Seven Hands

and I had crossed; so I cracked open the pot and—a little uncertain and a little afraid of what was about to happen to me (for I had never done this before)—I selected a small one of the black granules and swallowed it.

A little bit later my footsteps slowed as I approached an enormous maple that shaded the way. The sound of the wind in its branches grew slow also, and low, like a moan, and then slower, till it was too low to be heard. The sound of the birds slowed, and the movement of the leaves; the sunlight dimmed to a blue darkness that was still daylight, like the light of an eclipse; one branch of leaves absorbed my attention, and then one leaf; I had leisure between one footstep and the next to study it quite intensely, while the sunlight on it didn't change and the low call of a bird extended note by note infinitely. I was waiting with enormous patience for my raised right foot to fall, which it seemed it would never do, when the leaf and the birdcall and the soundless moan of the wind went away, the footfall struck and I found myself standing before That River, downstream from the iron bridge, watching the sun go down. I laughed, amazed. Lighten my load! I had traveled the whole of an afternoon, miles, and hadn't noticed it. I suddenly understood the chuckle of old men when they look, a little startled, at some day-long task they have completed after taking one of these black cinders to lighten the load.

I looked back the way I had come, the trees turning their leaves in the evening breeze, and regretted missing the journey. You lighten a load, I saw then, which you have carried a hundred times before; or to go a journey you must make but would rather not. It wasn't for new journeys or new saints. There's a lesson, I thought, and spun the little pot so that it skipped across the brown swollen river and sank.

Across That River the sun still lit the tops of the hills, but down amid the weeds and roots at the water's edge it was growing dark and a little cold. A frog plunked. I put my hands in my armpits and watched the current go by; I was tired—I really had come a long way—and I wondered if I had put match to more than I could smoke. There was a gurgle and splash of water then, and out on the river a man strode by. Strode: the water came up to his chest, and his shoulders made the vigorous motions of a man striding; a wake flowed out behind him. He shot on past me without seeing me in the shadows; he was moving quickly on the current.

Amazing! Without exactly knowing why, I ran along the riverbank following him, stumbling on roots and plunging my feet in mud. I lost sight of him, then glimpsed him through the trees floating away serenely, a fair pigtail and his wet white shirt flapping. I was some time crashing through the willows and vines at the river's edge, the mud sucking at my boots, till I saw him again, standing up as ordinary as any man, on a wooden wharf built out over the water, laughing with a woman who was toweling him vigorously as he squeezed water from his pigtail. Just as they turned to see what was clambering through the bushes, I lost my footing and slithered like an otter into the muddy river.

They helped me out, laughing and wondering how I came to be there, and it was a moment—a spluttering moment—till I realized they were truthful speakers. They took me up onto their wharf, which connected by a set of stairs to a house built into the bank of the river. And tied up to the wharf, riding high out of the water without his weight on it, was what had allowed him to walk the river: two big cylinders of light metal, with a seat attached between them, and handholds, and broad foot pedals to make it go. He was Buckle cord, I knew then. I was going to tell him about my amazement at seeing him on the river, but just then a boy burst through the door that led out of the house, stopping when he saw me. He was a couple of years younger than me, tanned already, and his hair sun-streaked. He carried a stick and was naked except for a blue band around his neck.

I was thinking how I might explain myself to him, but at that moment a boy came out the door behind him, stopping when he saw me. He was tanned, and his hair sun-streaked; he carried a stick and was naked except for a red band around his neck.

They were the only twins I have ever seen. It was hard not to stare at them as I wrung out my wet clothes. They stared at me too, not that there was anything remarkable about me; they stared with a look I didn't understand then, but know now is the look of people who don't see strangers often.

"This is Budding," said the man, "and that is Blooming." I couldn't help laughing, and he laughed too. "My name is Sewn Up, and she is No Moon. Come in and get dry." Buckle cord, as I supposed; and the woman must be Leaf; the two boys were harder to tell, maybe because there were two of them.

Inside the house, the sunset over the water glinted and glittered on the ceiling and across the dark, rug-hung walls so that it felt as though we were under water too. The gurgle of the river made me sleepy, and sitting with the water-walker and his family made me feel like a fish visiting fish friends. Sewn Up talked as he lowered and filled a glass pipe;

his voice was a good one, with odd insides that made me laugh, and made No Moon laugh even more. I asked him why he didn't live in Little Belaire.

"Well," he said, motioning to the two boys with a spoonful of bread, "they liked the water, and the stream that runs through Little Belaire wasn't enough water for them. Their Mbaba said they moped a lot, so I said if they liked water, they should come back and stay here; and if they liked people—other people besides us, anyway—they should stay at Little Belaire. Well, they get along best with each other, so here they stay."

"We were born here," Blooming said, and Budding said, "This is our spot."

"I took them back, you see, for a while," No Moon said; "it's their home, in a way, as it was mine and still is. But they like it here."

"Aren't they going to be truthful speakers?"

"Well, if we're truthful speakers, so will they be, won't they? There are two truthful speakers in the river house and no river in Little Belaire, so it all works out fine."

And it was better for them, too, Sewn Up said; people would always make much of them, there were people who came a great distance just to see them, and he didn't want it to go to their heads; he had pointed out to them that there was nothing really so remarkable about them. They said nothing to this, only smiled the same smile; they knew there was something very remarkable about them, and so did we.

There was a thick, dry smell of smoke in the cool room, easier to breathe almost than air. When Sewn Up talked, puffs of smoke mimicked his words from his nose and mouth. "Odd you should find it odd to leave Little Belaire," he said, sprinkling new bread onto the blue ashes. "It seems you've made the same choice yourself, and younger than we were by quite a bit."

"Oh no," I started to say, but thought that, yes, I had, and had no intention of returning, not for years and years; yet I had been feeling sorry for Budding and Blooming, who couldn't stay there in the best place in the world all the time. "I'm just, well, ranging; I'll go back, one day. It'd be terrible if I couldn't ever go back." And terrible it did seem to me for the first time.

"Well," No Moon said rising, "stay here anyway as long as you want. We have room."

So when I could think of no more news of the warren to give them, and the lights No Moon lit were growing low, I followed the two boys up a winding flight of stairs to a room with glass windows all around, open to the clear night which Little Moon sped across. But sleepy as I was, it was a long time before we were quiet under our shaggy blankets. I lay amazed and listened to Budding finish Blooming's words and then Blooming Budding's, as though they were one person. Giggling and laughing at things I didn't understand, they rolled over each other like otters; they had looked tan in the sun, but in the pale night light they were white against the dark covers.

They had treasures to show me, tucked away at the bottom of the bed and in boxes, an empty turtle shell, a twitch-nose mouse in a nest of grass. And, taken carefully from its hiding place in the wall, their best thing. It was a little cube of clear plastic; inside the plastic, poised for flight, a fly. A real fly. A cube of plastic with, who could tell how, a fly right in the middle of it! We turned it in the moonlight, our faces close together. "Where did it come from?" I asked. "Is there a story? Where did you get it?"

"The saint gave it to us," said one, and the other was drawing out something else for me to see, but I stopped him at hearing that.

"A saint gave you that? What saint?"

"The one we know," said Budding.

"You know a saint?"

"The one who gave us this," said Blooming.

"Why did he give it to you? What is it?"

"I don't know," said one. "It's a lesson, he said. The fly thinks he's in the air, because he can see out all around, and can't see anything that holds him back. But still he can't move. And let that be a lesson, he said."

"It was just a present," said the other one.

"Can I see him?" I asked, and they must have been surprised at the urgency in my voice. "Is he far away?"

"Yes," said one.

"No," said the other. "He's not too far. Walk all morning. We can take you. He might not like you."

"He likes you."

The two of them looked at each other and laughed. "Maybe that's because," said Budding, and "there are two of us," said Blooming, and they stood with their arms around each other, grinning at me.

With true Leaf cord politeness, they let me choose where I would sleep, but I lay awake a long time, listening to the gurgle of the brown river, with a saint to see tomorrow, already, so soon!

THIRD FACET

In the morning, Sewn Up ferried us across That River on his contraption, laughing and making jokes: I've never seen anyone as happy to be up in the morning as he, except maybe myself on this morning, off to meet a real saint. Budding and Blooming wore thick shirts against the morning chill and the mist that lay thickly over the river and its fragrant tributaries, and I shivered. No Moon had given me more bread, and a nice plastic bottle full of grape soda she'd put up in the winter, and a kiss.

"I'll go to the warren in the fall," she said. "I'll tell them I saw you, and that you were well."

I thought of a thousand messages she might bring for me—gone only a day!—but I kept quiet and only nodded, an adventurer's uncaring nod, and climbed behind Sewn Up.

The twins and I followed a rushing tributary of the river for some time till it ran quietly between its wooded banks; when the sun was high and hot and the mist gone, we came to an inlet where a little dish of a boat was tied up among the saplings at the water's edge. It was something angel-made of white plastic, and (like so many things in the world) put to a use the angels surely never intended; certainly, with its odd ridges and projections and strange shape, it had not been made for a boat. So hot and still it had become that Budding and Blooming threw their warm shirts into the bottom of the dish, and I sat on them and watched the twins pole along. Some white water-flowers came away with the boat from the inlet, and the twins pulled them out of the water to wear for hats; naked, they poled upstream, the leaf shadows flowing over them, wearing flowers in their hair.

When the stream became shallow and poured fast over shadowed rocks, we tied up the boat and followed the stream up its narrowing rocky bed. The breath of it was cold in the warming woods, still fed by snow melting in far-off mountains. When we had tramped through the new ferns at its side for a long way, Budding and Blooming signaled me to be quiet, and we climbed the bank. Past the trees that bordered the stream was a small sunny pasture full of small white flowers; and on a slope amid them lay the saint.

He was fast asleep. His hands were crossed over his bosom, and he snored; his feet, clad in big boots, stuck up. His white hair lay all around him on the ground, and his beard spread out around his small brown face so that he looked like a milkweed seed. We crept up on him, and Budding whispered something in Blooming's ear that made him laugh. That woke up the saint, who sat up suddenly, looking around confused. Seeing us, he sneezed loudly, got up grumbling, and stumbled off toward the woods across the pasture. Budding cried out and started chasing him as though he were a bird we'd raised; Blooming followed after, and I hung behind, embarrassed at how they approached him.

When they had been some time crashing around in the woods into which the saint had gone, they came back to me panting.

"He's in a tree," said Blooming.

"We'll never find him now," said Budding, licking his finger and wiping a long scratch on his thigh.

"Why didn't you just leave him alone?" I asked. "He would have waked up, we could have waited."

"Blooming laughed," said Budding, "and he woke up . . ."

"Budding made me laugh," said Blooming, "and he ran off."

"He saw you, is why," said Budding. "He's not scared of us."

I wished I could have approached him alone; now I could never get into his good graces. The twins didn't really care about saints; they chased a grasshopper now with the same enthusiasm they had chased the little old man. They sat for a while poking each other and whispering together, and then came to the log I was sitting on.

"We're sorry about the saint running off," said Blooming. "But you saw him anyway, and now you know what one looks like. Let's go home."

He spoke kindly, because he could see I was disappointed; but he said too that even if we left now it would be long after dark when we got back, day was going.

"I'm going to stay," I said.

They looked at me blankly.

"Maybe he'll come down from his tree in the morning," I said, "and I can talk to him, and apologize for waking him and all. I'll do that."

"Well," said one of them, "I suppose, if you want to. But we brought you here. Do you know how to get back?"

With a sudden decision that startled me as much as I hoped it would startle them, I said: "I'm not coming back." I'm not coming back, twins, so go chase your grasshoppers. "I guess I'll just stay here, and wait for him, and stay and live with him, and I guess be a saint."

The twins thought about that for a while, sitting down again and looking from me into the woods and at each other. Then Budding came and gravely kissed my cheek; and Blooming took the cue and kissed the other cheek. They brought my pack to me from where I had left it at the pasture's edge and put it by me. And without another word they turned back to the brook and disappeared in the aspens at its edge.

One thing about Leaf cord, they're very down to earth, but if an occasion comes up, they'll rise to it.

Evening gathered as I sat, and a stack of new midges danced in the still air of the little pasture. The more I thought about my decision the more sensible it seemed to me; but the more I thought how sensible it was, the less I felt like getting up and going into the woods that breathed at the edge of the pasture to look for the saint.

I practiced what I would say in apology to him—no more than "Hello there" or the like, but I practiced till I felt it had enough weight to be convincing. (You practice just by meaning it harder.) But in the end, what got me into the woods were the twins' kisses burning on my cheeks, and the thought of how I would feel if I went back—if, that is, I could find my way back at all. Of course they're Leaf cord, it wouldn't matter to them, they'd just be glad to see me—and somehow that made it worse.

So I got up in the growing gloom and went into the woods, quietly so as not to disturb him should he be around. It was almost dark already in the woods, and grew darker as I went deeper in, and a breeze whispered and creaked in it warningly, and soon it was impossible to take steps without tripping. I had come on an enormous old oak as wide as a wall, which it seemed the woods must have started with, and sat down amid its sheltering roots.

Too dark now to string my hammock, but there was a star caught in the web of leaves, and the air was still; I could spend this night here. It was no good thinking of the water house, or of Belaire, if I wanted to be a saint as much as I said, but it was hard not to think of them as I sat with knees drawn up. I rolled some smoke, carefully picking up the crumbs I dropped. I had enough for several days, and there were always roots and berries that Seven Hands had taught me about, though there would be no berries ripe yet; and if I really got hungry I could kill some little animal and toast it over a fire and eat the meat, as they did in ancient times. And, I thought, if he's a real saint, he won't let me starve to death, right in his own woods.

And if I did starve: perhaps something like that was what was in store for me. It would be sad, but maybe in future times people would learn from it; perhaps I would become a part of this saint's story, and so never die—was that what Painted Red had meant? I thought of Once a Day, and how she might someday come to hear the story; she would know, then—know something. I sat and looked at the blue glimpses of heaven revealed by the moving leaves and thought about being dead.

"If you're going to sit there all night," said a small voice over my head, "you might go and get me some water." I jumped back from the dead and looked upward into the darkness. I could just make out the whiteness of his beard in the dark leaves of the oak I had been leaning on. I couldn't remember what it was I had planned to say. The beard disappeared, and a dark object was thrown at me, and I ducked as it clattered near me. It was a plastic bucket. I stood holding it and staring up at the tree.

"Well?" said the small voice.

I picked my way out of the woods and down the hill, and filled the bucket from the black water of the brook, and came back with it, stumbling through the woods. When I stood again at the foot of the oak, a rope fell from its branches with a hook on the end. I attached the bucket and watched it hauled up into the darkness.

"You've gone and spilled most of it."

"It's dark."

"Well. You'll have to go again."

The bucket came down again and I went to refill it, trying to be careful. The face didn't reappear. I stood looking up into the oak till my neck hurt; I heard some splashing and knocking but the saint didn't speak again.

In the first light of morning, when I woke stiff and chilled, and looked upward, it was all clear: what had been a massy darkness in the tree was a little house built in the broad arms of the oak with great care, of woven branches and pieces of angel-made this and that, with small windows and a smokestack that leaned out away from the branches. A rope ran from a window to a convenient branch, and from it hung two long shirts.

It hadn't once occurred to me, you know, that perhaps the twins were mistaken, and their little old man wasn't a saint at all; I had just assumed that somehow they knew. And looking up now at his tree house, I had no need for doubt. It was just such houses that the saints lived in so many lives ago, when we wandered; St. Gary's great beech and the oak of St. Maureen, and the tree whose stump is still marked in Little Belaire's woods, where St. Andy went to live after St. Bea died. "Saints in the trees!" I said aloud, as old people do when something astonishes them.

Should I call out to him? I didn't know his name; and now in the daylight, despite the errand I had run for him, it was clear to me that he didn't want me there, squatting at the foot of his tree. No doubt he was sitting in his little house waiting for me to go away. In my excitement at having so soon in my journey come upon a real saint from whom I could learn, I hadn't considered his feelings in the matter at all—and I Palm cord, too! I felt a hot flush of shame, and went quietly away from his oak, though not so far that I couldn't observe him. I sat on a patch of moss there, and smoked some, and waited.

In not too long a time I saw his door open, and from it fell a rope ladder ingeniously made, and slowly but confidently the saint climbed down. He seemed to be speaking to someone not present, agreeing, disagreeing with gestures; he carried a brush and a ragged towel.

Gone for a bath. And there was the rope ladder to his house, still moving from the last step he had taken from it.

Did I dare? I would only take a brief peek while he was gone; I would go only to the top of the ladder and look in. But when I got to the doorway and looked in, I forgot that resolve and climbed inside.

And where to begin to describe what I saw once I had got myself inside! The walls of wattle were chinked with mud and moss, and a big limb of the oak, running up through the house at an angle, made a low arch that divided the house in two; the floor was uneven, and stepped up and down to fit itself to the branches it was built into. The ceiling was low, and peaked at odd angles, and everywhere, hung from the ceiling, on shelves built into the wall, in cubbyholes in the corners, on tables and chests, were things I knew nothing about but knew were treasures: things angel-made, by skills long gone from the world, their purposes still potent in them if only you knew enough to discover them. There were more old mysteries and angel-stuff crammed into that little house, it seemed, than in all of Belaire itself.

So absorbed was I in all this that I failed to hear the saint returning till the house creaked and moved with his climbing up the ladder. There was nowhere to hide; I picked up my pack quickly and slung it over my shoulder, just leaving, and stood fearful and embarrassed as his head—at first astonished, then displeased—appeared in the doorway.

He gave his attention to getting in the door, and when he stood inside—shorter than I was—he considered me. I was too embarrassed to speak. He caught a thought then, and came to me smiling, holding out his hand to me.

"Good-by," he said politely, and I shook his brown hand. He turned away then and stood in the low arch made by the limb with his back to me, waiting for me to be gone. But I couldn't bring myself to leave. His hands behind his back clasped and unclasped impatiently. Inspired, I reached into my pack and pulled out the bottle of grape soda that No Moon had given me; and when he peeked around to see if I had gone, I showed it to him, smiling, still afraid to speak. His gaze stopped on the bottle for a moment, and when he looked away he began to rock back and forth on his big boots. I waited. At last he edged away from the arch, ducked down beneath a cluttered table, and drew out an old glass, lumpy and full of bubbles. Without looking at me, he put the glass on the table, and I brought the bottle to him. He looked up then suddenly, smiling as broadly as his small face could. "My name is Blink," he said. "What's yours?"

"My name is Rush that Speaks." I put the bottle on the table, and we both watched a bit of sun from the window stab through its purple heart. St. Blink broke the seal and the bubbles crowded to the top. He poured out a foaming, hissing glassful, recapping it tight quickly to keep the bubbles in. He picked up the glass and drank two long noisy gulps. A moment later a small musical belch escaped him, and he smiled at me fondly. "Did you know," he said, sitting down slowly in a creaking chair of bent wood and rushes and turning the glass in the sun, "that in very ancient times, to keep summer fruits, they would boil them down into a thick paste, like honey, very sweet, and eat them that way?"

There was another chair there like the one he sat in, and gingerly I lowered myself into it. "No," I said, and felt a strange lump in my throat. "No, I didn't know that; but now I do."

"Yes," he said. He looked at me curiously, nodding his head and sipping his soda. I allowed my arms to rest on the arms of the chair. I knew—though I was afraid, as yet, to let myself wholly believe it—that I had come to a place I had long sought, and could stay.

FOURTH FACET

And I thought, as that summer went on and I was not sent away, when I would come through the woods with water and see the tree house amid its speaking leaves, that perhaps Blink had found me just as I had found him: someone whom he had long waited for. I would smile at our luck even through the complicated task of getting myself up, and then the water up, and then the water inside and into Jug.

Jug on its table stood as high as my chin; made of plastic, bright yellow, sleek and edgeless. It had a top that fit snugly, which had once been clear but was now cloudy. Water from its little tap, though it had been standing all day, tasted as fresh and cool as though you drank it from the stream. Painted or somehow sealed on its front was a picture of a man, or a creature like a man, with thick square running legs and arms thrown wide. One fat hand held a glass from which orange liquid splashed; the other hand thrust up one clublike finger. His head, orange as the liquid in his glass, was immense for his body, a huge sphere, and bore an expression of wild glee, of unimaginable shrieking joy. That was Jug.

I asked if it was one of Blink's souvenirs from the city. He had made a trip to the city when he was young, and he would tell stories about it at night. "I took it to carry the rest of the things I found," he said, "because it was light and big. I strapped it to my shoulders." And he would tell about the silent city, more silent than anywhere, because almost nothing lived there to make noise. In ancient times there had been not only the men but the populations that lived on men, birds and rats and insects; they all disappeared when the men left. He had walked through the silence, and climbed into buildings, and took Jug to carry the things he found.

When he told stories of the city and the things he had found there, I thought Blink might be Bones cord, or even Buckle, though Buckle cord has no saints at all in it. But I wasn't satisfied with this. When I saw him with his specs on, at the table working at his crostic-words, absorbed in their mystery, and beautiful in his absorption, brushing away a fly and crossing and uncrossing his big feet in perplexity, I was sure he was of St. Gene's tiny Thread cord. But still it wouldn't do.

Why didn't you ask him?

Ask him what?

What cord he was.

Well, if I didn't know, how was he to know?

But you knew what cord you were.

Yes. And if I had known St. Blink in the warren, with his friends and his occupations and the places he chose to live, I would have known what cord he was, too. Your cord, you see, isn't something you discover just by examining yourself, the way you look into a mirror and discover you have red hair. In Little Belaire, you are in a cord, and a cord is—well, a *cord*, like a piece of string, not like a name you bear. That makes it clearer, doesn't it?

Well. Just go on. What was it you said he was doing, so absorbed, that made you think he was Thread cord?

He was at his crostic-words.

When St. Ervin came to learn to be a saint from St. Maureen in her oak tree, he was never once allowed up into the house she had built there, never once, though he stayed for years. She would dispute with him sometimes, and tell him to go away and leave her alone; he wouldn't go, he insisted on staying, he brought presents and she threw them away, he hid and she discovered him and ran him off with a stick, well, the story is very long, but the end is that when St. Maureen was dying and St. Ervin came to her as she lay too weak to run him off, and wept that he could not now ever be a saint, she said, "Well, Ervin, that's a story; go tell that." And died.

When I had been a few days in the tree house, I told Blink, in some embarrassment, why I had come, and like St. Maureen, he only said, "You want to be a saint? A saint? Then why are you here? Why don't you be about it?"

"I thought," I said, head down, "that maybe I could stay here with you, and listen and watch, and see how you became a saint, and learn to do the same."

"Me?" he squeaked in consternation. "Me? Why, I'm not a saint! Whatever could have given you that idea? Me a saint! Boy, didn't they teach you to speak truthfully in the warren? And couldn't you have heard it in all I said? Do I sound to you like St. Roy?"

"Yes," I said truthfully.

Abashed, he turned to look at his crostic-words. "No, no," he said after a little thought. "I'll tell you what. A saint will tell you stories of his life, and . . ."

"And so do you, about going to the city, and all the things you found there."

"There's a difference. The stories I tell are not of my life, but of our life, our life as men. It's the difference between wisdom and knowledge. I'll admit to knowledge, even to a lot of it, if it makes you happy to have found me; useless knowledge though it is. But wisdom—I'm no angel, I know this much, that wisdom need not come from knowledge, and sometimes can't at all. If it's knowledge you want, well, I haven't had anybody to tell about it for years, so I'm glad you've come; if it's wisdom, then you'd better be about it any way you can find; I'll be no help."

"Would it be possible to have knowledge and still be a saint?"

He hmmed a bit over that. "I suppose," he said; "but being a saint wouldn't have anything to do with how much knowledge you had. It would be like, you can be tall, or fat, or have blue eyes, and be a saint—you see?"

"Well," I said, relieved, "maybe then I could start with getting knowledge, and take my chances with being wise as I go along."

"It's all right with me," said my saint. "What would you like to know?"

"First of all," I said, "what is it that you're doing?"

"This? This is my crostic-words. Look."

On the table where the morning sun could light it lay a thin sheet of glass. Below it was a paper, covered minutely with what I knew was printing; this took up most of the paper, except for one block, a box divided into smaller boxes, some black and some white. On the glass that covered the paper, Blink had made tiny black marks—letters, he called them—over the white boxes. The paper was crumbled and yellow, and over a part of it a brown stain ran.

"When I was a boy in Little Belaire," he said, bending over it and brushing away a spider that sat like a letter above one white box, "I found this paper in a chest of Bones cord's. Nobody, though, could tell me what it was, what the story was. One gossip said she thought it was a puzzle, you know, like St. Gene's puzzles, but different. Another said it was a game, like Rings, but different. Now, I wouldn't say it was only for this that I left Belaire to wander, but I thought I'd find out how it was a puzzle or a game, and how to solve it or play it. And I did, mostly, though that was sixty years ago, and it's not finished yet."

He ducked his head beneath the table and searched among the belongings he kept there. "I talked with a lot of people, went a long way. The first thing I found out was that to figure out my paper I had to learn to read writing. That was good advice, but for a long time no one I met knew how to do it." He drew out a wooden box and opened it. Inside were dark, thick blocks that I had seen before. "That's Book," I said.

"Those are books," said St. Blink.

"There's a lot there," I said.

"I've been places," he said, lifting the top Book, "where books filled buildings as large almost as Little Belaire, floor to ceiling." He lifted the cover to reveal the paper sewn up inside, which released the peculiar smell of Book, musty, papery, distinct. "The book," he said slowly like a sleeptalker, drawing his finger under the largest writing, "about a thousand things." His fingers wandered over the rest of the page, while he said "something something something" under his breath, and came to rest on a line of red writing at the bottom. "Time, life, books," he said thoughtfully, and lowered the lid over it again.

"There are people," he said, tapping the gray block, "and I found some of them eventually, who spend their whole lives with this, peeking into the secrets of the angels. They're turned around, you see, and look backwards always; and though all I wanted to do was to solve my puzzle, the more I learned to read writing, the more I got turned around myself.

It's endless, the angels' writing, they wrote down everything, down to the tiniest detail of how they did everything. And it's all in books to be found."

"You mean if we could read writing, we could do all those things again that they did? Fly?"

"Well. They had a phrase, they said, 'Necessity is the mother of invention'; and I can imagine that there could come a time again when some inner necessity makes us begin all that again. But I can more easily imagine that all that is done with, put away in these books, like toys that don't amuse you any longer but which are too much a part of your childhood to pitch out.

"Those old men, you know," he said, putting away all the Book and sliding it back into place under the table, "they wouldn't dream of actually trying to follow the instructions in any of the million instruction books. That it was once all like that is sufficient for them. That it could ever be like that again—well, it's like smiling over the sadnesses of your youth, and being glad they're all quite past."

He bent again over his ancient puzzle. He sighed. He wet a finger and wiped a mar on the glass. "You put letters in the boxes," he said, "according to instructions written here. But the instructions are the puzzle: they are clues only, to words which, when broken up into letters, will fill the empty boxes. When every clue has been deciphered, and the word it hints at guessed, and all the letters rearranged rightly and put in their proper boxes, the letters in the boxes will spell out a message. They will make sense as you read them across."

That may not have been exactly what he said, because I didn't ever really understand how it worked. But I understood why he had spent so many years at it: to have been hidden so well, what at last appeared in the boxes must be of vast importance. I looked down at what composed the message, filled with gaps like an old man's mouth. "What does it say?"

THERE ARE COS   KS IN SAN DI   O CZ RS
OF THE STRE TS TH   ALL THEMSELVES
PR TTY NAMES LIKE TH CI IZE S COMM
      TEE BUT THEY ARE THE   TIR   TS
OF EU   PE SPROOT NG A   N IN THE
SWEWT SOIL OF THIS FREE LAND

77777777777

He was right, that it was a puzzle or a game; you were wrong to think it must be important, to be so well hidden. It was one of thousands like it; the angels solved them or played them in a few minutes, or an hour, and tossed them away.

Angels. . . . If I could believe only a part of what St. Blink told me, the hundred years or so before the Storm must have been the most exciting to be alive in since there have been men. I spent a lot of time daydreaming about those times, and what it would really have been like. The stories to furnish my daydreams poured out of Blink like water; I think he had been like me when he was young, and still was in a way, though he snorted when I talked about how wonderful it must have been. "Wonderful," he said. "Do you know that one of the biggest causes of death in those days was people killing themselves?"

"How, killing themselves?"

"With weapons, like the ones I told you about; with poisons and drugs; by throwing themselves from high buildings; by employing oh any number of engines that the angels made for other reasons."

"And they did that deliberately?"

"Deliberately."

"Why?"

"For as many reasons as you have to say the time they lived in was wonderful."

Well, there was no convincing me, of course; I would still sit and dream away the hot sleepy afternoons, thinking of the angels in their final agony, their incredible dreaming restless pride that covered the world with Road and flung Little Moon out to hang in the night sky and ended forcing them to leap to their deaths from high buildings still unsatisfied (though I thought perhaps Blink was wrong, and it was only that they thought they could fly).

Oh, the world was full in those days; it seemed so much more alive than these quiet times when a new thing could take many lifetimes to finish its long birth labors and the world stay the same for generations. In those days a thousand things began and ended in a single lifetime, great forces clashed and were swallowed up in other forces riding over them. It was like some monstrous race between destruction and perfection; as soon as some piece of world was conquered, after vast effort by millions, as when they built Road, the conquest would turn on the conquerors, as Road killed thousands in their cars; and in the same way, the mechanical dreams the angels made with great labor and inconceivable ingenuity, dreams broadcast on the air like milkweed seeds, all day long, passing invisibly through the air, through walls, through stone walls, through the very bodies of the angels themselves as they sat to await them, and appearing then before every angel simultaneously to warn or to instruct, one dream dreamed by all so that all could act in concert, until it was discovered that the dreams passing through their bodies were poisonous to them somehow, don't ask me how, and millions were sickening and dying young and unable to bear children, but unable to stop the dreaming even when the dreams themselves warned them that the dreams were poisoning them, unable or afraid to wake and find themselves alone, until the Long League awakened the women and the women ceased to dream: and all this happening in one man's lifetime.

And it all went faster as the Storm came on, that is the Storm coming on was the race drawing to its end; the solutions grew stranger and more desperate, and the disasters greater, and in the teeth of them the angels dreamed their wildest dreams, that we would live forever or nearly, that we would leave the earth, the spoiled earth, entirely and float in cities suspended between the earth and the moon forever, a dream they could not achieve because of the Wars starting and the millions of them falling out in a million different ways and all at each other's throats. And the Long League growing secretly everywhere as the desperate solutions fell to ruins or exploded in the faces of their makers, the Long League in secret struggle with the angels, who hardly knew of its existence in their midst till the League was the only power left when the Law and the Gummint had exhausted themselves with the Wars and in the struggle to keep the world man's; and for that matter the truthful speakers beginning the speech over the thousand phones of the Co-op Great Belaire; and while the million lights were going out, and the mechanical dreams fading and leaving the angels alone in the terrible dark, the Planters, thousand-armed and -eyed and wiser than any human being, searched other skies and suns at the angel's bidding, and brought home the trees of bread and who knows what else now lost; and nobody able to comprehend everything going on all at once, and no wonder either; and then the Storm, as Seven Hands said, which anybody could have seen, and it all began to stop, and kept stopping till all those millions were standing in the old woodlands which they had never been in before and looking around in wonder at the old world as though it were as strange as their dreams had truly been.

Blink said: "It was as though a great sphere of many-colored glass had been floated above the world by the unimaginable effort and power of the angels, so beautiful and strange and so needful of service to keep afloat that for them there was nothing else, and the world was forgotten by them as they watched it float. Now the sphere is gone, smashed in the Storm, and we are left with the old world as it always was, save for a few wounds that can never be healed. But littered all around this old ordinary world, scattered through the years by that smashing, lost in the strangest places and put to the oddest uses, are bits and pieces of that great sphere; bits to hold up to the sun and look through and marvel at—but which can never be put back together again."

We lay stretched out in the late-summer yellow meadow and watched the solemn clouds go by. There had been a chill that dried out the woods and left them dusty and odorous, rustling and tinted brown, but summer kept on: engine summer.

"Blink," I said, "are there cities in the sky?"

He scratched behind his ear and settled back with his hands behind his head. "The angels' cities in the sky. That's what Little St. Roy called clouds like those. But there's a story. It's said that at the time of the Storm the angels built cities covered with domes of glass, which by some means could float like clouds. I don't know. I don't doubt they could. And they used to say that one day, after thousands of years perhaps, the angels would come back; the cities would land, and the angels would come out and see all that had been going on while they floated. Well. Hmmm . . . Nobody, no angel's returned. . . . I don't know. . . . Maybe they got it mixed up with Little Moon, which really was a city in the sky, where angels did live, though all there are dead now, caught in the Storm they were with no way to get home—still there, I guess. Who knows? The milkweed's breaking, see there?"

The brown seed floated near him, which looked so much like him; I thought that if I could get close enough to it, it would have a long nose, little features, like Blink's. It rolled across his wrinkled white shirt and got off again, going elsewhere. The air would choose.

"Bits and pieces," Blink said sleepily. "Bits and pieces."

He slept. I watched the clouds, peopling their valleys and canyons with angels.

FIFTH FACET

B its and pieces: a silver ball and glove. An angel picture of St. Gary's Uncle Plunkett. A house in which two children and an old woman told about the weather, and the stone dead men in between. A false leg; a clear sphere with nothing at all inside it except all of Dr. Boots; a fly caught in plastic; a city in the sky. No, it can't be put back together, he was right about that, and I never wanted to put it back together; but it seemed that each of these things in turn gave me a message, a sign, pointed a finger toward the next, and that somehow, at the end of the series, I would find something precious which was lost—perhaps only knowledge, but something which I wanted above all else to find.

You have found it.

Have I? Who is this I? Didn't Mongolfier tell me that it wasn't I at all that would come here, that what would come here was no more than a reflection, an unvanished dream, no more I than the angel picture of Uncle Plunkett, made by no human hand, was Plunkett himself? Then why do you say I have found anything at all?

Because no one else found the silver ball and glove—this silver ball and glove. No one else searched for it. No one else followed the series from begin-

ning to end—and then took the last step. Perhaps anyone else could have—but no one did. So it is you that found us. You that I speak to now: you alone who speaks to me. Now: were you going to tell about Plunkett?

I . . . yes. Yes: I was going to tell how I saw the picture, and what Blink said. . . . Do you know this story better than I do?

Go on. It's not for my sake you tell it.

I had asked Blink about the little house Once a Day showed me, and the four stone dead men. "I know about four stone heads," he said, "four heads that are a mountain; but they aren't the four dead men in the story I know. Perhaps the four stone heads picture the four dead men; or perhaps it's a joke of Whisper cord's. What was it she said of them? 'Are they mad.' Well. Who can follow Whisper? But there is a story:

"At the time of the Storm, when at last the lights and phones of the Co-op went off for good, and Great St. Roy led us away to wander, there was a boy, Gary, among us, who would become St. Gary. St. Gary had been raised by his aunt, who was a speaker, and by his uncle, who was named Plunkett. Plunkett's work, secret in nature, was one of those last plans of the angels spoiled by the Storm: a plan for immortality. The secret slipped out through Plunkett's wife, who revealed to Gary that although his uncle was dead and buried, which she didn't dispute, he was also alive in an underground place near Clevelen, far west, near the place the Co-op had been.

"So St. Gary turned back from the speaker's flight to return to Clevelen to see if he could find his supposed uncle still alive, though as he went west he passed the grave where he had seen his uncle laid. After a long search, Gary did find the place Plunkett's wife had told him of; and by that time so had others, some desperate to learn what the angels knew of immortality, others wishing to destroy the work as they were intent on destroying all that the angels had done.

"What they had found, and now kept constant watch over and had fierce disputes about, were five clear spheres without any openings and with, it appeared, nothing at all inside them. Attached to four of these five were angel-pictures, gray and shiny, of four faces. One of them was St. Gary's Uncle Plunkett.

"There was a lot of resistance among the others there to St. Gary taking his uncle away with him. For some time he argued with them, defending Plunkett from those who wanted to smash the spheres, if they were smashable, and from those who wanted to open them, or operate them, if that could be done. Then the Long League intervened there.

Women of the League came, and said they would decide the matter—as they were just then deciding so many matters—and that no one should touch the spheres or investigate them further but they. St. Gary wouldn't agree; and by stealth one night he made away with the sphere that was in some sense Plunkett, and fled.

"For many years and through many hazards, Gary kept Uncle Plunkett with him, though the speakers laughed at him and the sphere that was so obviously empty. He became a great saint in his old age, and lived in a beech near the camp the speakers had then near New Neyork in the days of the Long League's power; and he lived with Plunkett at that time. And if Plunkett ever said a word, nobody heard it.

"After Gary's death, Uncle Plunkett went into St. Andy's wagon with other stuff, precious and useless; and like so many other things, the silver ball and glove they tell about, the spectacles to see at night with, the dream machine, it was lost eventually, or perhaps sold, no one remembers, as no one then cared much. The Long League indeed did care: rumors came that they were searching for the last of the four dead men, some said to destroy it as they had the others, or to keep it out of the hands of their enemies as others said, but the speakers had little to do with these disputes. And then no more we heard about it."

I had questions, but to all of them Blink only shrugged and shook his head: why were there five spheres, and only four pictures? If the five spheres were all alike, why was it said there were only four dead men? How could they be what they were said to be, alive? "Ask the angels, ask the Long League," he said. "They alone know. All I know is Gary's story; if Whisper cord knows more, it's their secret—but somehow I think they don't, and their four dead men are only a game, like the three dreams of Olive, the seven wandering stars, the nine last words of Little St. Roy. There is, though, one thing; one tangible thing, and by a path I won't describe to you, I come to have it. Look . . ."

And like Mbaba going to her chests to prove a story of when-we-wandered, Blink got up and searched among his belongings, and from a cranny in the wall he took out the cracked angel-picture of Uncle Plunkett which Gary had found attached to the clear sphere, and taken away with him when he took Plunkett. In the picture, Plunkett wore a shirt with buttons and had almost no hair, only a gray burr all over his head. Under his shaven chin he held a card with writing on it. He wasn't looking right out, but a bit to one side, as though he had heard someone call to him. The crack in the picture made white seams across his face like the scars of a terrible wound; he was smiling a big smile, and his teeth shone like the fits-all teeth. For some reason the picture made me shiver violently.

"Maybe," I said at last, "they had it all wrong. Maybe the spheres were something else altogether, and there never really were four dead men; they'd got it mixed up with some other story, or got it wrong somehow. Probably."

Blink smiled at me and patted my cheek. "Probably," he said. "Let's go look for mushrooms."

I didn't think that a man as old as Blink would spend the winter in a place as exposed as his house in the oak, but though autumn came on faster now he showed no signs of moving. He pottered around working in Book or staring glumly at the glass which covered his crostic-words, as nights grew colder and cold mist filled the house in the mornings so that we sat wrapped to our ears late in the Three Bears, as Blink called the sewn-together shaggies and skins we kept warm in. We wrapped up early in them too, and smoked and talked through the long evening while we watched his little charcoal fire go out. "That fire," I said, "won't be much help soon."

"No," he said. "Good thing we won't need it."

The woods became transparent. From the windows of the house you could see now all the way out to the pasture and nearly to where the brook ran chilly between its frosted rocks. Blink and I worked at making the house secure: we chinked cracks with mud and moss, hung the walls with thick rugs he had stored all summer. We closed up the fire's mouth and blocked its chimney. We made a new front door to fit over the old one, and bickered over how the two could best be fitted together to keep out the cold. On a day when the stillness and the curdled darkness of the clouds all day suggested a heavy frost, Blink drew out from where they were stored several thick sheets of plastic, unclouded, great treasures; a thickness went over the outside of each small window, and another on the inside. When this was done, he arranged the two bed-chairs so they faced the windows. "Is Jug filled right up to the top?" he said.

"Yes."

"Then I guess we're ready."

In a little brazier he lit twigs and started small lumps of charcoal going; while these caught, he found a small jar made of angel-silver, tightly sealed, and opened it. From it he took a big pinch of black powder, looked at it, frowning, and shook some back in. The rest he scattered on the glowing charcoal. It didn't smoke, but the smell was pronounced, a dense and penetrating odor like no other I have ever smelled. We made some last preparations; Blink carefully resealed the jar and put it by him; he looked around, finger to his lips, satisfied that all was ready. I had begun to feel deliciously warm and sleepy, but alert as well, as though I could go to sleep and stay awake at the same time. That seemed to be Blink's idea too, and we crept into the Three Bears, made even warmer with silver cloths Blink had attached around them, made ourselves comfortable, and sat there for three months.

On the evening of that first day we talked little; we grew silent and still as though asleep, but watching the clear cold sunset fade behind the fuzz of black trees on the mountains beyond the pasture. Later, that month's full moon lit the bald, still earth and we listened to the cracks and snaps of its freezing. Clouds gathered, moving fast over the moon's white face. By morning the year's first snow was falling, dusting the ground with a fine cold powder which the bitter wind blew around like dust.

Jug kept water as warm in winter as it had kept it cool in summer. Once a day perhaps, I would fill a pipe with St. Bea's-bread, all flaky with cold. At full moon time, St. Blink would climb complaining from his Bear, and light charcoal, and burn more of the black powder. When there was a warm spell, we would sometimes crawl out and open the two front doors and climb down the ladder, moving with careful gravity like two ancient invalids; and then back up in a short time utterly exhausted, though having seen a great deal.

We slept a strange, utter sleep, coming out only past noon as winter truly took hold, and passing back in again as evening came; many days passed without comment, only glimpsed between one doze and another. Snow choked the woods deeply; we sat all day once absorbed in the progress of a fox across the trackless pasture, and watched the doings of jays and sparrows, falling asleep when they did. Two chipmunks of the oak at last found a way into the tree house, and would run cheerfully over us, breathing our heated breath; they slept in Blink's lap for three days of blind violent storms that sheathed the forest in ice, which seemed to make music in the fine blue morning that followed, music too blinding to look at. The chipmunks slept. We slept, dust and loose bits of moss and spines of leaves blown up around our feet by drafts. We had become a part of Blink's beloved sleeping oak, hearing its branches creak and snap in wind, grieving when a great weight of ice broke one fine limb. Snow fell from its branches to thud on our roof, and then slide from our roof to the ground. I blinked less often, I came to notice; and when I blinked, often I slept. My left hand lay on my right for half a month.

On a white afternoon sometime in that endless season, a warm day when Blink had struggled out to take powder from the jug to steam us into our deep hibernation again, I asked, "Where does it come from?"

"Where does what come from?" he asked, looking around to see if I meant some beast.

"The powder," I said. "And how does it do that?" Already it had begun to do it; the penetrating smell was in the air, sharp and metallic, like the warm breath from a brass throat, and I felt my haunches wiggle more comfortably into the seat I had sat in so long.

"Ask the angels how it does what it does," he said. "They'd tell you, but you wouldn't understand. Can't you tell how it does it? Listen to it work; you've got time." With great care he worked himself back into his chair as I tried to listen to the powder work. I could begin to tell what he meant; and I knew that by winter's end I *would* know how it did what it did, though I wouldn't be able to explain it to anyone who hadn't spent a winter with it.

"And where it comes from," Blink was saying, finding a way to sit he liked well enough to stay in, "well . . . that's a tale . . ."

I said we slept a lot; but awake, I felt strangely clear and smart, as though everything were taking its time to reveal itself to me with slow precision, to surprise me that it contained more than I'd thought it had: not only the hunting fox's every movement, but St. Blink's long tangled histories, unfolding meantime, twisting but patent, as the peach-colored brook was patent at sunset running through the black and white pasture.

He went on, talking about the powder, and about other powders and medicines the angels had made; about how the angels, not content with altering the world for their convenience, had altered men too to fit the altered world, paving and remaking their deepest insides as they had the surface of the earth. About medicine's daughters: he said, "Medicine is to medicine's daughters as a dry stick is to a tree. Medicine is like paint; medicine's daughters are like the change of color in a crystal. Medicine changes you, fights your diseases, drowns your sorrows; medicine's daughters make you a suggestion that you change yourself—a suggestion that you can't refuse. A medicine lasts as long as a meal; medicine's daughters leave you changed long after they've disappeared from your body."

Four of medicine's daughters are contained in the Four Pots, the first to cause you to throw off nearly every disease, and the last, the bone-white pot and its white contents, was made to solve a strange problem that was caused by the first. "The angels learned to heal the things that kill men young," Blink said, "and hoped therefore that they might live forever. They were wrong in that, but so successful at keeping men alive that it seemed that soon there would be in the world far too many healthy people, as good as immortal, unable to be killed by anything but their own stupidity, flowing from the wombs of women like ants from an anthill, and no food and no room for them all. Think of the fear and revulsion you feel when you kick into a nest of ants and see them swarm: men felt that for their kind, and the Law and the Gummint most of all, who most of all bore the burden of keeping the world man's.

"And so, by a means we have forgotten, a means like medicine's daughters but far more subtle even, they made themselves childless. It took some generations, but at last they made this childlessness perma-nent: it would be passed on then, from mother to child. And they made the medicine's daughter which is in the fourth of the Four Pots to start up again the inside goings-on which their means stopped. When it's taken, a woman can for a while conceive: but her child will be childless, until she too makes the choice to take the medicine's daughter. It's as though we were born without eyes, as though our eyes were not stuck in our heads but passed down from mother to child like a treasure, and every child had the choice to take them up or not.

"And it would have worked out, perhaps, if the Storm hadn't come; men would have chosen their numbers as they chose to build Road and put up a false moon next to the real one. But the Storm did come; and who can say it wasn't hastened by this terrible choice of theirs? And in the winters that came after, in the Wars and catastrophes, millions died by all the old means the angels thought they had removed forever from the world, and few were born by this new means of theirs.

"And we are left now, we few, unable to reverse what they did; carrying a part of ourselves outside ourselves, in the white pot; left with their choice still."

There was a winter when I was five or six, when I had gone looking for my mother, Speak a Word, and come upon her in a curtained place; I had come up quietly, and she didn't see me, for she was intent on what the old gossip Laugh Aloud was saying to her, which I couldn't hear. I saw then that Seven Hands was with them, and so I came no closer—this was when my knot with him was most tangled. I knelt there and watched them in the winter light. Laugh Aloud had the box of pots open before her, and with one finger she moved the white one across the table to my mother. My mother's nose was shiny with sweat, and she had an odd, fixed smile on her face. She picked up and put down again the fourth pot.

"No," she said. "Not this year."

Seven Hands said nothing. Did he wish it? Did it matter? He said nothing, for the angel's choice was only for Speak a Word. "Not this year," she said, and looked only at Laugh Aloud, who pursed her lips and nodded. She placed the pot in its fourth place in the holder, and returned the holder to its box. The top of the box closed with a little noise.

At my dream of that noise, I woke.

"The angels," Blink was saying, "with their phones and their cars and their Road, they used to say: 'It's a small world. Getting smaller every day.'" He shook his head. "A small world."

He went on, after we had smoked, talking of winter. Of the winters of the Wars, and this black powder that had kept the fighters against the angels alive, and how he came to have it now; and the winter the Long League was made manifest; and the winter Great St. Roy locked the door of the Co-op Great Belaire, and the speakers began their long, hunted wanderings, and about his lost leg; about the rest of the world, beyond the oceans, from which no word came any more . . .

"His lost leg?" I said.

"From cold," said St. Blink. "Frozen, and rotting from it, and had to be cut off. In years before, the angels' science could have replaced it, made him a whole new one, a real one; but he had to be content with a false one."

Patent as sunset water . . . "Which is in the warren now," I said.

"So it is." Interminably the snow continued its silent, blind descent. "You cry, Roy said, just after, and brood, and think you might as well be dead. But you get an artificial one, even if it's not like the angels could make, it's wood but it works; and you force yourself to get up and walk, feeling foolish with it as much as hurt. But you set to, and one day you can keep up. You can't dance, maybe, and it's a long time before you make love again, but you get along. You learn to live with it. You even laugh; for sure Roy did. But still he always had one less leg. No matter how good it got.

"And what Roy thought, who saw the Storm, was that from then on we would all be as he was—all legless men. Whether it was the choice of childlessness, or further back, in the angels' decision to hammer the world into a shape convenient for men, no matter what the cost—whatever it was, we lost that terrible race.

"And it left us legless men." Twilight would be forever today, starting almost as morning ended and sliding imperceptibly into moonless night. "And we can laugh. We have our systems, and our wisdom. But still only one leg. It doesn't get better, a lost leg, like a cold. We learn to live with it. We try."

He shifted, ever so slightly. "Well, these are winter stories. . . . See how gray the light is today, the world's as sleepy as I am. Little Belaire's closed up now, they're all close inside, and the old stories told . . . and spring comes, when it comes."

And we slept again, not having moved. The days went by full of blown snow, the sun's trip quick and cold and veiled. No stars, no moon for days: the fox: the birds.

Sixth facet

There was a day, after gray rain had melted the last hillocks of black-peppered snow, and many birds had come home, and the woods were filled with new smells as with a stretch and a yawn, that Blink and I crept down the ladder and stood in the new air burdened with odors, looking around blinking and trying to stand up straight.

At the last full moon Blink, after judging the weather and counting something twice on his fingers, had put away his jar of black powder; but the first warm days found us still sleeping out the last of our long sleep, staying in bed as you do on a fine morning when you know you should be up, but perversely roll and toss under your untidy blankets until the sun is high. Now we wandered slowly in the woods, greeting the others who had come from hibernation, a snail and a basking turtle, a woodchuck so lean he seemed to be wearing someone else's baggy clothes, and the trees too; and as Blink and I stopped to watch the woodchuck sniff the air I was filled with gratitude that I had made it, made it through another winter through which many had not, a winter that was over now, a winter which is half of life. Life is winter and summer, a day is half asleep and half awake, my kind is man and they have lived and died; and I have come through

another winter to stand here now on the winter-turned earth and smell the
wet woods. I thought of Once a Day, I saw her vividly on travels far away.
St. Roy had lost a leg to winter, but had lived to see spring. I sat down with
the weight of all this, and looked up at Blink, ancient and lined, whom the
winter despite his powder had weakened and aged, and knew there were
those in Belaire who hadn't lived. I knew that what the powder Blink
burned had done was to *stop:* stop all this that I felt now rush over me
intolerably. It had started again as the powder wore off, and it was enormous. I sighed to breathe it out but could not; and wept suddenly, big
panting sobs where I sat on the bursting earth.

At Little Belaire they would be making new rooms from old in honor of
spring. Buckle cord would be shifting walls and opening doors all along
Path, new dirt would be walked into hard floors, sun would be let in.
Belaire opens like a new insect in the warmth, and Leaf cord trims and
decorates and invites people to watch it unfold. Insulation is taken down,
rooms swept of leaves and winter, favorite chairs lugged along Path to
favorite bits of sun; and a new word that makes all the cords hum with
thought and laughter.

"And you want to go home to it," said St. Blink.

"What? Go home? Why do you say that?"

"You don't answer when I speak to you, you can't hear what I say.
You've been staring out the window all morning when there is a way out
of the house, and things to do too, I don't just mean hauling and fixing,
there are things abroad now to see and flowers blooming. And you sit
instead indoors."

"It's not really indoors here."

"You know what I mean. You itch all over, but there's no place to
scratch."

"Well, I can't go back," I said. "Of course."

"Of course."

There would be the bees swarming and the expeditions out beyond
Little Mountain to see the new bread, and Mbaba's birds returning; and
soon the travelers from the List coming, and perhaps she among them
this time, and so much to tell her.

"I suppose," I said, "there are other places in the world."

"Yes," Blink said, "I suppose there are; other places, and just as nice."

I got up from my window and hustled down the ladder, almost angry with him. Because he was right: I went out to sit in the blooming meadow and let myself think Yes, I want to go home, now, in spring, now, I want to go home; my throat was hard and painful with it. I wanted to go home so badly for such a long time that day that I was only a little surprised when my wanting summoned from the leafy trees by the brook two pale boys, lankier than they had been, one with a red and one with a blue band around his neck. Among other more important things, I had forgotten, during the winter, which was which.

They climbed the bank in their dawdling way, stopping to poke into bushes for animals; when one saw me he waved, and I waved back. It was as though they had been waiting all winter just around the turn of the brook for the first hot day of spring.

"Hello," said, I think, Budding. "Are you a saint yet?"

"No," I said. "Not yet."

"Well," said the other, coming up behind, "they'd like to see you back in Little Belaire."

"No Moon went in the fall," said the first, "and again in the spring; your mother misses you."

His brother hunkered down on the meadow and ran his hand through his lank blond hair to find a leaf. "Maybe," he said, "if you had a whole year, and you're not a saint yet, you should go home and start again later."

"Maybe," said the other.

"Maybe," I said, thinking of my mother, and of the little that No Moon could tell her, and how easily I had left and how little I had thought of hers or anyone's feelings. A hot wave of shame and impatience made me jump up with clenched fists. "Yes. Yes, I should," I said. "Maybe I should . . ."

"Where's the saint?" the twins said, almost in unison.

The saint. I turned from the twins and looked back toward the woods, where from the cover of the hawthorns a brown face ringed with white hair peeped out at us like some shy wild thing, and disappeared into the shadows when he saw that I saw him. I stood half-way between the woods and a fallen log where the twins sat absorbed in something they had found. "Wait!" I shouted to the twins, who looked up, surprised. They were in no hurry.

I remembered the spring before, when I had crashed through these trees in search of him; it had been just a wood then, like any wood. Now, like a face you've learned to love, it had grown so familiar that the first wood was gone forever, and I knew this one only, which had a path through it, secret like Path, by the split birches, around the dense ever-greens and down the bank to the mossy, ferny places and the black fallen trees where mushrooms grew, up the slate outcropping splashed now with clinging green, and up the sloping, brambly ground to where the old oaks grew, and to the oldest oak. To Blink, who sat at its foot, looking down it seemed in sorrow.

I crept up slowly to him and sat by him without speaking. He didn't look up at me, but now I saw that it wasn't sorrow that made him look down, but something in the grass at his feet which he watched intently: a black ant of the largest kind. It struggled through the bending grasses, its feelers waving unceasingly.

"Lost," Blink said. "Can't find his nest, lost the path. Nothing worse than that can happen to an ant. For an ant, being lost is a tragedy."

"What is that? Tragedy."

"Tragedy, it's an ancient word; it meant a description of a terrible thing that had happened to someone; something that, given circum-stances and some fault in you, could happen to you, or to anybody. It was like truthful speaking, because it showed that we share the same nature, a nature we can't change and so cease to suffer. If this ant ever finds his nest again, and could tell about his experience and the suffering he felt, they'd have a tragedy. But he's unable, even if he does get back. In a way, no ant has ever before been in the tragedy of being lost; this one's the first, because ants have no way of telling about such things, and so being forewarned. Do you see?"

"I think I do."

He raised his eyes from the ground and regarded me calmly. "Well. I think my stories are all told, Rush, the important ones; and now that those two look-alikes have come back, you'll be going home, I suppose."

Old Blink! I had learned truthful speaking in that winter with him, and the weight and tenderness in his words made no answer possible. I only knelt by him and waited. He said nothing more, though; only watched the ant struggling through the grass like a man in the dark.

"Tell me what I should do," I said at last.

"No, no," he said, as though to himself. "No. . . . I guess, you know, all your foolish talk about me being a saint did affect me a little. Enough so that I wanted to tell you a story you would remember, and could repeat. But it's no story, is it, only 'and then, and then, and then' endlessly. . . . A saint, no. If I were a saint, I wouldn't tell you, now, what you should do. And since I'm not a saint, I can't."

I thought of Seven Hands, and the day we had gone to see Road. He'd said: "If you're going to go somewhere, you have to believe you can get there. Somehow, some way." I thought of Sewn Up and No Moon, living at the river house but tied to the warren by strong cords. I thought of Once a Day. No: though Belaire tugged at me, I couldn't go home again. Not yet.

"Blink," I said. "You said, about the four dead men, that if I wanted to know more, I should ask the Long League, or the angels."

"Both gone."

"Dr. Boot's List is a child of the League. And knows things the League knew."

"So they say of themselves."

"Well," I said, and took a breath. "I'll go ask them, then."

He sat silent, blinking at me as though he had just then noticed me kneeling by him, and wondered how I had got there.

"Maybe," I said, "I'm not to be a saint. Maybe not. But there are still stories to learn, and tell." I reached down with a finger and made a path through the grass for the ant, who stopped his labors, bewildered. I wondered if I would weep. I had wanted to be a saint.

"I know the way there," Blink said. "Or I knew it once."

I looked up. His brown face was creased in the beginnings of smile-wrinkles. He hadn't wanted to tell me what to do; but I had chosen as he would have chosen for me. "I wonder, though, if they'll tell you what you want to know."

"There was a girl," I said, "a Whisper cord girl, who years ago left Belaire, and went to live with them. If I could find her, she'd tell me."

"Would she?"

I didn't answer. I didn't know.

"Well," Blink said, "if you listen now, I'll tell you how to reach them. That's the first thing."

I couldn't think, at the same time, of Little Belaire, of Once a Day, and of the directions Blink would give me, so I held up my hand for a moment, palm toward Blink, as gossips do before they hear a tale, and made myself as much as I could an empty bowl; and Blink told me then how I must go from here to where the List lived; and he told it in such a way that I couldn't forget it: because in a way he was a saint, he was: my saint.

We rose, and linked arms, and walked out into the blinding meadow strewn with new flowers. The twins came to their saint, who patted them and giggled, become again the little old man they knew. We sat and talked, and his eyebrows danced up and down and his tiny hands slapped his knees. The twins supplied news from the warren, what little they knew. He listened, and yawned in the heat; finally he lay down, his feet up, on the slope. "Yes, it goes on there as always. . . . No new thing, and if there were you wouldn't know of it . . . well. And then, and then, and then. Another spring, and getting hot too. . . . Quick enough it comes and goes . . ." He was asleep, hands behind his head, breathing quietly in the warming south wind.

We went away quietly. I gathered my pack, but left the fine string hammock for Blink: a small enough gift.

"We'll be at the river house tonight," Budding said; and Blooming said, "Then you'll get home tomorrow."

"No," I said. "I'm not going home. But I'll go with you as far as the river. I'll find Road there."

"I thought you weren't going to be a saint," Budding said.

"I don't know about saints." We had reached the edge of the little brook. "But I decided to leave home, and I think I ought to stay left." I looked back as we went into the woods and caught a glimpse of Blink, asleep in the meadow. I wondered if I'd ever see him again.

I wonder if I ever did.

SEVENTH FACET

I stood next dawn at a great joint of Road, kicking apart the pink embers of the night's fire. Southward, Road fell away to woodlands gleaming in a clear morning, westward it led into lands still night. Above my head, spanning all of Road, was a great green panel supported on rustless pillars, that creaked and swayed in the rising wind. It was lettered, meaninglessly to me, except for two arrows of stained white: one pointing south, one west. I packed my little camp and went south.

In the afternoon I came into the wooded country I had seen. Road entered the forest; and the forest too entered Road. The forest stepped down steep inclines in great trees, and gracefully out onto Road in saplings and weedy trees which tore up the gray surface as spring breaks ice on a river. The liquid slide of the big trees' shade was over it, and when I waded a stream that had cut a deep wound across it, I saw that among the stones in the stream were pieces of Road. And will it all one day be washed away? I thought of Blink talking about the bits of the great angel sphere.

I was in the forest seven days without it thinning or breaking, only growing deeper and older (though not as old as Road). It was an ancient place, and nice to be in—nice to follow Road through, anyway. Night made it different; it made you think that a thousand years ago there had been no forest here; there might have been houses, or towns, and now there were only trees, huge and indifferent, the undergrowth thick and impassible except by animals. Only Road here was for man any more; and Road would be conquered in the end. The fire I built made a great vague hole in the dark, and kept animals away, though I heard noises; and the nations of the insects made their songs all night. I slept lightly through them, waking and dozing, my dreams like waking and my waking like a dream, all filled with those ceaseless engines.

It was as though I had been taken in, by the forest, and forgotten that I had ever been elsewhere. I continued to be afraid at night, but that seemed proper; in the day I walked, turning my head side to side to see only trees. I even stopped talking to myself (which truthful speakers do all the time, alone) and just watched, as the forest watched me. I had become part of it. So much so that when between waking and sleeping in a moonless night I heard two large animals pass near me, and one come close on padded feet, I only waited, absolutely still like any small prey, alert but somehow unable to wake fully and shout or run. And they passed. And next morning I was hardly sure they had been there. I sat smoking in the morning, wondering if I should be grateful I had escaped; the forest had so far convinced me that I was the only man in the world that it was not until I heard human voices singing that I realized it was a man who had passed me in the night.

The birds talked to each other and even the sunlight seemed to make a noise as it fell unceasingly, but the human voices were another kind of noise, which sorted itself from the forest's as soon as I heard it. For a reason I remember but can't quite express, I hid when I heard it was coming closer, coming from the way I had come. From within the great ferns at Road's side I watched; and along the broad gray of Road came, not men but one, then two, then three enormous cats. I had seen cats before, shy feral faces in the woods, and one or two who lived at Belaire and caught mice and moles. These cats were not of that kind; it wasn't only that they were huge—if they had stood on their hind feet like men, they would have been nearly my height—but that their soft, padding motion was purposeful and their lamplike eyes so observant, so calmly smart. I had heard of one cat like them: the cat that came to Belaire with Olive.

They sensed me, and without altering their steady padding came toward the place I hid; I was afraid for a moment, but they were not threatening, only interested. And now down the road those singing came into sight: ten or so, in black, with wide black hats that shaded their faces. When they saw that the cats saw something in the ferns that interested them, the singing died away, and, as interested as the cats, they came toward me. I stood up and stepped out onto Road. They were more surprised than I was, because of course it was they I was looking for, though I hadn't expected to find them so soon.

I greeted them as they gathered around me, and smiled. One said: "He's a warren boy."

"How did you find our camp?" another said.

"I didn't know I had."

"What do you want with us? Why have you come here?"

The urgency and hostility in their voices made it hard to say, hard to say anything at all; I stammered. The first who had spoken, tall and long-limbed, strode over to me and took my arm, holding tight and looking hard into my face. "What are you?" he said, low and insistent. "Spy? Trader? We want nothing more from you. Did you follow us here? Are there others hidden in the woods?"

They all stood close around me, their faces secret and blank. "I've come," I said, "to—to see you. Visitors to Little Belaire aren't treated this way. I didn't follow you, I was ahead of you. I don't mean any harm to you, and I'm alone. Very much alone." It was amazing to see them pause and puzzle over this, and look darkly at me; because of course I had spoken truthfully. And with the force of a blow I realized that none of those I faced did. Perhaps Once a Day, supposing I found her, no longer would; nobody that I would meet, for hundreds of miles around, spoke truthfully. My throat tightened, and I started to sweat in the cool morning.

Another man, whose beard was grizzled gray and whose movements were as graceful as the cat's beside him, came up to me. "You have your secrets, there," he said. "You guard yourselves. We have our secrets. This camp is one of them. We're surprised, mostly."

"Well," I said, "I don't know where this camp is you talk about, and if I went on now, I'd never be able to find it again. If you want, I'll do that."

We had nothing further to say, then. They wanted to go on to this camp, and I didn't want to lose them; they didn't want to take me to it, but didn't know how to part from me. I was a real wonder.

The cats had started to go on, having grown bored with me, and some others drifted after them as though summoned. The question of me wasn't resolved, but the cats seemed to make up everyone's mind. The big man took my arm again, more gently, though his look was still black, and we started down Road after the cats. (There would be a lot of arguments and hesitations resolved that way among the List, I would come to find; the cats decided.)

Soon a spur of Road fell away from Road itself, and led downward in a sharp curve, broken in places and seeming about to lose itself in woods; and only when, at the bottom, it straightened itself and joined Road again, but Road going in another direction, under a bridge hung with ivy as with a long garment, did I realize we had gone around one of the great somersaults I had seen Road do so many years ago. Through the trees we could see its broad back humped as it made its big circles; no doubt the whole forest was seamed with Road, if you knew where it ran. Where does it go? I'd asked Seven Hands. Everywhere, he'd said.

We left Road then, and went through what seemed impassible woods, though there were hidden paths, and came to a small stone clearing, and nestled in the woods at the edge of the clearing was their camp: a low, flat-roofed building, angel-made with wide windows filled in now with logs. Before it were two ranks of decayed metal piles, almost man-high, that had once been engines of some kind, of which I could make nothing.

Before the door sat a bony, black-hatted old man, who waved to us slowly with a stick. The cats had found him already, and sat in the sun by him switching their tails and licking. The tall man who held me showed me to the old one. "He stays outside," he said, and looked at me; I shrugged and nodded as though that would be all right with me, and they went through the door.

I smiled at the old man from where I stood on the stone clearing, and he smiled back, seeming not in the least surprised or apprehensive, though he was clearly the guard and the doorkeeper. I noticed leaning against the building's side a huge square cake of plastic, sleek as Blink's Jug, dirty and cracked, but its red and yellow colors undimmed, that bore a picture of a shell. The sun was getting hot; finally I ventured over to sit with the old man in the shade of the building.

We exchanged further smiles. He was no more doorkeeper than the rotting rows of angel engines before us. I said: "Years ago . . ."

"Yes, oh yes," he said, nodding reflectively and looking upward.

"Years ago, there was a girl, who came to you from Little Belaire. A young girl, named Once a Day."

"Swimming," he said.

I didn't know what to say to that. Perhaps he was senile. I sat for a while, and then began again. "This girl," I said, "came here, I mean perhaps not here, but came to live with you. . . . Well. I'll ask the others."

"Not back yet," said the old man. "Is she back yet?"

"Back yet . . ."

"She went off to the pool in the woods, a while ago. That's the one you mean?"

"I don't know, I . . ."

He looked at me as though I were behaving oddly. "She went out to meet you last night," he said, "when Brom knew you were close. Isn't that right? And came back early, early this morning, after greeting you. Then she slept. Now she's at the pool. I think."

He thought I had come with the rest, from far away. And that I must have seen her. . . . And I had: between wake and sleeping, two had passed me. A man, and another, who must have been a cat. I jumped up, startling the old man. "Where is this pool?" I said loudly. He pointed with his stick toward an opening in the woods that showed a path. I ran off.

How huge the world is, and how few in it, and she passed me in the darkness in the forest and I hadn't known. I was hurrying through the woods as though to a long-lost friend, but thought suddenly that perhaps I shouldn't rush on her: she may not be the person I knew at all, might not know me at all, why am I here anyway, and yet I rushed on as fast as I could. The path went straight up a mossy rocky ridge; on the other side I could hear water falling. I climbed, slipping on the moss, and scrambled to the top, and looked down.

A deep rippled pool of water that leaves floated across. A little falls that poured into it chiming and splashing; the rocks were wet and shiny all around it, black and green and bronze. And at the water's edge, a girl knelt to drink, her hands under the clear water and her breasts touching its surface. Beside her, drinking too, was a great white cat marked black in no pattern. He had heard me; he raised his huge head to look, the water running down his white chin. She saw him look, and rose to look too, wiping her mouth and her breasts. Her face made something like a smile, quick, with open mouth, and then was still, alert as the cat's, watching me climb carefully down the rocks to the pool's edge opposite her.

But this is not she, I thought; the girl I had known had not had breasts, her dark aureoles were like small closed mouths, like unopened buds. This one's thick hair was black, and her eyes startlingly blue, her down-turned eyebrows made an angry sulk; but it wasn't she. Six springs had passed; there was a light beard on my face. I wasn't I.

"Once a Day," I said, at the edge of the pool, my hands on its wet rocks as hers were. Her eyes never left mine, and she made again the smile I had seen from above, but now, close to her, I could hear her quick exhalation as she made it; and when the cat beside her made it too, I saw that it was a cat's smile, a smile to bare teeth and to hiss.

I could think of nothing to say that she would hear. The cat had made himself clear, and she had made herself as the cat. I tore off the pants and shirt I wore and stepped down into the icy water. She watched me, unmoving; in two long strokes I reached and touched the rocks where she sat. When I grasped the rocks near her feet, and began to say a word about cold water, she rose and stepped back, as though afraid I would touch her. The cat, when I drew my numb body out and water streamed from me, turned and loped away silently. And then she, deserted and pursued, without a word turned on her toes and ran from me.

I called after her, and almost followed, but felt suddenly that that would be the worst thing I could do. I sat where she had sat and watched her wet footprints on the stone dry up and disappear. I listened: the woods had stopped making noise at her passage; she hadn't run far. There was nothing I could do but talk.

I don't remember now what I said, but I said my name, and said it again; I told her how far I had come, and how amazed I was that she had passed me in the night; "come more miles than I thought I could hold," I said, "and I don't have any other gift for you than that, but as many more as you want . . ." I said that I thought of her often, thought of her in the spring, had thought of her this spring after a winter in a tree and the thought had made me weep; but, but, I said, I haven't chased you, haven't followed you, no, by the Money you gave me I said I wouldn't and I didn't, only there were stories I wanted to hear, secrets I learned, from a saint, Once a Day, from a saint I lived with, that I wanted to hear more about; it's your own fault, I said, for setting me on a path I've walked ever since, and you might at least say my name to me now so that I know you are the girl I remember, because . . .

She stood before me. She had put on a coat of softest black covered with stars, black as her hair. "Rush that Speaks," she said, looking deeply into me, but like a sleepwalker, seeing something else. "How did you think about me when I wasn't there?"

She spoke truthfully, I thought, I hoped, but her speech was masked, masked with a blank face like a cat's or like the blank secret faces of the ones who had found me in the woods. "You never thought of me?"

The cat came from the woods, warily, and passed us. "Brom," she said, not as though to call to it but only to say its name. It glanced once at us as it passed, and started up a path toward the camp. She watched it for a moment, and then followed. She glanced back at me, her arms crossed, and said, "Come on, then," and all the years between now and the first day I had seen her folded up for a moment and went away, because it was just that way she had said it to me when I had followed her to Painted Red's room when we were seven, as though I needed her protection, and she must, reluctantly, give it.

She didn't ask how I came to be here, so I told her.

"Are you a prisoner?" she said.

"I think so," I said.

"All right," she said.

Something more than years had happened to Once a Day, more than a mask put over her speech. The girl who had kissed me for showing her a family of foxes, and lain down with me as Olive had with Little St. Roy, was gone, gone entirely. And I didn't care at all, at all, so long as I could follow this girl I had found, this black-robed starred girl, forever.

EIGHTH FACET

At evening I sat alert among them, though they were easeful, resting their backs against the walls of their camp in the gathering dusk. For what they were discussing, they didn't seem fierce enough.

"We could tie him to a tree," said one of them, moving his hands in a circle as though tying me up, "and then hit him with sticks till he's dead."

"Yes?" said the older one, the one with gray in his beard. "And what if he doesn't hold still while all this tying and hitting is going on?"

"I wouldn't," I said.

"We'd hold him," the first said. "Use your head."

Once a Day sat apart from me, with Brom, looking from face to face as the others spoke, not concerned in it, it seemed. I would never be able to run from them in their forest.

"If we had a knife," said another, yawning, "we could cut his tongue out. He wouldn't be able to talk then."

"Are you going to be the one to cut it out?" Once a Day said, and when he didn't answer, she shook her head in some contempt.

"We don't have a knife, anyway," he said, not much cast down.

They were afraid, you see, that I'd go back and tell everyone where their camp was, and that they would be invaded or stolen from; there were thieves still; they had no reason to trust me. They just didn't know what to do.

"If we were nice to him," Once a Day said. "And gave him things."

"Yes, yes," said a voice, someone lost now in darkness, "and one day he's dark, and then what does any kindness mean?"

"He's not like that," she said in a little voice. And no more was said for a long time. I jumped when someone near the door got up suddenly; it was the old doorkeeper, who went inside and came out a moment later pushing before him a white ball of light, cold and bright, which when he released it floated like a milkweed seed and shone softly over the men and women seated there. My mind was set on my fate, but when he released the Light and it floated, I thought of Olive and the full moon; I looked at Brom, and the other cats there, who regarded me with the same frank candor that was in the faces of those discussing hitting me till I died. And in Little St. Roy's ear Olive whispered her terrible secrets.

"I have an idea," I said, trying to keep the quaver out of my voice. "Suppose I didn't leave." They all looked at me with the same graceful indulgence they granted one another. "Suppose I just stayed on with you and never went back. I could help out; I could carry things. Then I'd grow old, and die naturally, and the secret would be safe." They were silent, not thoughtful particularly; it was as though they hadn't heard. "I'm strong, and I know a lot. I know stories. I don't want to leave."

They looked at me, and at the Light that moved slightly when the breeze pushed it. Finally one young man leaned forward. "I know a story," he said. And he told it.

So I spent that evening between Brom and Once a Day, not sleeping, though they were asleep in a moment. Nothing further had been said about hitting me or cutting me; nothing further at all had been said, except the story, which I smiled at with the rest, though I hadn't understood any of it.

And not long after I had at last fallen asleep, before dawn, she woke me. "The cats are walking," she said, her face dim and strange; I forgot, for a moment, who she was. I stumbled up, shivering, and smoked a little with her, and drank something hot she gave me in a cup; it tasted of dried flowers. Whatever it was, it stopped the shivers, that and a long cape of black she gave me, giggling when she saw me dressed in it. The others were laughing too, to see me in this disguise. In the long night while my fear passed, I learned something; that the truthful speakers have little need to be brave, because they always know where others stand. It had been only that these people couldn't speak that way that had made me afraid of them when, in fact, they would do no harm to me. I had been afraid of men for the first time in my life, and I saw that it would happen often from now on—fear, confusion, uncertainty—and I would just have to be brave. Odd to find it out, old as I was, for the first time. And to think of the warren, where old people died peacefully, never having learned it.

The cats were walking: it was time to go. There was some discussion over who was to carry what of the things that had been packed the day before; I shouldered a big shiny black pack whose rustle told me it was full of dried bread, enough to last many through a year. It seemed right that I should carry it. And we set off along still-dark Road, in a long line, the cats dim in the distance and the sky beginning to glow to the left through the forest.

When the sun was high and the cats had had enough walking, we found a place to stop for the rest of the day, to sleep and dawdle through the afternoon with them, till evening when they were restless to move again. In a mountain meadow where tall feathery grasses grew up between dark pines and birches, Once a Day and I lay on our stomachs with our heads close and drew out sedges from their casings and chewed the sweet ends.

"When I was a little kid," I said, "I thought I would leave Belaire to go find things of ours that had been lost, and to bring them back to put in their places in the carved chests. . . ."

"What did you find?"

"Nothing."

"Oh."

"I found a saint, though; a saint in a tree. And I thought I would stay and live with him, and learn to be a saint too. And I did."

"Are you a saint?"

"No."

"Well," she said, smiling, with the grass between her teeth, "that's a story."

I laughed. It was the first time since I had found her again that Once a Day had been the girl I had known in the warren.

"And he told you to come here to find us," she said.

"No. There was a story, a story you started, about four dead men . . ." A cloud passed over her face, and she looked away. "And my saint said the League knew that story. But that's not why I came."

"Why?"

"I came to find you." I hadn't known that, not truly, till I had seen her at the pool; but all the other reasons were no reasons at all, after that. I drew another sedge squeaking from its fibrous case. Why are they made like this, I wondered, in segments that fit together? I bit down on its sweetness. "I used to think, in Belaire, that maybe you had gone to live with the List, and it hadn't suited you, and that one spring they'd bring you home dead. From homesickness. I saw how you would look, pale and sad."

"I did die," she said. "It was easy."

The puzzlement in my face must have been funny to see, because she laughed her low, pleased laugh; pushing herself forward on her elbows, she brought her face close to mine, and plucked the grass from between my teeth, and kissed me with eyes and mouth open. "It's nice you thought of me," she said then. "I'm sorry you were dark."

I didn't know what that meant. "You thought of me," I said. "You must have."

"Maybe," she said. "But then I forgot how."

The cat Brom beside her made an immense sharp-toothed yawn, his rough tongue arching up in his mouth and his eyes crossing; she pillowed her head on her hands, as the cat did. "Nice," she said; and slept.

That journey lasted many days, mornings and evenings of long walking and hot, vacant middles when we slept. Walking, the List sang their endless tuneless song, which at first I could hear no sense in, but which came to seem full of interest; I began to hear who was good at it, and waited for the entrance of their voices. Their singing was a way to lighten a load, I saw; it was like the second of the Four Pots I had used: it stretched time out so endlessly that it vanished, and the miles fell behind us without our noticing them. It was only when, one dawn, we came out upon a great spiderweb of Road, where huge concrete necks and shoulders supported the empty skulls of high ruined buildings from which the glass and plastic had been stripped hundreds of years before, that they stopped singing; they were nearing home, awaking from the dream of motion.

They didn't stop when the sun was high, but hurried on, pointing out to one another the landmarks they saw, ruins great or small in the forest; and, at a wide sweeping curve of Road, cheering, they caught sight of their home. Once a Day pointed. I could see, far off, a black square; a square so dark black it made a neat hole in the noonday.

"What is it?" I said.

"Way-wall," she said. "Come on!"

We left Road on a spur of concrete, and came out suddenly onto one of those wide naked plazas, vast and cracked, windy, useless, as though the angels had wanted to show how much of the world they could cover with stone at once. Buildings stood around the stone place, some ruined, others whole; one was the odd blue and orange that are the colors of the first of the Four Pots, and had a little steeple. The largest building, in the center, was made of huge arched ribs rising out of the ground to a great height; and taking up most of its flat face was the square of utter blackness. The ivy that covered the building like a messy beard didn't grow on this blackness, and no daylight shone on it; it seemed to be a place that wasn't there; my eyes tried to cross in looking at it.

There were others, people and cats, coming out of the buildings toward us, greeting and shouting; one was an old woman, taller by a head than I, striding ahead of the others, a huge tiger cat rubbing herself against her skirts. Her long arms used a staff, but she walked as though she didn't need it; she motioned Once a Day to her and wrapped her in her long arms with a laugh. Once a Day hugged her and said a name like a sigh: Zhinsinura. The old woman's eyes fell on me, and she raised her staff to indicate me. "And where did you find him?" she said to Once a Day tucked under her arm. "Or did Olive Grayhair send him to us, to tell us we're all dead?" Once a Day snuggled laughing within her arms and said nothing.

"I came to stay," I said.

"What? What?"

"I came to stay," I said loudly. "And Olive's dead many lives herself."

She laughed at that. "You're carrying," she said. "Bread, is it? Come, put it down; we'll taste it. If I were dark now, I'd question you. Staying is one thing, but . . . anyway, welcome to Service City." She raised her stick and swept it around to indicate the buildings that stood on the stone plaza. "Well. Come, warren boy; we'll think awhile, and see."

She put an arm around me as strong as the bearded man's who had taken me in the forest, and we walked together toward the black hole in the wall that Once a Day had called way-wall. Zhinsinura's long strides took us directly toward it, and though I tried to make us turn away, she gripped me and we kept on till it loomed above us, making me dizzy with its unseeable no-place. I had a moment to feel limitless fear, that if we walked into it we would be lost in its blackness, blind, and we struck it. Or didn't strike: there was a moment that felt like a cracked knuckle all through me—and we were inside, not in darkness but in the hugest indoors I had ever been in, vast, glittering with light; as though there were a raindrop on my glasses, there was an odd shimmer and sense of refraction everywhere and nowhere. I looked back at the black wall I had passed through and was looking outside. The light that lit this place fell through that wall. Way-wall!

And the place that black wall lit, the house that housed Dr. Boots's List: I stood still in wonder at it. Zhinsinura walked away with Once a Day across the black and white tiles that made the vast floor, and their heels clacked and their voices echoed, for the place went up, up, up to the metal ribs that made the roof's curve. In that huge echoey space, so different from the warren's hivelike insides, there were enough people it seemed to fill a city. At the back of the place a great shelf jutted out and made a second floor, reached by a wide sweep of stairs cable-flown from the ceiling; people sat on the shelf's lip and on the stairs with legs dangling and called down to those below; the travelers piled up their goods and sat on them, talking to friends who embraced them, and children ran with drink for them across the tiles. Clouds of bread-smoke arose from groups visiting, and the big cats sniffed the air and mewed. The whole place hummed and buzzed with the purr of the List's ancient speech (though some fell silent as they turned to see me) and none seemed surprised in the slightest to have stepped through Night and fallen into a treasure house of the angels.

For that's what it was. Once a Day ran across the floor to me, skipping away from friends who reached out hands to her, and came to take me in amid it all.

All along the long, long sides of that place were bins and chests and cases, angel-made; some were waist-high to me and made of glossy white plastic, others were tall, with hinged doors of glass and made all, all of angel silver—there were so many of these there that the dull glow of them seemed to lower the heat in the place and make it cool. Some of the open low bins had mirrors above them, slanted in such a way as to make what was inside seem twice as much as it really was—only the angels would have thought of that.

Once a Day ran from one of these cases to another, showing me

things kept in them which she had told me about while we walked—
"and here's this that I told you about and here's that that I told you
about," and her eyes were wide and bright and she was light and I loved
her intensely. She took me by the hand to see the huge pictures fixed all
along the sides above the bins; though they were so large I couldn't have
missed them, she felt I must be shown, and stood pointing them out. The
colors of them seemed as bright as the day the angels made them: one
was carrots, beets, and beans; another had eggs and white bottles; one
was a cow, with a smile like a man's, which was ridiculous. As she stood
solemnly pointing to the cow, she saw someone, and said softly, "Zher."

It was a name. A boy, pale blond and with a pink tint of sunburn on
his shoulders and nose, sat in a circle of people, mostly older, who
seemed to keep a distance from him, though they smiled at him, and
occasionally one reached out to stroke his arm or touch him. Once a Day
went over to them. The boy Zher looked up at her, who was known to
him, and at me, who was a stranger, and his look was the same. Once a
Day went through the circle and knelt before the boy; he looked at her,
his eyes searching her but seeming to look for nothing. She touched his
face and hands, and kissed his cheek, and without a word came back and
sat with me.

"What is it?" I asked.

"Zher," she said. "Just this year come of age, and got his first letter
from Dr. Boots today."

"What's that?"

"It's a letter. And it's from Dr. Boots."

"Why is he naked?"

"Because he wants to be."

Zher smiled a little, and then more; a laugh seemed to be within him,
and those around him smiled too, and looked at each other and at him,
and he did laugh, and they laughed with him. Somewhere someone
dropped something with a clang, and the cats' ears all rose, and Zher's
head snapped around with eyes wide.

"Have you had this letter from Dr. Boots?" I asked.

"Yes. Every May month since I was his age; the first, the summer
after I came; and just before I went out to the camp, and met you, this
year."

"Was it like that for you when you got your letter?"

"Yes. Just the same. I felt that way."

"Were you silent? Do you have to be?"

"You don't have to be. You just are, especially after the first. You don't have anything to say. It's all done. It's all like it will be. Talking, after that, is just—just for fun. Just something to do."

"When you talk to me—is it like that?"

She brushed her black hair with her hand and said nothing, and I didn't dare talk more about it. Evening was falling in the room; the blue daytime shimmer turning dusty gold.

"Doesn't he look beautiful?" she said.

"Yes."

"Beautiful."

"Yes."

As the sun set, the singing began, low and quiet, touched off by the purring of some cat, Brom or Zhinsinura's tiger, and taken up by one group of them, and then by another, a low sweet chuckle and drone and growl, each voice finding room in the medley to purr; and, as night came on, left off, voice by voice, Once a Day's high sad sound nearly the last, until they were all silent. And the Lights were let out.

Perhaps the angels knew a way to make the cool globes dark in the day; the List just keeps them in black bags, and lets them out at night. There were many there, but still in that great place there were pockets and vague places of darkness. No one around Zher moved to bring a Light near him, and in the gloom I could see his fair body glowing as though a lamp were lit within him.

THE THIRD CRYSTAL

A LETTER FROM DR. BOOTS

FIRST FACET

● ● ● A nd wait till I've inserted it.
               What? Shall I begin again?

No. It's all right. Here is the second crystal; see how tiny: yet it's all there. Blink and Budding and Blooming, all that part.

How many more? The sun is setting. Look: the clouds below us are all pink and yellow.

The third is the last, usually.

Angel . . . tell me this now . . .

No. Not yet. Tell me: what happened next day, at Service City?

Well, that night we slept; she took me up the wide flight of stairs that led to the big platform which covered the back part of the place—the mezzanine, they called it (the List knew such words, words that rang like ancient coins flung down angelstone—mezzanine). There, rooms had been made with curtains and low walls, and it reminded me a little of home. Once a Day found us an empty nook piled with pillows, and we lay together there, she talking all the while as though to pull me into her List's arms by strength of stories, until she was yawning too much to talk. She was so happy to be there, and so glad I was with her to see it, that it made me ache with some unnamable feeling—oh, Dr. Boots, you make them—no, you let them make themselves—so happy, so seldom!

Dr. Boots's List can do a thing that I never could, that Once a Day had learned in her years with them: they sleep like cats. They cat nap. Once a Day would sleep for a time, and be up for as long, and sleep some more and be up again. All through that night I felt her get up and go and come back to watch me, impatient for me to get done my long sleep; but I was in the middle of thick dreams, the dreams a sleeper in a strange house has, and couldn't wake. When I did, it was with a cry that woke me from some adventure; I lay staring, trying to remember where I was. I stumbled out through the curtains and found myself on the very edge of the mezzanine, looking out over the vast hall lit by a clear morning turned faintly blue by way-wall. Once a Day stood by it, bent over with her hands on her knees, by a little muscled brown man who sat holding up a ball of clear blue glass, turning it so the light shot through it; he bit on a tiny wooden pipe from which rose a fine white smoke.

When I reached them, stumbling past groups that fell silent when I smiled at them, I saw that on the brown man's wrist was the bracelet of blue stones which Once a Day had given to him on the day of the trading at Little Belaire. His name was Houd, but when he said it it was as soft and long and unspeakable as a cat's sigh. Others gathered around us, and I was made much of; they stared as frankly as cats at my pigtail and my spectacles and marveled at my ignorance of Dr. Boots and the List; and I couldn't understand much of their talk, though I knew the words. Outside in the morning, Brom the black and white cat walked across the wide stone, and Once a Day and the others turned to watch me do what I had to do, being new to way-wall: I tried to walk out there. It doesn't work that way; I could get close to it (always from it a hot breath blew, smelling of metal somehow) but—it doesn't work that way. I looked around at them, and they were all smiling the same smile.

"It doesn't work that way," Houd said around his pipe, and Once a Day came and pulled me away. "It's only one way," she said laughing. "Don't you see? Only one way."

She took my hand and we went across the black and white squares of the floor and out the heavy glass doors ranged all along the back of the place, and around to the front through the real morning light, and then ran together headlong across the stone, with Brom beside us, and we must drown in its limitless blackness, but of course didn't, and we were inside again, panting and hugging. "One way," she said, "only one way! I learned that, I learned that; it's all only one way, don't you see?" And the brown man Houd seemed to watch me to see if I had heard in her words all that she said; and I knew I hadn't.

There was one other thing that one new to way-wall has to do: I tried putting my arm through and then drawing it back out. I never tried it again.

In Little Belaire we said a month the same way we said a minute or a mile: to the angels they meant exact things, so that every month and minute and mile were the same length. To us, they just mean a lot or a little, depending. The List is the same, about minutes and miles, but they know how long a month is. They count it off in a number of days, thirty or so to the month, twelve months to the year, and you are back at the beginning again; and for a reason they explained to me but which I can't remember, to every fourth year they add one winter day that has no number.

To me, the name of a month is the name of a season. I've been in years with two Marches and no April, or where October came in the middle of September; but I loved the List's calendar, because it didn't only count the days for some reason you might want them counted, it told too about the twelve seasons of the year.

The building at Service City that had the orange roof and the little white steeple was called by them Twenty-eight Flavors, and it was there they made most of the medicines and doses for which they're famous. Once a Day took me there, and we sat at two seats that enclosed a little table, private in the dimness (Twenty-eight Flavors had once had big windows of glass, but most had been broken and filled with sticks and plastic). There were many tables there like the one we sat at, angel-made with a false wood grain and not even marred in how-many-centuries. On the table was a beautiful box such as the List makes for precious things, and with a reverent care Once a Day took off its cover.

"The calendar," she said.

Inside the box were shiny square tiles, a pile of them face up, and another face down, about this size: two hands would just have covered their faces. The one showing, the one on top of the pile that was face up, was a picture, and below the picture were ranks of squares, a little like Blink's crostic-words. The picture showed two children, younger than

Once a Day had been in our first June, in a meadow impossibly full of pale blue flowers, which they picked with faces quiet and absorbed. He wore short pants, she a tiny dress of the same blue as the flowers they picked.

Once a Day touched a black word below the picture. "June," she said. There was a small stone, made sticky with pine gum, in a square below the picture; she plucked it off and moved it to the next square. Ten days in June. The bell which hung before the way-wall house sounded four times, clear in the dimness, and we went to the great room for evening.

When twenty days had passed, and the stone had made its way through all the squares, we sat again in Twenty-eight Flavors. There were others there that day to watch, and they stood in the heat as Zhinsinura's big hands moved the June tile to the face-down pile and showed the next. When it was revealed, they all made a satisfied sound, like *aaaah*.

That picture let me know, and laugh to know, that however strange and old the angels were, still they were men, and knew what men know, if they could make this. The same two children, she still in her blue dress, lay on green grass darker than June's, older with length of hot days, and looked into a sky my great changeable clouds were piled up in, cities in the sky. But what made me laugh: the grass and they were at the top of the picture, and looked down into the clouds which floated below: and that's how it feels, in summer, to watch clouds.

"July," Once a Day said. The evening bell rang.

In July I went with her on expeditions to gather things, plants and rocks and soils and funguses the List uses for their medicines; and when we grew tired of searching, we lay to watch clouds.

"What are dark and light?" I asked. "Why do you say someone is dark, and another time that he's light?"

She said nothing, only pillowed her head on her hands and closed her eyes.

"Is it a game?" I asked. "I remember Little St. Roy said, about Olive, that when she was dark she was very, very dark, and when she was light she was lighter than air."

She laughed at that, her flat stomach shaking. "I heard that," she said.

"What did he mean?"

She lay silent for a time, and then rose on one elbow to look at me. "When will you go back to Little Belaire?" she said.

The name in her mouth sounded odd; it was the first time I had heard her say it here, and it sounded like a place impossibly remote. "I won't," I said. "I promised I wouldn't."

"Oh, they've forgotten that. If you left, no one would mind; no one would ask you where you went."

"Would you mind?" I said, for I hadn't heard in her speech that she would, or that she wouldn't; had seemed to hear only that there was no minding in her, which couldn't be so. For a moment my heart felt cold, or hot, and I quickly said: "Anyway I don't want my tongue cut out."

"Tongue?" she said, and then laughed. "Oh, they were dark. Now . . ." And she looked away from me, closing her mouth, as though she had told a riddle wrongly, so that its answer was revealed. But nothing had been revealed to me.

"It was a joke of Roy's," Once a Day said. "A joke is all; an old joke. Look, look, we're falling!"

Below us—yes, below—the sky was tumbled full of clouds. By some magic we stuck to the grass, we were even cross-legged and calm, but we were falling endlessly into cities, faces, monstrous white animals, holding hands to hold onto the roof of the world: strange, when the clouds roll close below you and the sky is grass.

And July's tile turned at the time table made seven in one pile, five in the other.

The calendar's two children lay in deep shade; the boy was asleep, a straw hat over his face and a long yellow straw in his mouth, his small bare feet wide apart. She in her blue dress sat beside him looking over a field of the same yellow straw to a red angel's tower with a conical top; and the gray clouds of a summer storm grew far off. August.

We had a shade house we shared for summer, under two maples that grew together on a hill, and we could see far off too, though all the angels' works were gone, and Once a Day wore no blue dress; no dress at all. The edges of our house changed as day went on, and the brown bodies of our guests moved with the shade.

"Four doors along the spine," Houd said. One of his skinny legs he dangled over his knee, and a wide hat shadowed his face, from which his wooden pipe protruded. "And press with all your might against them, you wouldn't be able to open them. That's my opinion."

"That's because they *are* open," Once a Day said, yawning. "The heat makes me sleepy."

"Just as hard to shut them," Houd said.

"No," she said. "They blow open; as doors are blown open one by one down a corridor by wind; and that's the end of that; they're open."

"You're light to think so," Houd said, and Once a Day yawned again and stretched out her little tawny body on the matted grass so her breasts were nearly flat; she smiled me a sleepy smile.

"Sun's come around," someone said. "Everybody move one place."

Shade.

At evening one let out a light he had brought, but the air drew it away toward Service City, and one by one they followed it there. We lay together as the moon rose and remade our shade house all different.

"Do you think," she said then, moving away from me by a series of slow changes of posture, "that there are four doors along your spine? And how do you think they open?"

"I don't know," I said, following her.

"Neither do I."

There was a faint rumble of thunder, like someone huge, over the horizon, grumbling in his sleep; and as we lay together our moon house too gradually moved away from under us, leaving us splashed with still, cold light.

And September's tile shown at the time table made eight in one pile, four in the other.

"I know her," I said when I saw it, "and now I know those two as well."

"How could you know them?" she asked.

"Because you showed them to me. Look: there's the old one, who comes out when it's dark; and see? she waits now, inside, in this month, and the two children are out . . ."

"No, you're wrong."

"And in the next months she'll be out, and they'll be hid."

"They won't," she said. "They're just two, like any two . . ."

"Dark and light," I said, "just as you said, don't you remember . . ."

"No!" she shouted, to silence me.

The tile we looked at showed a golden engine-summer day. The two children walked together with shining faces; slung over his shoulder by a strap was some Book, and she carried proudly a bright September apple. In all this it was like every other tile, he and she, she in her dress of blue, in a day just the color of the month it pictured, as though squeezed from the month as from a fruit. But in this month only, there was somebody else: the children walked smiling toward a tiny red house with a peaked roof, in whose door could just be seen a small and aged woman.

And yes, it would grow dark, though it was nice now; the old woman would come out, and the two children must retire to wherever they could, to wait out the dark months, isn't that right? The angels, even in their covered cities without weather, would not have forgotten that, that in warm perfect engine summer the old woman waited . . .

"No!" she said, and ran from me.

"I want to understand," I said, when I found her amid her pillows on the mezzanine. "You have to speak truthfully to me. There was the house on the wall you showed me, where St. Roy's leg was kept. The children came out when it was light, and the old woman when it was dark. In between were the four dead men, who never changed. It was about the weather. So are the tiles."

"Yes. About the weather."

"Yes. But, when we saw it, a cloud passed overhead, and the old woman didn't come out; and the last time I saw it, on the day you left, it was spring, and yet the old woman stood there . . ."

She lay face down away from me, her head on her arms like a cat; now she turned her face to see me. "Then," she said, "was it about the weather?"

"I don't know. What else was it about? Why can't I hear it in what you say?"

She turned her face away again. "The tiles are about the weather. The angels made them to tell the months, and they are very true. That's all."

"Then why did you run from me?"

She said nothing, and though she lay still I felt her run from me further. I wanted to pursue her where she ran, and I took her shoulders in my hands as though to stop her, restrain her: but she had fled.

There's a certain kind of dream, the kind where you set off to do an urgent errand, or a task, and directions are given you, but as you go on the places you have been sent to are not the places you intended to go, and the nature of the task changes; the person you set out to find becomes the one who sent you; the thing you were to do turns into a place, and the place into a box of treasure or a horrid rumor; and the goal can never be reached because it's never the same goal; and yet you search on, never surprised by these changes, only persistent, only endlessly trying to do the changing thing set before you.

Until you wake, and there is no search after all.

"Once a Day," I said, and laid my cheek against her hair, which hid her face; "Once a Day, tell me there's no winter; tell me winter never comes, and I'll believe you."

SECOND FACET

On a blowing, rain-swept day which I would have called the first day of November but which the calendar called the twentieth of September, I went to Twenty-eight Flavors, summoned by Zhinsinura. She sat at the time table with September's tile before her.

"Did you wonder who they are?" she asked me.

"Yes," I said.

"Just two," she said. "Like any two in this month. The other is an old woman, to whom in this month they go for counsel." She smiled at me. Her big solemn head was made bigger by her wide gray hair, and her eyes were many-pouched and always sad; but her smile was quick and real. "And how do you get on, now, warren boy?"

"Fine," I said, and would have said nothing more, but that Zhinsinura wouldn't hear in my speech just what I meant, what was fine and what not. "Can you tell me, though, what a letter from Dr. Boots is?"

There were others there, working and sitting, some I knew. I had got used to being stared at around Service City; I would have preferred now to be alone with Zhinsinura, but that's not the List's way. The others looked at me with great interest.

"It's a letter," she said. "And it's from Dr. Boots."

I felt their eyes on me. I looked down at Zhinsinura's long hands feeling the smooth edges of the tile. "There's something," I said carefully, "a thing, that I don't know."

"Always, I should hope."

"That's what she seems to mean. Your dark and light, you know, it's not an easy thing to understand. I thought I'd seen a path, that it was about winter coming; but that was only another riddle; and she seems to say the riddles are answers."

"Every riddle is its own answer," said Zhinsinura. "That's easy. But how could a riddle know its own answer? Don't think I mock you. I don't mean to, a bit. It is a secret thing. The truthful speakers haven't much believed in such secrets, is all. You ask for her secret, though you may not know that's what you're about; and she can't tell you without learning it herself. And she wants not to learn that secret."

"How can you have a secret you don't know?"

The others there looked away now. They didn't like this conversation, not the younger ones; the older weren't listening any more; but Zhinsinura only laced her fingers together and leaned toward me smiling. "Well, how do you speak truthfully?" she asked. "Let's both tell a secret."

"That's not a secret," I said. "It's something you learn so well you forget you know it."

"Well then," she said, opening her hands, "there it is."

Painted Red had said: for Whisper cord a secret isn't something you won't tell, but something that can't be told. "There's something," I said slowly, like someone stupid, "I don't know. I want to know it. There must be a way to learn it, because you all know it. If it can't be told, I'll learn it any way there is."

Zhinsinura's steady eyes seemed hooded and pouched from so much seeing. "Do you know what you ask?" she said gently. "You know, a thing about secrets is that once you learn one, you know it for good. It's your secret. You don't go back out and stand outside again not knowing. There's no way back out."

"Like way-wall," I said.

"Way-wall?" she said smiling. "There's no such thing."

Everybody laughed gently, as though an old joke had been told at just the right time. Their laughter woke the tiger cat named Fa'afa, who was always near Zhinsinura. She touched its head and it rested again.

"You know," she said, "the League had no love for the truthful speakers. Perhaps it was that their women wouldn't join the League in the very ancient times, or then help out after the Storm when they might have, but only kept to themselves. Then perhaps it was the League's pride, that you all had survived without their help. It was only long after women had gone to others to tell them the League was dissolved that Olive went to the warren. The League thought never to make peace with you; and there were some, to the League's shame, who tried to prevent Olive. Well. All that is old.

"But we have grown old differently, in all those lifetimes since then. I know how differently: I visited your warren often, oh, so long ago it's neither light nor dark now. There was a boy there—well, a boy, an old, old man now if he's lived—who asked me to stay there with him, with you all. I wanted to, though I was afraid; in the end he was more sensible; but I think we both knew we would end up in a corner. And even so, I think the harder way is to come here from there. Your girl could because she is a cousin; you . . . well. I don't say it to frighten you."

She looked away, raising her long bony arm to shake down her bracelets. The evening bell rang. She thought; then said: "Yes, there is a thing you don't know. Yes, there is a way to learn it, though not this time of year; and it's too soon for you, anyway. Stay; listen and learn; and don't ask for what's not given you." She moved the sticky stone from the twentieth to the twenty-first day. "You say she ties riddles for you. Well, I'll tie you another. I'm not afraid to tell it because *ay,* though it's not a riddle at all you'll think it's one; and *bee,* if you're going to stay here I think it will have to be by your way and not ours; and *see,* it's the day and the time for it anyway.

"This is the riddle: you can tie a string around your finger to remember something, until you forget there's a string tied around your finger. Then you will have forgotten doubly, and for good. This calendar is the string tied around our finger—and the letter from Dr. Boots is how we forget it, doubly and for good.

"You can look for a path through that. I know your famous Path. If you want to find it here, think this: *path* is only a name for a place where you find yourself. Where you're going on it is only a story. Where you've been on it is only another. Some of the stories are pleasant ones; some are not. That's dark and light."

I sat with my head bowed before her and the September tile between us and listened; and I might have understood, too, if I had ever in all my growing up been told a story that wasn't true.

"Did she send you away?" Once a Day asked. She sat amid baskets of apples that were being brought in through the way-wall, helping the children sort from them the bad ones, which would spoil the others.

"No," I said. "I don't think she did."

She polished on her starred robe and held up for me an orange apple that blushed red like a cheek. "I'm glad," she said.

I had been wrong about her speech. There was no mask put over it to hide from me; only an opacity filling it up, from within, filling up its transparency as fog fills up transparent autumn mornings. Yet overhead the sky is blue. Zhinsinura had offered me every way not to enter into their secrets; what she didn't know was that I had already gone in, by the pool in the forest, no, long before then, in a game of whose-knee in Little Belaire that seemed now as long ago as a time when angels flew; and I had always known there was no way out. I had never truly looked behind me to see.

She was right, you know, I think, about way-wall: that there's no such thing.

Yes?

I mean it wasn't a thing, like a door; only a condition. A condition of the air in the doorway, air altered, as ice is only altered water.

Was it?

I think it had been done long before, in order to heat the place. You said a hot breath blew from it. I think it was just an engine, to make heat . . .

Maybe so. And the little house on the wall, in the warren, was only a bombom, a barom, a thing to tell the weather. Is it all only and merely and just? Why is it you know so much and understand nothing at all?

I'm sorry.

No; no. It's only that this is the hard part of the story, the part that was hardest to live through, the part hardest to tell rightly; and if you don't understand it, the story won't make sense. You must try to imagine me there, angel; you must imagine me, because if you don't imagine me I won't exist. None of it will exist.

Yes. Go on.

In October Twenty-eight Flavors was an argument of odors. There was a long counter there, wood-grained like the tables, behind which rose a great mirror, black-flecked and dull: and on it were drawn in white two people, a man with an apron and a tall hat, and a boy to whom he offered what looked like a giant version of the Four Pots. It was in Twenty-eight Flavors that the List kept and made their medicines. From the ceiling hung brown roots strung in loops, and on the plastic were heaps of wrinkled leaves and the crushed buds of flowers; in the great stainless-steel ovens and sinks behind the mirror, things were baked and washed and mixed: the kitchen, they called it. Brown Houd, who knew much of such things, went among them with a confusion in his cup, looking and grinning.

A confusion?

They made confusions from leaves and such, boiling them with water. There were confusions to wake you up, others to put you to sleep. There were confusions that made you strong or weak, stupid or smart, warm or cool. "It confuses the dark and light," Houd said, "and gives you a pause: for a while you think only about the confusion, and not about everything."

"Everything?"

"That's Relativity," he said.

In that crowded house were also hung the long golden leaves to dry, which Houd and others there smoked in little pipes, racks and racks of it, smelling as it looked, dry and golden. It hung near the calendar, whose October tile of the two children raking orange leaves to burn was changed by Houd to November's: those two walking arm-in-arm, scared perhaps, past leafless trees through which black crows cawed. One curled brown leaf was tossed past them, on a curved black line that meant Wind.

I think Houd was a child of November, like me. Often he would sit much of the day on a huge stump on the edge of the stone plaza Service City occupied, well wrapped up, and there he could be visited. The white smoke from his pipe was like the smoke from the orange leaves the calendar children burned, but the leaves that piled up around his stump were gray, and he himself was the color of November: nut-brown and whorled like wood.

"It's not like your bread," he said to me; "it won't do you any good to inhale it; inhale it enough and it'll kill you, so the angels said, who smoked it by the bale. . . . I only tell you that because it does taste good, once you get used to it." He offered the pipe to Once a Day, who refused it with a grimace, and to me. It was an acrid, harsh taste, that fit the day, autumnal and burnt and brown.

He sniffed the air and put the pipe back between the teeth that liked it. "You know things now that you won't know again in the year. It's in this month, they say, that you can see the City."

"The City," someone said, in a low tone of delighted horror, and the children said, "Tell it, tell the City."

"Say on a day like this," Houd said, raising his yellow palm to us, "in a big sky like that deep with clouds that turn in the wind, a wind you can almost see, that you know will bring cold rain again soon. See there? Where that gray knot of cloud is like a tabby face? It could yawn—it could yawn now—and out of it would come, of a color like it of gray stone and frozen earth, the City. The City that the angels plucked out of the earth like a root. It'd be far away and high, floating, but still you would see the high square towers on it like crystals growing on a rock; and below, the whole plug of earth that came away with it, and tree roots feathering the top and bridges hanging torn away, and tunnels from which roads run out to nothing. And the clouds would wind and stream around it, that might be its own ancient smoke, and half-hide it; until it grew closer (if it weren't quickly swallowed up again to leave you wondering), close enough for you to see the glitter of its uncountable glass, and the bits of rock and earth that fall ceaselessly from its base; and you would see that the vast wind turns it, makes it revolve ever in the sky like a great wheel.

"And in its square streets where nothing lives the dead men walk, made too of stone or worse; and, stuck in life like death, and dreaming, make no motion.

"That would make you shudder."

"Just the story does," said Once a Day, and clutched herself.

"That's like this month," Houd said. "It's the world's shudder that winter is coming."

Just the story does . . . Little St. Roy called the clouds Cities in the Sky; and Houd called the City a cloud, and put the four dead men there to make the children shudder, a November shudder. And long ago Seven Hands had said all lost things end up in the City in the Sky, to make Mbaba laugh when her spectacles were lost. Somewhere a burnt sun was beginning to set; the sky and the afternoon were smoky with it.

"Then winter does come," I said.

"Oh, winter comes," Houd said. "But only when it comes." He puffed his pipe and grinned. "That's Relativity," he said; and everybody laughed, of course, except me, of course.

The great forest which circled around the stone plaza where Service City
sat, two fingers of a gigantic hand about to pinch Service City out like a
bug, didn't seem to grow and thin insubstantial in winter as Belaire's
woods did. It was much greater than that woods, and seemed to grow, as
Belaire's did not, at a great rate: the ivied buildings seemed now more
settled into the forest even than when I had come in the spring. You
could still see Road through the black trees; but it wouldn't be so forever.

The forest was strong; the world was slow but strong. As Service City
fell back into the forest, so Road was drowned in brooks and broken by
winter weather. And so too, I thought, was Belaire drawn in; the bridges
around it fell, and its paths to the great world were blocked, slowly for
sure, but for sure. All our men's places were stained and whelmed by the
world and winter; the leaves piled up behind Service City and littered its
stone plaza, they found their way into Blink's tree house; and on the roofs
of Little Belaire they were bound up in hoarfrost with bird droppings and
last year's nests.

Yet at Belaire the ancient war of man with the world was if not still
fought at least remembered. Maybe it was because Dr. Boots's List lived
not in a gentle river valley but in a great and impatient forest, but it
seemed they had forgotten such things; they no longer struggled to hold
back the world, nor even much remembered how the angels had fought
and won and lost against it. But there it is: the whole tangle of their lives
was based on something they were trying to forget.

For the doctor was there, indoors for winter, along those walls; she
could climb the stairs to the mezzanine, way-wall admitted her, and she
looked out all the eyes which I looked into, though I didn't see her.

They should have seemed childlike, the List, with their changeable
sadnesses and enthusiasms, their dark and light, their endless, pointless
small bickerings. But they weren't childlike; they seemed old—not aged,
but like grownups, with histories, with old knowledge, old manners, a
careful, circumspect way—and how could that be, I wondered, that they
could change like children and play like kittens, that yesterday and tomorrow could be real for them only as a dream is real, and yet seem
circumspect?

Like a dream, yes . . . I thought winter would make Once a Day
sad, you know, dark; but she was the same, or never the same the same,

and whatever the game or trick of dark and light was it was a thing which happened day to day, moment to moment, and not by seasons. In the mezzanine we made private places for ourselves where we spent the long, long twilights; sometimes the sadness of them would make her sad—no, in the sadness of them she would happen to be sad—and we would let out a Light early to pretend it was already night. Her summer-tawny body grew pale again, and the light hair that downed her limbs dark. And we dreamed together amid the crowd there. I thought it was for shame, a shame like their old manners, that she never spoke of these things elsewhere, and never wanted them spoken of, as though they hadn't happened. But it wasn't shame. It was that she wanted to mark nothing: wanted to make each time the only time, as pastless as a dream. There were no words: she wanted none.

And then I woke. And now I only know I dreamed, and am awake.

THIRD FACET

The big snows fell in that month in which the calendar children, bundled up, made a faced pile of snow with twigs for arms and a hat like the hats the men of the List wear. On a day in the month that followed, February, we lay on the mezzanine and watched snow fall, turning to rain; through the veil of it the black trees seemed to proceed slowly toward us, though they came no closer. Once a Day lay against Brom, carefully biting her nails to the length she liked them and filing them smooth on the rough stone of the wall. Around us we heard tiny winter stories told, stories of doors in the forest, tiny doors at the top of worn steps, a light inside; they open a crack, and eyes look out.

This was the time of the List's long laziness; if it could be said they ever waited for anything, you could say they did little in this time except wait for spring. It was now that most of their children were born, the time carefully calculated; below, a group was cooing over a new child, a girl I supposed by the way they made much of it. Two older children stood at an open bin of the long white bins in an endless game of changing clothes; one stepped out of a black, shimmering belt and changed it for the other's frayed wig and false fur. They dangled jewels and stained ribbons, arm-clocks and rags of shirts, each twirling for the other's criticism and grudging admiration. I watched them, enjoying their moments of pale nakedness; their voices rose up to where we sat, low and indistinct.

"The door in the elbow," the sleepy storyteller near us said, "the door open a crack, through which winter comes, blowing on the heart."

I thought of Blink, bundled and sleepy, saying *It's a small world.*

And yes, you see: circumspect, as I said, and careful for themselves: for they won't disappear, the List would never choose that, though it sometimes seemed to me that disappearance was what they aimed at in the end—no, but they will be wholly taken in, because they have forgotten, doubly and for good, the ancient struggle of man against the world, forgotten doubly and for good the string once tied around all men's fingers; and in the forest, like shellfish in a secret shellfish bed, they will move only for the current's sake, and keep their counsel as close as cats, endlessly counting off the twelve seasons of the year while the forest and the water and the winter eat up the angels' works and Road and perhaps even Little Belaire . . .

"The shortest month is February," Once a Day said, testing her filed nails against her cheek for smoothness; "or the longest too."

The floor below belonged as much to the cats who walked it as to the people they walked among. I said there were cats who lived at Little Belaire; but the List seemed to live with their cats and not the reverse. They were deferred to. Houd had told me that the cats of the List were not of the same family at all as the cats I had known; these great, pacific, wise animals were descended from a race the angels invented, so to speak; a race they made out of the old race of cats, altering them by the same means we men had been altered, and for the same reason—convenience. And in the thousand generations that came after, they had been altered further by careful selection of mates. They hunted little, but ate the food made for them in the kitchens of Twenty-eight Flavors; almost never did I hear them make that eerie, tormented cry I had used to hear, like a lost baby, in the woods near Little Belaire. I said the List were grownups: but now looking down at the floor where the cats walked I thought it was the cats who were the grownups, and the people their children. And as children learn their manners from watching grownups, so the List learned theirs from cats.

I was proud of this small insight; I had no notion how close I was to the truth, and therefore I was as far away as ever.

Zhinsinura came through the way-wall, and others after her, dressed in their raggedies—winter warm-clothes piled on however to keep the cold out.

"We're going to the forest," she called up to us. "You come."

"Why?" asked Once a Day.

"A cat's lost. Help find her."

The cat's name was Puff, a very old and tired orange female with a big scruffy mane, blind in one eye. She'd been gone two days, Zhinsinura said as we struggled into warm-clothes, which wouldn't have worried anyone if it was Brom or Fa'afa, but Puff in the winter . . . She hurried our dressing.

It was wet, black, and hopeless in the forest, a thin rain still falling, and I didn't know how they thought they would find anything but mud and old snowbanks to fall in, but they kept on through the day just as though they had a path. We spread out, and soon lost sight of each other, and I found myself struggling along beside someone I didn't know, bound up to his eyes in gray. He slashed at the dirty snow with a stick, breathing wet clouds from his nose.

"Help me here," I said, my foot caught in something beneath the snow.

"Dog days," he said.

We pulled me loose. "What did you say?"

"Dog days." He waved his stick, indicating the forest. "February's the lean month for them. They're said, when they find nothing at all to eat, to run around in a circle till the weakest drops, and then he's it. I don't know. I guess that's fair. But usually they find something."

Like Puff, I thought, old and cold as she was. The story at Little Belaire was that all the dogs had long ago been eaten or killed, but in this forest . . . "Dog days," he said again, his eyes shifting from side to side above the gray scarves covering his mouth. We stopped to get our bearings. The relentless drip seemed to fill my ears, making it hard to hear other sounds. The high trees' tops were lost in fog, and their black trunks seemed rotten with wetness. The forest crackled suddenly quite near us, and we spun around: two of our number came out of the trees toward us, dressed in black like the day. We called out and kept on; and now my eyes were shifting around like my gray friend's.

For a long time we tore through a thicket of harsh bushes, clawed at by springing limbs and tripped up by roots. Beyond it the ground fell away sharply into a sort of depression in the ground, whose lowest part was filled with dark water edged with papery ice. As we came out on the edge of this bowl, he saw one thing on its far side, and I saw another.

He saw Puff, off to the left, struggling up through the snow to reach the crest on the other side.

I saw Once a Day, off to the right, also climbing, trying to reach Puff. We both pointed and said, "Look!" at the same time. Once a Day must have been to the cat's blind side, because the cat kept on, desperately, up to her chin in snow; and just then we heard what she was running from. The noise tore through the fog, a sharp, snarling yelp made again and again that made me freeze in terror. Once a Day stopped too, but Puff kept on; the woods crackled and thrashed to the left, and there burst from cover an animal. The man next to me bared his teeth and hissed out in fear, and the animal—a dirty-yellow, skinny, big-headed thing—stopped and with great snaps of his head looked from Once a Day to Puff who was disappearing over the ridge. The woods behind him spoke, and a red one charged out; he didn't stop at all, but hunched his skinny back up through the snow. The yellow one followed. Bursting from the woods, a spotted one slipped into the water and slopped out again, climbing after the others.

Once a Day had got to the top and over, beating the snowbound dogs, and the man with me was halfway to the pool's edge, shouting and waving his stick, before I unfroze and slid after him. As we circled the pool, stepping up to our knees in black water and muck, two more dogs came yelping from the woods, and stopped when they saw us. They backed and ran to and from us as we tried to climb the bank, we not daring to turn our backs on them, shouting at them as they shouted at us. Two men now came from the woods following Once a Day's foot-prints, and my stick friend tore the gray scarf away from his face and waved to them, and the dogs, seeing them, ran off in another direction.

Heavy with water, sobbing painful cold breaths, we got to the top. Puff, Once a Day, and the dogs were gone. The snow, stirred and foot-printed, melted out in hillocks along the wet black ground; and across the snow, starting at my feet and running crazily away in drops, was a long stripe of blood.

Cat's blood: I grasped at that. Puff's blood. Poor Puff, but old after all, still too bad, anyway it's cat's blood. . . . The two in black passed me, hurrying on, pointing out the signs of the trail to each other. I still stood stricken. Stick came up next to me, his sodden boots squishing.

"Dog days," he said; "a lean month, and nothing's that large, if they're together they'll try it . . ."

"No," I said.

He went off, following the others, his head nodding rapidly side to side. "If she stayed with the cat," I heard him say, "they'd take them both, oh yes, drag them to the woods, you hear the silence now, you see what that would mean . . ."

No, no, no, he's not kept his head, I thought, starting after him, then turning back to look again at the snow, not kept his head about the cat's blood that it was, why does he go on like that?

"Dogs are dogs are dogs are dogs at least," said Stick.

"Why don't you just look?" I shouted at him, my feet numbly plucking mud. "Why don't you just be quiet about it and look?"

"Wood smoke," said Stick, stopping still.

I smelled it and saw it at once: a dark smudge in the woods, browner than the gray day. He ran on toward it, calling out to the others; I only stood, still trying to speak truthfully to myself, scared, not knowing what a fire in the forest would mean anyway. Stick turned and waved to me, and disappeared in a clump of trees.

There was a path through the clump of trees, and at the end of the path a cabin of logs built against an old angelstone wall; ashy smoke rose up through a hole in the roof of wattles. The yellow dog, the first one Stick and I had seen at the pond, paced back and forth before the door until he saw us, and backed away and ran as we came close. From another direction the two in black came up to the cabin, and disappeared into the darkness inside, as though walking through way-wall; they seemed to be laughing. Stick went in. I came up last, and heard them talking inside.

I went in.

In the flare of firelight and smoke, the black-cloaked people sat laughing softly, relaxing in the warmth. Zhinsinura was laughing too; beside her old Puff lay asleep; and within her arms Once a Day lay, her eyes bright in the firelight, smiling. I crept to her, my fear still a hard knot in my stomach, to touch her, to know for real it was she.

"You're all right," I said, and the others laughed.

"Yes," she said. "The doctor was there."

"What doctor? What doctor?"

She only shook her head, smiling.

"How, what happened? How did this fire get here? How, what . . ."

Zhinsinura put her hand firmly on my wrist. "Hush," she said. "It's nice now."

The others had fallen silent, and for a moment Puff awoke and eyed me with her one eye. I saw that I wouldn't learn now, probably would never learn, what had happened, whose blood was on the snow, because it was then not now; it was nice now. I was not to ask for what I wasn't given. I sat slowly, thinking: if it had been I among the dogs, I wouldn't have found this nice place, because I would have looked for it.

"Yes," I said. "Yes, it is nice now; with the fire and all, yes."

"*He* was dark," said Stick, whose face I could see across the fire grinning widely. "Dark even to shouting." He laced his hands comfortably behind his head and showed more teeth. "Dog days," he said, pleased.

And that's how I found out what dark and light are.

You didn't tell about February's tile.

I don't remember it well. I remember that it was "crazed," you know, heat or something had made it a web of fine cracks. I remember that it was black, mostly, like the month. They stood on a bridge, I think, over a cold river; there was something huge out on the river. I don't remember.

In March's pale tile the hem of her blue dress curled with the same curl that marked the dead leaf's path in November: the curved line that meant Wind. They stood in the wind atop a brown hill that looked to be the top of the world—nothing could be seen around them but a big sky, pale and purplish. The wind that blew behind them tangled their curls and held their kites high up, so high they seemed tiny.

In the still-roofed part of one of Service City's ruined buildings, amid piles and bundles of the List's things stored there, Once a Day found her kite. We sat amid the clutter and listened to Zher as she tied, with infinite absorption, a new tail for it. Her eyes were cast down, and her mouth seemed to obey the same commands that her hands were following: closing firmly to tighten a string, opening then pursing to find the next rag; when she made a knot, her tongue peeked out.

"When the moon is full in March," said Zher, "the hare goes crazy." His eyes grew wide and fierce. "He stamps his feet." Zher's leg kicked the ground with a thump. "He balls his fists and can't *stand* it, can't *stand* it."

He stared around him, his leg twitching to kick again. "When another comes, he shouts out, 'No room, no room!' even if there's plenty."

Once a Day laughed at his craziness, and then returned to her work. Of any there at Service City I found her absorption most beautiful, because I loved her, but they were all like her in it. On each thing they did their attention was complete. It was as though the thing to be done directed the doer, as though the task were master.

Of course there weren't many things the List did. One of them was to fly kites in March. There were many in that building, broken and whole, hung between a pile of plastic boots and gray capes and a stand of furled umbrellas. On the right day, chill and blowing, a day like a stiff new broom for winter, they would all be scattered across a brown hilltop with their hats tied on and their raggedies snatched at and billowing, and all their bright-tailed kites aloft. Or then again maybe they wouldn't.

Anyway. On a day still and odorous, with pale things sprouting in the forest, the kite tile was moved, and there were three in one pile and nine in the other; the ones who stood to see it turned made their small sound of satisfaction as April was revealed.

A silvery, sidewise-falling shower struck splashes from puddles. The puddles, silver-edged, reflected a soft green that was indistinct, rain-shrouded, all around. In this tile only was the girl not in blue; she and he were identical in shiny yellow coats, and her calves curved gently rising from the wide mouths of yellow boots. Her umbrella, though, was blue; and though it rained in other months, it was only in April that the List took out their umbrellas to water them.

On a showery day I watched them through the way-wall, strolling across the wide stone with their umbrellas in bloom. Some were patched, some bent and with missing struts, some stretched wrong on the frame and looking like bats' wings. Houd was among them; his gray and green barred umbrella was larger than the others and had a strangely carved grip, and he grinned at me just as though he could see me through the way-wall as I could see him.

They began to come in when the bell sounded five times, not for evening but in the middle of the day. They shook water from their hats and from the flapping umbrellas—not allowed taut indoors, for some reason—and they smelled of the warm wet day, and brought in green things, ferns and shoots and blossoms sparkling with drops. As they collected around the floor, Zhinsinura, who had had a high seat brought out for her, watched them as the cats did, and her gaze was the same, a mild and accustomed curiosity. She sat them down without words, her big hands lightly guiding them; children were shushed and the milling subsided as people found seats facing her, arranging themselves with the List's patience for such things. After a time two rough half-circles had been drawn up, one closer in all of women and girl children, and an outer one of men and boys.

Once a Day went past me, brushing the clean rain from her face, smiled at me and went to sit with the women. I would have liked to sit by her, but this was the day the List remembers the Long League and Mother Tom, and on such a day the men know their place, sit back and hold their tongues.

Beyond the way-wall, the rain grew strong for a moment, like a fit of sobbing, then lessened. We were silent. Zhinsinura began speaking, and the cats grew curious.

FOURTH FACET

"In the last month of winter," she began, almost as though she were talking only to the cat at her feet, "which is the first of spring, the ice on the river, which had been solid and could bear weight, broke up and floated away in great clashing chunks, which makes a pretty sight.

"The ice asked: How is it that the river could accomplish such a thing? And the river might answer: Ice set itself a task it could not finish, and all that was left undone remained the river; and for the undoing of what you did do, well, it wasn't I at all but time and changes, and I am left.

"I say the river might answer so, but it doesn't answer, there being no ice left to answer to.

"If we were to tell a story about ancient times, we would say that the men were angels who could fly: they were the ice's brittle, still surface. The river flowing quick unseen beneath we would name the women and their League. And as for time and changes, well, they have always been the same, without another name.

"Now the men in those times said to the women, 'See: we have thrown Little Moon into the sky, our planters have escaped the sun, and we must struggle to further these works forever. Men have things to do, and must use their time properly; any of you who can do so may help in these tasks. But while we build a new moon and get it put up next to the old one, you are still controlled by the old moon; you can't use your time properly; that is your greatest weakness.'

"And Mother Tom said to the League: 'That is your only strength. Spring is coming, and the ice must break on every river. Time is in need of you, and, dark or light, will put you to its use.' "

She reached behind her chair and took up a tall box which she set before her. The front of the box was made to look like a sort of archway; and when Zhinsinura turned something at the back of the box vigor-ously, the archway brightened, and it seemed we looked into a garden where a fruit tree flowered, and where a huge, fat woman waved. She waved: I mean it wasn't a picture of her waving, she waved, her hand rose, made a hello, and returned to her side; then it rose again, waved again, came down again, then rose again and waved. While she waved, Zhinsinura spoke, her hands resting lightly on the box.

"Mother Tom said: 'I'm part man, part cat, part dream, and All Woman.'

"Mother Tom had had an Operation, you see. She had been a man, and then been turned into a woman. And very well, too, these were the days of every possibility and contrivance. Her female parts were real, as real as her man's parts had been; she named her female parts Janice, after a woman murdered on Road, from whom they had been taken. She said, 'Janice would be glad, if she knew.' The doctors then could just replace one set of parts with another, easy as that, and in their angel way thought that was the end of it; but Mother Tom's female parts began to grow a person outward from them, a woman, that dark by light outgrew the old man Mother Tom had been. Mother Tom said, 'Janice is changing my mind.' Mother Tom weighed as much as any two women, and had a voice like a loon, and wanted to be a Woman entirely, even to being in the women's League.

"The angels had a joke, in those days, about the League. When the League meets, they said, women with breasts like pigeons fold their hands before them and speak to other women from between bowls of cut flowers. They all wear flowered hats, and they speak only foolishness." Zhinsinura took a nut, and a cracker for it, from within her deep pocket. "It was a good joke," she said, "but the angels didn't know why it was funny.

"I have wept," she said, "to think of their struggles to use their time properly; and I have thought of them weeping. Mother Tom wept often after those meetings, when once again the women had struggled more with one another than with the angels; wept when she heard in her dreams their voices, abused and frightened and angry and silly and above all Feminine. 'Feminine!' Mother Tom would weep. 'Feminine!' She was beginning to learn, I guess, what she had let herself in for, and was glad to know it. 'I wouldn't be a man again for all the planters in the universe,' she said, 'or all the Money in the bank or all the cities in the sky.'

"Mother Tom confused the League, and for a long time she was not allowed among them, but she wouldn't stop talking, whenever she was let to, and as the years went by her story grew longer: about what was to come, as much as she could see; about men, for she had been one; about dark and light, though what was there to say? The women began to listen, some of them; and understand; but sometimes they would only look away, and smile, and not listen, and wait for it to be nice again.

" 'Nice!' Mother Tom would shriek. 'Nice!' For as she grew older, and as more and more of the League's women listened to her, the less Mother Tom wept and the more she shouted.

"The angels made a mistake, then. They had always thought the League was funny, and they thought Mother Tom was funnier still. But Mother Tom knew men, and kept on talking, and grew older and louder, and the more listened to the older and louder she got; until men were like someone who had a bird in his hand that is struggling to escape: squeeze tight, and the bird dies; don't squeeze tight, and the bird escapes. The angels squeezed tight, and the bird escaped. It was ever their way."

Zhinsinura broke and ate her nut with calm absorption. "You see," she said, "the angels at long last got the joke: that as long as women struggled to use their time properly and join the terrific enterprises of the angels, there was nothing to fear, but as soon as the women shut up, as Mother Tom told them to shut up, then the angels' enterprises were in terrible danger. So what they did was to send some two or three to Mother Tom's garden, this garden, and kill her. Mother Tom was near eighty then. And they killed her.

"If you were to tell a story about ancient times," she went on, "you would say that the day the angels killed Mother Tom in her garden was that day in winter which is the shortest, the day on which winter begins in earnest, but the day too after which the days, however slowly, begin to lengthen toward spring. Because, in her long life, Mother Tom had finally got herself understood by the women she loved, the angels for a long time thought the bird was dead. The ice grew thick—but the river was deeper; the ice was silent, and the river spoke only to itself, all unheard.

"The river spoke about Mother Tom. It was in those days that this picture was made, to remember her by, and a thousand like it, which women kept. They said of Mother Tom: when she was dark she was very, very dark, and when she was light she was lighter than air.

"About the things Mother Tom had said. About what was to come, which their men came home every night from planning for and struggling with and failing against and using their time properly to defeat: and they remembered Mother Tom's advice, when the men talked: shut up.

"About gardens and clothes and the difficulties of food and how the lights kept going out. About their children and which was most beautiful, and Money stories, and what to do when the lights went out for good. About the latest of the angels' wonders and how it seemed that soon there would be nothing impossible and their men could give them everything they wanted.

"Everything they wanted." Zhinsinura passed her hand over her eyes and touched the box in which Mother Tom waved endlessly. "I would have been dark, dark, dark, then; am dark to think it. How hard, how hard! To be time's tool when those who think themselves time's masters tell endless, useless tales to bind it, tales which even if the women understood they could never contradict. To watch your kind like a sick cat eat and be not satisfied, to gorge and cough up worms. And still shut up. And never know, any more than any tool can, when the need for you will come—or if perhaps you have been wrong, and your task is not after all simply the satisfaction of that endless angel hunger, is not after all Everything you Wanted. It wasn't Mother Tom, no, and she had known it wouldn't be—it was that long fire that made time's tool, endlessly shaping it in the flame of dark and light until its task was ready.

"To the angels, the Storm was the darkest time since our kind began: for what does ice know about spring? And though the League was full-grown then, and all their stories learned by heart when they gathered here for the first time after the fall of the Law and the Gummint, here on this floor in Service City and in a thousand places like it; and though they remembered Mother Tom, and knew now what she meant, and knew somewhat what to do to begin to help—though they knew all this, yet they were not light then. For remember, children, remember: for all that the women of the League knew better, for all their dark and light, *they too were angels themselves.* Never forget that, for it is their greatest glory. I have felt them meeting here then, in those days: and I know that whatever skills they had, it was terror, dark, and panic that they felt; and that whatever they created later, they knew that their task just then was mostly to watch the angels die. For with a sound like weeping and laughter, the ice had parted in the sun."

The women before Zhinsinura, some of them, had listened intently, chins in hands; others had been preoccupied with hushing children, or nudging cats away, or changing their places for better ones. The children played at distracting each other, as children do when serious things are said. For it was an old, old story, after all, and heard hundreds of times; this was only the day in April when the List chose to tell it all together. I had listened perhaps more intently than any of them.

Mother Tom in her garden raised her hand, waved, lowered her hand.

"We who are the League's child," said Zhinsinura, "and who remember Mother Tom—we who feel those ancient women still to be here, here, where they guarded and dispensed the food that once burdened the thousand shelves long since gone; where they made medicines to save lives now long over; to where they returned from their journeys with stories and angels' things which remain here still; where their plans were laid, and where the old agreements were come to which made the world the way it is today; and where in the end that struggle was resigned—we don't forget, though we regret nothing, as no one in old age regrets the death of a parent long ago.

"If you were to tell a story of the days in which the League grew to be the Long League of famous memory, you would say that a cat is curious when it's not comfortable. That their curiosity found the secrets of medicine's daughters and all the angels' medicines, we are grateful. That it uncovered the four dead men, most horrid of all the angels' secrets, and destroyed them, we shudder at: and praise their courage. That it learned Dr. Boots and so came to know dark and light as we do, well, what is there to say? But the League as it was is gone; the curiosity is satisfied; the struggle over. Dark or light, the world is lighter than it was."

She shook her head, smiling, and brushed shell crumbs from her lap. "Yet think of it," she said, smiling wider and looking out over them, who caught her smile, "only think of it long enough to feel how odd it is, children, how odd in the end, far, far more odd than either happy or sad. May comes now, and that communion: the oddest of all. I want no one's secret: only think a moment that we are here now, and that that was then, and it has come to this, and how odd, odd, odd it is!"

On the faces around me, as Zhinsinura asked, it seemed to dawn on them: the one thing I had known and they had not, seemingly. There was even a ripple of laughter that rose here and caught there, grew deep among the men and died away as our evening song did. Their laughter at the oddness of it was the first time they had seemed like ordinary people —I mean like truthful speakers—since I had come there.

In their laughter, it seemed, that day came to an end. The rain would go on till night, or through the night; in the silver glimmer of it the afternoon was already dark. Zhinsinura still sat, with Mother Tom before her, and broke nuts to eat, while the rest of us stretched and moved, walked and talked again.

I made my way to where Once a Day sat before the box inside which Mother Tom stood waving. It had grown dimmer in that garden, and Mother Tom's eternal wave moved more slowly. Because Once a Day still watched it, I watched it.

"What did she mean," I asked, "when she said 'May comes, and that communion'?"

"She meant our letters from Dr. Boots," Once a Day said, her eyes not leaving the box.

There was a flowering tree in the garden, and now, close to it, I could see that there was a tiny cat curled up at her big feet. Mother Tom's hand rose, and a petal began to drift from the tree. Her hand rose high and waved; the petal reached the ground; Mother Tom smiled, and the cat at her feet closed its eyes peacefully. Mother Tom lowered her hand; her smile faded as her hand came to rest against her side. Then the whole garden seemed to give a minute shake. Mother Tom's face became set and grim and apprehensive, the cat's eyes were suddenly open and alert. Her hand rose, in the same way; her face lightened to a smile, the cat's eyes began to close—and another petal fell from the tree, exactly then.

When she was dark, they said, she was very, very dark, and when she was light she was lighter than air.

She waved, and waved again. Each time, her face would be dark and apprehensive, then lighten to a smile; each time as she smiled the cat would close its eyes. And each time another petal would drift in rocking lightness to the ground.

"If we watch long enough," I said, "there will be no more petals. The tree will fruit."

"No," said Once a Day. "No, it won't."

There was a puzzle that St. Gene made: he took a strip of paper, and half-twisted it, and sealed it in a loop. Now, he said, trace the outside of the loop with your finger. But don't trace the inside. But the beginning of the inside always came before the end of the outside; the loop always began again before it came to an end.

"That's a riddle," I said. "You promised me, last month, you wouldn't set me riddles any more."

"I don't remember riddles," she said.

Mother Tom waved. The cat slept. The petal fell. With a sudden suffocating sense of having discovered myself to be in a small, closed place for ever and ever, I understood: all the petals that fell were one petal. Mother Tom's wave was one wave. Winter never comes.

FIFTH FACET

"When do you go?" I asked her.

May had rebuilt our shade house on the hill; the grass we had beaten down there had sprung up golden-green again.

"Soon," she said. "They'll come to tell me."

They had been going away, one by one, down toward the river, and returning, naked many of them, from Dr. Boots, the old looking like children and the young ancient. The letter was got by each, and their secrets grew strong and sure, and intersected me everywhere. I turned to them, one by one, to the friends I had made, and found they had disappeared, though they looked at me still; and the greeting died on my lips. Even the youngest children, though left out as I was, seemed more still, and played games I didn't know with cats who seemed restless and watchful. And though it was the List that had become—become disembodied, in a way, yet it seemed that it was I who was not there, who was only a flicker of memory and misunderstanding amid the solid weight of their magic.

"What if," I said to her, "what if you didn't go, this year?"

"What do you mean?" she said, not as though she truly wanted to know, but as though I had said something without any meaning at all, which hardly interested her. A thick wave of despair came over me. She could never, even Whisper cord as she was, have asked me that question in Little Belaire: what do you mean?

"I mean what I say," I said softly. "I really mean what I say."

She looked at me, the blue of her eyes as blank and opaque as the sky behind us. She looked away, at the hoppers that hopped in the damp grass; at Brom, who chased them, daintily for one so huge. She couldn't hear. I would have to say it all in words.

"I don't want you to go and get this letter," I said.

Through the year I had lived with her, she had come slowly to be someone I knew; not the girl I had once known, but, month by month, someone I knew. I hadn't asked for what wasn't given me; yet she had given me herself. And I knew that when she got her letter she would be abstracted from me again as surely as if she fled from here to Little Moon. "Listen to me now," I said, and took her thin wrist. "We could go away. You said they wouldn't care, and surely now of any time they would care least. We could go tonight."

"Go where?" She smiled at me as though I were telling some fantastic tale, one of their jokes.

"We could go back to Little Belaire." I meant: to Belaire, where we were born, Belaire and the saints and the Filing System and the gossips who untie knots instead of tying them tighter as the old ones here do, Belaire where every story has a proof and all the secrets have names at least; I meant *We could go home.*

"It wasn't my home," she said, and my heart leaped, for I heard she had heard me. "It wasn't my home, only a place I found myself in."

"But, then, anywhere, anywhere you like, only . . ."

"Don't," she said gently, looking at the grass, at the glitter of the hoppers. She meant: don't darken me now, not now of any time.

Far off, we saw someone coming toward us, in a sleeveless black coat and a wide hat. Houd. He stopped some way off and watched us for a moment. Then he raised the stick he walked with, summoning her, and turned and walked away.

"I'm to go now," she said, and rose.

"Do you know I lose you by it?" I said, but she didn't answer, only started after Houd toward Service City.

I put my head on my knees and looked at the grass between my feet. Each blade of grass, tiny bud, tinier bug, was clear, clearer than I had ever seen them before. I wondered at that.

No! I leaped up, and Brom stopped playing to watch me. I caught up with her as she started across the wide, sun-heated stone plaza. Winter had cracked it, adding minute wrinkles to its face as years add them to a human face.

"Once a Day," I said to her back, "I'm going away. I don't know where, but I'm going. In a year, I'll come back. But promise me: promise you'll think about me. Think about me, always. Think about . . . think about Belaire, and the foxes, about the Money, think about how I came and found you, think about . . ."

"I don't remember foxes," she said, not turning to me.

"I'll come back and ask you again. Will you think about me?"

"How can I think about you if you're not here?"

I grasped her shoulder, suddenly furious. "You can! Stop it! Speak to me, speak to me, I can't bear it if you don't. . . . All right, all right," for she was closing her face against me, turning away, taking my hand from her as though it were some accidental obstruction, a dead branch, an old coat, "only listen: no matter what you say, I know you can hear me: I'll go away now, and we can both think, and I'll come back. In the spring."

"This is spring," she said, and walked away across the plaza. I watched her, vivid, white, and living for a moment against the immense absent blackness of way-wall; and then gone. Blink: gone. As though she hadn't been.

And what if, I thought, my heart a cold stone, what if she had spoken truthfully to me, what if she had heard in all I said that I could no more go away from here for a year—for a month, for a day—than Brom could speak or St. Blink tell a lie?

I don't remember the rest of that day, what I did with myself. Perhaps I stayed where I had been left, on that stone. But at evening, before I could see her return, I went to Twenty-eight Flavors to find Zhinsinura.

She stood with other old ones at the long counter, pondering with them a great piece of smooth slate which had been carefully coated with beeswax, so that signs could be made on it. After some thought, she brought forward one woman and gave her a pointed stick; as the others smiled and nodded, she bent and made a sign on the wax. Zhinsinura hugged her then, and she departed with one or two others.

"I want to go too," I said, and Zhinsinura turned her hooded eyes on me. "I've passed all your tests. I haven't asked for what wasn't given me: but I ask now for that."

She held up her hand for the others to wait, and took me by the shoulder to the time table, where we could talk alone. "No tests were set you," she said. "But I will ask you this: why did you come here?"

There were a lot of answers to that, though only one that mattered now. "There was a story," I said, "about four dead men. A wise man I knew told me that you here might know the ending to it. I suppose he was wrong. It doesn't matter now."

"The four dead men are dead," she said, chin in her hand. "The League destroyed them, the four clear spheres with nothing at all inside them; they destroyed all but one, which is lost for good, as good as destroyed . . ."

"There were five."

She smiled. "Yes. So there were, five." In her hooded eyes were answers to that mystery; the last test was not to ask for them.

"I don't care now. I only want to stay, here, with her. I can't, unless I know what you know, unless I understand. . . ."

"What if it doesn't help? I think you truthful speakers put too much faith in knowing and understanding and such things."

"No. Please. It's not even understanding I want. She . . . I want, I want to be, *her*. I want to be her. I don't want to be me any more. It doesn't help. Nothing I know helps a bit. I don't know if being her is better than being me, but I don't care any more. I give up. Help me. I have no more reservations."

Zhinsinura listened. She chewed a finger and thought. We were alone now in the place, except for the cat Fa'afa, who wasn't interested. I looked down at May's tile between us: the children (who had not grown older in a year) stood in a wooden house with a wide door, a house filled with cut yellow grass in piles—the sun shone from it and lit their cheeks and placid downcast eyes. Hands on their knees, they looked down at a cat, a tiny tabby lying on her side, at whose nipples sucked three, four, five kittens. More than any cat mother and her children I had ever seen, it looked like the family of foxes I had found for Once a Day. Would I forget them too?

Zhinsinura leaned toward me and stroked my cheek; I felt her rings catch at my beard. "I love Boots," she said quietly. "I'm as old as anyone I ever heard of, and I would not have had it any other way. I love Boots; so I will grant your request; and I hope you will be done by as I have been.

But remember: there is no hoping for it to do anything. It will do as it does, and is not accountable: not Boots, not me or your young girl, not even, as you will see, you.

"But that's too many words already. They won't help." She rose, and led me to the counter where the slate slab covered with wax lay. "Be alone tonight," she said. "Come early tomorrow and find me. I'll take you. You'll have your letter from Dr. Boots." She gave me the pointed stick. "Now sign the List."

All their marks were there; Once a Day's was there. I had no mark, so carefully and clumsily I scratched on the List the palm sign of my cord.

I was alone that night, though I didn't sleep. I lay thinking that however much it had been Once a Day that had brought me to this, it must anyway have lain on the path I had walked from the beginning. I had seen the four dead men, and Once a Day had whispered Olive's inaudible secrets in my ear; I had gone out to be a saint to solve those mysteries, and learned that winter is half of life, though I could come no closer to Once a Day's heart than that—could come no closer ever, unless I took this last step. I thought of Zher, as I had seen him the first day I had come to Service City, and thought that now Once a Day sat among the old ones as he had, as though a lamp were lit within her. Tomorrow I would be as she was. And my only regret, now, is that I didn't pack my old pack that night and leave Service City forever.

I came early to Zhinsinura, shivering and yawning with morning chill and expectation, and followed her through the forest to the river's edge. There was a log raft there lashed with plastic closeline; a man and a woman my parents' age sat within it waiting. He and I, when Zhinsinura was seated, untied the boat and poled it with poles worn and smooth out onto the May-quick river.

Silent but for the spank of the river on the raft's sides and the chuckle of the forest, we followed the current. Zhinsinura smoked tobacco, and continually changed the pipe from place to place between her teeth. "About the letter," she said once, "we have only an old joke. The angels said every letter has three parts: the Salutation, the Body, and the Complimentary Close." I listened to the roll of the ancient words and said nothing. The gullied banks were tumbled with ruined places, mostly become forest now, revealed only by an angel-made angle or straight line in the moss. We glided past them, passing through drooping willows as through thin draperies, and after a time came up against a wharf in the river, swung the raft around and tied it up.

A path from the wharf led up to a—what was their word—*glade:* a
kept place of young willows and soft grass, which the sun reached into.
Some of the List were there and watched us approach, but gave no sign;
some were naked. In the center of the glade stood a small house of
angelstone, which over time had sunk and was now partly buried in the
soft earth; a narrow path led down to its low door. Zhinsinura took aside
the two we had come with; they nodded together, looked at me smiling,
and sat to wait. As she had before way-wall, Zhinsinura took my shoulder in a firm grip and led me down into the darkness within the little
house.

There was but one small window. For a moment the dimness was
spangled with the sunlight still in my eyes. I saw that the small square
place was empty; then I saw that it was not. There stood there a box, or
pedestal, as clear as glass or clearer; inside it, silver and black balls or
knobs were suspended in rows as though in water. And on top of the box
was a clear sphere, the size of a man's head, with nothing at all inside it.

"The fifth," I whispered.

"Boots," she said. She was drawing on her hand a silver glove, a silver
glove that glowed like ice. "Sit," she said. I sat; I didn't think my knees
would hold me anyway; Zhinsinura with her gloved hand pretended to
turn one of the knobs within the box. The knob turned. The clear sphere,
with a small noise like a shocked, indrawn breath, changed instantly to
black: black so black it appeared no longer a sphere, a black circle cut
out of the world.

"Now close your eyes," Zhinsinura said; "It's best to close your eyes."
I did; but not before I saw that with her silver glove she was pretending
to turn another of the knobs within the box; and that the black circle was
rising from the pedestal, moving like a Light; and that it came toward me.

And then there came the time that I must tell you of, but can't; the
time when Boots was there, and I was not. When I was not in Rush that
Speaks, and Boots was; when Boots lived; when she was Rush and I was
not; when I was not at all. I remember nothing of it—I wasn't there—and
though Rush was stained with Boots's being, stained and colored with it
forever, he remembers nothing, forgot all even as I returned to him:
because though Boots has many lives she has no memory. I know only
the last thing Boots did: and that was to close her eyes. And then she left
him. It was in that moment, when Boots left, that I got my letter: my
letter was myself.

"Open your eyes," said Zhinsinura.

That—"open your eyes"—entered in at the doors of Rush. I was not, and that entered nothing; but still as quick as ever it found and ran along the old path which such things had taken countless times before. Only this time, as though it were a Light, it was able to see the path, infinitely long, which it took. The path was Rush: the walls and snake's-hands were his stuff, the countless steps and twists and false ways and rooms were him, chest full of Rush, it was all Rush: all along, Rush was handholds, ways, stairs, a path for that to get deep in. And I—I was nothing; but when Zhinsinura said that, "open your eyes," I uncurled outward from some tiny center of not-being and built Rush to receive it: the path those words took and the place the path led through spun out both together. The words watched me watch myself make a place that held a path which the words took through the place to where I built it. A place like spheres, like the trees of bread, but all within each other, spheres of bright complexity made only of making, each sphere fitting within a larger just in time to let "open your eyes" escape into the smaller, until the words and I had made up Rush to hold us both; and we all three, in a silent swift coupling, laced all our ways together. And I opened my eyes.

The black sphere was retreating from my face, returning to the pedestal to perch. Zhinsinura with the silver glove pretended to turn knobs. The sphere settled; Zhinsinura turned a knob. The sphere was clear again. Boots slept.

Zhinsinura said, "Can you go? We'll go now."

The whole great place I had built to hold Open Your Eyes vanished like a cloud, and just a little more quickly than I had built it, I built a new Rush with a new path to receive these new words. And I knew then (unmoving, unable to, hands gripped around my updrawn knees, mouth wide as my eyes were wide) that I had built oh how many million before, and lost each, changed from each, they were less real than clouds, I was less changeless than a banner in the wind, and I knew that I would build a million others, each as different as this one was from . . . what? How had I been, a moment before? What was the huge thing I had only just learned? Gone . . . I tried to grasp at something to Be, some house to Be in, and could not; and Dread came chasing out through all the spangled spheres of Rush, and I felt myself building a house for it to live in, and as soon forgetting I had ever lived in any other thing than Dread. I struggled to rebuild, remember, but struggle only enriched Dread's house, and I was only Rush here now afraid.

But sunlight happened then, for Zhinsinura led me out.

And the house of Dread was less than memory because Sun took up all my room.

I almost wept and almost laughed to think how I must build a house not just for every word but for every thing at all that has a name. A Willow happened, and Walking on the Grass; a Person I Knew happened. Each time I turned my head a thousand things ordered their paths and chattered with each other about whose would be next, and each time I turned a thousand Rushes were made and fell away tinkling, sighing, whispering, crashing.

I stopped, stock still. Zhinsinura's tug on my hand made me recoil. I must be careful. Surely, in this rush, something, something is bound to lose its way. I must be careful not to draw Path wrong for any name to lose itself on. Wait, wait, I pleaded; but they wouldn't wait, and how had I ever been able to build fast enough for Everything? I was tense as stone with effort, and Dread was all I knew how to accommodate: but at Dread's door I stopped: something was rising in me, something was rising to meet all that I could not meet.

What rose was, I will say, Boots. I will say that though Boots had left, she had also stayed. I will say that Boots rose, and that out of her house deep within me she spoke and said: *Forget.* Forget you were ever other than the perfect house you are forever building, and whether it is a house of dark or light it will build itself. As for any name that enters there, it couldn't lose itself; for if the house is whole, why then isn't Path drawn just as wholly on its feet?

I will say Boots said this, I will say that this was what her letter said; I will say even that at her words the stone tension went out of me, I fluttered like a banner in the wind, and wept and smiled at once. I will say so: but the secret, oh the secret is that Boots has nothing, nothing, nothing at all to say.

SIXTH FACET

Time, I think, is like walking backward away from something: say, from a kiss. First there is the kiss; then you step back, and the eyes fill up your vision, then the eyes are framed in the face as you step further away; the face then is part of a body, and then the body is framed in a doorway, then the doorway framed in the trees beside it. The path grows longer and the door smaller, the trees fill up your sight and the door is lost, then the path is lost in the woods and the woods lost in the hills. Yet somewhere in the center still is the kiss. That's what time is like.

I know that at my center now is the time I was not there and Dr. Boots was. That's the kiss. The letter came, not then, but in the first step I took away: when I returned, as though new-born, to the place I had always lived: Rush and this world. Yet Boots is there, at the center; sometimes, in a moment that makes my heart beat slow and hard, or a dream shatter, or a present moment fall to bits, I can remember—taste, more nearly—what it was to have been Boots. I think that if I had lived on at Service City, and every year repeated that kiss, I would have come to be as much Boots as myself, to share Rush with Boots—as all the List shared themselves with her. And even as it was I knew, as I sat on the pier waiting for the raft to return, that I would carry Boots forever.

I say waited: I did for a moment try waiting, but couldn't for long; I became instead a pier man, who waited for nothing. I had no meanwhile.

"Can someone pole?" Zhinsinura said to some others who sat there with me. "He can't."

Slipping through the brown current the raft came to the pier; it struck, wet wood on stone, and swung about. The two on board stood up with its motion and looked at me from beneath their wide hats; one flung a white rope to me, and I stared at it where it lay without taking it. I heard them laugh, and I laughed too, but then forgot why in the task of watching the long poles laid up with a great wood sound. I sighed a huge sigh, as though I had just done sobbing; a sigh for the vast richness of it all.

They put me on the boat, and Zhinsinura came on; and the turning of it upstream turned the world in my eyes dizzyingly.

I suppose it was they, the two in the boat, who brought Zhinsinura the news about Once a Day. I think I can remember them talking with her, and they all three turning to look at me. If I heard them say her name, I could not then build a house large enough to hold it; and watched instead the ripple of the water by the boat, the sun's countless bright eyes in the leaves overhead. I couldn't have known, wouldn't have guessed, that to be absent for a time, to be for a time inhabited by a creature simpler, less confused, more simply wise than I, could so alter me, could so alter the world that I am made of: but with growing joy I learned. I learned, as the raft moved and I slid through the day, as the day slid through me, to let the task be master: which is only not to choose to do anything but what has chosen me to be done. Without any suffering every cat knows how, every living thing but man, who must learn it. Letting the task be master is a hard task for men, hardest of all for the angel's children, however distantly descended. But it could be learned: learned is the only way it could be learned, for I am a man. Far away and long ago the angels struggled in great anguish with the world, struggled unceasingly; but I would learn, yes, in the long engine summer of the world I would learn to live with it, I would. It was after all so simple, so harrowingly simple. I felt my sweet taskmasters multiply, and from my eyes the salt tears fell, even as they do now from yours.

Zhinsinura crossed the raft and sat by me. Unable to speak to express my gratitude to her, I only laid my head in her lap. She stroked my hair.

"Once a Day," she said, "has gone this morning with some who are gone trading, to the west. She wasn't chosen to go; she chose herself. She said to Houd: I won't return until Rush is gone, and gone for good."

Doubly and for good. There are houses outside houses over time, far, far harder to live in than the million small ones within them; just then I was enjoying a little one about the intersecting ripples of the water skiers in the river shallows.

"If I had known this," Zhinsinura said, and then no more; for what is there to say? Then: "Rush," she said, "you must stay as long as you have to; but we want her to come home, sometime."

How wise of her to say it to him then! For I was light, and she knew it; and though I felt for sure a distant dark house begin to assemble itself around all I did, I was light then, and watched the water skiers. I sighed, and perhaps it was for a vast and hopeless burden in this way lifted from Rush's back, and from Once a Day's back too. I thought, content, how sad it would be never to be able to go home again. I think I slept.

I'm very tired, now, angel. I have to rest.

Rest.

Take out your crystal, there's nothing, nothing more to tell.

Only the end. That won't be long.

The moon has risen. It's crescent now. It was full when I chose to come here. Is that how long I've been here?

No. Longer.

The clouds are thick. I suppose, below, they can't see the moon. . . . Oh, angel, take it out, stop, I can't any more.

THE FOURTH CRYSTAL

THE SKY IS GRASS

FIRST FACET

nd begin again with another, the fourth.
. . . A   Perhaps you shouldn't waste them. We didn't finish the last.

It's all right. Can you go on now?

Did you tell me why you need such things, these crystals I mean? If
you did I've forgotten.

*Only to see . . . to see how strong you are. I mean whether the story will
change, depending on who . . .*

Depending on who I am.

Depending on who tells it.

Has it changed?

*Yes. In small ways. I don't think . . . I don't think any other loved Once
a Day as much as you, I mean as much as in this story. And I never heard of
the fly caught in plastic before.*

Will you tell me about him, the one who I am? Is it a man?

It is.

Do you love him?

Yes.

I wonder why I thought so? Because you remind me of her? . . . No, well, I'm not to know, am I? Well. I'll go on.

I'd tell you about how I passed the time at Service City with Once a Day gone, except that I remember almost nothing of it, and that's not surprising. I remember only how it seemed at once empty and full. And I remember the cats: changing places around the floor, arguing and forgetting arguments, stepping down (by steps that were clearer to me than words) into rest, and from rest into sleep, and from sleep into deeper sleep. Watching them made me sleep too.

And then I left. I don't remember how I chose a day, or if I was dark or light; or how I chose a direction, except that it wasn't west. I do remember, in July, sitting on a rock far from Service City and making friends with a cow.

My beard was longer; I hadn't clipped it short in the warren's way. Beside me was my camp: a big square of something not cloth but like cloth, which Zhinsinura had given me out of the List's treasures. It was silver on one side and black on the other, and wrapped in it, though it was as fine as their finest cloaks, I was warm, and dry on wet ground. In my pack was bread, enough to last a year almost if I was careful, in a dry pouch the List makes; and Four Pots and some other doses; and a handful of fine blue papers made by hands I knew of Buckle cord; and matches, that fizzled out as often as not, not as good as my people make. And on my silver camp next to my pack Brom sat, watching the cow warily and ready to run.

Would you have thought Brom would have followed Once a Day? I would have. But he followed me. Or I followed him: it's easier that way with a cat, and I had no place to go; he was the adventurer. We ended here, in July, in grasslands, good for walking in, where there were mice and rabbits for Brom to chase, and cows seen far off. I wore a wide black hat. In all the time I had lived at Service City, I hadn't worn a man's hat, but the day I left Houd took this one off his head and put it on mine. It fit. It wasn't as though I had earned it, though I hadn't worn one because I felt I hadn't earned it. It fit, is all.

The cow had seemingly lost her kid. Her great teated breast was swollen, and she made lamenting sounds because of it. Because I had camped there quietly for a few days, or because of Dr. Boots, the cow came close to me. I didn't move, but sat and smoked, and Brom hissed and she moved away. She came back and went away again in a little dance. Well, I thought, there's no way I can suck for you, friend. She came close enough finally for me to touch, though she threw off my hand when I tried. She had amazing eyes: great, liquid, and brown, like a beautiful woman's in a way that was almost comical, and long silky lashes.

After a day of this (Dr. Boots's endless patience!) I learned, and the cow allowed me, to stroke and squeeze her teats so the milk ran out. Once I started, she stood calm as a stone and let me, must even have sighed (can they sigh?) for relief at it. The milk ran out in quick, thin streams. As she was running dry, I took off my indestructible hat and laid it on the ground below her, and the last of the milk made a little pool in the bottom of it, and with some misgivings I tasted it. Warm, thick, and white it tasted; I wondered if I would remember the taste from when I was a baby, but I didn't, or perhaps I did, since I liked it. On my way to the brook to wash my hat I thought that if she stayed around, it would make a nice change from bread and water, and I supposed it wouldn't hurt me; it tasted good, and that's the best sign.

She did stay, and Brom stopped hissing when she came close, though I can't say they ever became friends. When I moved (I mean when Brom moved, and I followed) she followed me. I named her Fido, which Blink had said was a name the angels gave their animals in ancient times. Traveling with the two of them was a little tedious, but have I said I was patient? If I lost them, I would stop and sit, and in an afternoon or a day they would both have returned to me.

You would think I would be dark, darkest then of any time. It's not so. I was happy. It was summer, and a fine hot dry one; the sea of grass was endless, and ran silver in little winds, as though fish darted through its pools. For companion I had another cat, Brom, and a cow for milk; for amusement I had Rush. In the hours when Fido ate grass and Brom hunted or slept, I would walk along his paths, which Boots had showed me. I liked him. There seemed to be endless insides to him, nooks and odd places where he attached to the world and to words, to other people, to the things he knew and liked and didn't like.

It was only later, in the winter, that I grew afraid of him.

When October or so (without the List's calendar, I was back to my old judgments) made the grass sea brown and rain fell in banners across it, I began to look for a place to spend the winter. It was the first thing I had chosen to do since I left Service City; I thought perhaps I had forgotten how. Anyway, the place really found me: all I did was to find Road, and walk it for some days, and then go off on a little spur that (I knew) would lead back to Road again; and found myself looking into his face.

He was a head only, about three times my height, and his thick neck sat on a small square of stone cracked and weedy; all around the woods grew rank and full of falling leaves. Perhaps he had once been painted, but now he was a dull white save for dark streaks of rust that ran from his eye-places like grimy tears. Since he grinned from great ear to great ear, it seemed he wept from some unbearable joy.

It was for sure a head; there were two bulging eyes, and a ball of a nose; the grinning mouth had once been an open space, the lower lip ran broad and flat like a counter, and the rusted metal plates that filled it were like a mouthful of bad teeth. Only, for a head, it was absurdly, perfectly globular. Standing before it, I had the impression I had seen it before, but even now I can't remember where.

There was a door of metal in the back, rusted as thin as paper, and I broke through it. Inside it was dark and close, with the smell of a place closed for who knew how long, and of small animals that had found a way in; they fled from Brom and me, who took possession. With the door open, I could see what sort of place we had: it had been, of all things, a kitchen. It looked like a miniature of the one in Twenty-eight Flavors. And for what, here, in the middle of nothing, where only Road ran? Maybe the angels had wanted to show they could build one of their kitchens anywhere. . . . A ceiling cut the place in half, at about nose level, and there was a door in it, and by piling up things I clambered up through it. Very dark, but I could make out the curve of the skull, which I stood inside, and the concave eye sockets. After a lot of tripping through ancient mess and new nests, I found a length of something metal, pipe perhaps, and with it I whacked out both great round pupils and let in light.

It took a day or two to pitch out all the ancient junk, and find the floor was sound and the skull leakless. I built a stair for Brom and me to climb up into the skull, and fixed the door in the neck, and made shutters for the eyes, to close at night. I have some skill in ancient ways, you know, and I knew enough to spend some days gathering in what dry grass and other eatables I could for Fido when winter came. (Of course I gathered in too little.) It surprised me that though for sure the time must be past when any child she had would be grown, still as long as I plucked her milk ran.

Downstairs in the tubs of angel silver I could make fires; there was even a hood of angel silver over them, and a hole to the outside, so it wasn't too smoky; the heat rose up, and up above I made a bed of boughs and leaves and pine needles, covered with my black and silver. And so I had my hat hung up there as winter began.

If you had been there, if you'd stood at the bottom of the woods and looked up through the leafless trees slick with rain (it seemed to rain every day now), you would have seen the head we lived in, bone-white in the drizzle, grinning idiotically with rusted teeth; and looking down at you (but not at you; at nothing; at no one) would have been Brom, in his left eye, and me, in his right, peeking out. I had a lot of time, as I sat, to think about what my head could possibly have been for. I was alone for all that winter there, and many explanations occurred to me. Once I scared myself dark by coming to the sudden conclusion that what I lived in wasn't something the angels had made but one of the angels themselves, buried up to his neck in stone in this desolate place, dead grinning weeping with a kitchen in his mouth and me in his brain—it was all I could do to keep from running out in terror.

Well, I got over it. I had to. I had no place else to go.

It was in this winter that I took up avvenging for a living. In a way, everyone who lives now is an avvenger; certainly the List with its treasure house of angel stuff, and the warren with its chests; Blink was an avvenger if you count knowledge. But there are some whose sole occupation it is: like Teeplee.

There was a day when I thought I would see if I could find some glass to replace the wooden shutters I had made for my eyes, or perhaps even some nice clear plastic. I had passed a great ruin coming to the head, and I took the day to go there and see if I couldn't find something I could use. It was a warm Decembery day, clear and brown and cheerful; I had just passed my birth-time; I had turned seventeen.

The ruin had been one of those places the angels made countless thousands of something in, a place huge enough to raise its head or heads above the woods that grew around it. One tall wall stood alone, like a cutout, all its windows empty; strange, but though the sunlight passed more easily now through all those windows, it seemed only more blind. Big trees had gotten fingers and toes inside the walls of other fallen buildings, though they had left the wide stone plaza (which all must have) mostly alone; spiky brown grass grew over the odd hillocks made of fallen walls. It was no more still there, I suppose, than any place; jays screamed at me, and chipmunks whistled; but it seemed stiller. You could see where paths had crossed between the buildings at proper angles; the broadest of these led up to the largest and least ruined of the buildings, and I went up to its wide dark mouth. I almost went in, but stopped to blink in the darkness—and saw that the place had no floor. I stood on the edge of a drop several times my height. Far down, something scurried; one of the animals that had found living room there. The tiny sound echoed hugely.

The dusty shafts of light from the empty windows didn't illuminate the dark tangle below, but I made out that there were ways to climb down. I had got some way down when I wondered if I could get back up, and stopped. I kicked something off the ledge I stood on, and listened to it clatter down in the depths; I sat and brushed away something that had fallen on my shoulder.

I turned. What had fallen on my shoulder was a glove, and inside the glove was a hand. I cried out, but couldn't stand, because the ledge was too narrow. The hand was attached to a whole long body topped with a pale face, whose curly-browed eyes looked down into mine bright with suspicion.

"Now," he said, and his grip tightened on my shoulder. The glove his hand was in was shiny black plastic, with a big stiff cuff from which plastic fringe dangled. On the cuff was printed or painted a dim white star. I didn't know whether to be afraid or astonished: head to foot he was cloaked in a thick, shiny stuff caught in a hood with string; it was broad-striped in red and white, except over his shoulder where there was a square of bright blue crossed by even rows of perfect white stars. From out of the red and white hood snaked his long neck, so long it bent in the middle as though broken; his hair was a fine stubble of metal color, cropped nearly off. In spite of myself, I smiled; and though his grip didn't lessen, he smiled too. His teeth were even, whole, and perfect; and as green as grass.

"Avvenger?" he said.

"I don't know," I said, though the word sounded familiar to me. "I was looking for some glass. I thought I might find some I could use here, some glass or clear plastic . . ."

"Avvenger," he said, nodding and grinning greenly. He released my shoulder and drew his hand out of its glove. The hand was pale and sparkled with rings; he held it out to me and said "Shake." I thought he meant to help me stand up, but when I took his hand he just—shook it, quickly up and down, and let go. Was this a warning or a greeting or what? He was still smiling, but the green teeth made it hard to tell the reason, for some reason. He slipped past me, gathering in his barred skirts, and began to climb down quickly on handholds I hadn't noticed, then turned and waved at me to follow him.

He wasn't easy to follow. He went like a spider or a squirrel down the wall and over the vast nameless piles of rust and collapse. Now and then a great window far above threw a block of December light over him, and his gorgeous robe shone for a moment and went out, like a barred lamp. And I remembered: "I'm not an avvenger," I said. Then, louder, to be heard over the multiple echoes of our clambering, I shouted, "I thought all the avvengers were dead."

At that he stopped and turned to me, standing half in, half out of a window's light. "Dead?" he said. "Did you say dead? You did? Do you see this National thing here?" He flung the robe wide in the light. "This National thing here has been dead since it was made, and is still as good as new; and I suppose that long after I'm myself as dead as it is, somebody's body will be wrapped in its old glory. So don't say dead. Just follow me."

Second facet

"Avvengers," Teeplee said, "are like buzzers."

The room he had at last led me to, down in the bowels of the ruin, was small and lit by a harsh lamp. On the way here I had glimpsed a human face in a dark doorway, and a human back just retreating into another; and under the table we sat at, a child rummaged silently through things, learning his trade, I suppose, for the room was so full of old stuff that it was like sitting inside a carved chest, except that none of these things seemed to have any order at all.

Teeplee had told me—besides his name—that the others there were his family, and all the children there were his. All! "My gang," he called them. As I said, I had remembered: avvengers were men who, in the days of the League's power, wouldn't submit to the League, and went around taking what they could of the angels' ruin, and using it and swapping it and living as much in the angels' way as they could; and their chiefest treasures were women who could bear in the old way, without intercession, over and over like cats. Naturally, men who thought women of any kind were treasures were the League's enemies, and they were mostly hunted down; so sitting with Teeplee in his den of angel-stuff I felt as though it were hundreds of years ago.

"Buzzers?" I said.

"You know, buzzers. Big, wide-winged, bald-headed birds that live on dead things." He drew himself up grandly in his cloak. "Buzzers are National," he said. "They're the National bird."

"I don't know what National is," I said, "except that it was something about the angels . . ."

"Well, there it is," Teeplee said, pointing a long finger at me. "Haven't you ever seen angels? All bald-headed, or as near as they could get; just like buzzers."

For a moment I thought he meant he really had seen angels, but of course he meant pictures; and yes, I had seen one, the gray picture of Uncle Plunkett, bald as a buzzer.

He began going through piles of stuff in this room and the next, looking for the glass or plastic I wanted. "What an avvenger is," he said as he looked—and I began to see that there was a kind of squirrelly order to the place—"is someone, like me, who lives on what the angels made that doesn't spoil. 'Doesn't spoil' means it's not 'throw-away.' See, the angels once thought it would be good to have things you would just use once and then throw away. I forget why they thought so. But after a while they saw if they kept that up they'd soon have thrown away everything in the world, so they changed their minds and made things you would only have one of, that would last forever. By the time they were good at that, it was all over, but the things still don't spoil. . . . Hey, how about these?"

He showed me a box full of bottle bottoms, green and brown.

"I thought something bigger," I said.

He put them away, not disappointed. "Now I said, 'lives on,'" he said. "That means maybe you dress in it, like this National thing, or you swap it for things to eat, or give it to women for presents and like that, or maybe"—he leaned close to me grinning—"maybe you eat it. Find the angels' food, and eat it yourself."

He was looking so triumphant I had to laugh. "Isn't it a little stale?"

"I said, 'doesn't spoil,'" Teeplee said seriously. "I said, 'Avvengers are like buzzers'; I said, 'Buzzers live on dead things.' You see, boy—say here, look at this."

He had come up with some convex black plastic, warped and scratched. "I thought maybe something clearer," I said. He threw it down with a clatter and went on searching.

"You see," he said, "the idea of making things that don't spoil is to make them dead to start with, so they don't need to ever die. There's dead metal, that's angel silver, that won't rust or pit or tarnish; and dead cloths like this; and plastics like dead wood that won't dry-rot or get wormy or split. And strangest of all: the angels could make dead food. Food that never gets stale, never rots, never spoils. I eat it."

"I have food like that. I smoke it."

"No, no! Not that evil pink stuff! I mean food, food you *eat*. Look here." He stood on tiptoe and took down from a high shelf a closed pot of metal, with a dull plastic glow about it. "Metal," he said, "that won't rust, and a jacket of plastic over that. Now watch and listen." There was a ring attached to the top, and Teeplee worked his finger under it and pulled. I expected the ring to come off, but instead there was a hiss like an indrawn breath and the whole top came off in a graceful spiral. "Look," he said, and showed me what was inside: it looked like sawdust, or small chips of wood. "Potato," he said. "Not now, I mean, not just yet; but mix this with water, and you'd be surprised: a mashed-up potato is just what it is, and as good as new."

"As good as new? What does it taste like?"

"Well. Dead. But like food. Throw it in water and you've got something like a mashed-up potato that the angels made, boy, a potato that's a thousand years old." He looked reverently within the pot and shook the stuff; it made a dry, sandy sound. "Now even a rock," he said, "even a *mountain* changes in a thousand years. But the angels could make this potato that's dead to begin with, so it couldn't change. They could make a potato that's immortal."

He sat, suddenly lost in thought or wonder. "No glass today. Come back in two, three days, we'll see." He set the child to guide me out. "But remember," he said as I left, "it'll cost you."

I came back; I came back often. That was a long winter, and Teeplee was good to have for company. I talked about a dark house; I talked about forgetting over time. And it's strange: alone in my head, I would sometimes seem on the edge of losing myself altogether, but with old Teeplee I was comfortable—maybe because there's no one so different from everything I had grown up with than an avvenger.

What I mean about losing myself: when I was alone, still there seemed to be someone there to talk to. I would wake in my cold head (the fire long since out) and lie wrapped in my black and silver, and start a conversation with this other, and he would answer, and we would lie there long and bicker like two gossips trying to tell the same story two different ways.

What we talked about was Boots. At the heart of the story was her letter, but I had forgotten it, had forgotten that her letter was *Forget*. I would get up at last, and get milk from the cow and sit and smoke, and maybe then clamber back into my cold bed, and all the while chat endlessly with this other about something we couldn't remember to forget.

I really had wanted to be her, I explained; I meant that. I still do. I'm not to blame; no one is accountable, I said, not Boots, not her, not even me; I chose, don't you see, and what is there to say? But he said: then why are you here now and not there? You must not have tried hard enough. I know you're wrong, I replied; I can't remember why, but that's not it, it's just the opposite of that; anyway, I did try, I did. . . . Not hard enough, he said. And we would try to turn our backs on each other; that doesn't work.

What frightened me was that I had failed in the attempt to become her, and that in the attempt I had stopped being me. My earliest selves frightened me when they returned to me in the moments before sleep (have I told you I learned to summon them? Yes) and I felt that rather than learning anything, anything at all, I had instead suffered a grievous, an unhealable wound; that, try as I might, I could no longer really mean what I said, nor say what I really meant. And a hiss of fear would go all through me. I would stare out my eyes and wonder if it wasn't warm enough to go see what Teeplee was about today.

So we would spend the day together, wrapped to our chins in indestructible angel-stuff—he in his barred robe, I in my black cloak and my hat—and clamber over the old messes, and talk about ancient things until our hands and feet got numb; and in the crackling freeze, trudge back to his hole in the ruin to unload our treasures and talk about who should take what. Since I went mostly for the walk and the company, he always got the best things, though I would put up a show of bargaining so as not to hurt his feelings. He would deal hard for dead, useless contraptions, and only abandon them after long thought and much insistence that they could be put to some use.

Sometimes we would be gone two or three days, if Teeplee had discovered a good big stretch of Housing as he called it; sometimes he would bring along one of his boys, but never a wife. ("This is men's work," he would say, with his chin out.)

He knew a lot of angel lore, Teeplee, though I never knew how much of it to believe. I asked him why all the Housing I had ever seen was the same: each little tumbledown place the same, each with its room for a kitchen and a stone place for washing. Didn't any of the angels think of a different way of putting things together? He said that if what I had seen had surprised me, I should have traveled as far as he had, and seen it everywhere, Housing stretching as far as the eye could see was how he put it, and yes, everywhere fitted out exactly as the angels always did, so they could travel thousands of miles, from Coast to Coast, and have another box just like the one they had come from. He said some even trundled one around with them wherever they went, like a snail shell, just in case they ended up somewhere where everything was not just as they required. Think of them, he said, rushing over vast distances you won't travel even if you have many lives, and everywhere finding Housing exactly the same, and wanting it that way too.

Now, how could he know that? Maybe there was some other explanation altogether. Maybe it was a Law.

One rimy day, in a huge place of great fallen blocks sunken by their own weight into the earth—it looked as though the earth had taken a big, a too big, mouthful of the angels' works—I found a good thing: a big box of glittering screws, as good as new. "As good as new," Teeplee said trembling with cold and envy. All the way back, he kept asking if I hadn't lost them, if maybe it wouldn't be safer if he carried them, and so on; and when we were once again in the stuffy warmth of his hideout, and I put them on the table between us. Teeplee ungloved one hand and dipped it into the rustling bits; he felt their clean-cut spiral edges, stuck a thumbnail in their slots. "A screw," he said; "now a screw isn't like a nail, isn't like tying something on with string, boy. A screw, a screw has"—he balled his fist—"a screw has *authority.*" Then, as though the answer were of no real importance to him: "What do you want for them?"

"Well," I said, "I could use a pair of gloves."

He quickly gloved his bare hand. "Sure," he said. "Of course you'd want warm, good ones, not like these things." He raised his black plastic fingers and wiggled them. Why was there a star painted on each cuff?

"They look good to me," I said. "Indestructible."

"You say 'gloves,' " he said. "I've seen gloves compared to which these are bare hands." He looked at me sidewise. "Not a pair." He raised his hand to forestall some criticism I might have, and went to search in his other room.

He returned with something wrapped in a grimy rag. "There are gloves," he said, "and there are gloves." He unwrapped the rag, and laid on the table before me a silver glove that glowed like ice.

Will you believe, angel, that until I saw it there—like a hand more than a glove, like the bright shadow of a hand—I had forgotten that it was with such a glove that Zhinsinura had manipulated Boots, had forgotten entirely that it was a glove like the glove stolen from St. Andy which had replaced me with Boots? It's so: not until I saw Teeplee's glove on his cracked table, did I remember that other—no, more: when I saw it, that moment was delivered to me again, whole, in all its wonder and terror: I saw the small room, the clear sphere and its pedestal; I saw Zhinsinura slipping on her glove, and heard her say *Close your eyes*. Too many wonders almost immediately succeeded that one: I had forgotten entirely.

"I've seen a glove like that," I said, when the moment had—not faded, no—but passed.

"Seeing is one thing," Teeplee said. "Having is another."

"And I know a story of one like it, a story about this one, maybe." There was a place—a single small place, a point even—where everything in my life intersected every other. I felt my mind cross like my eyes can cross.

"About these screws," Teeplee said.

"Yes, yes," I said. "Take them," He did, slowly, surprised at my indifference, wondering if maybe he'd made a bad bargain for them. "Where did you find it?" I asked.

"Well, well, there it is."

"Was there, with it, anywhere near it, a ball—a silver ball, well, maybe not silver, but this color?"

"No."

"Are you sure? Maybe there was. Will you go there again? I could go with you."

He narrowed his eyes at me. "What about this ball?"

"I don't know what about it," I said, laughing at his confusion, and at my own. "I don't know. I wish I did. I only know I'd give everything I have to get it, not that that's very much."

He scratched his bald buzzer's head and looked down glumly at the glove. "It isn't even a pair," he said.

———

So I had this thing then to think about. For a long time I wouldn't put it on; it lay, stainless and impossible, amid my things, and no matter how I folded it, it took the shape of a living hand, though it was fine and nearly weightless to hold. When at last I did draw it on—it slid voraciously over my fingers and up my wrist, as though hungry for a human hand after long years—I took it off again almost immediately. I think I was afraid of what my hand within it might do. From then on I only looked at it and thought about it—thought in circles.

There were other things, too, to occupy the nights. The other would argue that it only made me want her more, and I would concede that; anyway, my reconstructions of our pale twilight dreams were feeble, we had marked too few. Sometimes I would lie with my skirts up working furiously with the useless thing and find myself at the same time shedding cold tears just as useless.

You really shouldn't laugh.

THIRD FACET

There came a day when I understood winter was forever; though there would be days when it didn't freeze and days when the sun shone, they would always be followed by cold and rain again.

That day had begun fair, but afternoon dragged the clouds back over and they began again their ceaseless weeping. Toward evening the drizzle subsided to a sniffle, but the clouds hung low and baggy with further business to do. I sat smoking, letting pile up on the inside of the concave eyeball a little pile of rose-colored ash which the wet wind played with. No, no spring this year; the wood was slimy with despair and chilled to the marrow. Not quite dead, not frozen; there had been little snow all winter. But hopeless.

Be thankful, he told me, that she wasn't there to go back to. She knew you wouldn't come back from Boots being as she was, only a poor cripple, not the one and not the other; not yourself whom she first loved, yet nothing other either.

I don't understand, I told him. I have understood nothing, and now I have nothing left. I overthrew my deepest wisdom for her sake, made myself a clear pool for her reflection. And now there's only empty sky.

Well, don't you see? he said. You tried to become transparent, and all the while she was working to be opaque.

Like way-wall, I said.

She must become opaque: you must become transparent. There's no force on earth left stronger than love, but . . .

Opaque, I said. Yes.

Transparent, he said.

Never a moment when I revealed to her I had seen something in her but she changed it at that moment to hide further from me.

She wanted not to know it herself, he said. There's no blame in that.

It was as though I went after her into a cave, marking my way with a long string; and just when I came to the end of the string, and so couldn't follow any further, Dr. Boots snatched the string from my hand.

It was only one way, anyway, he said. So there's no way out.

We agree, he said, on that.

Well then, I said, I think it's time to lighten that load.

I went to the pack that held everything I had and took from it the case that held the Four Pots. I took it back to the window, unsealed it and opened it. The first pot was blue and contained stuff colored orange —the two colors of the house called Twenty-eight Flavors; it was medicine's daughters for every sickness. The second pot was black and contained the rose-colored stuff that had dreamed me out of a knot with Seven Hands. The third was silver, and contained the black granules that lighten a load. The fourth was bone-white, and contained the white angel's choice I had seen Speak a Word refuse (no, she said, not this year). I picked up the cigar I had left burning on the edge of the window; I held it deep within two fingers, closing my eyes against the rising smoke, and thought·about them. I thought of Houd standing before that mirror which showed a tall-hatted man giving giant pots to a boy. "It confuses the dark and light," he'd said, "and for a while you think only about the confusion, and not about everything."

"Everything?" I asked.

"That's Relativity," he said.

Well, Relativity, then, whatever that is; we'll try a confusion. I opened the silver and the black pots; from the one I took a granule of black, like a cinder, and swallowed it. I wet my thumb and pressed it across the rose surface of the other, and then wiped the thumb inside my lip. And then went on smoking, building a pile of ash in the window, which the wind, grown harder, blew off into the wet.

———

There was just enough room inside my head for the game, though people standing in back to watch filled up the window-eyes and made it dark. The players sat cheek to cheek in a circle with knees drawn up. They played with only one ball, and though there was a lot of chatter, there was no argument about how to begin: the ball began on my mother's knee.

"Whose knee?" they said, and the gossip Laugh Aloud moved the ball to Mbaba's knee. "As for the silver ball and glove," Mbaba said, "they're gone; but for the rest, see here": and she opened her mouth to show a perfect set of teeth, as green as grass.

"Whose knee?" they said, and the ball moved to Painted Red's knee, and from hers to Seven Hands's, who said, "One day, big man, one day," and back to Painted Red, who was saying, "A knot in the cord—that makes me laugh." The ball in her long, sure tweezers paused in air. "Whose knee?" they said, and the ball went to Once a Day's knee. She raised her impossible blue eyes and said, "Ever after."

"Ask women," said Seven Hands, and moved the ball to In a Corner, who said, smoking softly, "Lighter than air, lighter than air."

"An old joke of Roy's," said Once a Day, and moved me to Painted Red. "Many lives," she said, "many lives in the moment between birth and dying."

"This is spring," said Once a Day, and with an unsure hand she moved tweezers toward the ball on Painted Red's knee. Zhinsinura shook her head slowly as the tweezers came close.

"How many lives does a cat have?" she asked.

"Nine," said Painted Red.

"Miss," said Houd, who wore a bracelet of blue stones; and with his yellow-nailed hand he put the dropped ball on his own knee.

"Whose knee?" they all said, and tweezers came for the ball. "Great Knot and First Trap make Little Trap, Little Trap and the Expedition make Little Second Gate, or Great Trap Unlocked in Leaf cord," said Painted Red, and the ball began to fly again from knee to knee.

"The fly sees out all around," said Budding, and moved me to Blooming's knee.

"And sees nothing that holds him back," said Budding; "and still he can't move."

"And let that be a lesson," said Blooming, and moved me to Blink's knee. "We're all legless men," Blink said, yawning. "It doesn't get better, a lost leg, like a cold."

"Are you a saint yet?" said Budding, and Blooming moved me back to Once a Day's sharp knee, and Blink said, "Bits and pieces," and moved me to the knee of another girl, a girl in a starred black robe with a great cat beside her, watching. "How can you think about me," she said, "when I'm not there?"

"Miss! Two misses," said the cat. The ball was retrieved and went to Zher's knee. Once a Day said softly: "Beautiful."

"After all," said Painted Red as they paused, "it's only a game."

"Whose knee?"

The ball started fast around. "The object," said Houd, "is to never discover you're playing it."

"To someday," said Painted Red, "become transparent; and in transparent life to be free from death."

"To learn to live with it," said Blink. "We learn to live with it; we try. We have our systems and our wisdom . . ."

"How is truthful speaking done?" asked Zhinsinura. "Let's both tell a secret."

"I don't remember riddles," said Once a Day.

"The Salutation, the Body, and the Complimentary Close. You can find a path through that."

"A path," said Painted Red.

"Is only a name," said Zhinsinura.

"Is drawn on your feet," said Mbaba.

"For the place where you are," said Zhinsinura.

"When-we-wandered," said Mbaba.

"Where you've been on it," said Zhinsinura, "is only a story."

"And then, and then, and then," said Blink.

"Some of the stories are pleasant ones . . ."

"That's Relativity," said Houd.

". . . and some are not. That's dark and light."

"*He* was dark," said Stick, and picked up the ball with tweezers of wet black wood. The ball slipped and bobbled within the twiggy tweezers. He could get no grip. And they had been doing so well.

"How many lives does a cat have?" asked Puff. "Quick."

"Many lives," said Painted Red, "many lives in the moment between birth and dying." Stick just managed to wiggle the ball to her knee, and everyone said *aaaah*.

"Whose knee?" they all said. "Dr. Boots's knee," said Once a Day softly; "this is spring."

"And truthful speaking is . . ."

"Transparent," said Painted Red.

"And dark and light is . . ."

"Opaque," said Zhinsinura.

The ball they played with was a hazelnut. Zhinsinura's tweezers that reached for it were like a nutcracker. "Opaque, transparent," said the ball. "Like way-wall."

"Miss," said Once a Day, a little sadly, but as though she'd expected it.

Zhinsinura, smiling, picked up the ball in her fingers. "Way-wall?" she said. "There's no such thing." She inserted the nut in her cracker.

"Three misses," Teeplee said. "Game's over." Zhinsinura calmly cracked the nut.

I looked up at that sound. Above me, a thin crack ran the width of the skull, making fingers.

The cigar in my hand had gone out. Brom lay asleep, but not in the bed where he usually lay. Through the door in the floor I could see the fire burning low and shadowy. Outside the sound of the evening was heavy, and I realized what it was—rain. The crack in the skull widened with a little noise, and I jumped up with a cry, which woke the doctor but not Brom.

What doctor?

"That's not right, though," I said. "It wasn't really three misses."

"Yes," the doctor said. She wasn't old, though her hair was white and the hands which held my black and silver cloth around her were lined. She moved, and the bed crackled beneath her. She looked at me with wide still eyes.

"Because," I said, "I *do* know how truthful speaking's done."

"Yes," the doctor said.

"It's done the same as dark and light."

"Yes," the doctor said.

"Yes," I said, "because when you speak truthfully, what you're doing is telling whoever can hear you about the dark and light, just then. The better you tell an old story, the more you are talking about right now."

"Yes," the doctor said.

'So I have always been dark and light. I never had to learn it, because I didn't know it."

"Yes," she said.

"And never stopped saying what I really meant or really meaning what I said, because how could I do otherwise?"

"Yes."

"Then there's no difference. They're the same."

"Yes."

"And is that what it means, then, that there's no such thing as way-wall?"

"Yes."

"So. All right. Two misses, then."

"Yes."

"The game goes on."

"Yes."

"So. All right. But," I said, sitting down, "if they're the same, then what's the difference?"

"Yes," the doctor said.

A loud crack overhead made me duck. I looked up. The split in my head was widening horribly. Rain seeped in, staining the white gray. Brom looked upward, and then at me. I went to my pack, tossed in the Four Pots, and found my specs. I put them on. "I think," I said, "that it's time to be going."

The doctor watched me as I came close to where she lay in the bed. "This will cover us, it's big enough," I said, and drew off the black and silver which covered her.

In the gloom I thought there was a cat with her in the bed; but of course she was the cat. She turned herself with careful grace and went on fours out of the bed and across the floor. Her tabby legs and thighs were like those of Fa'afa of the List; her hands helped her across the floor to look out the window. There she sat with knees up and her hands on the window ledge. Her tail swept around to cover her clawed feet. Above us the skull crunched and split; a fine white powder fell.

"Anyway," I said, my voice catching, "we have to go."

She looked from me to the rain, and then to the door in the floor. Soundlessly she padded to it and disappeared through it. Brom followed her. I shouldered my pack, and gathered up the black and silver, put on my hat. I glanced up: the skull was crazed.

They were waiting at the outside door, with the thoughtful reluctance of cats before rain. Brom would have to decide for himself; I moved hesitantly to the doctor and knelt before her. The wet wind from the door made her shiver, but when she saw I wore the silver glove—I don't know how I came to have it on—she grew calm and raised her arms slowly to slip them around my neck. With a soft cry that I don't remember, was it Yes or No, I put one arm beneath her and lifted her to carry. And we stepped out into the night and the rain.

The leaves oozed under my feet as I stumbled down the incline away from the head. Gusts of rainy wind blew across the way, and I nearly stumbled with my burden. Behind me, I thought I heard the head I had abandoned crumble to pieces; I tried to look back, but it was all darkness and woods, and the doctor's hands held me. I could feel her breath on me, gentle and warm, as though she were asleep and though my grip on her tightened at every stumble and lurch, she was easy; she even seemed to nestle against me under the robe which covered us.

When I came to broad naked Road I stopped. I looked both ways, but it was all wind and rain and stone and dim black-boned trees. "I think," I said, already panting, "I think I know a place where we might go."

"Yes," the doctor said, muffled by the black. She sighed; I sighed; and we started north:

That was a long walk. It had taken after all, some months to come this far south from home: the walk to Blink's woods, and south to Service City, and a summer after that, always going south; and this burden was heavy. "And what with the rain," I sobbed, my lungs aching, "what with spring not coming . . ." When at last drizzly dawn came, and I stood on a bare hill pied with snow and looked down into the wide valley of That River from whose hidden length white steam rose like winter breath, my arms and hands had been locked so long that I knew the hardest part would be letting go.

"Somewhere," I said to her, "down in those hills across That River is a wood; and in that wood, if you know it, is a path. The path gets clearer as you walk it, until it widens under the trees, and you see a door. The door will grow clearer as you come closer to it, until you are standing before it; and then you can step in, and look: a girl with blue eyes as opaque as sky is playing Rings, and looks up when you enter. But I can't go any further."

I sagged to my knees and let down my weight. Slowly, trembling, I uncurled my hands as my muscles snapped back on themselves with vengeance. I drew back the cloth and looked at what I had brought, and wondered if it had been worth it to carry this stuff so far.

There was a nice plastic jug and a funnel, which I had caught rain water in—scarce, they are. There was a spade blade, not too rusted, and a length of white close-line. There was some Book, mostly moldered, which I had thought to give to Blink if I ever saw him again. Angel silver bits and pieces—one of them Teeplee had called a dog collar; I thought that might be useful. And—heaviest of all—a machine, rusted where it wasn't plastic-coated, that looked something like a mechanical version of Blink's crostic-words: it had rows of little tabs with letters on them, and other inexplicable parts. Teeplee called it a spelling machine, with some contempt. I had kept it to see if I might learn to spell from it.

"It's all just too heavy to carry, though," I said. "Just too heavy."

"So your avvenging days are over?" Teeplee said. "I thought the speakers never threw away anything."

My heart slowed. The hilltop and the valley patched with fog seemed to thin, as though I could press upon it only a little harder with my senses and see through it. I did press: what I saw was the road leading into Teeplee's ruin, and the old avvenger himself in his stars and stripes. I had walked through the night and reached, not home, carrying the doctor, but this place, carrying a load of junk. Probably, behind me, my head was still whole. It didn't matter: I wasn't going back.

"No, not over," I said. My voice sounded thin and uncertain in this reality. "But they have a lot of stuff there already."

"Where are you going?" he asked.

"Home," I said, "now that spring's coming." And it was: the rain had foretold it and I hadn't known: but now where I knelt before that quiet pile it was quite clear: in the wet bushes around me each drop of water on each twig had within it an eye of green, and the wind that combed the dull grass showed tender new shoots starting. Of course Boots would never have told such a secret, would never whisper that spring was for sure until I had forgotten it was possible at all. That's dark and light, I thought; this is spring; it's nice now. I let go then of the doctor: and letting go felt like falling, falling gently backward into a waiting pair of hands I would never see but could not doubt were there.

"How about this, though?" Teeplee said, and from within his robe he took out something small, a piece of winter ice, no, something else. "I took a trip," he said.

It wasn't a ball at all; it looked like one of the knobs that hung suspended as though in water within Boots's pedestal. I raised the silver glove on my hand. "Give it to me," I said.

"It'll cost you," Teeplee said.

"Everything I have," I said. He made as though to hand me the thing, but released it; perhaps he dropped it, but it didn't drop: my glove began to sound, a strange whistle came from it yet not from it, and the ball came floating to it and landed in my palm as gently as a bird.

And joined, they made a double note, a note that some engine here, in the City, heard, isn't that right? Yes, some angel ear that had been waiting for how many centuries to hear it: and when it was heard, Mongolfier began to prepare.

"This stuff isn't much," Teeplee said, nudging my treasures with a toe. "Not for a good thing like that ball. That's a good thing, and in perfect condition."

"All right," I said; and I found and took from my sleeve a bright piece of ancient Money, the piece with which I had been *bot*. I held it for a moment, feeling under my thumb the upswept hair of the angel's face cut on it, but it no longer mattered to me. I had found what was lost and could take it to the warren and put it in its place again, and tell the long, the strange story of how I had come by it: and anyway, giving it to Teeplee in exchange for St. Andy's ball couldn't free me, for it's the same with Money as with anything, as with every other thing men do: it's all only one way.

FOURTH FACET

It was nearly summer when I stood for real on the hilltop that overlooks the valley Little Belaire lives in, for there really is such a place; it was more tricked out with details than in my confusion, and of course green, but I recognized it. It was just the time that I had left, three years before.

I had thought at first just to run down the hill as fast as I could and find the path to Buckle cord's door; but something stopped me there. I laid out my camp, as I had for every night along the way, and sat. Night came, and a moon near full; day again. I thought: when I go down the hill I will be as Olive was, arriving suddenly from far away, a great cat beside me with frank yellow eyes, and a terrible secret to tell.

I didn't tell you that at my first camp after I had left Teeplee's, Brom found me. He frightened me by sneaking up to the fire, and then I laughed aloud to see him. But after he'd smelled my breath, just to make sure I was I, and looked over the camp, he only lay on his feet with a sigh and went to sleep. A cat.

It was Brom who first saw my visitor. Another day had passed; I was still unable to make up my mind to go down the hill and across That

River, and lay on my back looking up at the gold-green new leaves thinking of nothing, when I heard Brom making that noise—ak-ak-ak-ak—that some cats make at birds or for no reason at the sky. I rolled over to see what made him snicker—a hawk, perhaps, hanging high up—and sat up with a cry.

Someone was letting himself down out of the clouded sky on a huge white umbrella.

It was a great half-globe of translucent white. Ropes ran from its edges, holding it taut over a ball of air; and in the ropes a man hung like a fly caught in a web, holding on, his feet moving idly as he descended. I leaped up and ran, following his long descent as it changed with the wind. As it came closer, it seemed to grow larger, an immense, undulating dome; I could see clearly the man in the ropes. He waved to me, and then gave all his attention to manipulating his thing by tugging on the ropes so that it would fall on the hillside meadow and not in the trees. I ran after him. He hurtled to the ground, moving fast and not gently at all, and it seemed certain he would strike the ground with tremendous force, despite his umbrella, which now looked like a very bad idea and not workable at all. I held my breath as his feet struck the meadow. He flung himself over just then, thinking, I suppose, to break his fall that way; and down after him came the dome, just cloth after all, collapsing and then billowing away outward in the breeze.

It tried, with great lassitude, to rise again on the breeze, but the man was on his feet, being walked away by it, struggling to untie himself from it, fighting with a fierce single-mindedness to stop it; got himself free, and began to haul his thing in with violent tugs as it rippled and rose across the ground like a compact fog. I came with a stone and threw it on top to pin it. It was easy then; he piled it up anyhow and turned to face me.

"Mongolfier," he said, and I didn't know what to say to that.

He was a pale, unsmiling man, with lank black hair that fell always over his eyes. Top to toe he was dressed in tight brown, a snug many-pocketed coat and pants, and strange glossy boots that reached to his knees, tightly thonged with yards of lacing. I smiled, and nodded, and made to come closer—at which he drew back, never looking away from me with eyes dark and wide, eyes such as I have seen only in wild things that have suffered some terrible hurt.

Just then Brom came warily out of the bushes behind me; and seeing him, the man cried out. He backed up, seemed about to fall over—there was a pack on his back as large as himself—and fumbled desperately for something in a holder at his side. He whipped it out: it was a hand-sized engine of some sort, with a grip and a black metal finger which he pointed at Brom. He stood stock still with the thing, staring. Only when Brom, sensing his fear, crept behind me and sat warily peeking out did he pocket his thing, and then without taking his eyes from Brom, he squatted, so that the bottom of his huge pack touched the ground. He pressed a black spot on his belt, and stood up. The pack remained standing in the meadow.

"Mongolfier," he said again. There were no straps at all attached to the pack, which was an irregular shape covered up in what looked like my own black and silver cloth, which clung closely around it as though wet, or as though wind pressed on it from all sides at once.

"How did you do that," I said, "with the pack?"

He held his hand up to silence me. With the other hand he reached into one of his many pockets and pulled out another small black machine. This one he fitted over one of his ears, fiddling with it to make it stay; it looked like a great black false ear. Which is just what it was. He made a "come here" motion with his hand, eyes cocked to the false ear, but when I stepped up to him he jumped away.

"You're jumpier than a cow I used to have," I said; at that he ducked his head and listened at his ear. He screwed up his eyes and bit his lip.

"More jumping," he said slowly, like a sleeptalker, and we stared at each other in confusion. He waved at me to come on again, and I was about to step toward him again when I understood what he was about. We didn't speak the same. He understood nothing of what I said, nor would I understand anything he said. But the false ear apparently could; it whispered to him what I said, and then he spoke back to me in my way, as well as he could. If that were so, it would be a long time before I could ask him what he had been doing up in the sky, so I sat down slowly, and started to talk.

He sat down too, after a while, and listened—to his ear, not to me, nodding sometimes, sometimes throwing up his hands in confusion; he clenched his fist in front of his mouth till the knuckles went white. He understood pretty quickly some hard things I said, but when I said, "Nice weather," he looked baffled. Late in the day, we were talking back and forth pretty well; he chose his words carefully and made sense as often as not. His eyes were never still, but darted always to the source of small noises, birds and bugs; a butterfly made him jump to his feet when it came near. Here he sat with me, not surprised at all by me, making me speak to him as though we had a long-standing agreement to meet here and do that, but every ordinary thing scared him. The only thing that distracted him from his fear was listening and speaking, which he struggled with fiercely.

Finally he waved me silent. He drew up his shod knees and closed his hands around them. "Yes," he said. "Now I must tell you why I am here."

"Good," I said. "You might tell me how, too."

He gritted his teeth with impatience, and I waved him calm. "I've come," he said, "to get back property of ours, which I think you have."

The strange thing was that "property" wasn't a word I had used to him. I don't think I've said it twice in my life. "What property?"

From another of his pockets he drew out a fine silver glove, dull in the sunlight. "A glove," he said, "like this one; and more important, another thing, a small thing, like a, like a . . ."

"Ball," I said. It was my turn to be afraid. "Could you," I said, and swallowed the fear, "could you answer a question for me?"

"Three," he said, holding up three fingers. "Three questions."

"Why three?"

"Traditional."

"All right. Three," I said. I counted them off in the List's way: "*Ay:* what is this ball and glove, and what does it have to do with the dead men, like Uncle Plunkett? and *bee:* how did you know I had it? and *see:* where did you come from?"

When he heard my questions, eyes toward his false ear, he began to nod; he looked at me, and for the first time since he had fallen, began to smile, a strange, dark smile that was more remote than his tightly closed face had been. "Very well," he said. "I answer them starting with the last —also traditional. I have come"—he pointed skyward—"from there. From a City there, some call it Laputa. I knew you had our property because of the sound it makes—not the sound you hear, but another, far subtler sound, which an engine in the City detected. And it has everything to do with the man Daniel Plunkett whom you call dead, and whom I have brought on my back from the City. That's that." And he pointed to the black shape which squatted amid the grasses of the meadow.

"You're an angel, then," I said, "to tell me such things." He stopped smiling to listen, and then made his gesture of not understanding. "I don't think," I said after a long time, "that three questions are enough."

He set himself, nodding, as though to begin a great task. He made a start three different ways, and each time stopped, strangled up; it was as though each word were a piece of him, drawn up out of his insides with pain. He told me there were not cities in the sky, only this one called Laputa, which the angels had built when the last days were at hand; it was a great half sphere a mile wide at its base, and all transparent—a fine lacework of triangular panes, he had a word for them which meant they were joined in such a way as to bear their own weight, and the panes not glass at all but something—nothing, rather—a thing or a condition that allowed light through but was not itself anything, but through which nothing could escape—

"Like way-wall," I said, and he looked at me, but didn't say there was no such thing. He tried to explain how the air inside was heated, and the air outside colder, and got confused, and I said I know: just because of that, the whole was lighter than air.

"Yes," he said. "Lighter than air." And so it rose into the sky, the whole mile of it, and, supported by its perfect simplicity, had floated ever since, while generations of angels had been born and lived and died there. He talked of engines and machines, and I wondered at first why they would choose to fill up their City with such stuff, until I saw he meant their machines were still perfect: still did what they were made to do. I looked at his false ear, and then at the pack in the meadow; he saw my look. "Yes," he said. "Even that still works."

He told me how after the Storm the angels had returned to find the four dead men, the greatest of their works, and how they found three of them destroyed by the League, and one lost; and they had followed that lost one, Plunkett, as the League had, but they found it first, and carried it away to the City in the Sky. Only, he said, there was a part missing: a ball, and the glove made to work it, which . . . which . . . And he stopped, and had to begin again another way, to explain Plunkett to me. It took a long time, because he must stop to think, and chew his knuckles, and slap his boots with impatience; and his tension affected me, and I interrupted with questions until he shouted at me to be quiet.

We began to understand each other when I told him I had seen a picture of Plunkett. He breathed deeply and told me: the sphere that was Plunkett was like that picture: but instead of being of his face, it was of his self. Instead of looking at his picture and seeing what his face looked like, you must take the sphere on your own head, and for as long as you wore that sphere, like a mask, for so long you would not be there and Plunkett would be: Plunkett would live again in you, you would look out Plunkett's eyes, no, Plunkett would look out yours. The sphere was solid with Plunkett, and only waited for someone to Be in; like, like the meaning of a word waiting for a word to be the meaning of . . .

"Like a letter," I said. He nodded slowly, not sure what I meant. "And the ball and glove?"

"To erase the sphere," he said. The sphere was a container only; now it contained Plunkett, but with the ball and glove he could empty it, Plunkett would be no more, the sphere would be as empty as a mirror no one looks into, and then could mirror someone else instead. The dead man would be dead.

"Doubly and for good," I said. "Is that what happened to the others?"

"I think so."

"Except the fifth."

"There were only four," he said.

"There were five," I said.

He stood and went to the pack. He had slipped on his silver glove, and with it drew away the black stuff that clung around his pack. There stood a clear box or pedestal, with rows of black and silver knobs suspended in it as though in water, and on top a clear sphere the size of a man's head with, it seemed, nothing at all inside it. "There were four," he said. "There was an experiment, with an animal. They did that because they didn't know if taking such a, such a picture of a man would kill him, or injure him; if it killed the animal, well, that didn't matter, but they would know not to do it with a man. But the experiment was a success. And they did it with four people." He sat again, and drew up his knees. "So the fifth you talk about: it was the experiment. It was a cat, a cat named Boots."

Evening had come. The valley below was dark, and trees' shadows reached across the sloping meadow, but we were still in light: he in his brown, clutching his knees, and I, and the thing which was Plunkett though Plunkett was dead.

"I have been that cat," I said.

His fear looked out his eyes; his pale face was drawn. "And I," he said, "have been Daniel Plunkett."

"And then returned."

"And then returned," he said.

"Angel," I said, "why have you come here?"

"I've answered your questions," he said. "Now you must answer one for me." He set himself, adjusted his ear, and asked: "How would you like to live forever, or nearly?"

FIFTH FACET

All night till moonrise I tried to answer him. I tried to tell him how I had seen the four dead men made of stone, and shivered in the warmth; how it had been to solve that mystery that I had followed Once a Day to Service City and been Boots: how the four dead men had always been the crossing place in my life where I turned further into darkness. And all night he tried to explain, and talked of processes and pictures and how painless and harmless it had been proved to be. We both talked, and despite his angel's ear, neither understood.

"You ask me," I said, "to be your dead man in Plunkett's stead. Even if I understood why you needed such a one, I couldn't choose to be one. Don't you see?"

"But I would take nothing from you," he said, trembling with effort. "No more—no more than a frosted glass takes anything from you when you print it with your thumb!"

"I don't know," I said. "Boots was there, when I was not. Alive as ever. She didn't mind, I don't think; but I think a man would. I think of a fly, stuck in a cube of plastic, able to see all around, but not able to move. It frightens me."

"Fly?" he said to his ear. "Fly?" He couldn't make it make sense. I rolled smoke for myself, and saw that my hands trembled. "Fly," he said desperately. I struck a match but the head flew off, sizzling, and struck Brom, who jumped up with a howl, and what with it all, the fly and the flame and Brom and me so stupid, he plucked the false ear from his head, flung it on the ground, and burst into tears.

What is it?

It's just . . . well, you make him sound comical. He wasn't. He was brave and fine and the best man of his time. When he came down, you know, he didn't know what he would find; he knew only the City—and the world Plunkett had lived in. For all Mongolfier knew, the land below him would swallow him like a mouth. Except for pictures, he'd never seen an animal. And yet he jumped from his home to change our lives. He wasn't comical.

I only meant to show my wonderment. I have no words for his sufferings: before them I felt thin and old, as you do before an angry child. I couldn't follow what he said, and it made him weep, is all I meant. . . .

If he could have spoken your way, he could have made it clear.

He would have told you that when the angels raised the City, it wasn't out of despair, or to flee the ruin they had created: they were proud of it, it was the last hope and greatest engine of man, and in it would be preserved the knowledge that led to its creation, preserved from the mass of men who wished insanely to destroy Everything they Wanted. Plunkett was the most complex and precious of all their works, and when they first used it, it was as they had used all the other things they had saved: to remember, in its use, the learning and skill that had made it.

But in its use they learned something unexpected, something terrible and wonderful: they learned what it is to be a man. As you learned from Boots what it is to be alive, they learned from Plunkett what it is to be a man: and it wasn't what they had thought, at all.

You see, you think all men who lived in Plunkett's time were angels, and could fly, and were consumed with fierce passions to alter the world and make it man's, without remorse, without patience, without fear. It's not so. The mass of men then were no more angels than you are. Unable to understand the angels' world, ignorant of how to do any wonders at all, they only suffered from the angels' hunger, suffered blindly in the wreckage of the angels' world. Plunkett was such a one. Zhinsinura said that even the League's women were angels: the angels learned from Plunkett that even they were men.

And the first of them to look out Plunkett's eyes and learn it, when he returned, never spoke again.

You make me afraid for this one who I am. How hard, how hard . . . Harder than Boots, it must be, far harder . . .

Yes: because though Boots has no memory, you have. And Plunkett had: they came away from him remembering everything, his shame, his hurt, his confusion, Everything he Wanted. Boots's letter was Forget: Plunkett's letter was Remember.

They said it made for madness, then, that it had been a mistake, that it shouldn't be used again. But it was used again. The bravest learned to bear Plunkett, and to speak of it. And while in the warren they told stories of the saints, and grew old in speaking; and as the List remembered the League, and grew old in Boots; so we grew old in Plunkett. All we knew was learning to live with his suffering: our suffering. We forgot our plans; the years came to the hundreds; our pride vanished, we studied Plunkett only, our hope became dread, our escape exile.

But why didn't you stop? Come back again? The City could return, couldn't it, if they'd seen they were mistaken?

No. The world they left was Plunkett's world: it was all they knew of earth. Plunkett taught them that the rule of men had not been sufficient; and if that were so, then the world beneath them must have died, and the men with it. It was the only possibility.

But it's not so. It got different, is all. You could come back; there's no hard feelings. You must come back. It's home.

Home. . . . Do you know how large the world is? I do. The winds blow always westerly around it, and the City is moved with them, and in a lifetime goes around to the place where it began. I was born over sea: when I was grown, still the sea was beneath us. When we pass through storms, they aren't the storms that fall on earth; we know them at their birthplaces; we pass through them and are not shaken. Do you know, when it snows here, the snow flies upward; lightning comes close enough to touch, and comes not from the sky but upward from the earth. It has never made me afraid.

Far off, when the clouds part, we see earth; vague and lovely and possible, I suppose the way you look at distant mountains, and wonder, but never visit. No: this is my home. It was Mongolfier's. For its sake, dark with Plunkett's fear and suffering, he jumped down to earth, to find you, who would heal us; you, who had found the ball and glove that could free us from Plunkett; you who would dry our old tears.

If he could have spoken your way, he would have said this to you. . . .
How is it you can speak my way, and he couldn't?
You've taught us. We are truthful speakers too now, Rush.
And you? Are you, angel? Do you know what it is to be . . . another, to return from not being, to tumble back through all your ways, as though you fell from a height, and see, and see. . . . Do you?
No. I only know what they've said: that the cruelest was to have been Plunkett; that heavy as you are, to put you down is joyful in the end, that after the days of silence, it's easy; that I could learn to live with you, as none ever could with Plunkett. Plunkett made us brave, they say, and you have made us happy. But I haven't, yet; I'm afraid to bear your weight.
And Mongolfier could? Did I make him easier?
No. He never dared, after Plunkett. He brought you here. They told him: he saw it work: but never dared.
You make me ashamed. Ashamed, with all that, of why in the end I did agree to let him take me, or whatever it was he wanted to take, with him.
Why?
It was just, well: ever since I was a kid I've somewhere in me believed in a City in the Sky. Not as Blink did, as a perhaps, or as the List did, as a story, or as Little St. Roy did, as a pretty thought, but that it was real. As real as clouds. And an angel had dropped from there, and said he'd take me. And however much he said that I, mortal I, would feel no change, that I would be left sitting in the meadow just as I was while he went off with—with something like a slide of the Filing System, if he could have thought to say that: still, I thought maybe I would get to see it, what it was like; that dome, those clouds. That's all.
But I slept, first. I was exhausted by our struggle. I wrapped up in my black and silver and watched the moon for a while; Brom lay next to me roaring. Mongolfier wouldn't sleep; he sat straight up, with his back against a tree, and watched.
I dreamed that night of the warren, of running on Path toward the inside, through great and little rooms where chests were kept and gossips studied cords, circling in a spiral nearer to the center past people smoking and kids playing, into narrow passages of angelstone in the dim small deep insides. I awoke without reaching the center, and thinking that after all I had never known where exactly the center of Belaire was, to see Mongolfier still sitting, paler with his vigil and with his, his Gun, as he called it, in his lap, waiting.

"All right," I said. "All right." I rubbed my eyes and sat up. He got up, stiff with tension, and held out his hand for the silver ball and glove. I searched in my pack for them; they called to me softly from beneath the raggedies piled on top of them. "Now," he said, when he had them, his voice hoarse with no sleep, but calm for the first time since I'd met him. He led me down through the pasture to where Plunkett stood amid the meadow flowers. "Sit, sit," he said, "and close your eyes."

I sat, but wouldn't close my eyes. I watched silver fog rising out of the valley of That River. I watched Mongolfier at the engine: he drew on my glove, and with it brought the ball close to the pedestal on which Plunkett sat, and then released it: as though thrown, it buried itself within the glassy box, lining up with the others there. Its whistle ceased as it entered. He pretended, with his gloved hand, to turn that ball, that knob, and it turned. The sphere on top of the pedestal, clearer than glass, grew clouded, as though filling with smoke; Mongolfier turned the knob until the sphere was black: as black as way-wall: a black no-place in the morning.

"Plunkett is dead," he said. "Close your eyes." With the other glove, the glove he had brought, he pretended to turn a black knob, and the sphere rose off its pedestal. "Close your eyes," he said again, worried, glancing from me to his machine.

"All right," I said, but didn't. I put my hat on. I took it off again. The black sphere came slowly before my face. I had a moment to feel the limitless fear I had felt before way-wall as it filled up my sight: and then I closed my eyes.

And opened them here.

Yes. And you must close them now again, the story's told. . . .

Wait. Put down the glove. I'm afraid.

Afraid?

Afraid for him, for me. What do I do, angel, alone, stuck like the fly, when I'm not here telling this?

Nothing. If you dream, they are the dreams you wake from having already forgotten. But I don't think you dream: no, nothing, probably.

It seems I'm still in that meadow, and that I, I mean my story, just got here to be told. But that can't be so. I've told all this before.

Yes.

Why don't I remember?

You aren't here, Rush. There isn't anything here of you but—but something like a slide of the Filing System, that can only reveal you by—

Interpenetration.

Interpenetration, yes. With another. Who is gone now, while you're here, who will return when you are gone. But nothing spoken to you while you are here can affect you, any more than the picture of Plunkett could smile back at you if you smiled at it; when you are in yet another, you will be surprised again to find yourself here, surprised that a moment ago you sat in the meadow with Mongolfier; and you'll marvel at the dome, the clouds; and tell your story again. What it is to be you when you aren't here but on your pedestal, we don't know; we only know that sometimes you come from that sleep asleep, sometimes awake . . .

How many times? How many?

. . . and each time ask that. When our son . . . when my son is grown, Rush, and takes you on himself, if he dares, you will have been awakened here three hundred times, in twice as many years.

No. No, angel . . .

Many lives, Rush. Painted Red said.

But she's gone. They're all gone. And I . . . what did I do, then, angel, in my life? Did I grow old? Did I ever go down the hill? And Once a Day . . . oh, angel, what became of me?

I don't know. There are those who, having been you, have guessed; have dreamed or imagined how you returned to Belaire, the saint you became. Mongolfier said he watched you, after the old copter had come for him, watched you marvel at it, watched you watch it fly off with him: that's all we know. We know nothing else, Rush, but what you tell us. It's all you here now, Rush.

And do I each time learn this? And then forget? As though I were Mother Tom in her box, like the strip of paper looped by St. Gene?

Yes.

Then free me now, angel. Let me sleep, if I can't die. Free me, quickly, while I can still bear all this. . . .

Yes. Sleep now, brave man; sleep again, Rush; close your eyes, close your eyes. Forget.

Only . . . wait, wait. Listen: the one who I am, you must be gentle with him, angel, when he returns, remember. Here, take my hand, take his hand. Yes. Don't let go. Promise.

Yes. I promise.

Stay with him.

Ever after. I promise. Now close your eyes.

wm WILLIAM MORROW 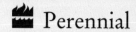 Perennial

New in Hardcover March 2002 from John Crowley:

THE TRANSLATOR
ISBN 0-380-97862-8 (hardcover)

In 1962, at a large college in the Midwest, Kit Malone, a young woman with
a troubled past, finds herself in a class taught by an exiled Russian poet,
Innokenti Falin. Over the course of the summer the two forge a friendship,
she becomes his translator, and a delicate love grows between these two
displaced people. Years later, returning from a convention on Falin in
Moscow, Kit realizes what really happened the last night that she spent with
Falin . . . while the country held it's breath against the threat of war, she was
helping him make a decision that would change the course of history.

Now Available in Trade Paperback:

LITTLE, BIG
ISBN 0-06-093793-9 (paperback)

The epic story of Smoky Barnable — an anonymous young man whose life
takes a magical turn the day he meets and falls in love with a unique woman
named Daily Alice Drinkwater. Daily Alice lives in Edgewood, a mysterious
place that cannot be found on a map, but where Smoky must travel in order
to take her as his bride. In this palatial manor lives a family with ties to other
worlds; as their history is revealed to Smoky, he discovers that he, too, is a
part of a much larger tale unfolding all around.

"Prose that Scott Fitzgerald would envy and a heartbreaking love story."
—Michael Dirda, *Washington Post Book Review*

OTHERWISE
Three Novels by John Crowley
ISBN 0-06-093792-0 (paperback)

Now back in print, this volume contains three of award-winning author
John Crowley's critically acclaimed short novels: *Beasts*, *Engine Summer*,
and *The Deep*.

Available wherever books are sold, or call 1-800-331-3761 to order.